6/20/14

WINFIELD PUBLIC LIBRARY

3 7599 00013 1993

P9-DYB-286

DISCARD

THIS ONE SUMMER

Mariko Tamaki
Jillian Tamaki

:01

First Second
NEW YORK

CRUNCH

CRUNCH

CRUNCH
CRUNCH

CRUNCH

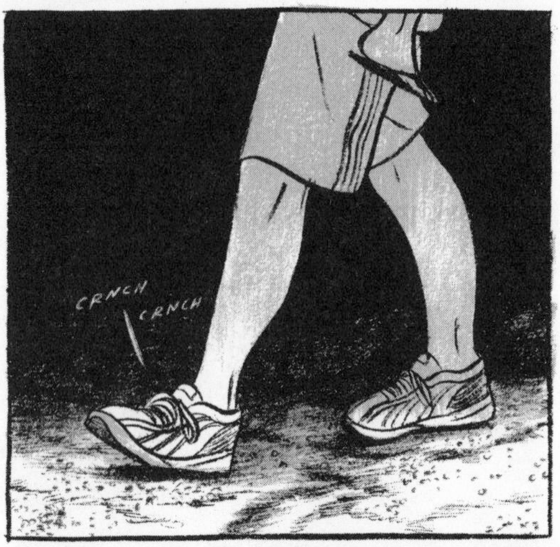
CRNCH
CRNCH

Okay.

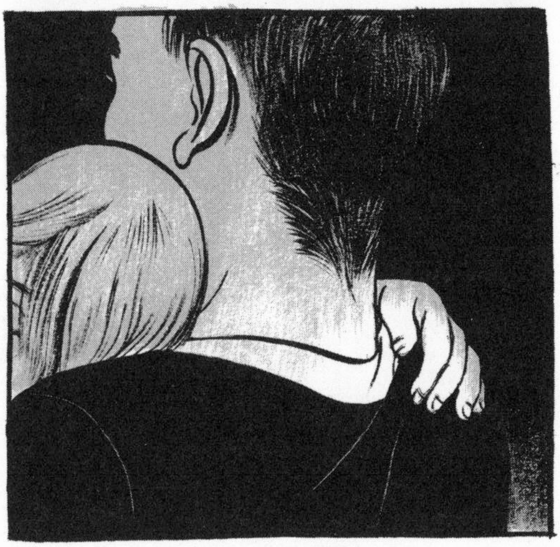

So.

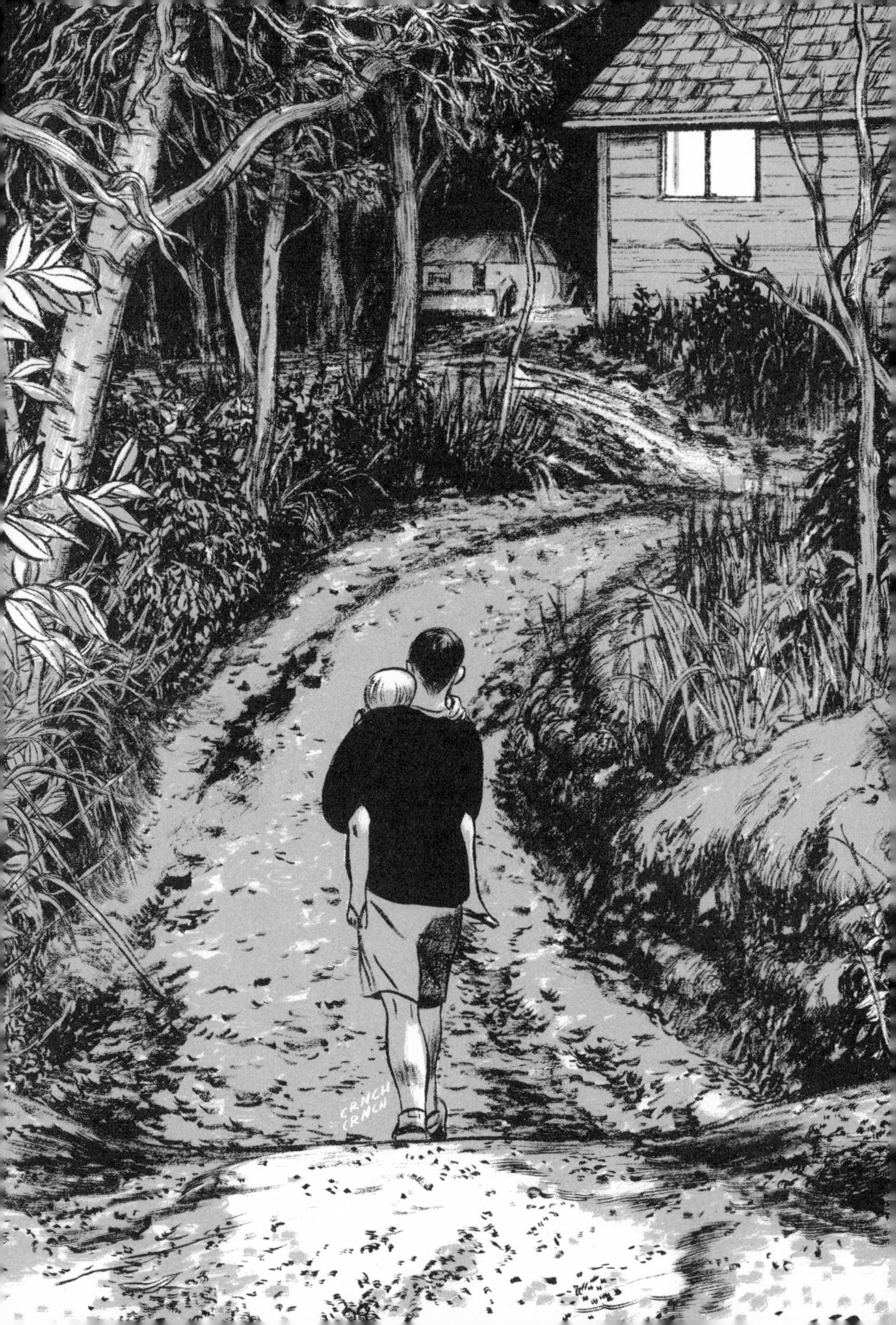
CRNCH
CRNCH

Awago Beach is
this place.

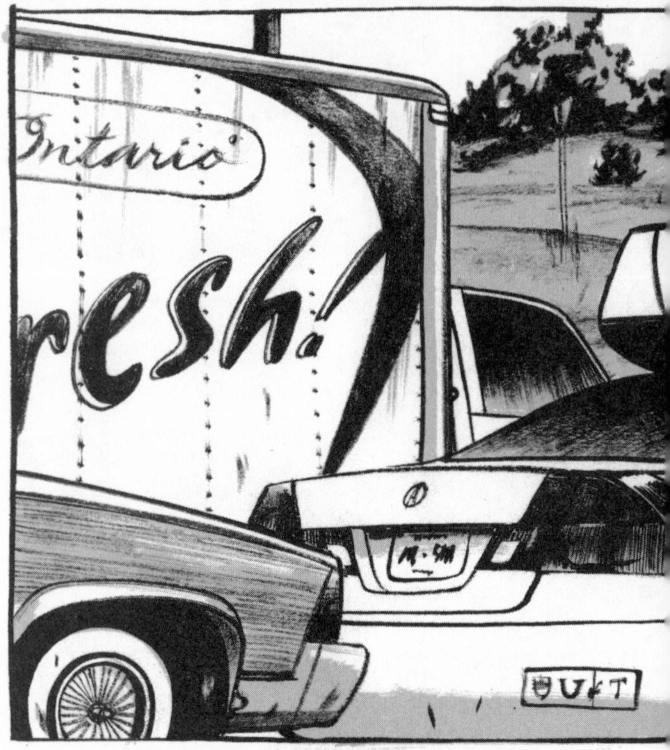

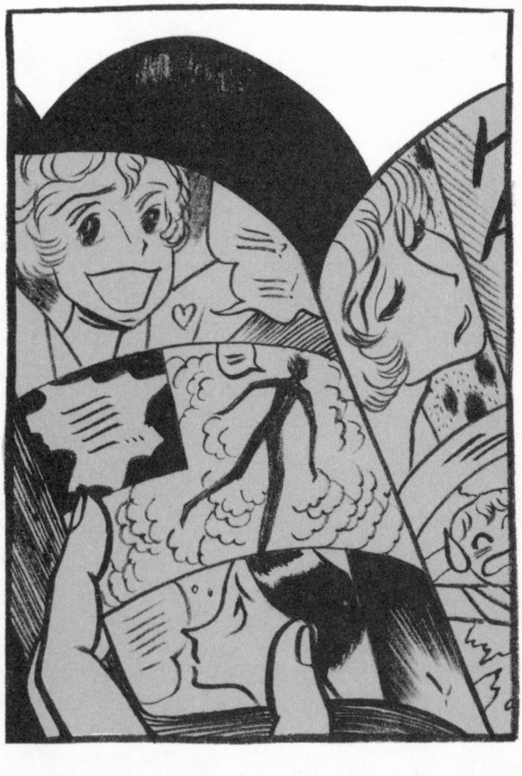

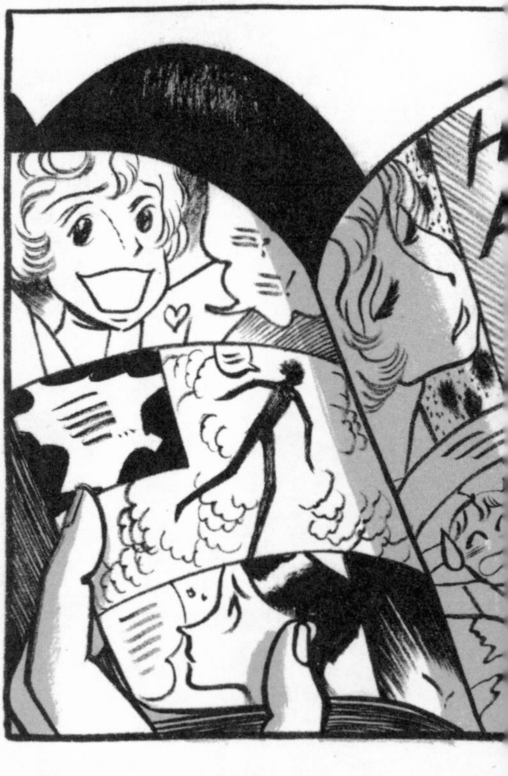

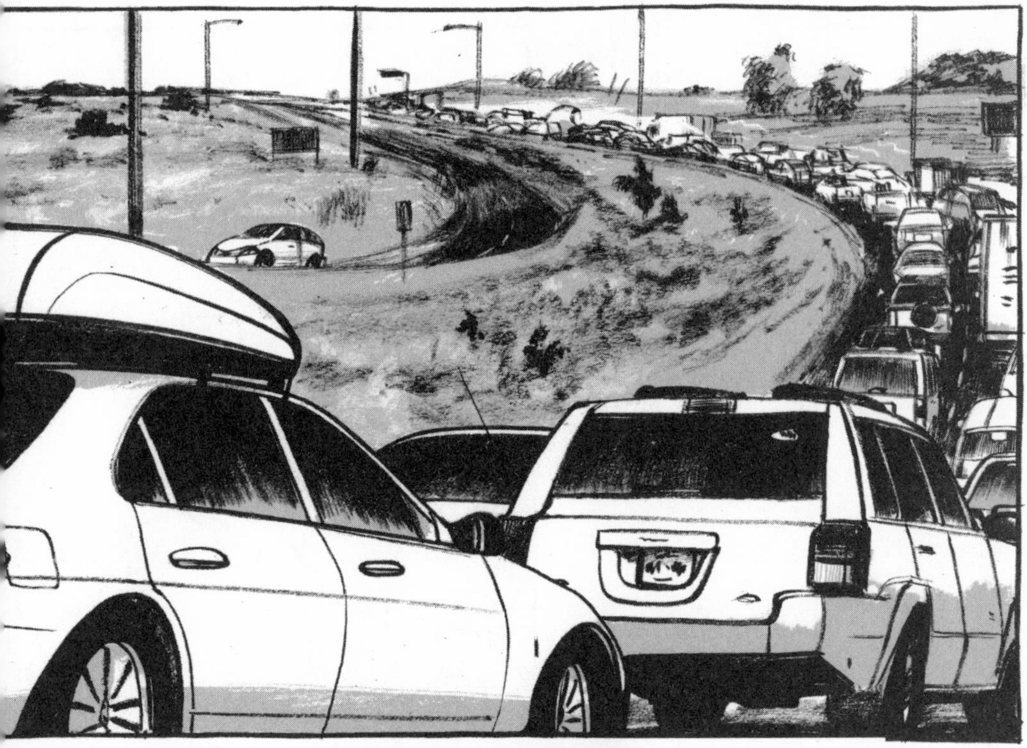

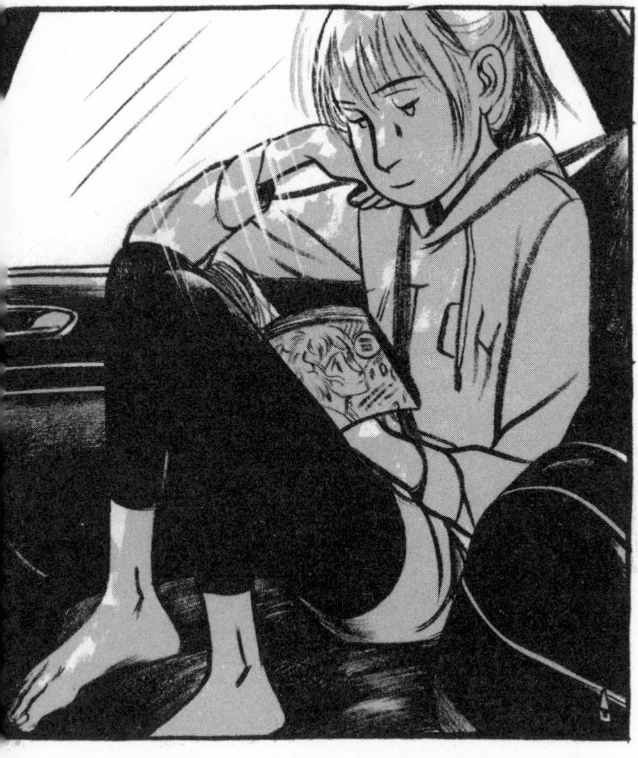

Where my family
goes every summer.

Ever since...

like...
forever.

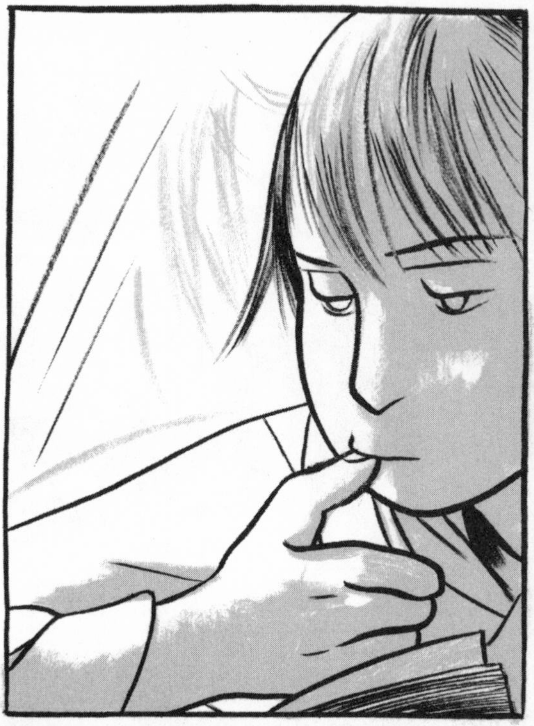

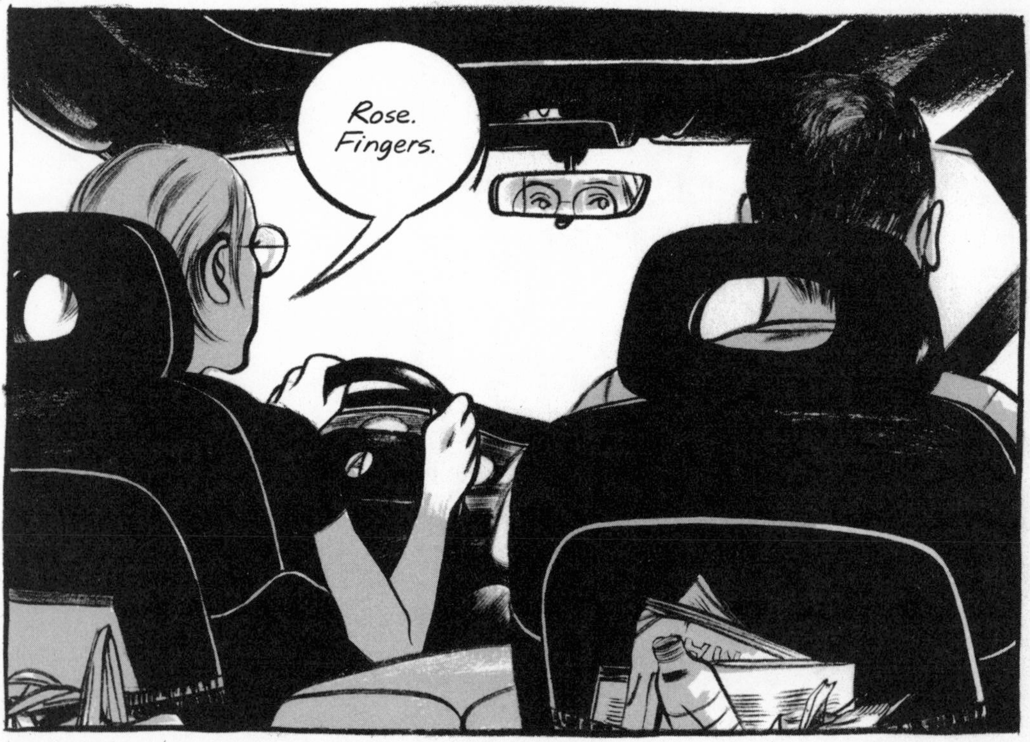
Rose.
Fingers.

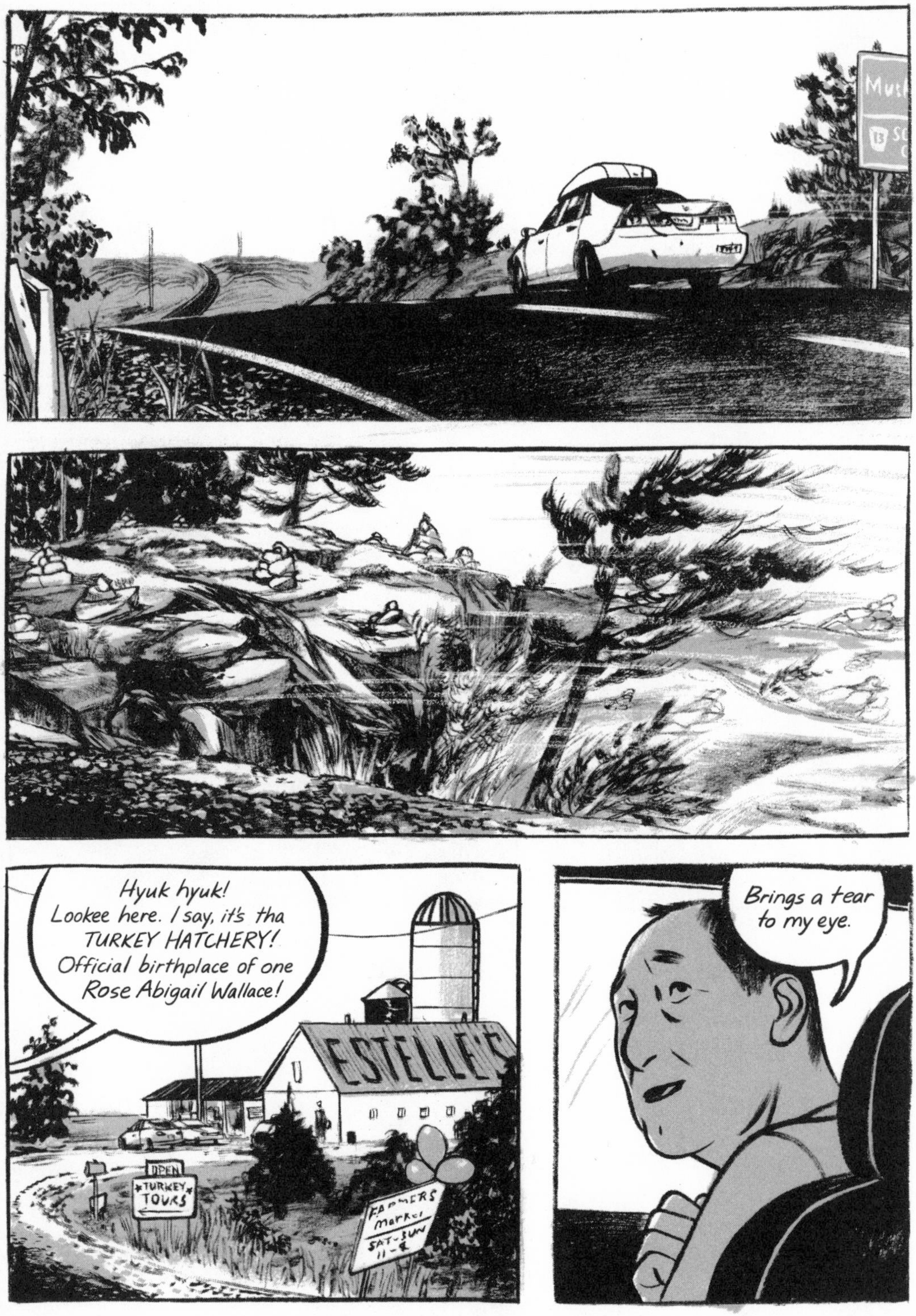
Hyuk hyuk! Lookee here. I say, it's tha TURKEY HATCHERY! Official birthplace of one Rose Abigail Wallace!
ESTELLE'S
OPEN
TURKEY TOURS
FARMERS Market SAT-SUN
Brings a tear to my eye.

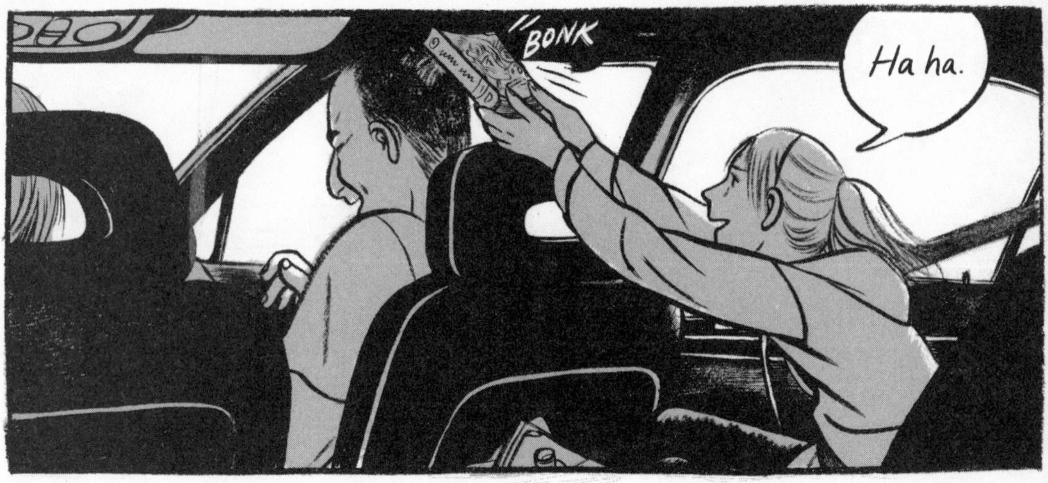
BONK
Ha ha.

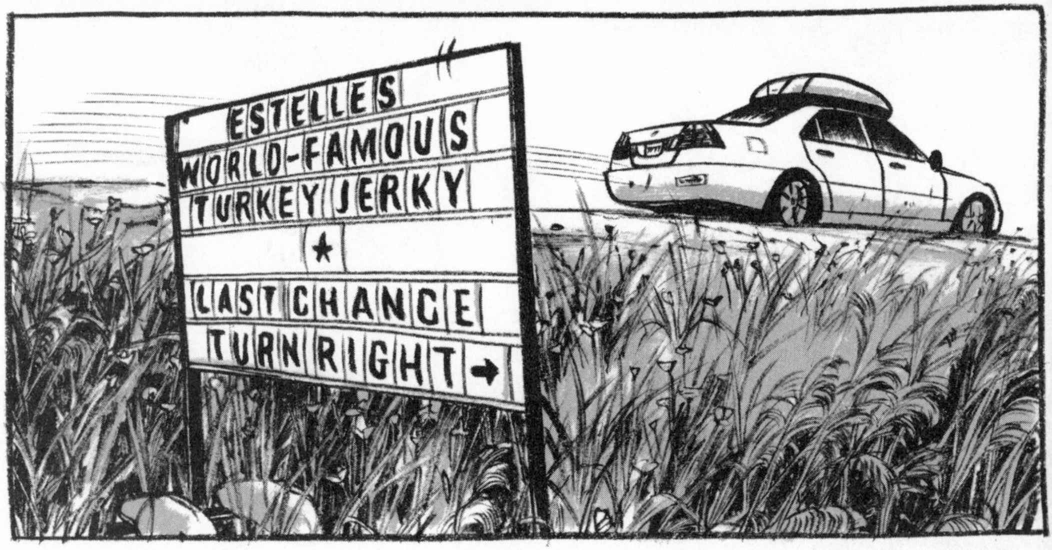
ESTELLES
WORLD-FAMOUS
TURKEY JERKY
LAST CHANCE
TURN RIGHT

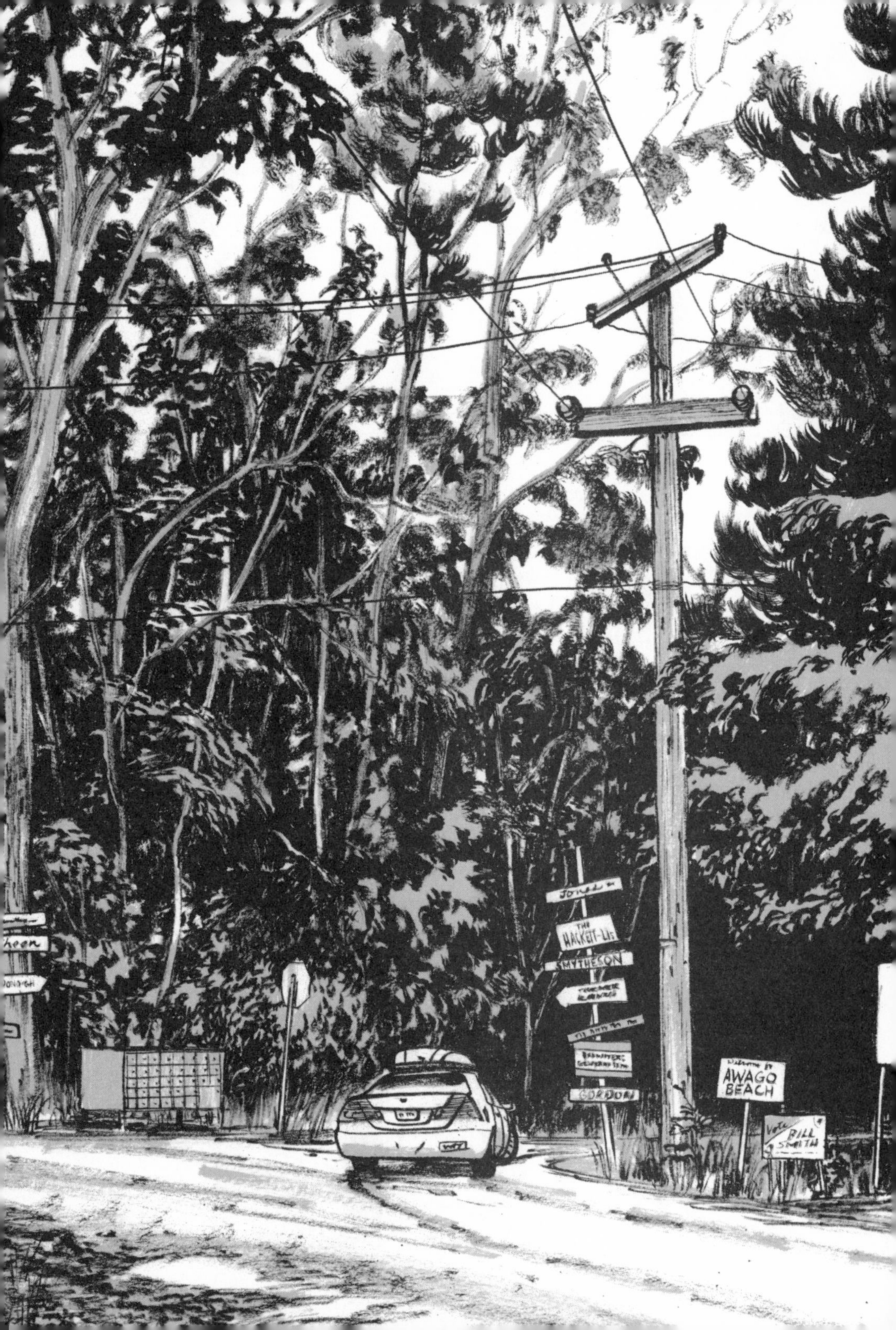
THE HACKETT-LIS
SMYTHESON
GORDON
AWAGO BEACH
Vote BILL SMITH

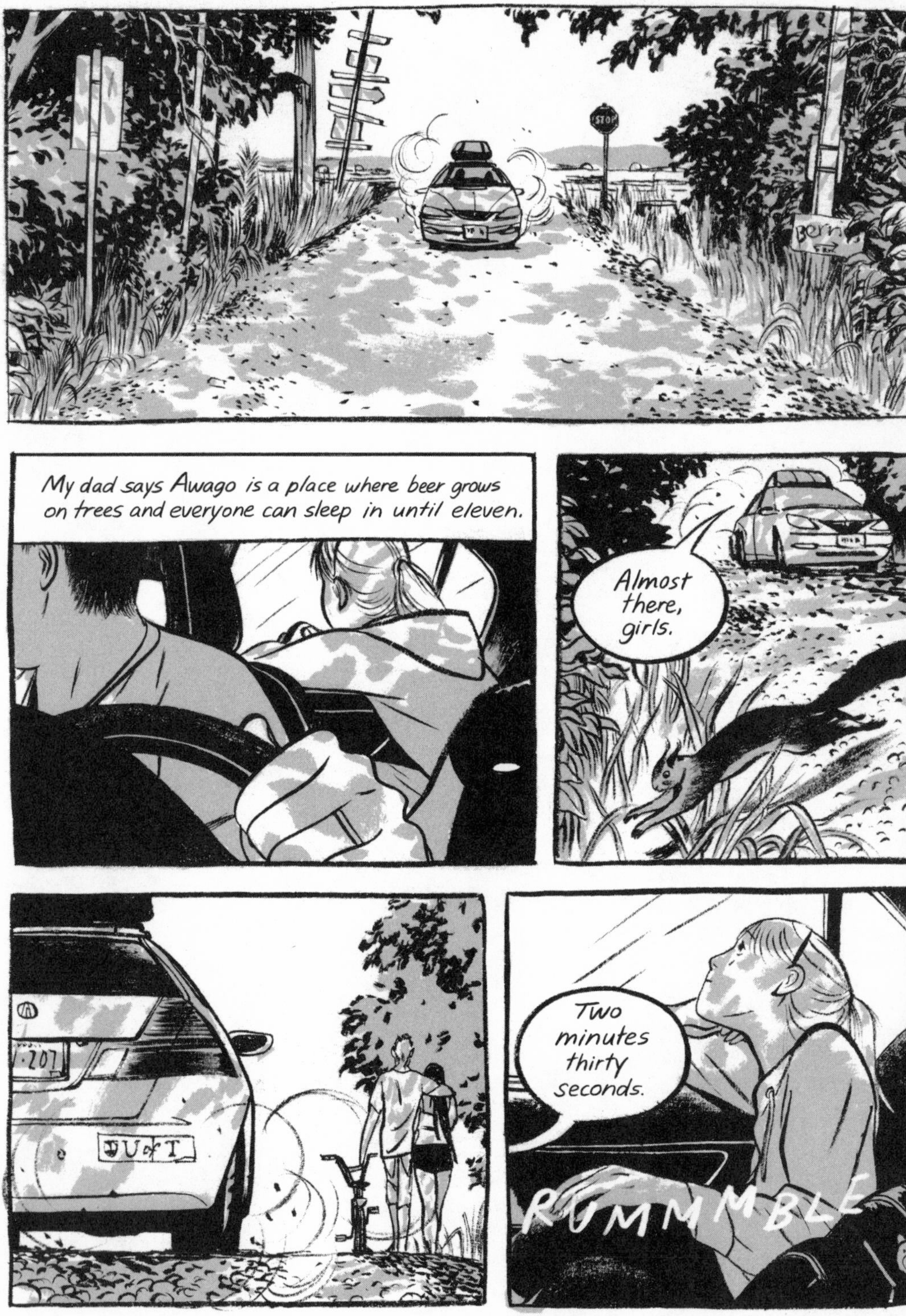
STOP
Bern
My dad says Awago is a place where beer grows on trees and everyone can sleep in until eleven.
Almost there, girls.
Two minutes thirty seconds.
RUMMMBLE

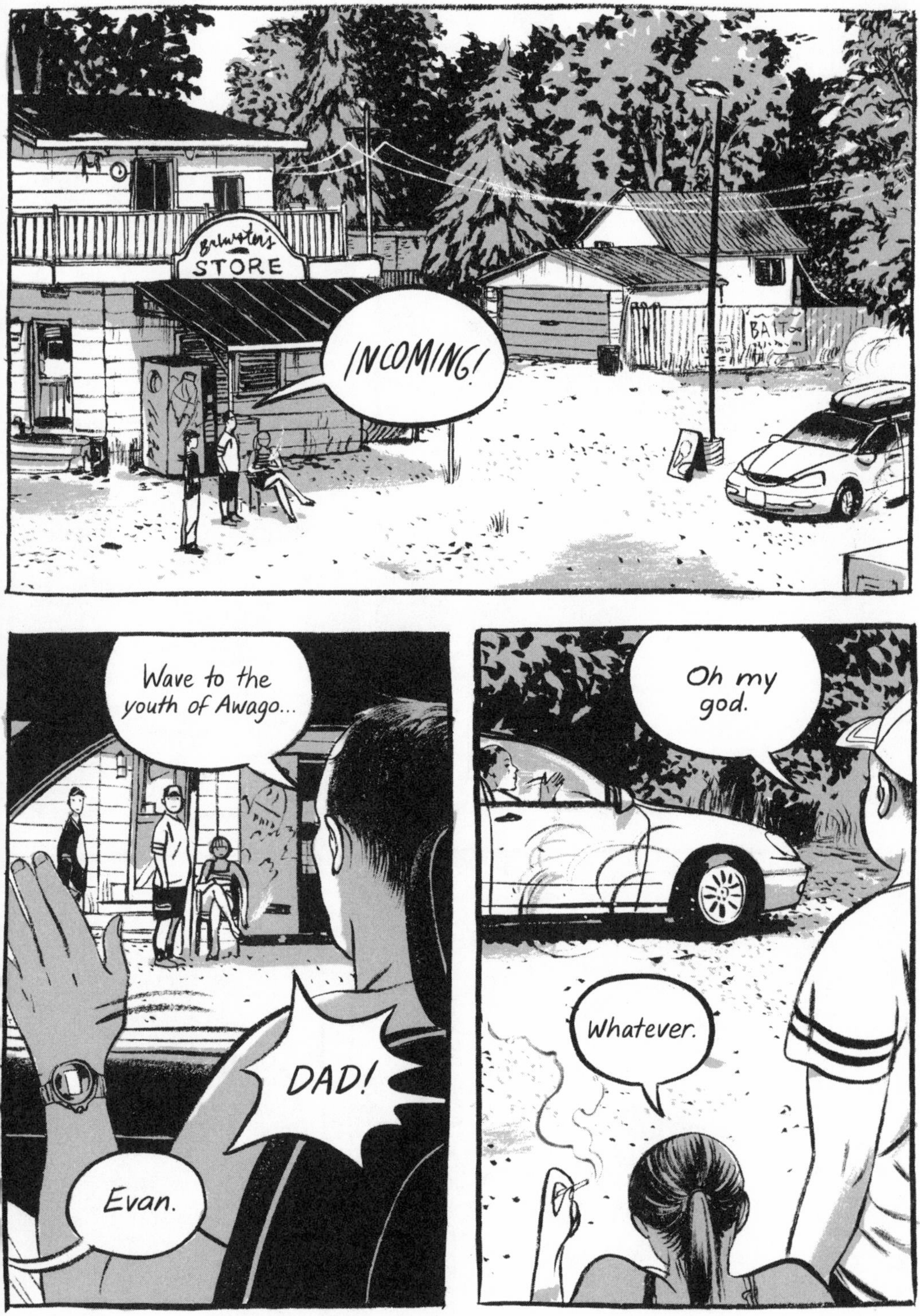
STORE
BAIT
INCOMING!
Wave to the youth of Awago...
DAD!
Evan.
Oh my god.
Whatever.

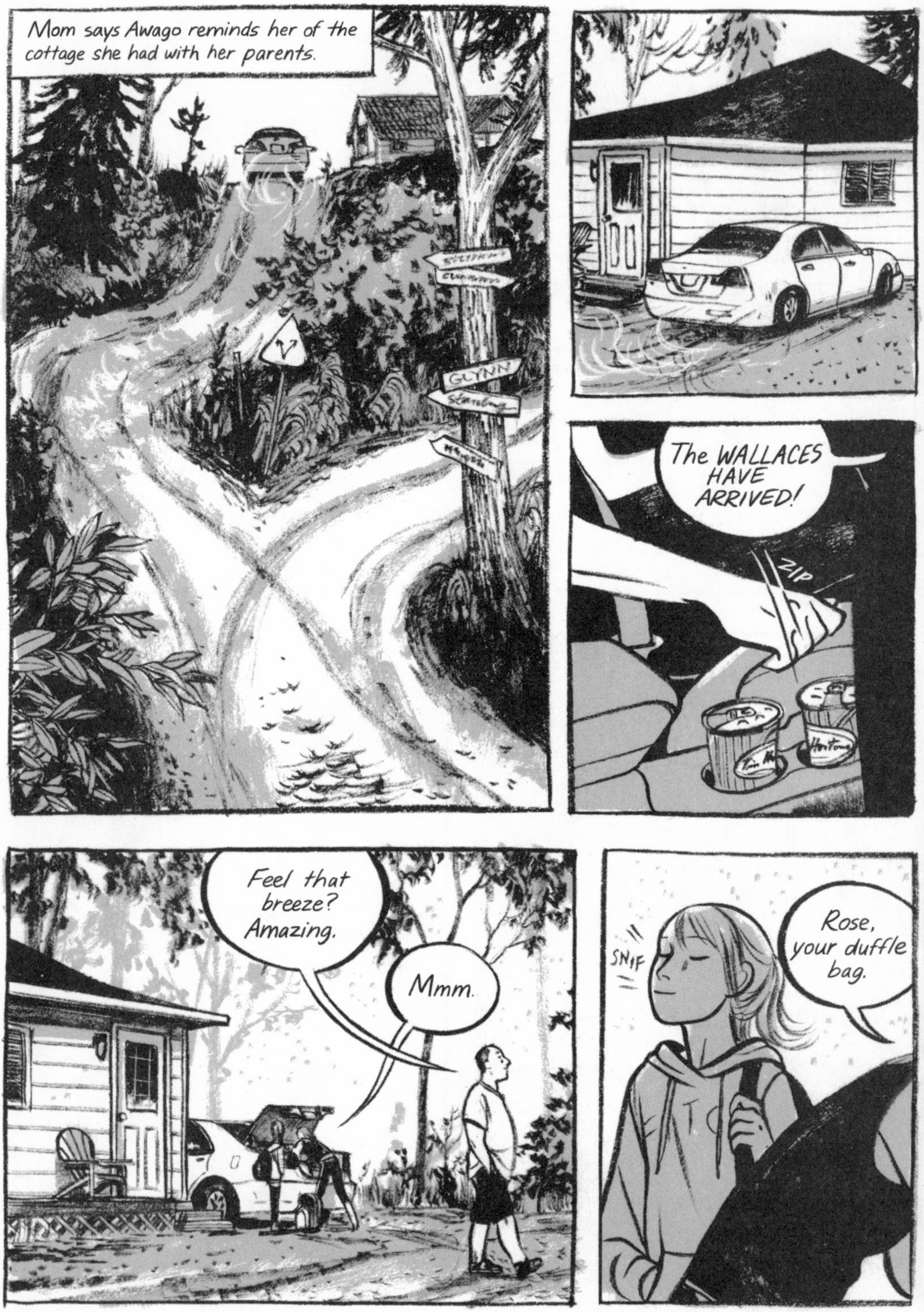
Mom says Awago reminds her of the cottage she had with her parents.
GLYNN
The WALLACES HAVE ARRIVED!
ZIP
Feel that breeze? Amazing.
Mmm.
SNIF
Rose, your duffle bag.

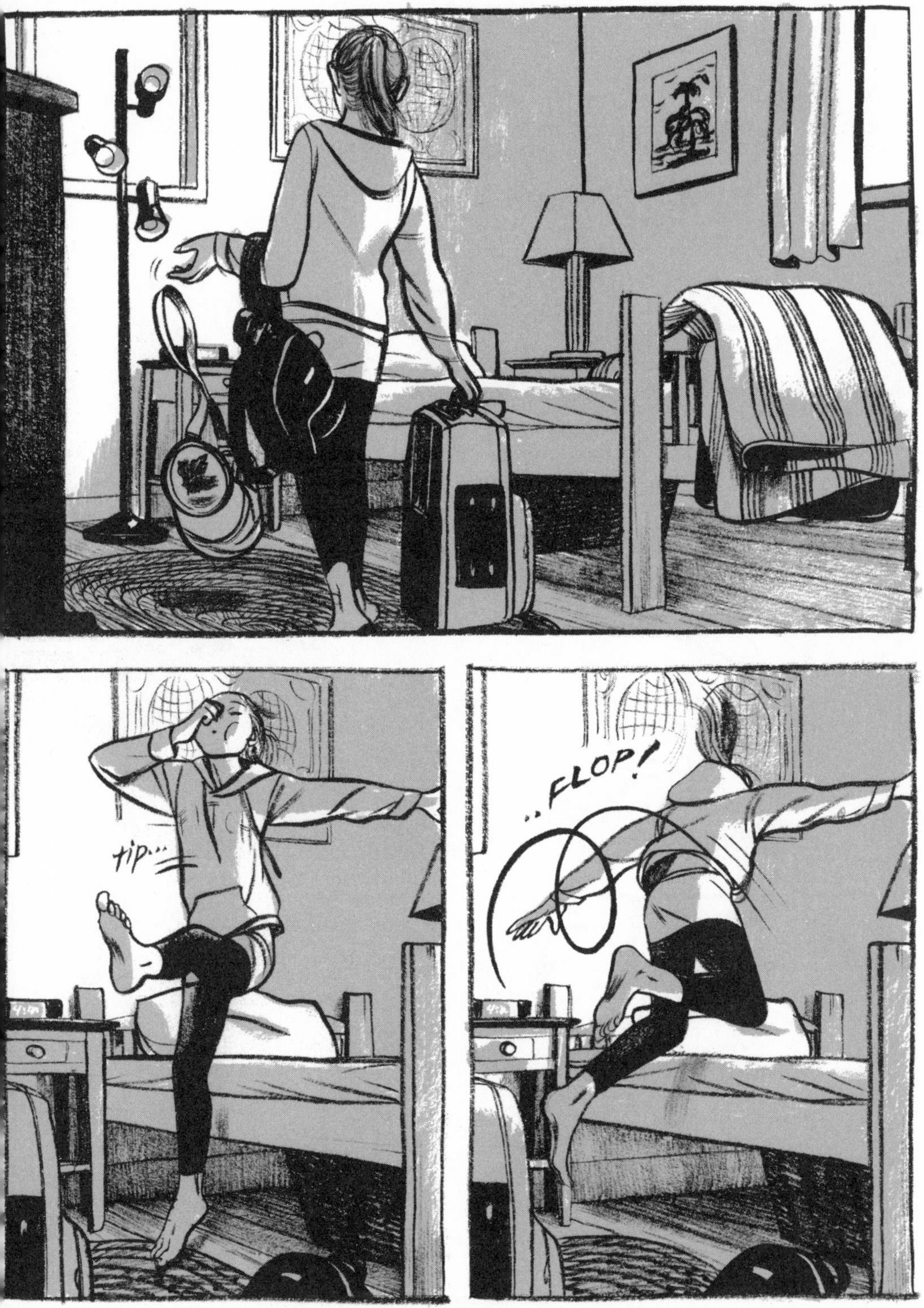
tip...
..FLOP!

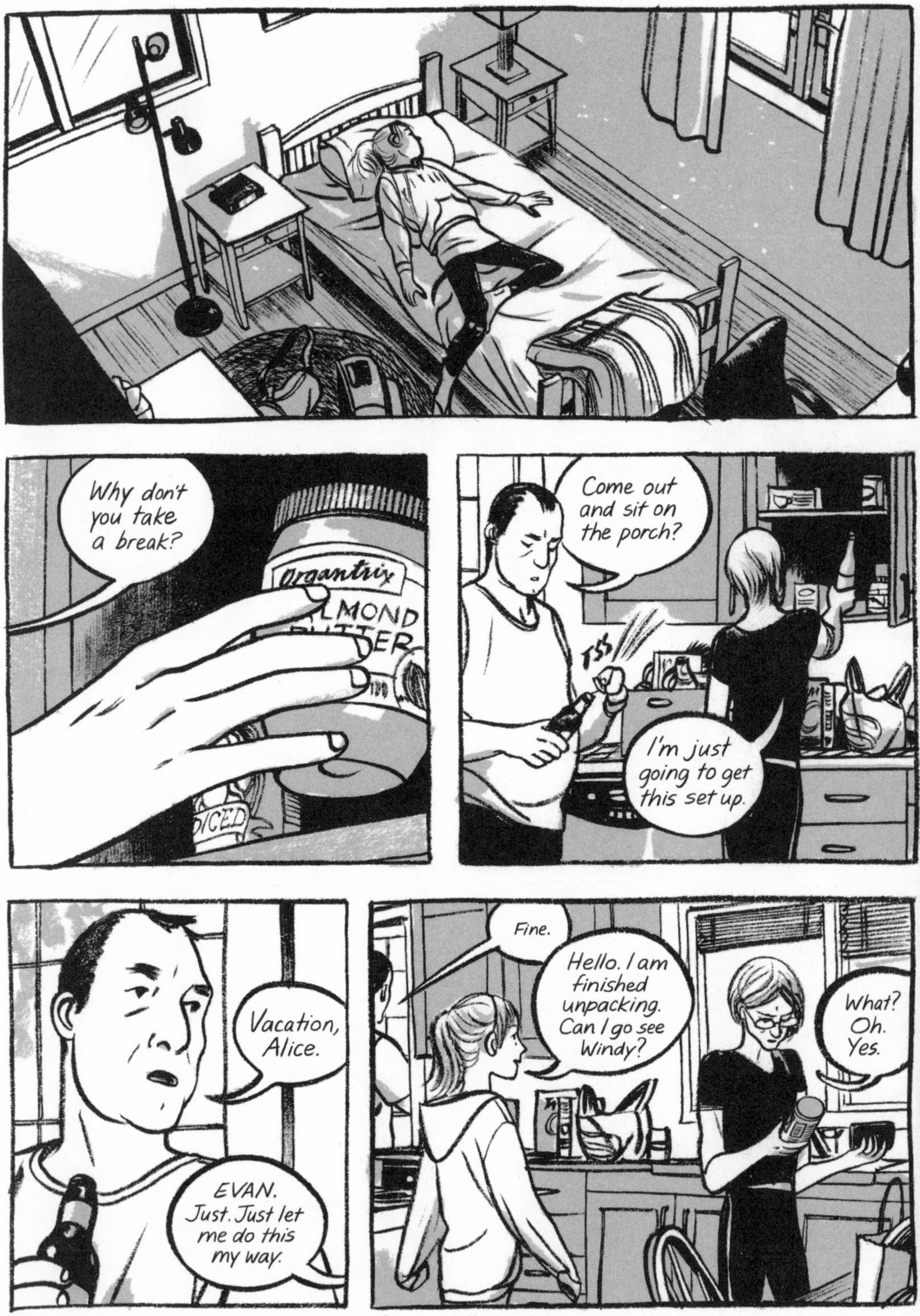
Why don't you take a break?
Organtrix
LMOND
DICED
Come out and sit on the porch?
TSS
I'm just going to get this set up.
Vacation, Alice.
EVAN. Just. Just let me do this my way.
Fine.
Hello. I am finished unpacking. Can I go see Windy?
What? Oh. Yes.

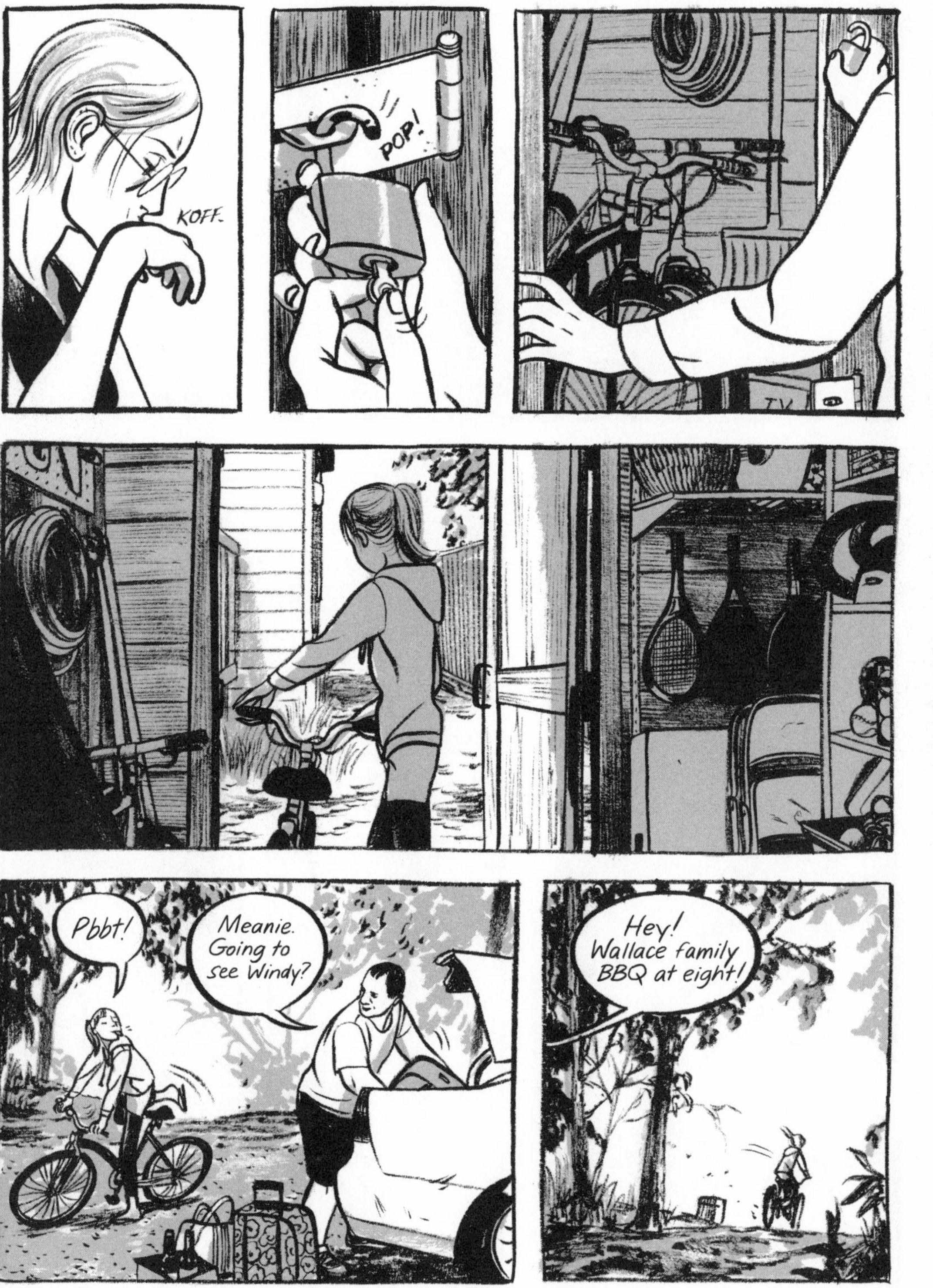
KOFF.
POP!
TV
Pbbt!
Meanie. Going to see Windy?
Hey! Wallace family BBQ at eight!

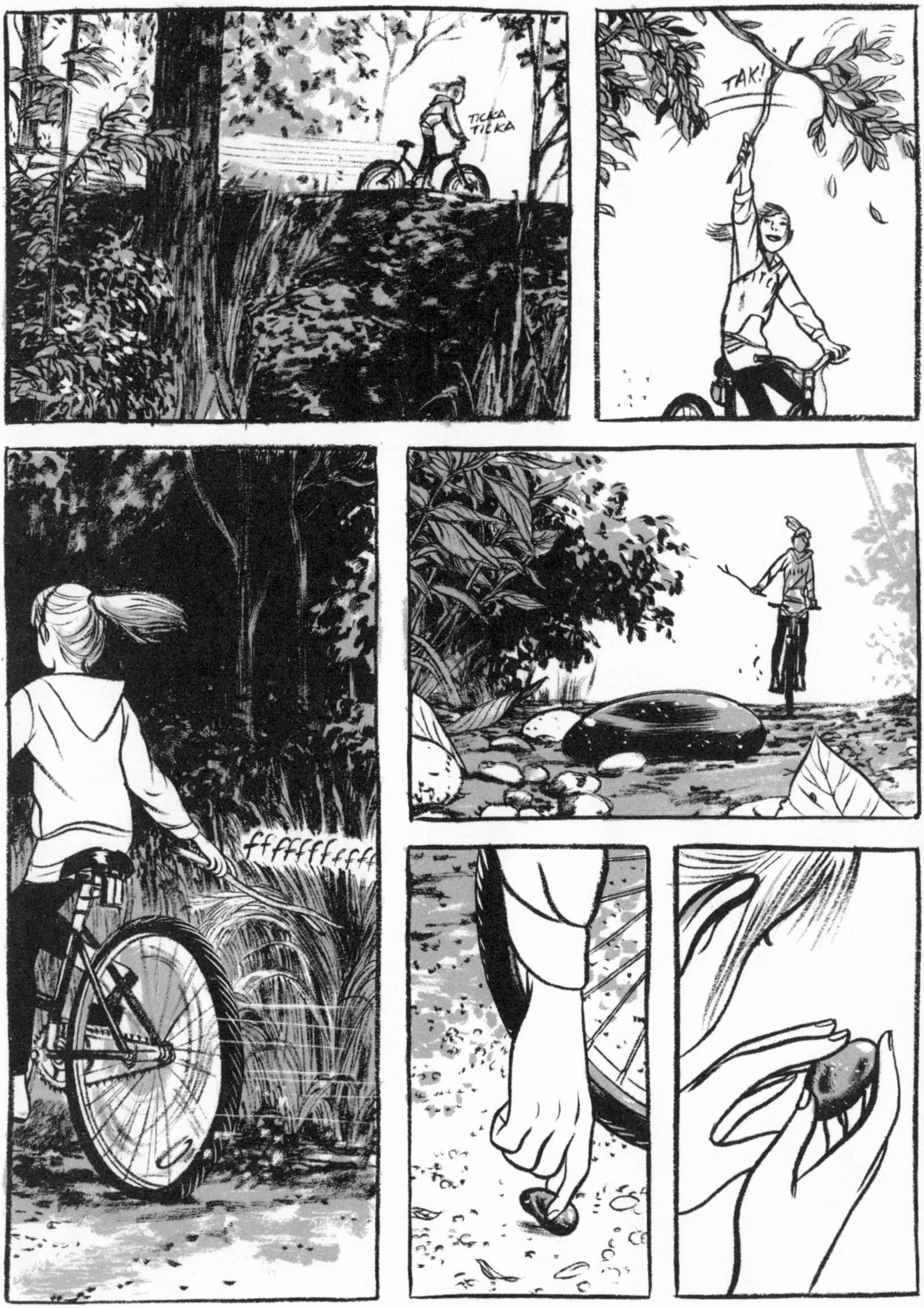

TICKA TICKA
TAK!
ffffffffff

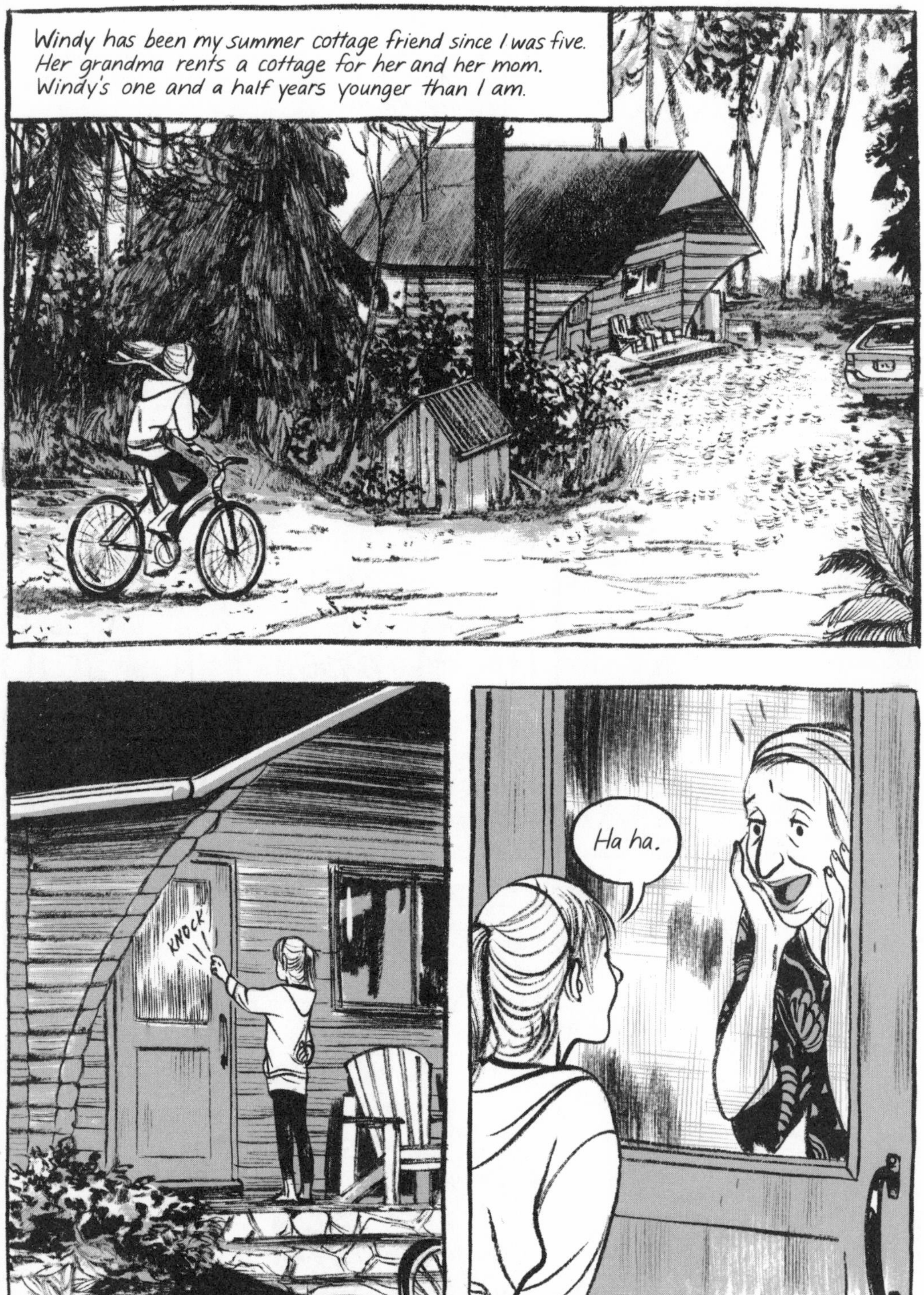
Windy has been my summer cottage friend since I was five.
Her grandma rents a cottage for her and her mom.
Windy's one and a half years younger than I am.
KNOCK
Ha ha.

Come in!

WINDY! Rose is here!

Hi Evelyn.

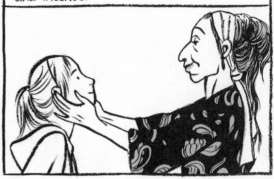

Windy's mother is a massage therapist and she runs a store with a bunch of other women. My dad says it's all vegetarian cookbooks and incense.

Mmmm. You smell like the trees.

Hey.

Do you want to go to the beach?

Sure.

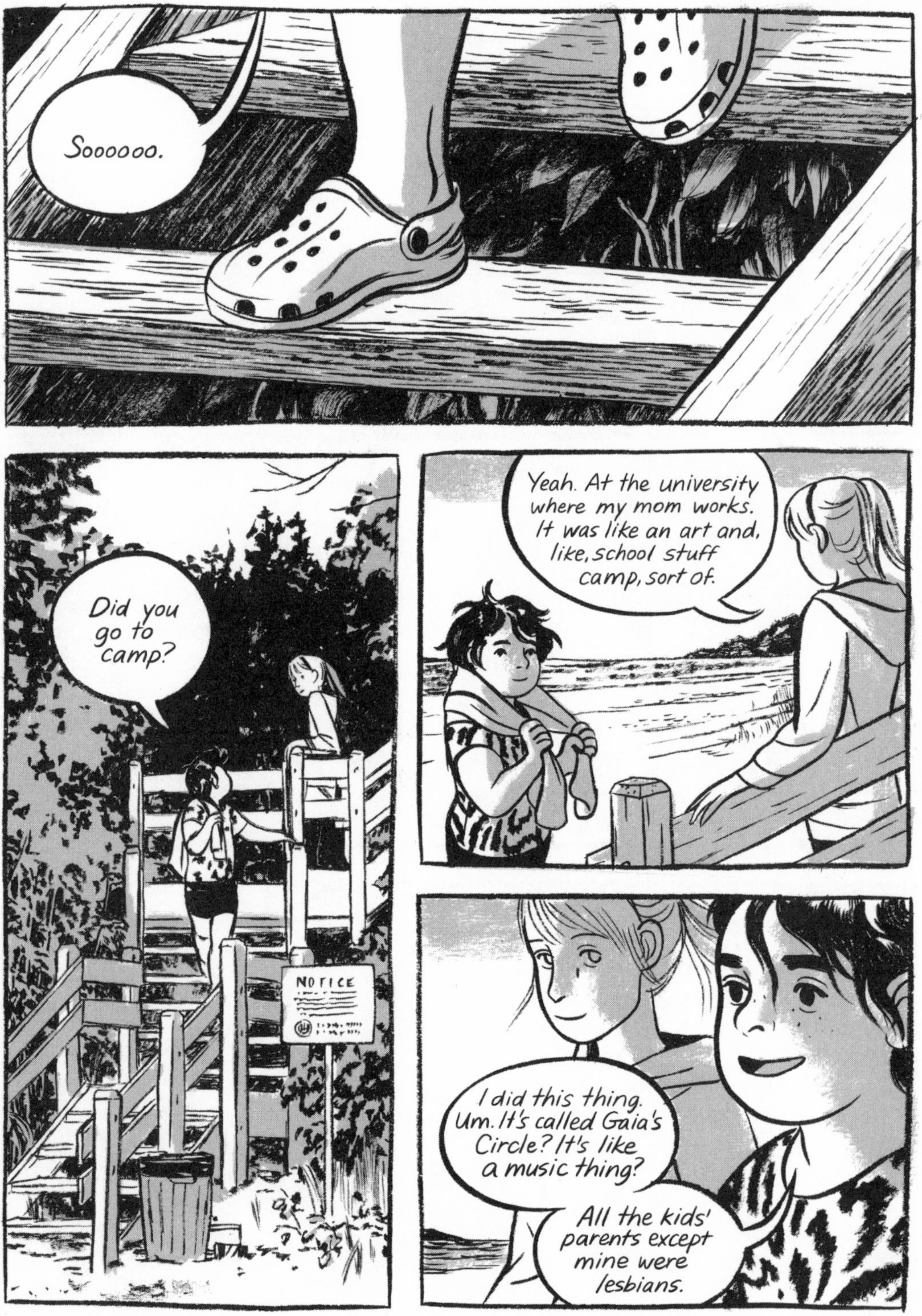
Soooooo.
Did you go to camp?
NOTICE
Yeah. At the university where my mom works. It was like an art and, like, school stuff camp, sort of.
I did this thing. Um. It's called Gaia's Circle? It's like a music thing?
All the kids' parents except mine were lesbians.

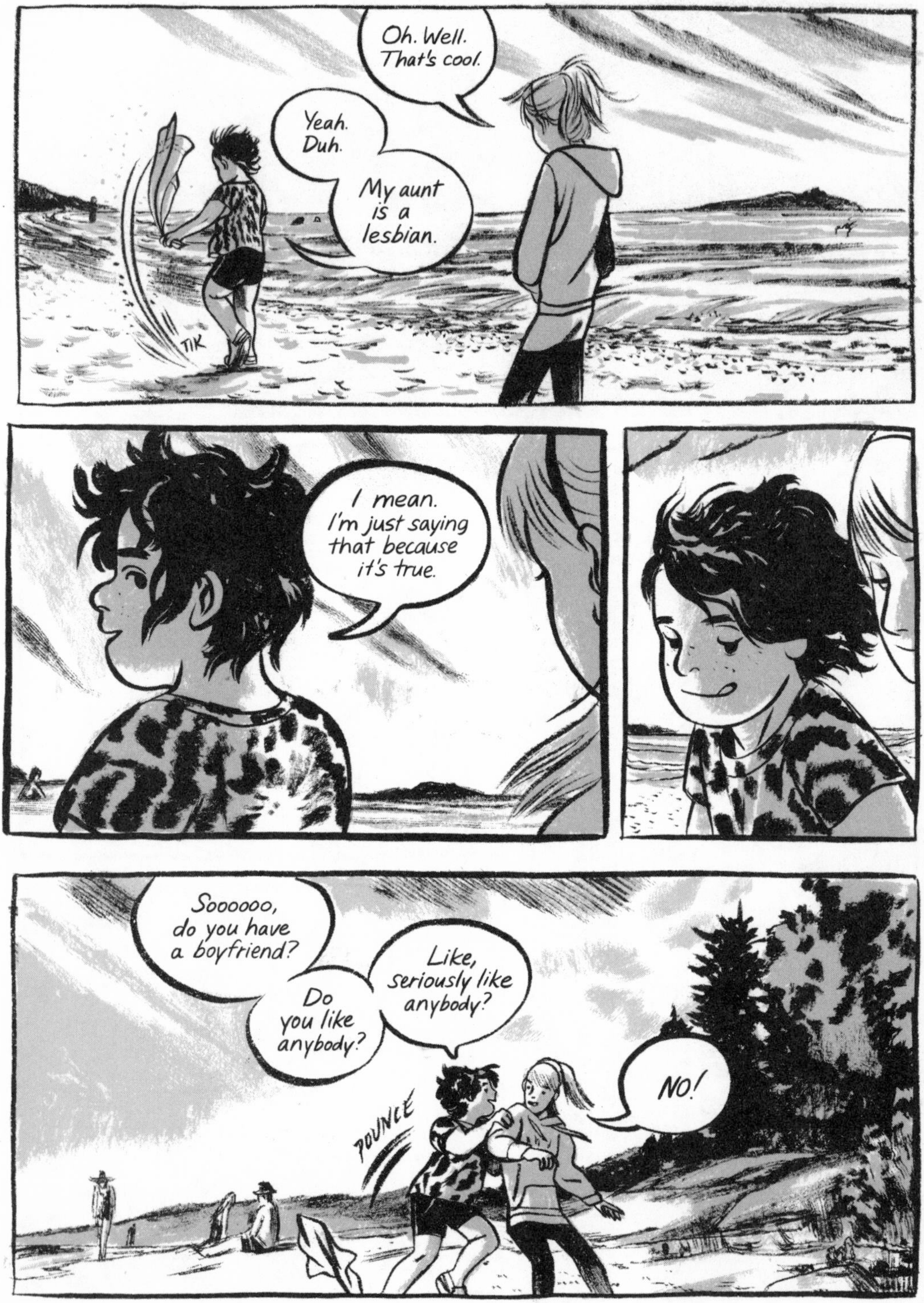
Oh. Well.
That's cool.
Yeah.
Duh.
My aunt
is a
lesbian.
TIK
I mean.
I'm just saying
that because
it's true.
Soooooo,
do you have
a boyfriend?
Do
you like
anybody?
Like,
seriously like
anybody?
POUNCE
NO!

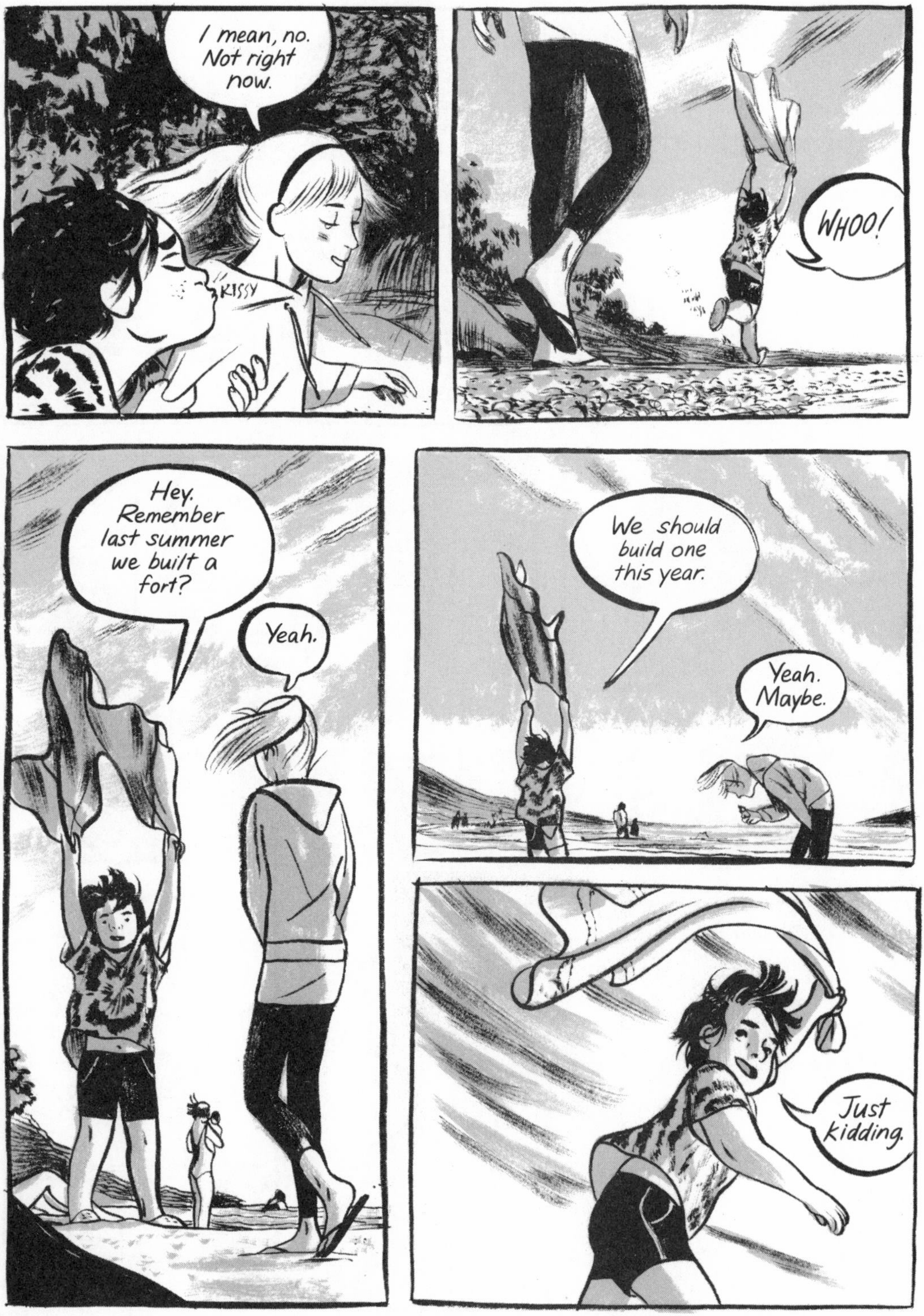
I mean, no. Not right now.
KISSY
WHOO!
Hey. Remember last summer we built a fort?
Yeah.
We should build one this year.
Yeah. Maybe.
Just kidding.

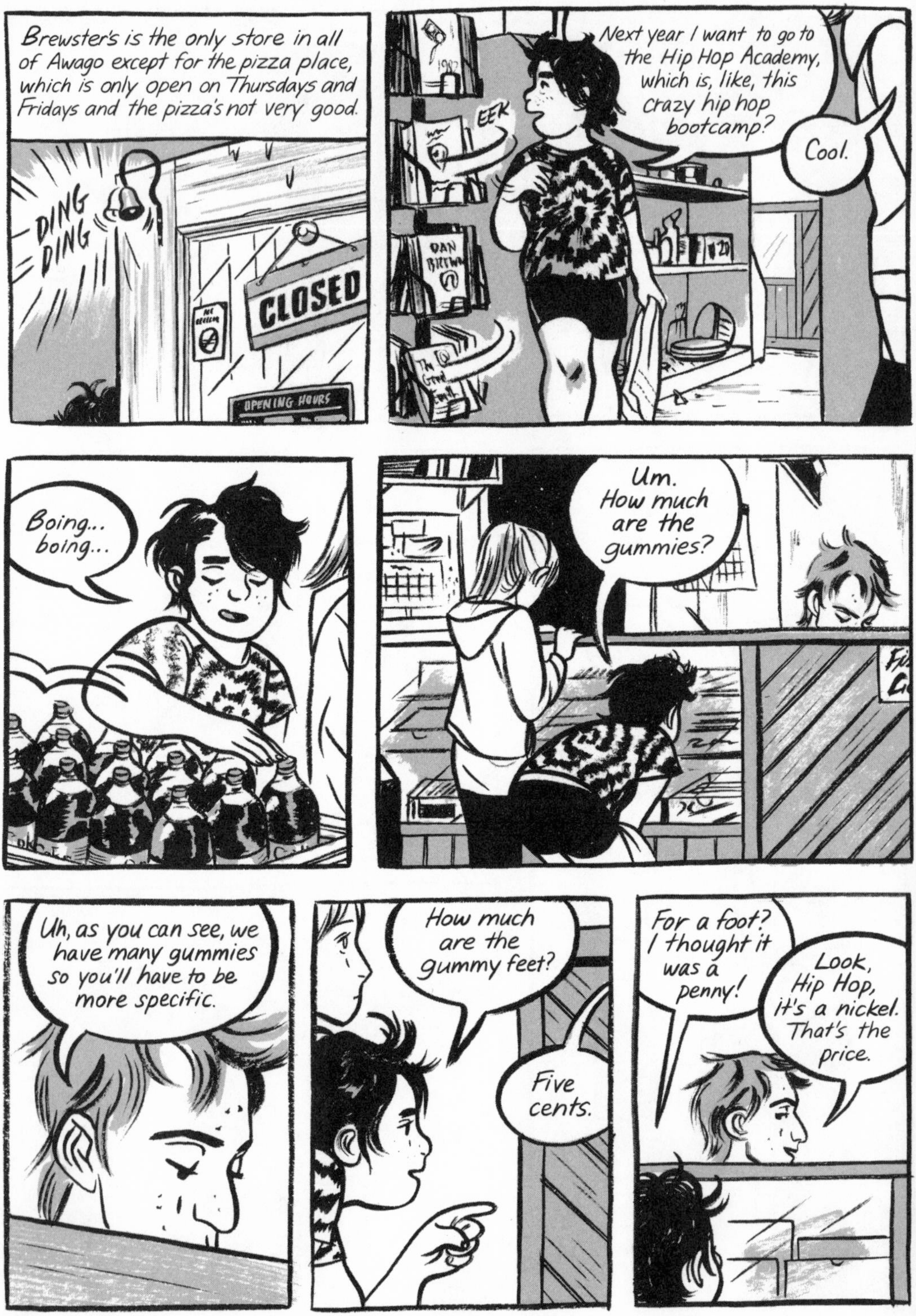
Brewster's is the only store in all of Awago except for the pizza place, which is only open on Thursdays and Fridays and the pizza's not very good.
DING DING
CLOSED
OPENING HOURS
EEK
DAN BROWN
Next year I want to go to the Hip Hop Academy, which is, like, this crazy hip hop bootcamp?
Cool.
Boing... boing...
Um. How much are the gummies?
Uh, as you can see, we have many gummies so you'll have to be more specific.
How much are the gummy feet?
Five cents.
For a foot? I thought it was a penny!
Look, Hip Hop, it's a nickel. That's the price.

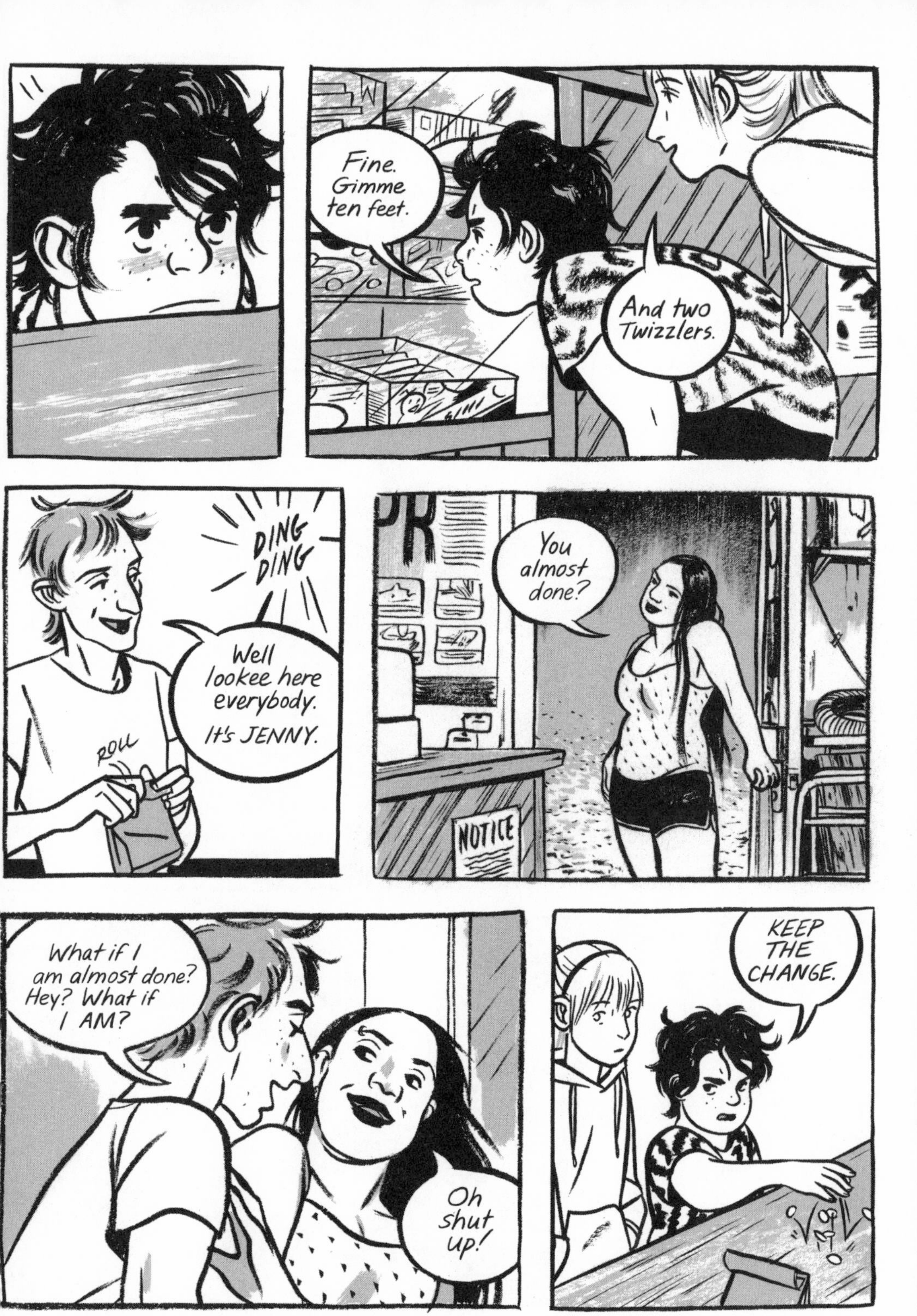
Fine. Gimme ten feet.
And two Twizzlers.
DING DING
Well lookee here everybody. It's JENNY.
ROLL
You almost done?
NOTICE
What if I am almost done? Hey? What if I AM?
Oh shut up!
KEEP THE CHANGE.

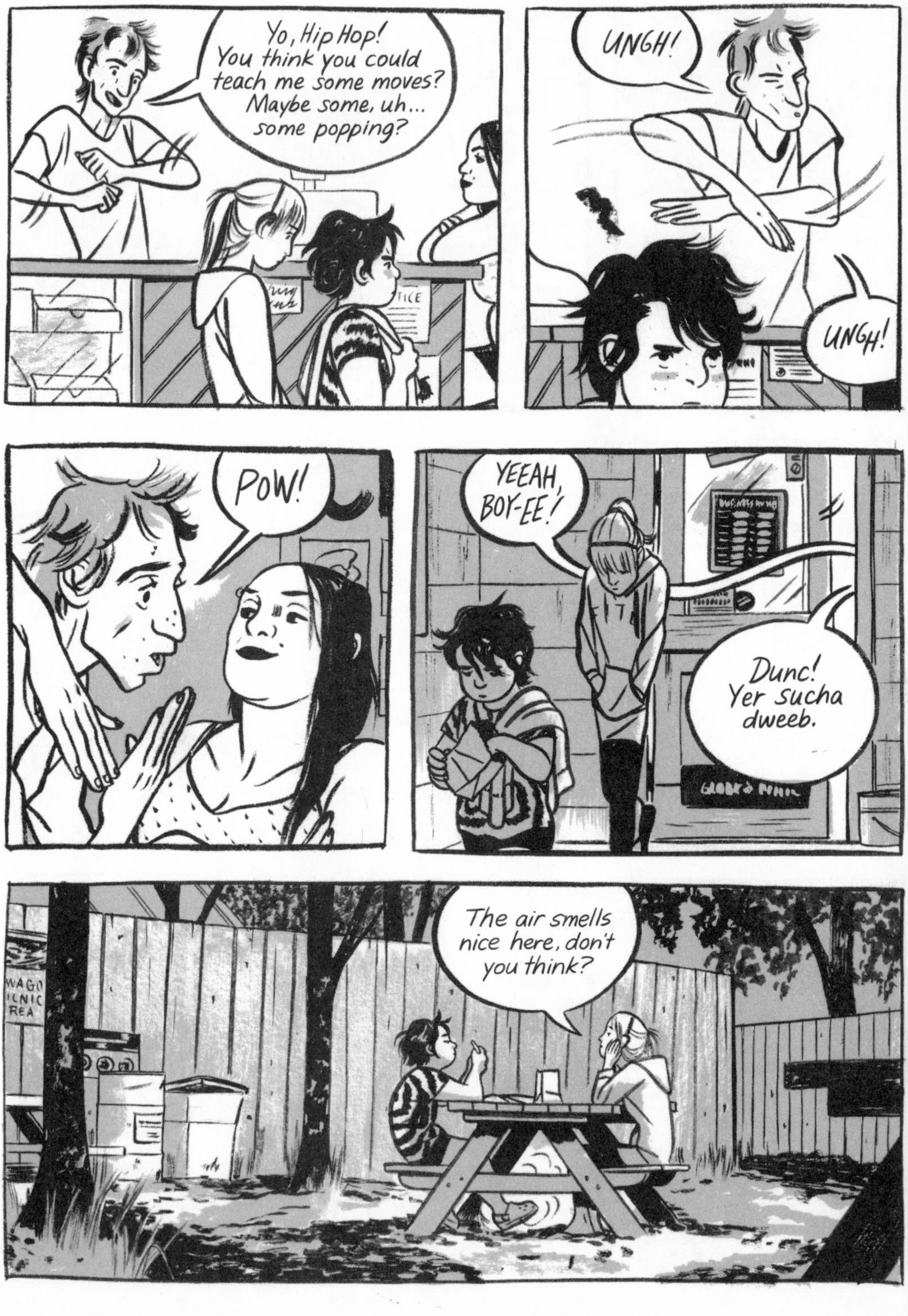
Yo, Hip Hop! You think you could teach me some moves? Maybe some, uh... some popping?
UNGH!
UNGH!
POW!
YEEAH, BOY-EE!
Dunc! Yer sucha dweeb.
The air smells nice here, don't you think?

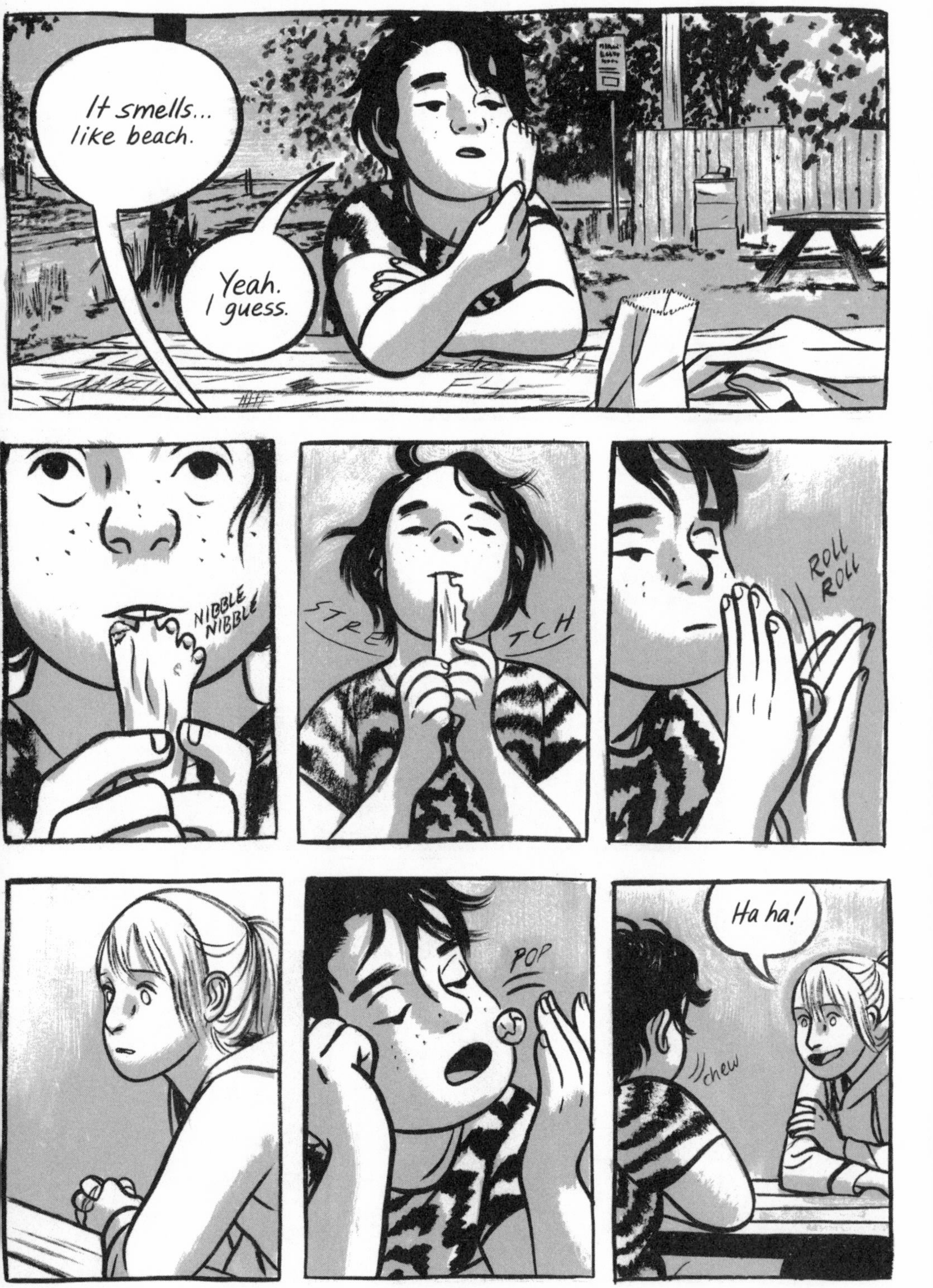
It smells... like beach.
Yeah. I guess.
NIBBLE NIBBLE
STRETCH
ROLL ROLL
POP
chew
Ha ha!

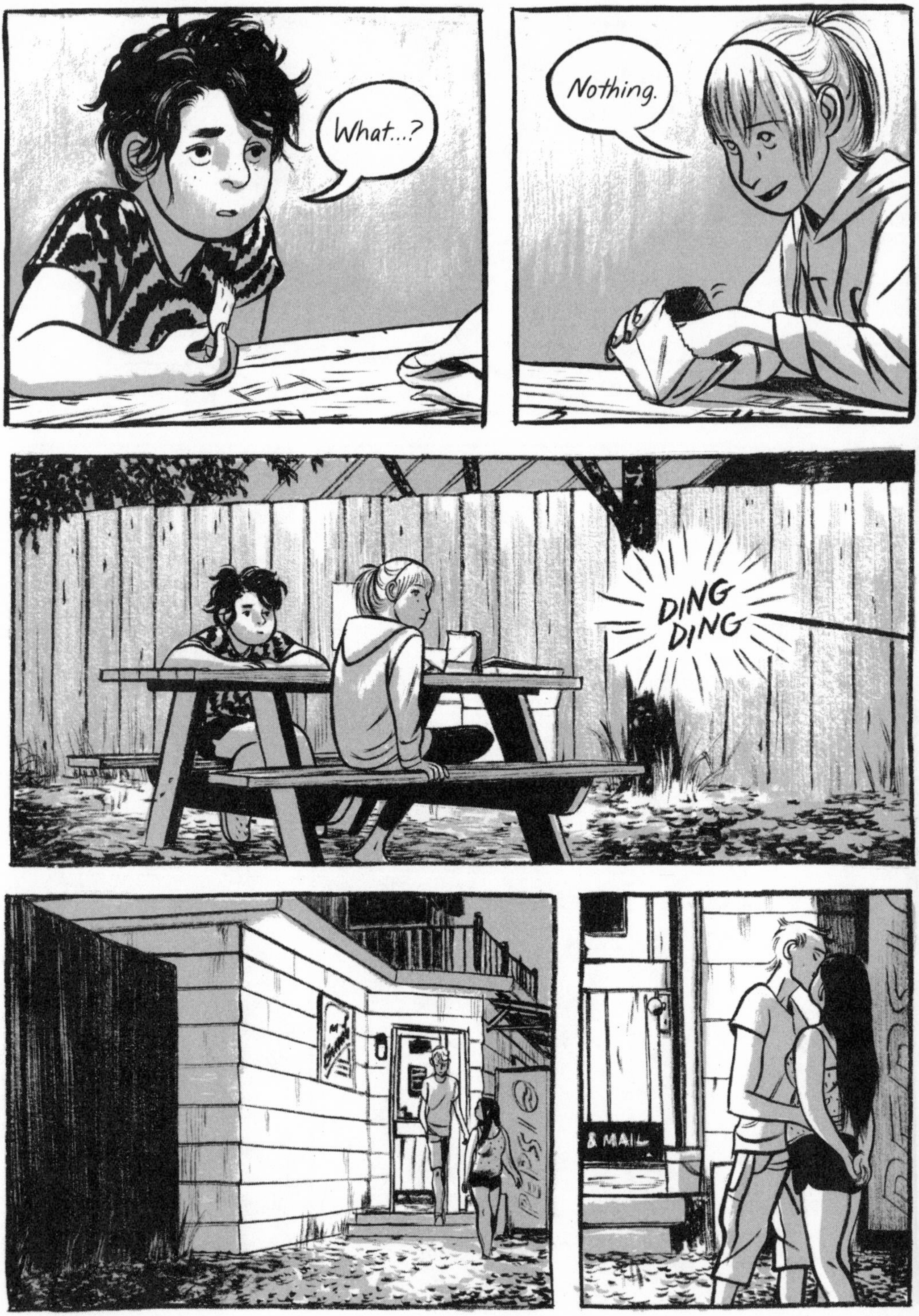
What...?
Nothing.
DING
DING
& MAIL

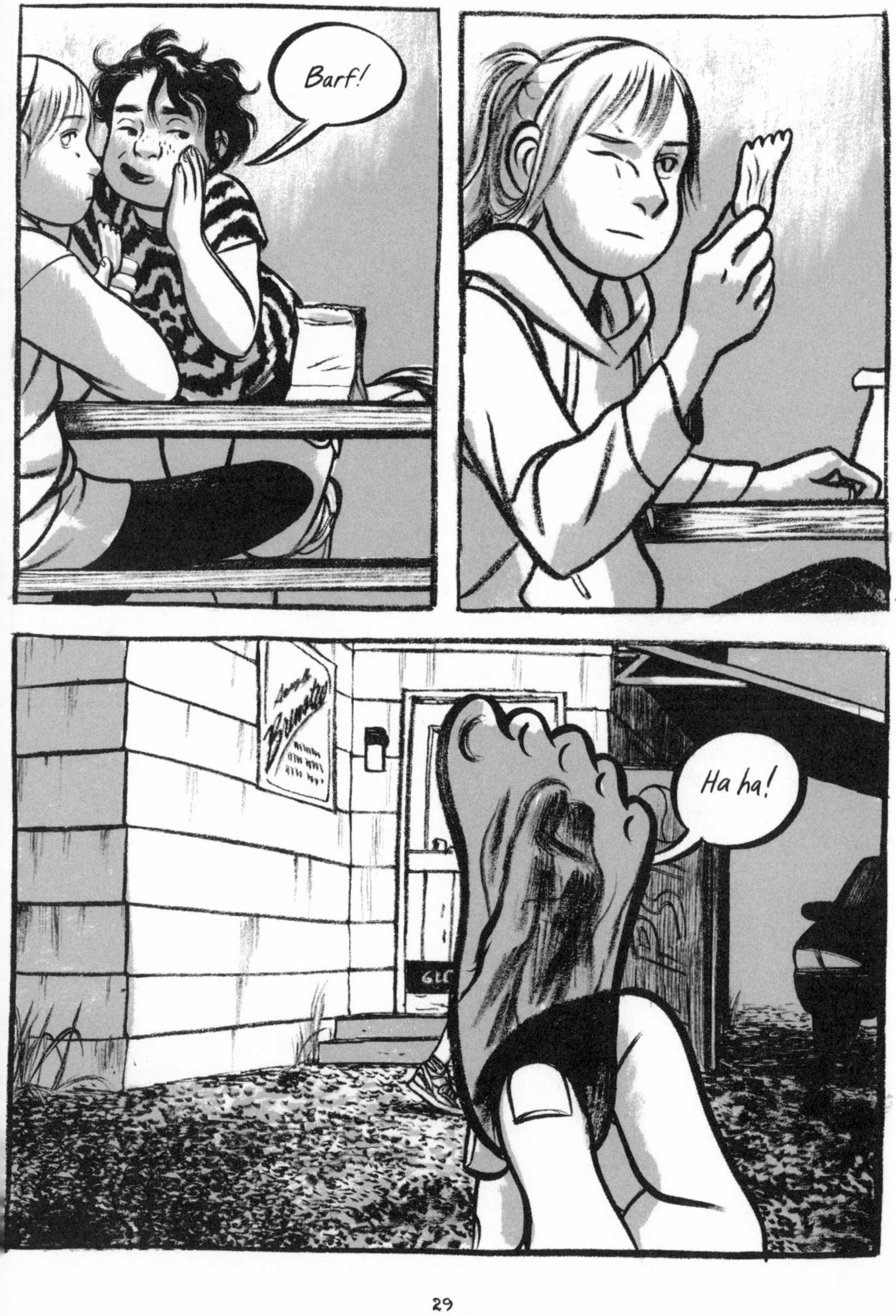
Barf!
Ha ha!

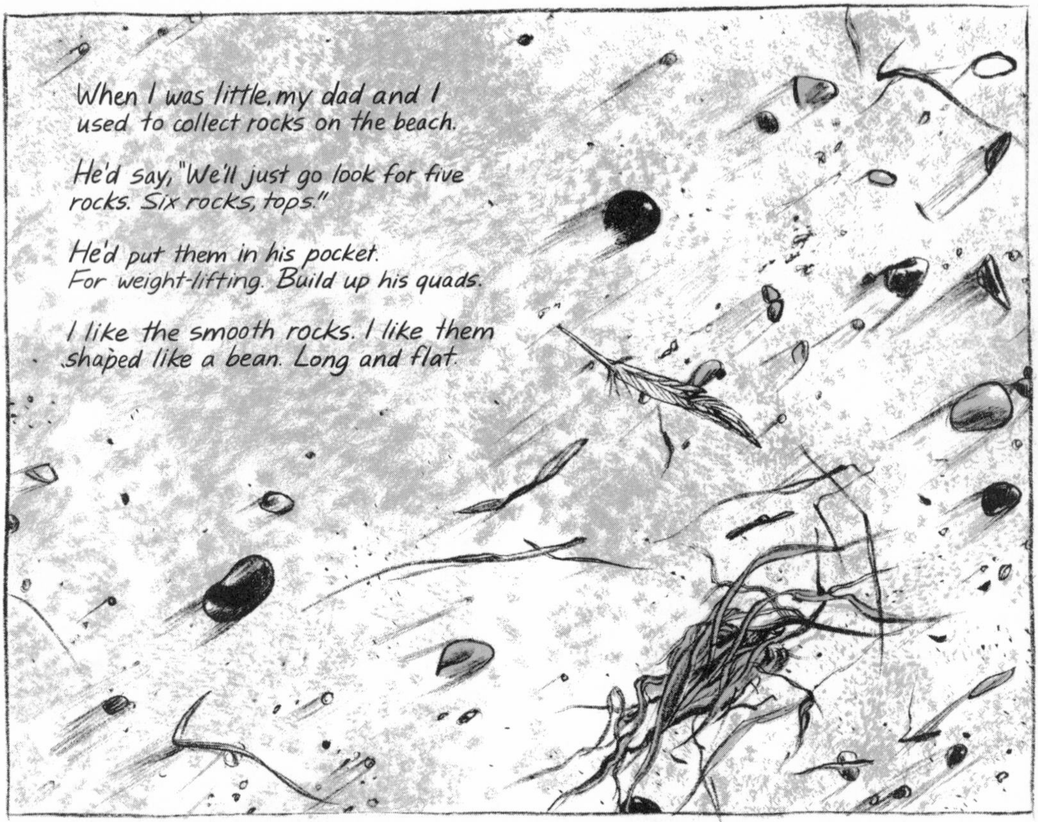
When I was little, my dad and I used to collect rocks on the beach.
He'd say, "We'll just go look for five rocks. Six rocks, tops."
He'd put them in his pocket. For weight-lifting. Build up his quads.
I like the smooth rocks. I like them shaped like a bean. Long and flat.

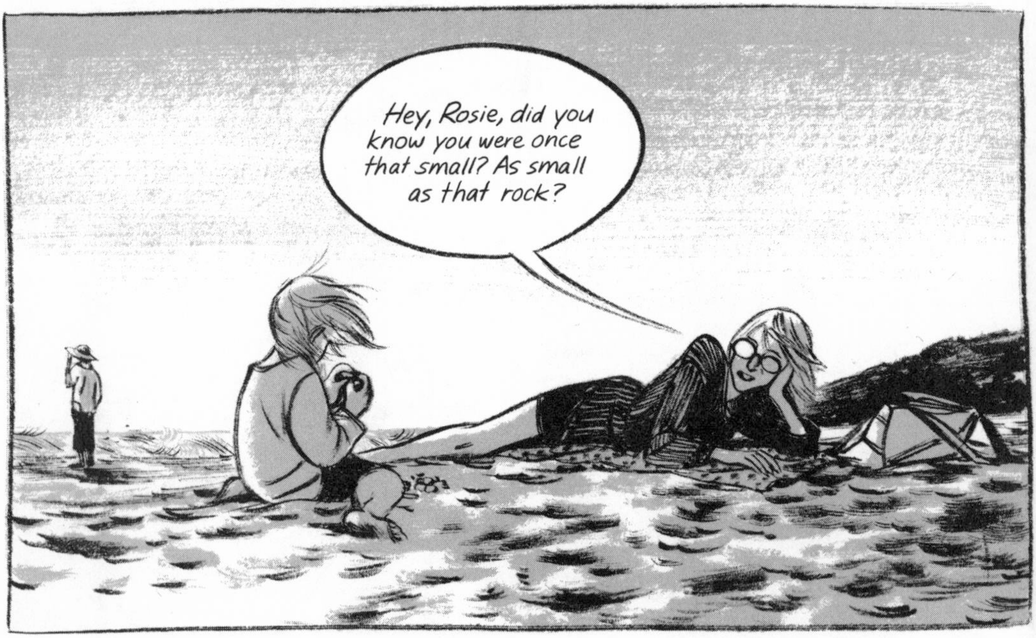
Hey, Rosie, did you know you were once that small? As small as that rock?

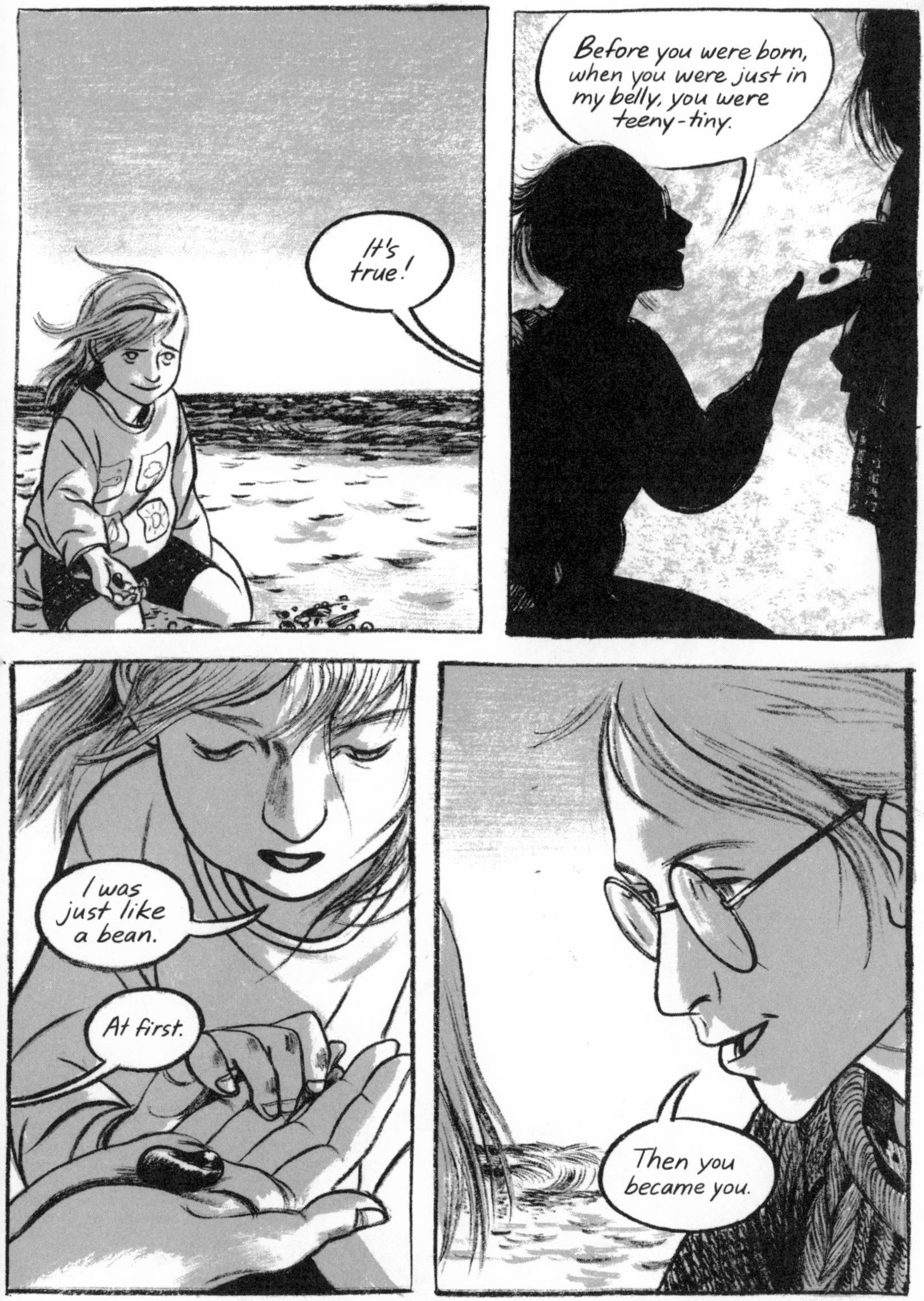
It's true!
Before you were born, when you were just in my belly, you were teeny-tiny.
I was just like a bean.
At first.
Then you became you.

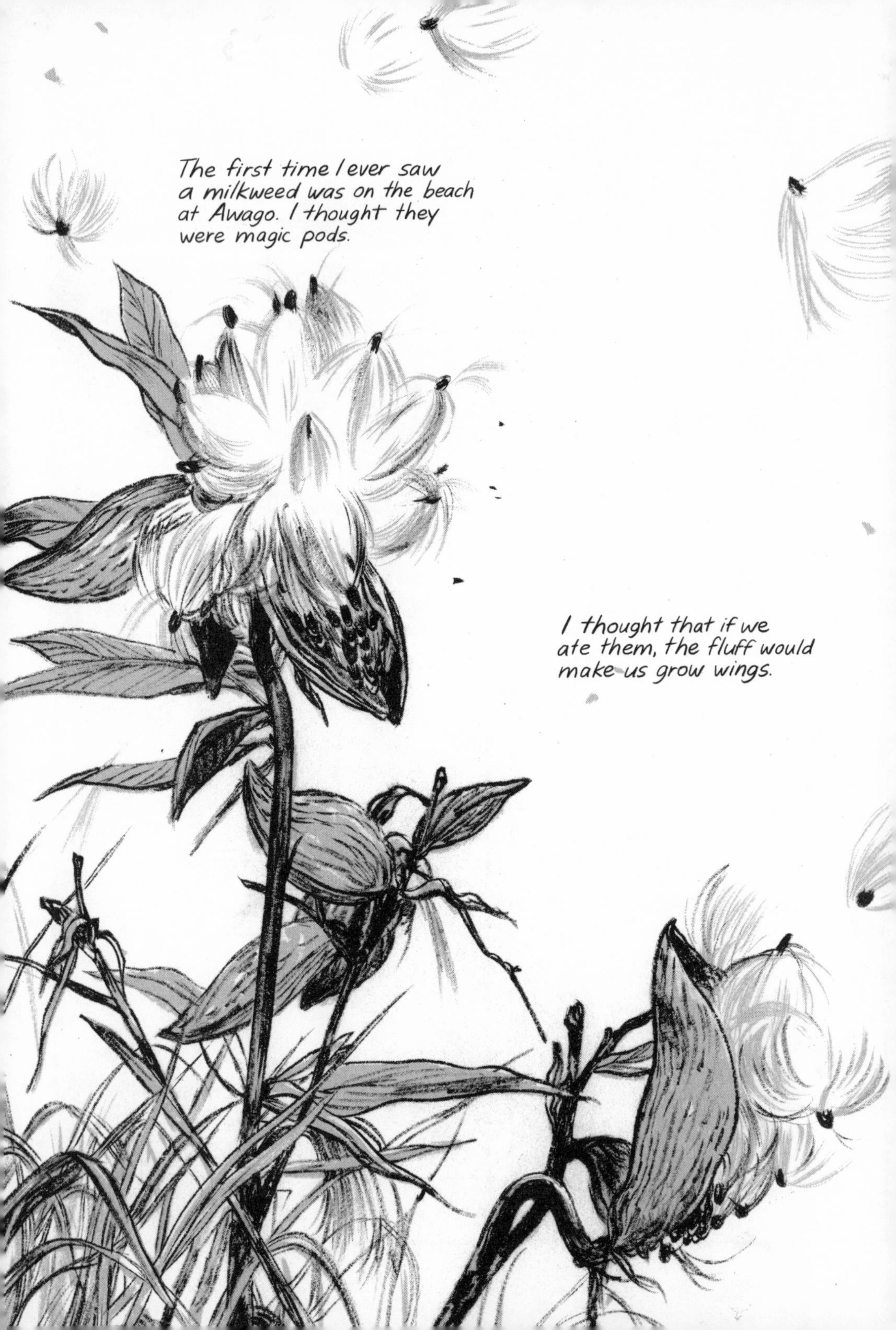
The first time I ever saw a milkweed was on the beach at Awago. I thought they were magic pods.
I thought that if we ate them, the fluff would make us grow wings.

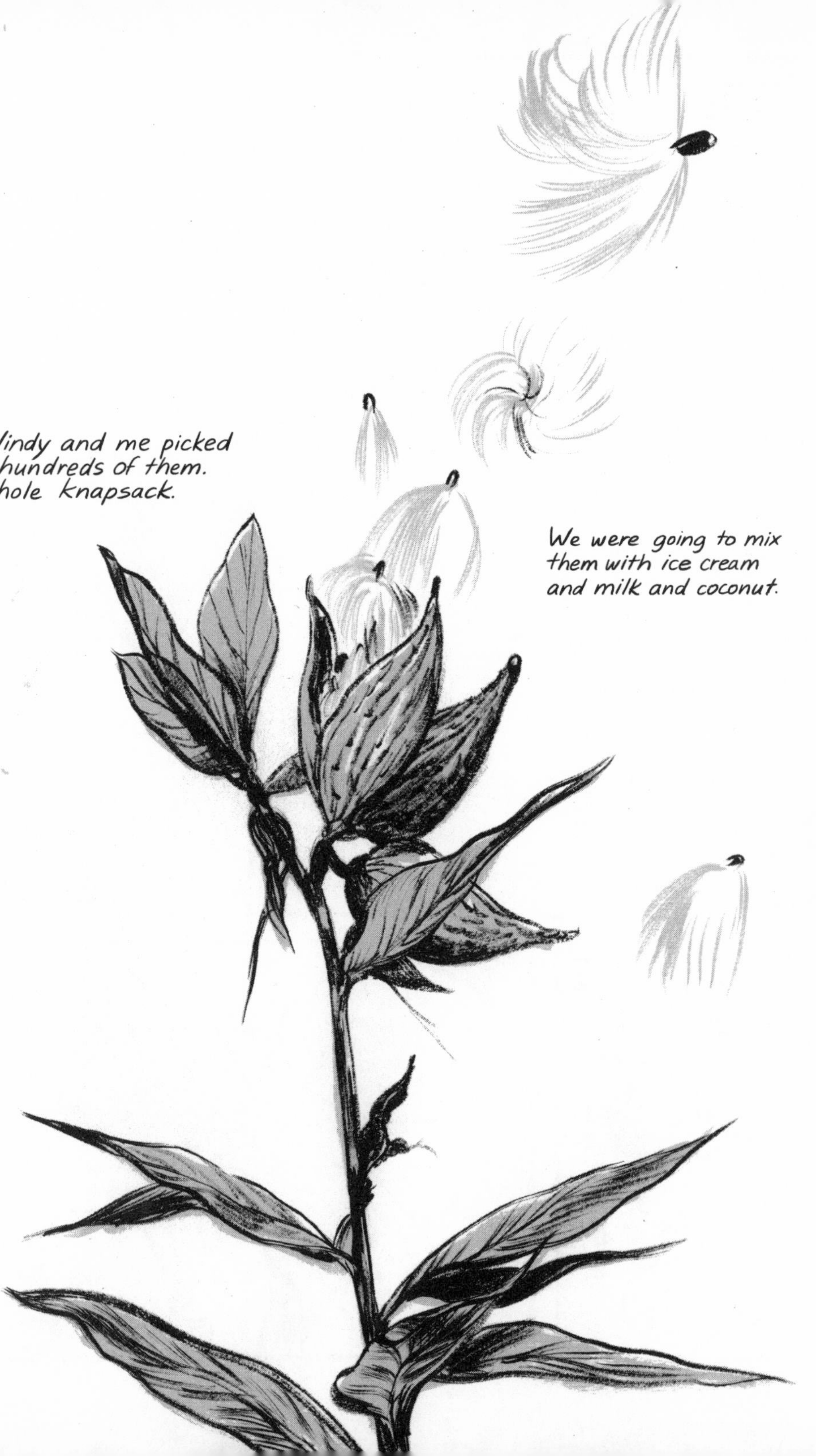
So Windy and me picked like hundreds of them. A whole knapsack.
We were going to mix them with ice cream and milk and coconut.

Then my mom found the knapsack and she told us milkweed is really poisonous.

Now every time she sees milkweeds, Windy makes a choking motion.

I still like picking them and tearing them up, though.

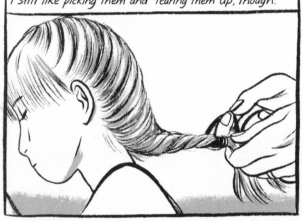

Are you coming?

No... I'll be down, all right? You go ahead.

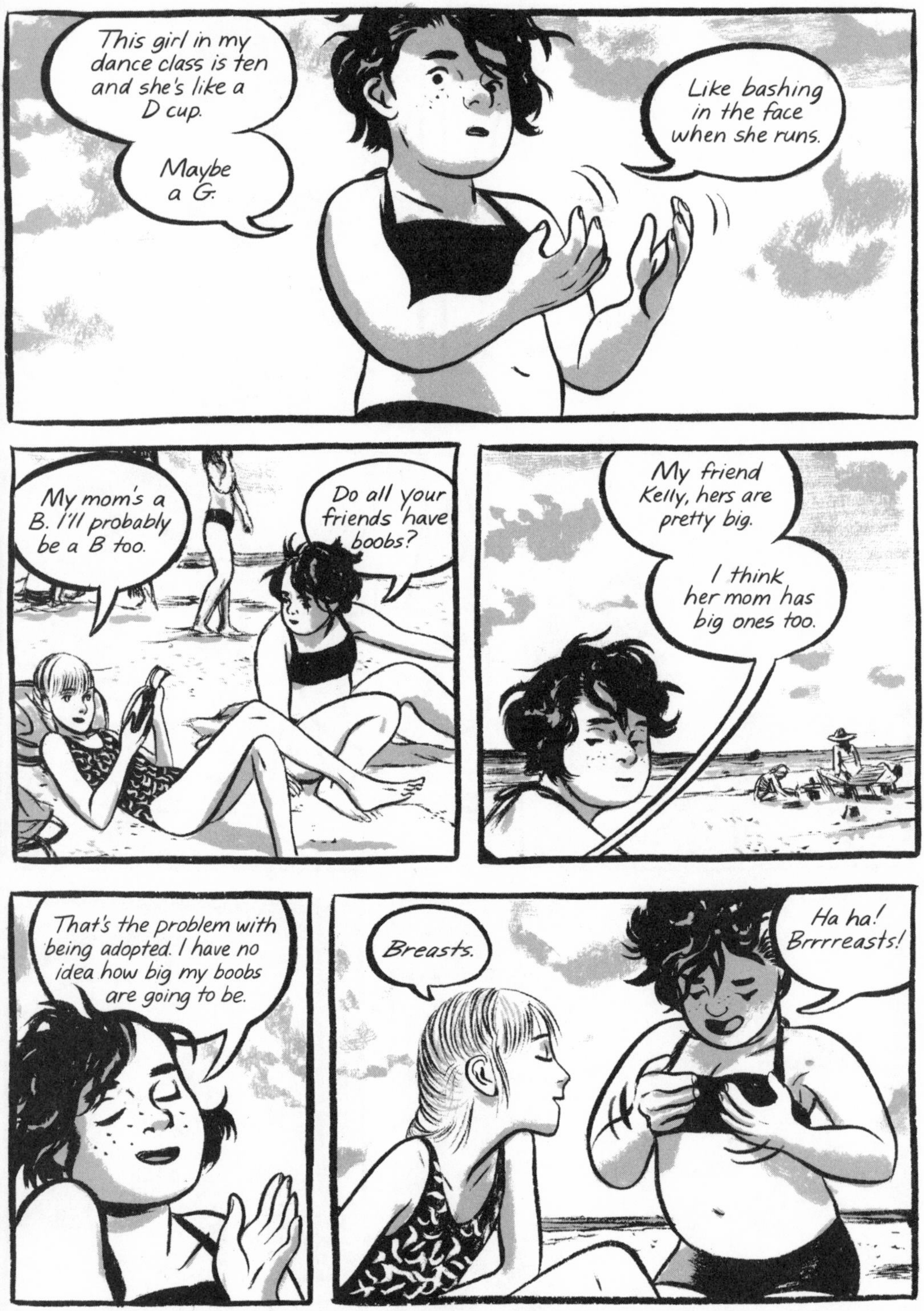
This girl in my dance class is ten and she's like a D cup.
Maybe a G.
Like bashing in the face when she runs.
My mom's a B. I'll probably be a B too.
Do all your friends have boobs?
My friend Kelly, hers are pretty big.
I think her mom has big ones too.
That's the problem with being adopted. I have no idea how big my boobs are going to be.
Breasts.
Ha ha! Brrrreasts!

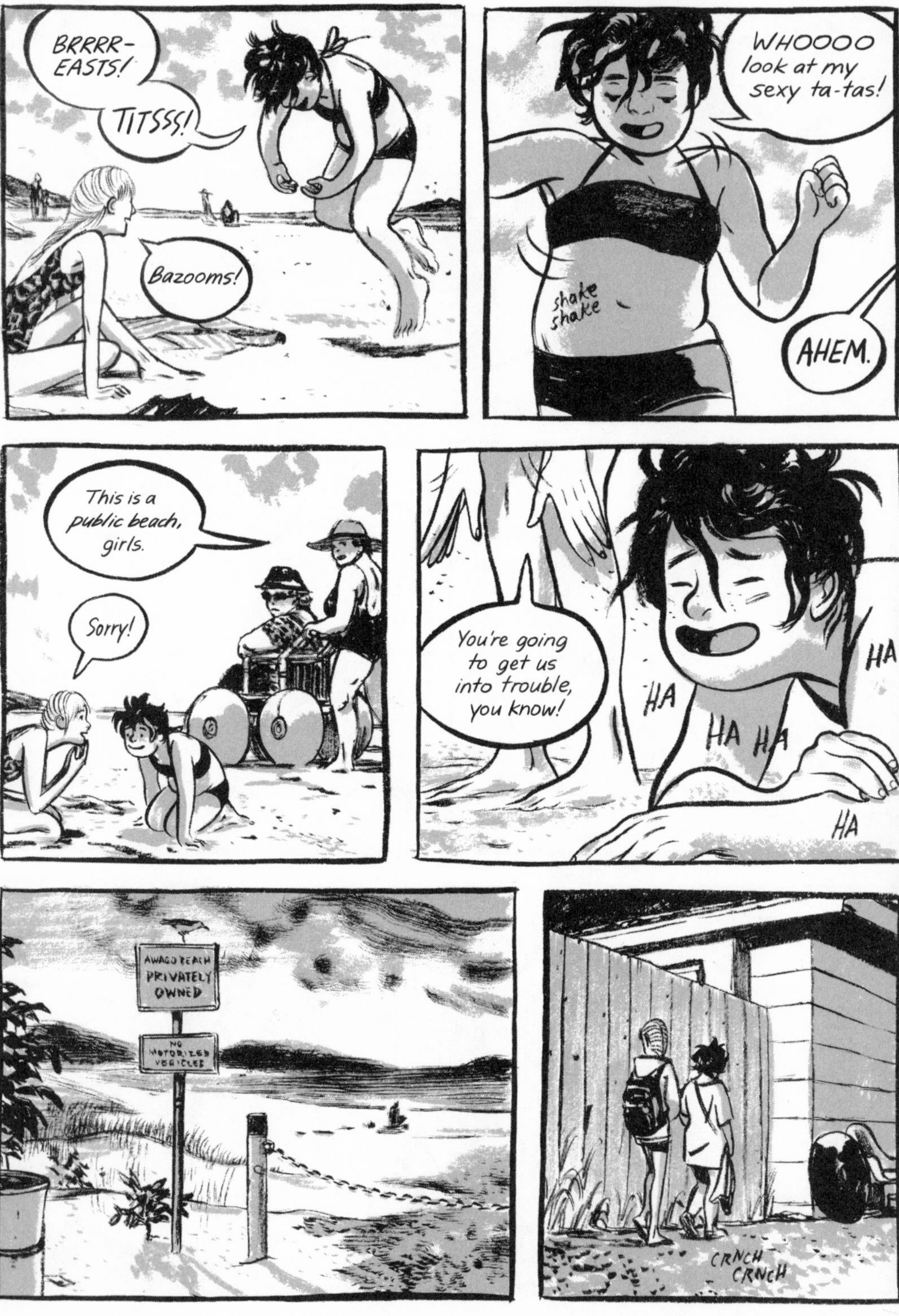
BRRRR-EASTS!
TITSSS!
Bazooms!
WHOOOO look at my sexy ta-tas!
shake shake
AHEM.
This is a public beach, girls.
Sorry!
You're going to get us into trouble, you know!
HA HA HA HA HA HA
AWAGO BEACH PRIVATELY OWNED
NO MOTORIZED VEHICLES
CRNCH CRNCH

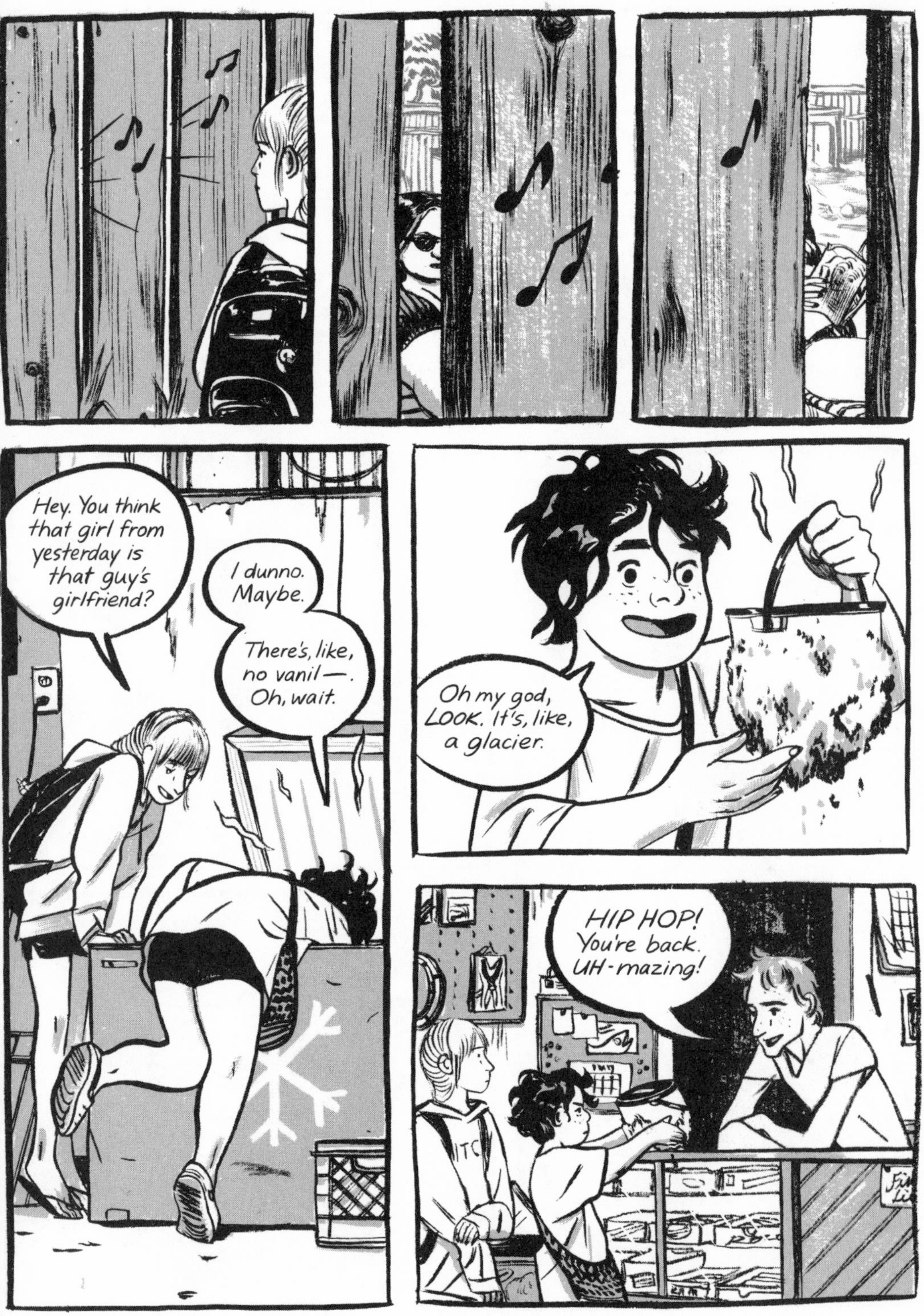
Hey. You think that girl from yesterday is that guy's girlfriend?
I dunno. Maybe.
There's, like, no vanil—. Oh, wait.
Oh my god, LOOK. It's, like, a glacier.
HIP HOP! You're back. UH-mazing!

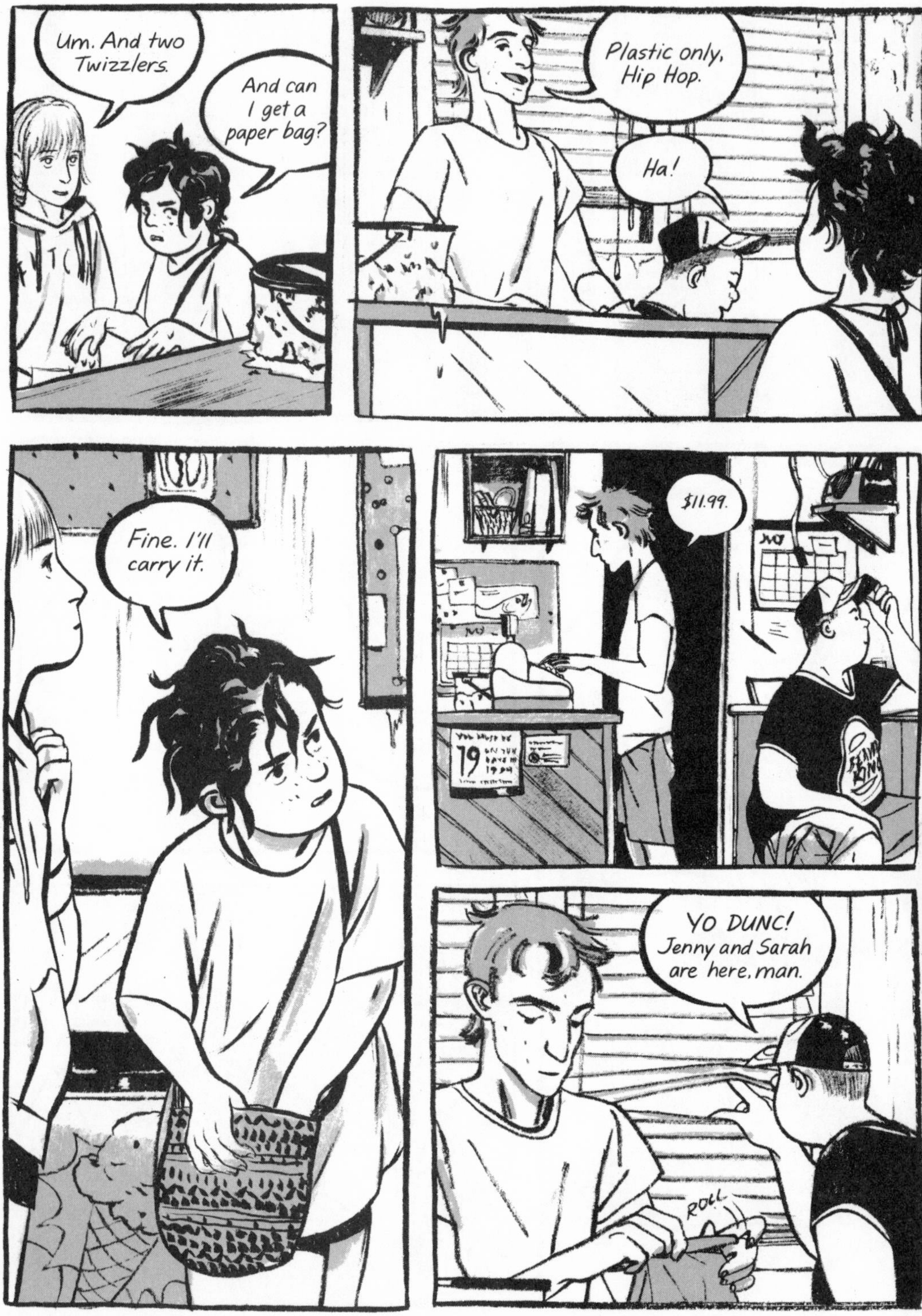
Um. And two Twizzlers.
And can I get a paper bag?
Plastic only, Hip Hop.
Ha!
Fine. I'll carry it.
$11.99.
YO DUNC! Jenny and Sarah are here, man.
ROLL

Yo
think y
brother
ID o

And
twoooo
Twizzlers.

DING
DING!

Okay, sluts,
let's go.

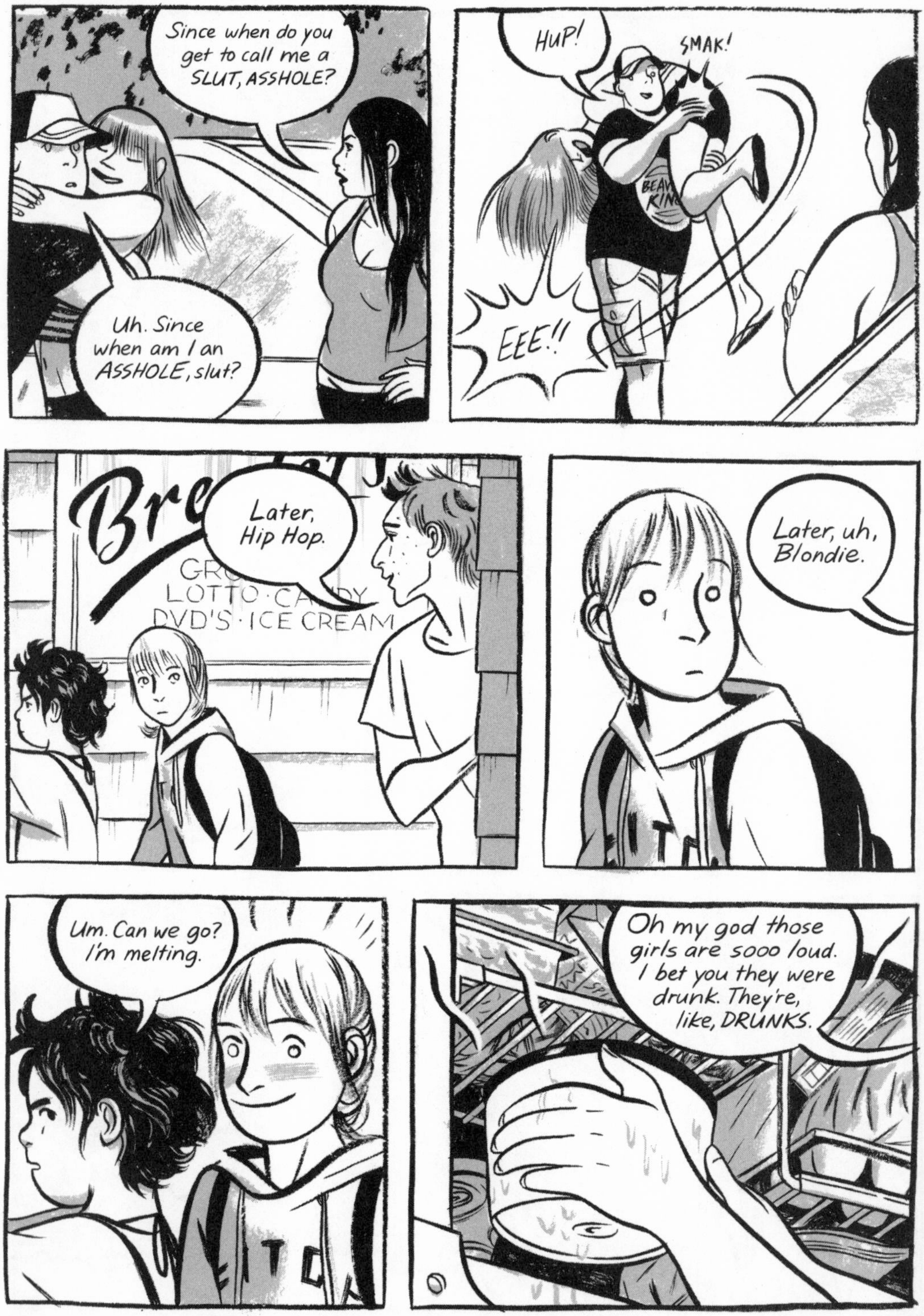
Since when do you get to call me a SLUT, ASSHOLE?
Uh. Since when am I an ASSHOLE, slut?
HUP!
SMAK!
EEE!!
Later, Hip Hop.
LOTTO · CANDY
DVD'S · ICE CREAM
Later, uh, Blondie.
Um. Can we go? I'm melting.
Oh my god those girls are sooo loud. I bet you they were drunk. They're, like, DRUNKS.

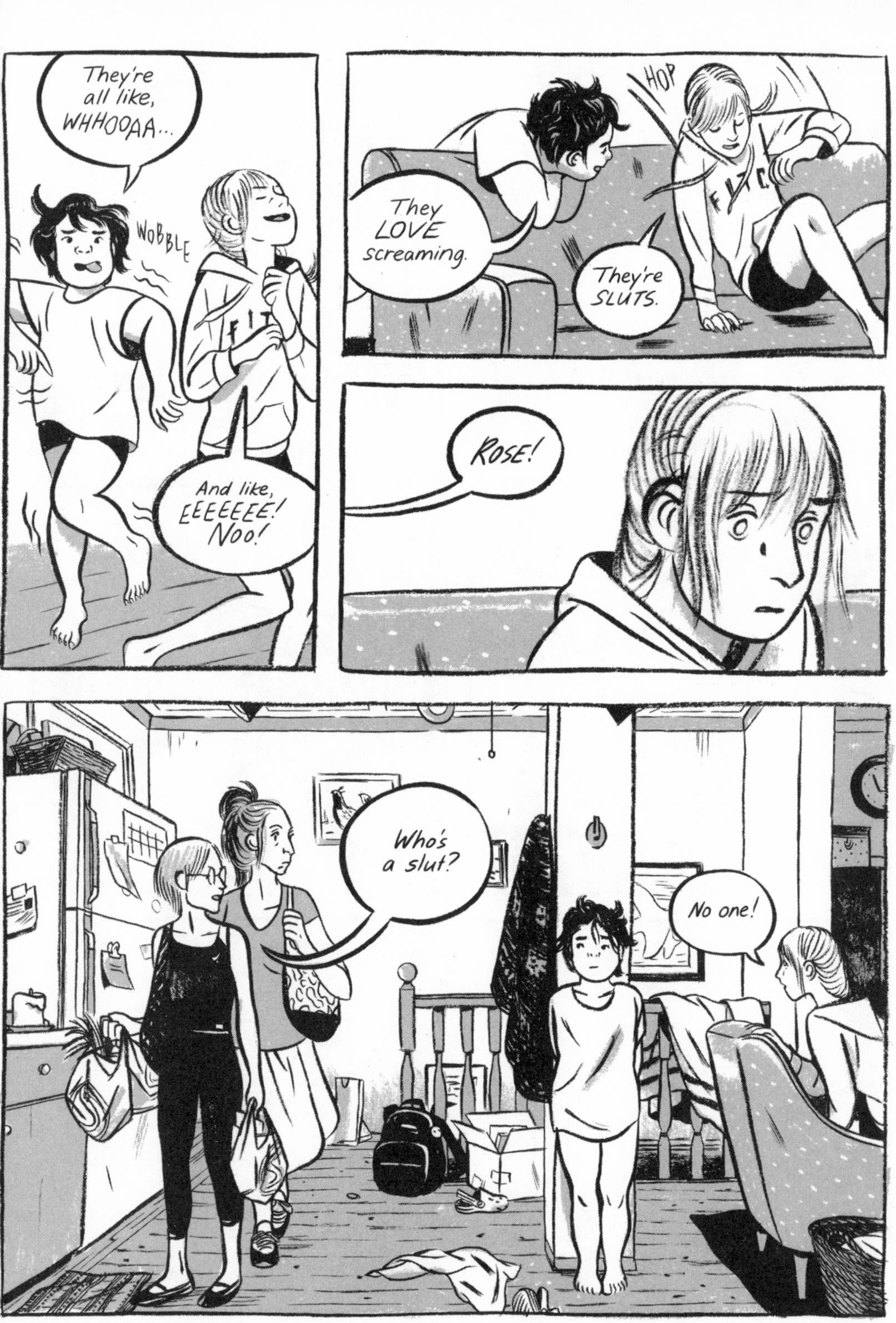
They're all like, WHHOOAA...
WOBBLE
And like, EEEEEEE! Noo!
HOP
They LOVE screaming.
They're SLUTS.
ROSE!
Who's a slut?
No one!

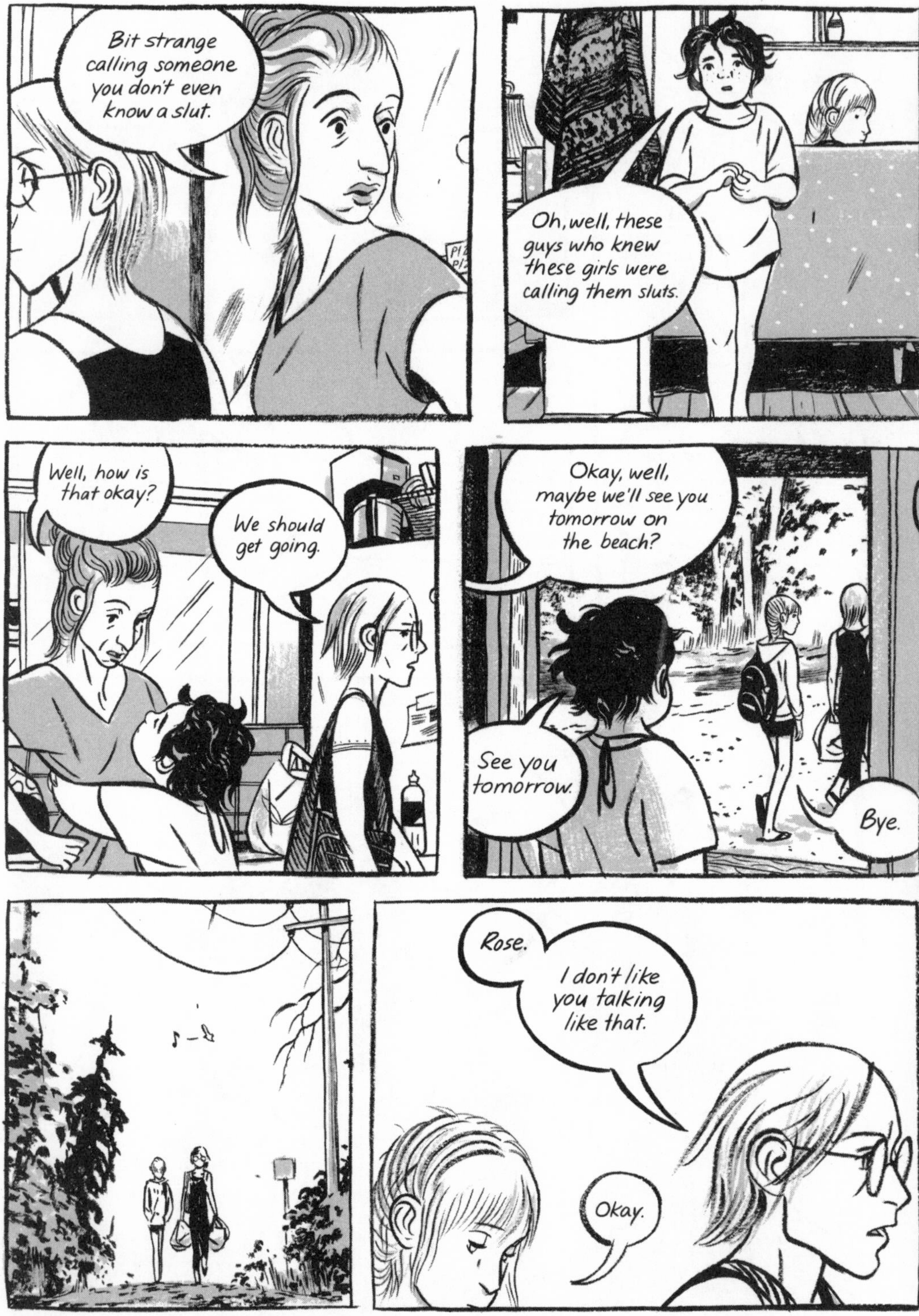
Bit strange calling someone you don't even know a slut.
Oh, well, these guys who knew these girls were calling them sluts.
Well, how is that okay?
We should get going.
Okay, well, maybe we'll see you tomorrow on the beach?
See you tomorrow.
Bye.
Rose.
I don't like you talking like that.
Okay.

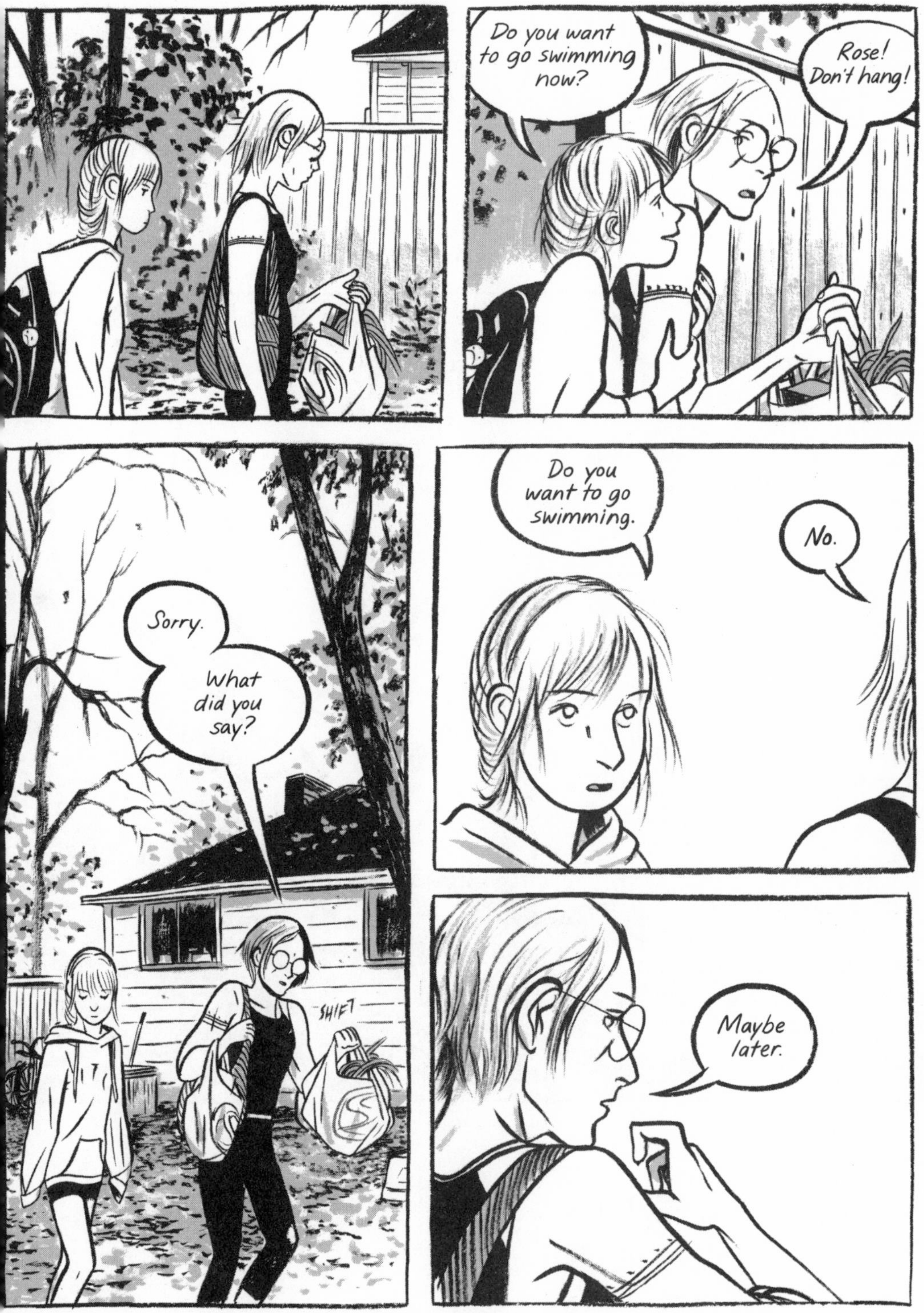
Do you want to go swimming now?
Rose! Don't hang!
Sorry.
What did you say?
SHIFT
Do you want to go swimming.
No.
Maybe later.

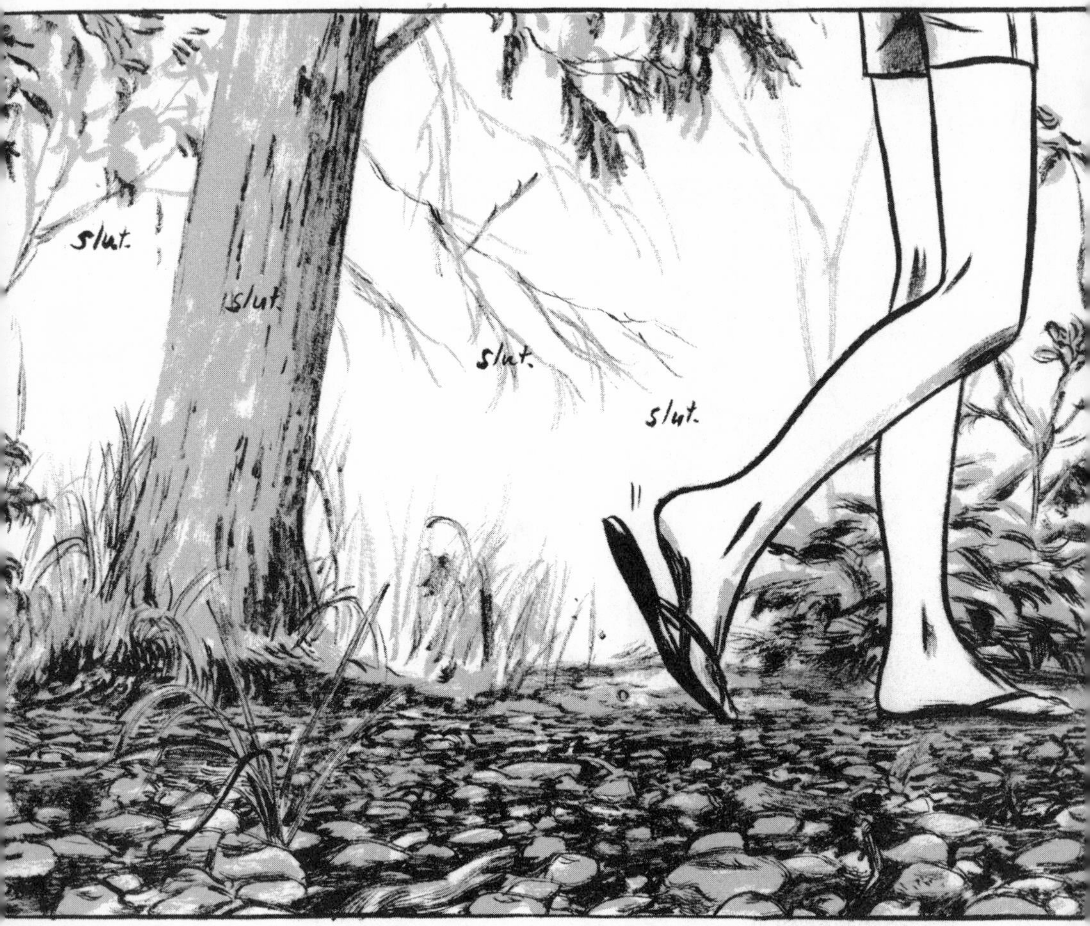
slut.
slut.
slut.
slut.

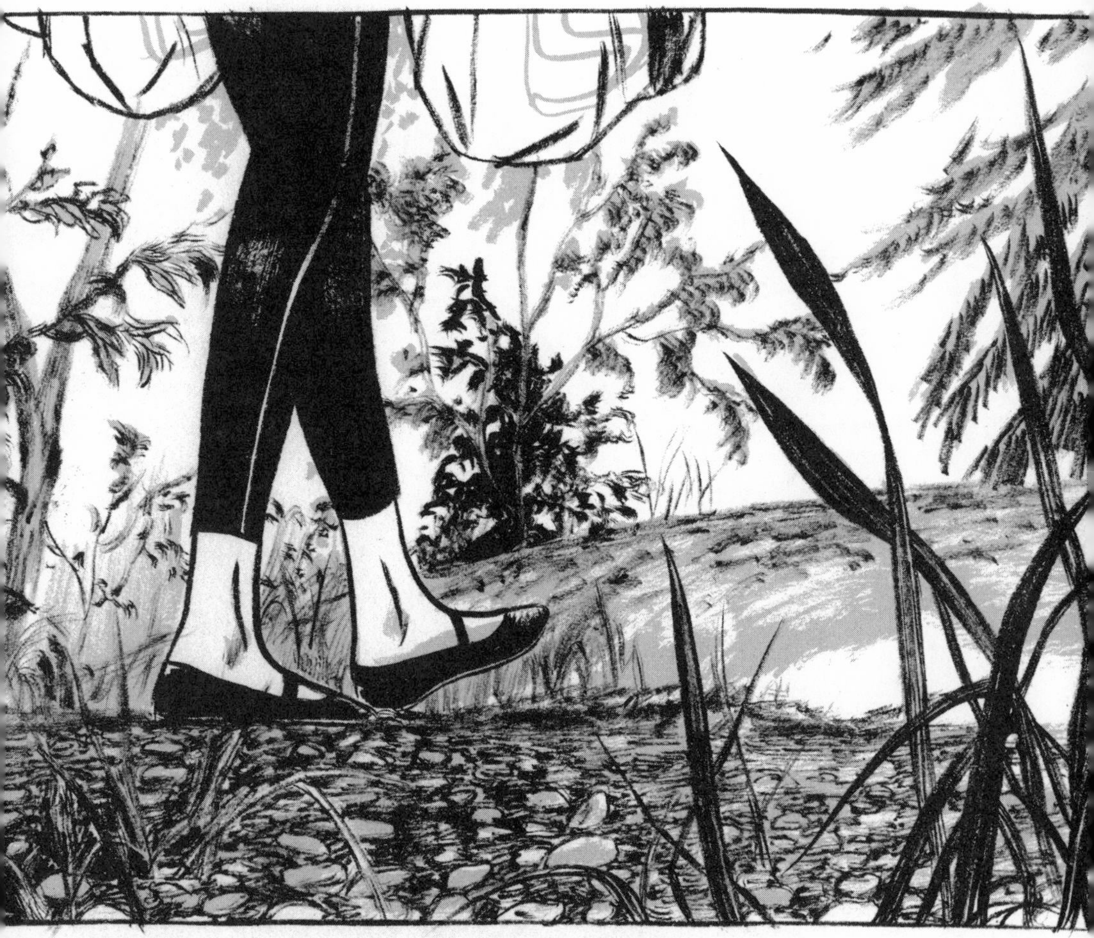

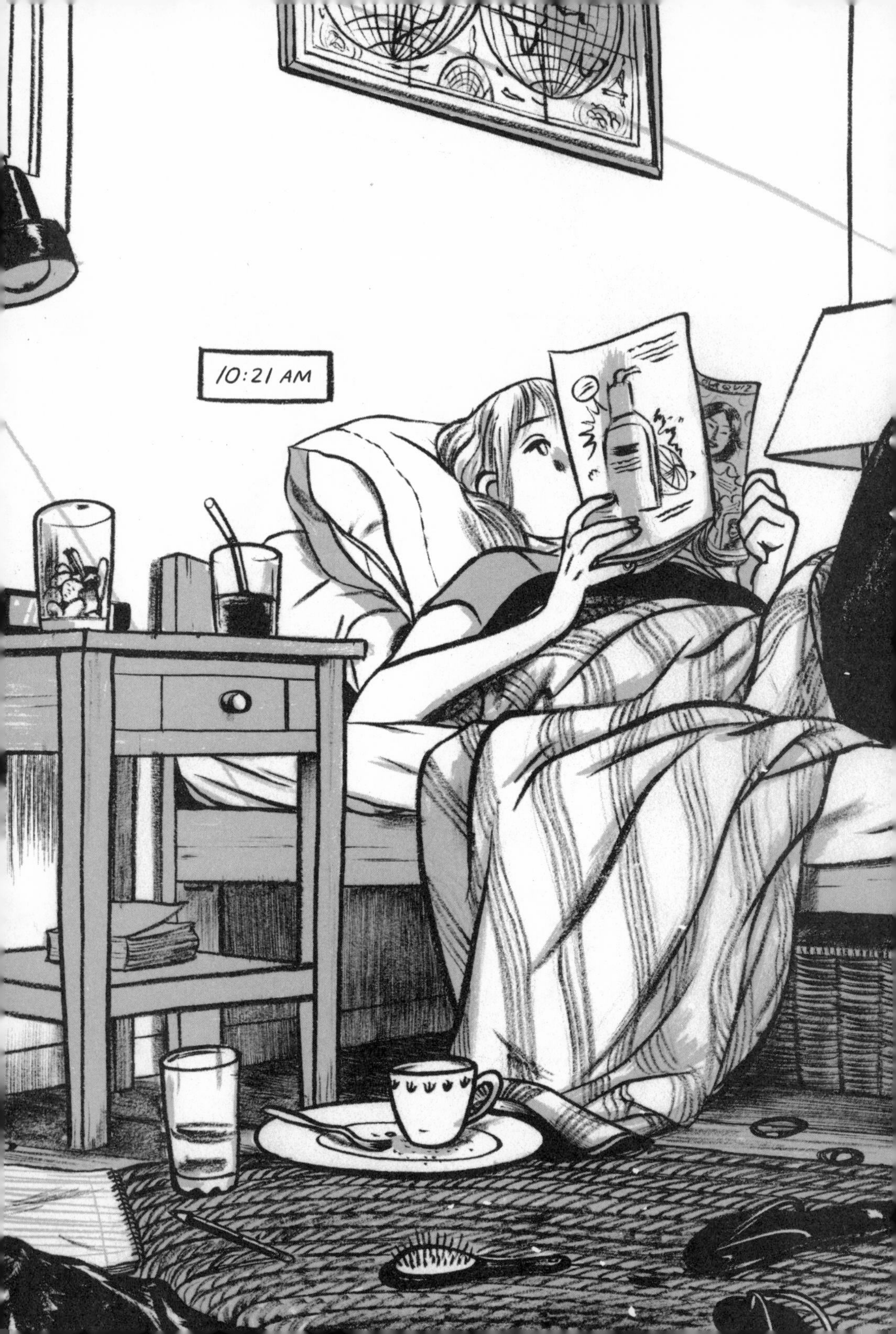
10:21 AM

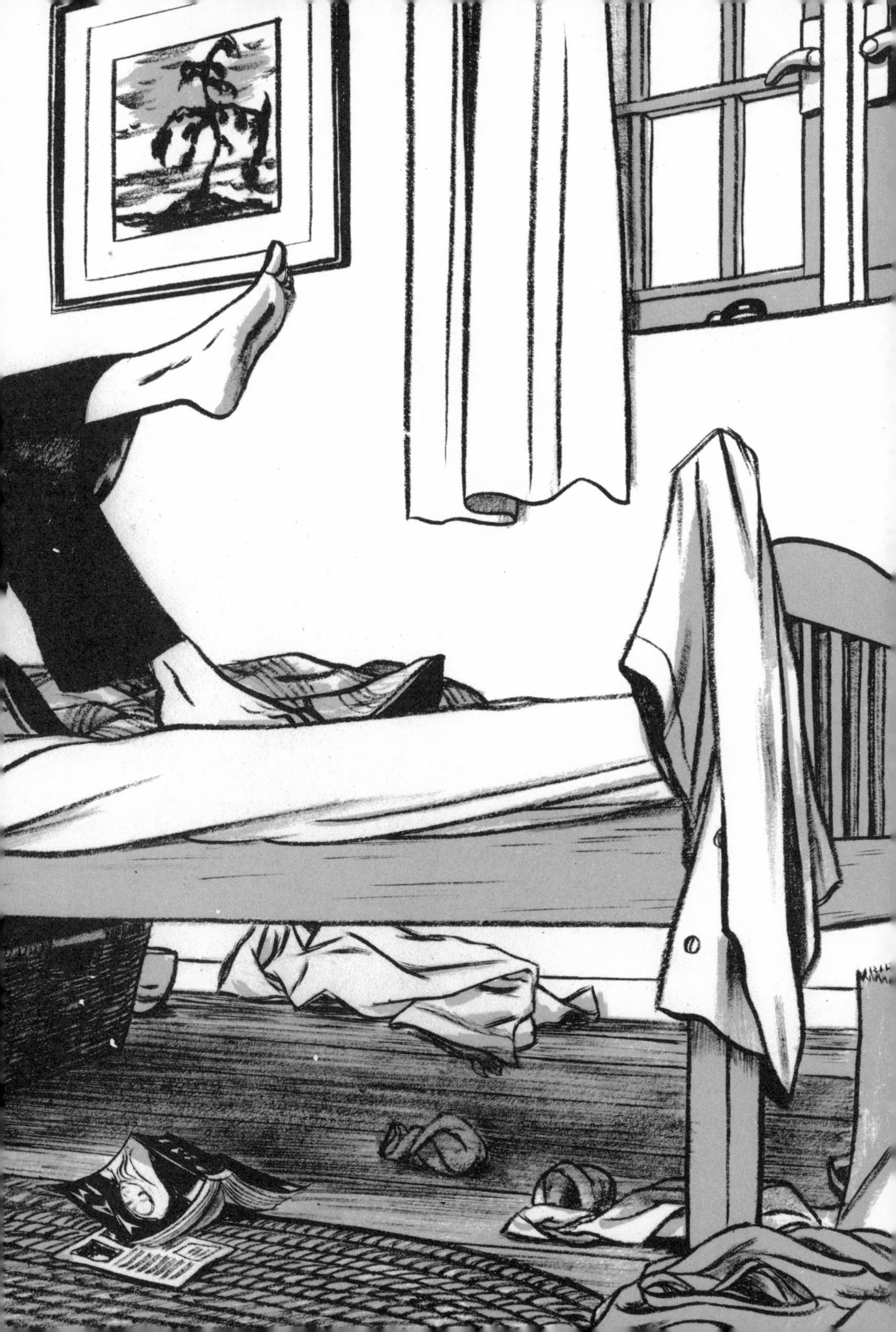

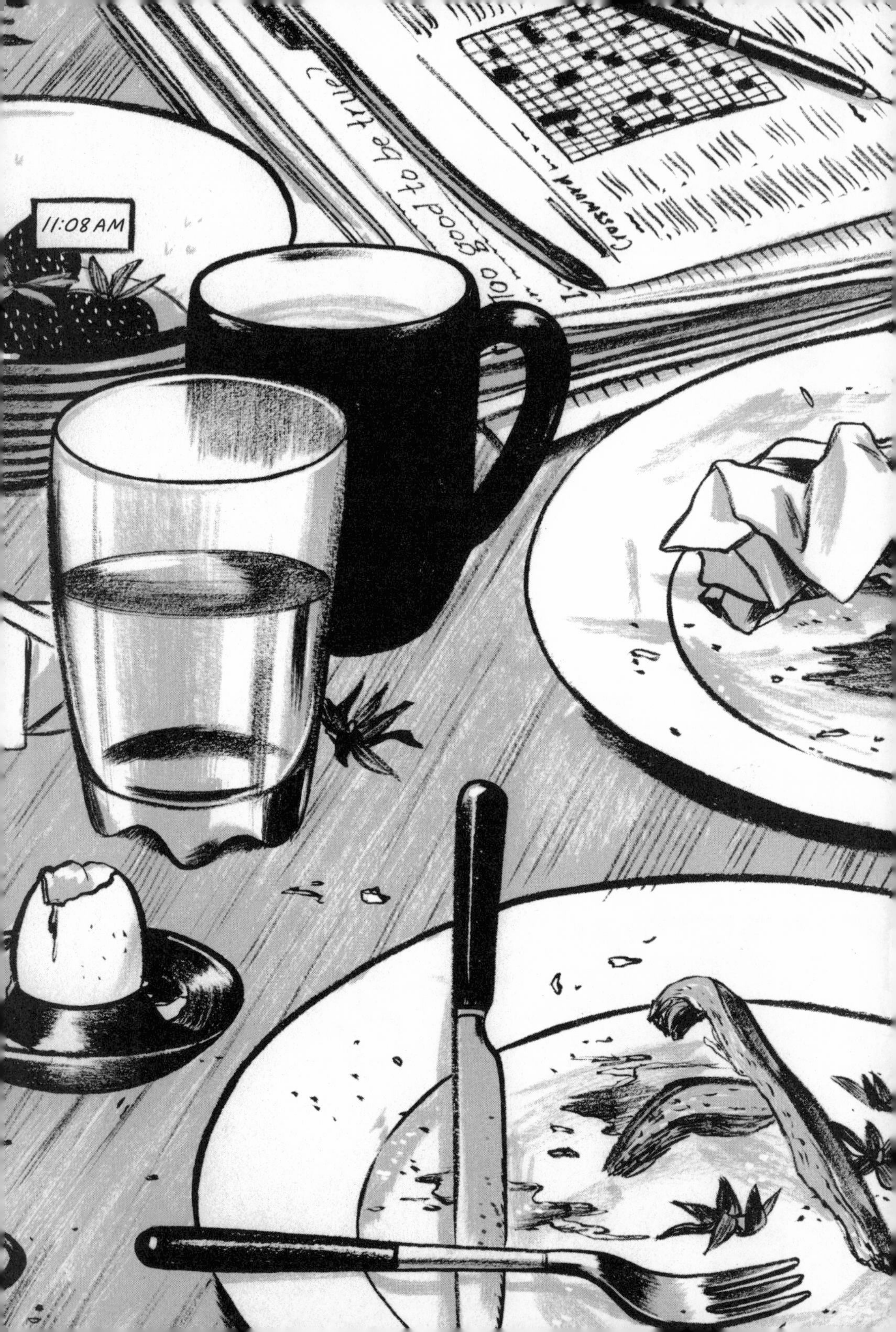
11:08 AM
Too Good to be true
Crossword

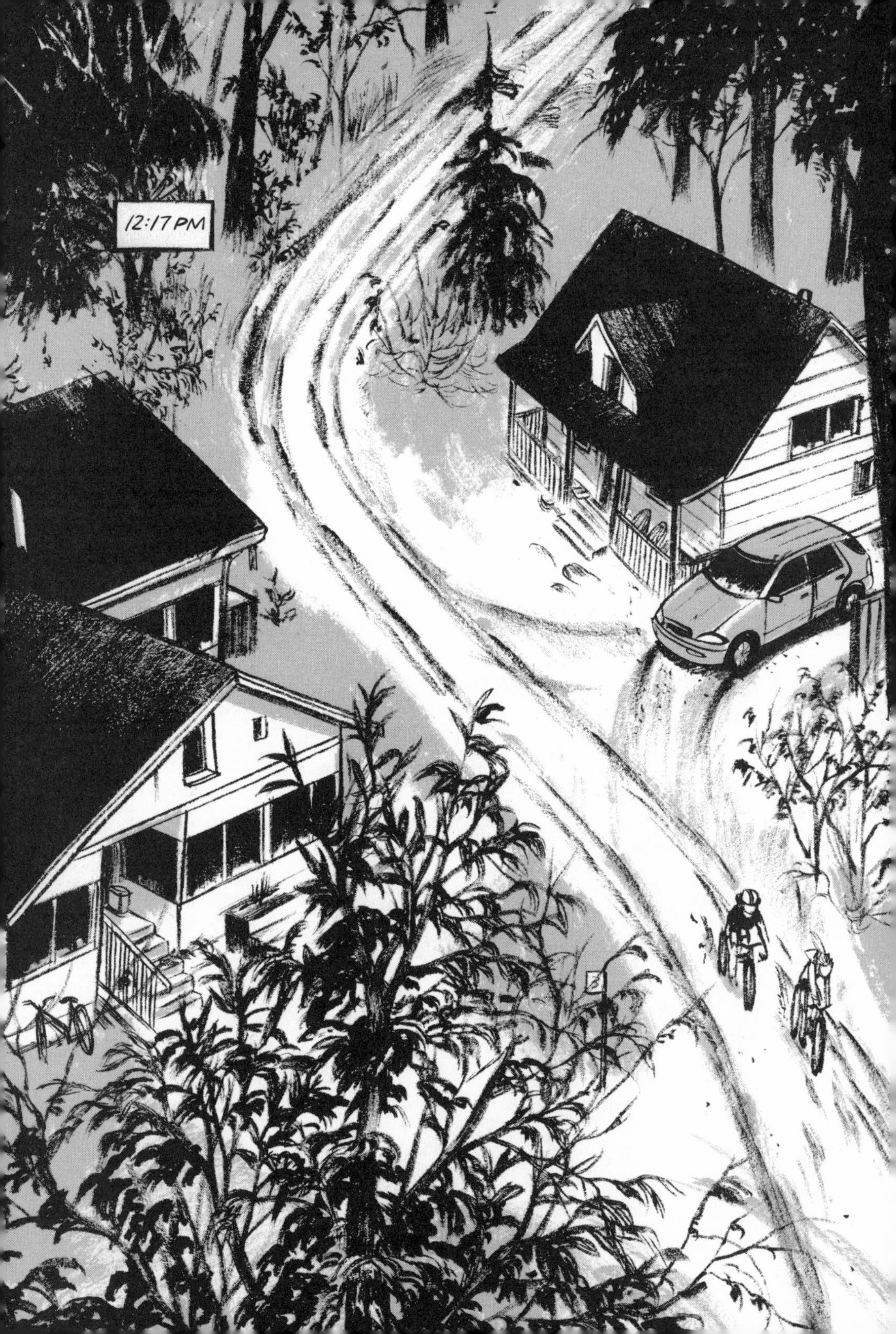
12:17 PM

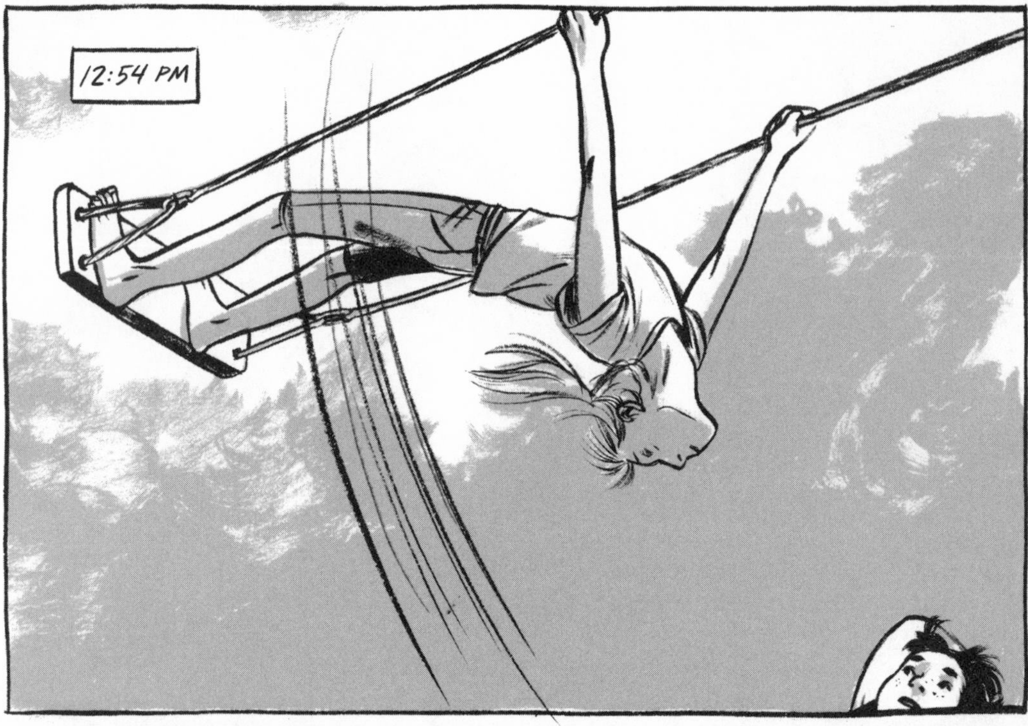
12:54 PM

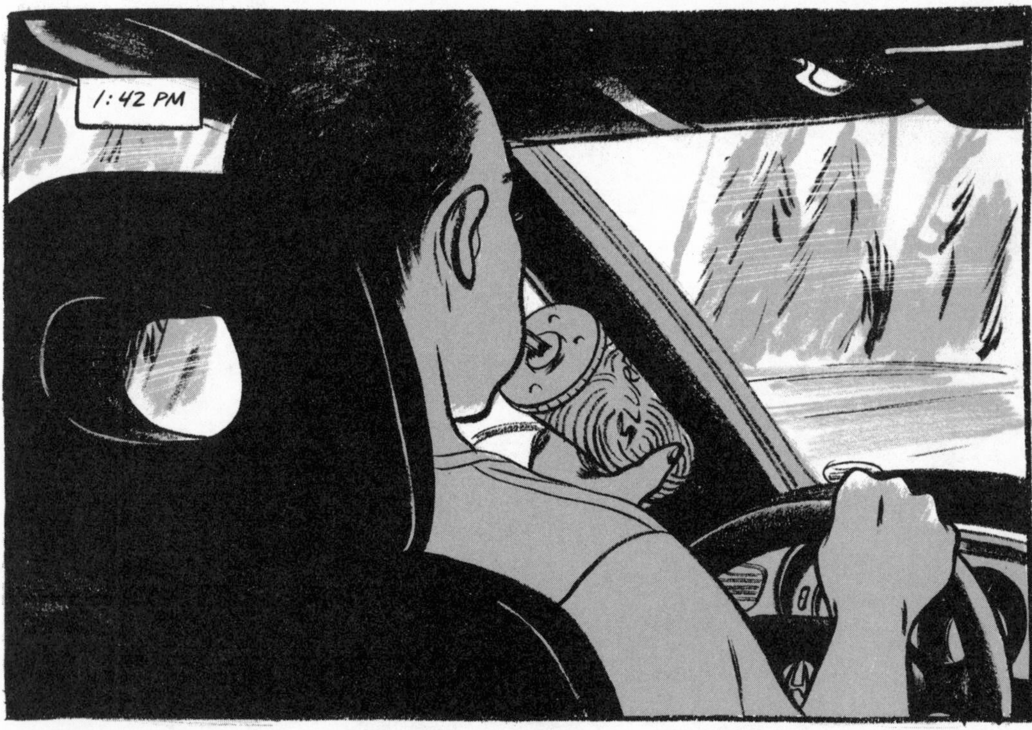
1:42 PM

2:12 PM

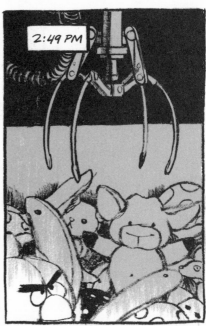

2:49 PM

3:22 PM

3:41 PM

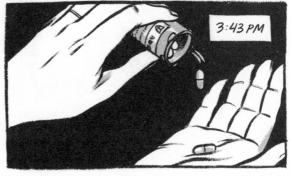

3:43 PM

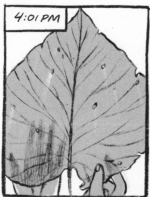
4:01 PM

4:37 PM

KTCH

5:02 PM

5:16 PM

5:15 PM

SPLASH!

5:46 PM

Facebook

6:11 PM

RIP

6:25 PM

6:30 PM

SMACK

6:47 PM

FWOOMP!

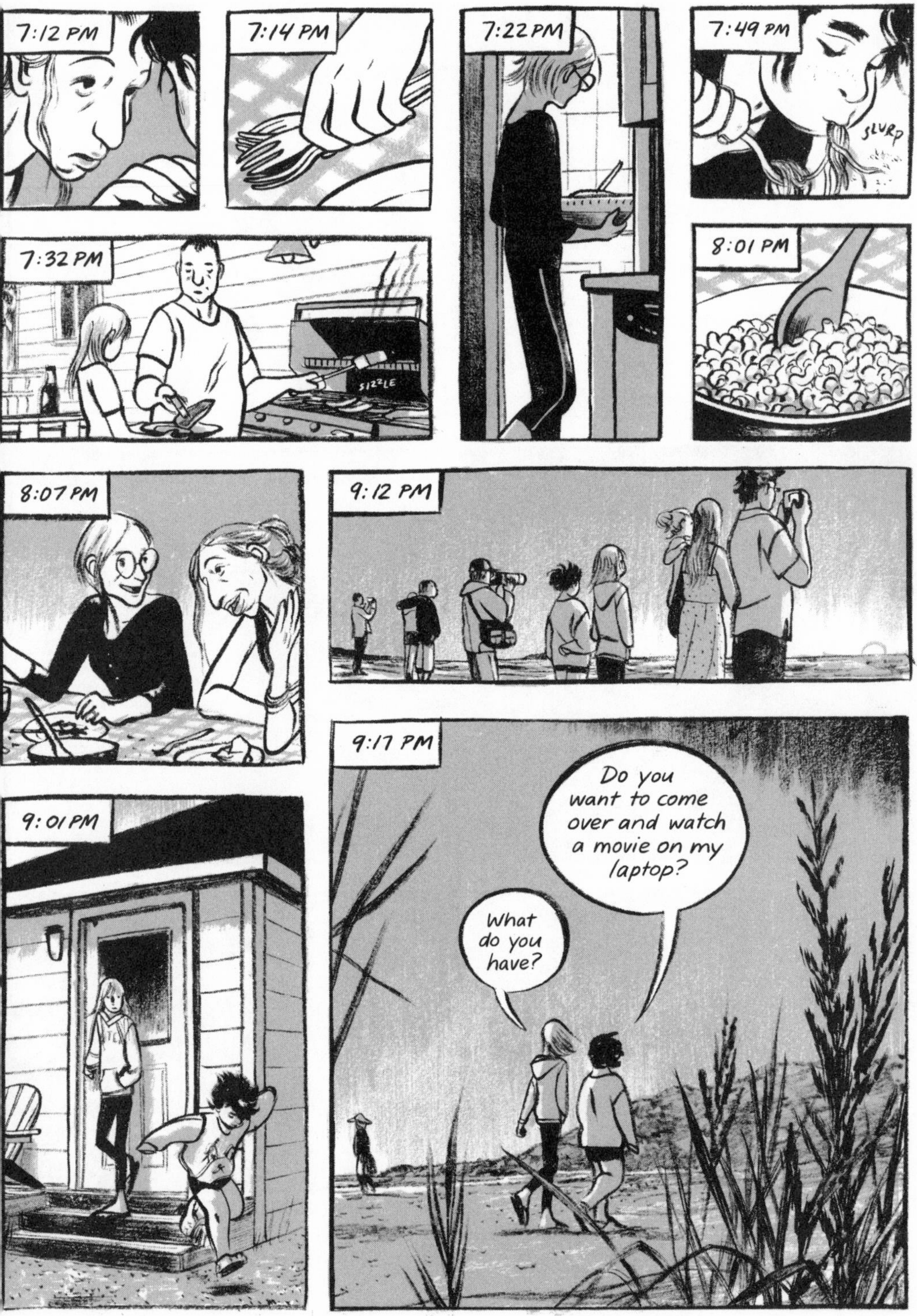
7:12 PM
7:14 PM
7:22 PM
7:49 PM
SLURP
7:32 PM
SIZZLE
8:01 PM
8:07 PM
9:12 PM
9:01 PM
9:17 PM
Do you want to come over and watch a movie on my laptop?
What do you have?

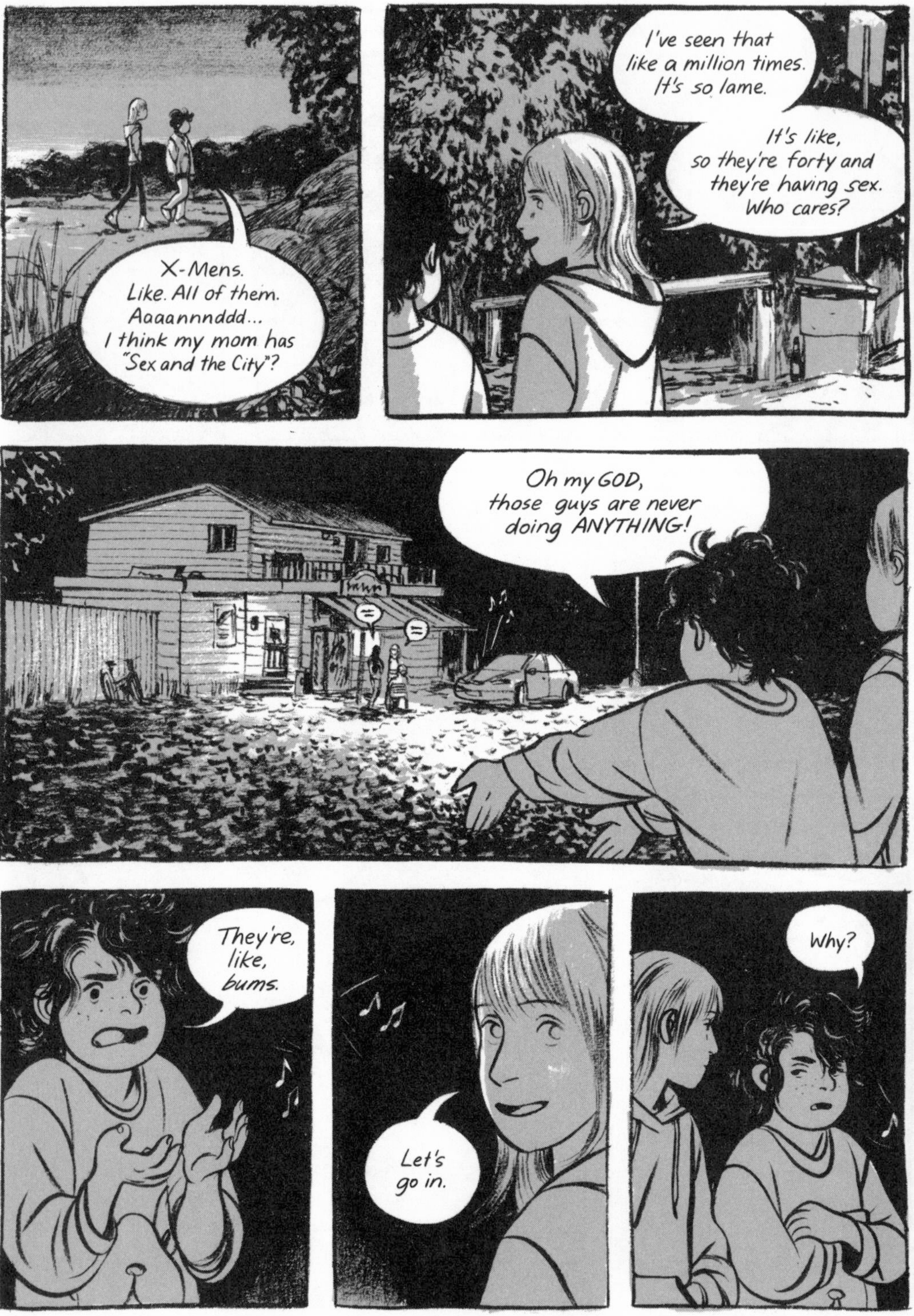
X-Mens.
Like. All of them.
Aaaannnddd...
I think my mom has "Sex and the City"?
I've seen that like a million times. It's so lame.
It's like, so they're forty and they're having sex. Who cares?
Oh my GOD, those guys are never doing ANYTHING!
They're, like, bums.
Let's go in.
Why?

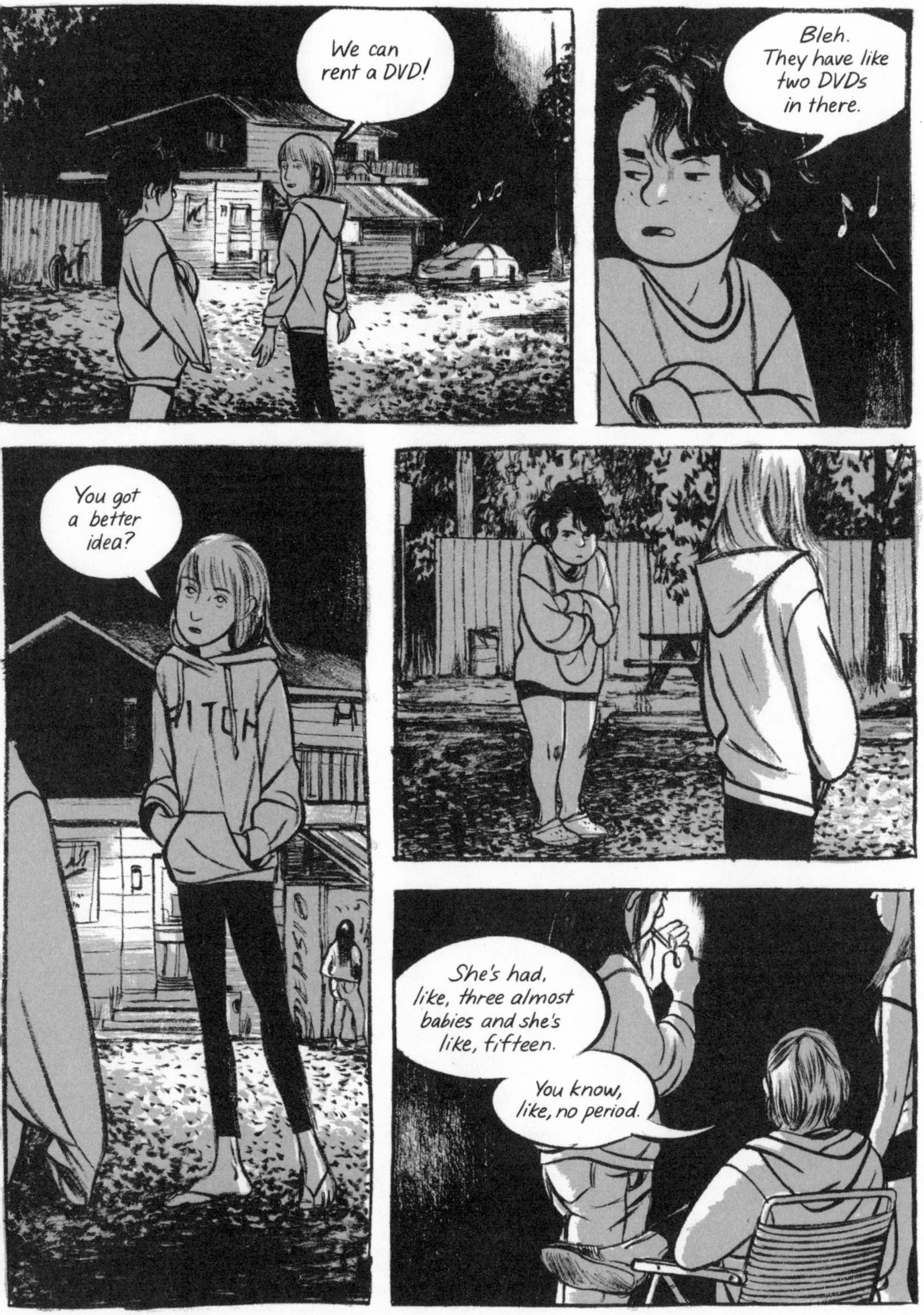
We can rent a DVD!
Bleh. They have like two DVDs in there.
You got a better idea?
She's had, like, three almost babies and she's like, fifteen.
You know, like, no period.

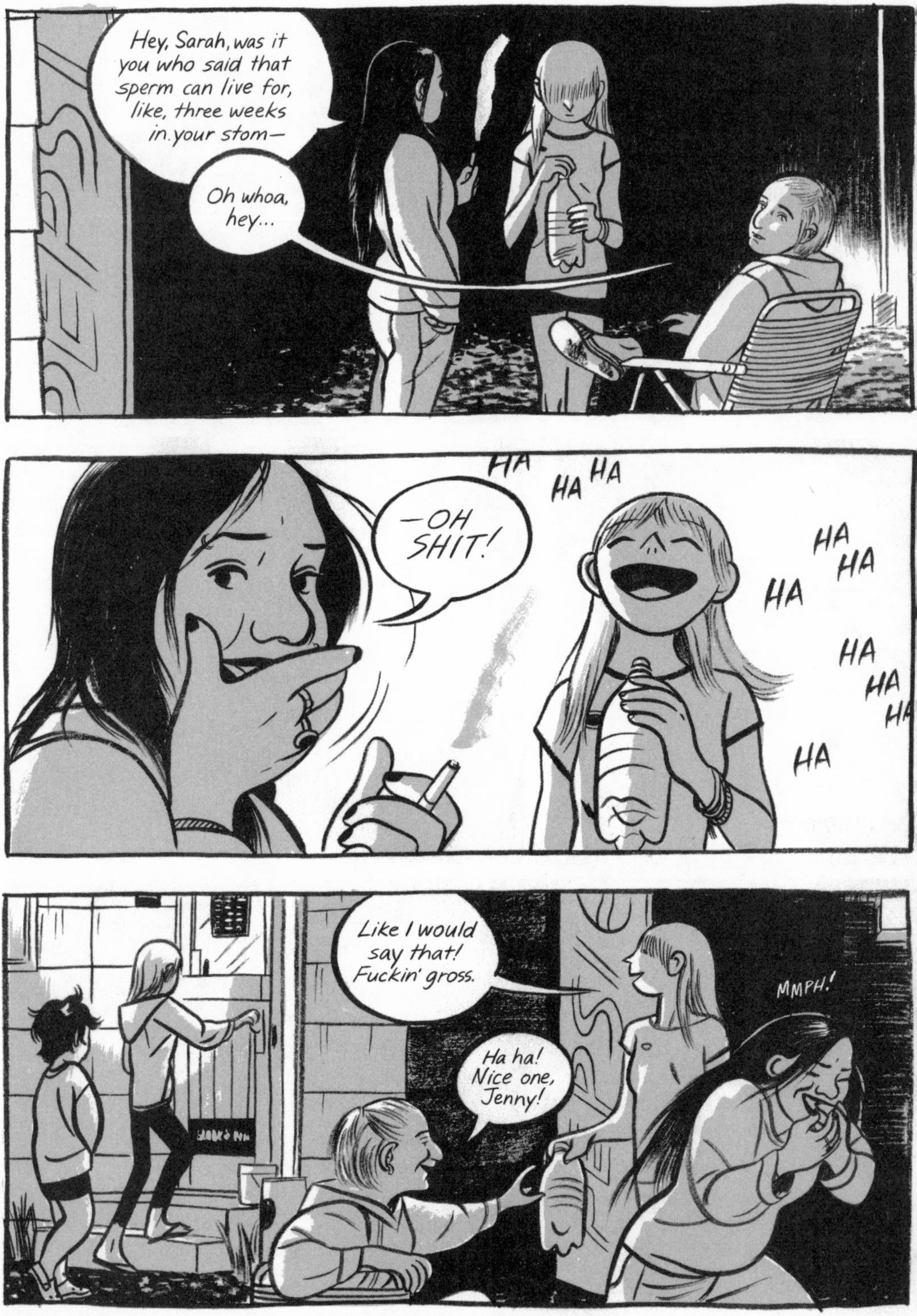
Hey, Sarah, was it you who said that sperm can live for, like, three weeks in your stom—
Oh whoa, hey...
—OH SHIT!
HA HA HA
HA HA HA
HA HA HA
HA
Like I would say that! Fuckin' gross.
Ha ha! Nice one, Jenny!
MMPH!

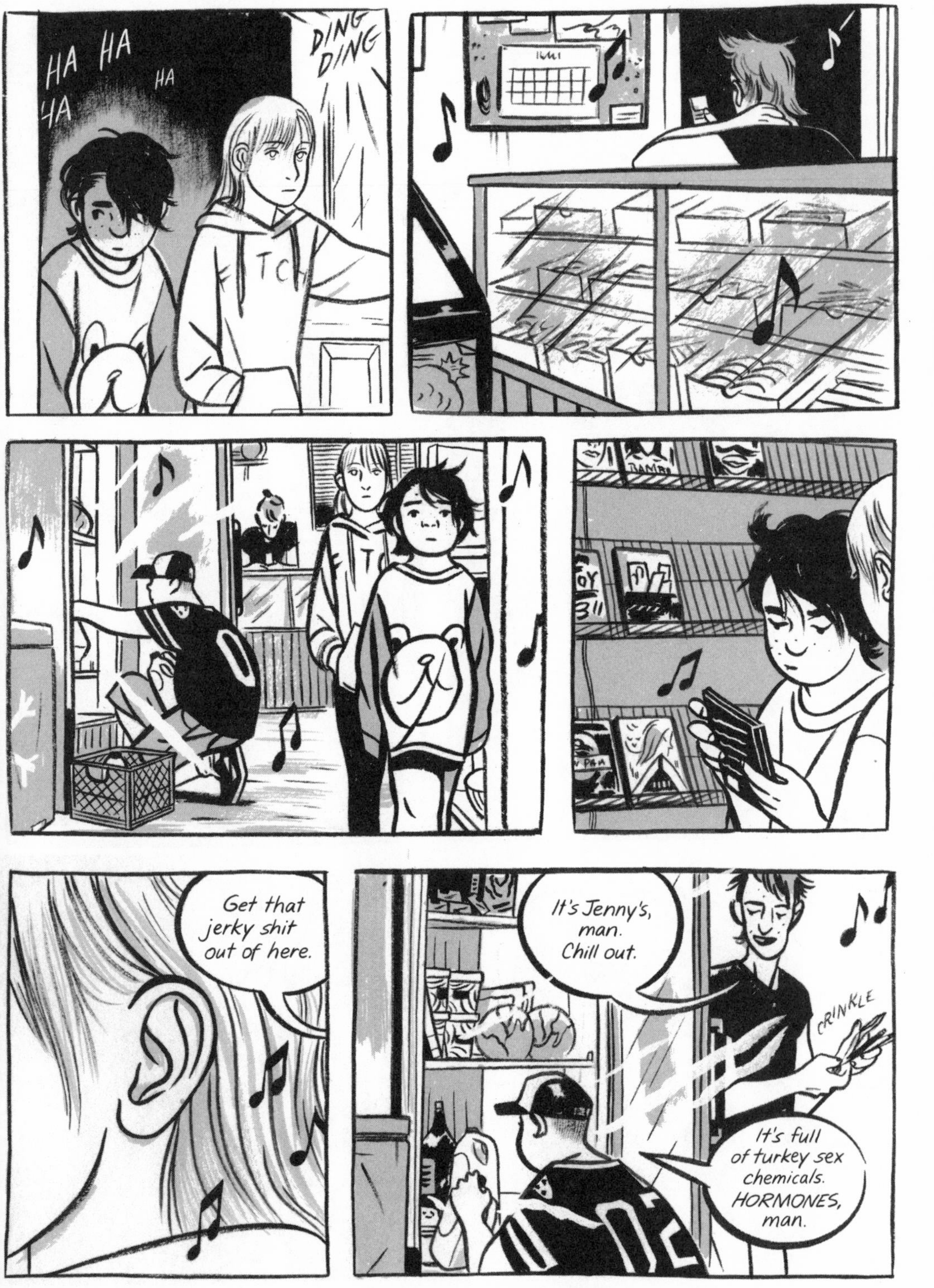
HA HA
HA
HA
DING DING
TCH
DAMBI
Get that jerky shit out of here.
It's Jenny's, man. Chill out.
CRINKLE
It's full of turkey sex chemicals. HORMONES, man.

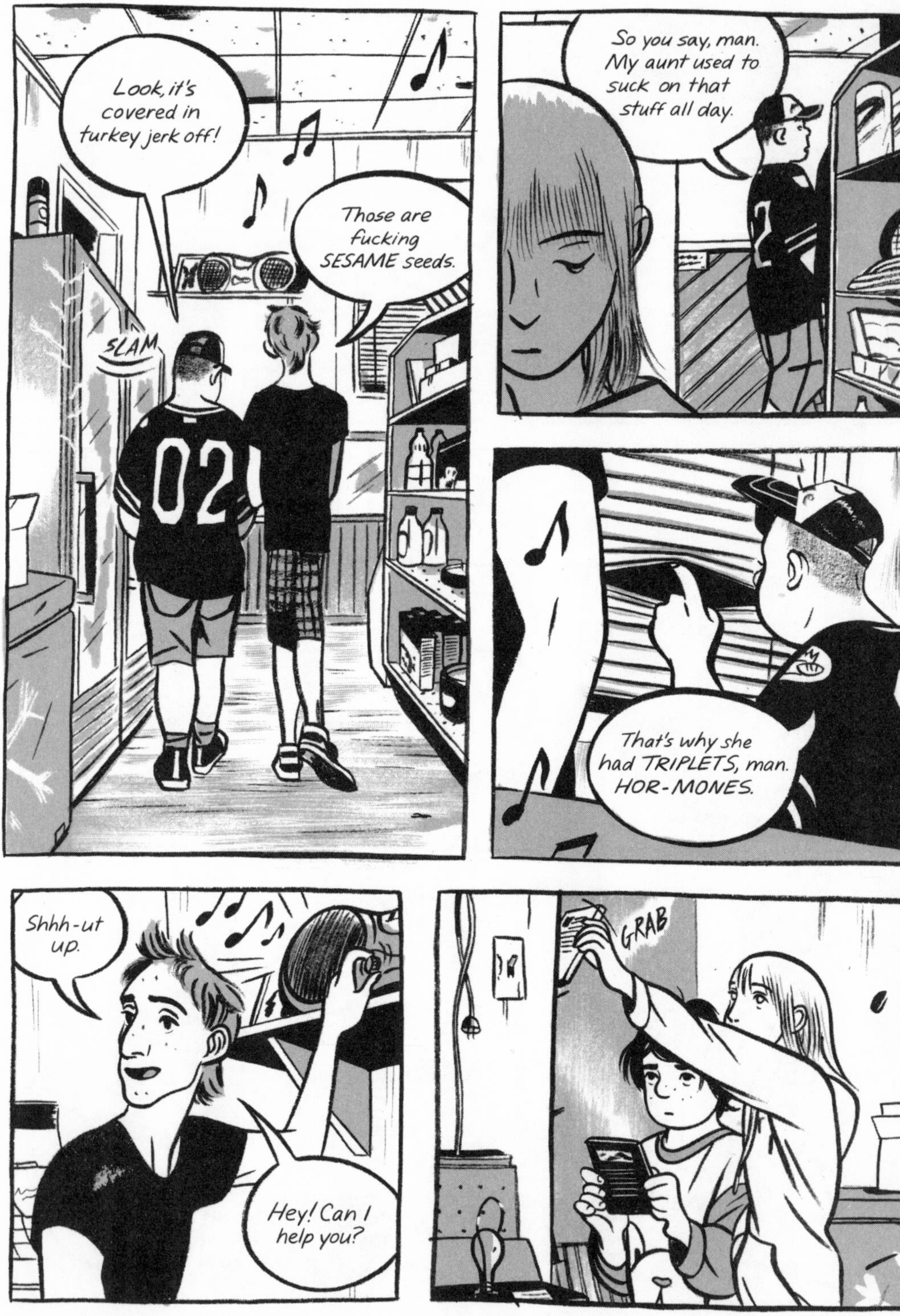
Look, it's covered in turkey jerk off!
Those are fucking SESAME seeds.
SLAM
So you say, man. My aunt used to suck on that stuff all day.
That's why she had TRIPLETS, man. HOR-MONES.
Shhh-ut up.
Hey! Can I help you?
GRAB

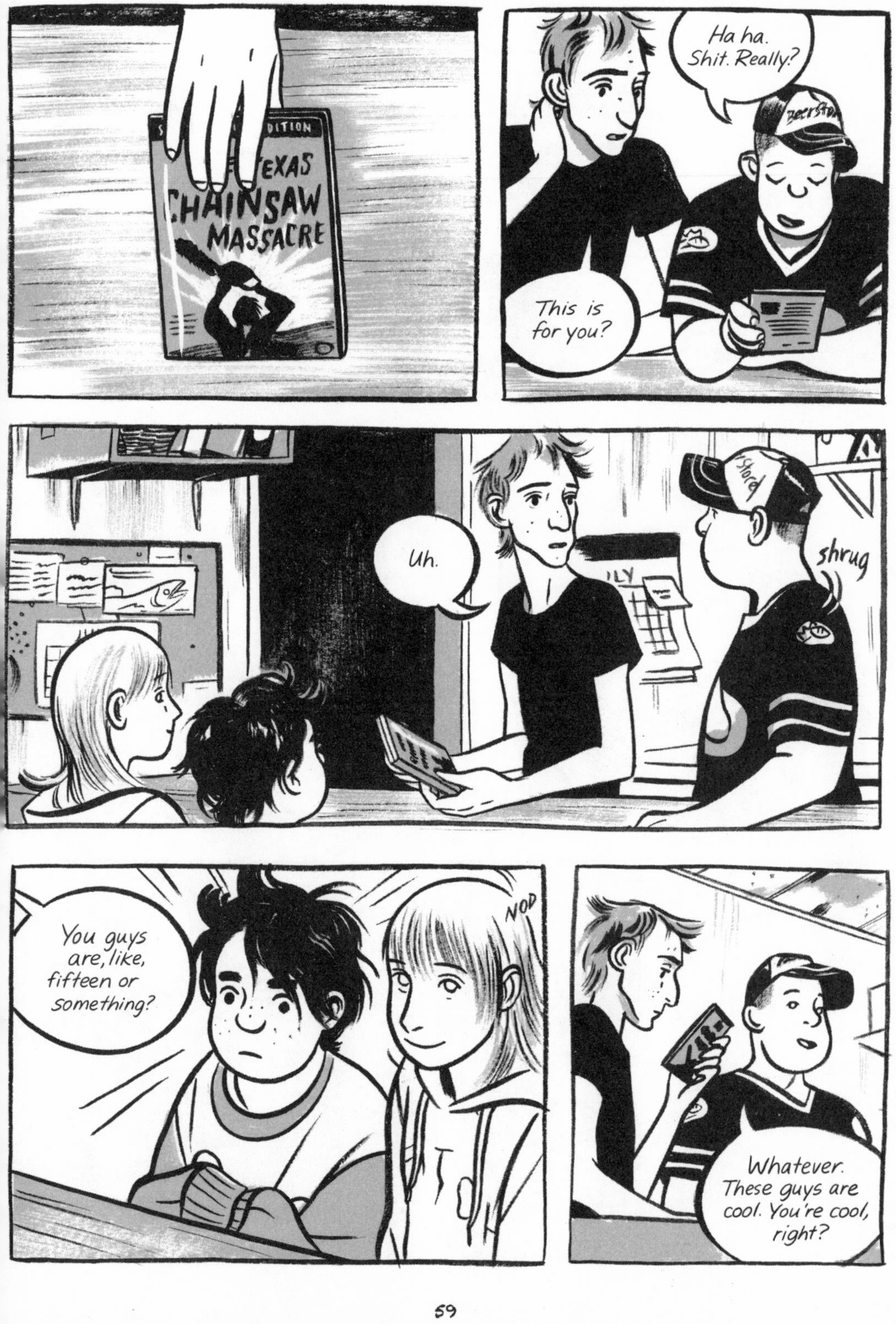
TEXAS
CHAINSAW
MASSACRE
Ha ha. Shit. Really?
This is for you?
Uh.
shrug
You guys are, like, fifteen or something?
NOD
Whatever. These guys are cool. You're cool, right?

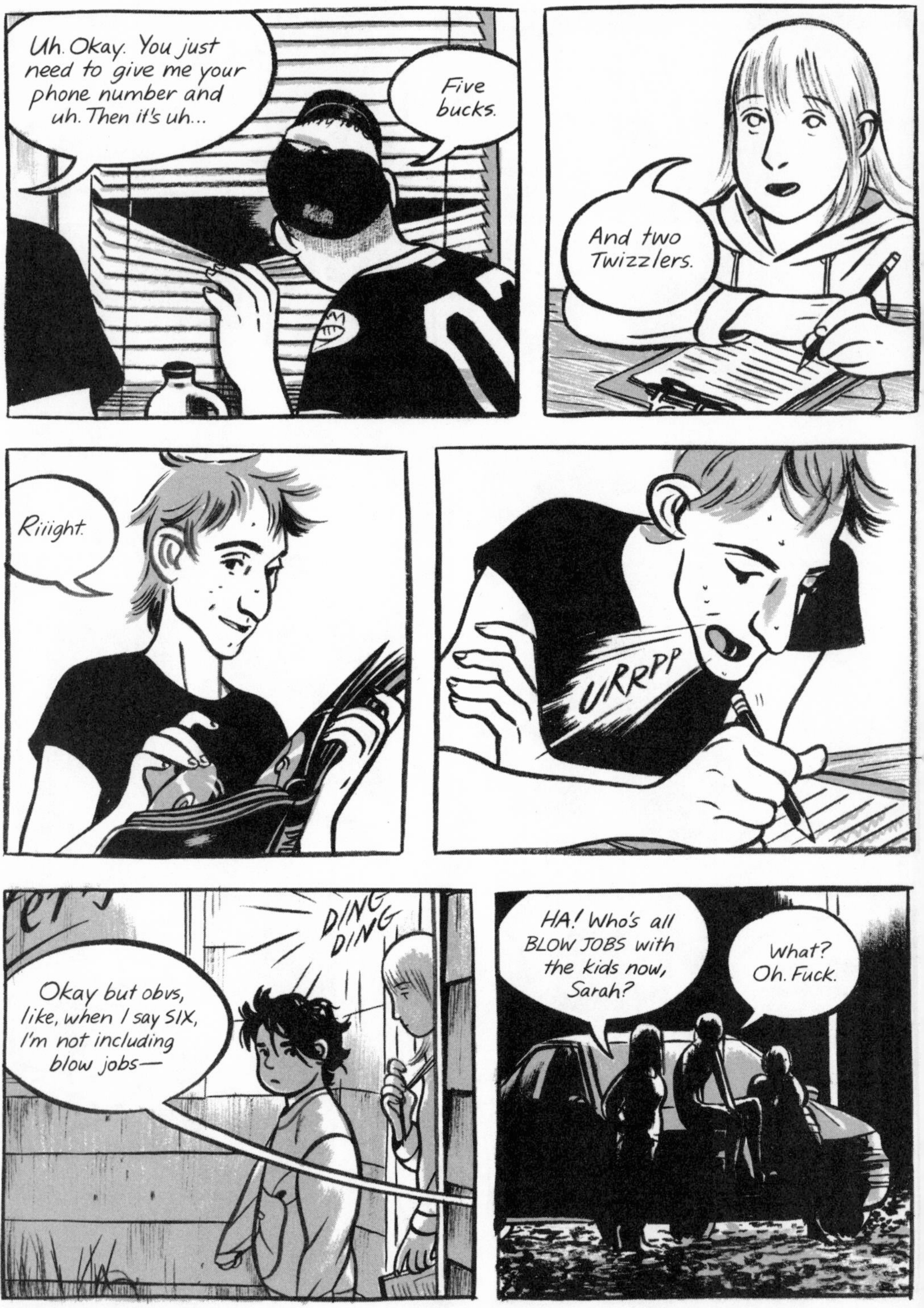
Uh. Okay. You just need to give me your phone number and uh. Then it's uh...
Five bucks.
And two Twizzlers.
Riiight.
URRPP
DING DING
Okay but obvs, like, when I say SIX, I'm not including blow jobs—
HA! Who's all BLOW JOBS with the kids now, Sarah?
What? Oh. Fuck.

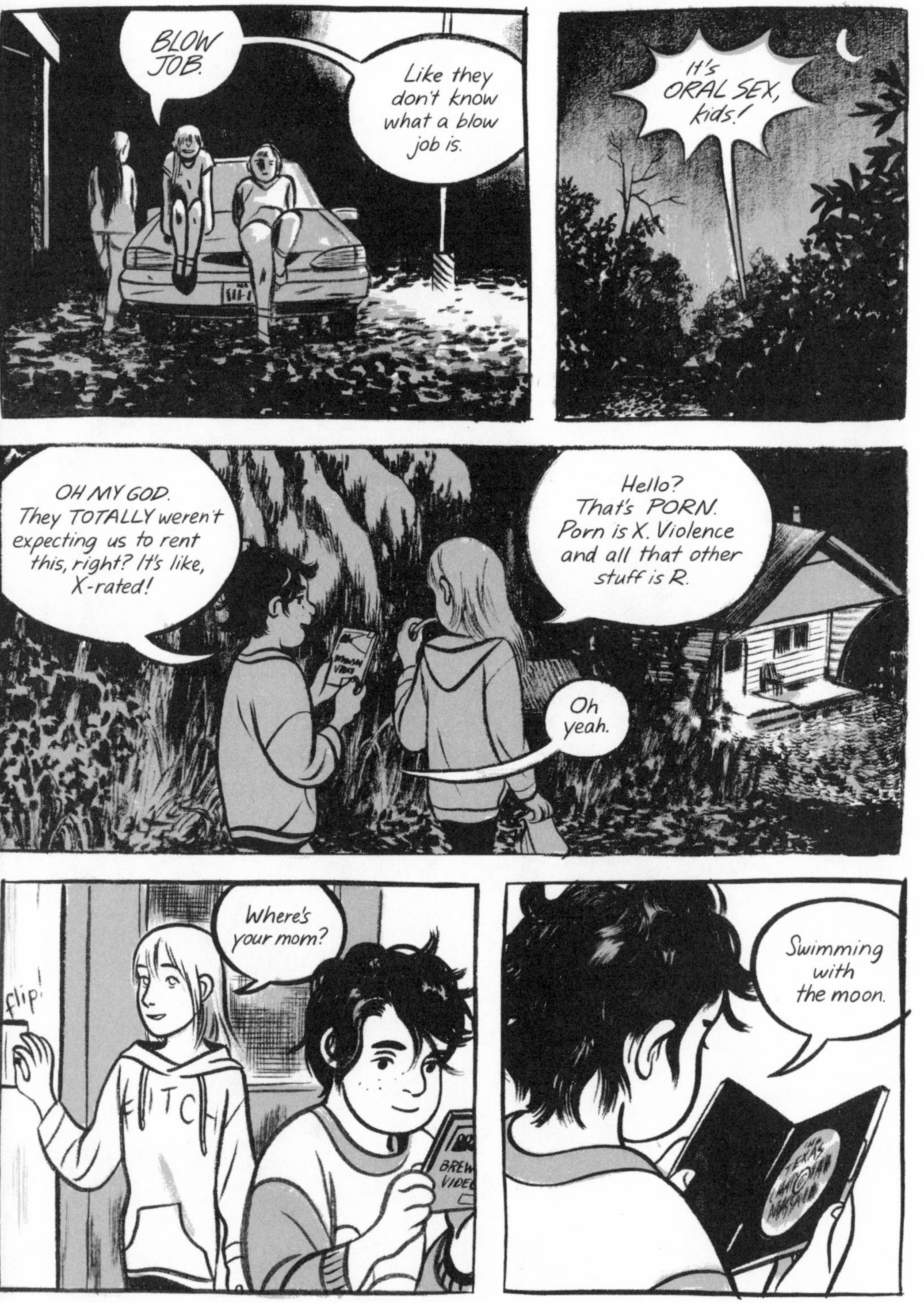
BLOW JOB.
Like they don't know what a blow job is.
It's ORAL SEX, kids!
OH MY GOD. They TOTALLY weren't expecting us to rent this, right? It's like, X-rated!
Hello? That's PORN. Porn is X. Violence and all that other stuff is R.
Oh yeah.
flip!
Where's your mom?
Swimming with the moon.

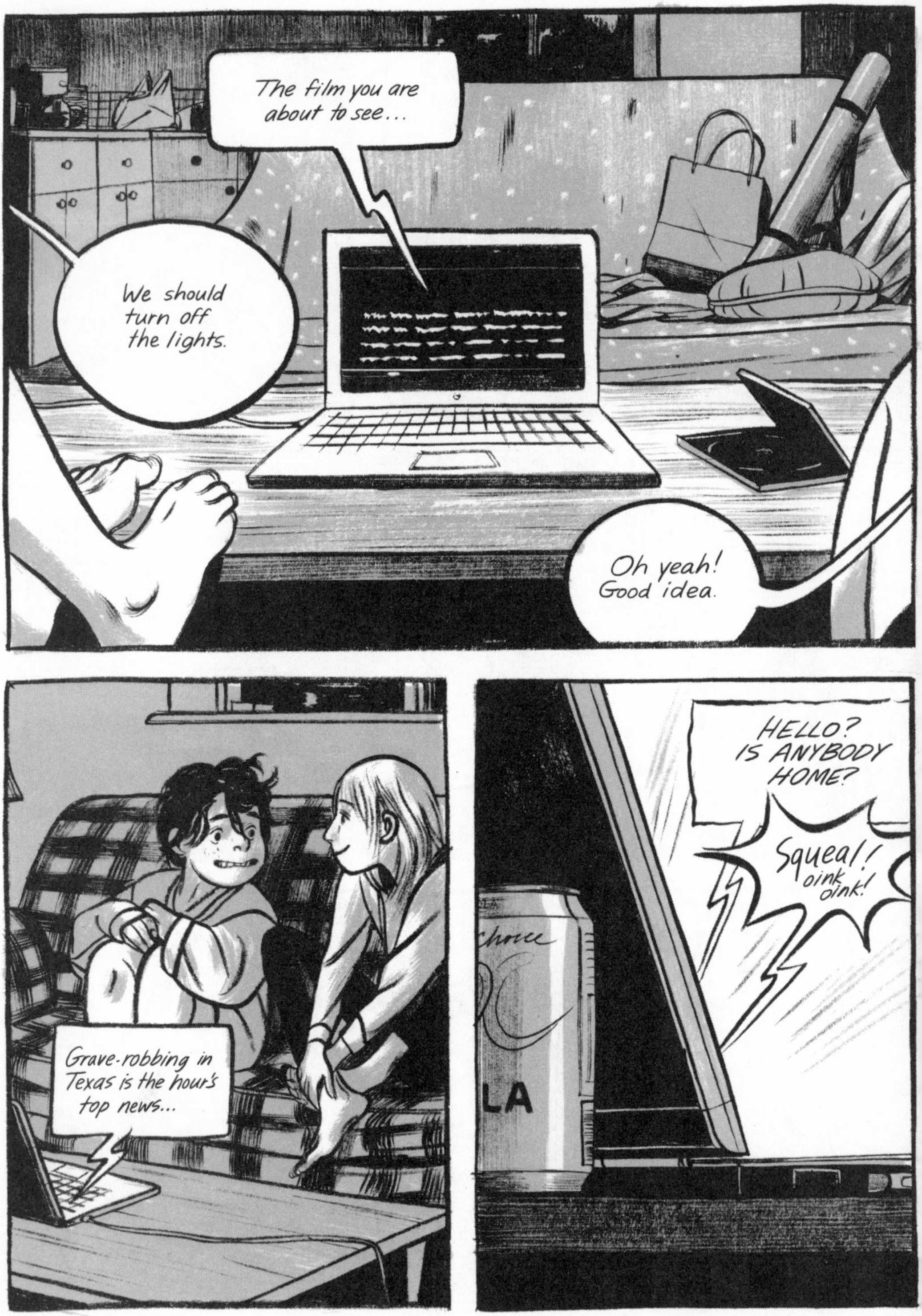
The film you are about to see...
We should turn off the lights.
Oh yeah! Good idea.
Grave-robbing in Texas is the hour's top news...
HELLO? IS ANYBODY HOME?
Squeal! oink oink!

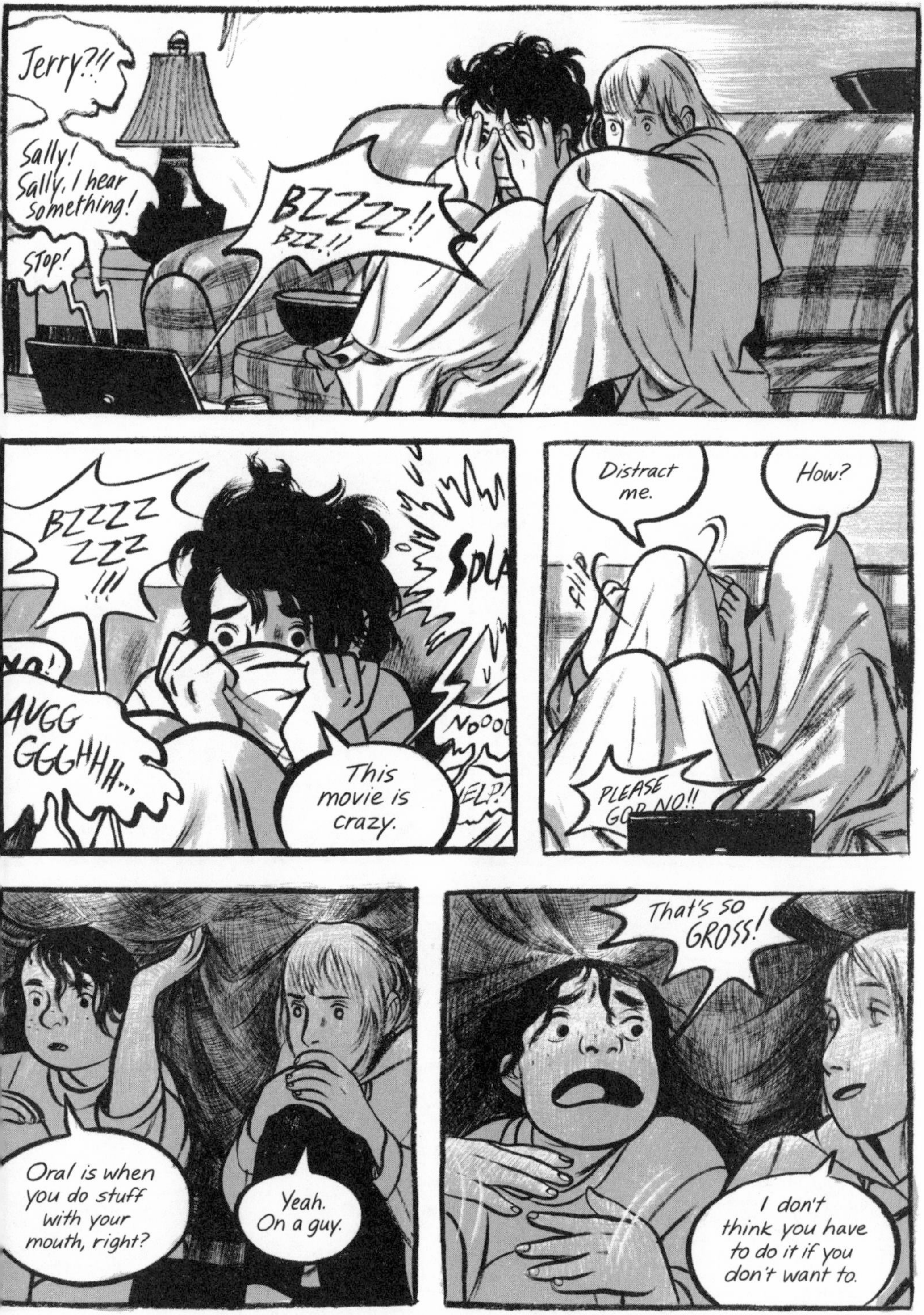
Jerry?!!
Sally! Sally, I hear something!
Stop!
BZZZZZ!! BZZ!!
BZZZZ ZZZ !!!
AUGG GGGHHH...
SPLA
NOOO
This movie is crazy.
Distract me.
How?
flip
PLEASE GOD NO!!
Oral is when you do stuff with your mouth, right?
Yeah. On a guy.
That's so GROSS!
I don't think you have to do it if you don't want to.

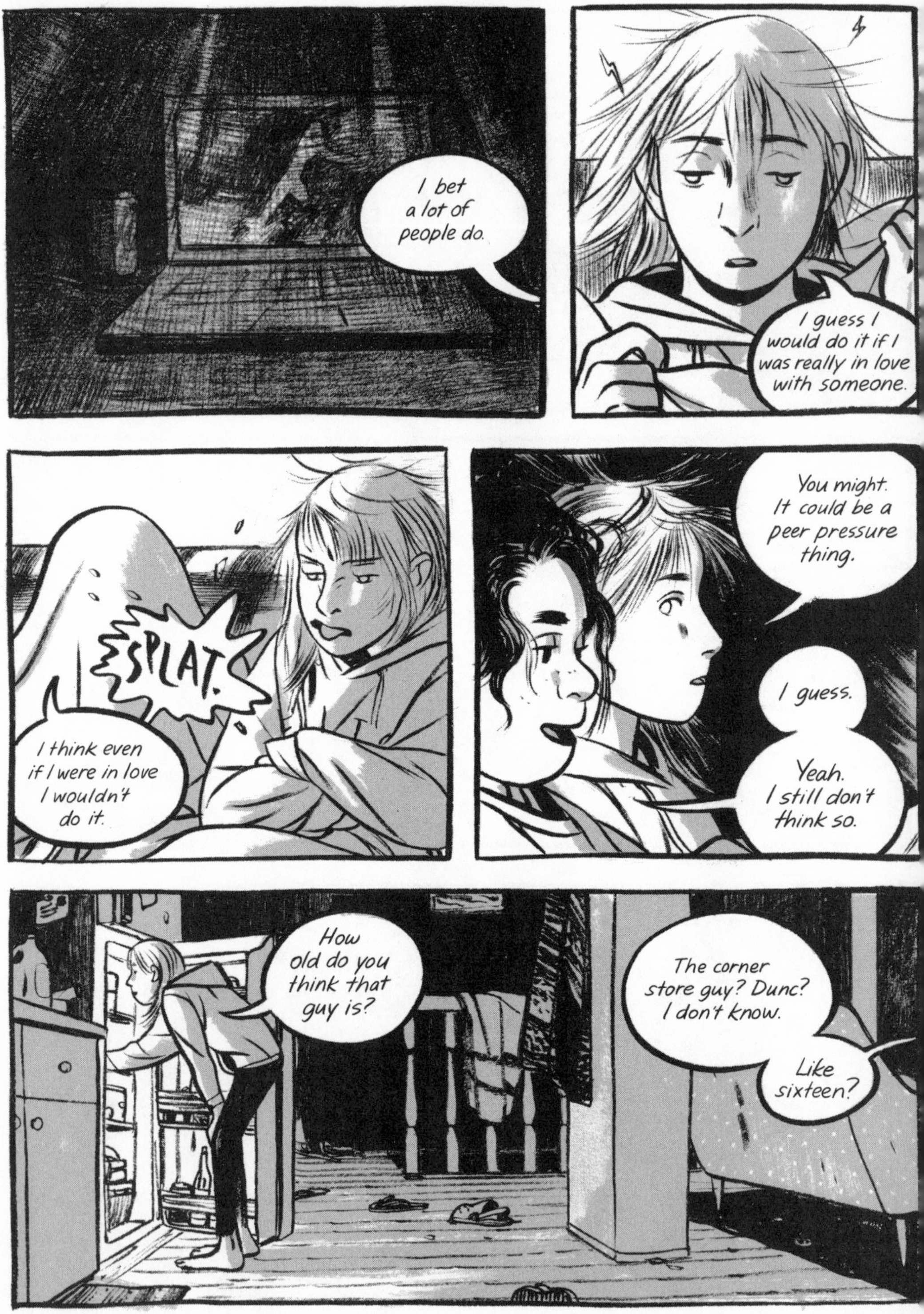

I bet a lot of people do.
I guess I would do it if I was really in love with someone.
SPLAT.
I think even if I were in love I wouldn't do it.
You might. It could be a peer pressure thing.
I guess.
Yeah. I still don't think so.
How old do you think that guy is?
The corner store guy? Dunc? I don't know.
Like sixteen?

I think he's like eighteen.

AAAAAAAAAAA AAAAAAAAAAA...!

BZZZZ ZZZ!

No way he's sixteen. He has, like, hair on his face.

BZZZZZ ZZZZ

HALP ME

SHIT!

Oh my goodness! What are you watching?!

OH MY GOD! AL

BZZZZ ZZ...

SQUIRT NOOO!

I know a little about sex.

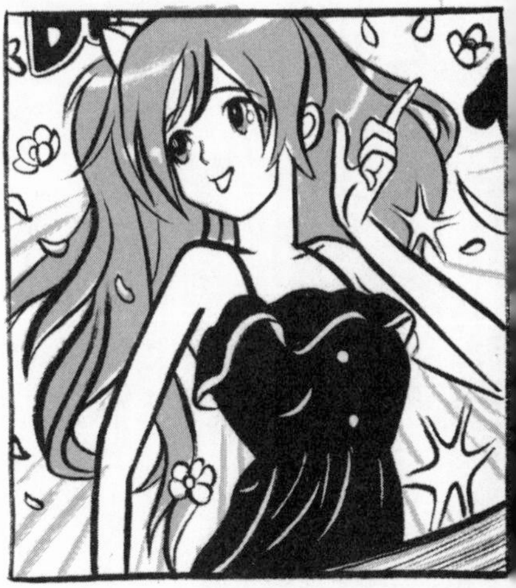

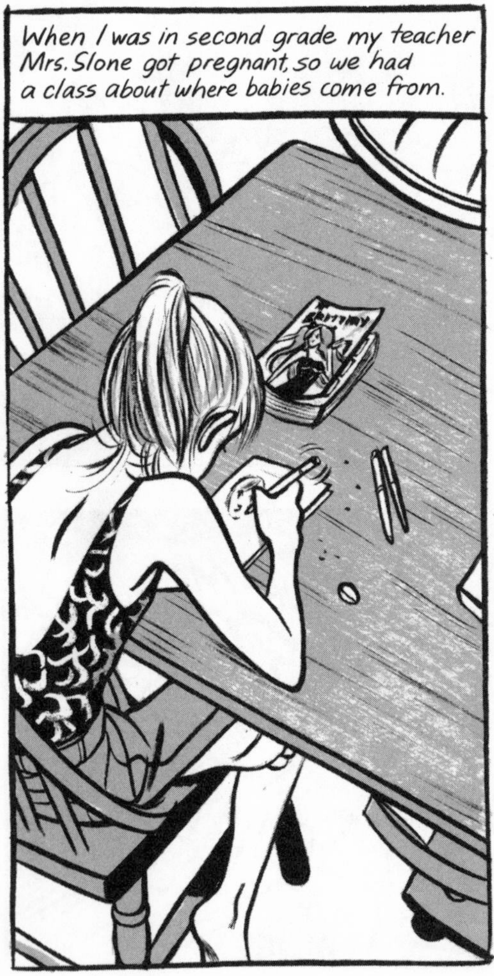
When I was in second grade my teacher Mrs. Slone got pregnant, so we had a class about where babies come from.

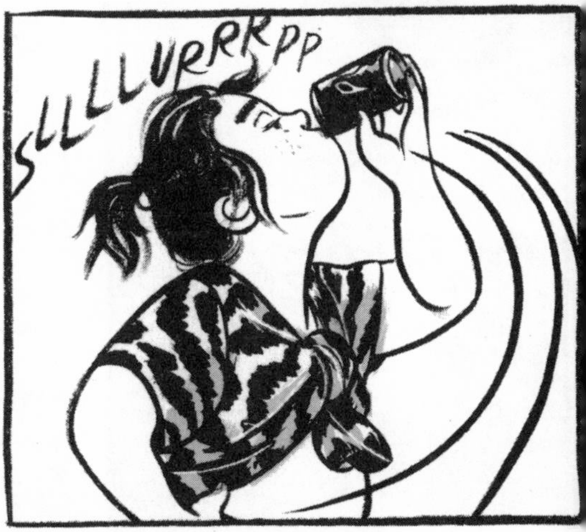
SLLLLURRRPP

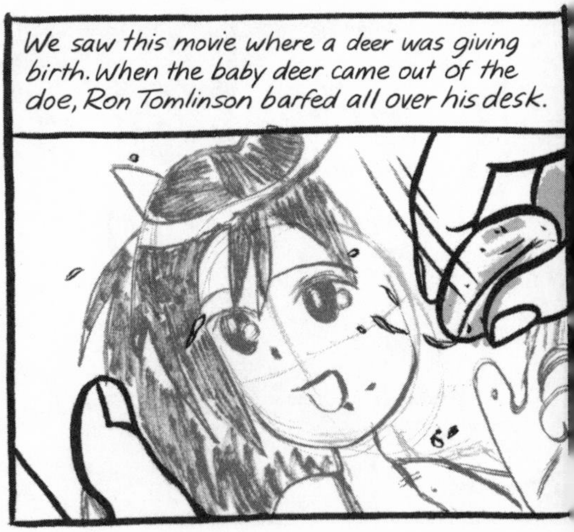
We saw this movie where a deer was giving birth. When the baby deer came out of the doe, Ron Tomlinson barfed all over his desk.

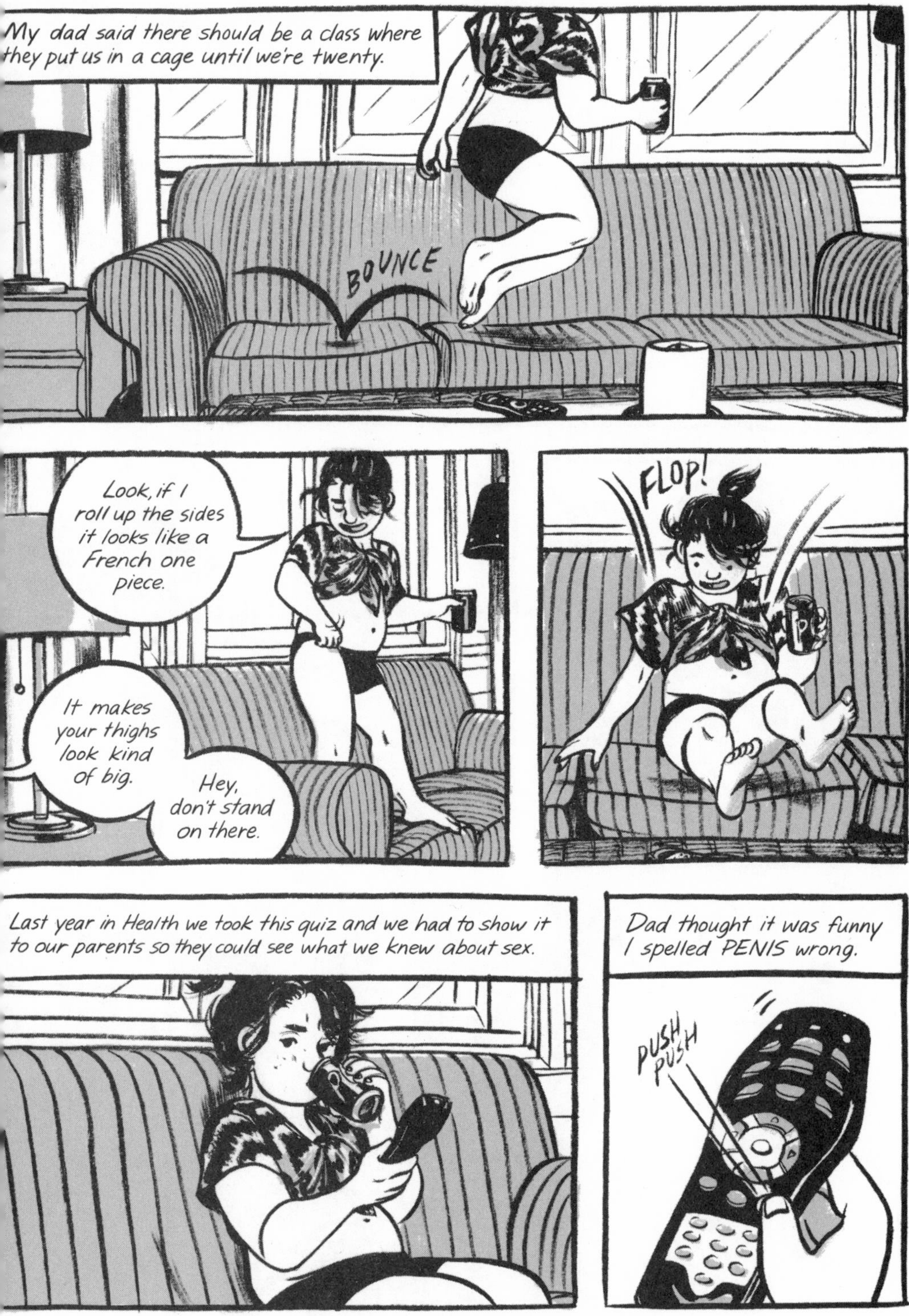

My dad said there should be a class where they put us in a cage until we're twenty.
BOUNCE
Look, if I roll up the sides it looks like a French one piece.
It makes your thighs look kind of big.
Hey, don't stand on there.
FLOP!
Last year in Health we took this quiz and we had to show it to our parents so they could see what we knew about sex.
Dad thought it was funny I spelled PENIS wrong.
PUSH PUSH

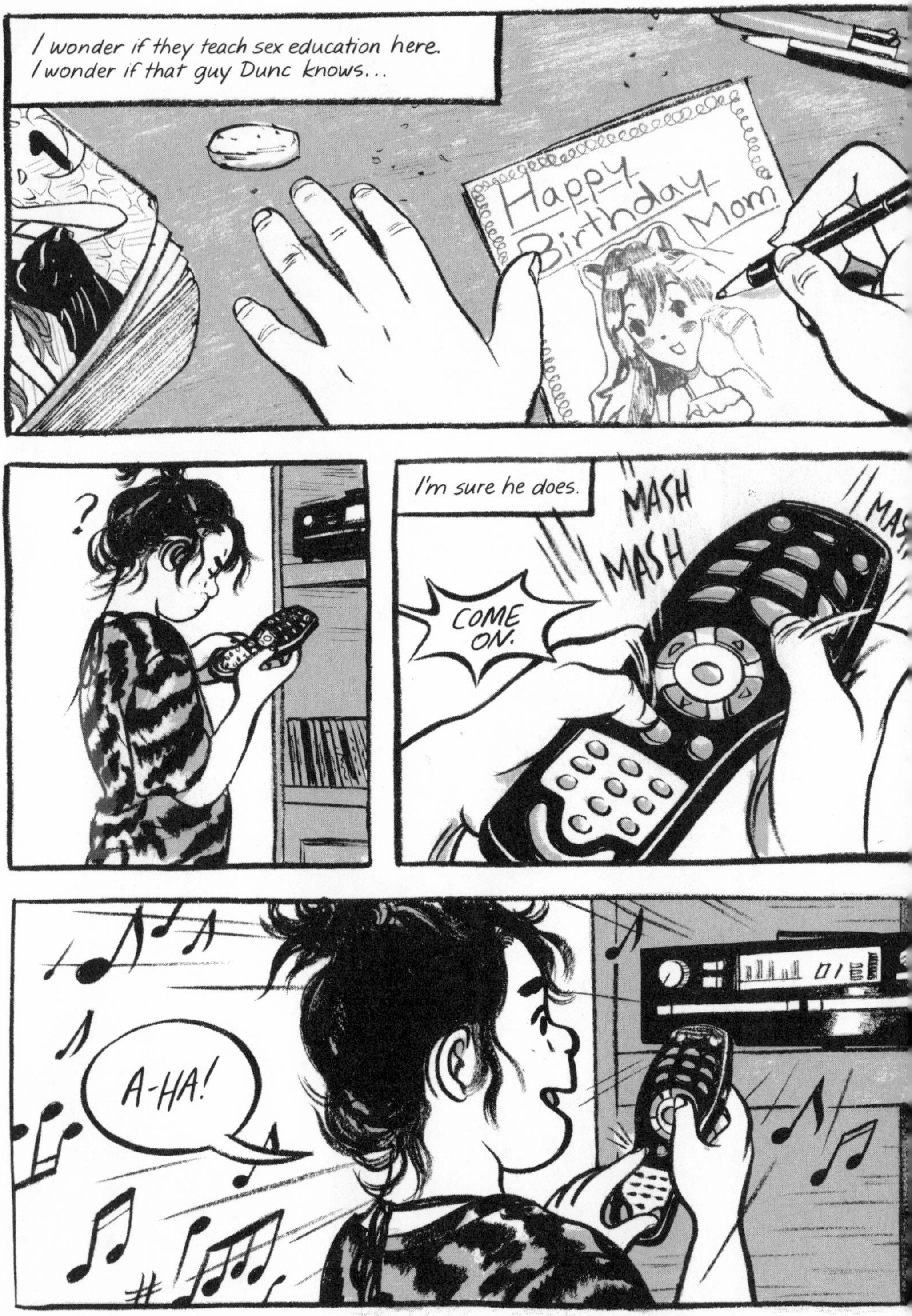
I wonder if they teach sex education here.
I wonder if that guy Dunc knows...
Happy Birthday Mom
?
I'm sure he does.
MASH
MASH
MASH
COME ON.
A-HA!
01

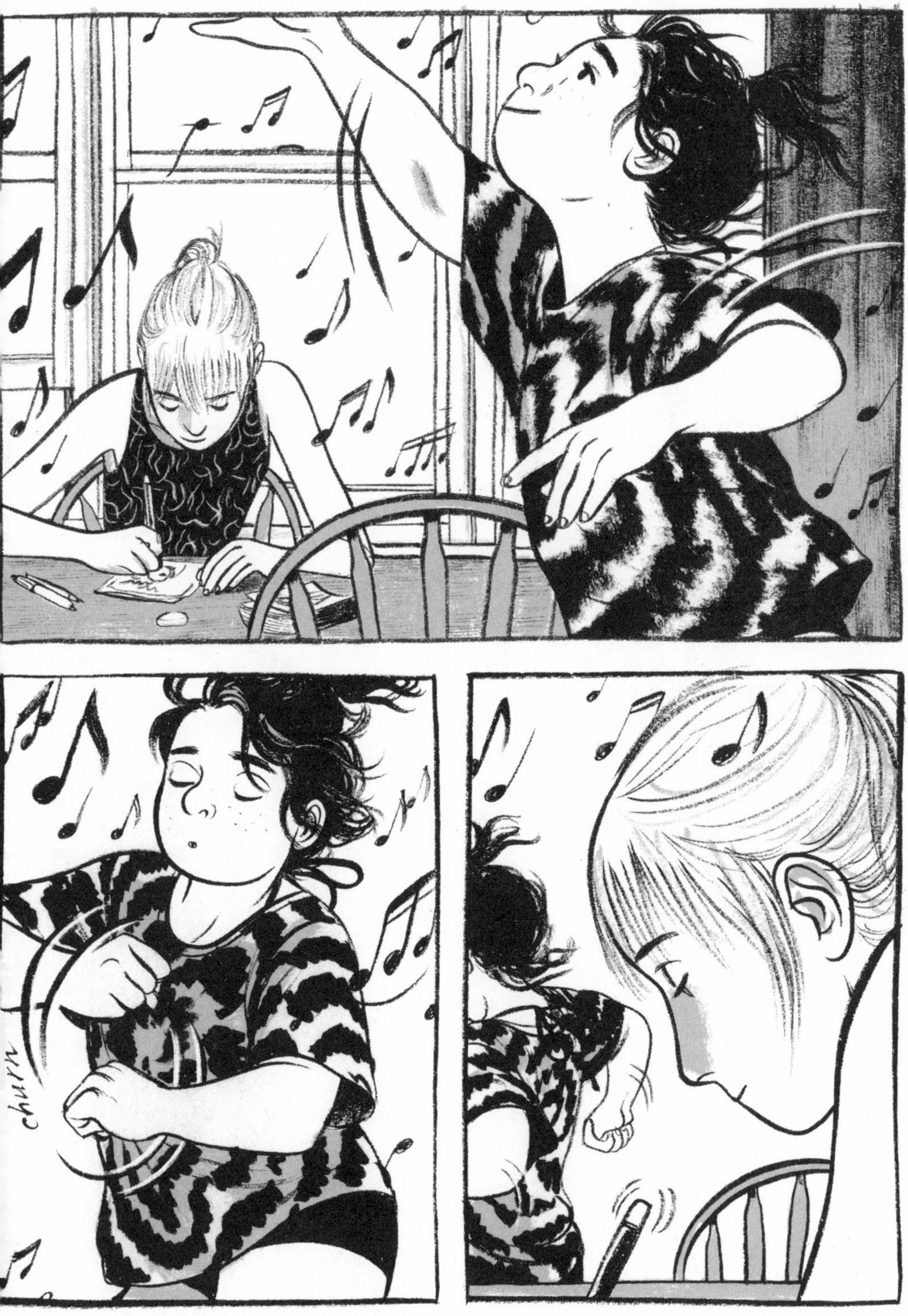
churn

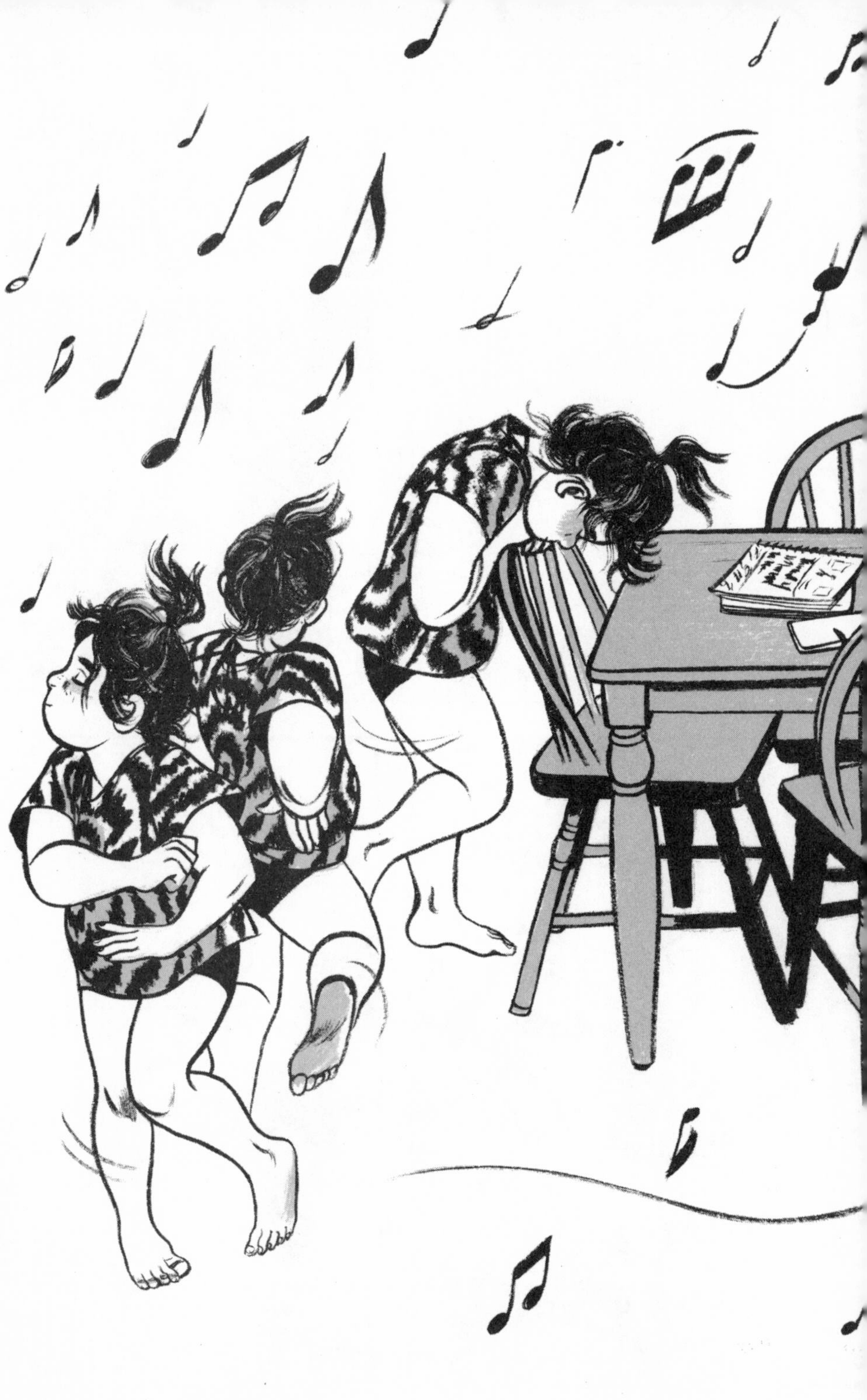

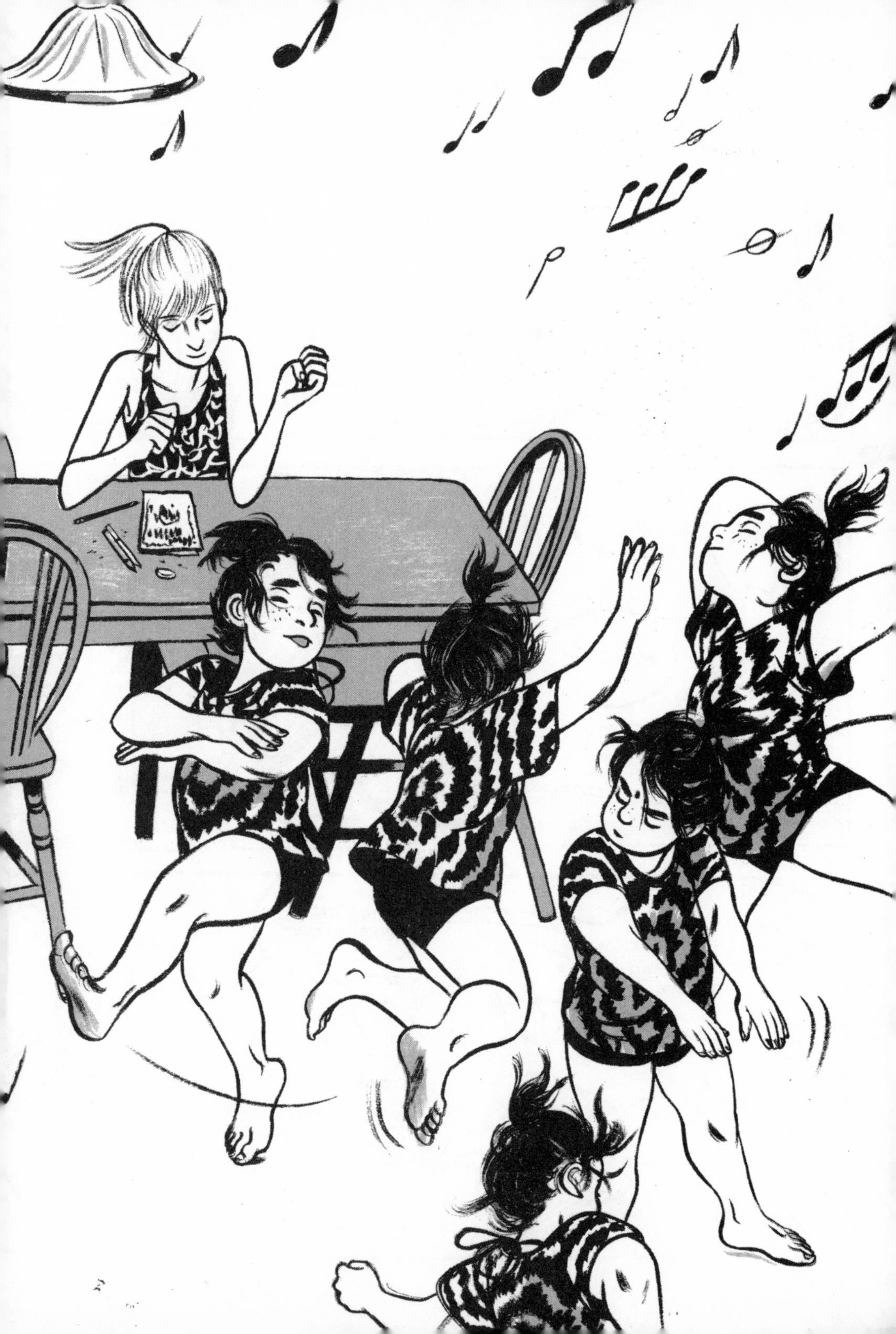

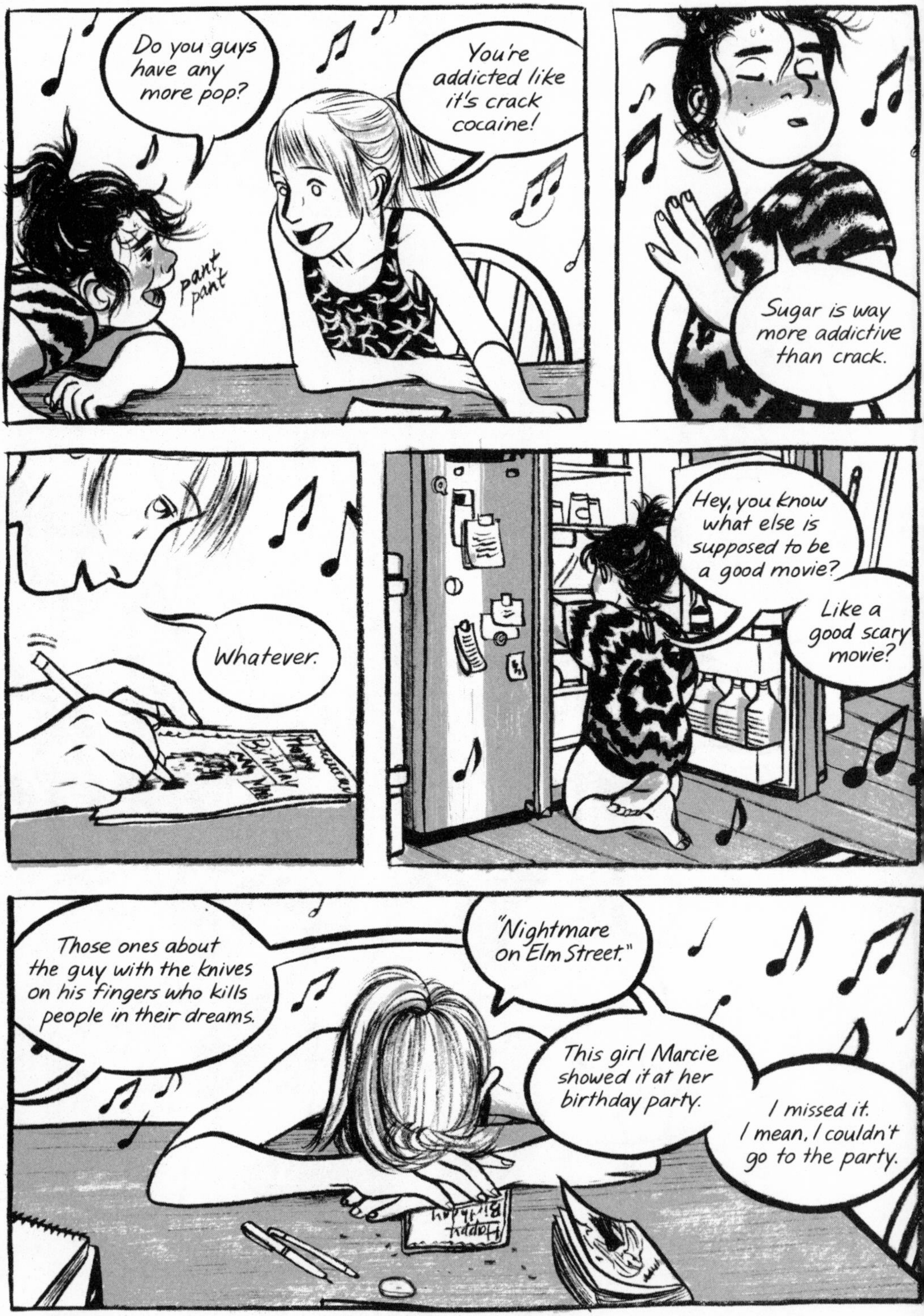
Do you guys have any more pop?
You're addicted like it's crack cocaine!
pant pant
Sugar is way more addictive than crack.
Whatever.
Hey, you know what else is supposed to be a good movie?
Like a good scary movie?
Those ones about the guy with the knives on his fingers who kills people in their dreams.
"Nightmare on Elm Street."
This girl Marcie showed it at her birthday party.
I missed it. I mean, I couldn't go to the party.

I think it's called "Nightmare on Elm Street"?

But.

It's supposed to be scary.

OFF

Like, really really freaky.

Windy, when's the last time you drank WATER?

NEW OBSERVATI

Journal of Pharmaceutic Sciences

Soooooo.

Do you do sleepovers still?

Sometimes. It's more like parties though. Not, like, sleepovers.

GULG

RO

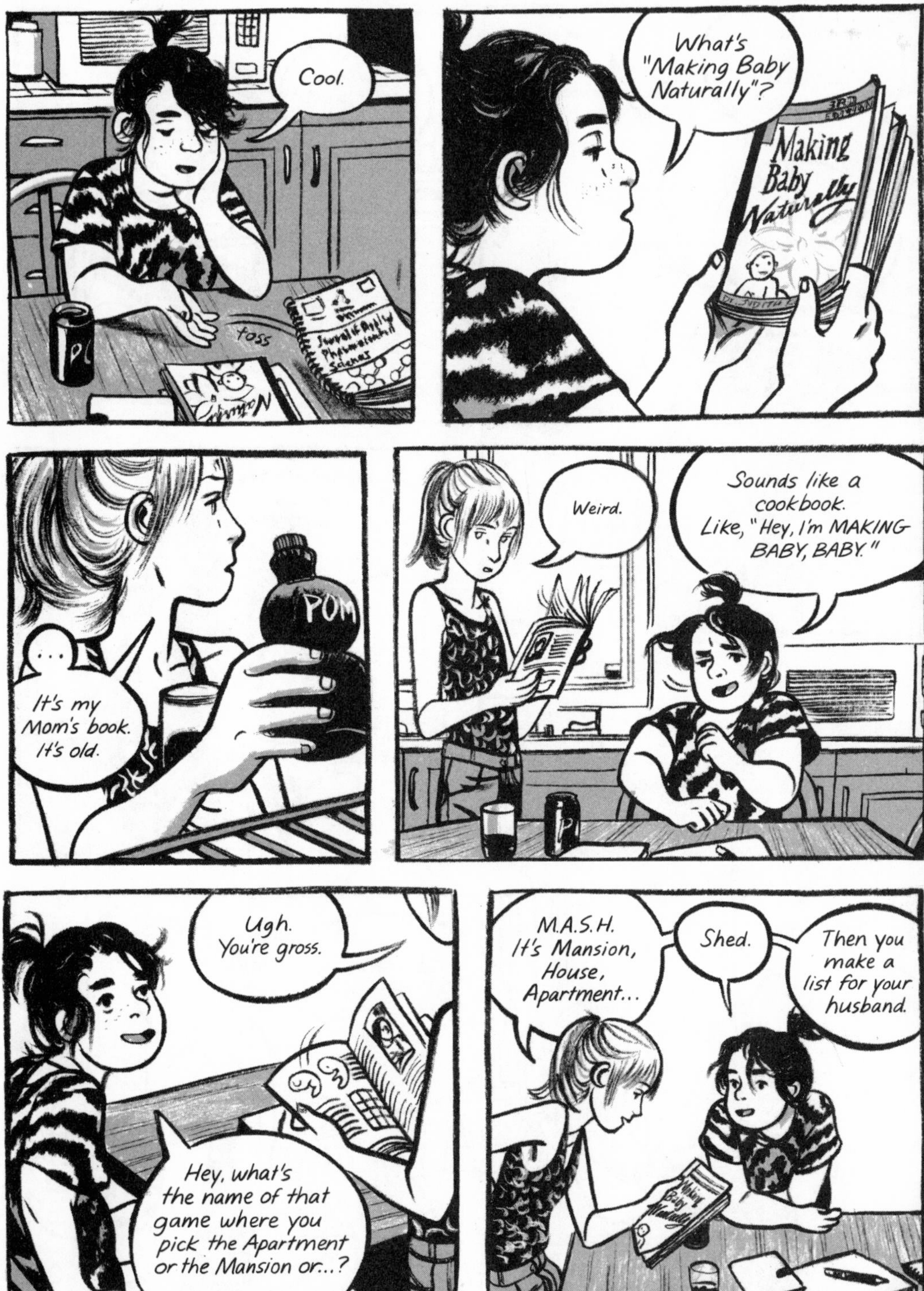
Cool.
toss
What's "Making Baby Naturally"?
Making Baby Naturally
It's my Mom's book. It's old.
POM
Weird.
Sounds like a cookbook. Like, "Hey, I'm MAKING BABY, BABY."
Ugh. You're gross.
Hey, what's the name of that game where you pick the Apartment or the Mansion or...?
M.A.S.H. It's Mansion, House, Apartment...
Shed.
Then you make a list for your husband.

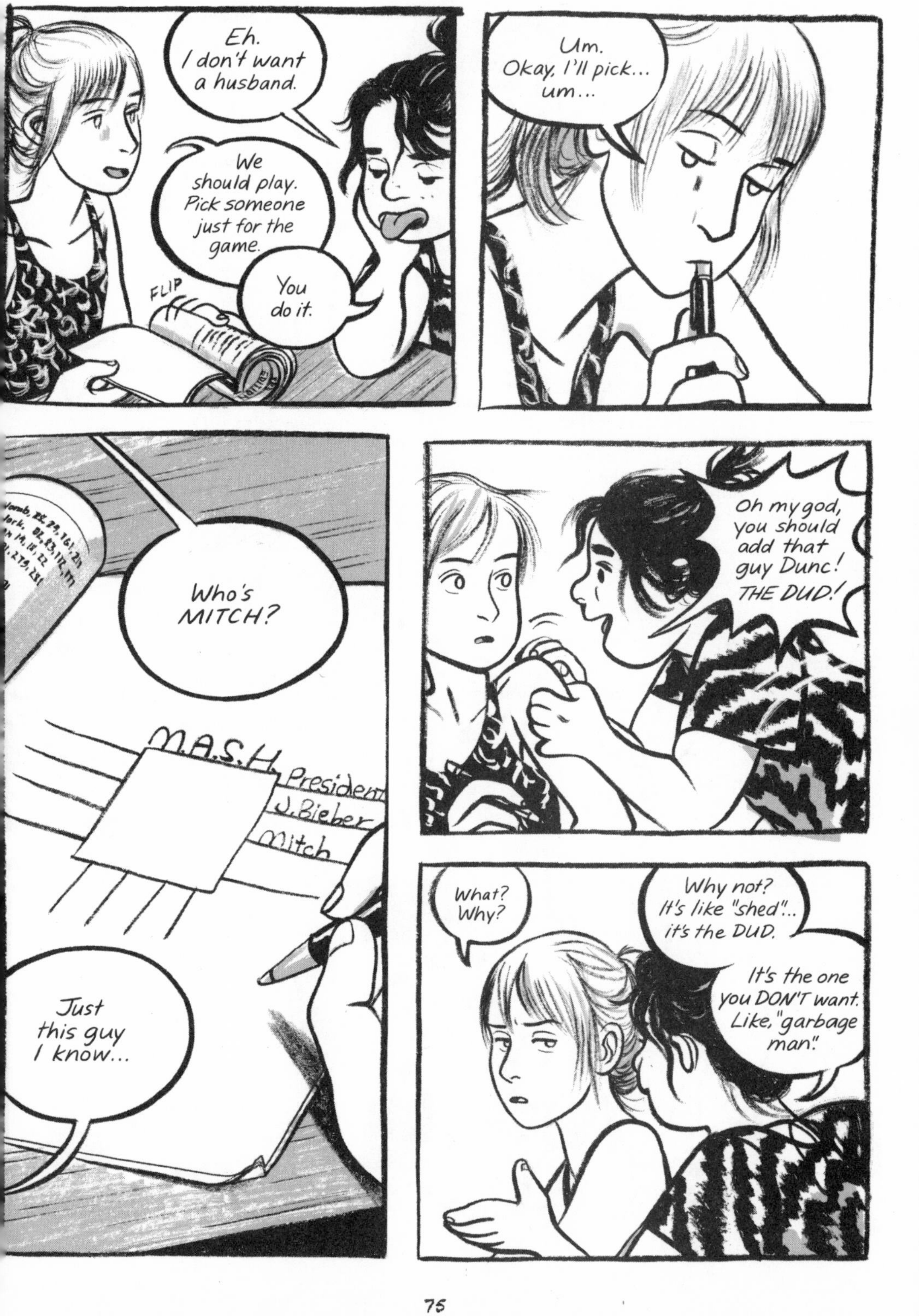
Eh. I don't want a husband.
We should play. Pick someone just for the game.
FLIP
You do it.
Um. Okay, I'll pick... um...
Who's MITCH?
M.A.S.H.
President
J.Bieber
Mitch
Just this guy I know...
Oh my god, you should add that guy Dunc! THE DUD!
What? Why?
Why not? It's like "shed"... it's the DUD.
It's the one you DON'T want. Like, "garbage man."

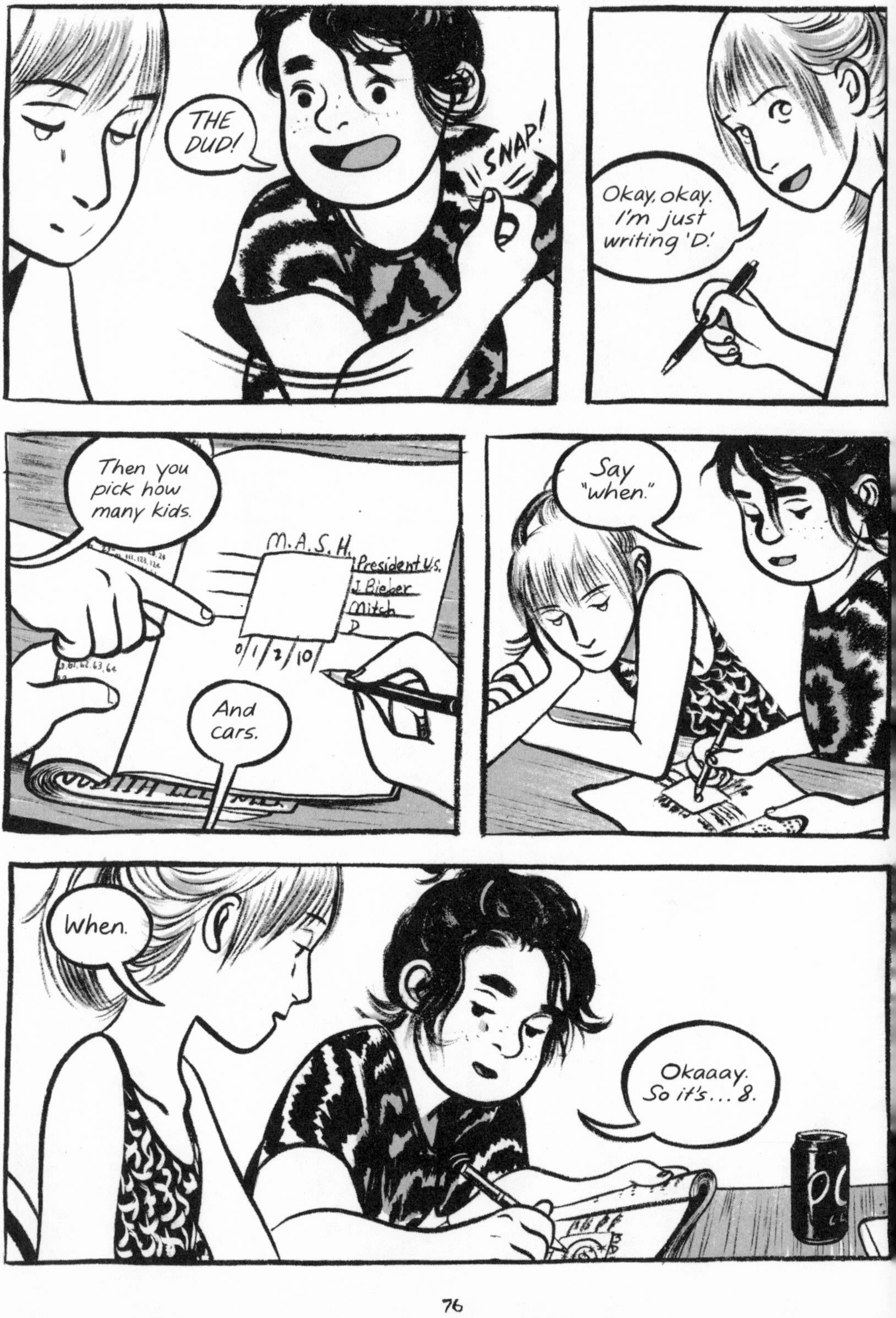
THE DUD!
SNAP!
Okay, okay. I'm just writing 'D.'
Then you pick how many kids.
M.A.S.H.
President U.S.
J Bieber
Mitch
D
0 1 2 10
And cars.
Say "when."
When.
Okaaay. So it's... 8.

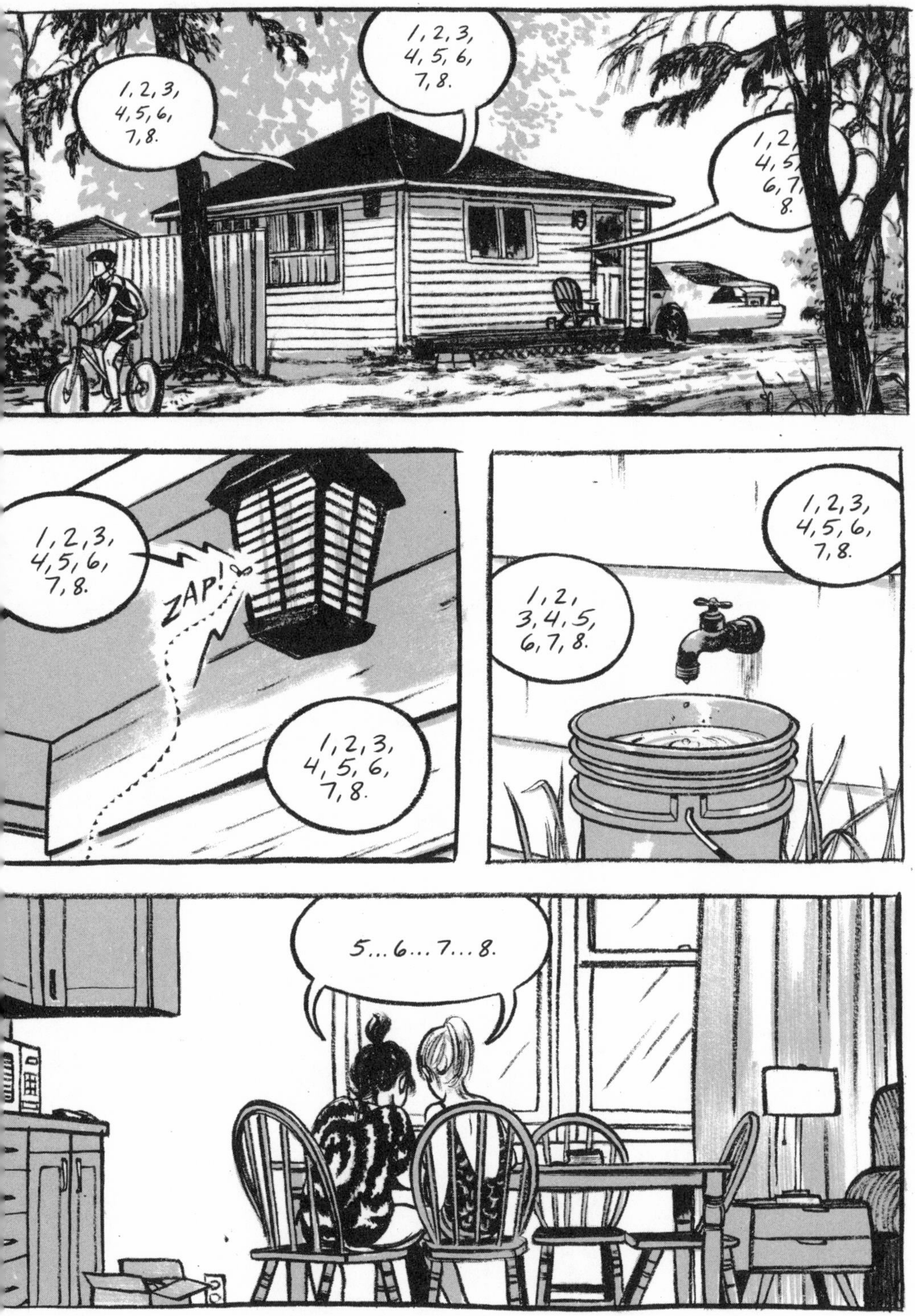
1, 2, 3, 4, 5, 6, 7, 8.
1, 2, 3, 4, 5, 6, 7, 8.
1, 2 4, 5 6, 7, 8.
1, 2, 3, 4, 5, 6, 7, 8.
ZAP!
1, 2, 3, 4, 5, 6, 7, 8.
1, 2, 3, 4, 5, 6, 7, 8.
1, 2, 3, 4, 5, 6, 7, 8.
5... 6... 7... 8.

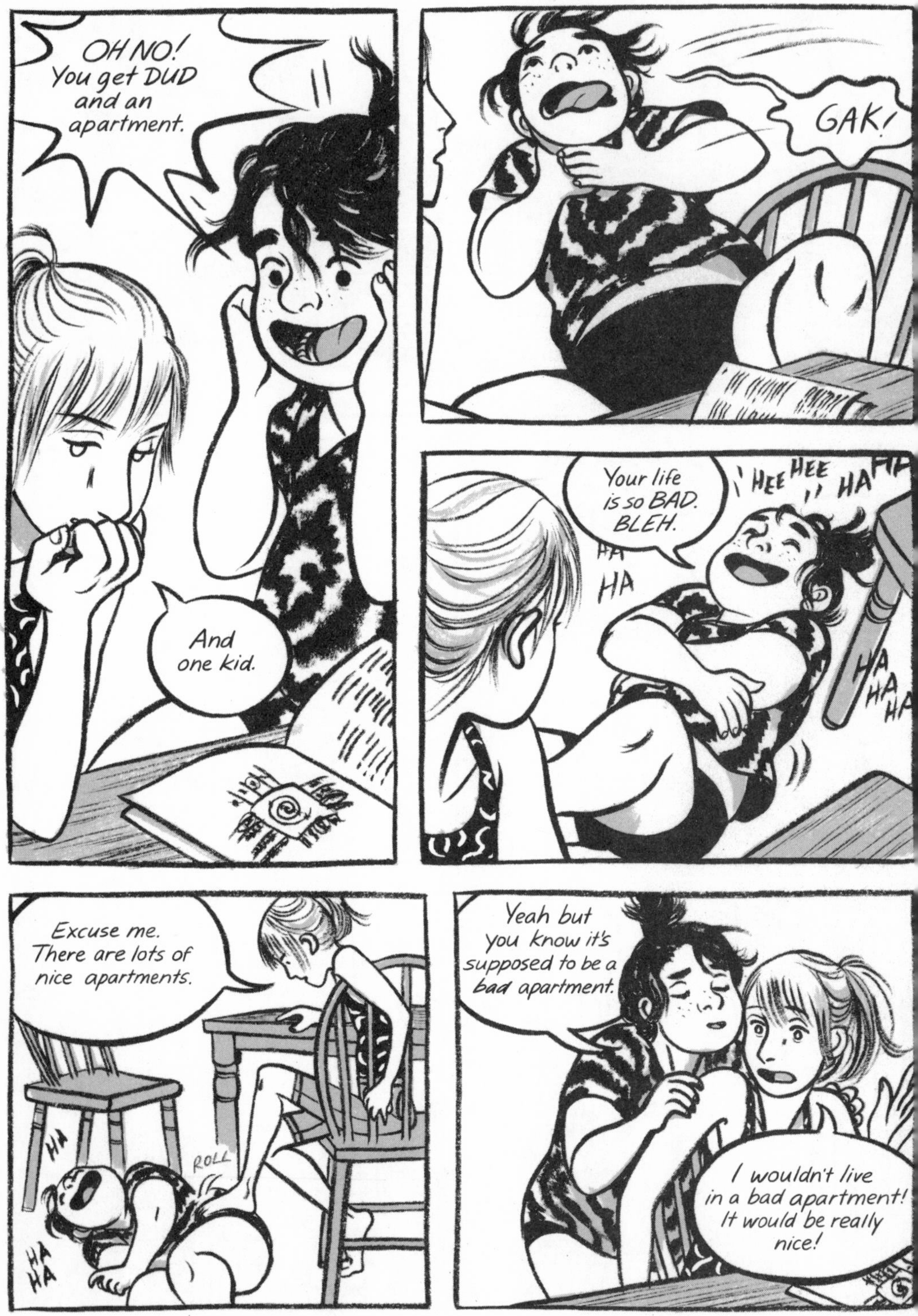
OH NO! You get DUD and an apartment.
And one kid.
GAK!
Your life is so BAD. BLEH.
HEE HEE HA HA
HA HA
HA HA HA
Excuse me. There are lots of nice apartments.
HA
ROLL
HA HA
Yeah but you know it's supposed to be a bad apartment.
I wouldn't live in a bad apartment! It would be really nice!

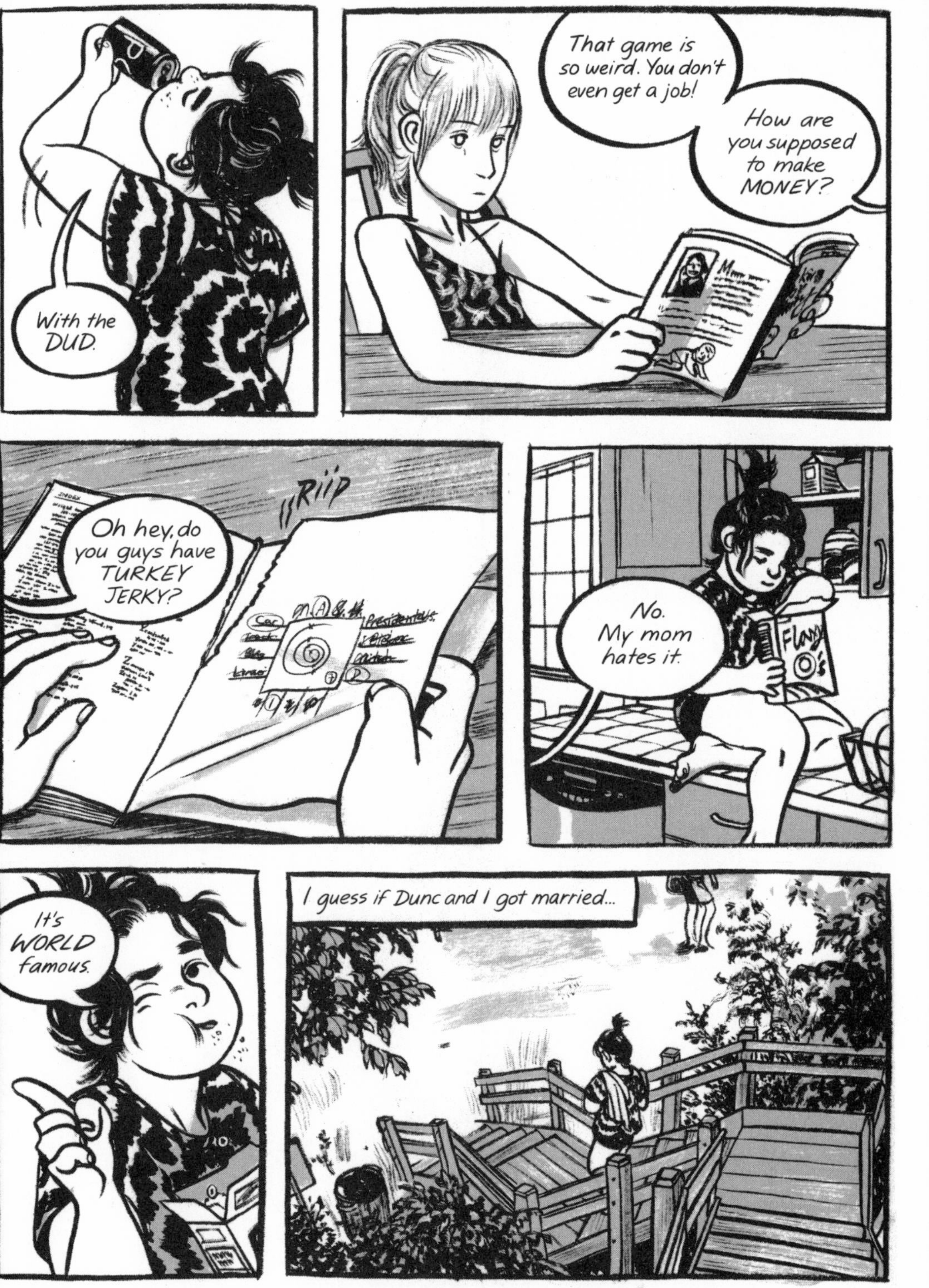
With the DUD.
That game is so weird. You don't even get a job!
How are you supposed to make MONEY?
RIIP
Oh hey, do you guys have TURKEY JERKY?
No. My mom hates it.
Flaxy O's
It's WORLD famous.
I guess if Dunc and I got married...

...we would live in an apartment first.
With regular jobs. Then.
Then we would get good jobs.
And.

And he would go to medical school.

Um.
And I would take time off to have one.

Perfect. Baby.

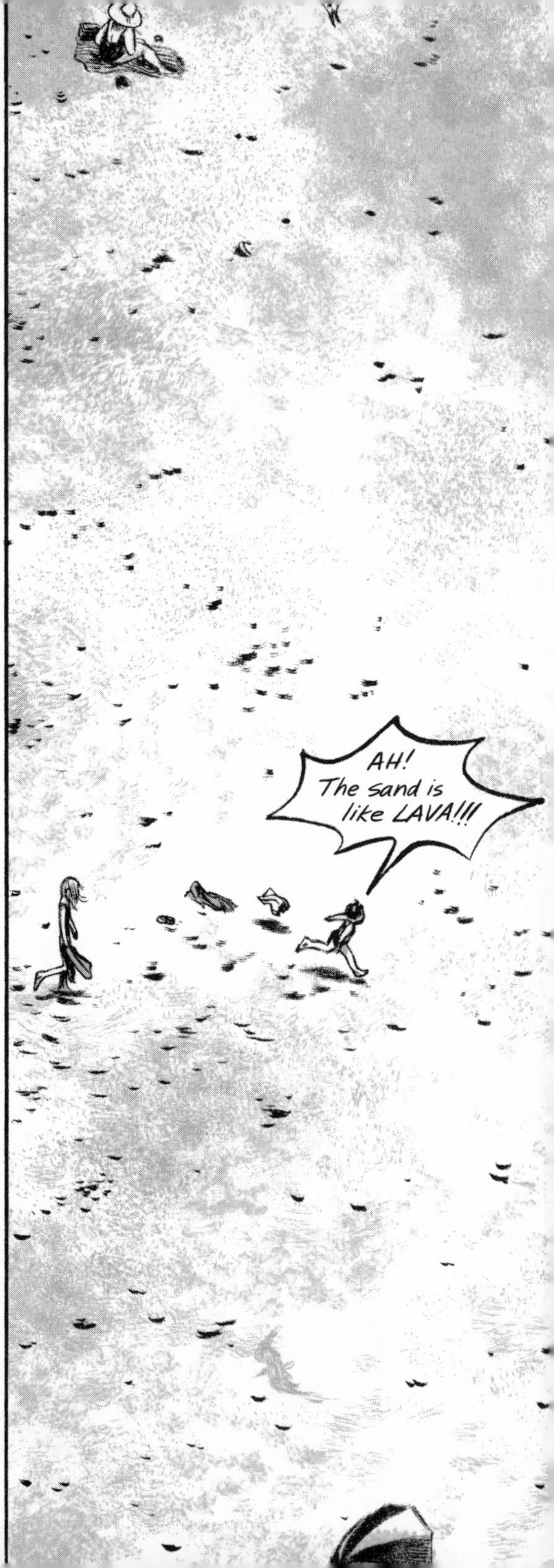
AH! The sand is like LAVA!!!

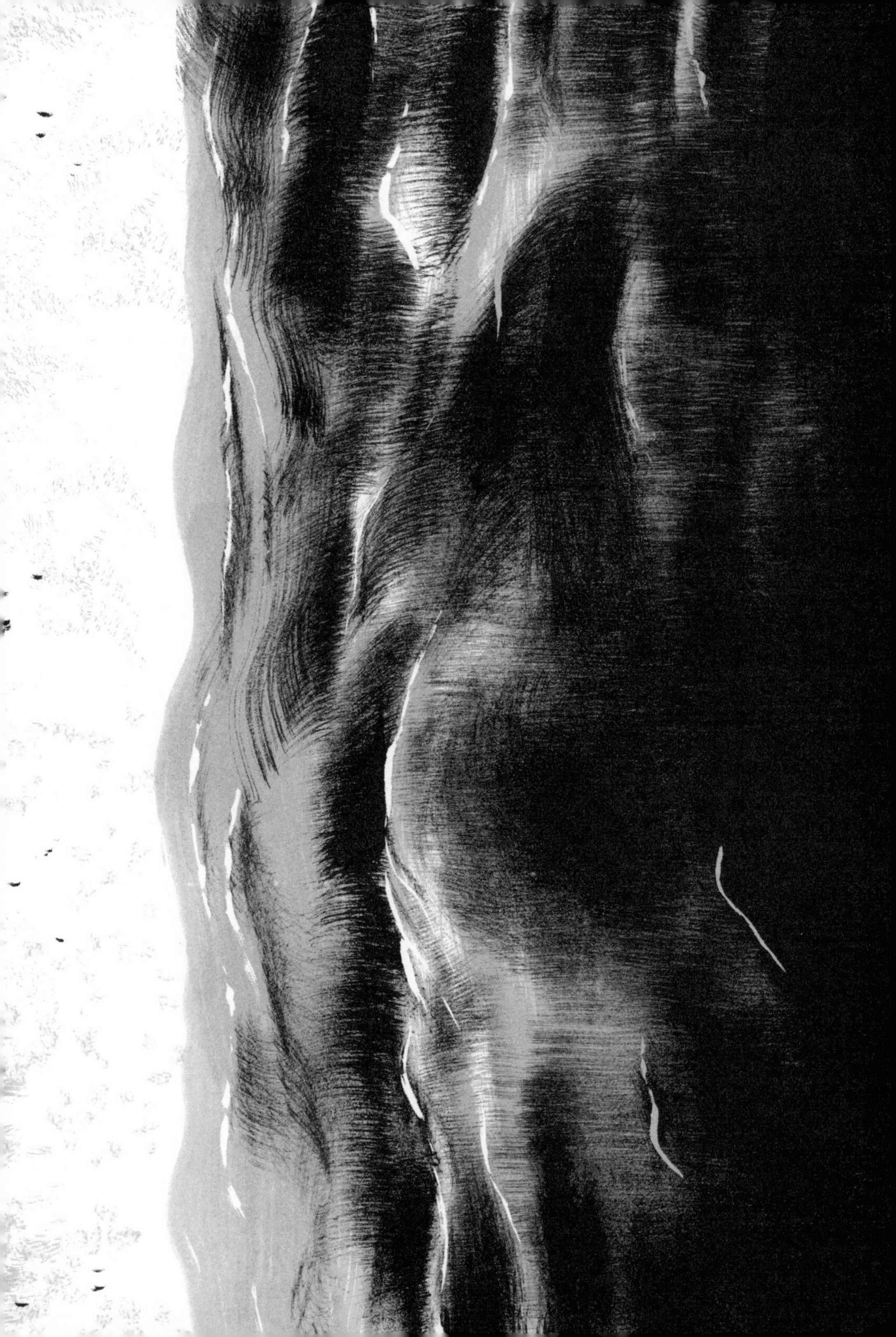

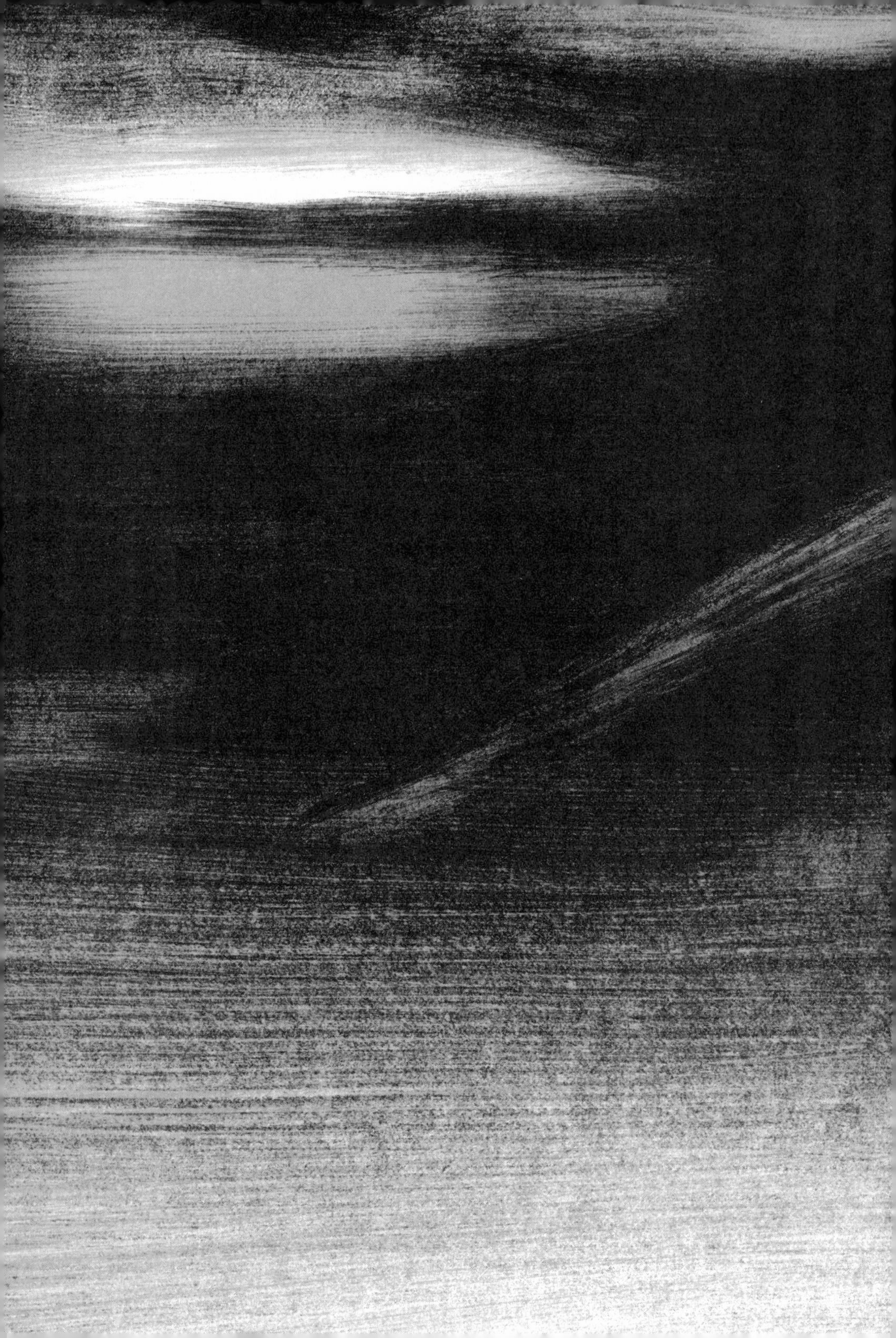

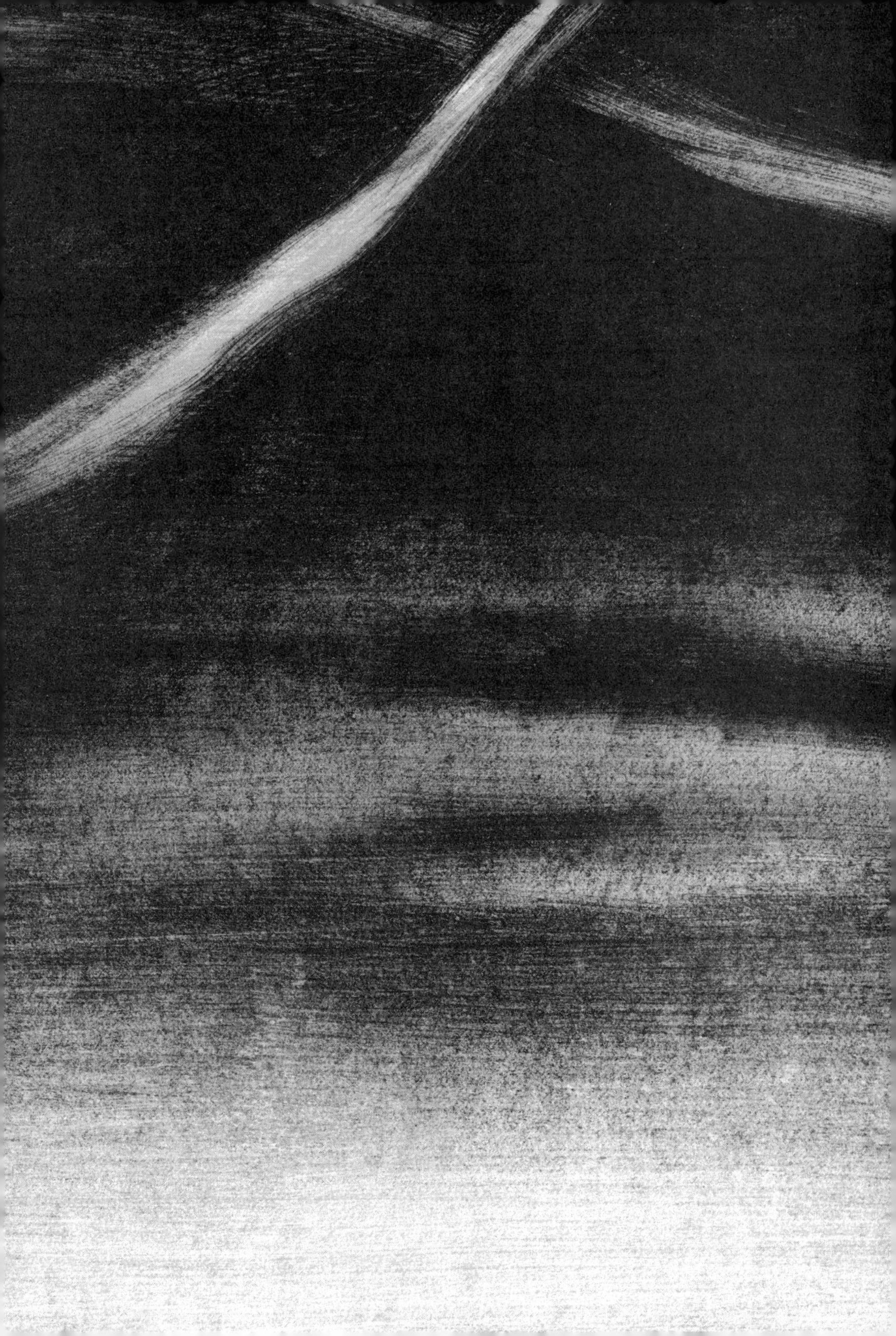

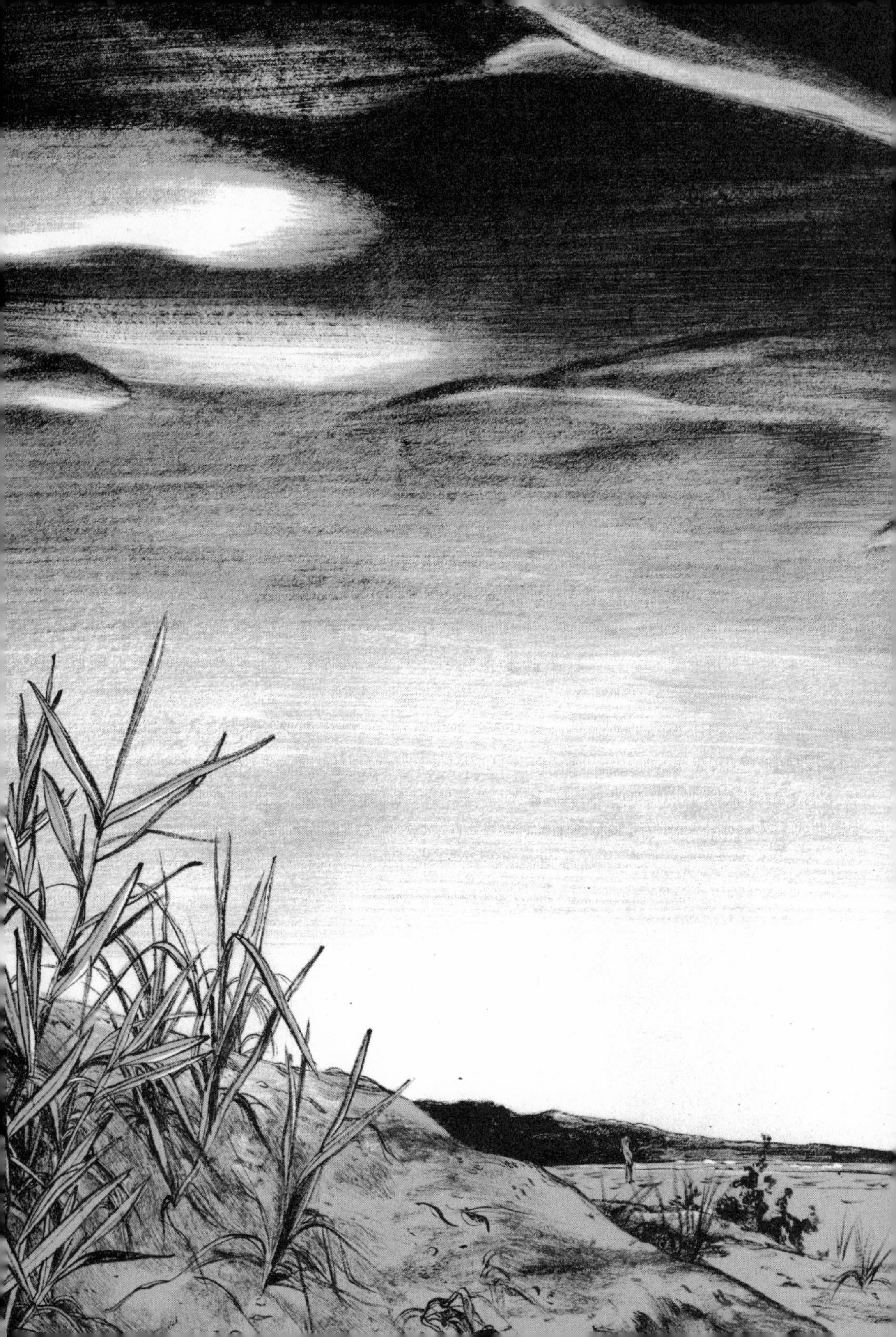

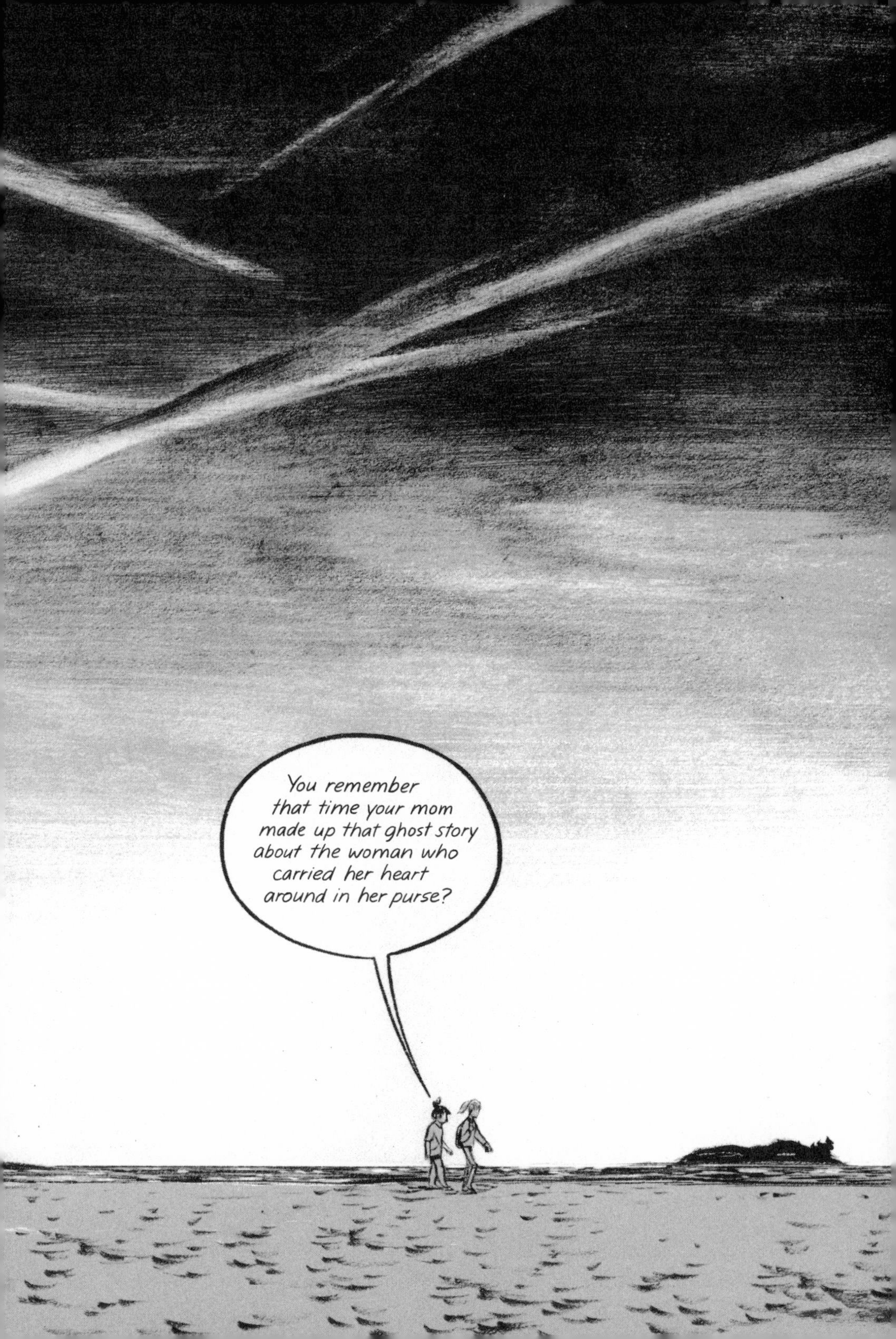
You remember that time your mom made up that ghost story about the woman who carried her heart around in her purse?

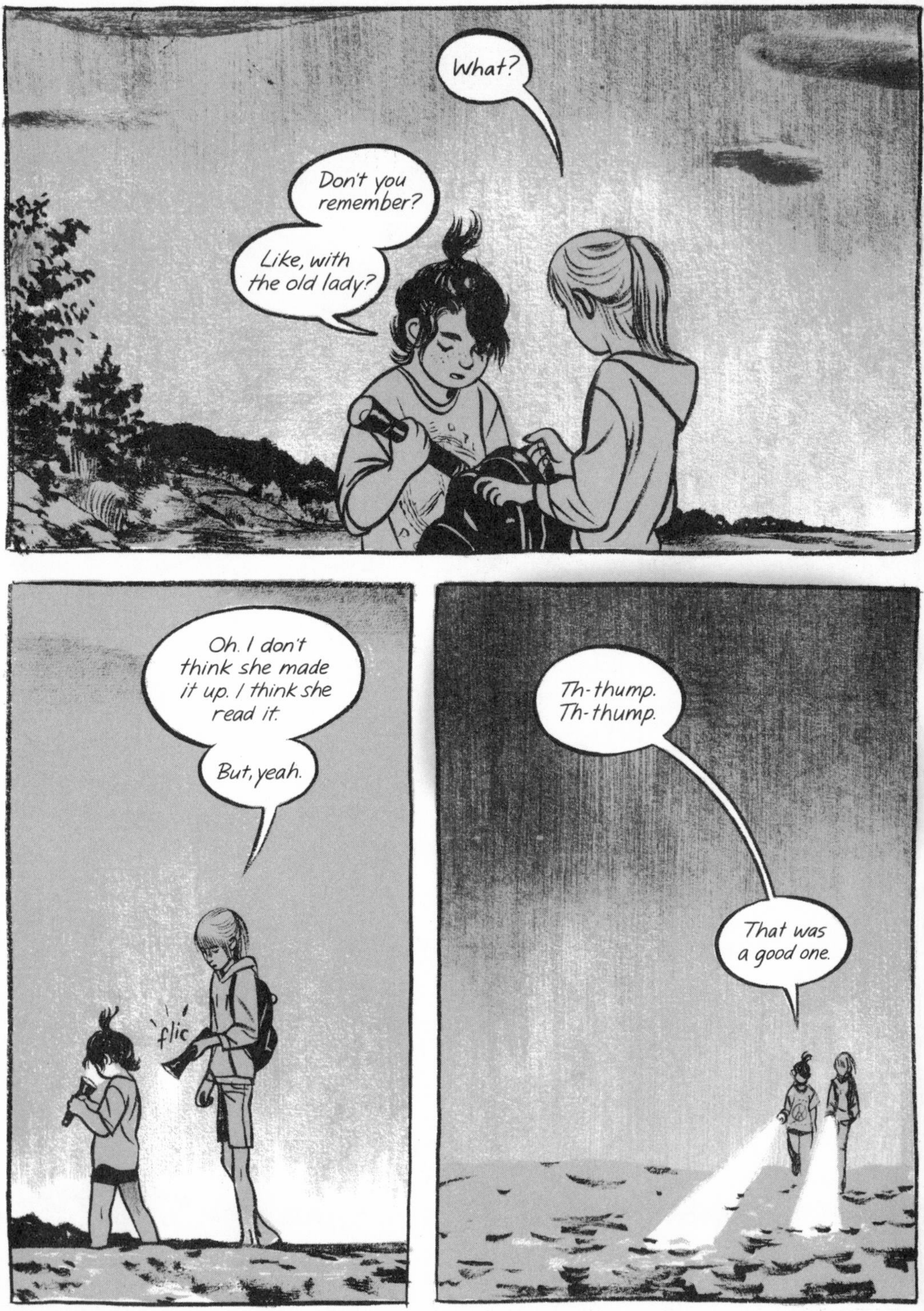
What?
Don't you remember?
Like, with the old lady?
Oh. I don't think she made it up. I think she read it.
But, yeah.
flic
Th-thump. Th-thump.
That was a good one.

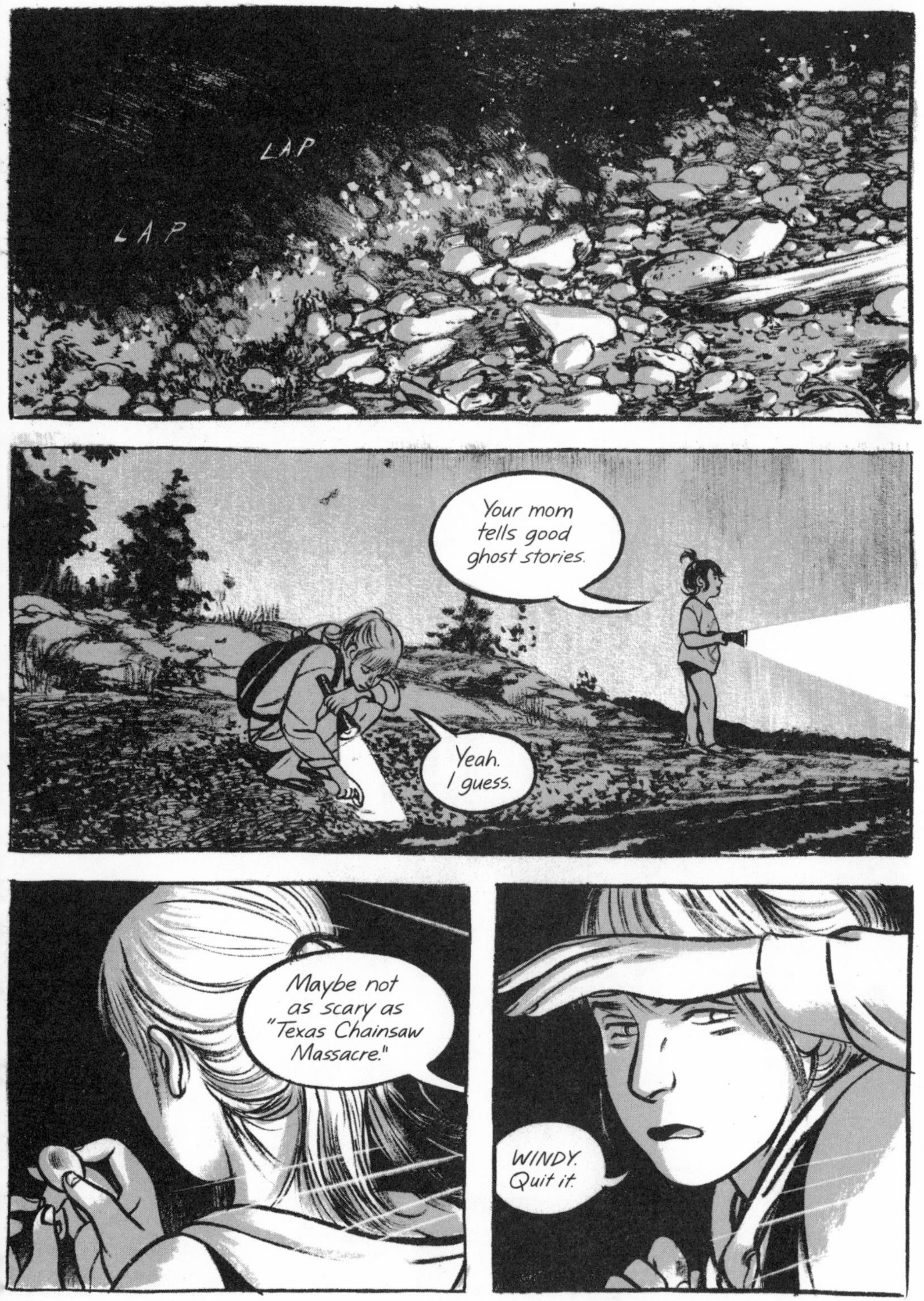
LAP
LAP
Your mom tells good ghost stories.
Yeah. I guess.
Maybe not as scary as "Texas Chainsaw Massacre."
WINDY. Quit it.

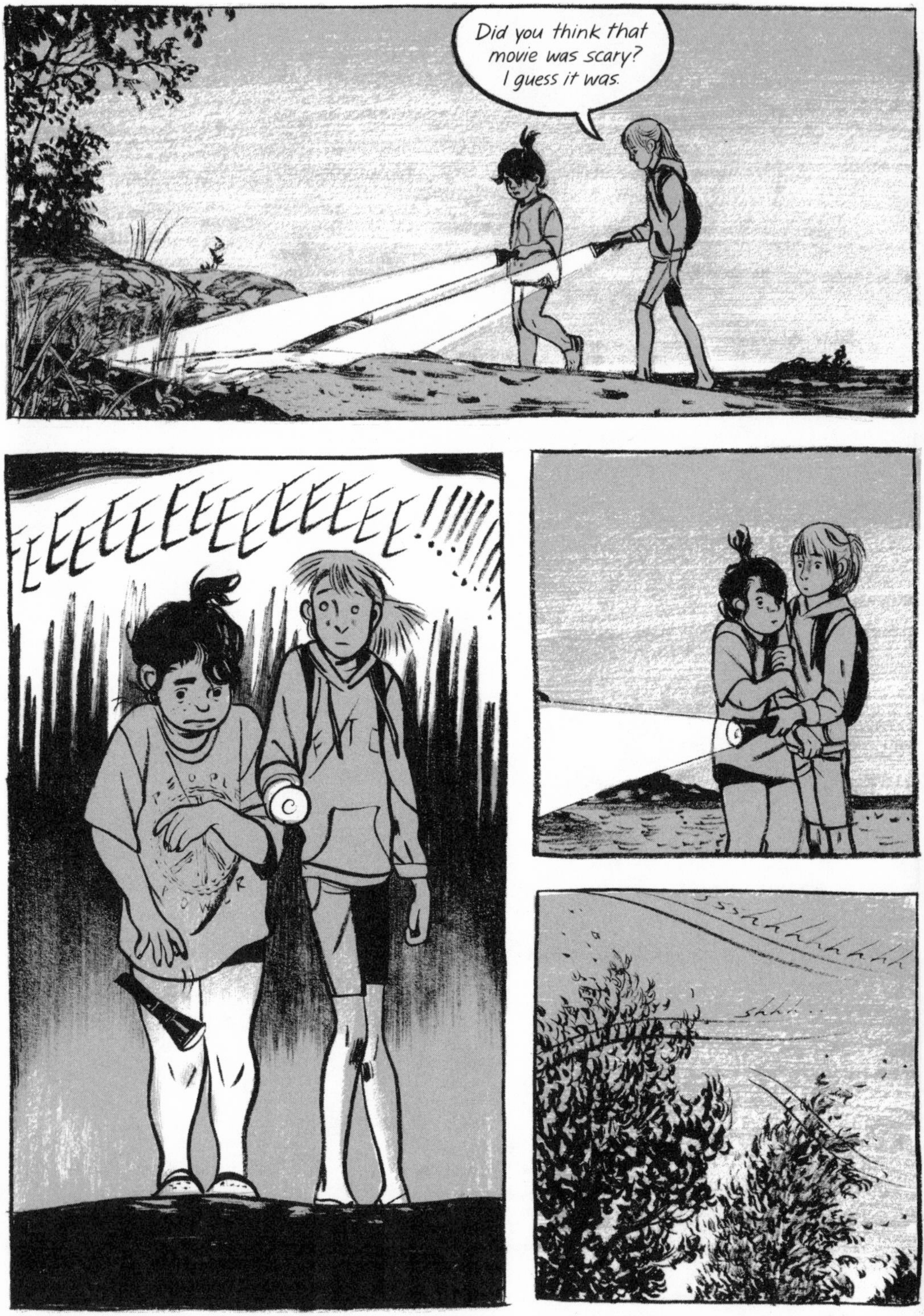
Did you think that movie was scary? I guess it was.
EEEEEEEEEEEEEE!!!!!
ssshhhhhhhh
shhh..

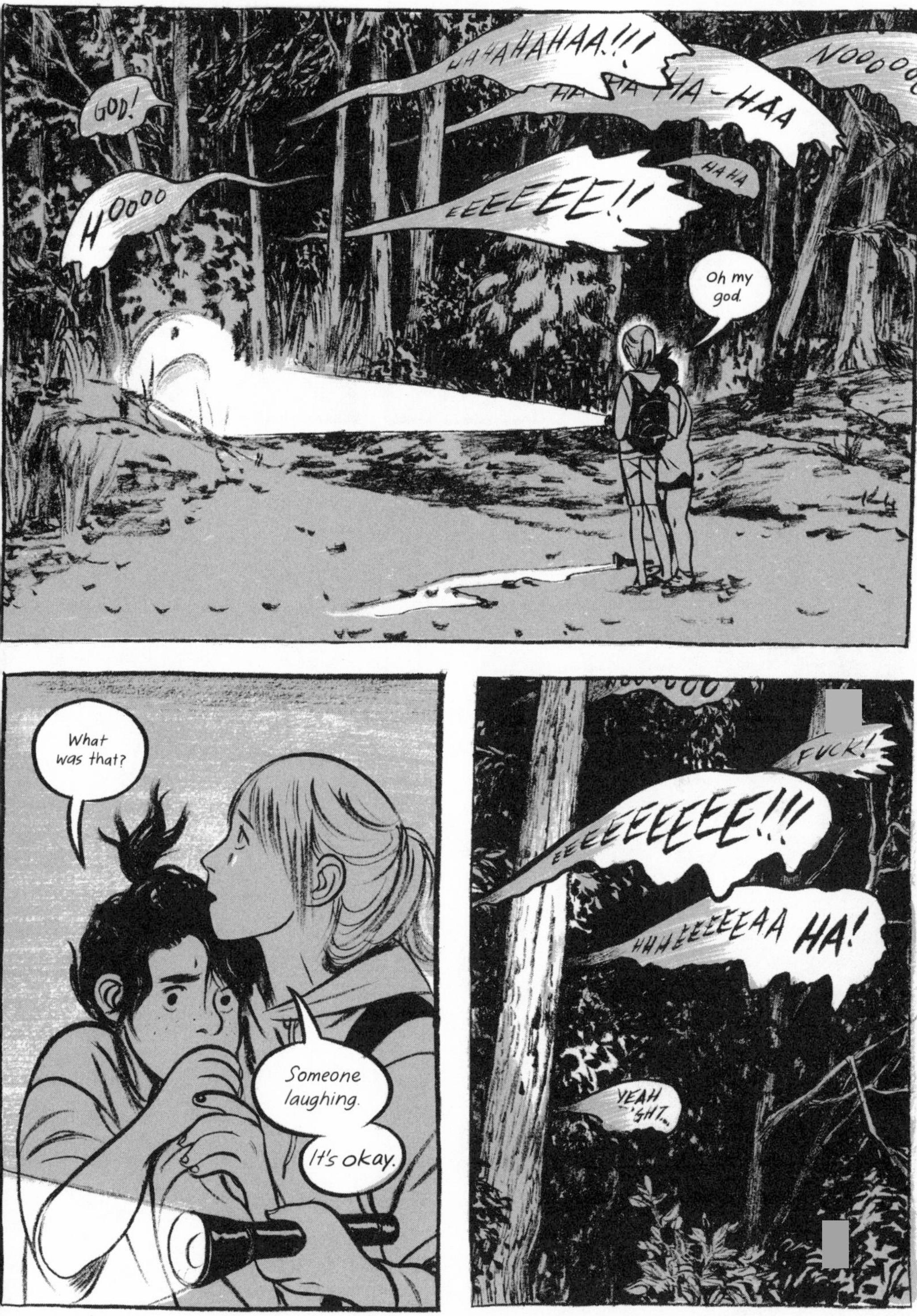
GOD!
HAHAHAA!!!
NOOOOOO
HA HA HA-HAA
HOOOO
EEEEEE!!
HA HA
Oh my god.
What was that?
Someone laughing.
It's okay.
FUCK!
EEEEEEEEE!!!
HHHEEEEEAA HA!
YEAH

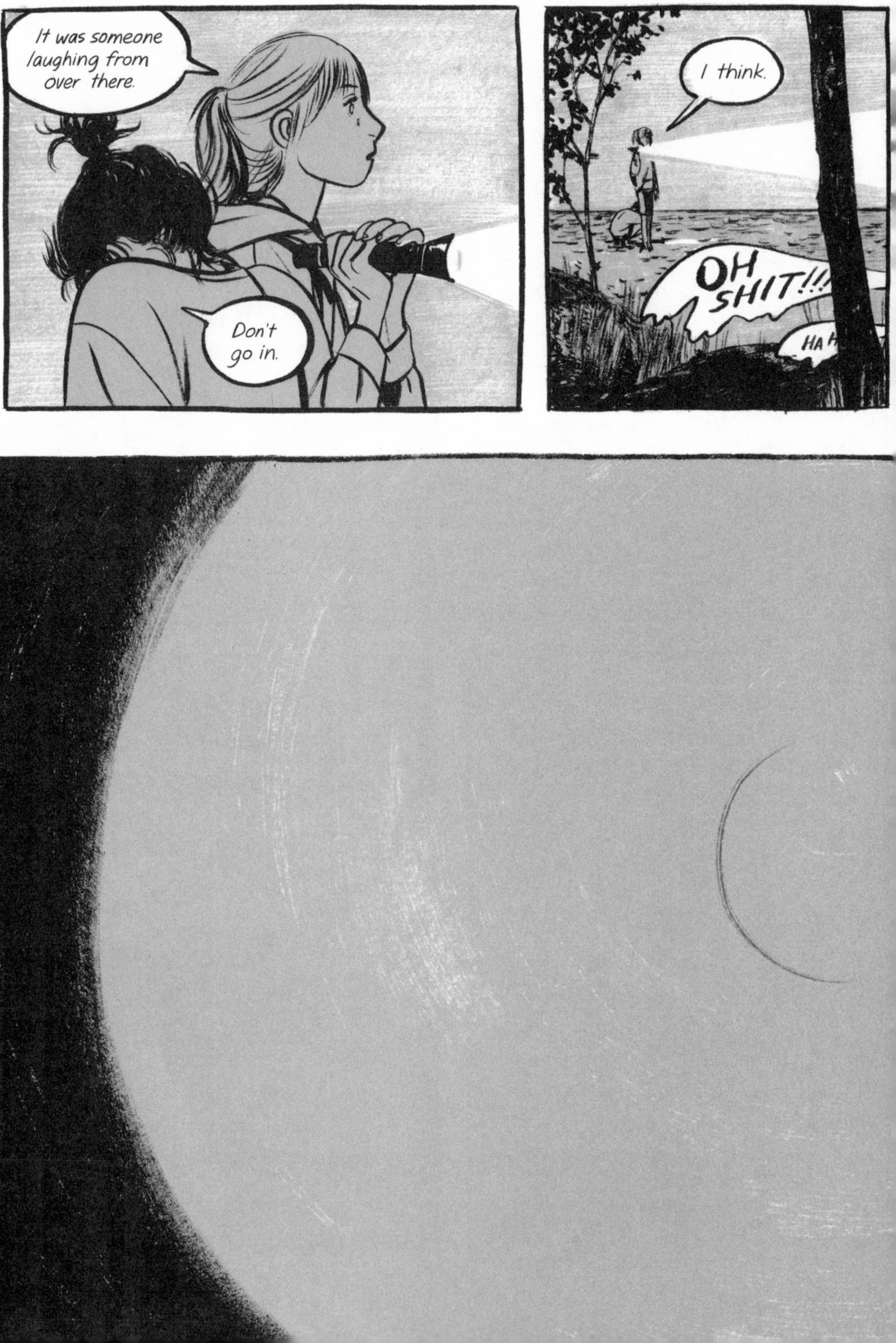
It was someone laughing from over there.
Don't go in.
I think.
OH SHIT!!!
HA H

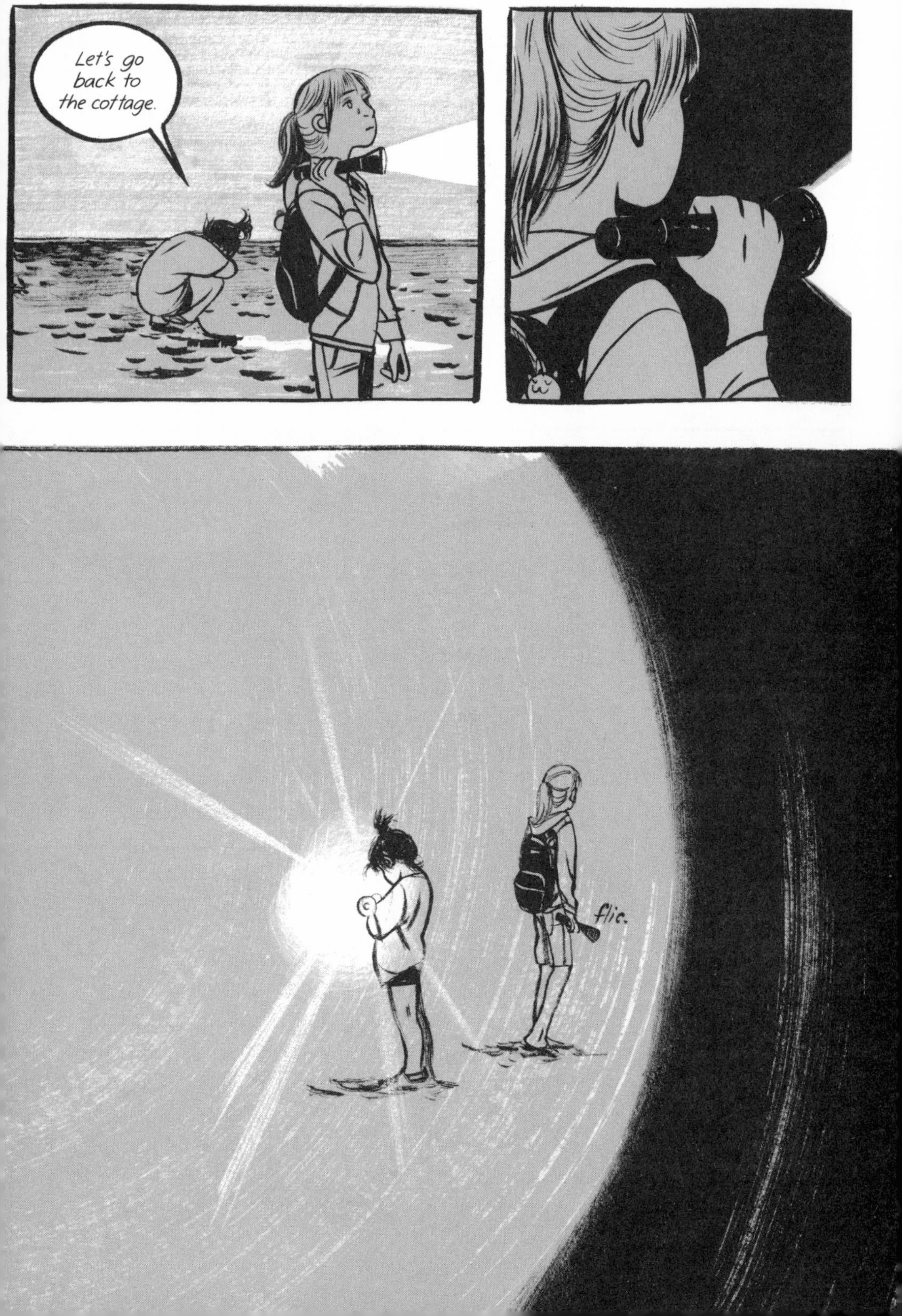
Let's go back to the cottage.
flic.

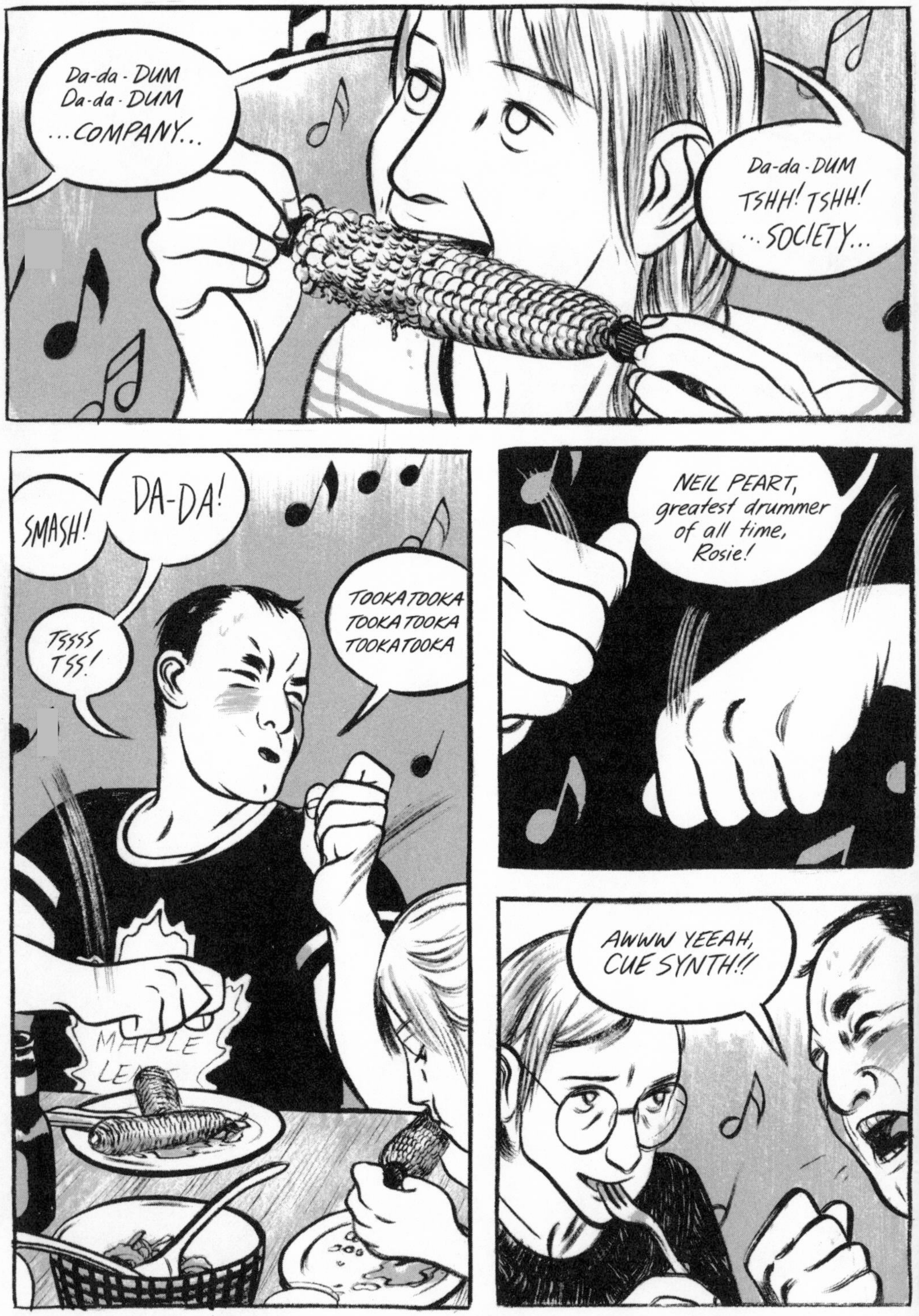
Da-da-DUM
Da-da-DUM
...COMPANY...
Da-da-DUM
TSHH! TSHH!
...SOCIETY...
SMASH!
DA-DA!
TSSSS
TSS!
TOOKATOOKA
TOOKATOOKA
TOOKATOOKA
MAPLE
NEIL PEART,
greatest drummer
of all time,
Rosie!
AWWW YEEAH,
CUE SYNTH!!

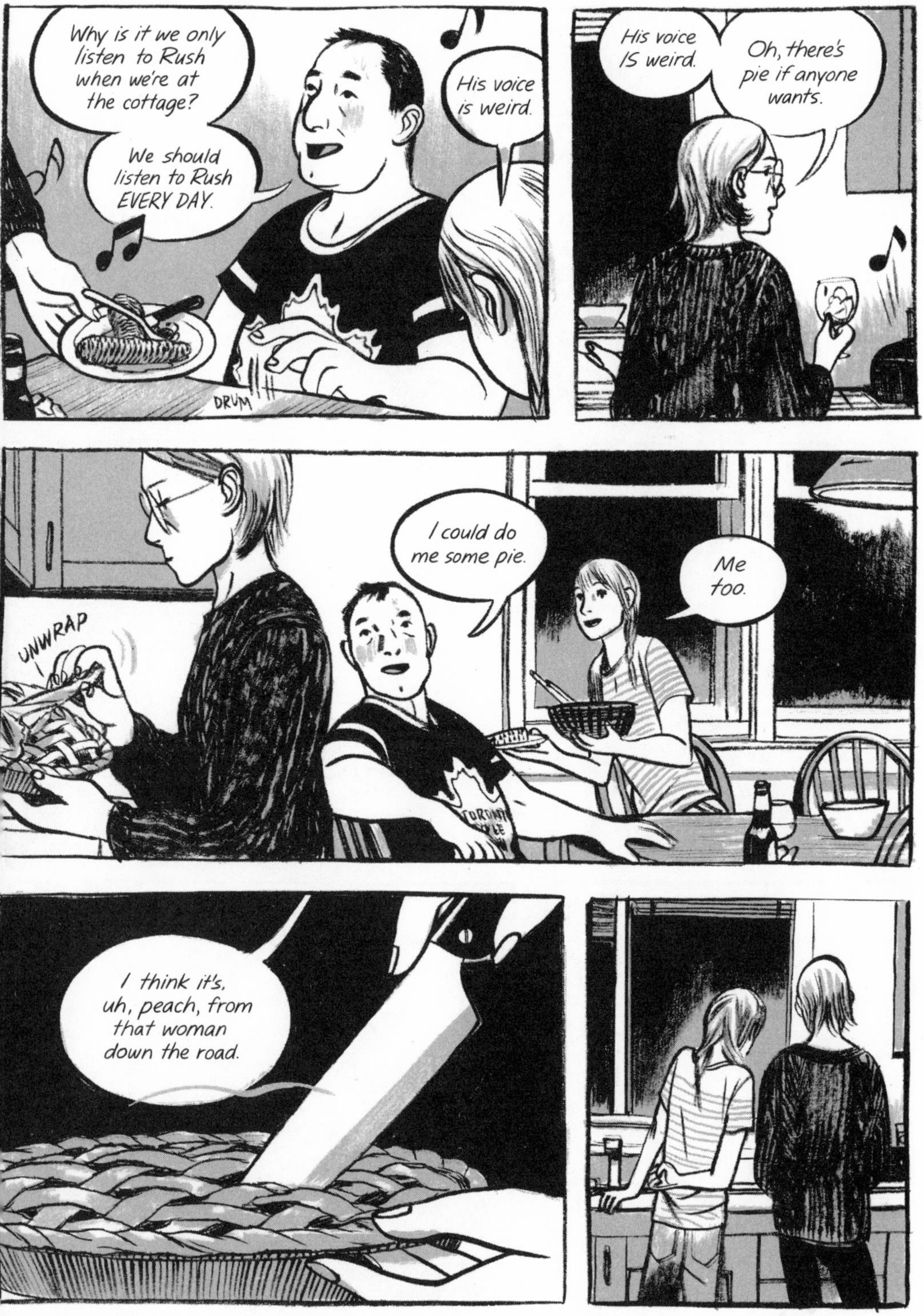
Why is it we only listen to Rush when we're at the cottage?
We should listen to Rush EVERY DAY.
His voice is weird.
DRUM
His voice IS weird.
Oh, there's pie if anyone wants.
UNWRAP
I could do me some pie.
Me too.
I think it's, uh, peach, from that woman down the road.

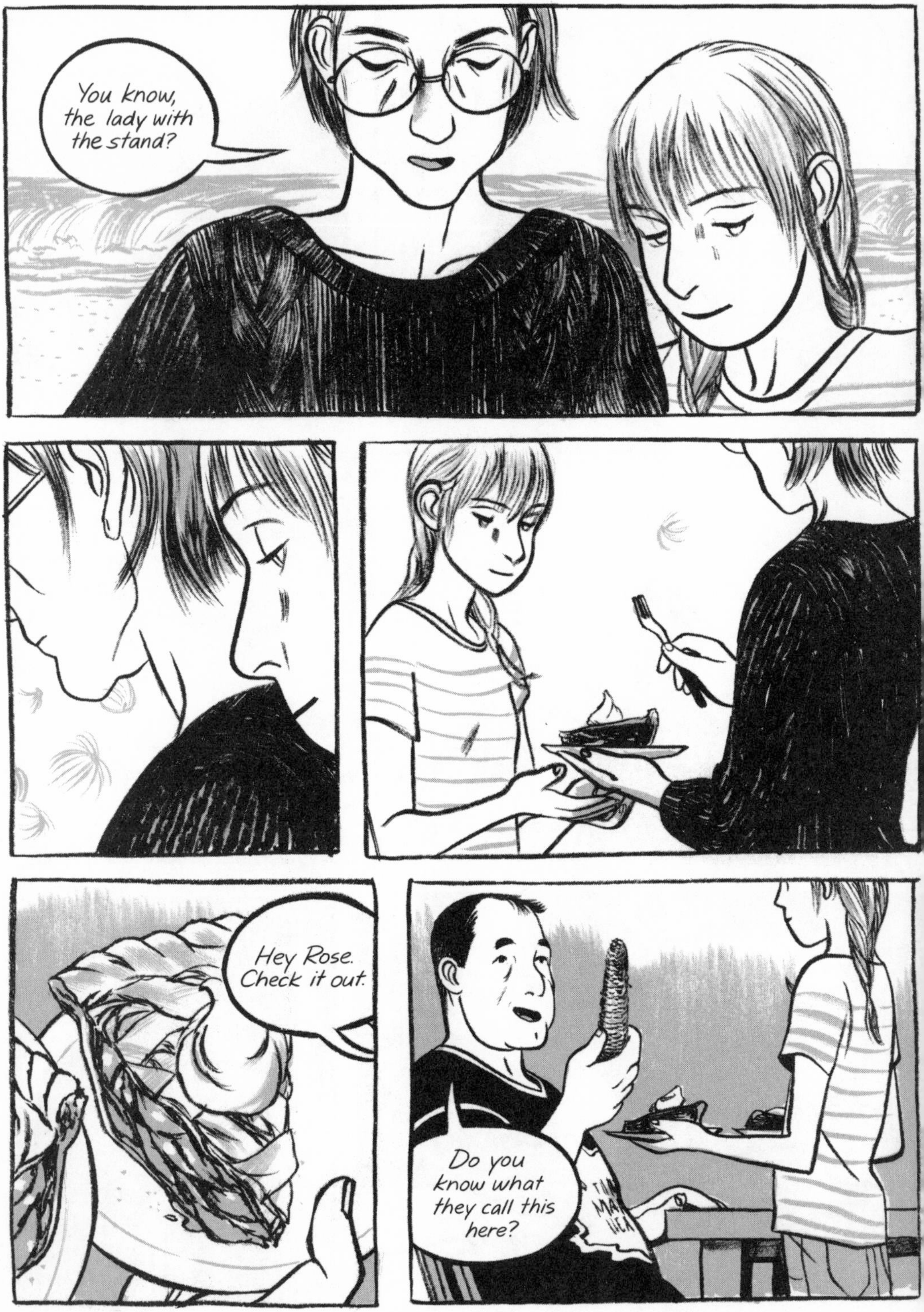
You know, the lady with the stand?
Hey Rose. Check it out.
Do you know what they call this here?

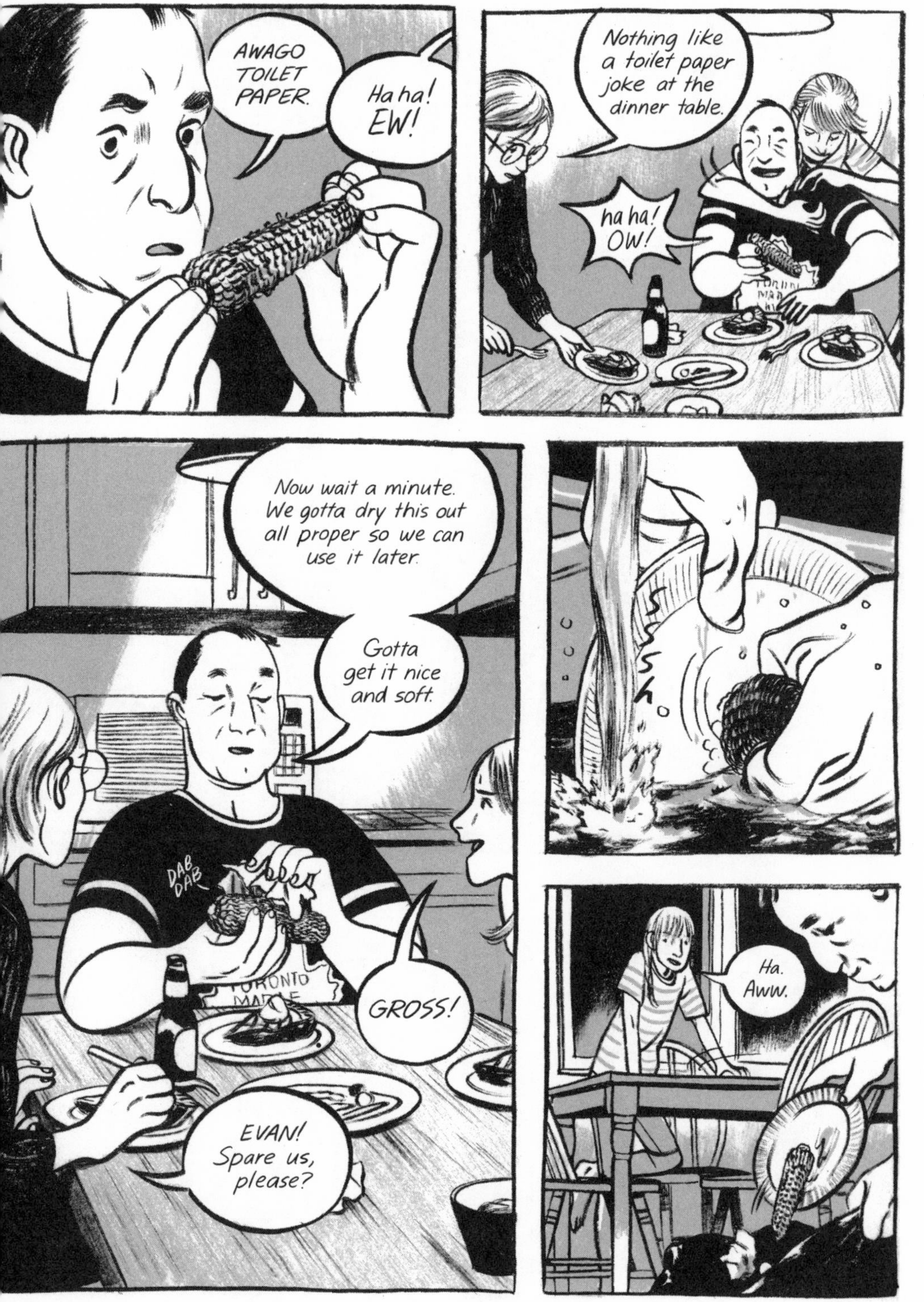
AWAGO TOILET PAPER.
Ha ha! EW!
Nothing like a toilet paper joke at the dinner table.
ha ha! OW!
Now wait a minute. We gotta dry this out all proper so we can use it later.
Gotta get it nice and soft.
DAB DAB
GROSS!
EVAN! Spare us, please?
SSh
Ha. Aww.

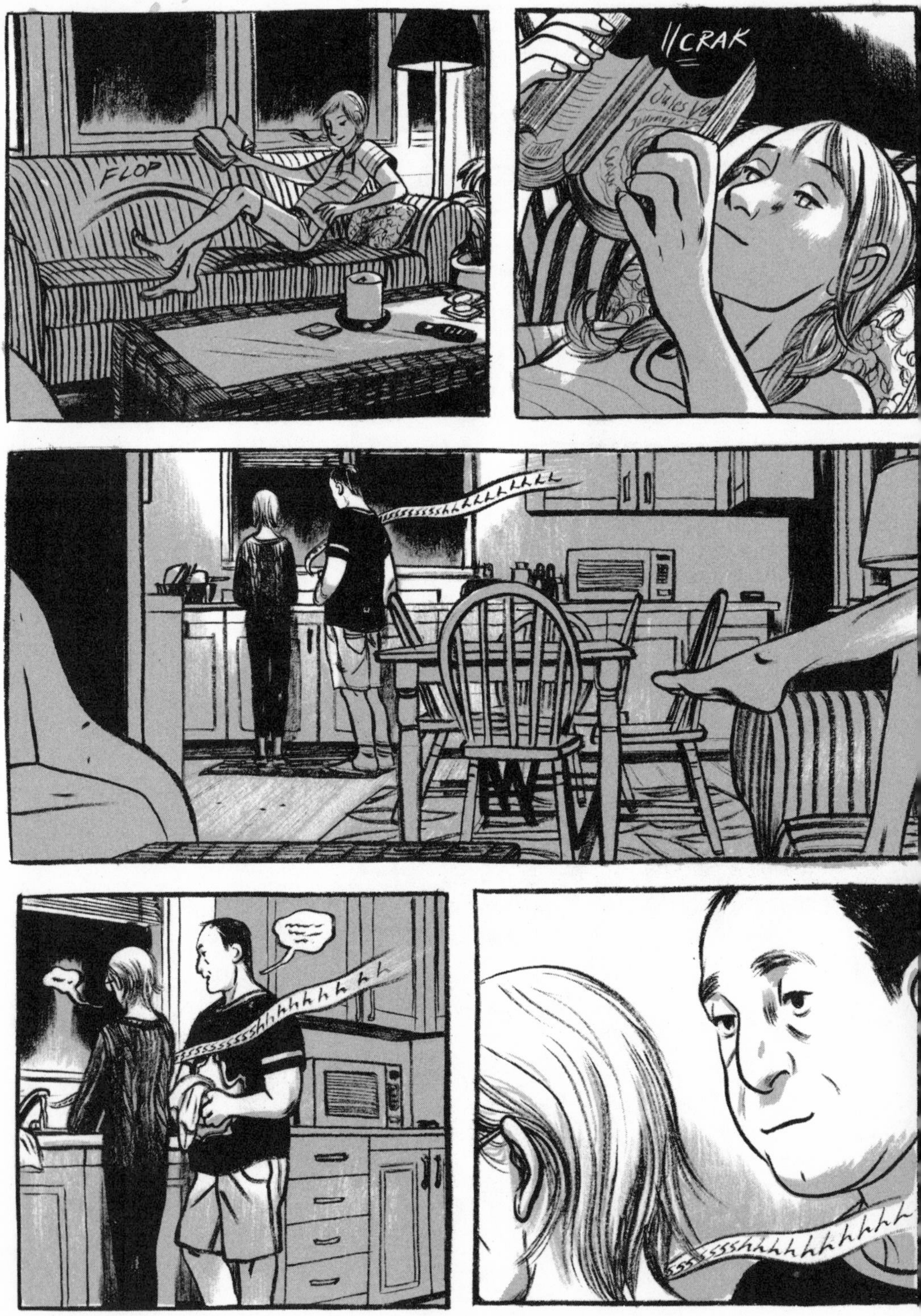
FLOP
CRAK

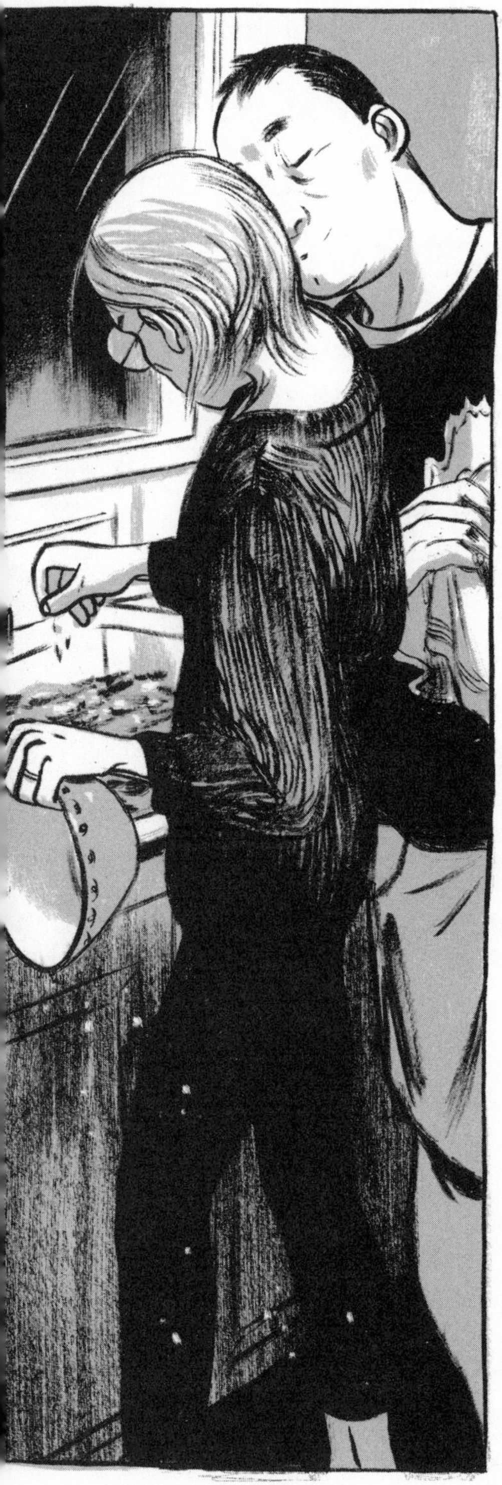

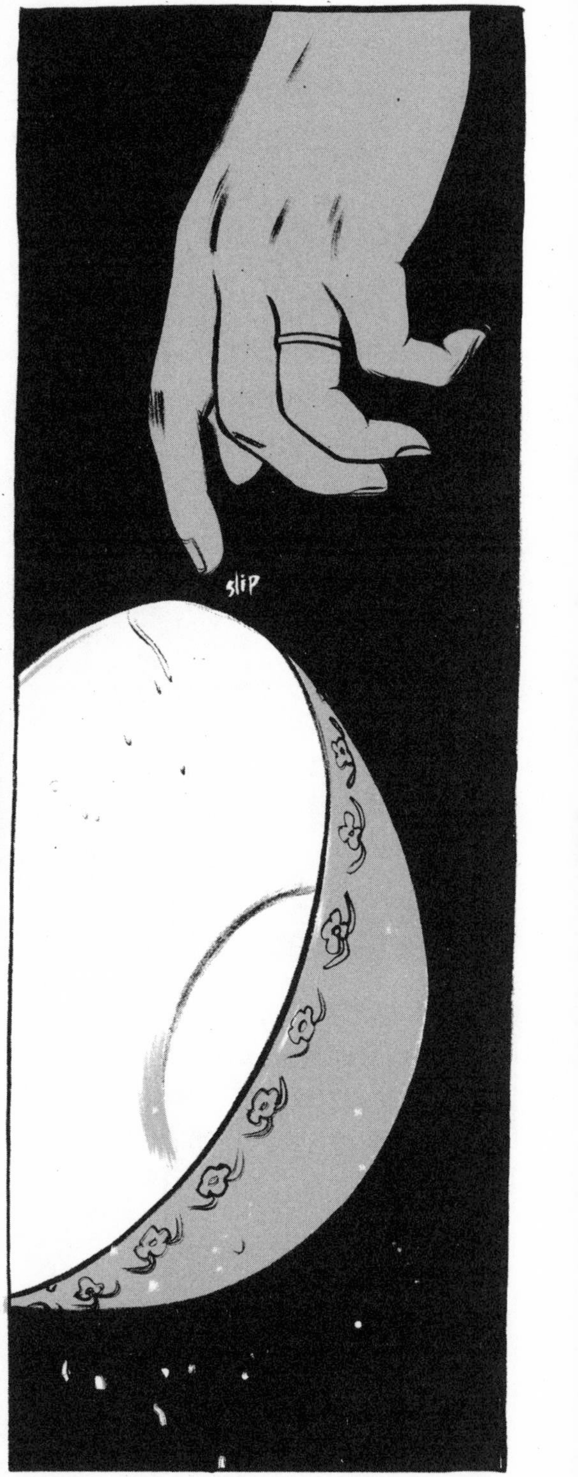
slip

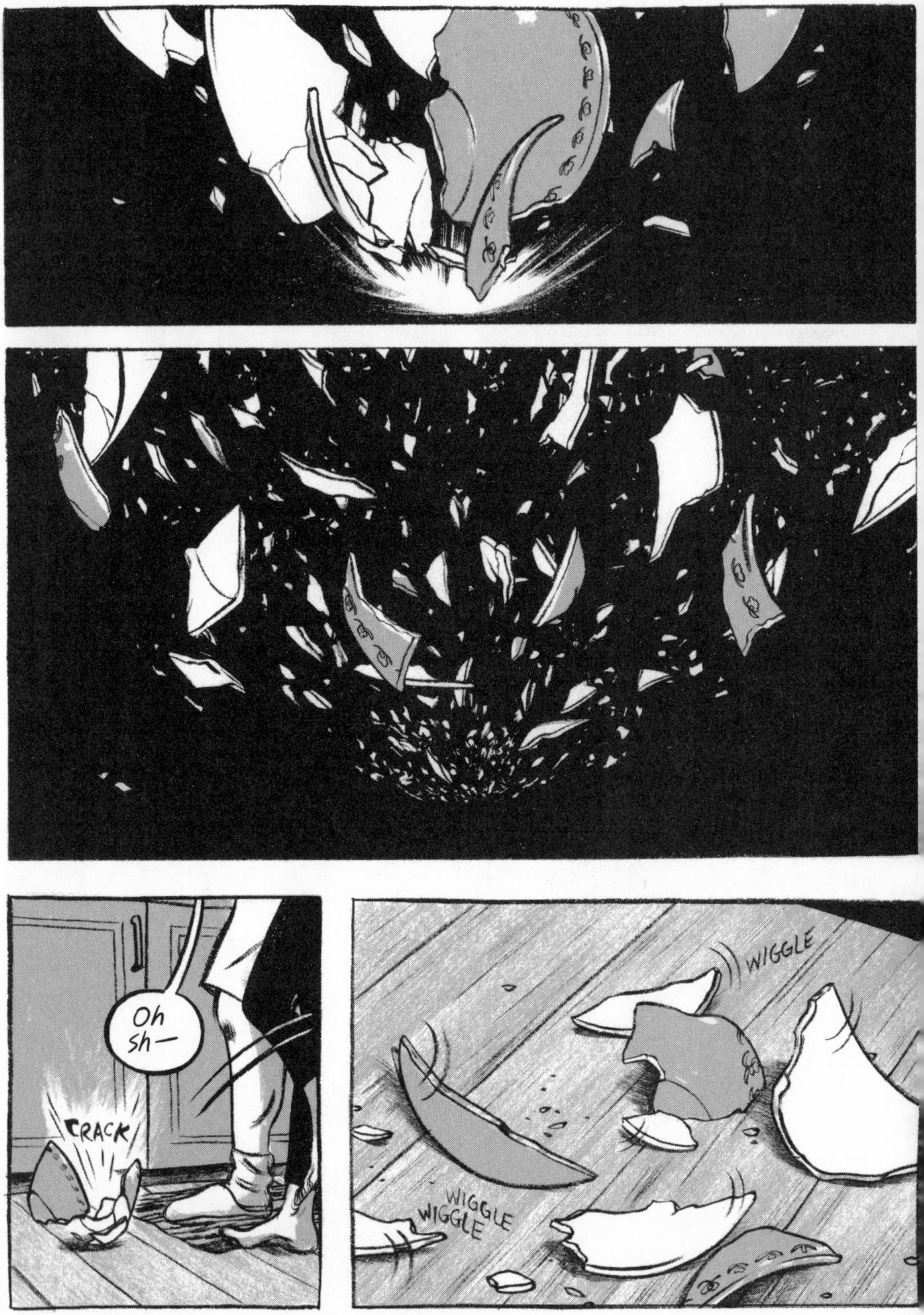
Oh sh—
CRACK
WIGGLE
WIGGLE
WIGGLE

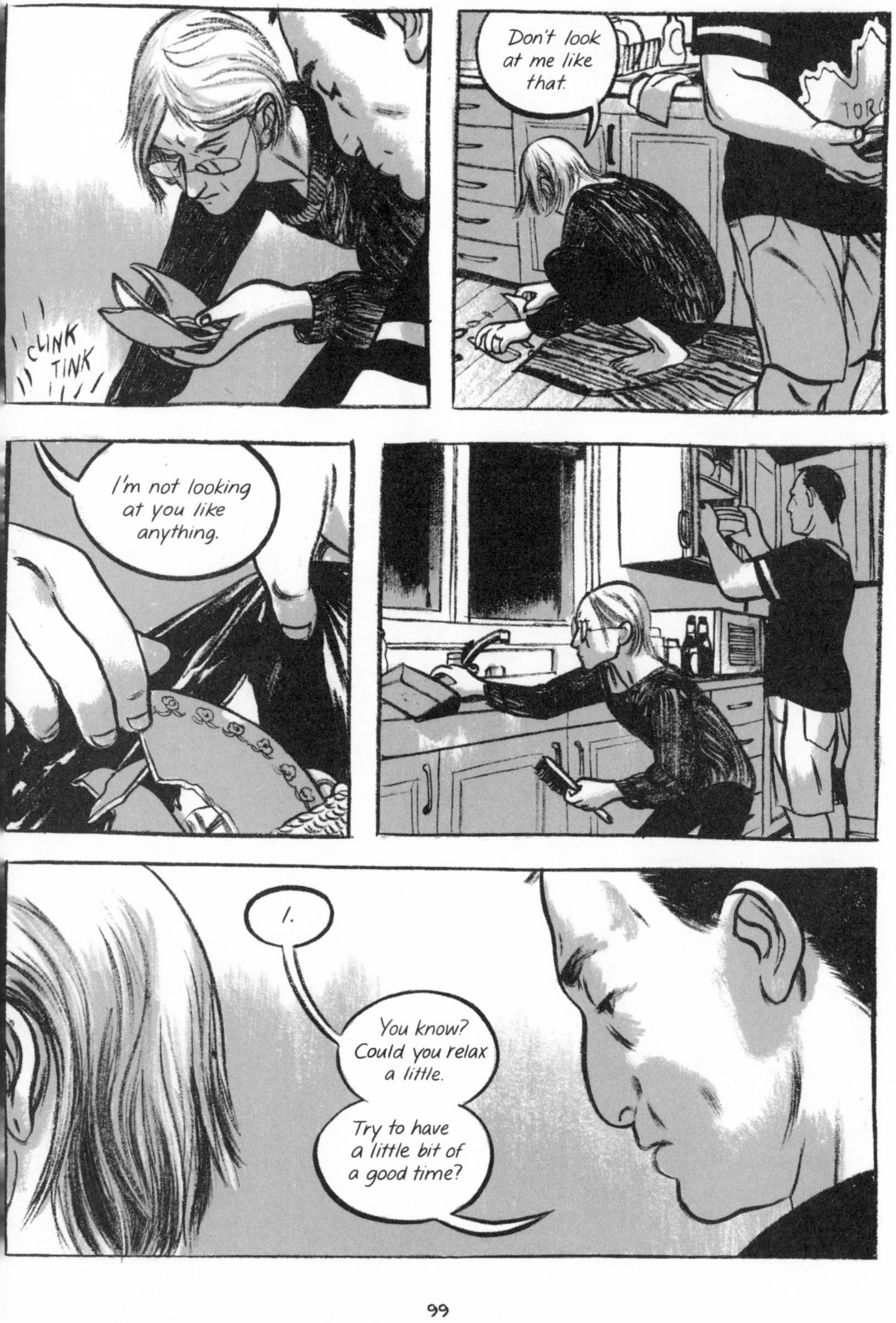
CLINK
TINK
Don't look at me like that.
I'm not looking at you like anything.
I.
You know? Could you relax a little.
Try to have a little bit of a good time?

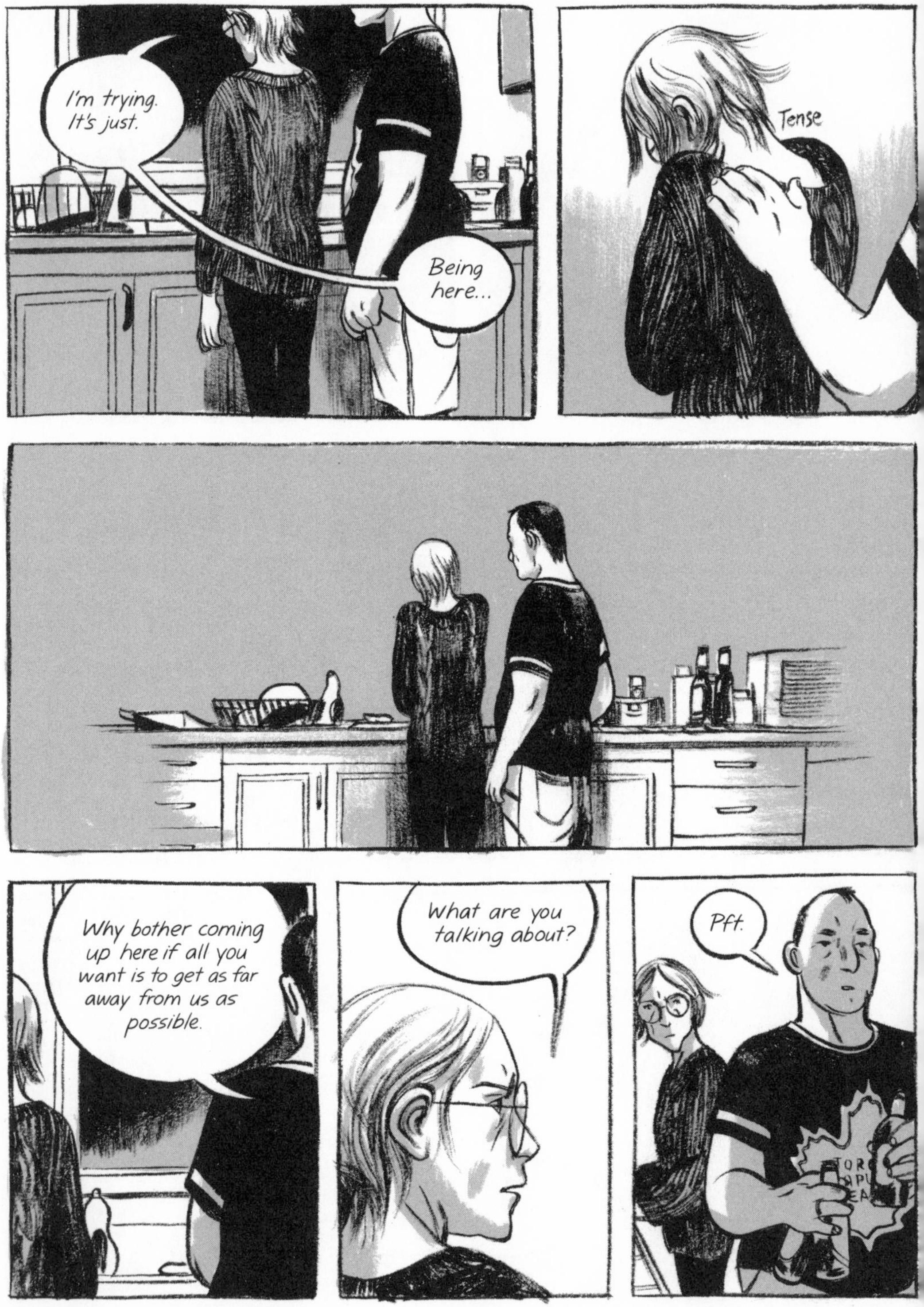
I'm trying. It's just.
Being here...
Tense
Why bother coming up here if all you want is to get as far away from us as possible.
What are you talking about?
Pft.

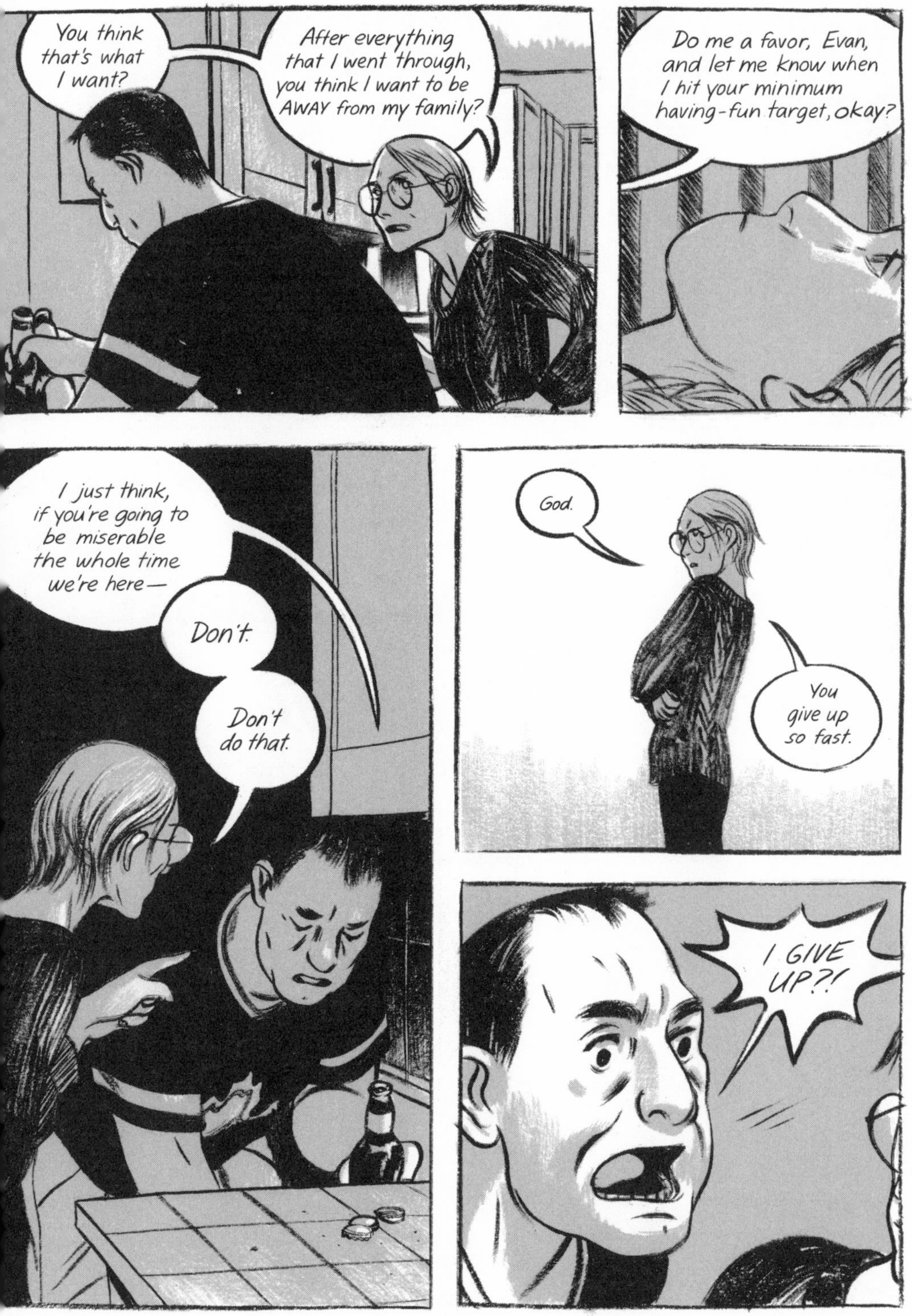
You think that's what I want?
After everything that I went through, you think I want to be AWAY from my family?
Do me a favor, Evan, and let me know when I hit your minimum having-fun target, okay?
I just think, if you're going to be miserable the whole time we're here—
Don't.
Don't do that.
God.
You give up so fast.
I GIVE UP?!

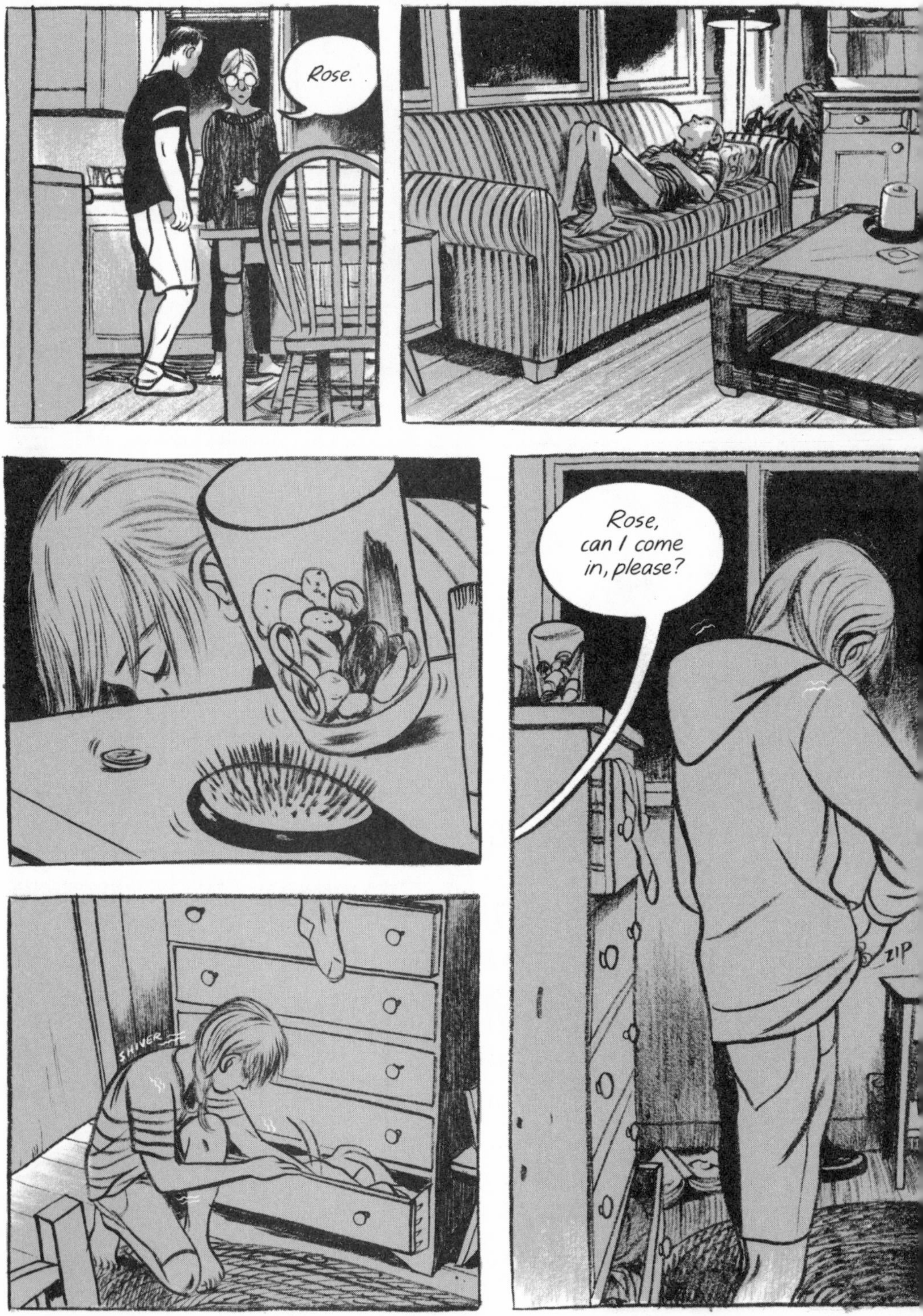
Rose.
Rose, can I come in, please?
SHIVER
ZIP

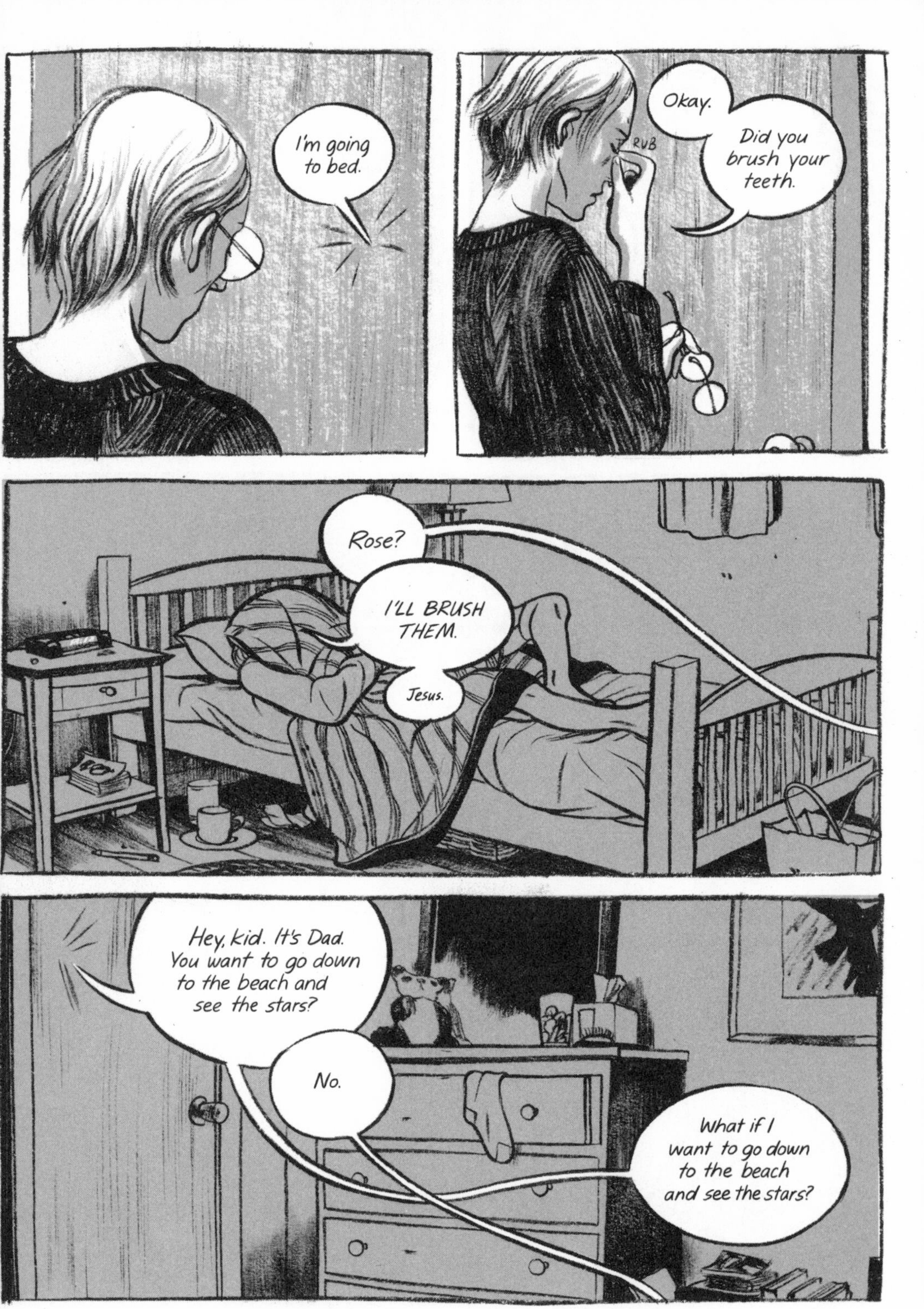
I'm going to bed.
RUB
Okay.
Did you brush your teeth.
Rose?
I'LL BRUSH THEM.
Jesus.
Hey, kid. It's Dad. You want to go down to the beach and see the stars?
No.
What if I want to go down to the beach and see the stars?

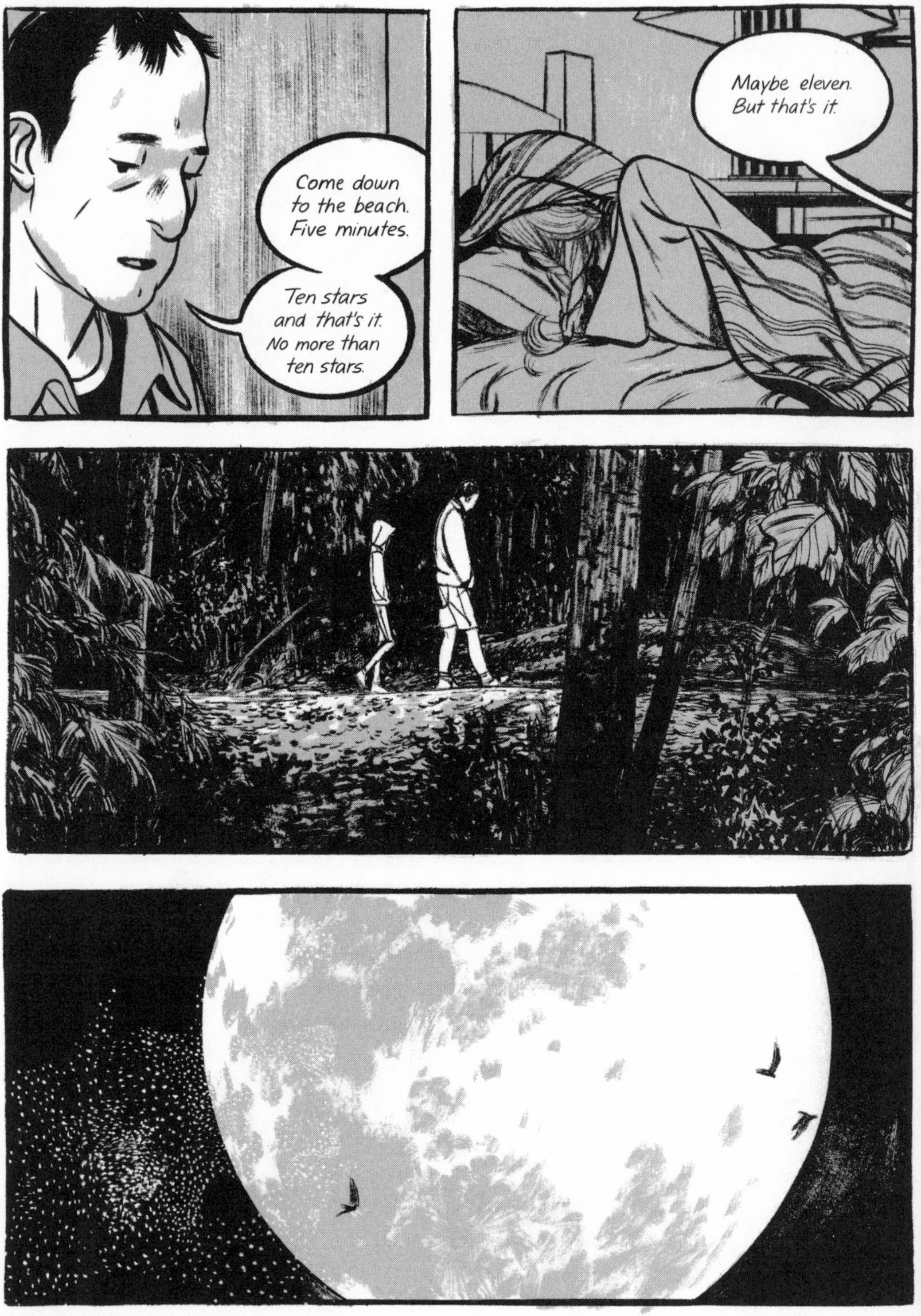
Come down to the beach. Five minutes.
Ten stars and that's it. No more than ten stars.
Maybe eleven. But that's it.

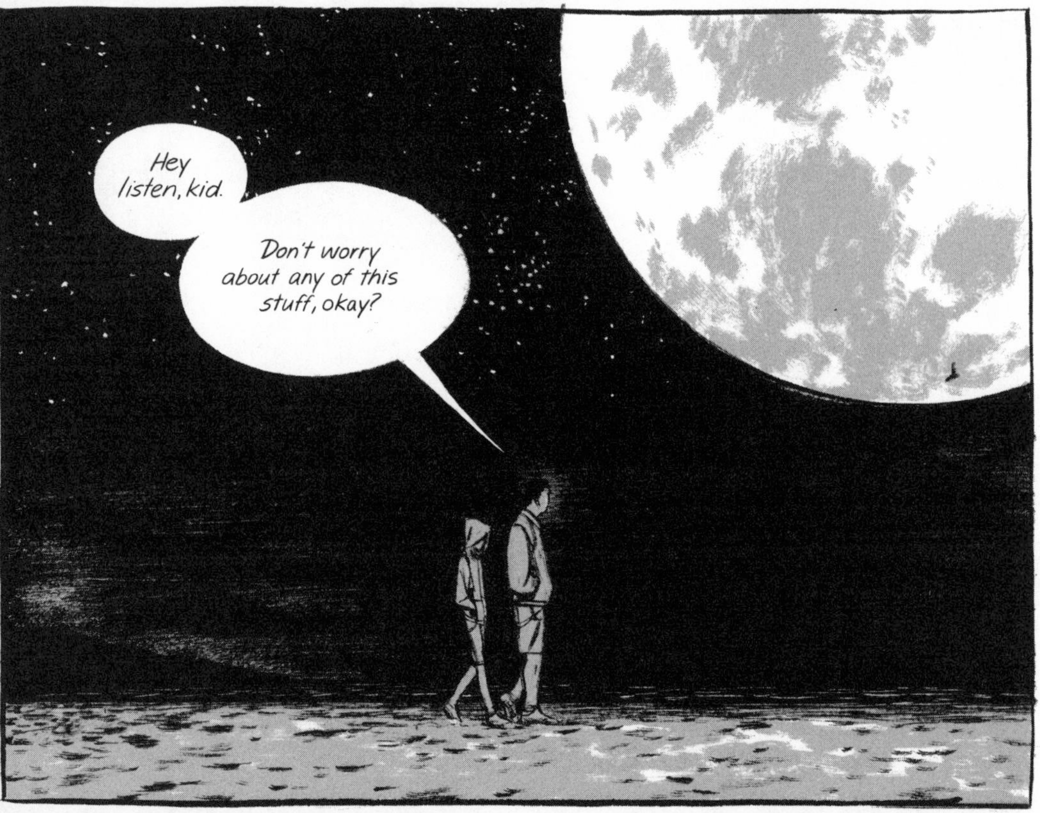
Hey listen, kid.
Don't worry about any of this stuff, okay?

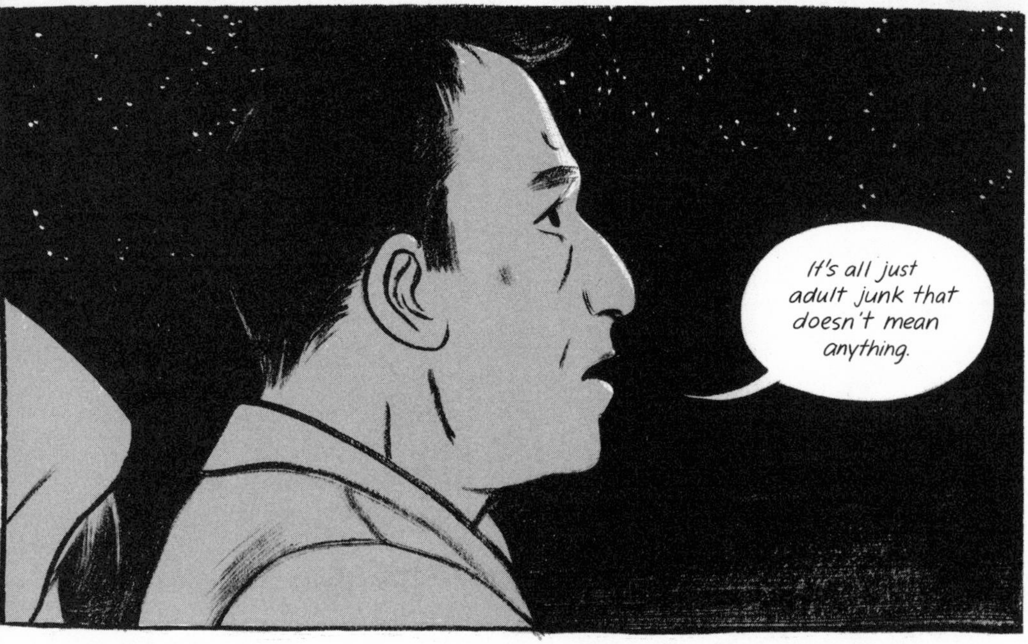
It's all just adult junk that doesn't mean anything.

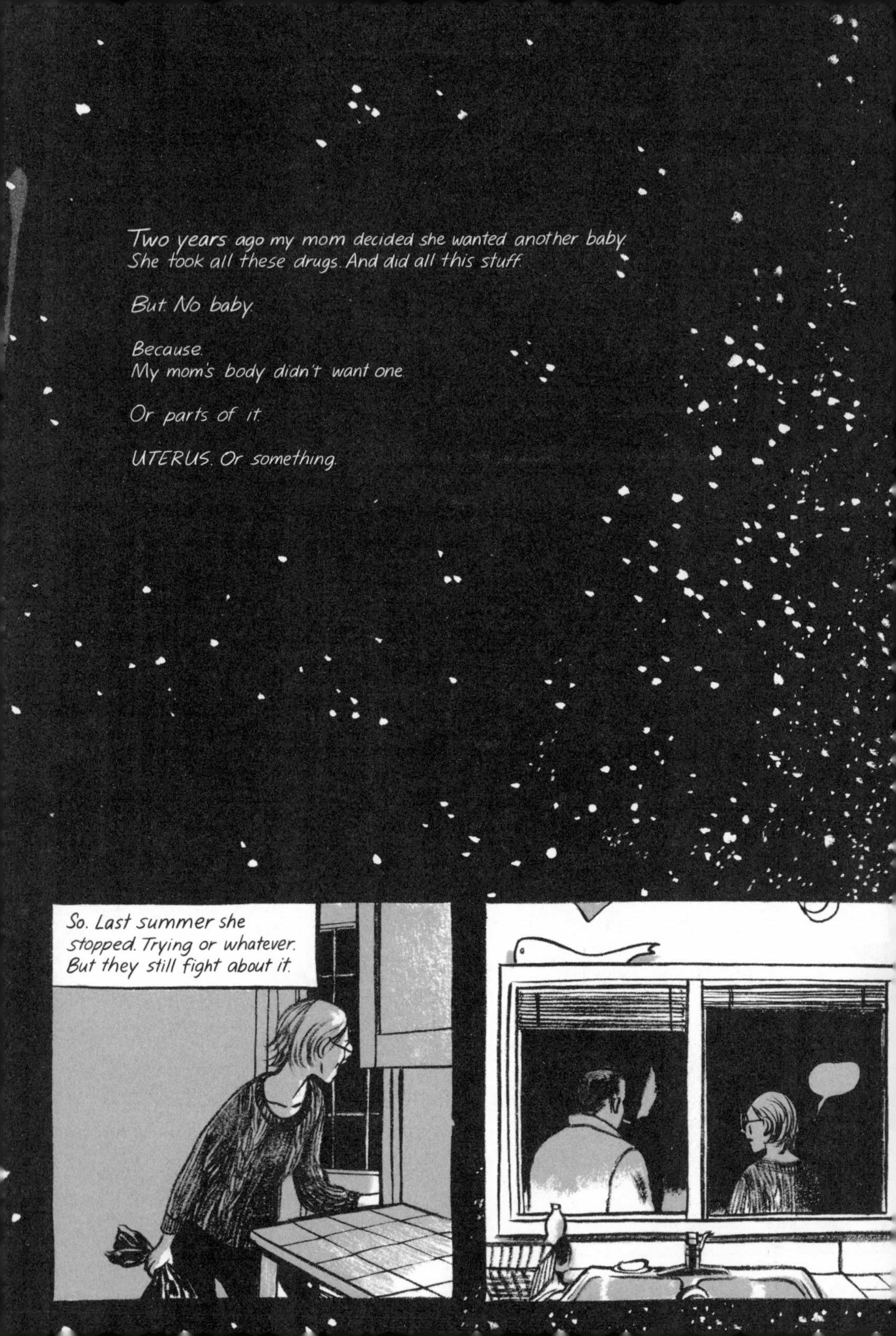
Two years ago my mom decided she wanted another baby.
She took all these drugs. And did all this stuff.
But. No baby.
Because.
My mom's body didn't want one.
Or parts of it.
UTERUS. Or something.
So. Last summer she stopped. Trying or whatever. But they still fight about it.

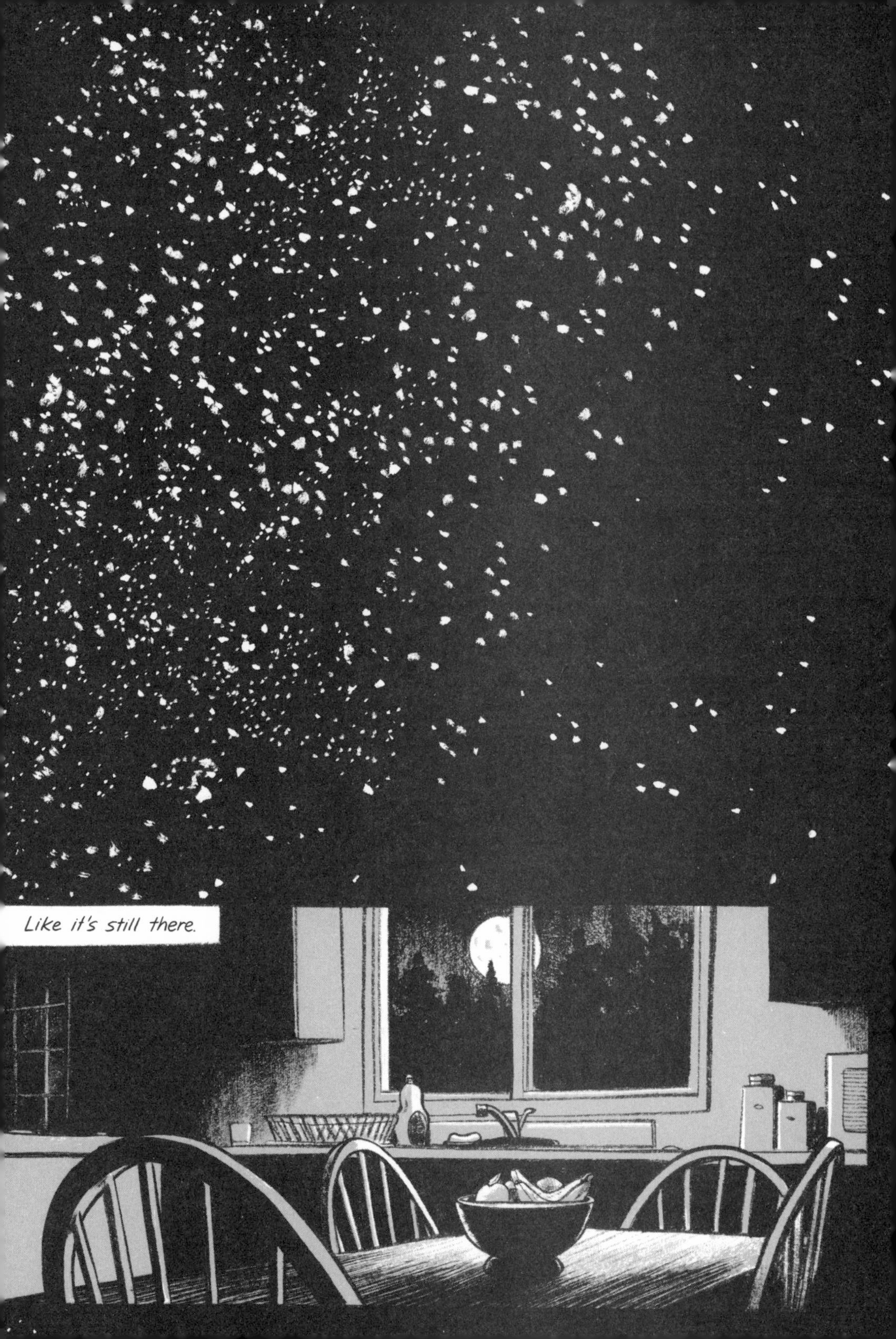
Like it's still there.

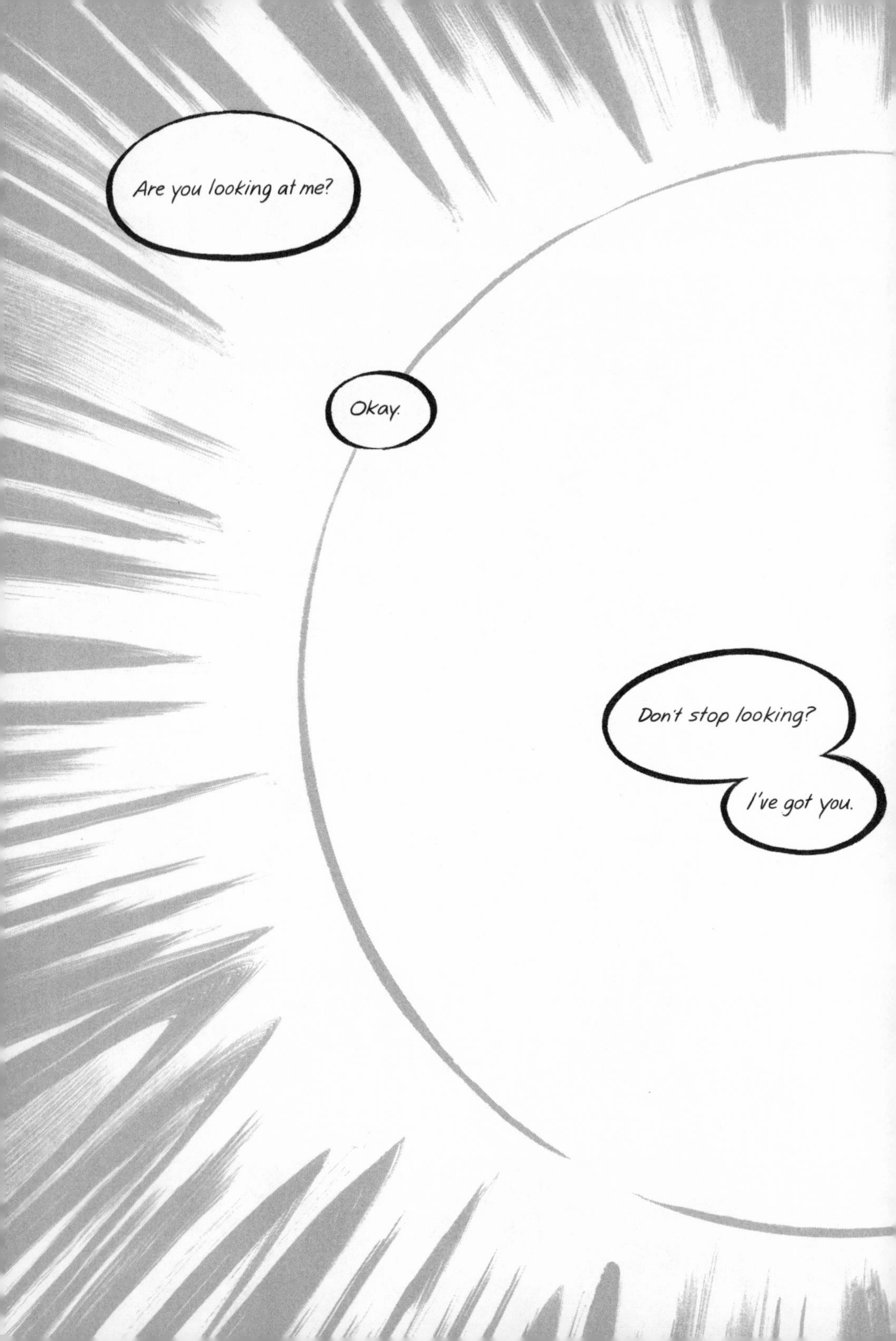
Are you looking at me?
Okay.
Don't stop looking?
I've got you.

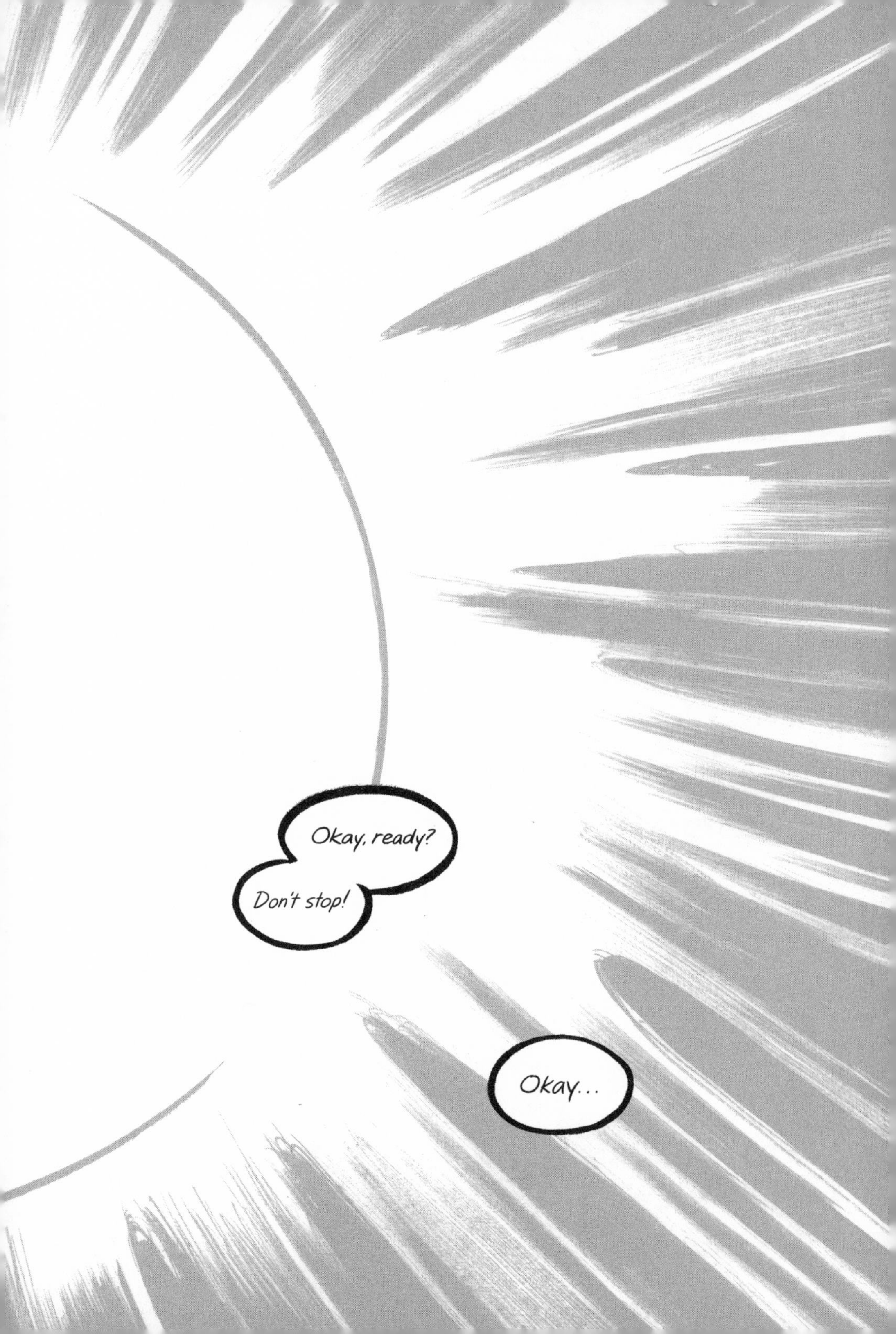
Okay, ready?
Don't stop!
Okay...

One...
Two...
Don't stop looking!
Three!

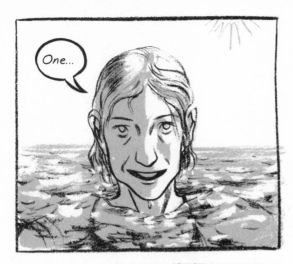

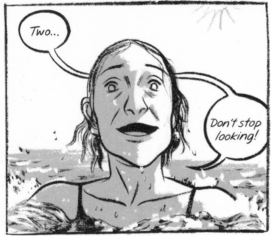

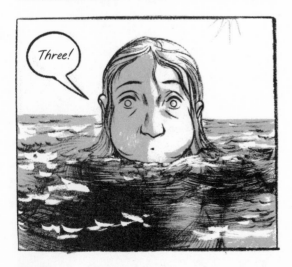

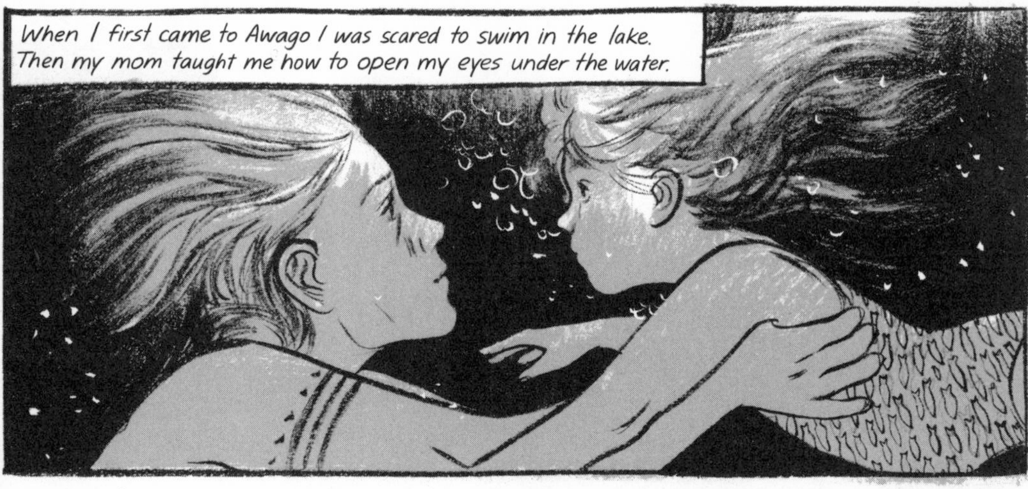
When I first came to Awago I was scared to swim in the lake. Then my mom taught me how to open my eyes under the water.

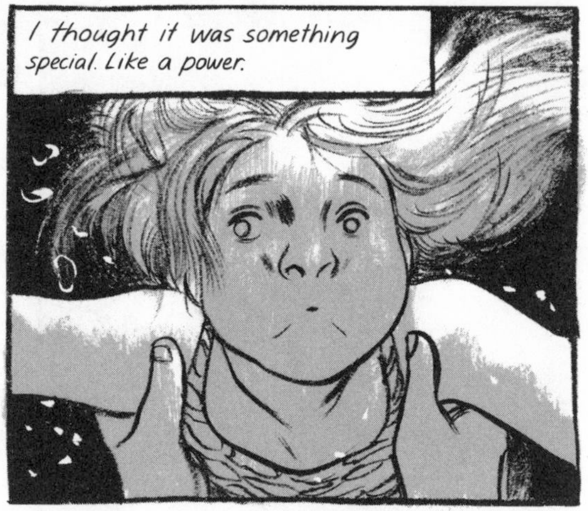
I thought it was something special. Like a power.

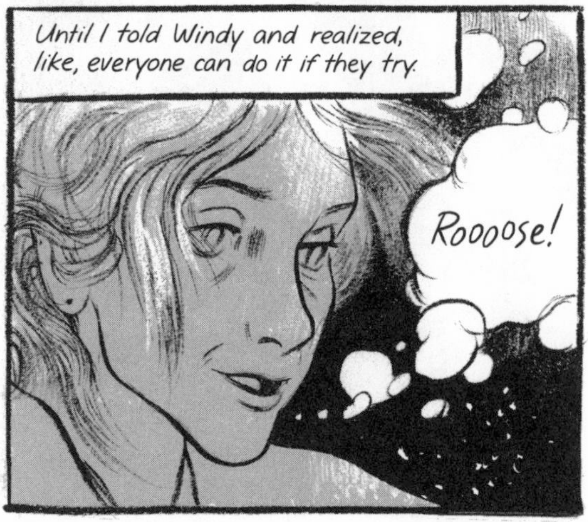
Until I told Windy and realized, like, everyone can do it if they try.
Rooooose!

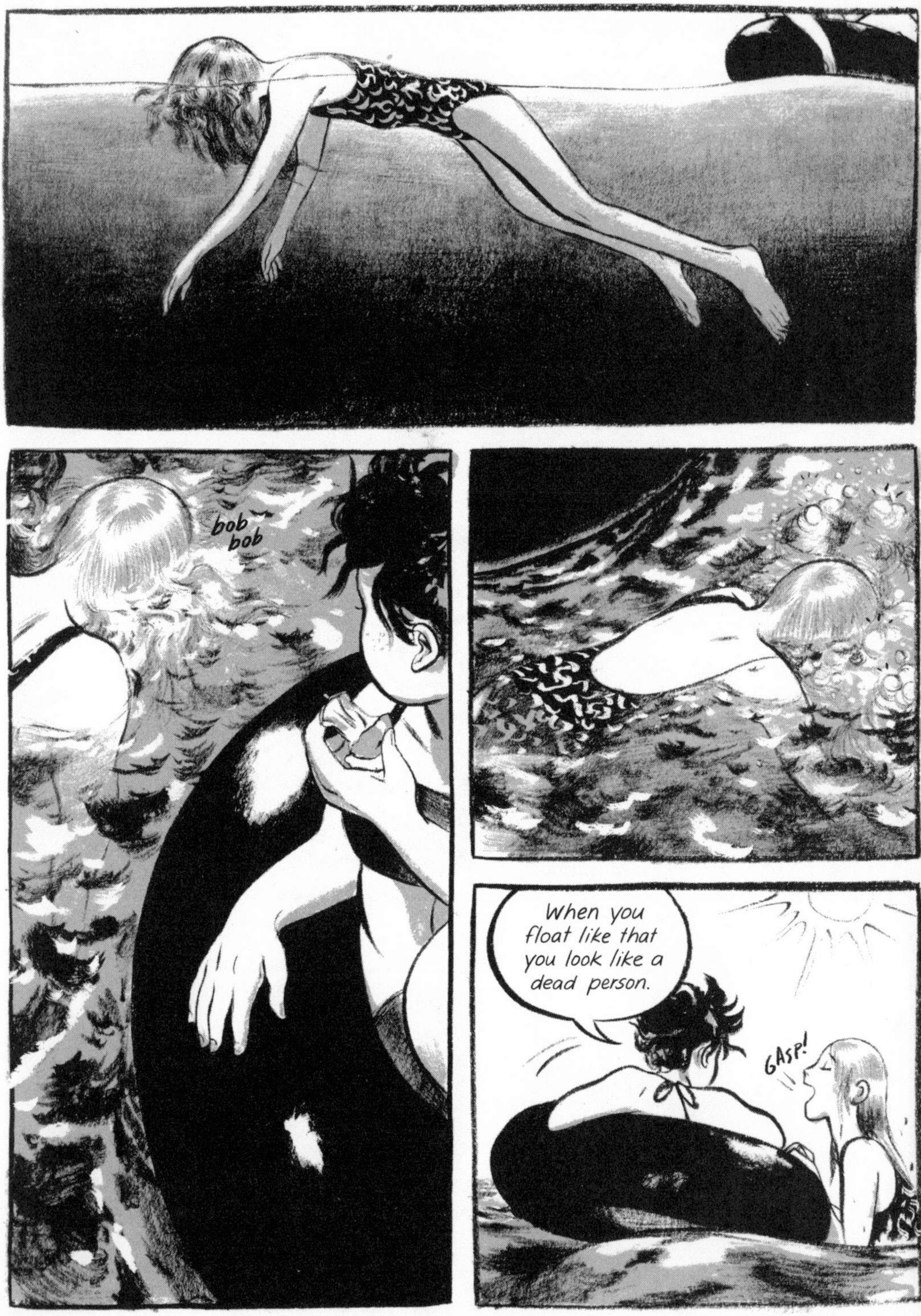
bob
bob
When you float like that you look like a dead person.
GASP!

It feels good. Floating.

It feels like flying.

How long can you hold your breath?

I can hold it for a pool length at school. I don't know how long that is.

Do you want me to time you? See how long?

Nope.

The best foods to take with you in a floatie are apples and chips in sealable containers.

Ahh!

Apples are better because you can just toss the cores into the water afterwards and the fish will eat them.

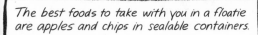

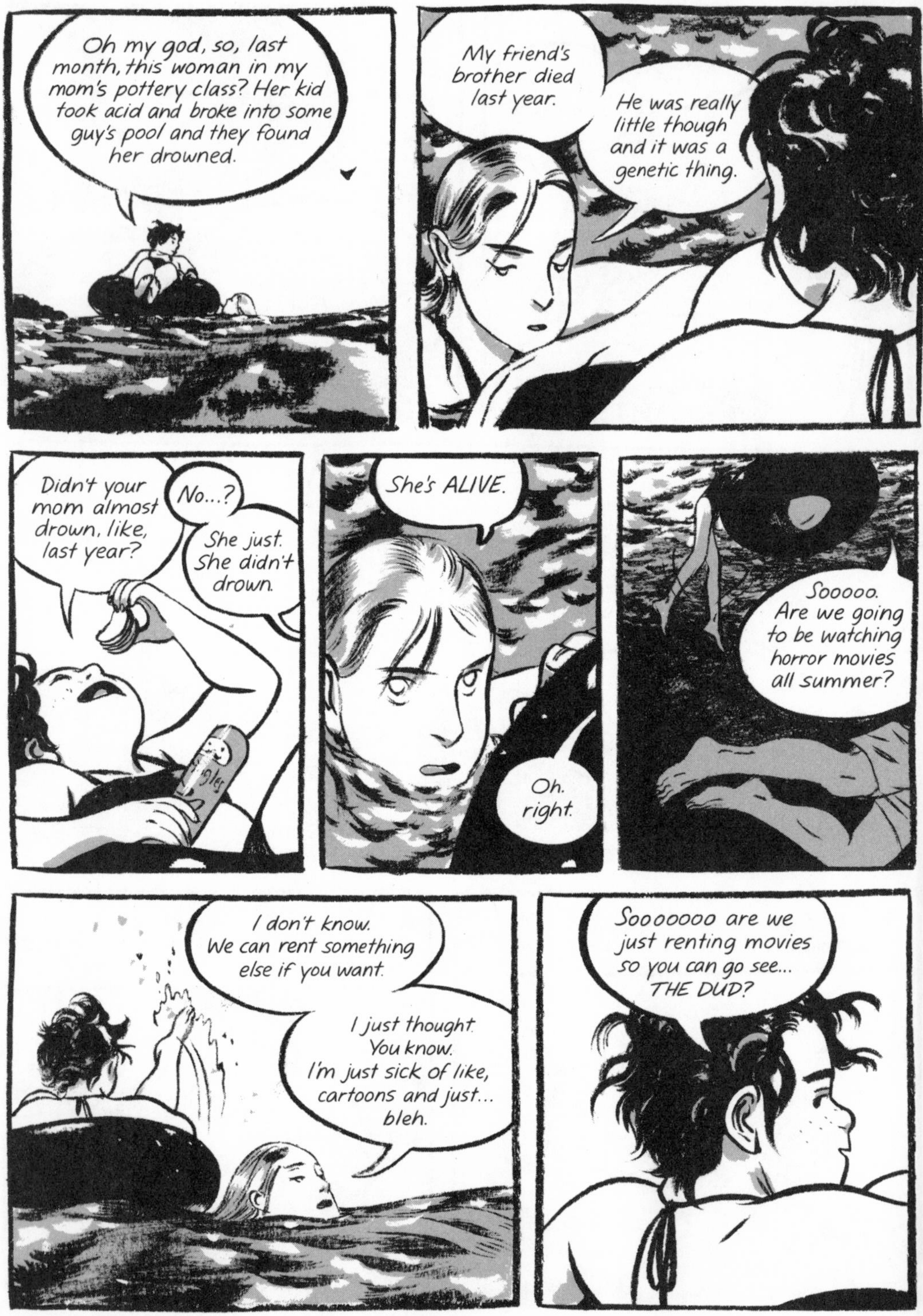
Oh my god, so, last month, this woman in my mom's pottery class? Her kid took acid and broke into some guy's pool and they found her drowned.
My friend's brother died last year.
He was really little though and it was a genetic thing.
Didn't your mom almost drown, like, last year?
No...?
She just. She didn't drown.
She's ALIVE.
Oh. right.
Sooooo. Are we going to be watching horror movies all summer?
I don't know. We can rent something else if you want.
I just thought. You know. I'm just sick of like, cartoons and just... bleh.
Soooooo are we just renting movies so you can go see... THE DUD?

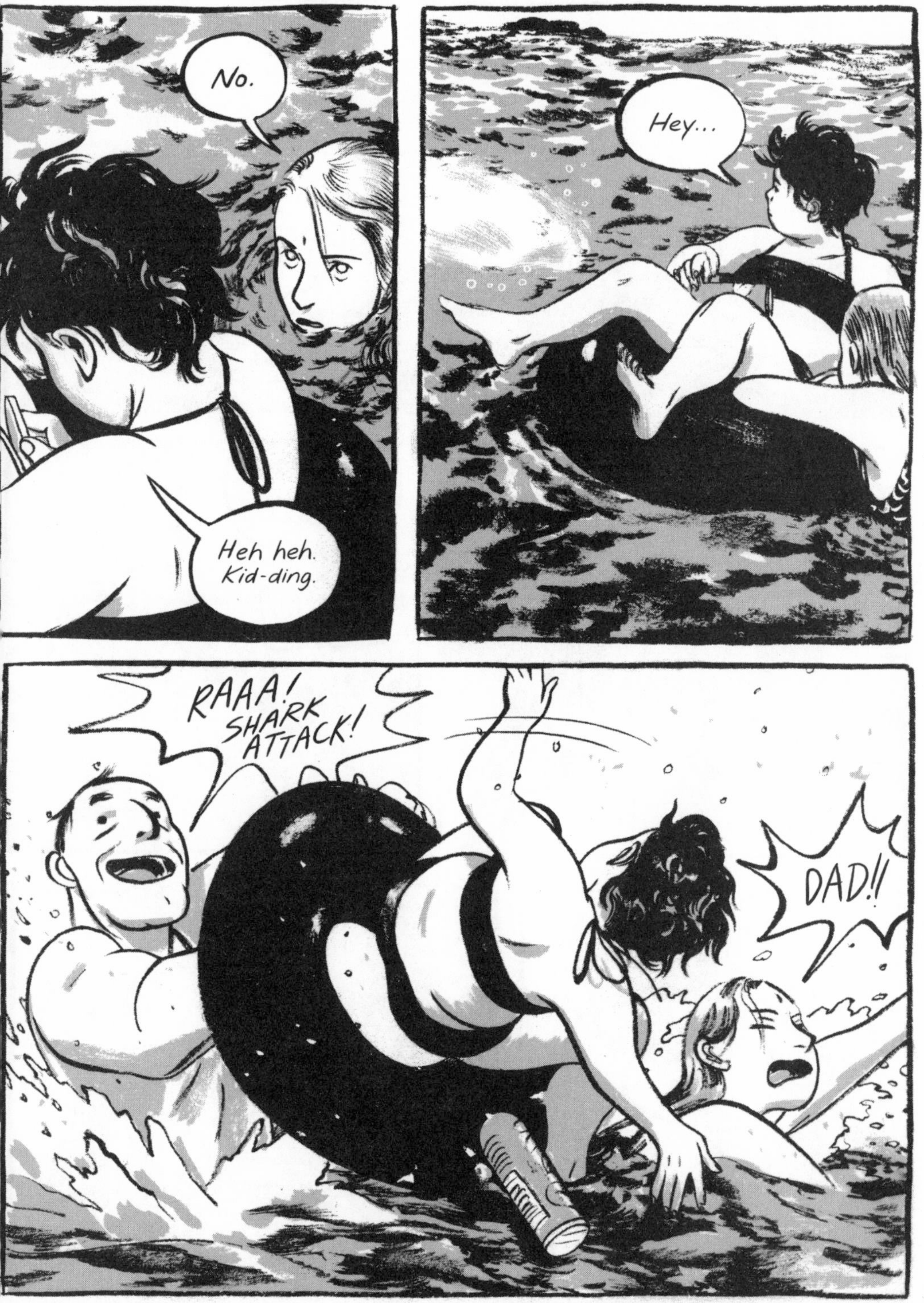
No.
Heh heh. Kid-ding.
Hey...
RAAA! SHARK ATTACK!
DAD!!

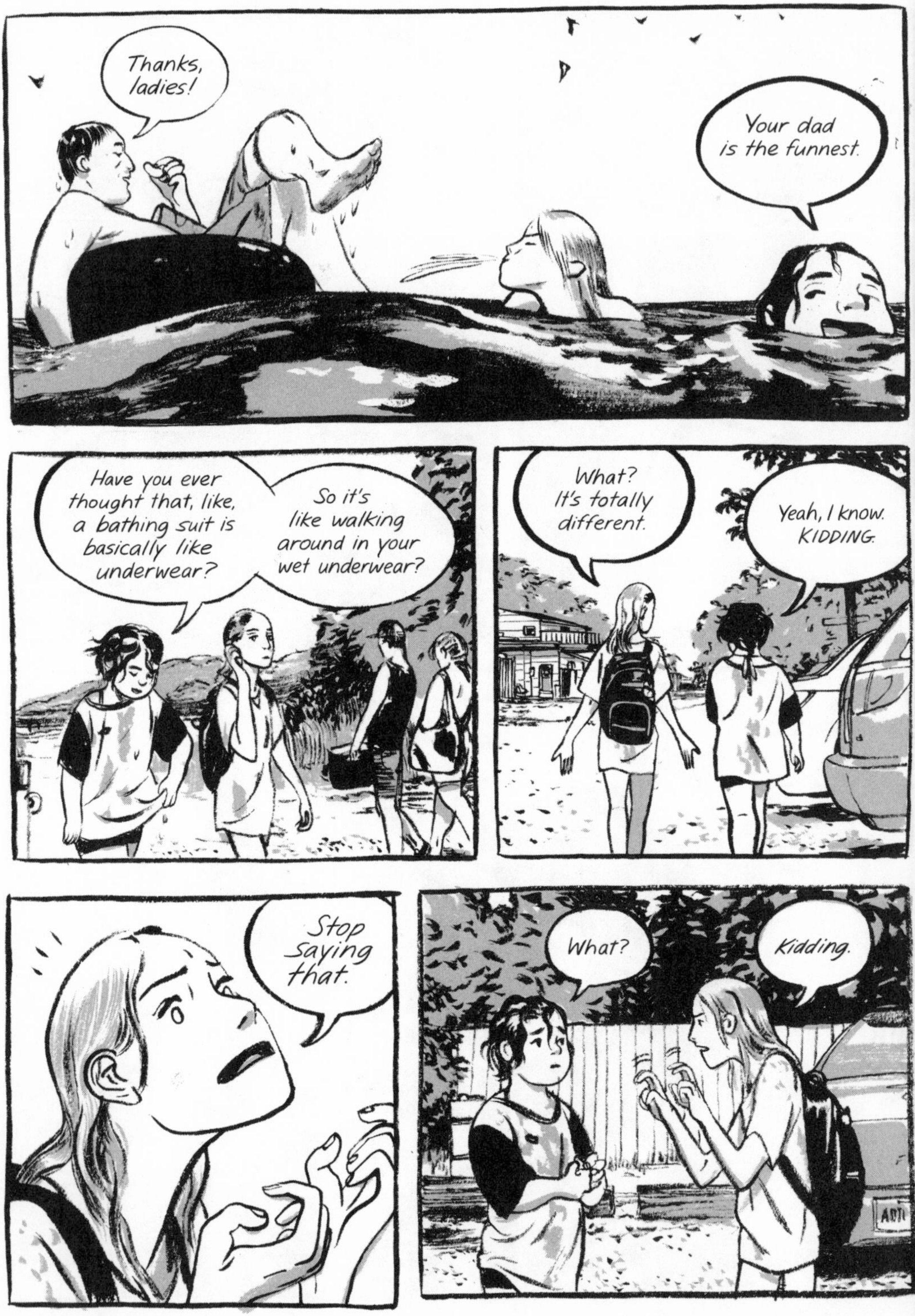
Thanks, ladies!
Your dad is the funnest.
Have you ever thought that, like, a bathing suit is basically like underwear?
So it's like walking around in your wet underwear?
What? It's totally different.
Yeah, I know. KIDDING.
Stop saying that.
What?
Kidding.

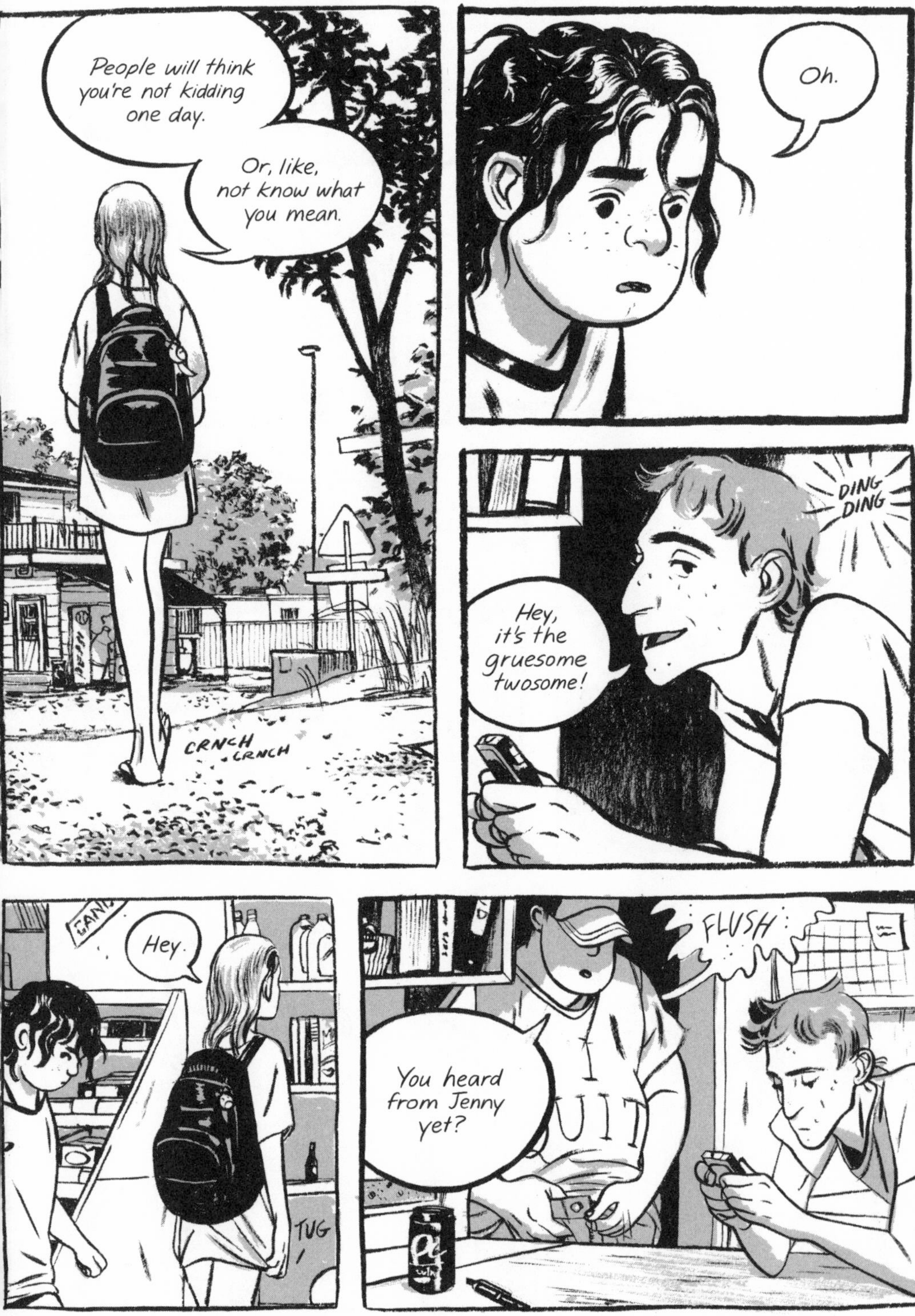
People will think you're not kidding one day.
Or, like, not know what you mean.
CRNCH CRNCH
Oh.
DING DING
Hey, it's the gruesome twosome!
Hey.
TUG
FLUSH
You heard from Jenny yet?

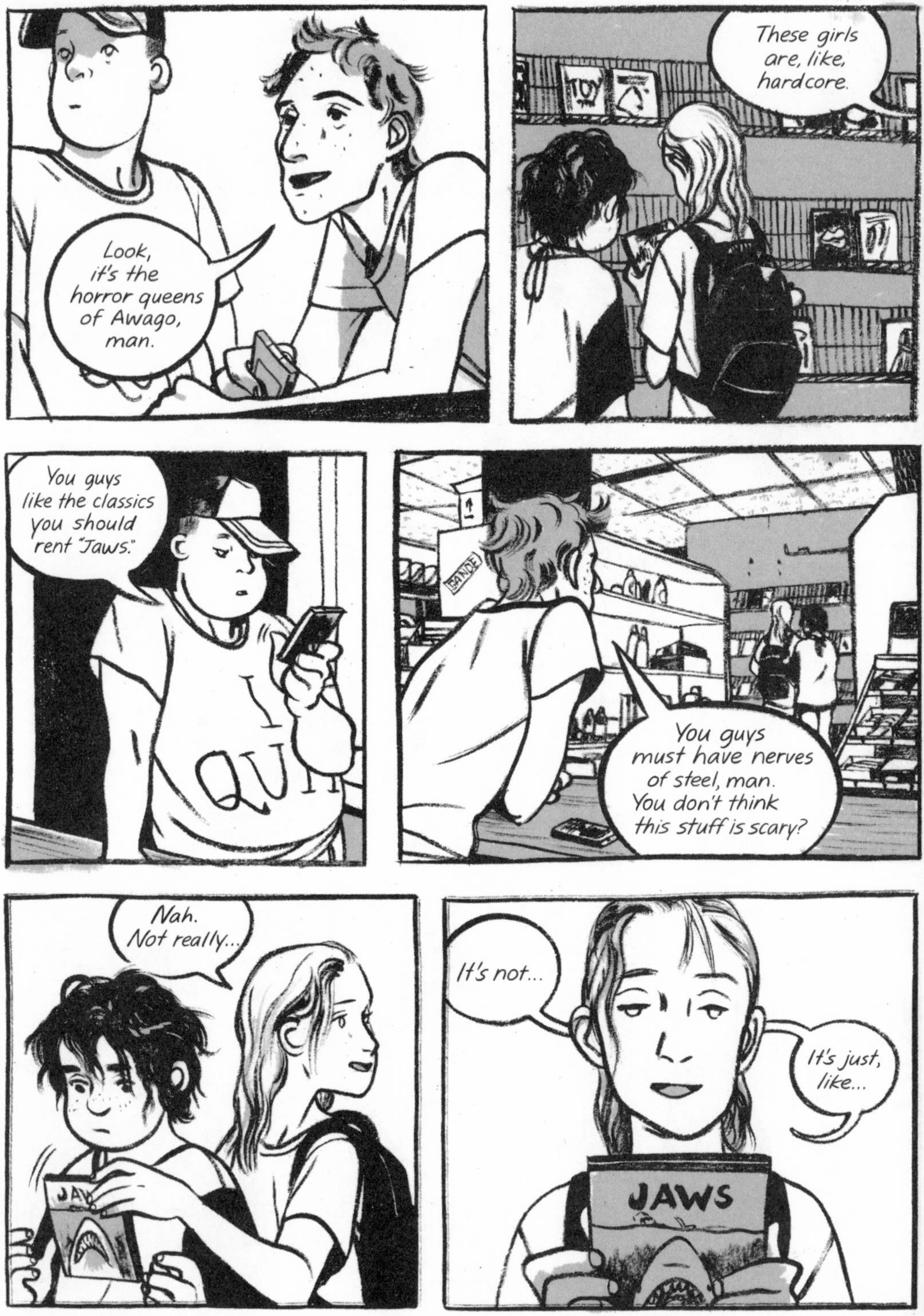
Look, it's the horror queens of Awago, man.
These girls are, like, hardcore.
You guys like the classics you should rent "Jaws."
You guys must have nerves of steel, man. You don't think this stuff is scary?
Nah. Not really...
It's not...
It's just, like...
JAWS

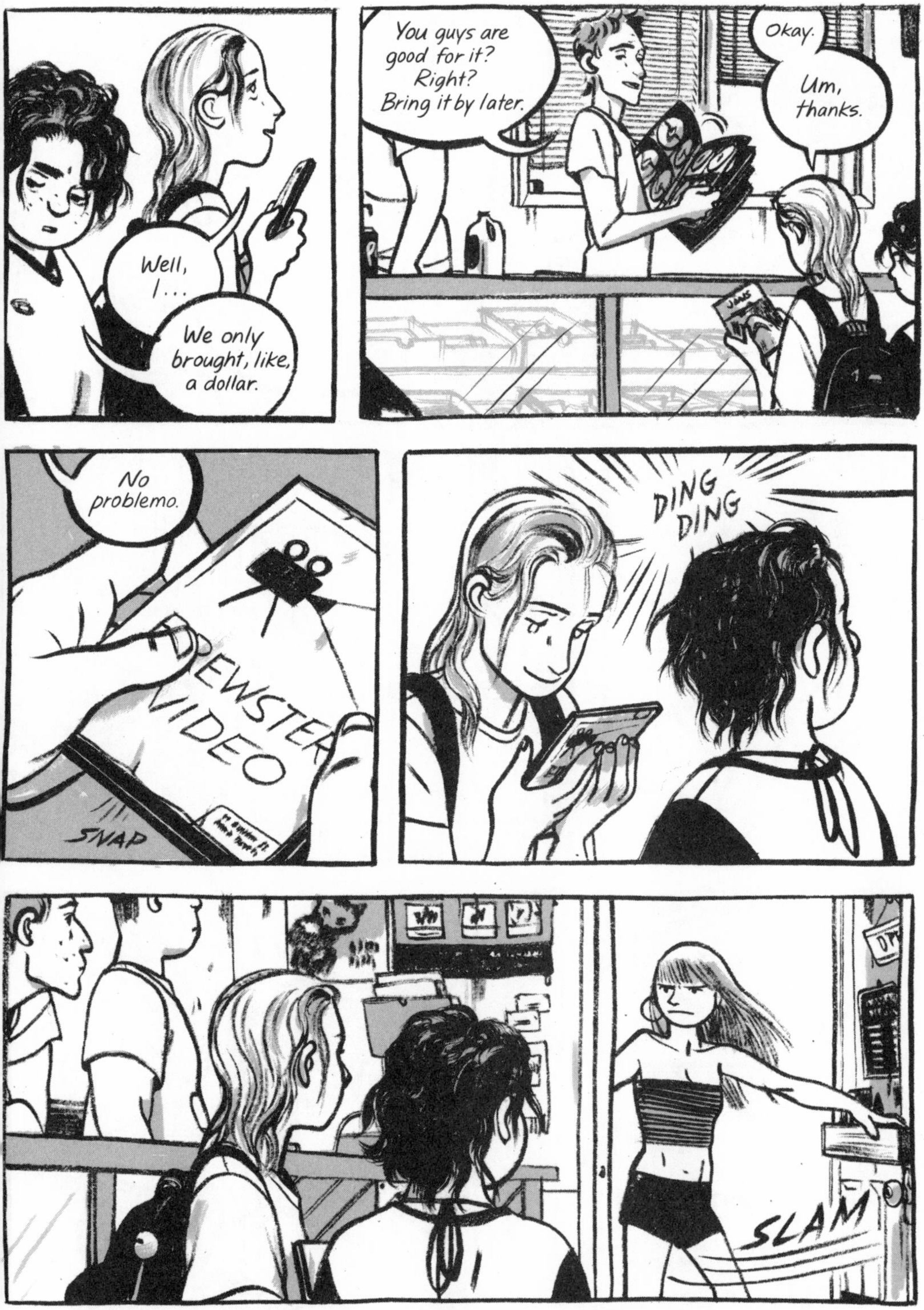
Well, I...
We only brought, like, a dollar.
You guys are good for it? Right? Bring it by later.
Okay.
Um, thanks.
No problemo.
EWSTER VIDEO
SNAP
DING DING
SLAM

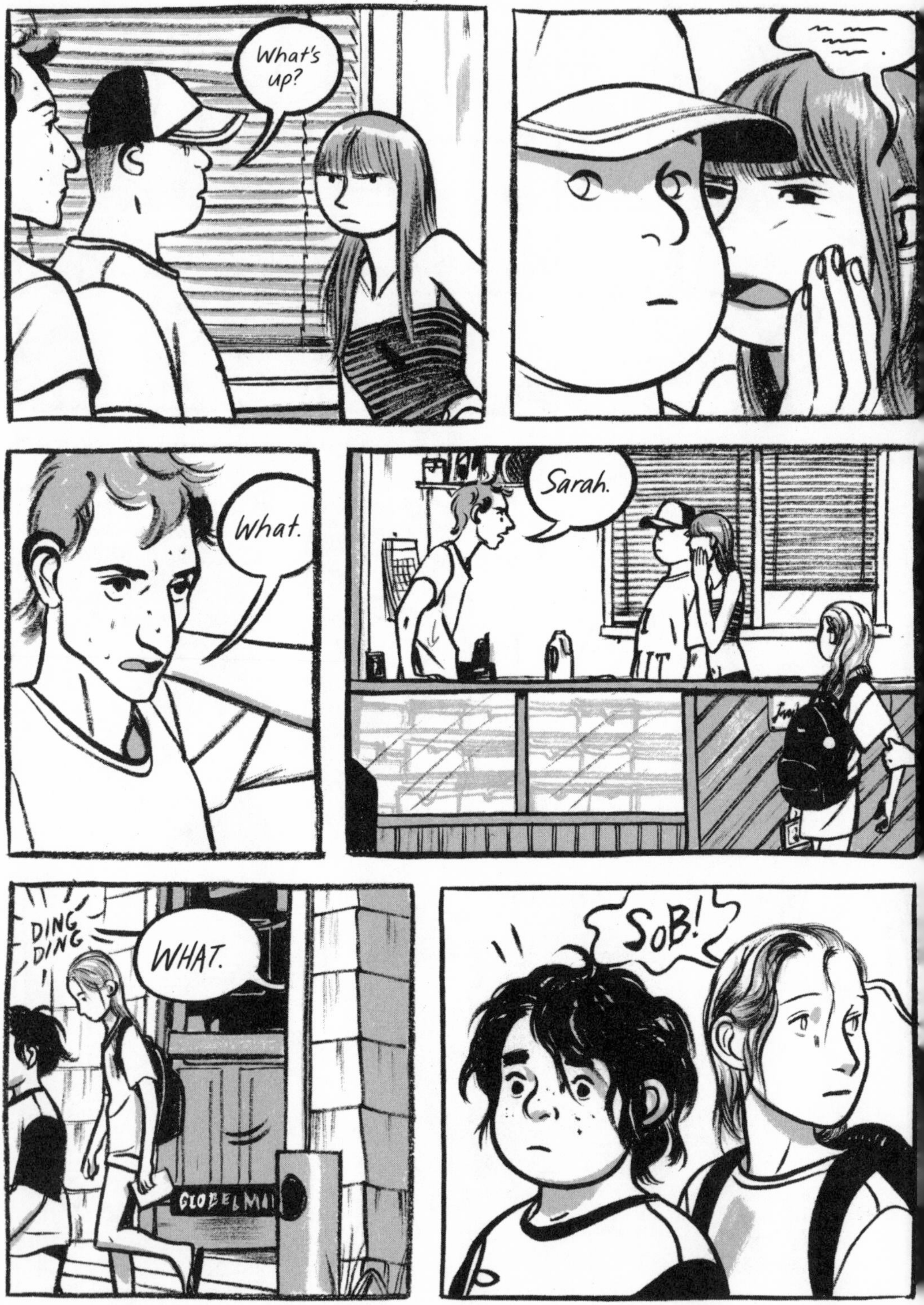
What's up?
What.
Sarah.
DING DING
WHAT.
SoB!
GLOBE & MAI

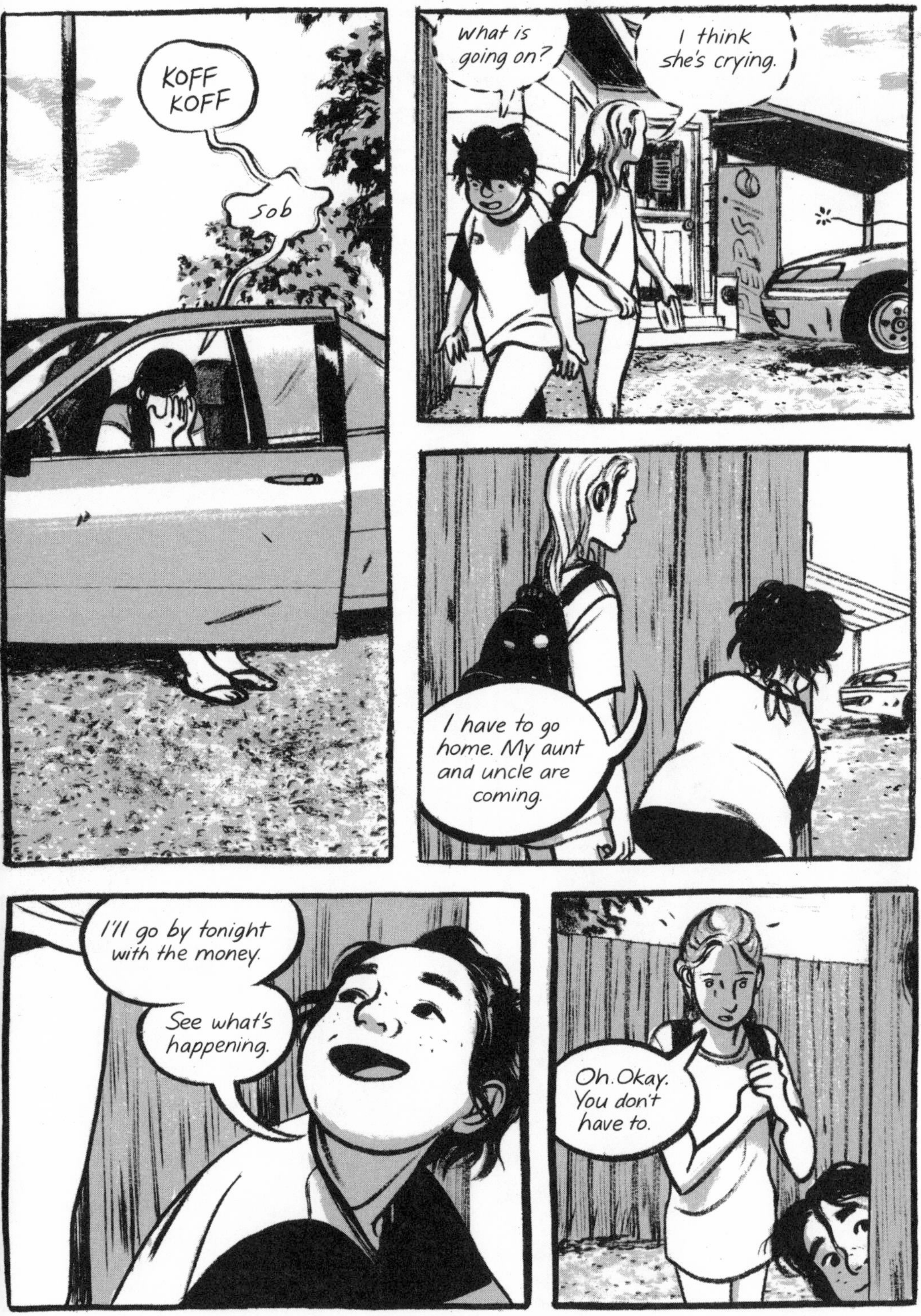
KOFF KOFF
sob
What is going on?
I think she's crying.
I have to go home. My aunt and uncle are coming.
I'll go by tonight with the money.
See what's happening.
Oh. Okay. You don't have to.

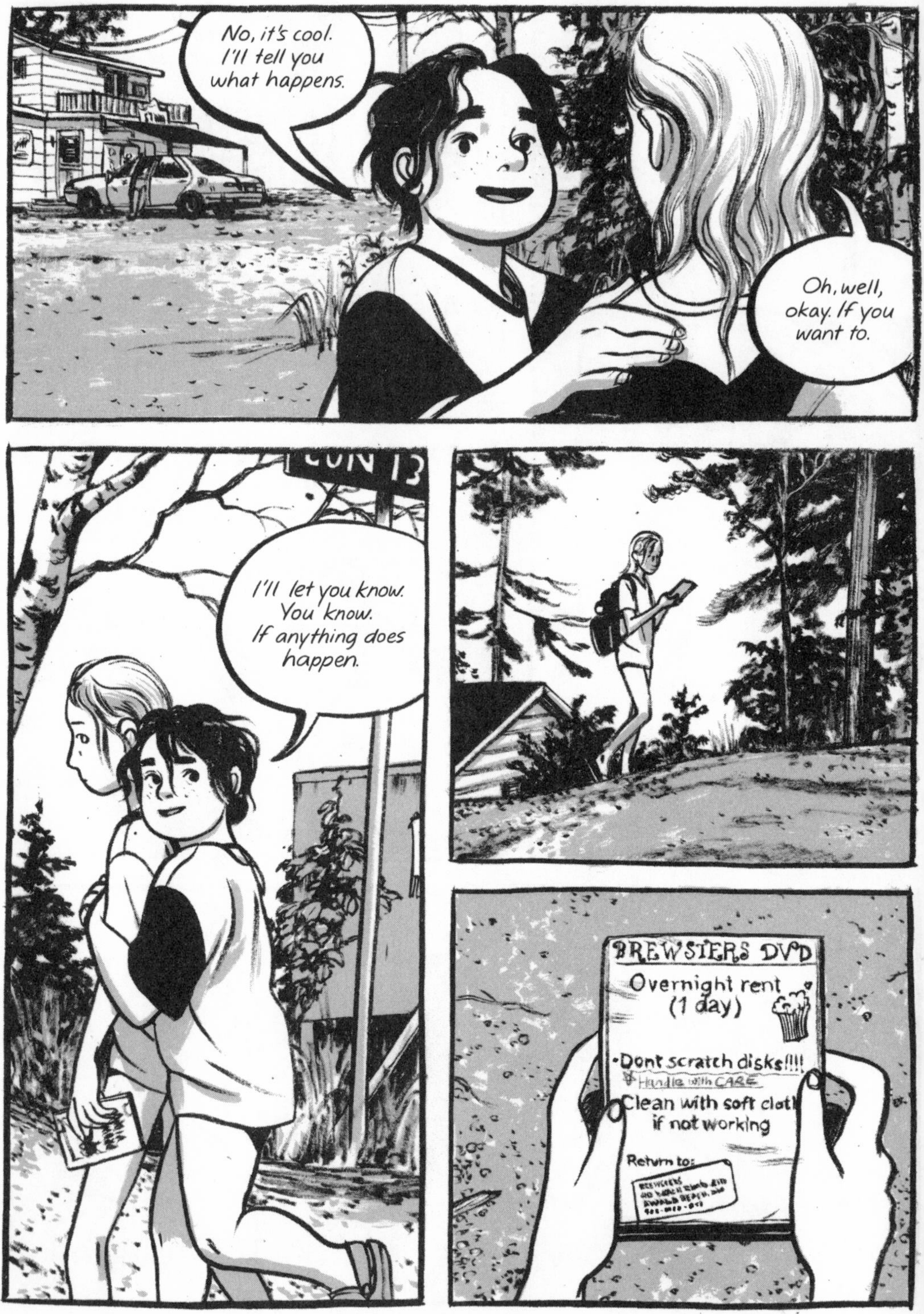
No, it's cool. I'll tell you what happens.
Oh, well, okay. If you want to.
I'll let you know. You know. If anything does happen.
BREWSTERS DVD
Overnight rent (1 day)
•Dont scratch disks!!!!
Handle with CARE
Clean with soft clot
if not working
Return to:

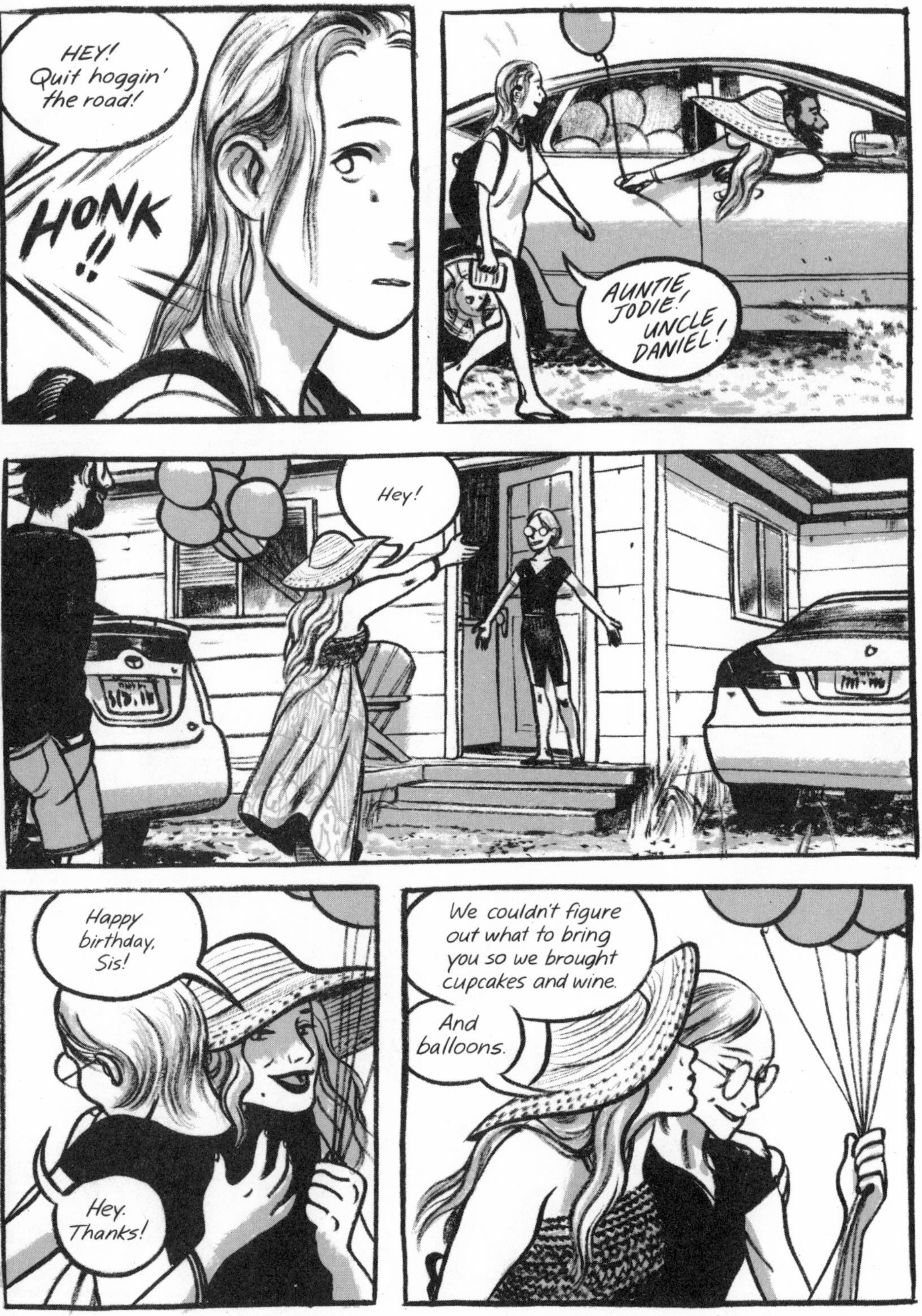
HEY! Quit hoggin' the road!
HONK !!
AUNTIE JODIE! UNCLE DANIEL!
Hey!
Happy birthday, Sis!
Hey. Thanks!
We couldn't figure out what to bring you so we brought cupcakes and wine.
And balloons.

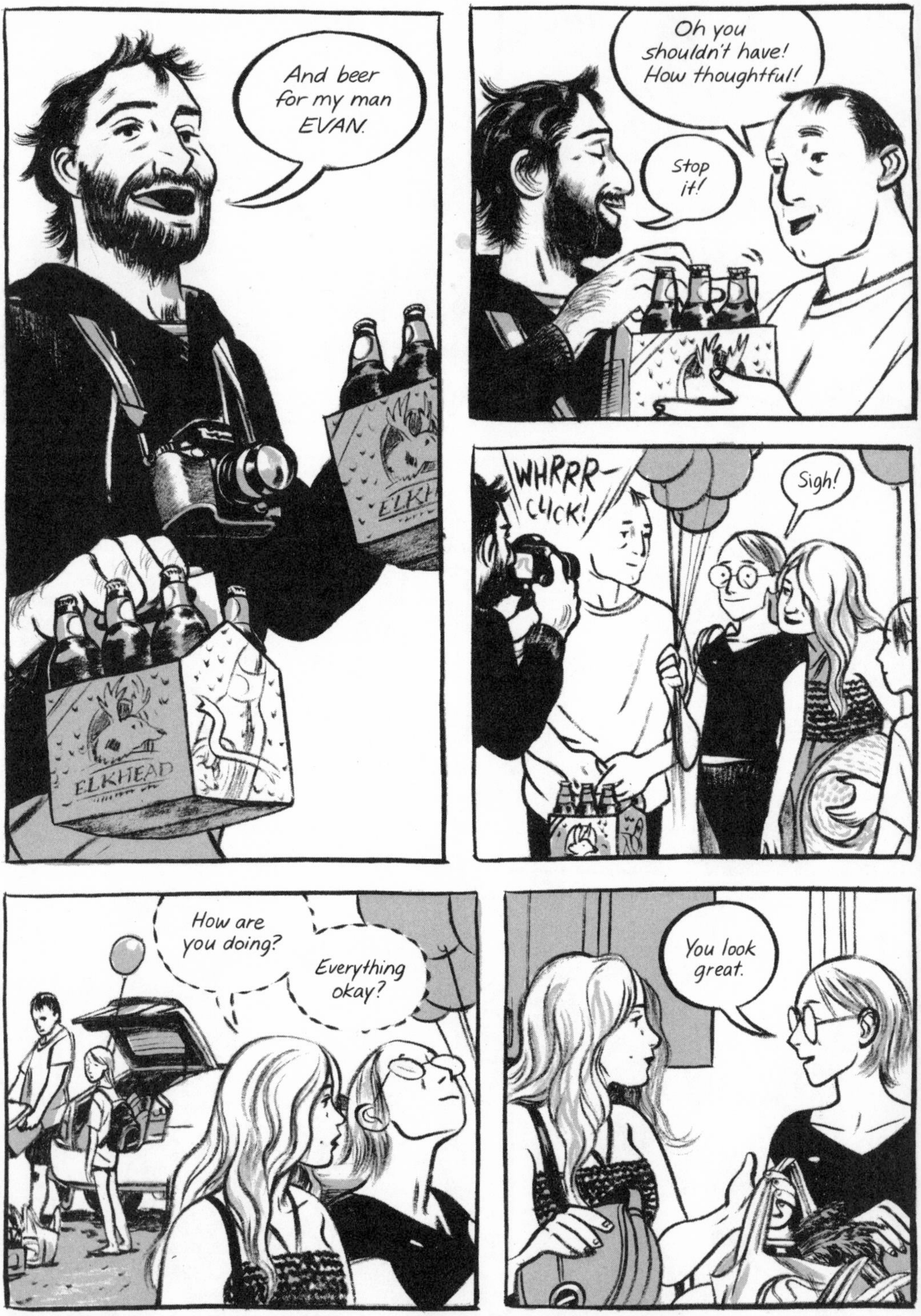
And beer for my man EVAN.
Oh you shouldn't have! How thoughtful!
Stop it!
WHRRR-CLICK!
Sigh!
How are you doing?
Everything okay?
You look great.

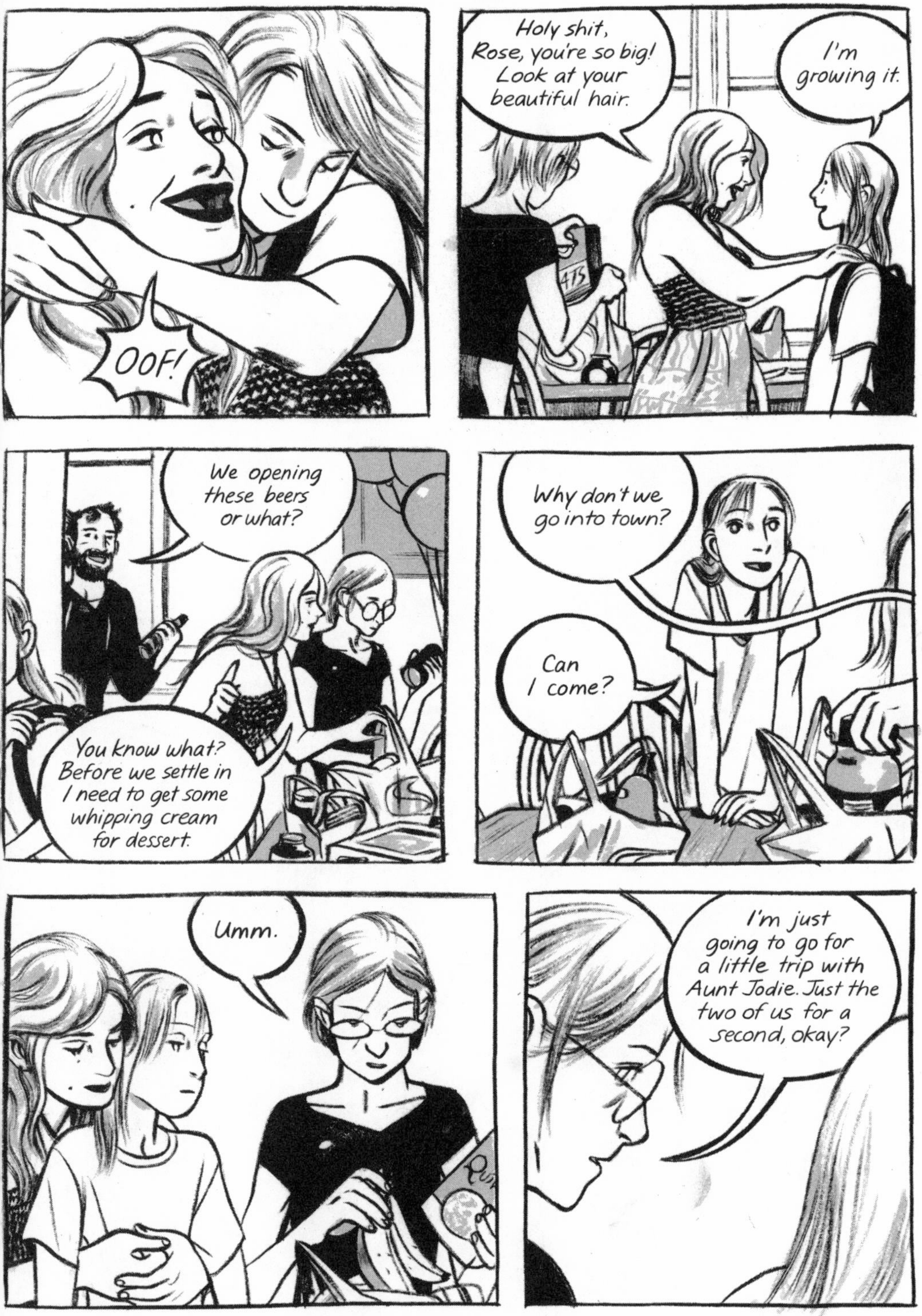

OOF!
Holy shit, Rose, you're so big! Look at your beautiful hair.
I'm growing it.
We opening these beers or what?
You know what? Before we settle in I need to get some whipping cream for dessert.
Why don't we go into town?
Can I come?
Umm.
I'm just going to go for a little trip with Aunt Jodie. Just the two of us for a second, okay?

We'll be right back.

Hey, Rosie, check it out. We brought WAGON WHEELS.

SCRAPE

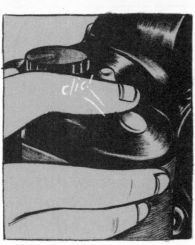

click

SCRAPE

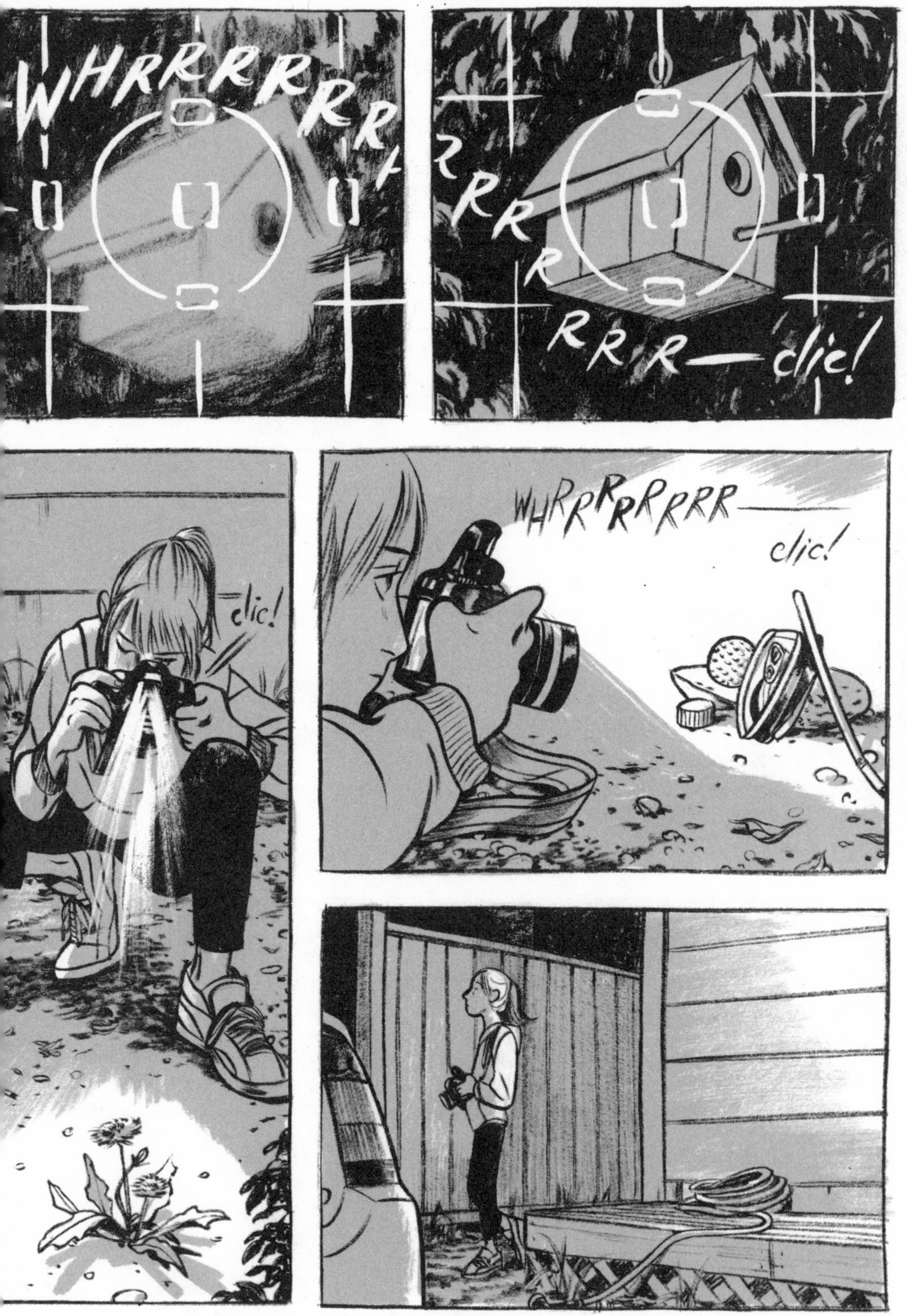
WHRRRRRRRRRRR
RRR—clic!
clic!
WHRRRRRRRR—
clic!

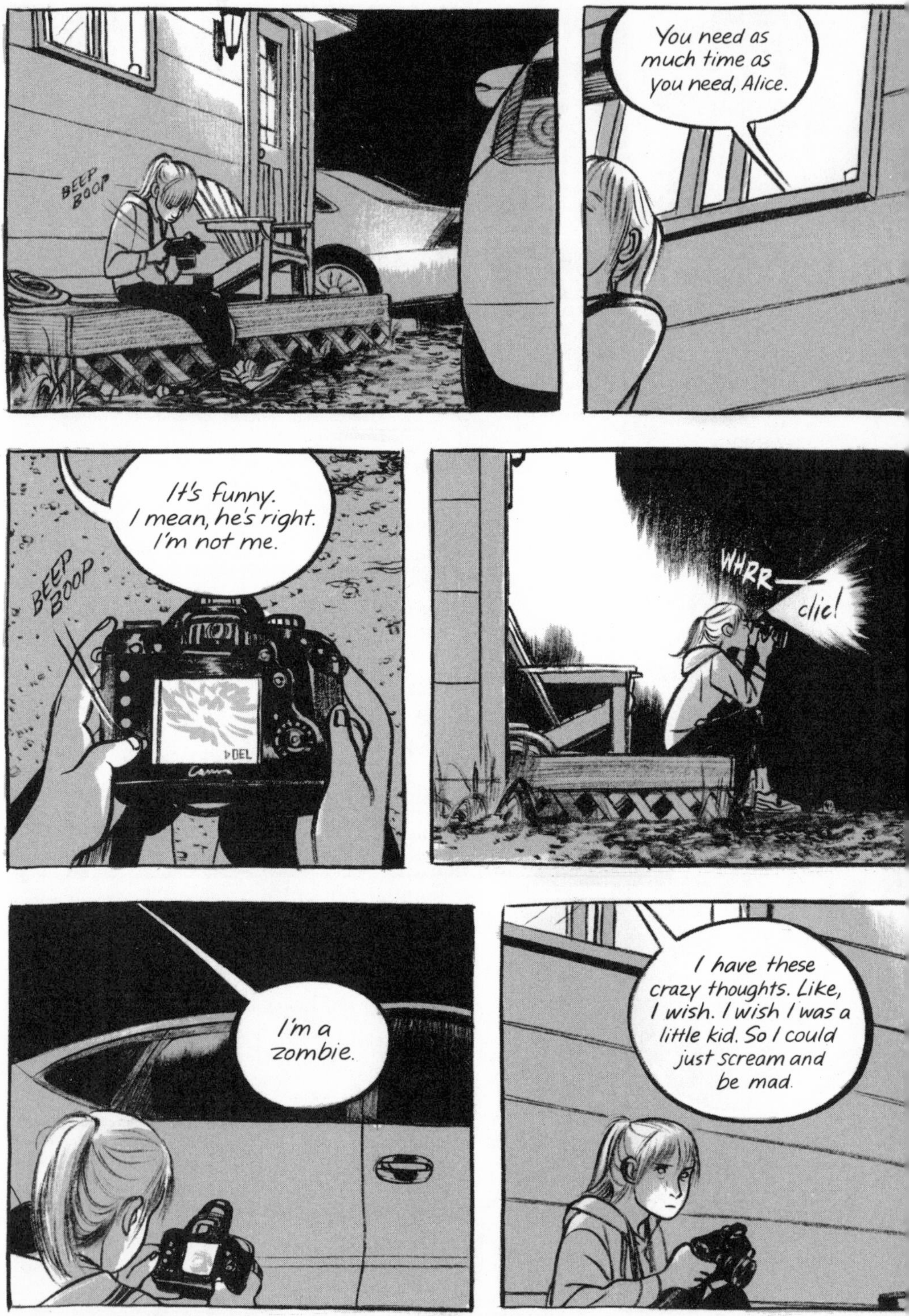
BEEP BOOP
You need as much time as you need, Alice.
It's funny. I mean, he's right. I'm not me.
BEEP BOOP
WHRR—
clic!
I'm a zombie.
I have these crazy thoughts. Like, I wish. I wish I was a little kid. So I could just scream and be mad.

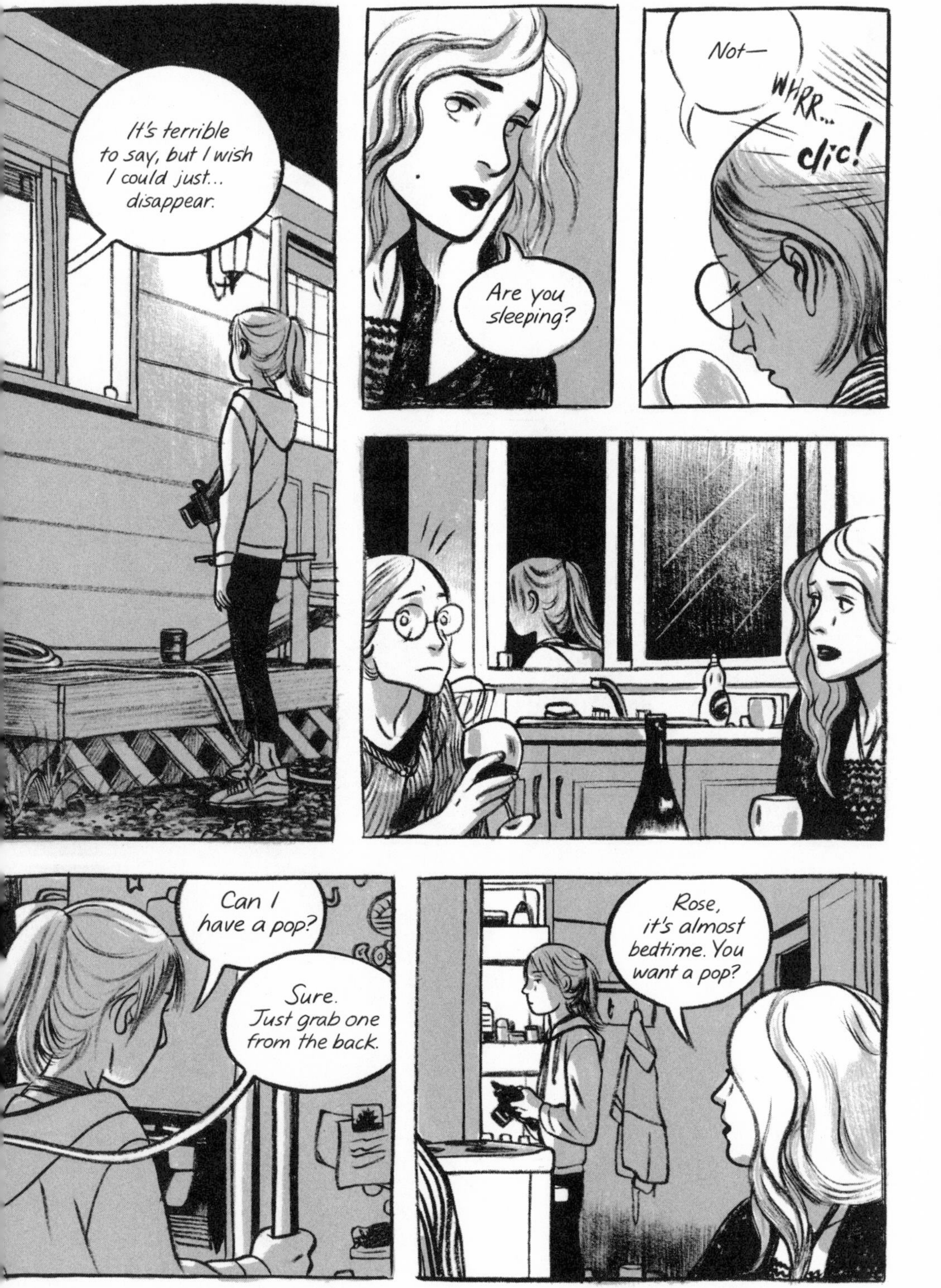
It's terrible to say, but I wish I could just... disappear.
Are you sleeping?
Not—
WHRR...
clic!
Can I have a pop?
Sure. Just grab one from the back.
Rose, it's almost bedtime. You want a pop?

Oh. Right.

Just have a glass of water.

sigh.

SLAM!

HELLO!

GRUMBLE

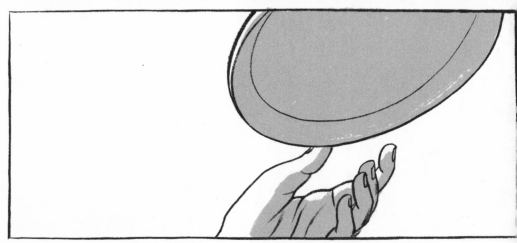

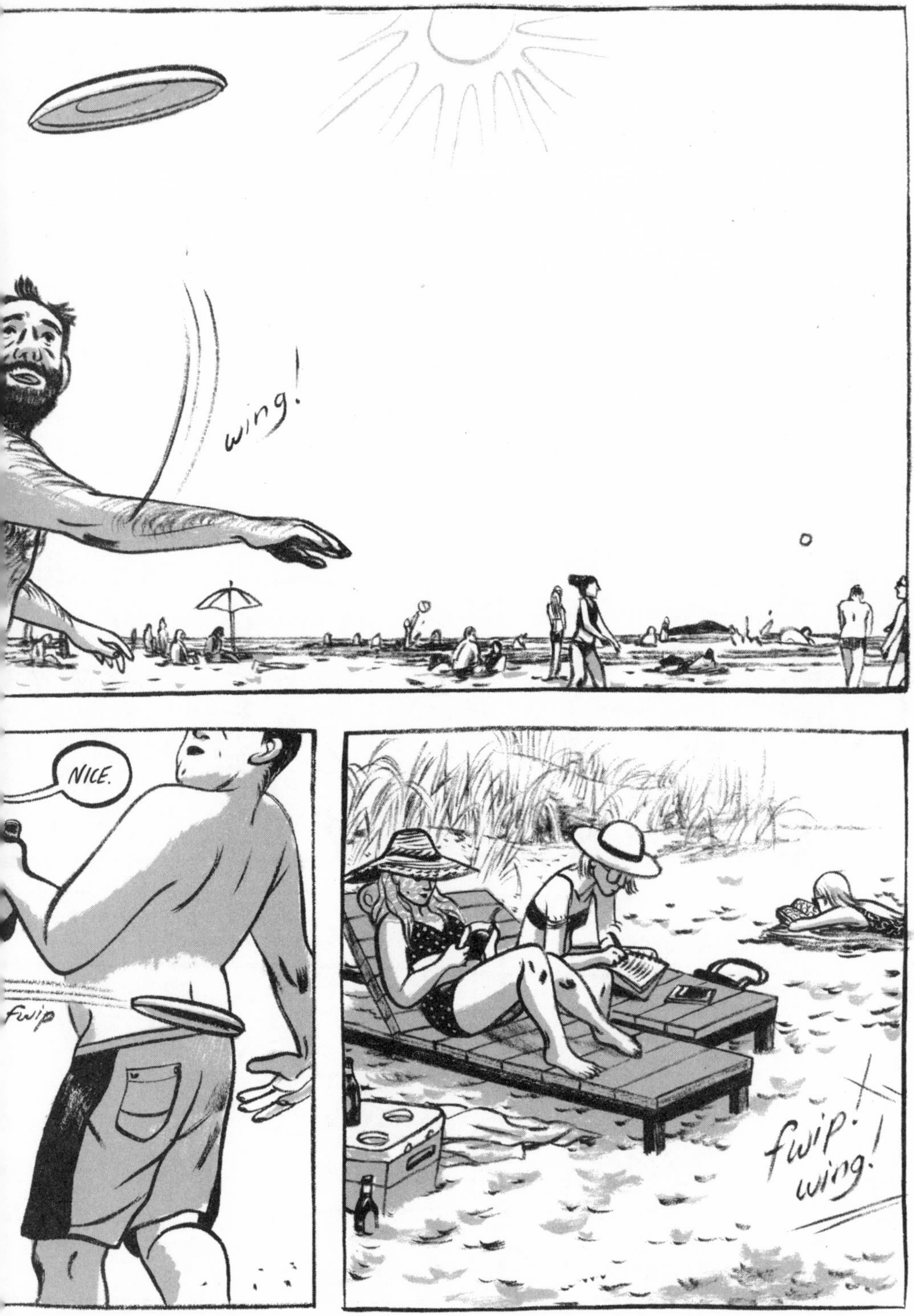
wing!
NICE.
fwip
fwip!
wing!

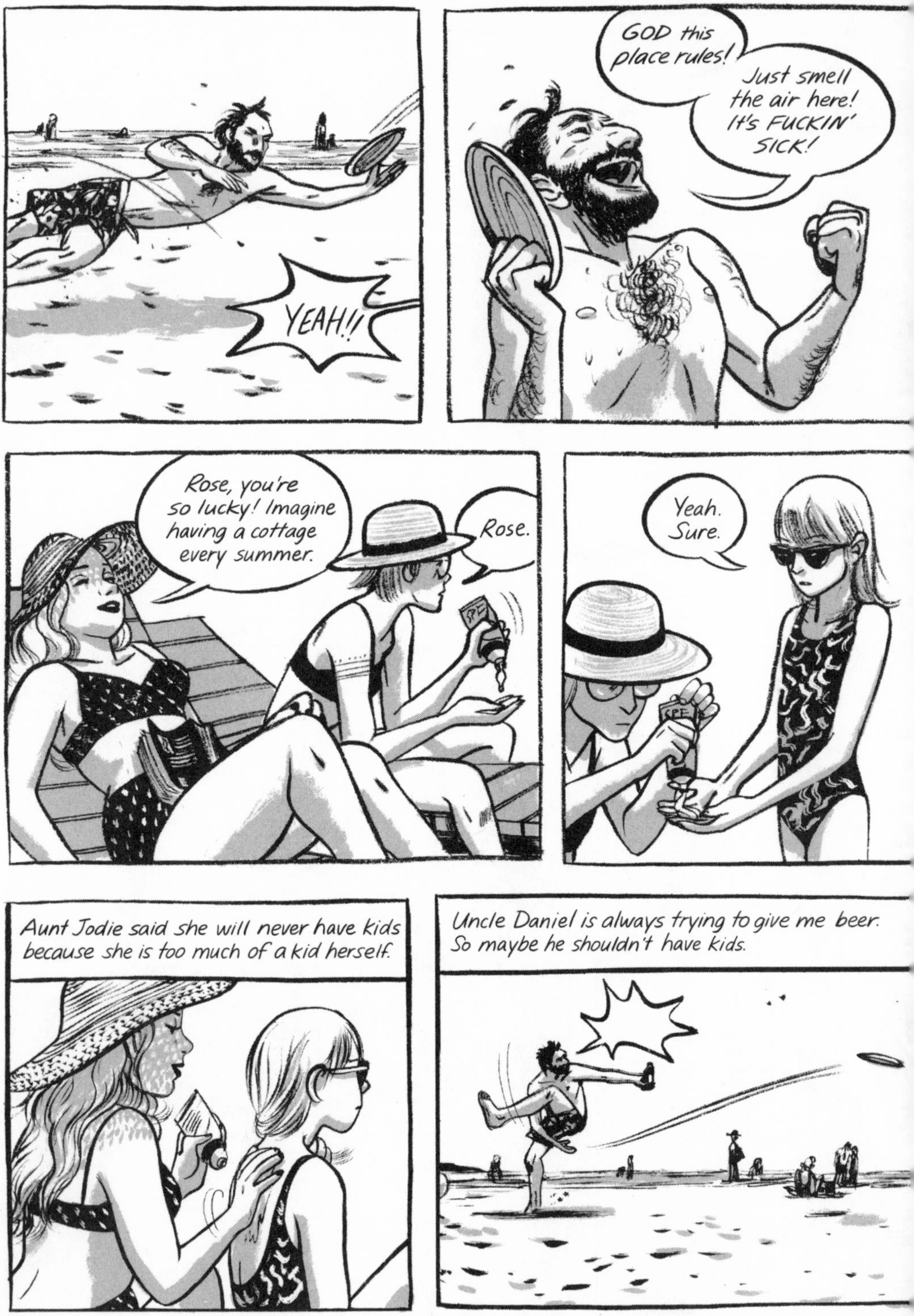
YEAH!!
GOD this place rules!
Just smell the air here! It's FUCKIN' SICK!
Rose, you're so lucky! Imagine having a cottage every summer.
Rose.
SPF
Yeah. Sure.
SPF
Aunt Jodie said she will never have kids because she is too much of a kid herself.
Uncle Daniel is always trying to give me beer. So maybe he shouldn't have kids.

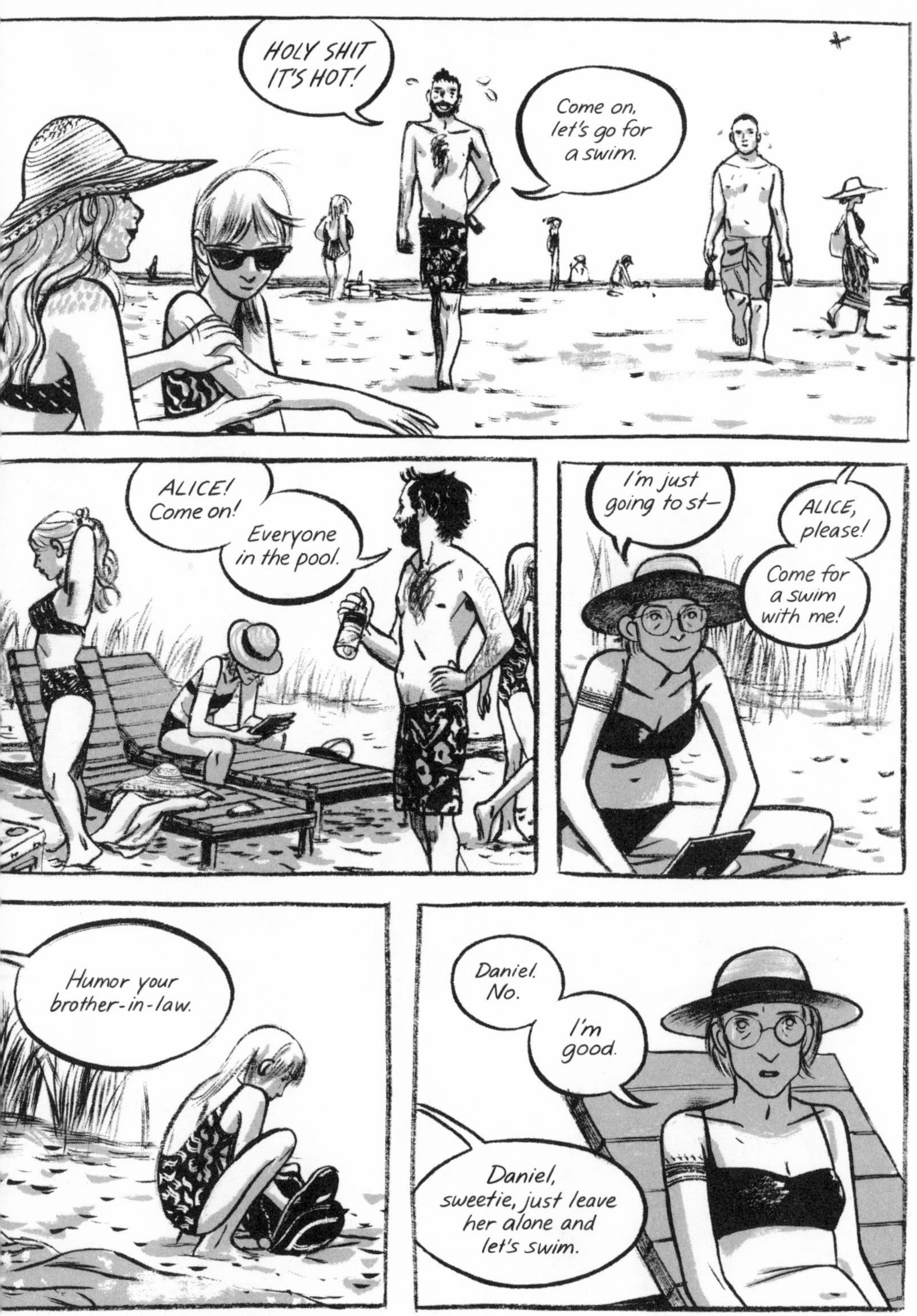
HOLY SHIT IT'S HOT!
Come on, let's go for a swim.
ALICE! Come on!
Everyone in the pool.
I'm just going to st—
ALICE, please!
Come for a swim with me!
Humor your brother-in-law.
Daniel. No.
I'm good.
Daniel, sweetie, just leave her alone and let's swim.

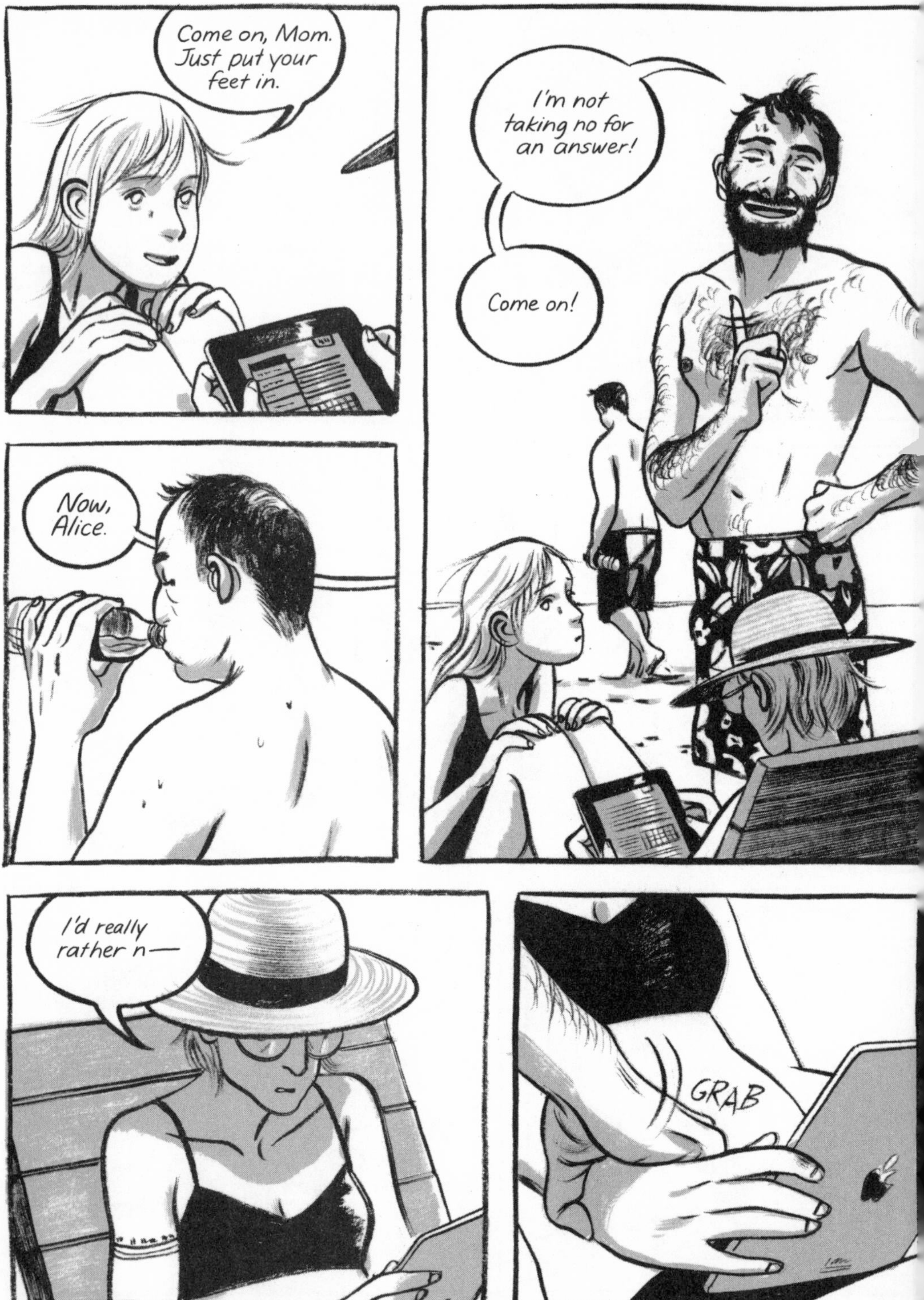
Come on, Mom. Just put your feet in.
I'm not taking no for an answer!
Come on!
Now, Alice.
I'd really rather n—
GRAB

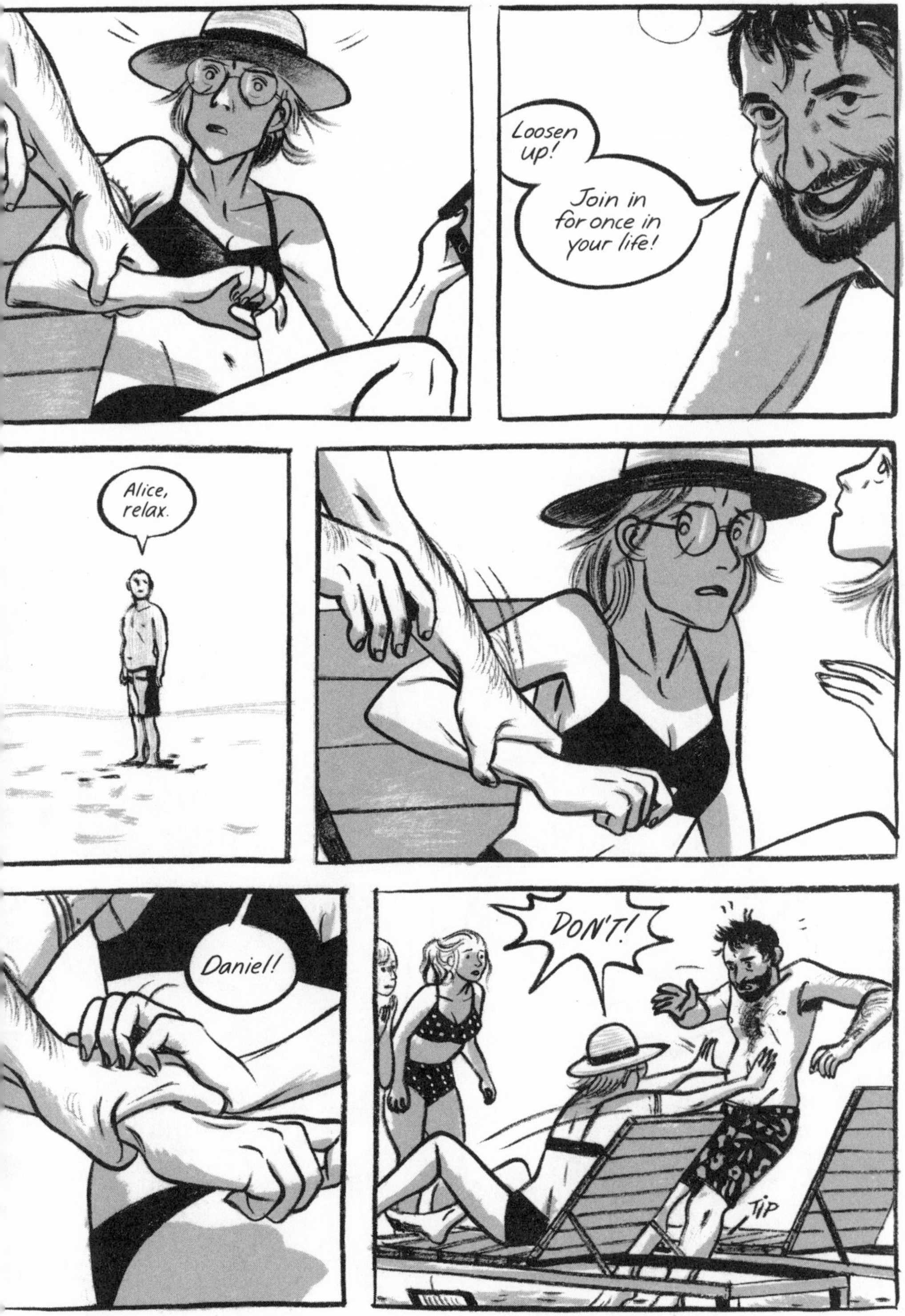
Loosen up!
Join in for once in your life!
Alice, relax.
Daniel!
DON'T!
TIP

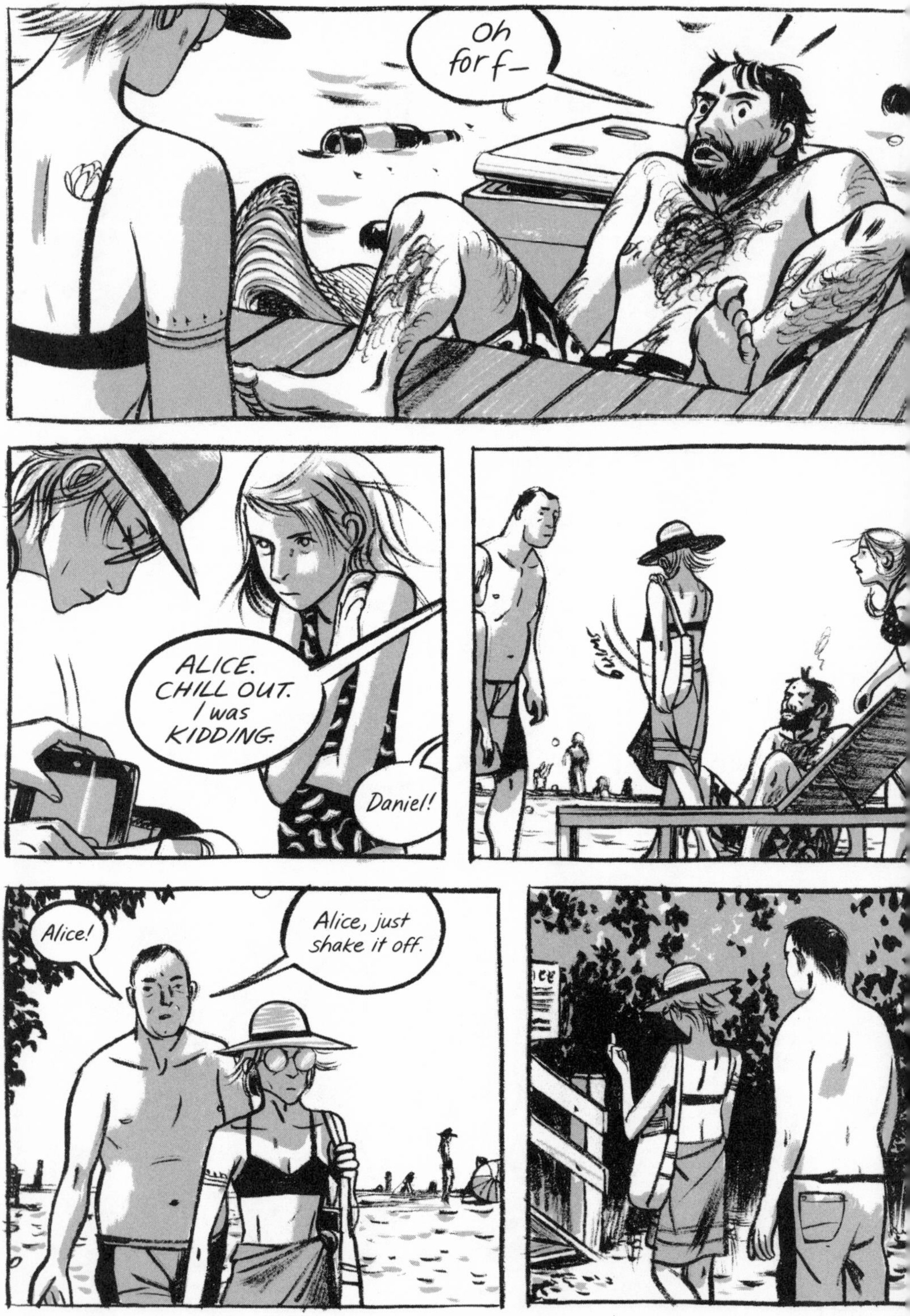
Oh for f—
ALICE. CHILL OUT. I was KIDDING.
Daniel!
Alice!
Alice, just shake it off.

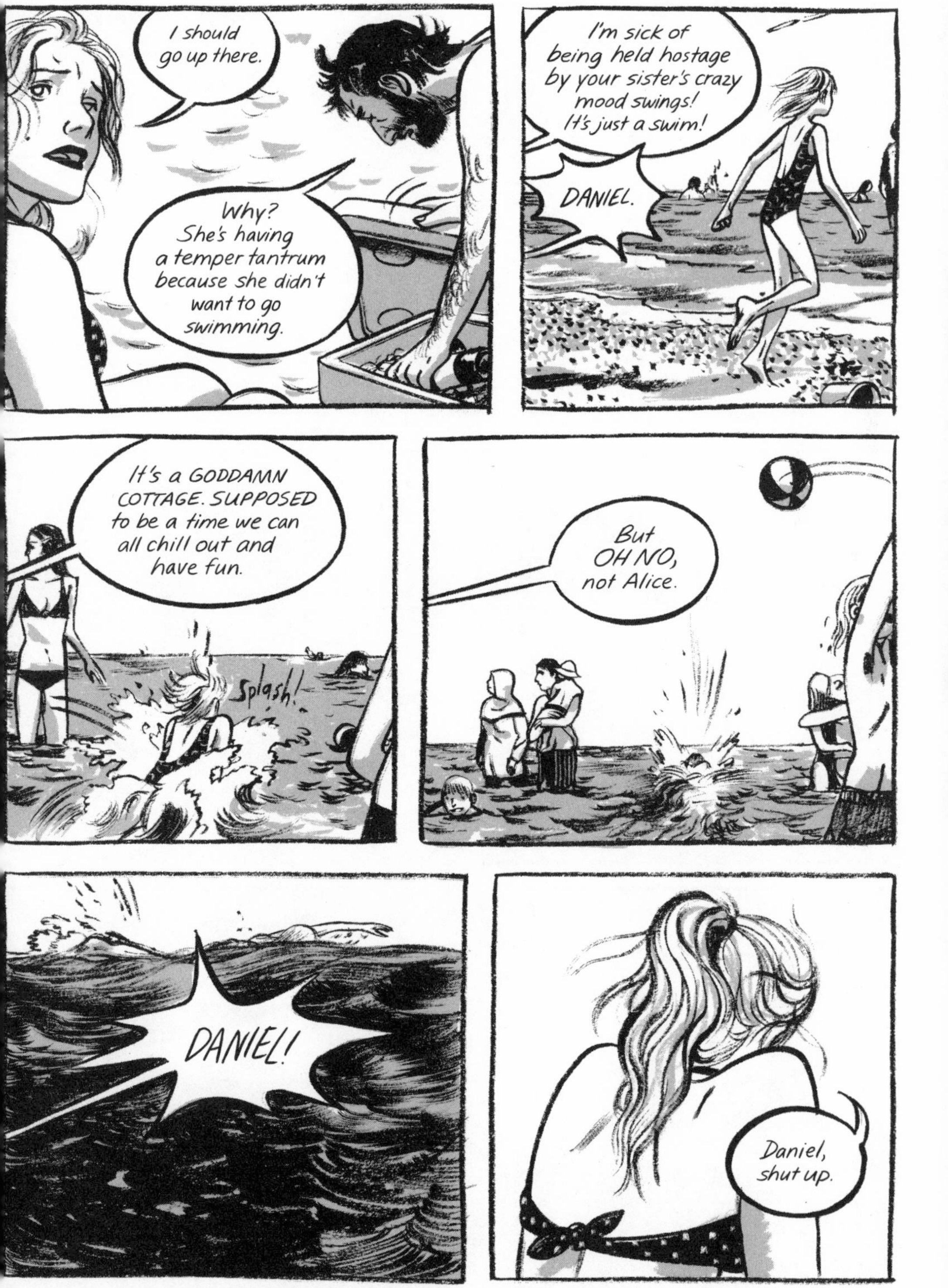
I should go up there.
Why? She's having a temper tantrum because she didn't want to go swimming.
I'm sick of being held hostage by your sister's crazy mood swings! It's just a swim!
DANIEL.
It's a GODDAMN COTTAGE. SUPPOSED to be a time we can all chill out and have fun.
Splash!
But OH NO, not Alice.
DANIEL!
Daniel, shut up.

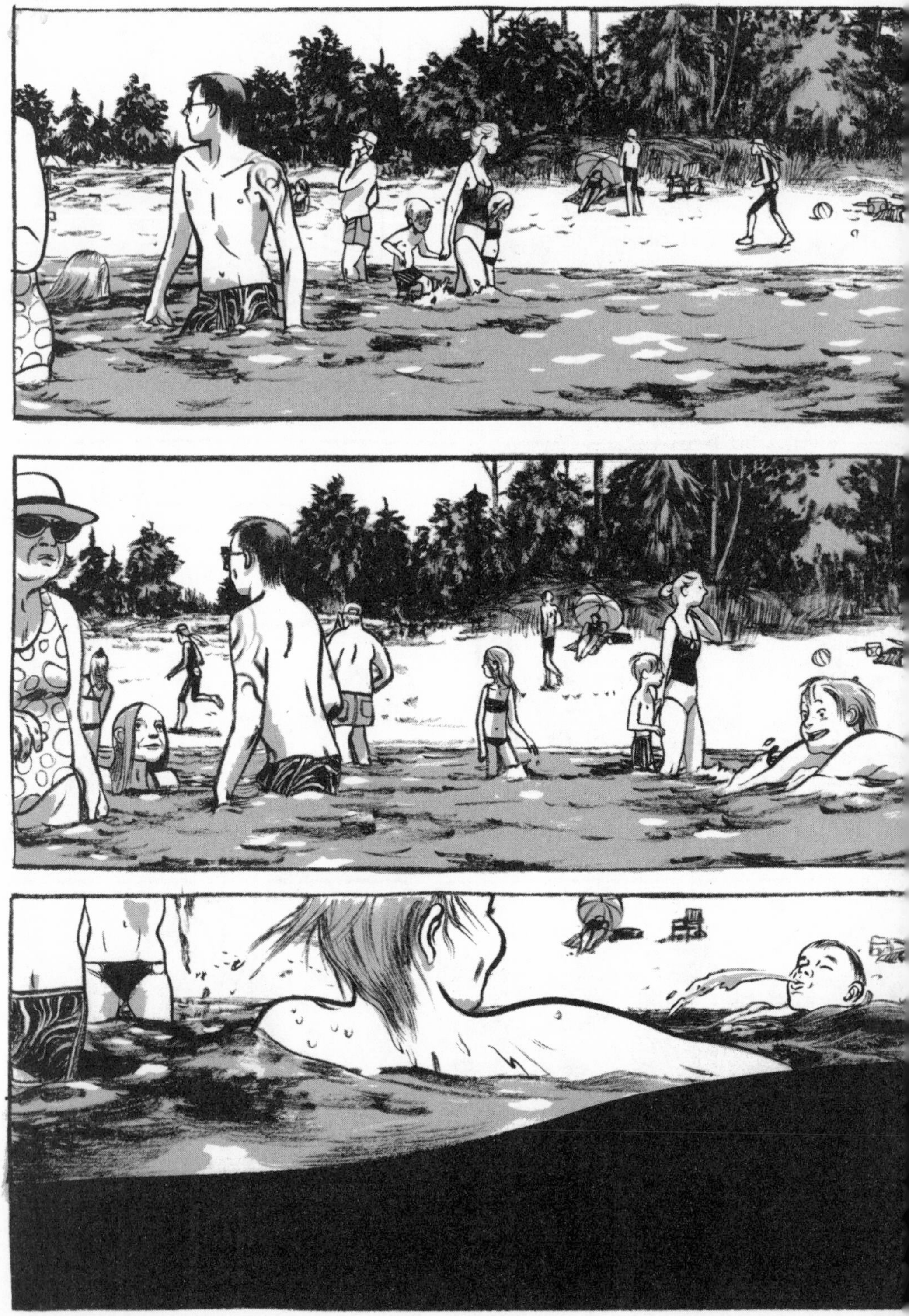

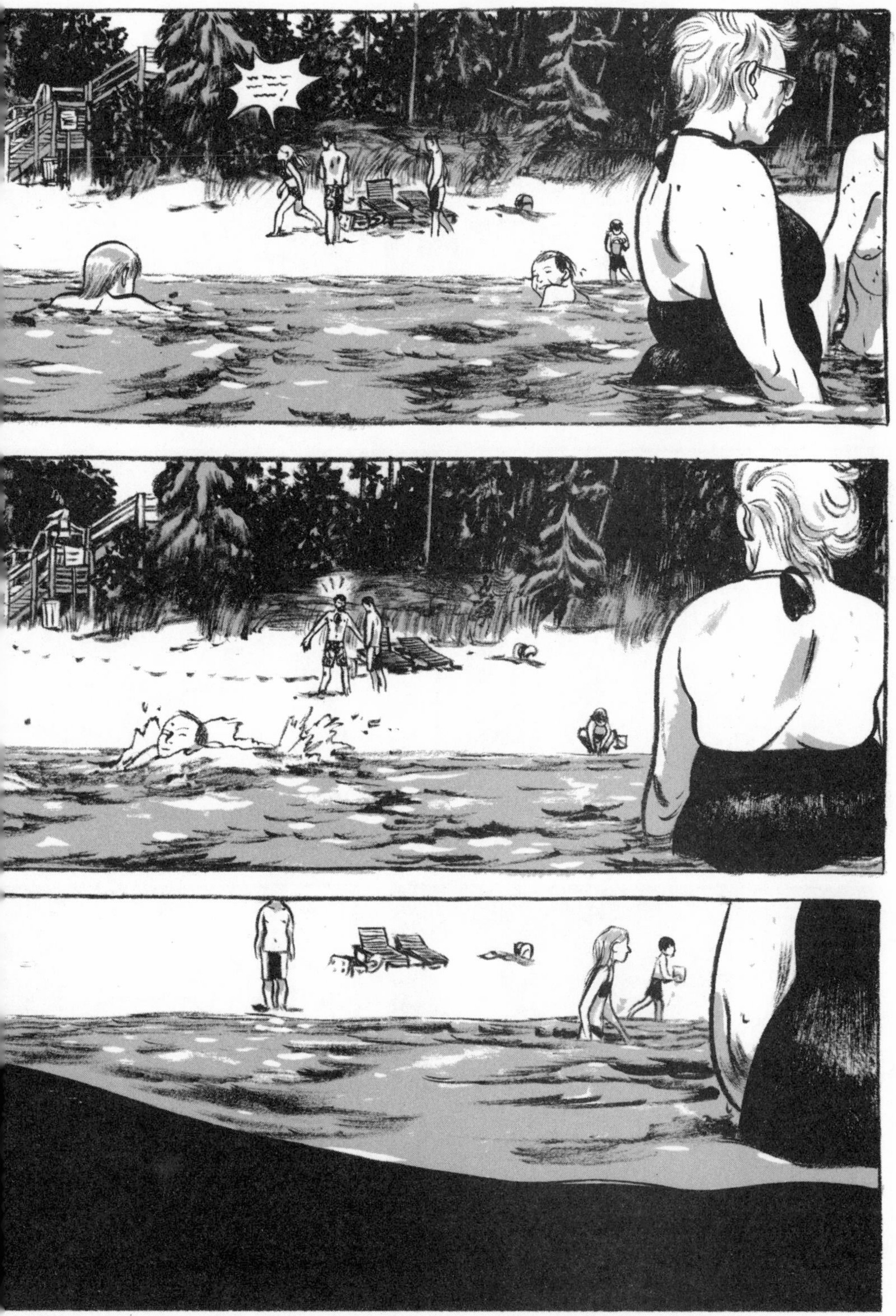

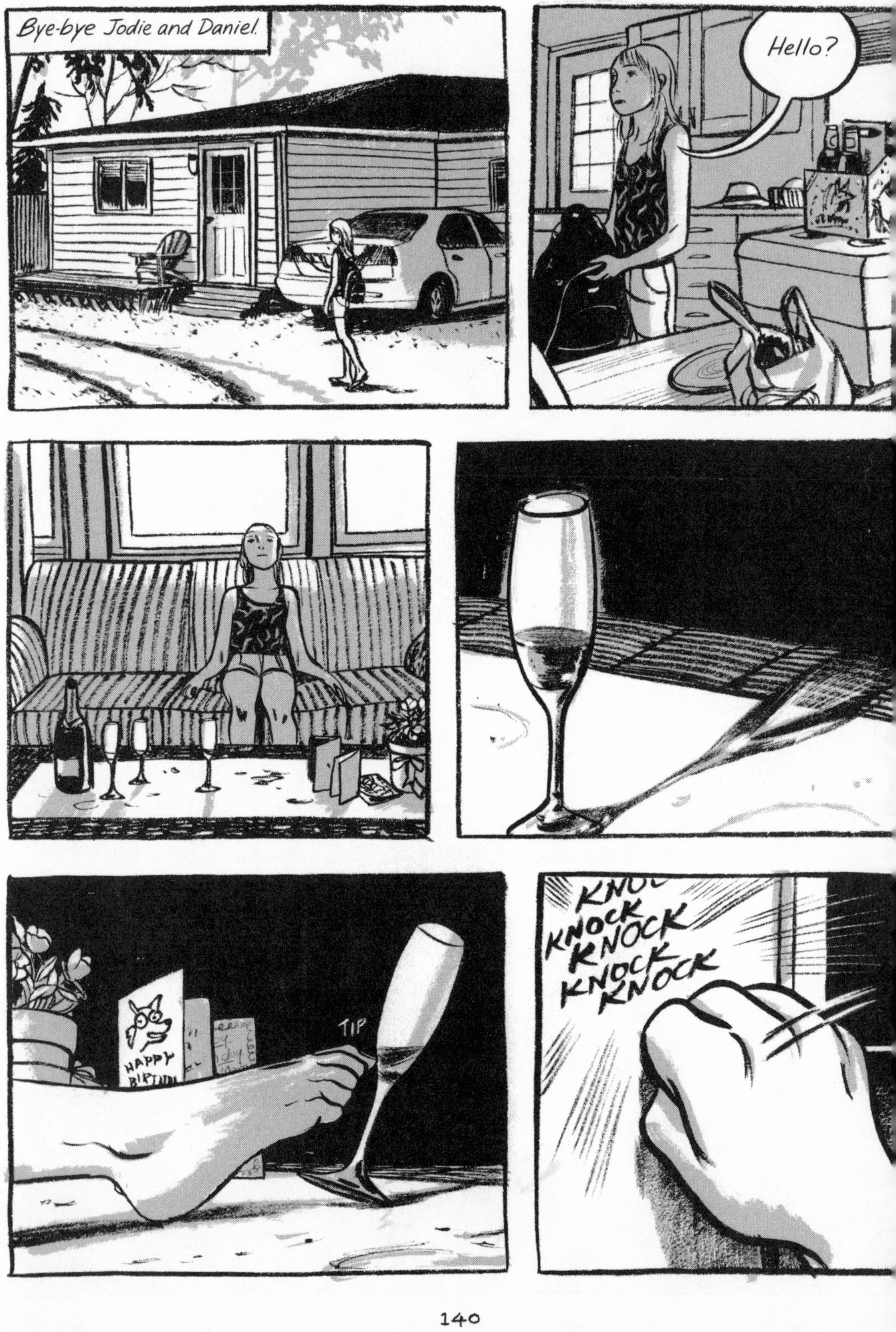
Bye-bye Jodie and Daniel.
Hello?
HAPPY
TIP
KNOC
KNOCK
KNOCK
KNOCK
KNOCK

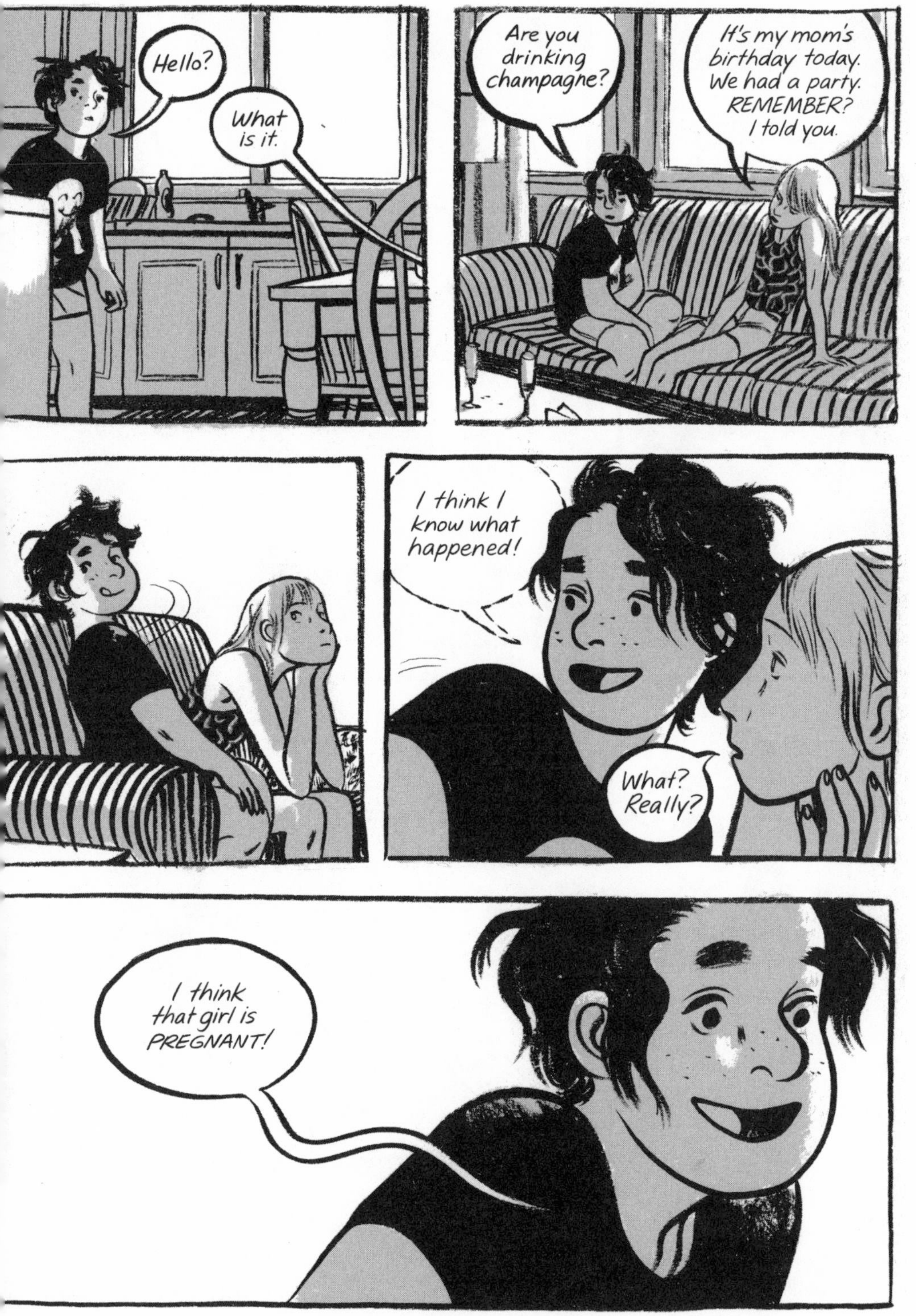
Hello?
What is it.
Are you drinking champagne?
It's my mom's birthday today. We had a party. REMEMBER? I told you.
I think I know what happened!
What? Really?
I think that girl is PREGNANT!

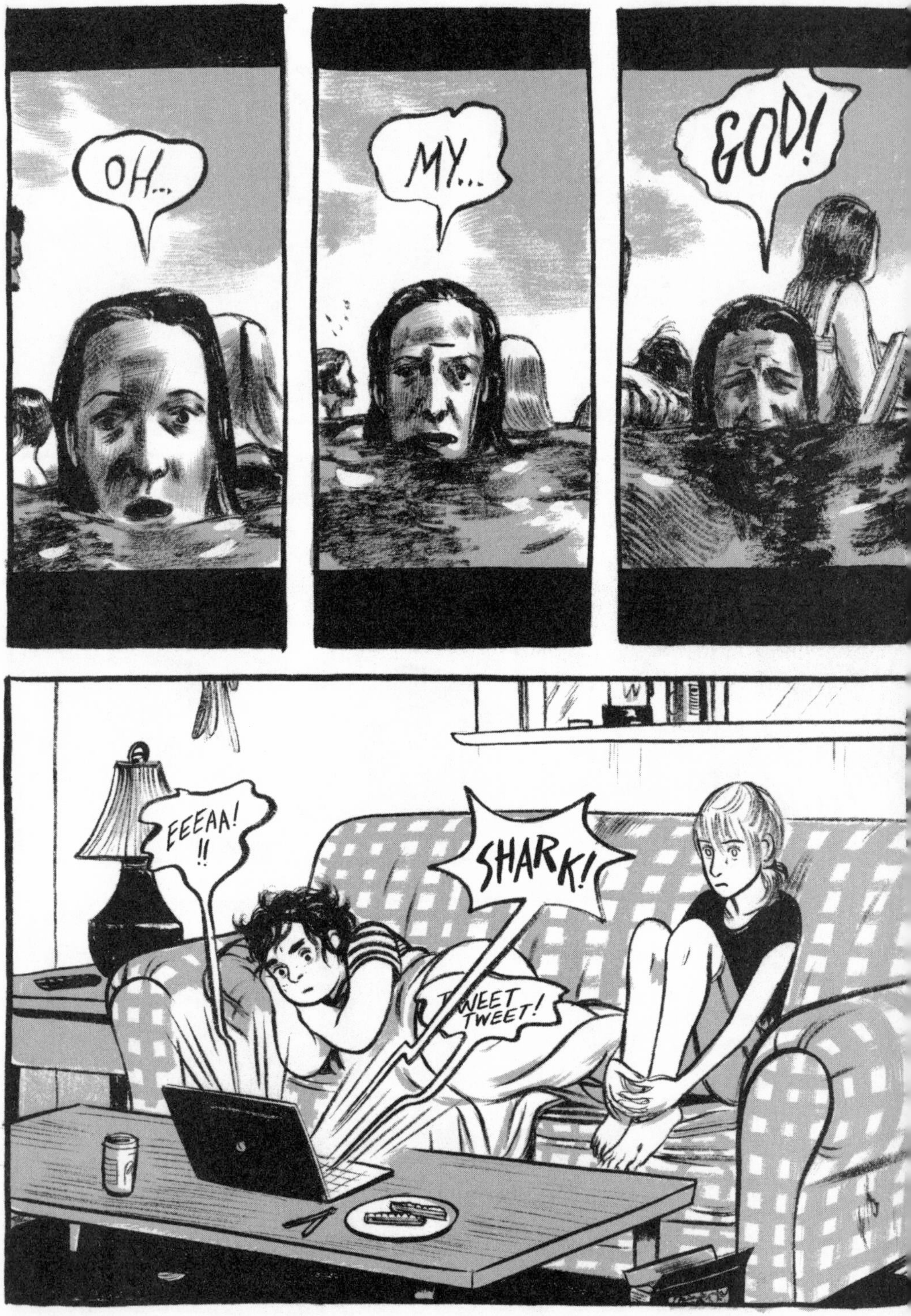
OH...
MY...
GOD!
EEEAA! !!
SHARK!
TWEET TWEET!

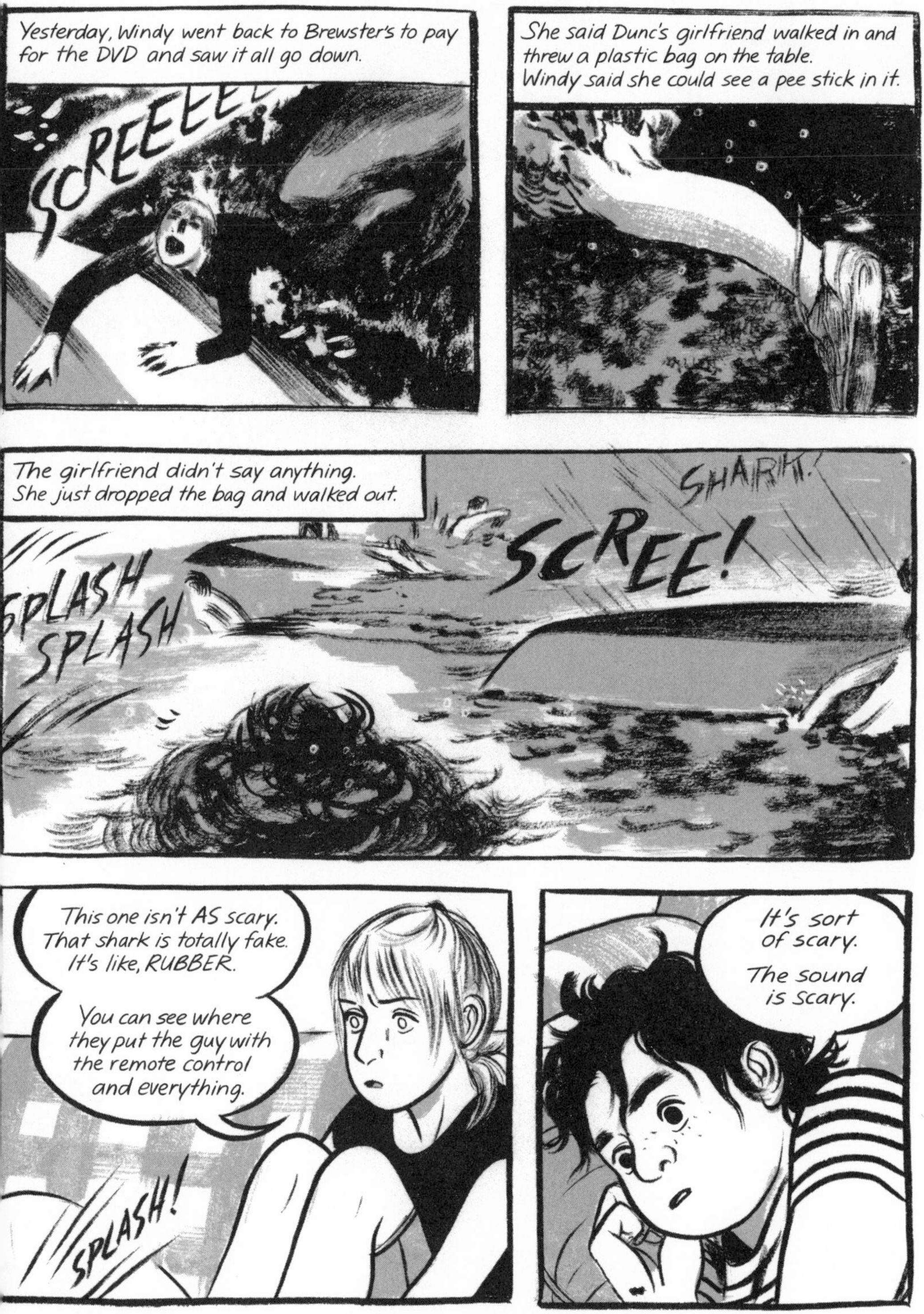
Yesterday, Windy went back to Brewster's to pay for the DVD and saw it all go down.
SCREEEE
She said Dunc's girlfriend walked in and threw a plastic bag on the table. Windy said she could see a pee stick in it.
The girlfriend didn't say anything. She just dropped the bag and walked out.
SHARK!
SCREE!
SPLASH SPLASH
This one isn't AS scary. That shark is totally fake. It's like, RUBBER.
You can see where they put the guy with the remote control and everything.
SPLASH!
It's sort of scary.
The sound is scary.

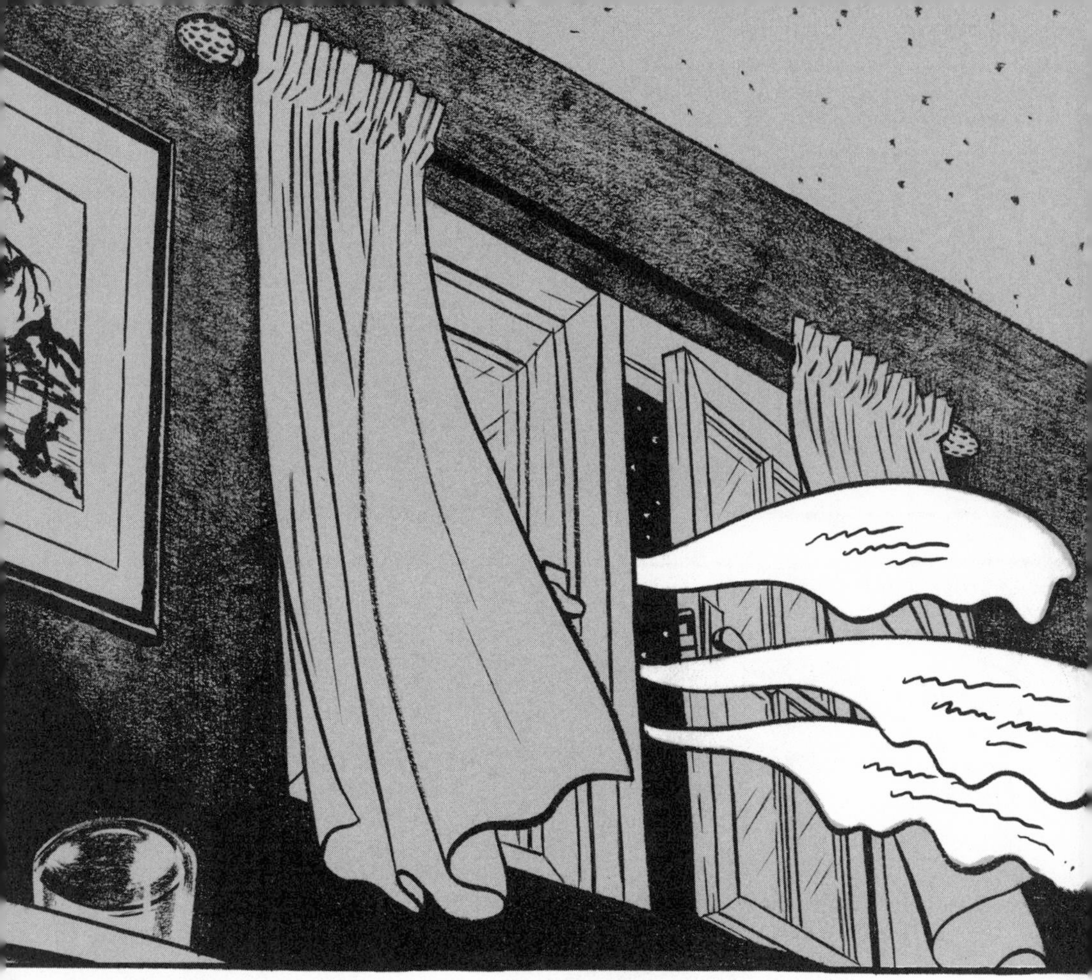

My mom screamed at my dad last night.
Like. SCREAMED. At my dad. They were outside in the car, but I could hear her through my window. My aunt and uncle left.

Then my mom stood outside by herself for a long time.

So today my dad is golfing and my mom is spending quiet time in her room.

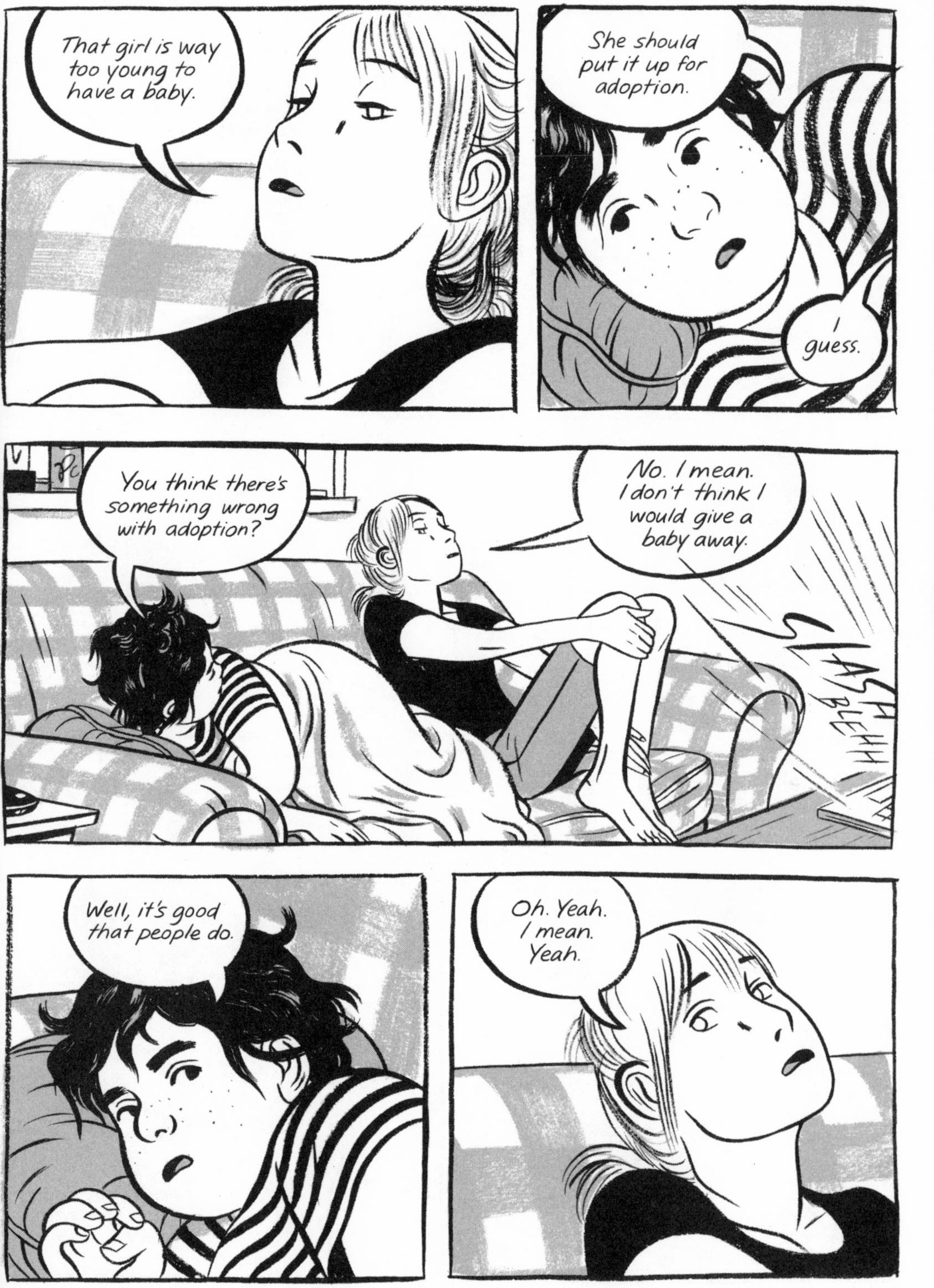
That girl is way too young to have a baby.
She should put it up for adoption.
I guess.
You think there's something wrong with adoption?
No. I mean. I don't think I would give a baby away.
SLASH
BLEHH
Well, it's good that people do.
Oh. Yeah. I mean. Yeah.

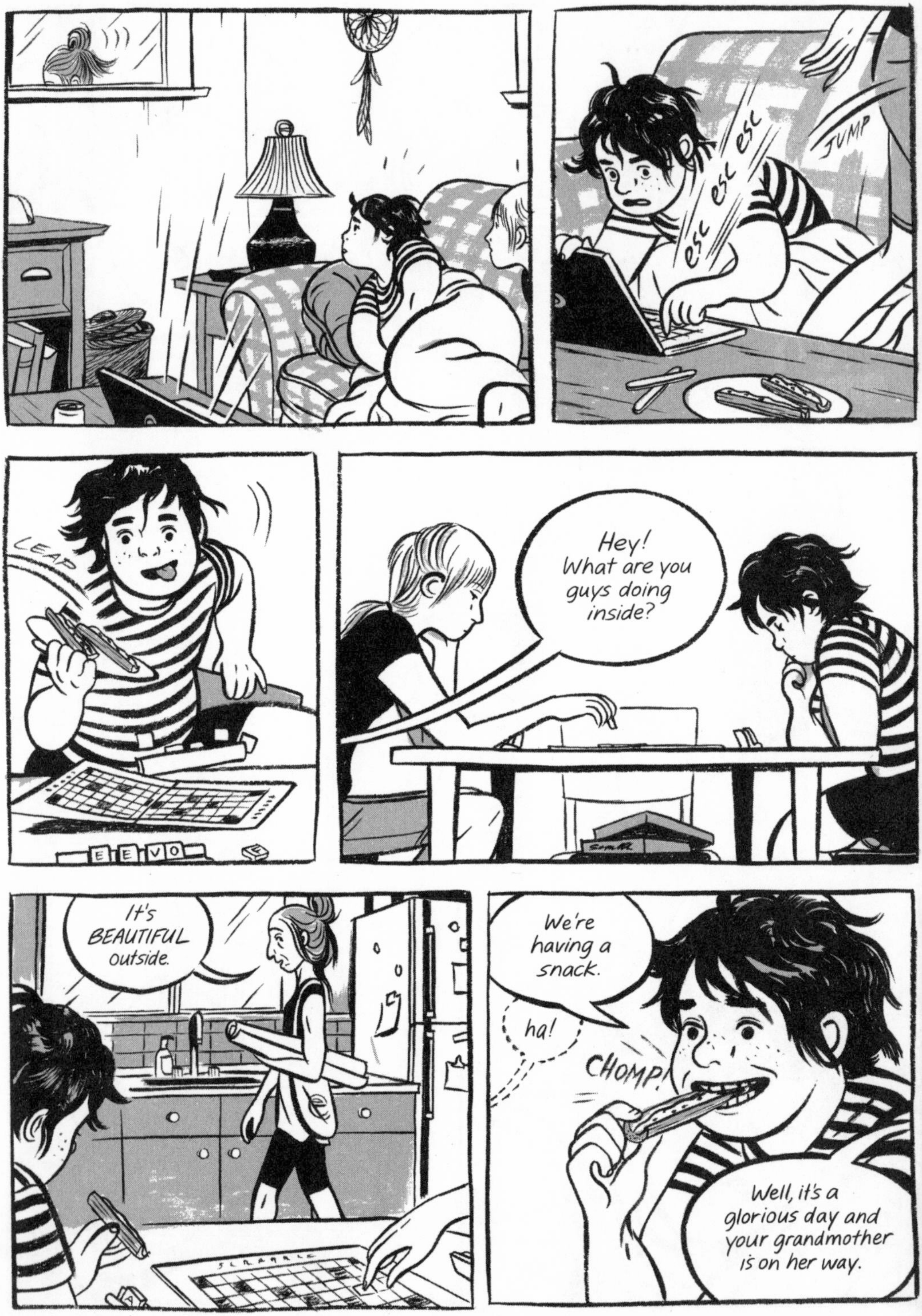
JUMP
esc esc esc
LEAP
EEVO
Hey! What are you guys doing inside?
It's BEAUTIFUL outside.
We're having a snack.
ha!
CHOMP!
Well, it's a glorious day and your grandmother is on her way.

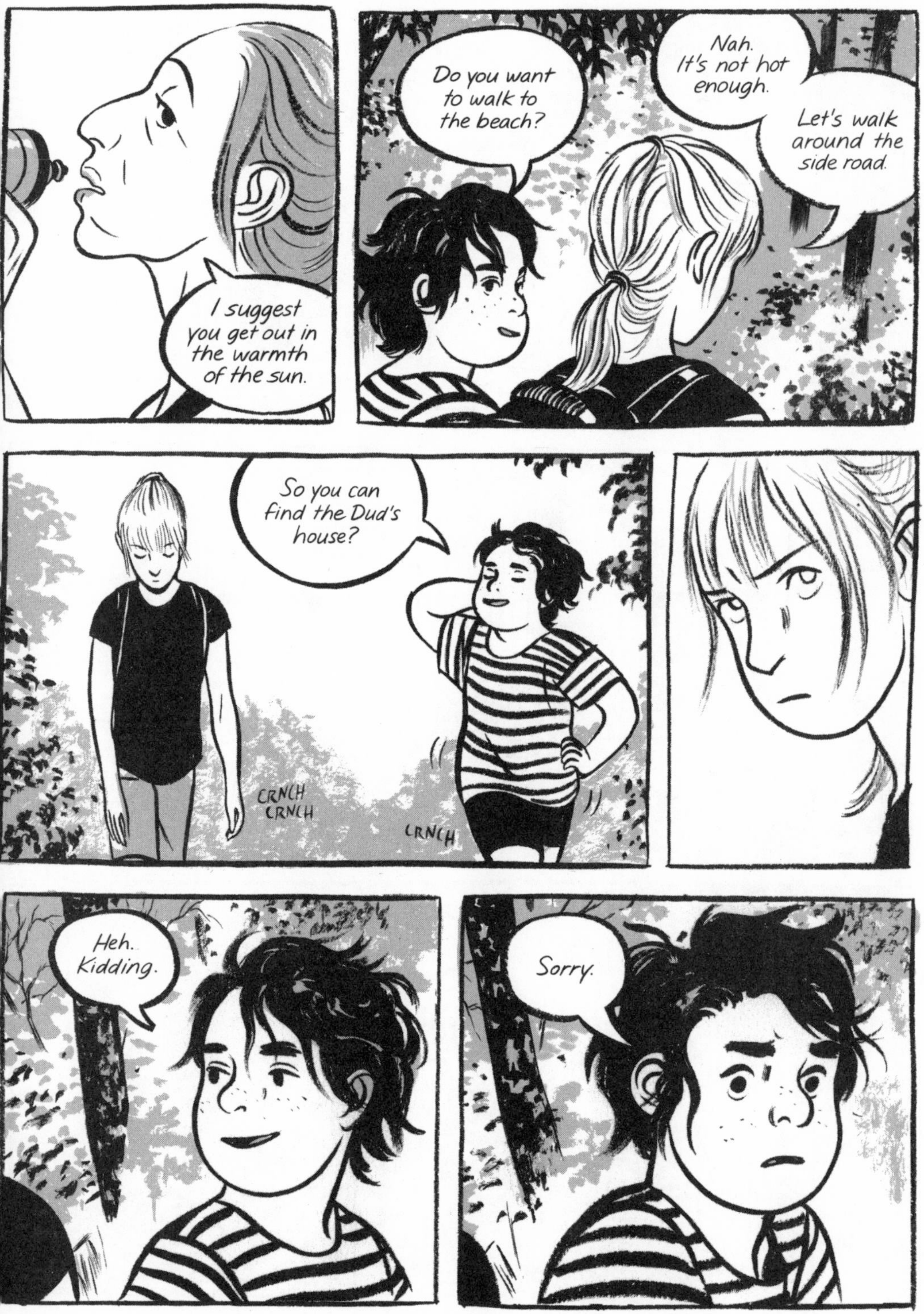
I suggest you get out in the warmth of the sun.
Do you want to walk to the beach?
Nah. It's not hot enough.
Let's walk around the side road.
So you can find the Dud's house?
CRNCH CRNCH
CRNCH
Heh. Kidding.
Sorry.

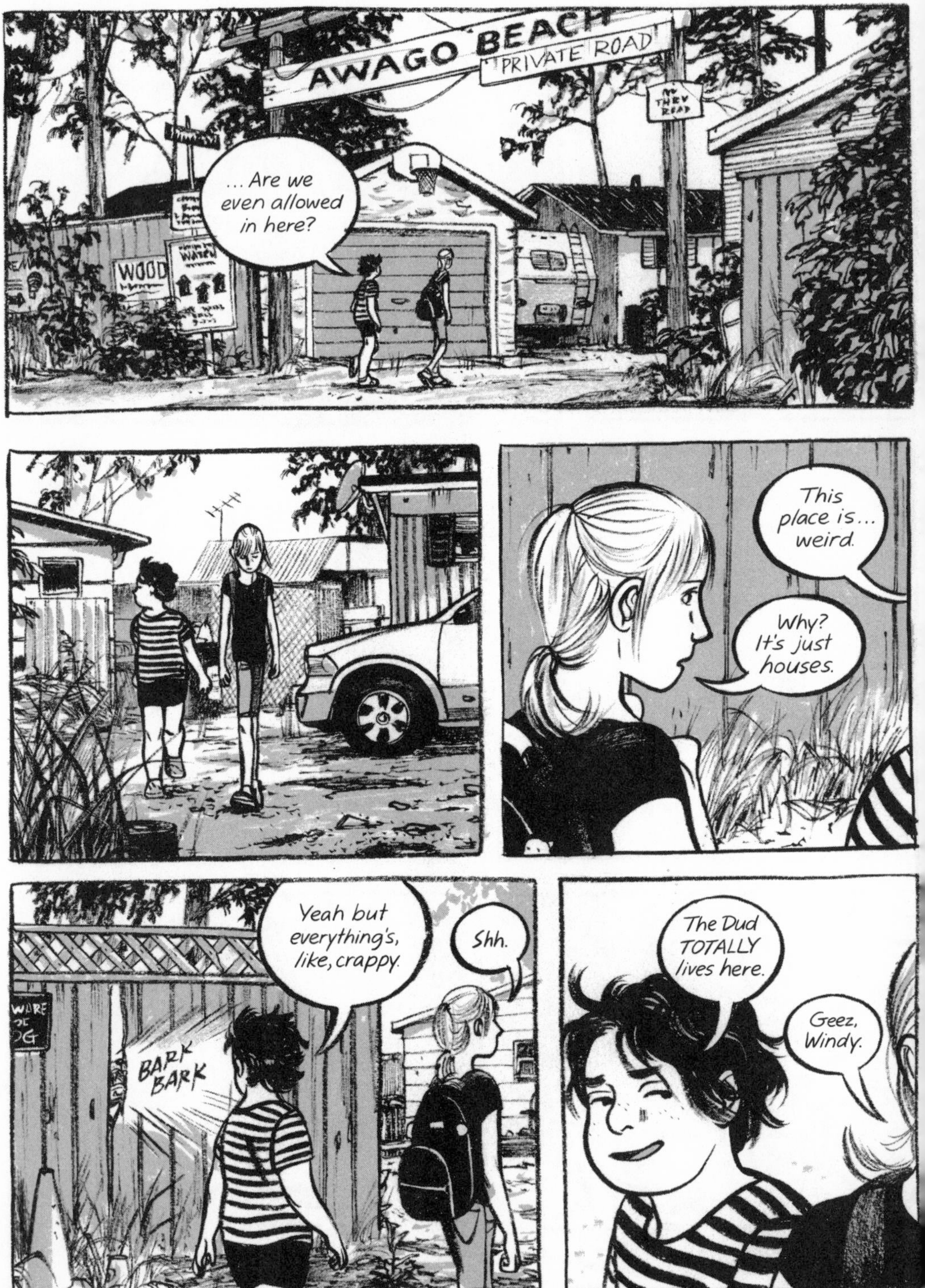
AWAGO BEACH
PRIVATE ROAD
WOOD
...Are we even allowed in here?
This place is... weird.
Why? It's just houses.
Yeah but everything's, like, crappy.
Shh.
BARK BARK
The Dud TOTALLY lives here.
Geez, Windy.

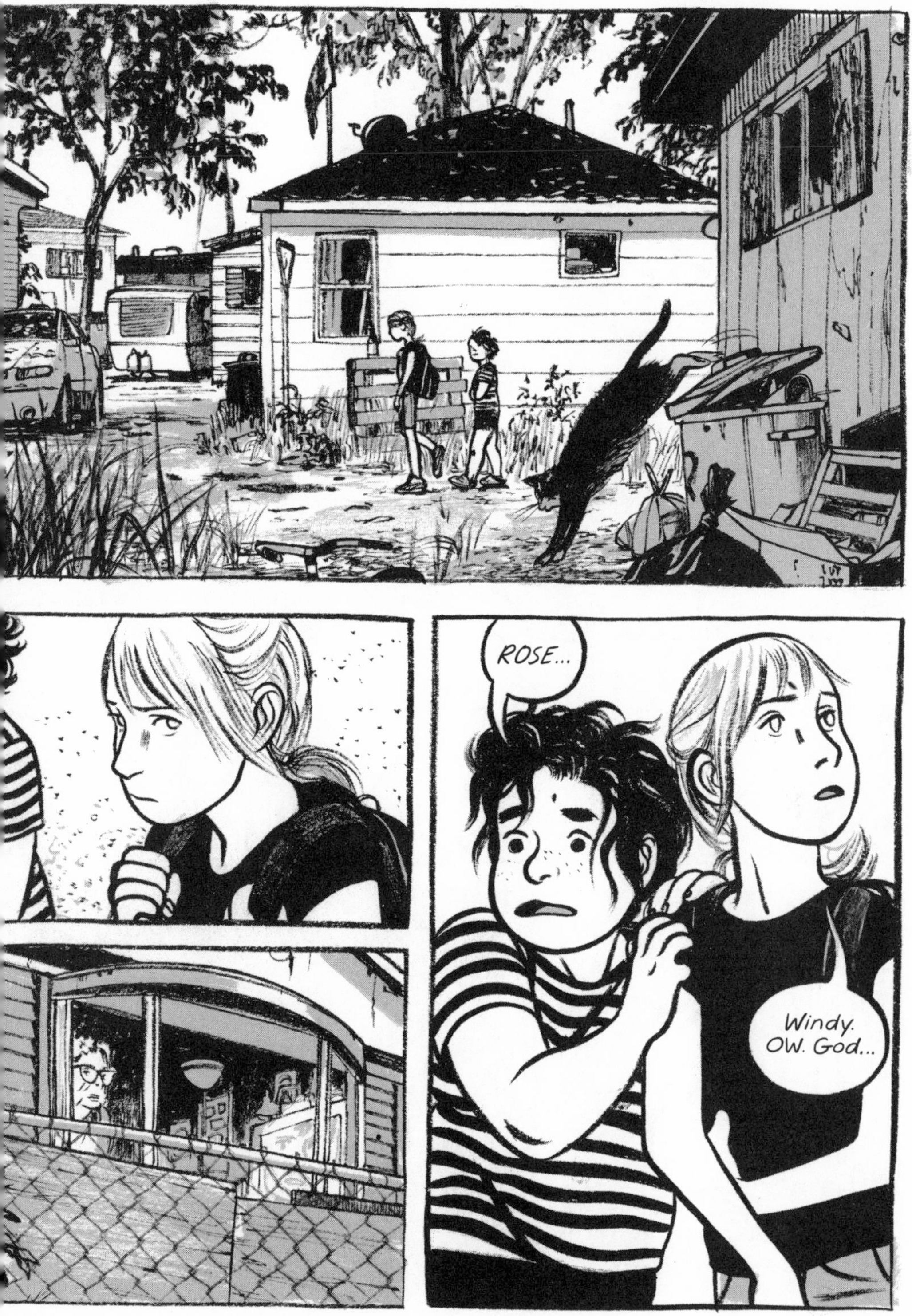
ROSE...
Windy.
OW. God...

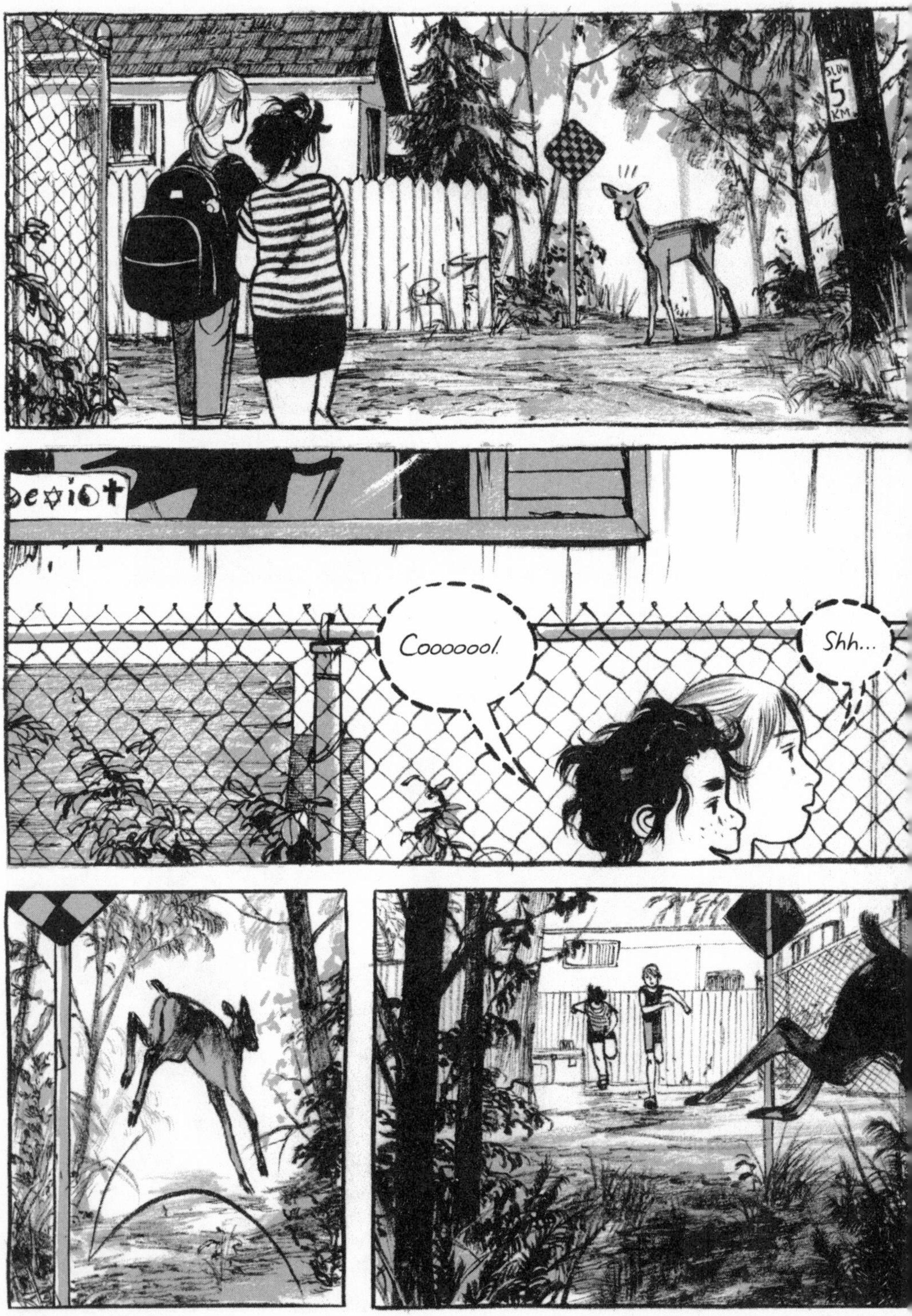
SLOW
5
KM
Coooooool.
Shh...

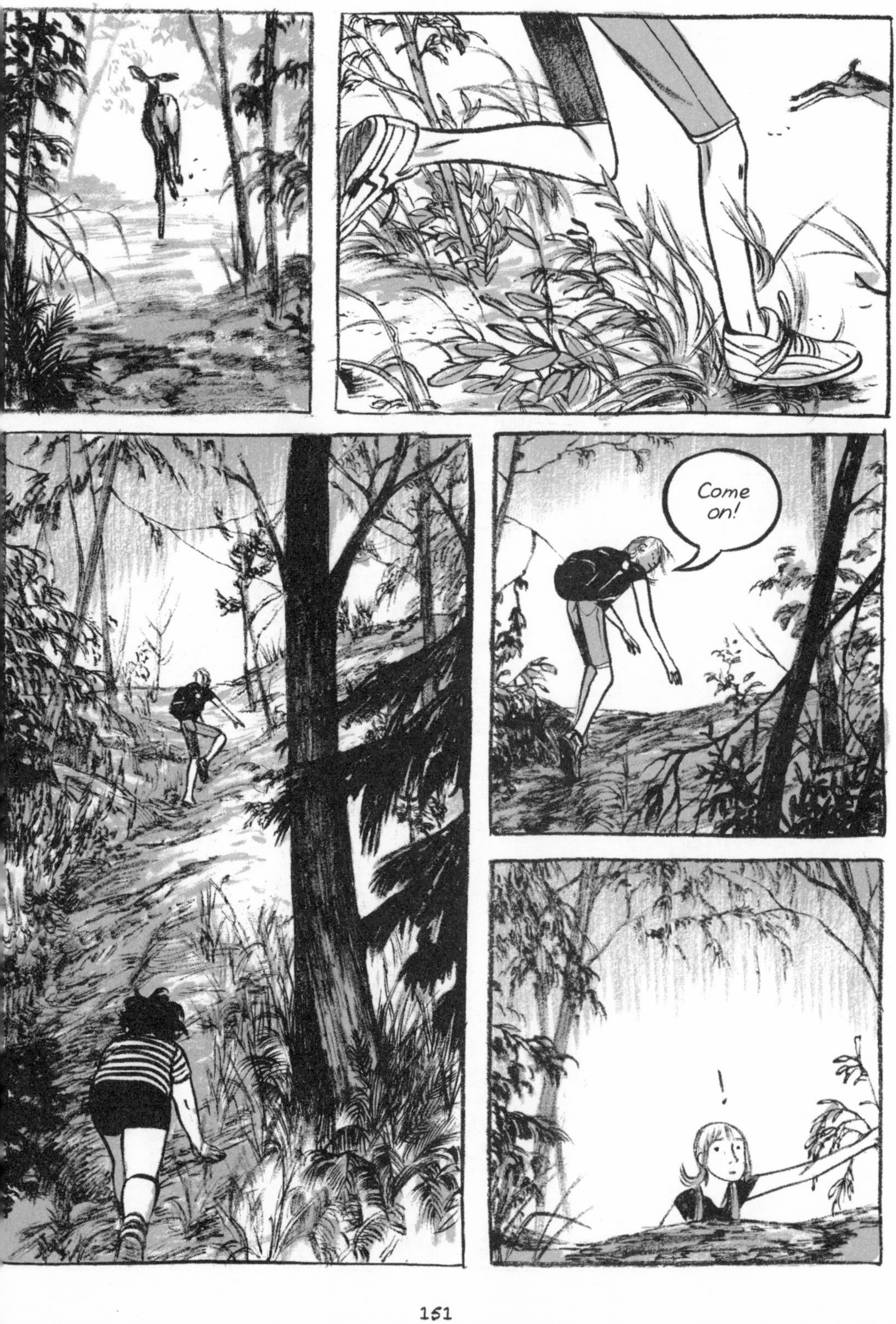
Come on!
!

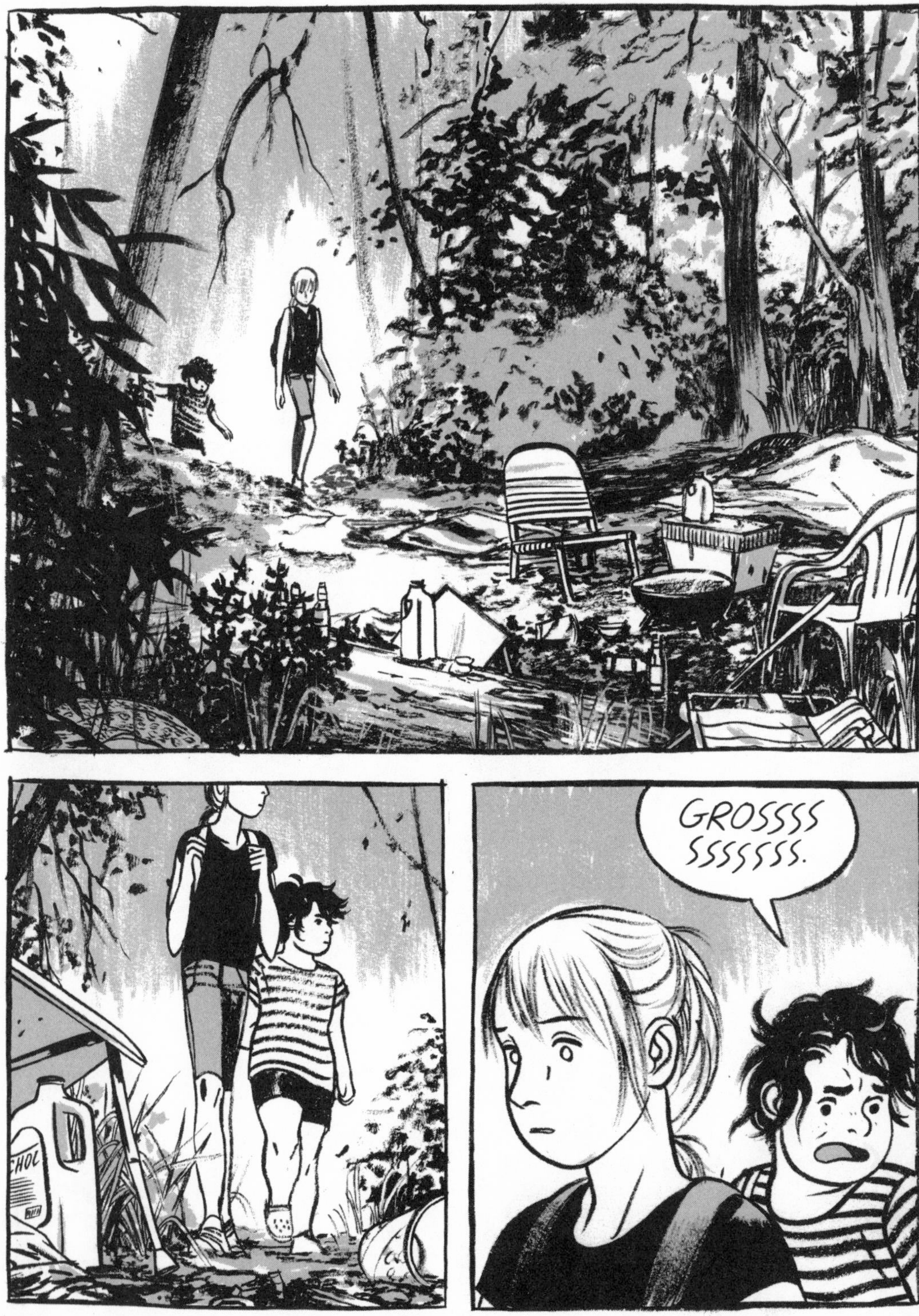
GROSSSS
SSSSSSS.

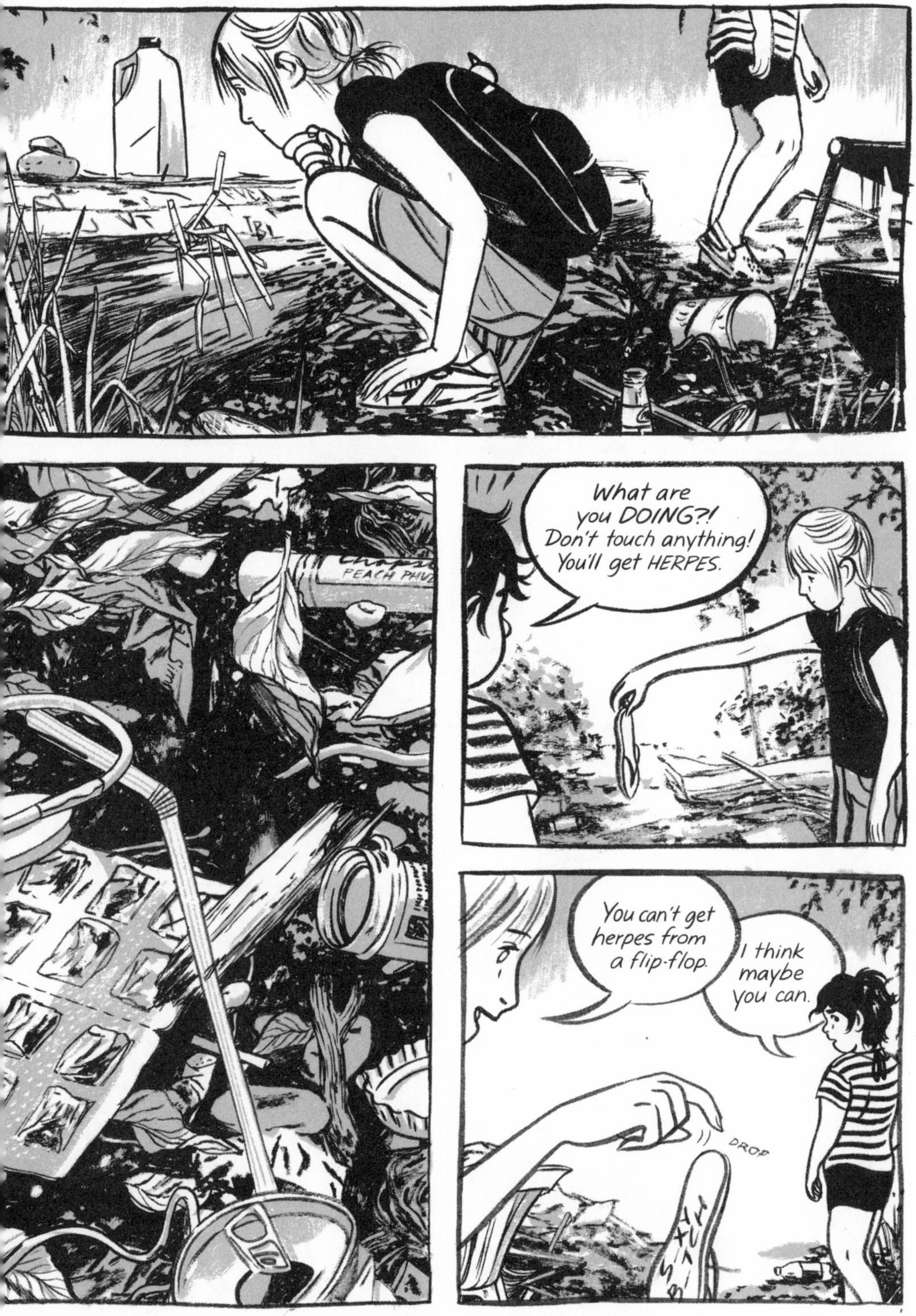
What are you DOING?! Don't touch anything! You'll get HERPES.
You can't get herpes from a flip-flop.
I think maybe you can.
DROP

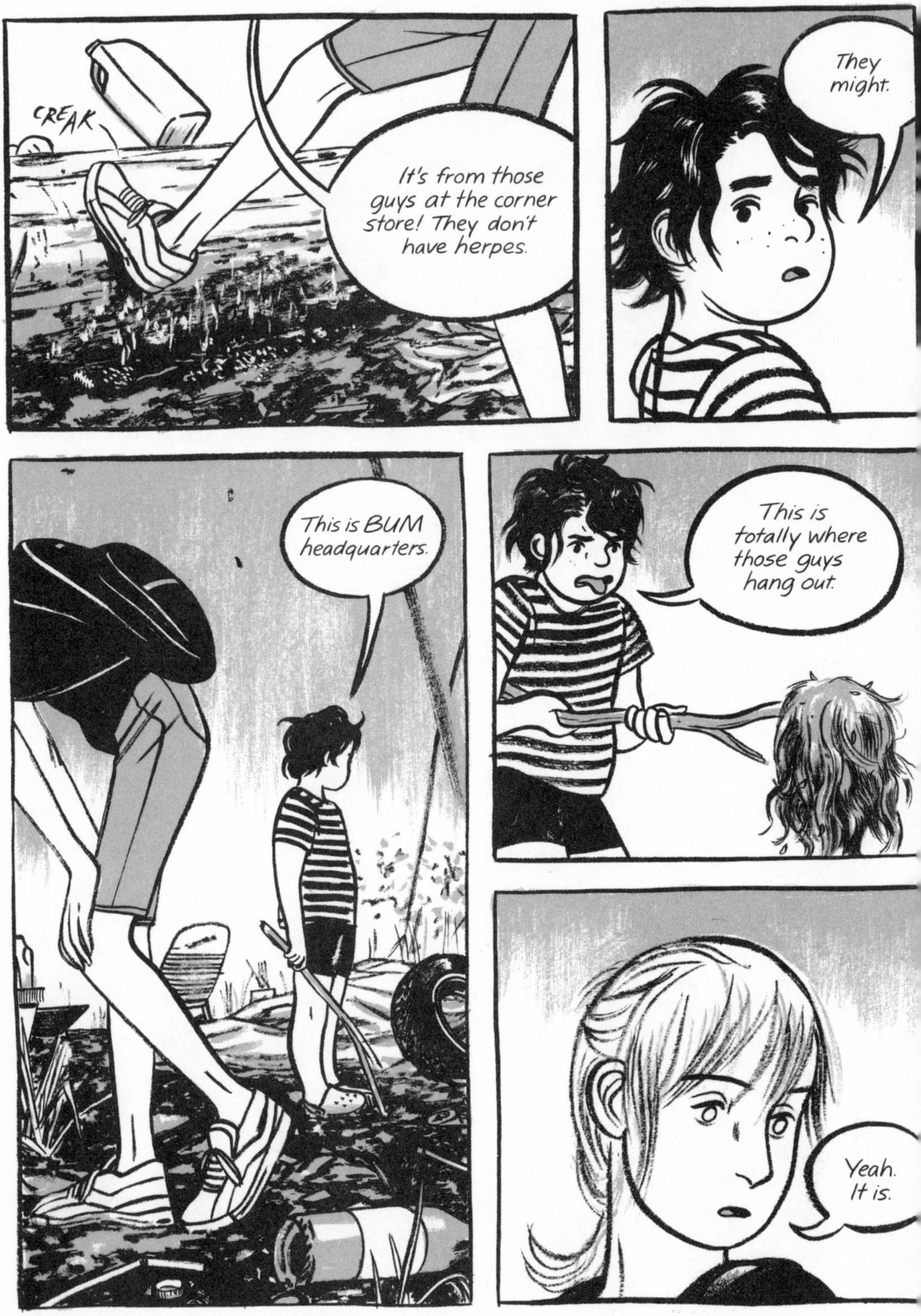
CREAK
It's from those guys at the corner store! They don't have herpes.
They might.
This is BUM headquarters.
This is totally where those guys hang out.
Yeah. It is.

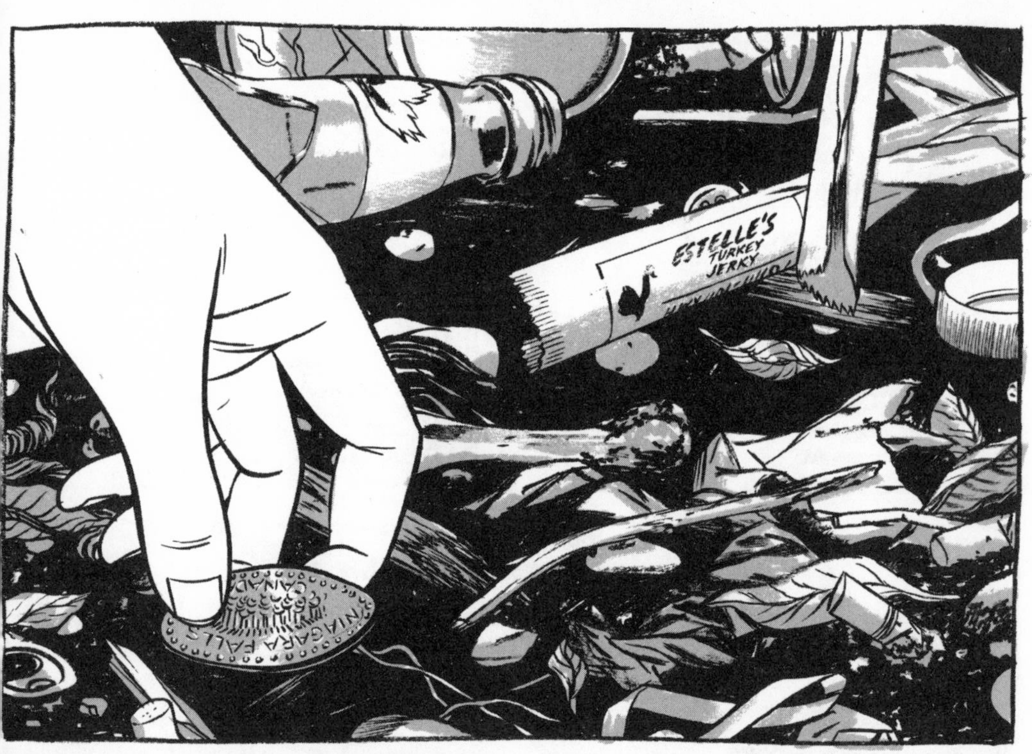
ESTELLE'S
TURKEY
JERKY
NIAGARA FALLS
CANADA

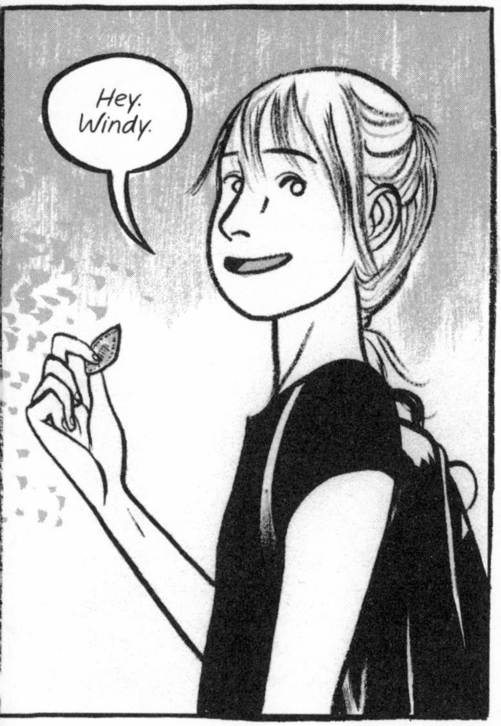
Hey. Windy.

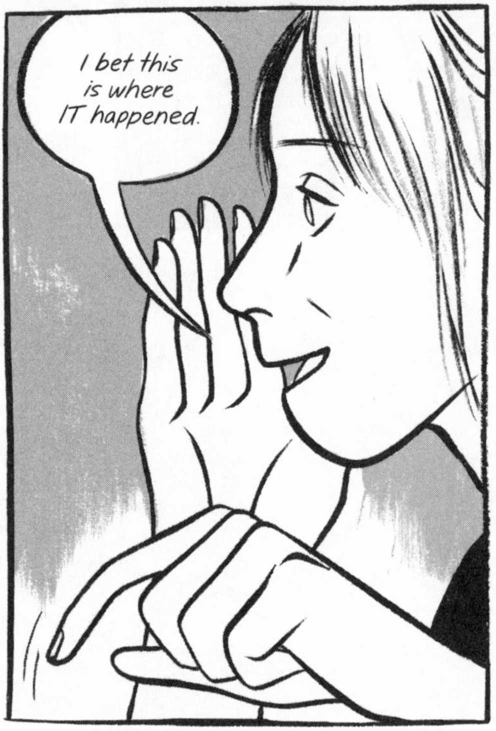
I bet this is where IT happened.

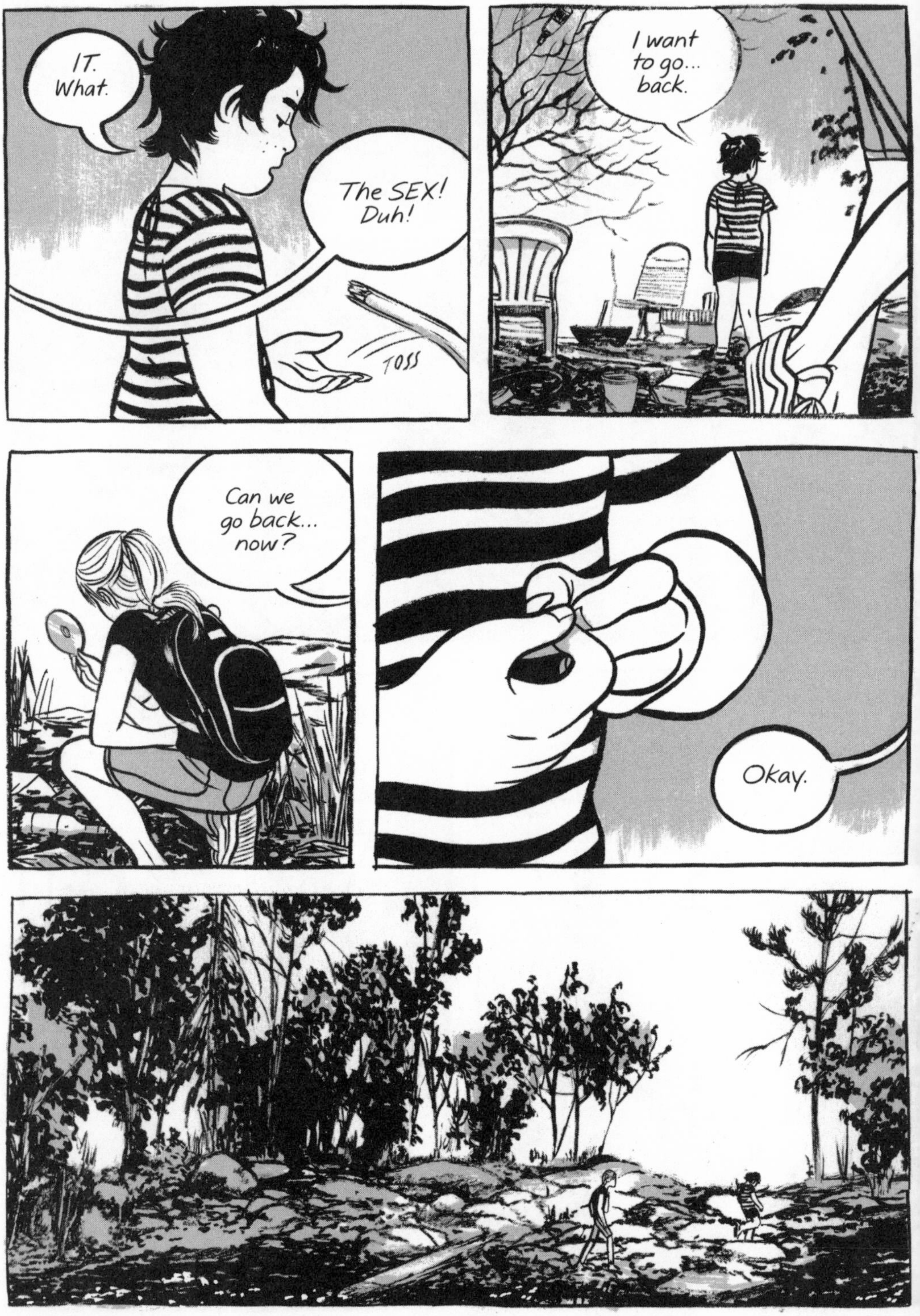
IT. What.
The SEX! Duh!
TOSS
I want to go... back.
Can we go back... now?
Okay.

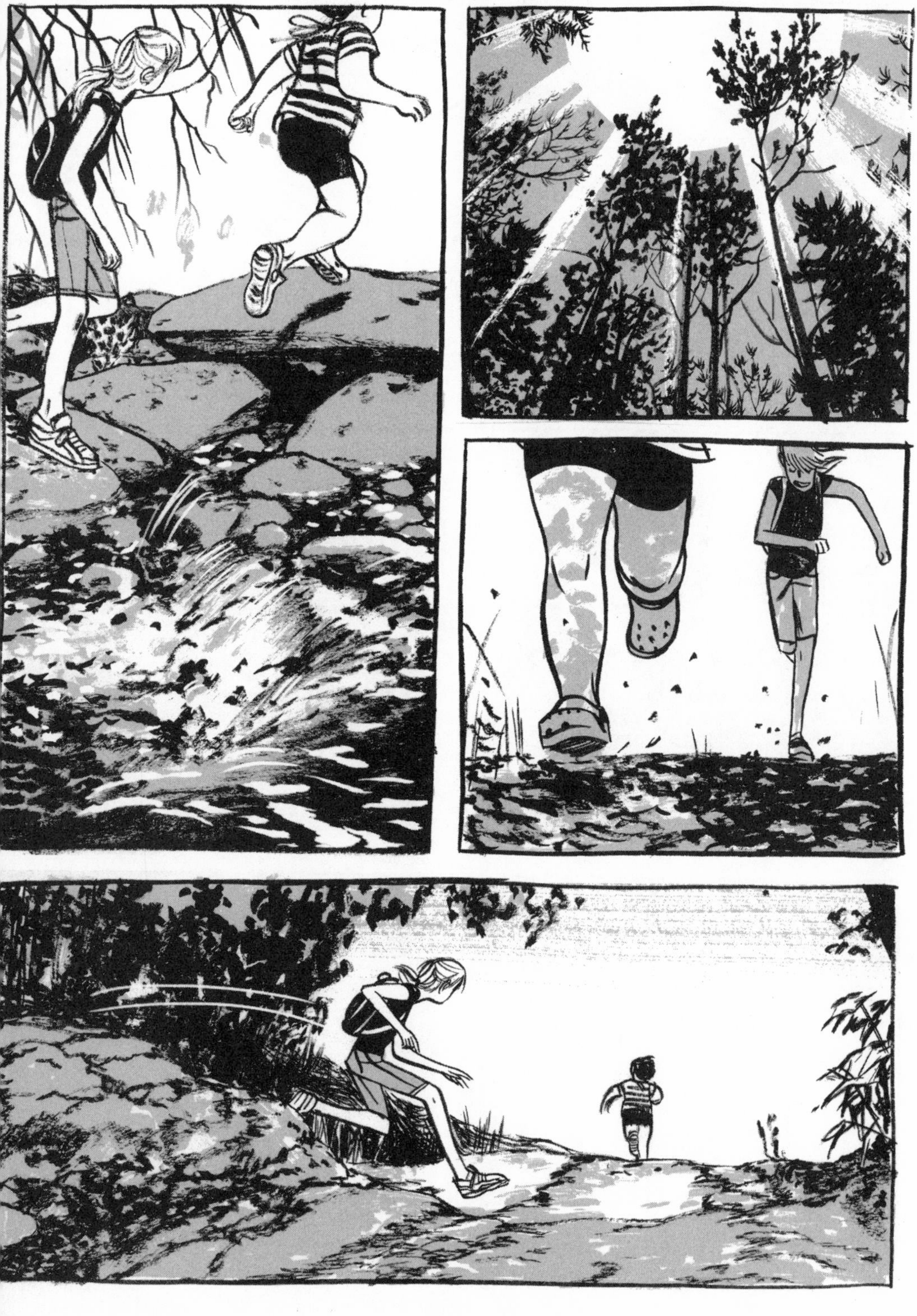

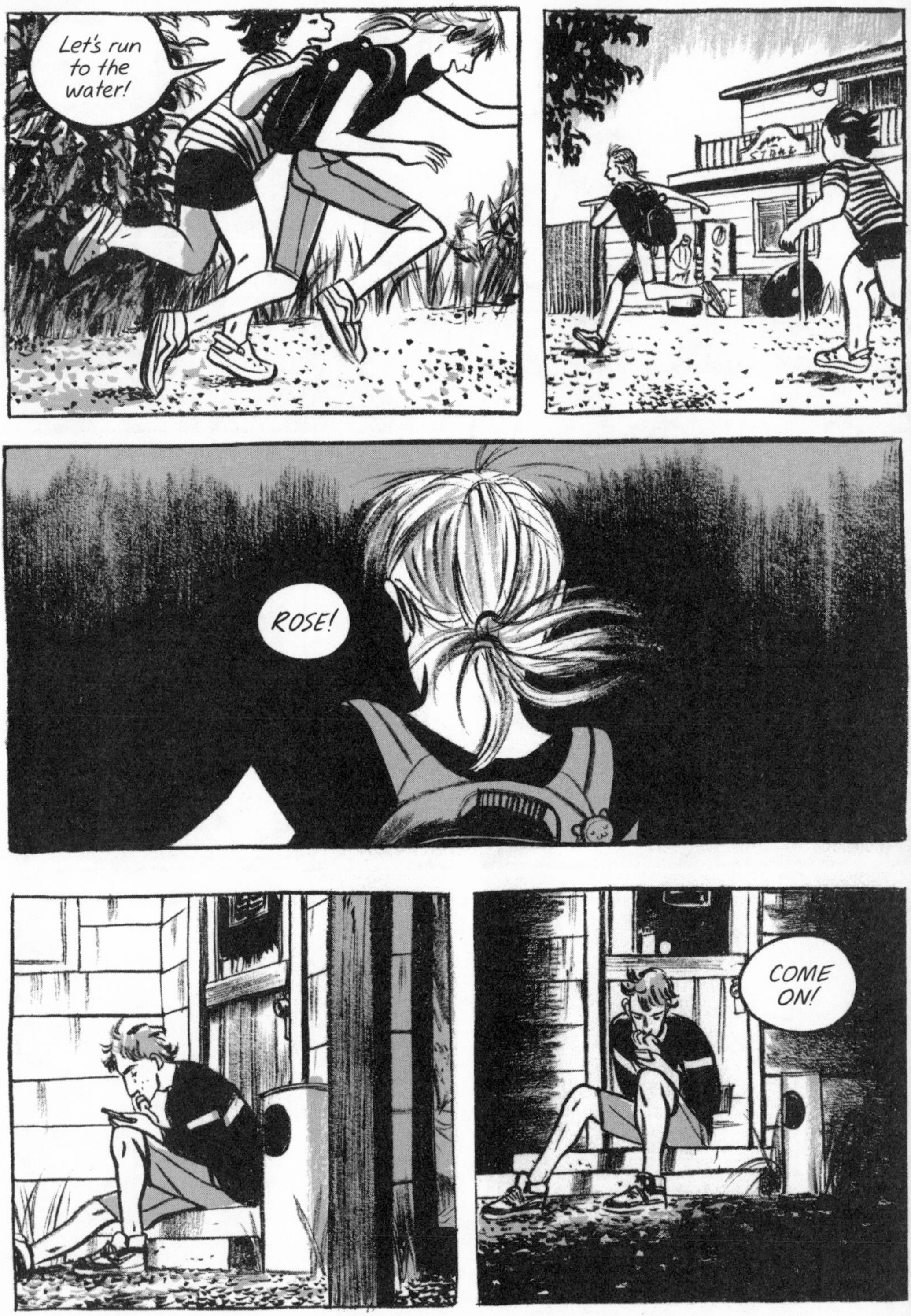
Let's run to the water!
STORE
ROSE!
COME ON!

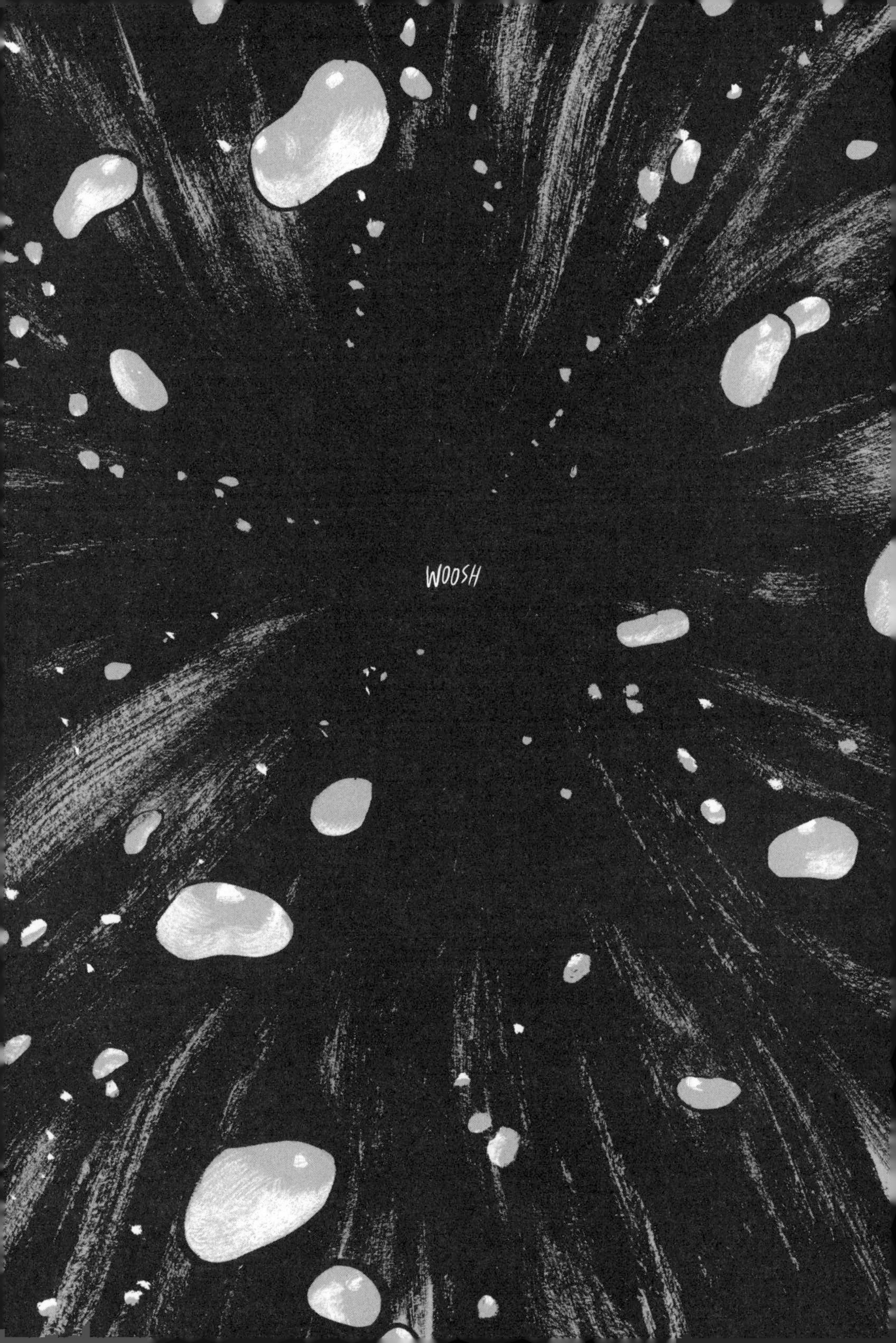
WOOSH

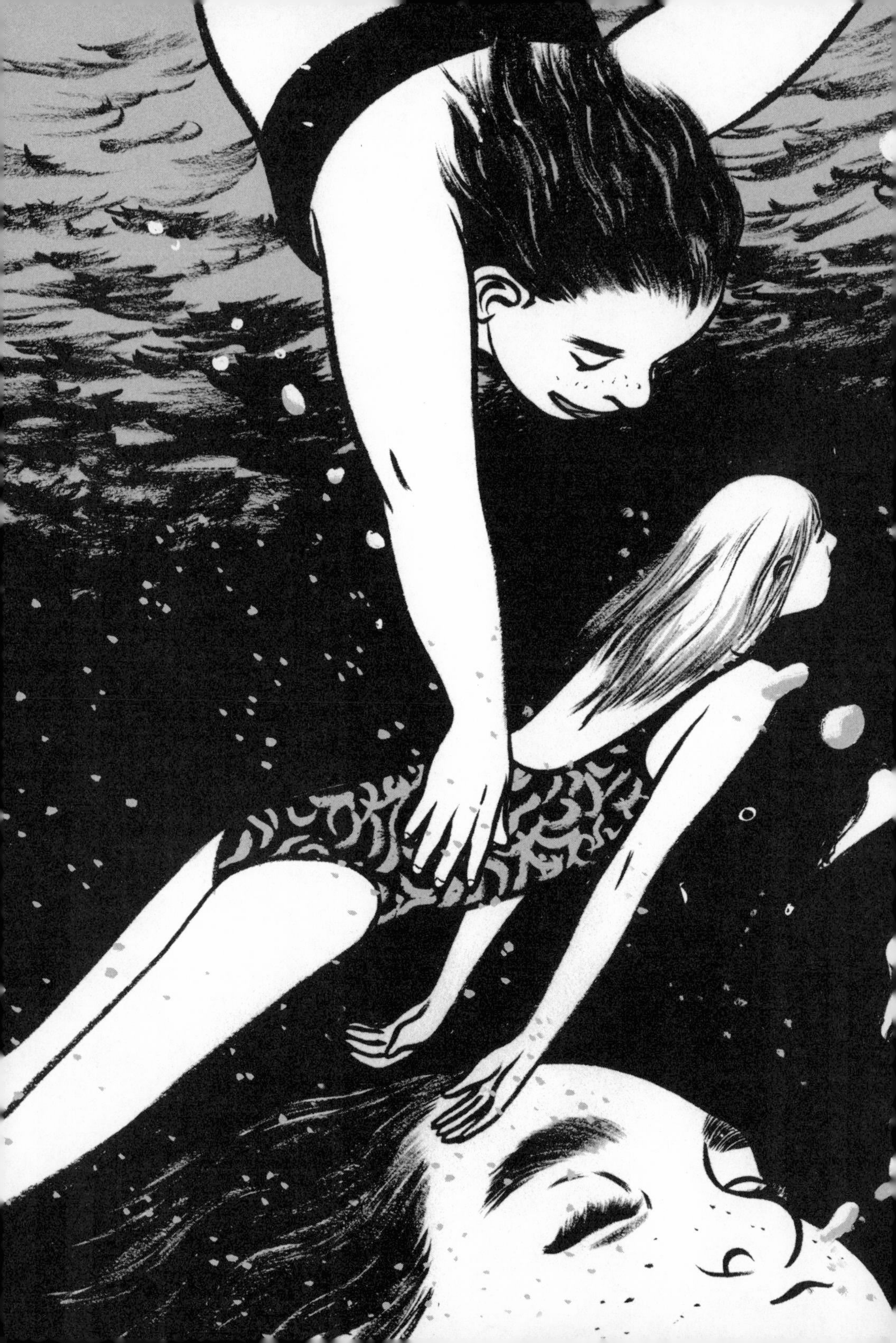

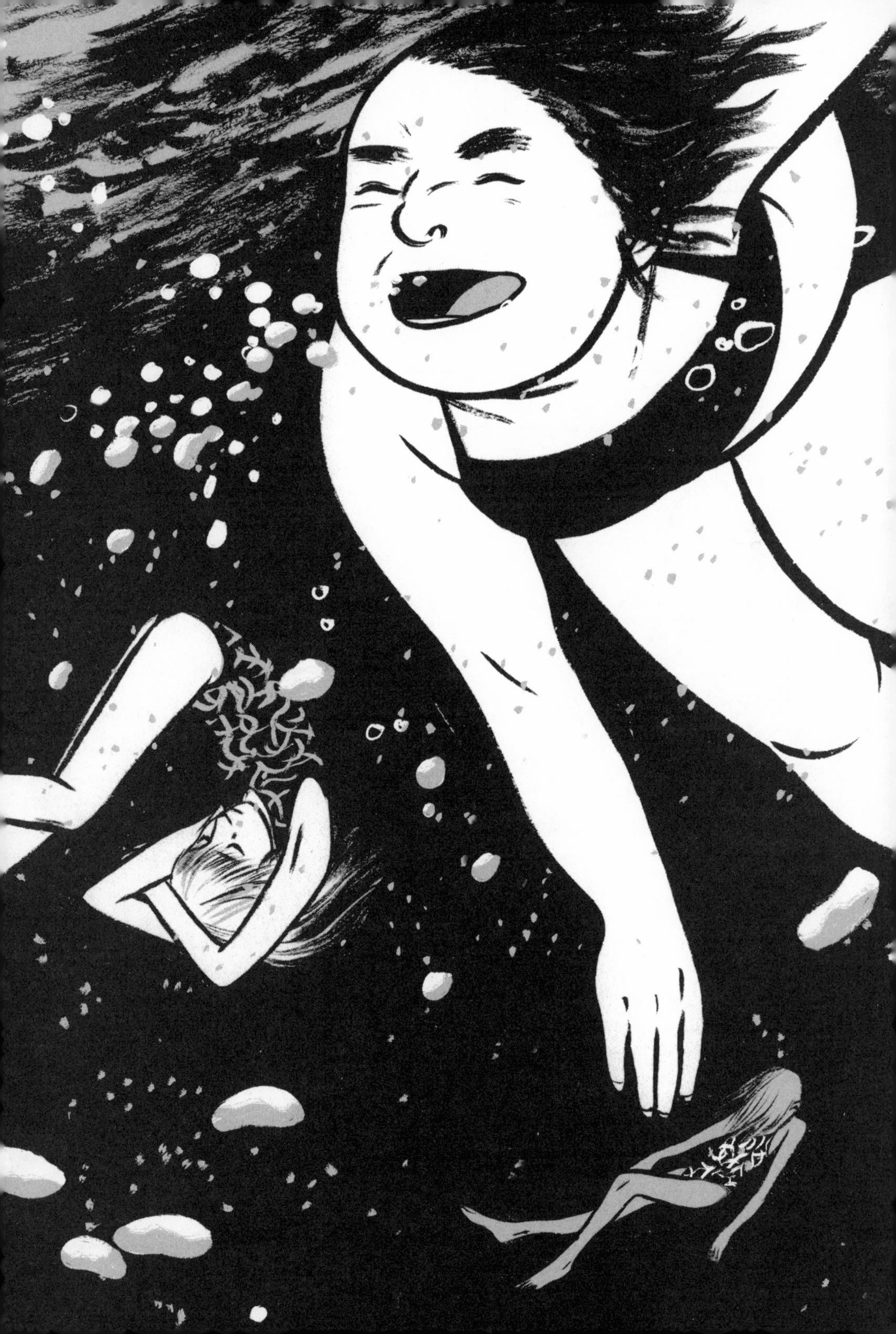

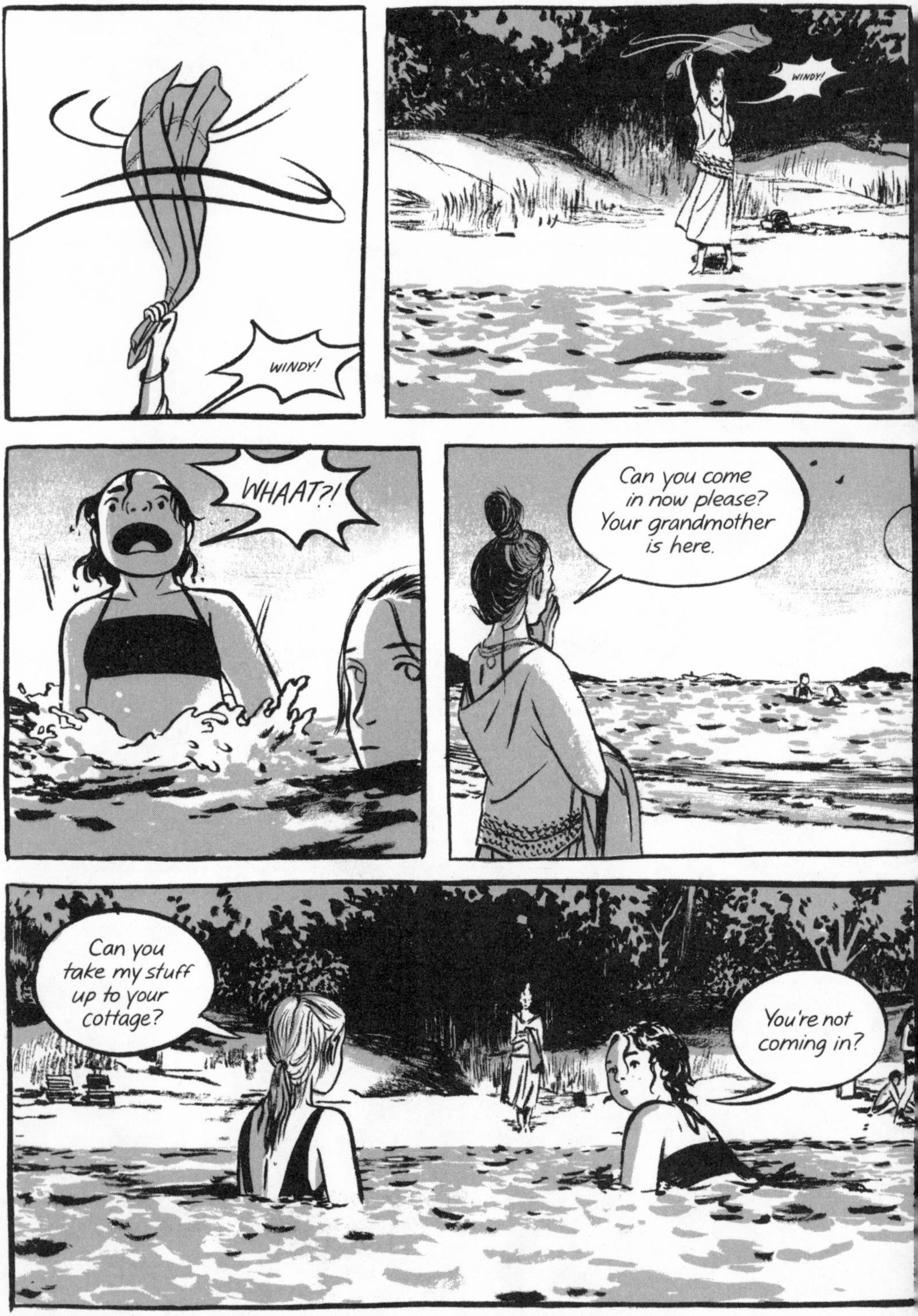
WINDY!
WINDY!
WHAAT?!
Can you come in now please? Your grandmother is here.
Can you take my stuff up to your cottage?
You're not coming in?

I'm going to swim along the beach. Home.

TIP!

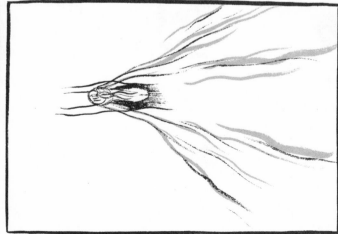

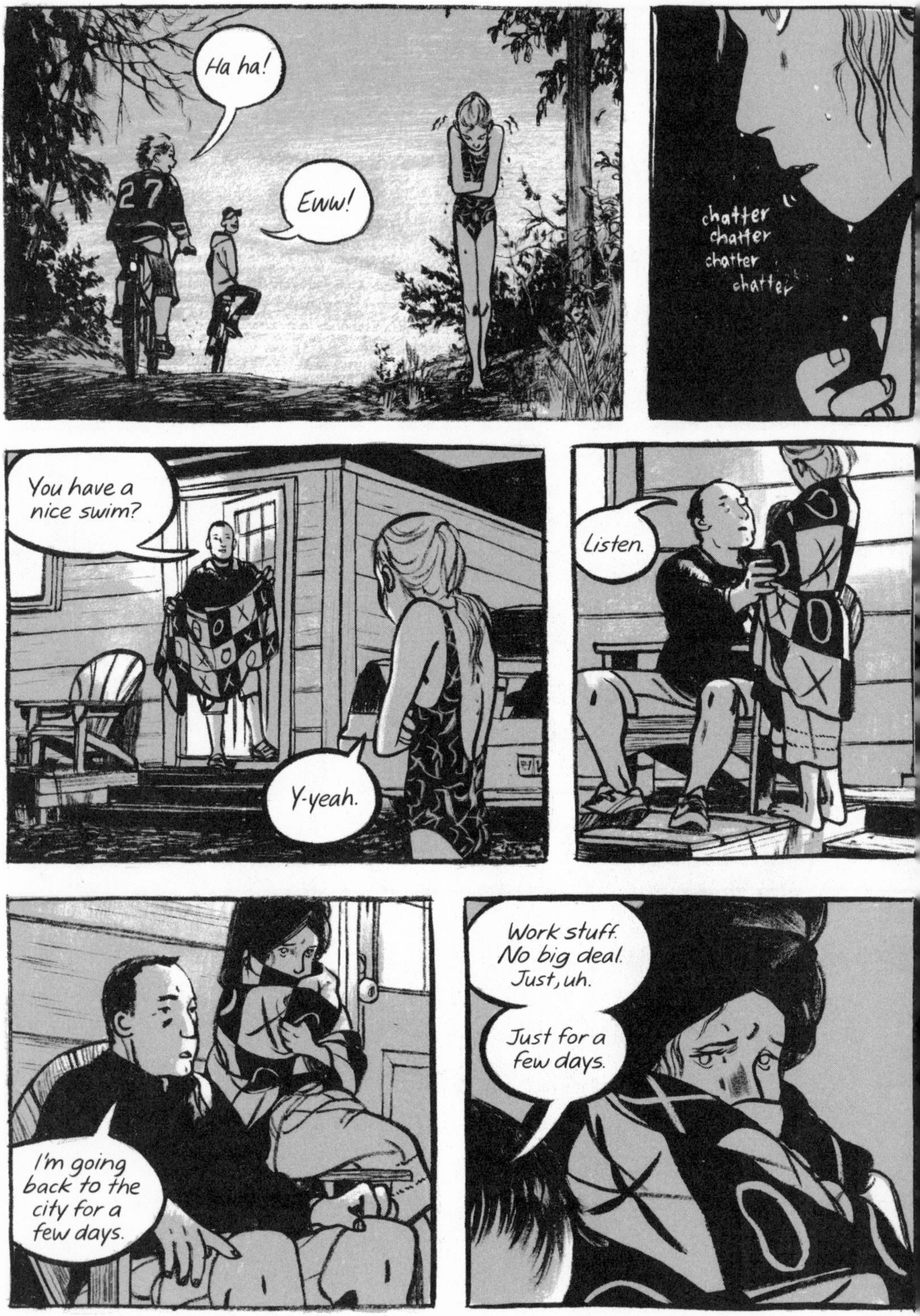
Ha ha!
Eww!
chatter
chatter
chatter
chatter
You have a nice swim?
Y-yeah.
Listen.
I'm going back to the city for a few days.
Work stuff. No big deal. Just, uh.
Just for a few days.

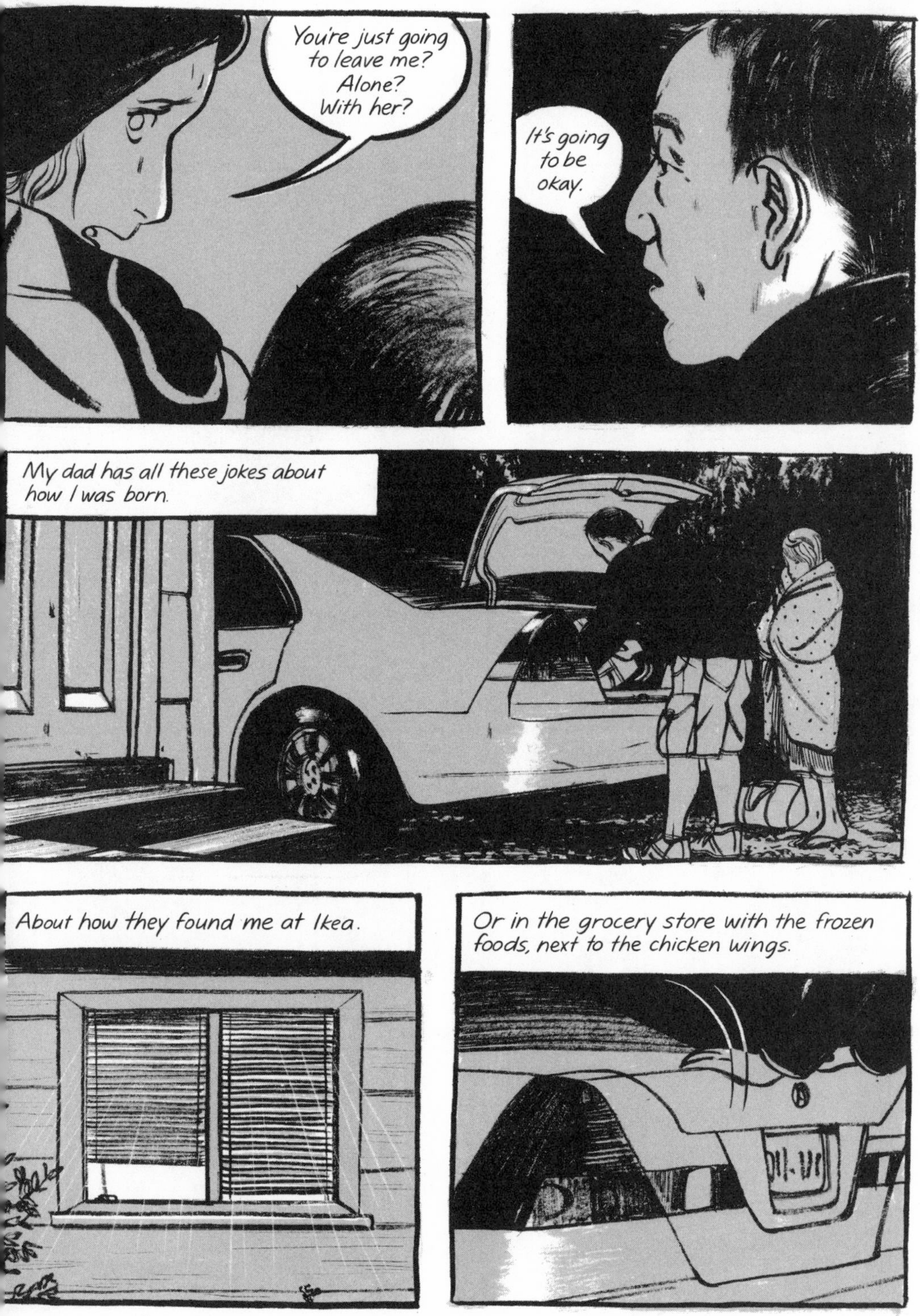

You're just going to leave me? Alone? With her?
It's going to be okay.
My dad has all these jokes about how I was born.
About how they found me at Ikea.
Or in the grocery store with the frozen foods, next to the chicken wings.

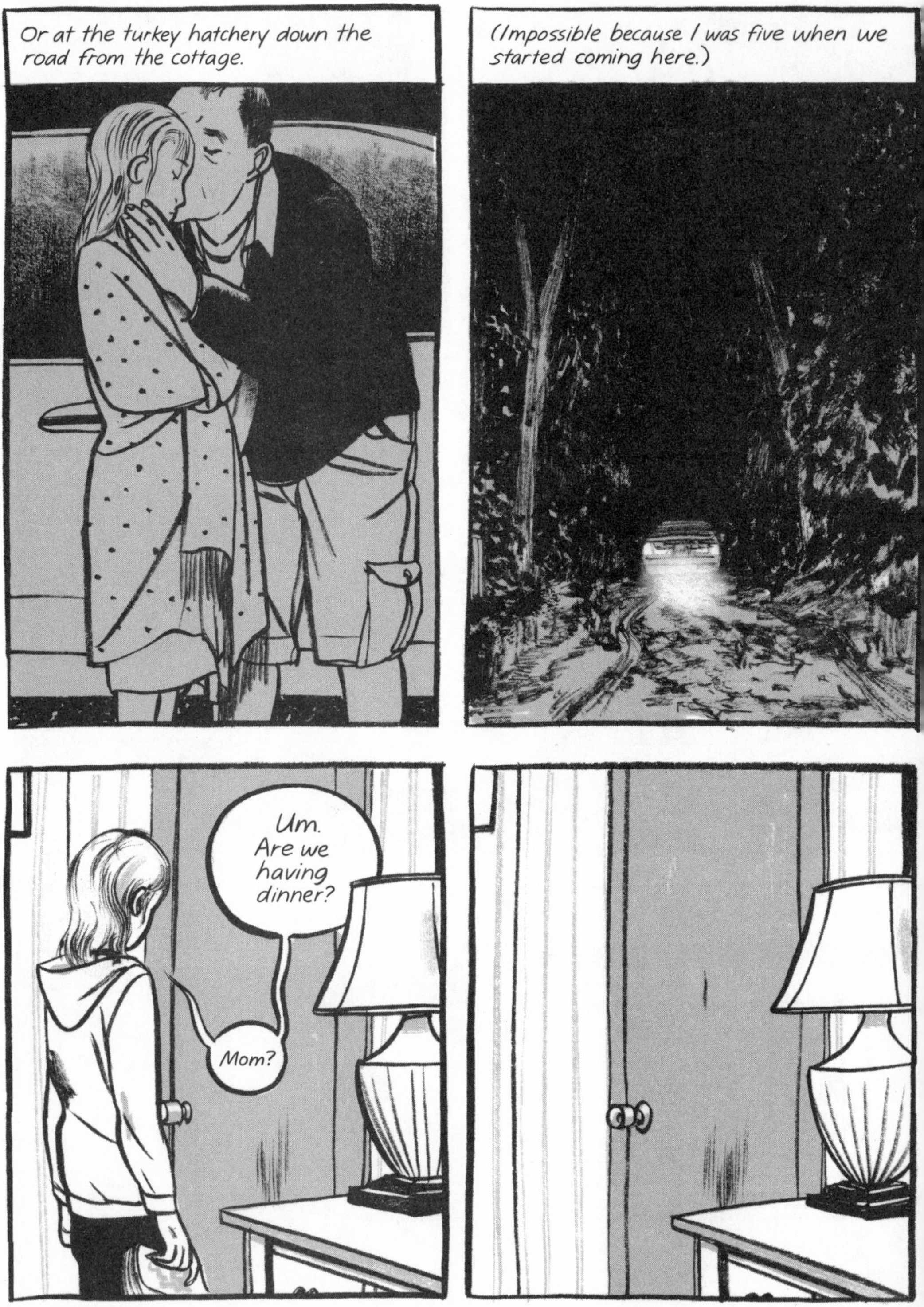
Or at the turkey hatchery down the road from the cottage.
(Impossible because I was five when we started coming here.)
Um. Are we having dinner?
Mom?

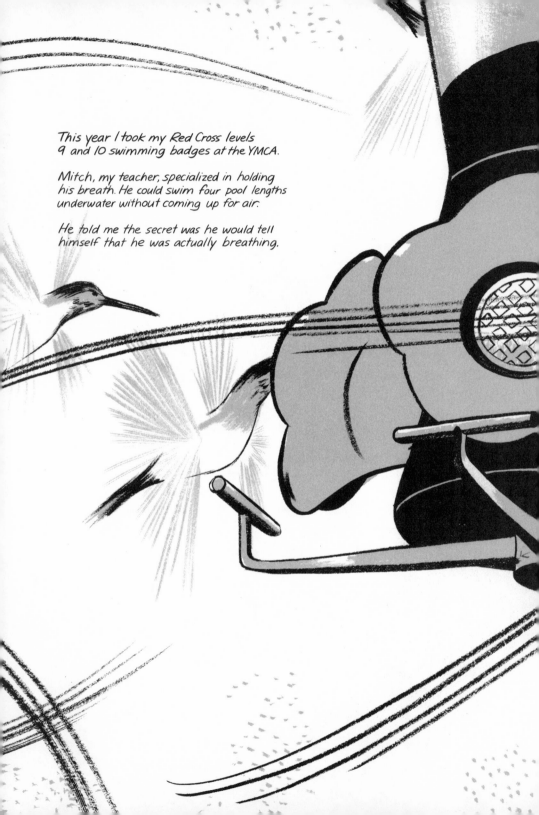

This year I took my Red Cross levels 9 and 10 swimming badges at the YMCA.

Mitch, my teacher, specialized in holding his breath. He could swim four pool lengths underwater without coming up for air.

He told me the secret was he would tell himself that he was actually breathing.

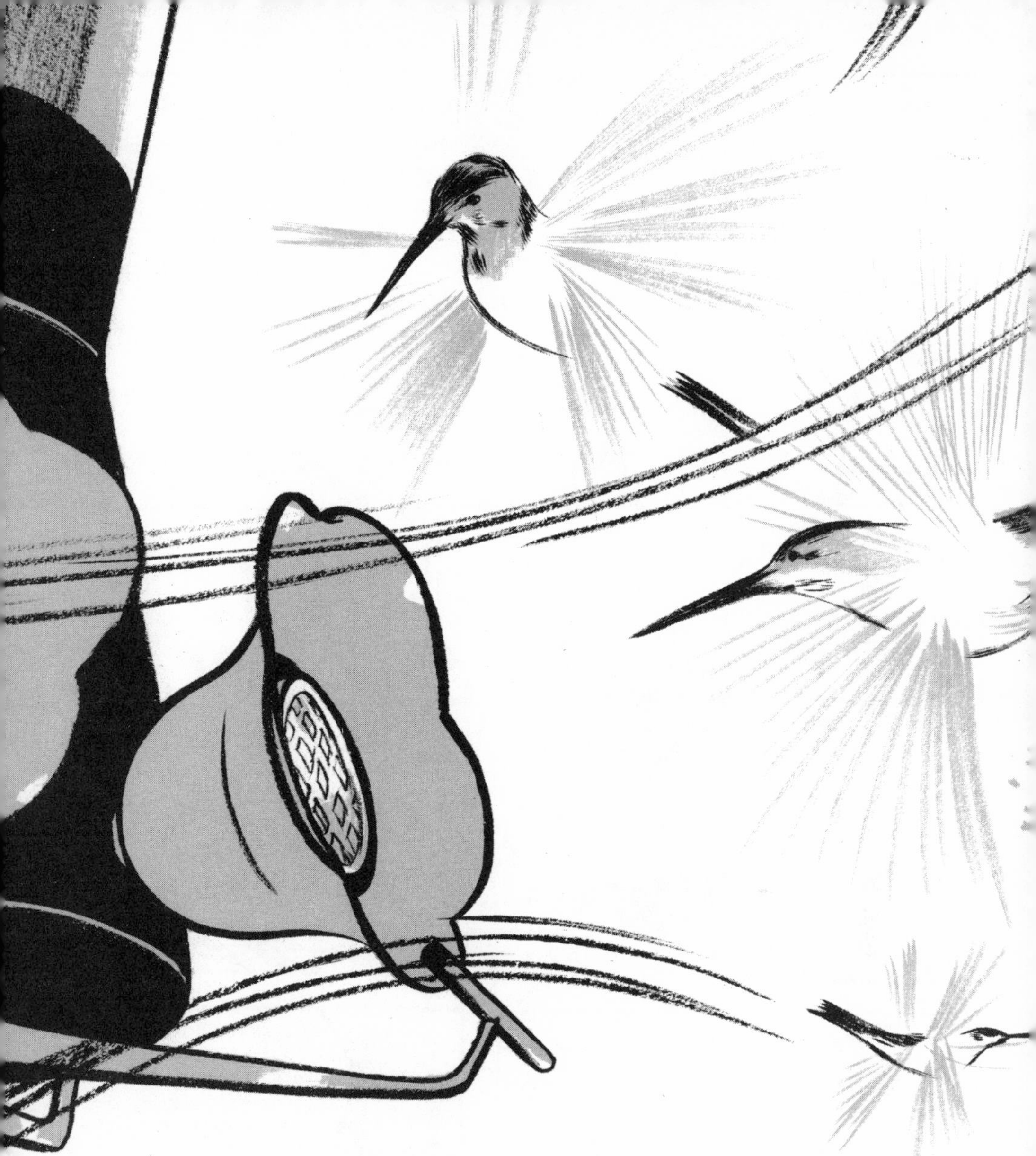

And he would just say to himself, over and over, "I'm breathing in, breathing out."

When my mom is mad at my dad, because my dad won't do something, or forgets to do something, she says, "You can say what you want, Evan, but I'm not holding my breath."

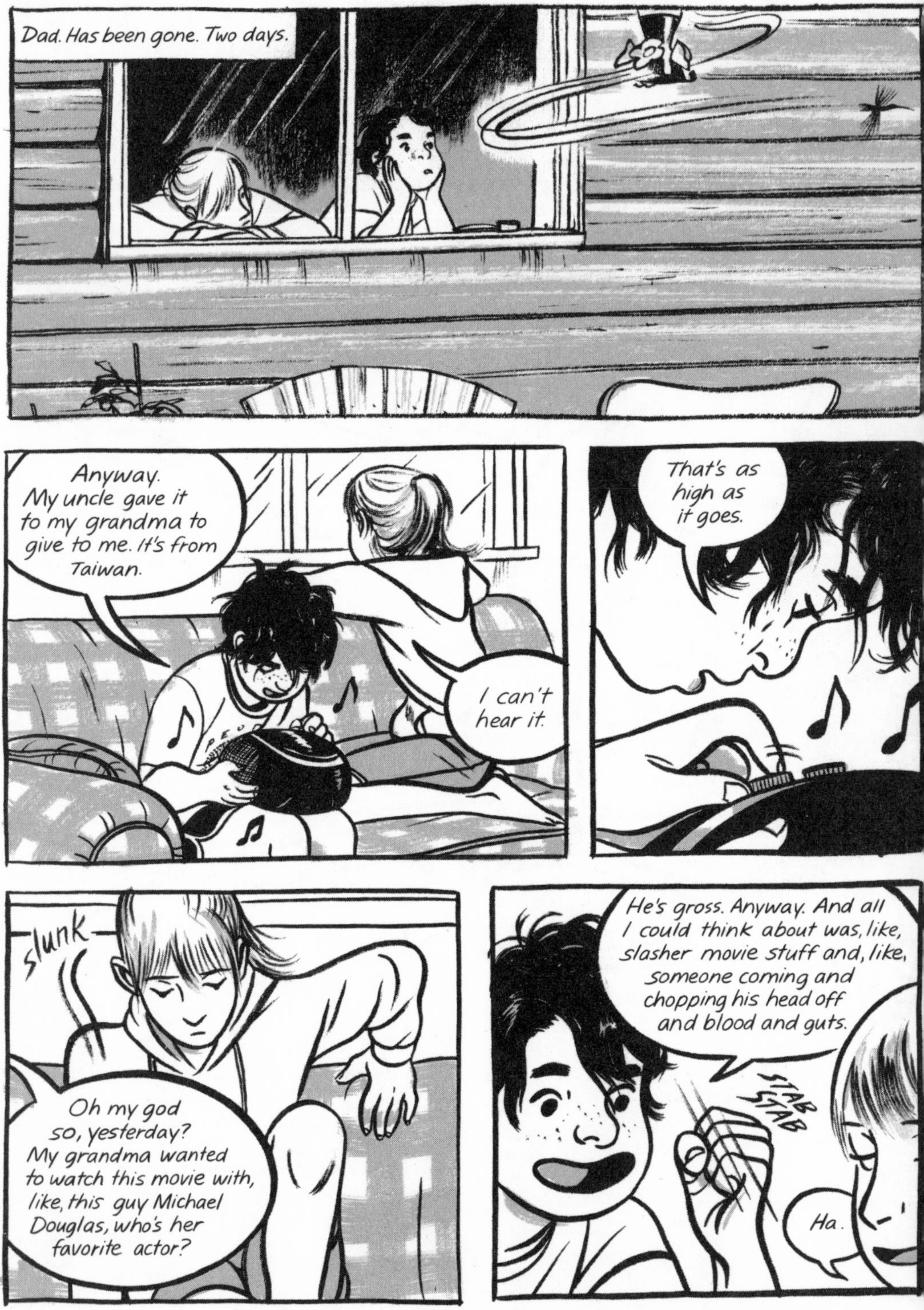
Dad. Has been gone. Two days.
Anyway. My uncle gave it to my grandma to give to me. It's from Taiwan.
I can't hear it.
That's as high as it goes.
slunk
Oh my god so, yesterday? My grandma wanted to watch this movie with, like, this guy Michael Douglas, who's her favorite actor?
He's gross. Anyway. And all I could think about was, like, slasher movie stuff and, like, someone coming and chopping his head off and blood and guts.
STAB STAB
Ha.

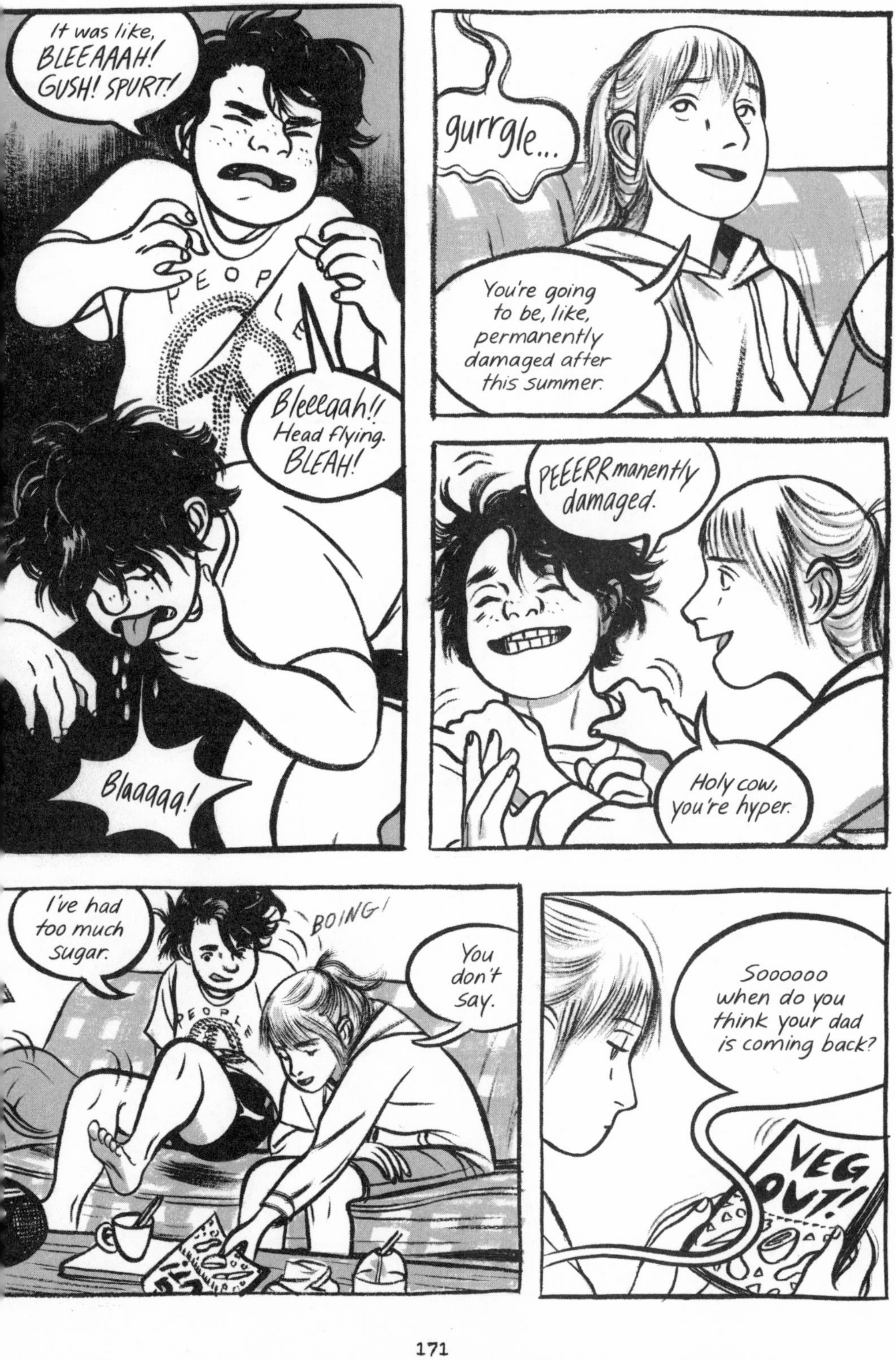
It was like, BLEEAAAH! GUSH! SPURT!
PEOPLE
gurrgle...
You're going to be, like, permanently damaged after this summer.
Bleeeaah!! Head flying. BLEAH!
Blaaaaa!
PEEERRmanently damaged.
Holy cow, you're hyper.
I've had too much sugar.
BOING!
PEOPLE
You don't say.
Soooooo when do you think your dad is coming back?
VEG OUT!

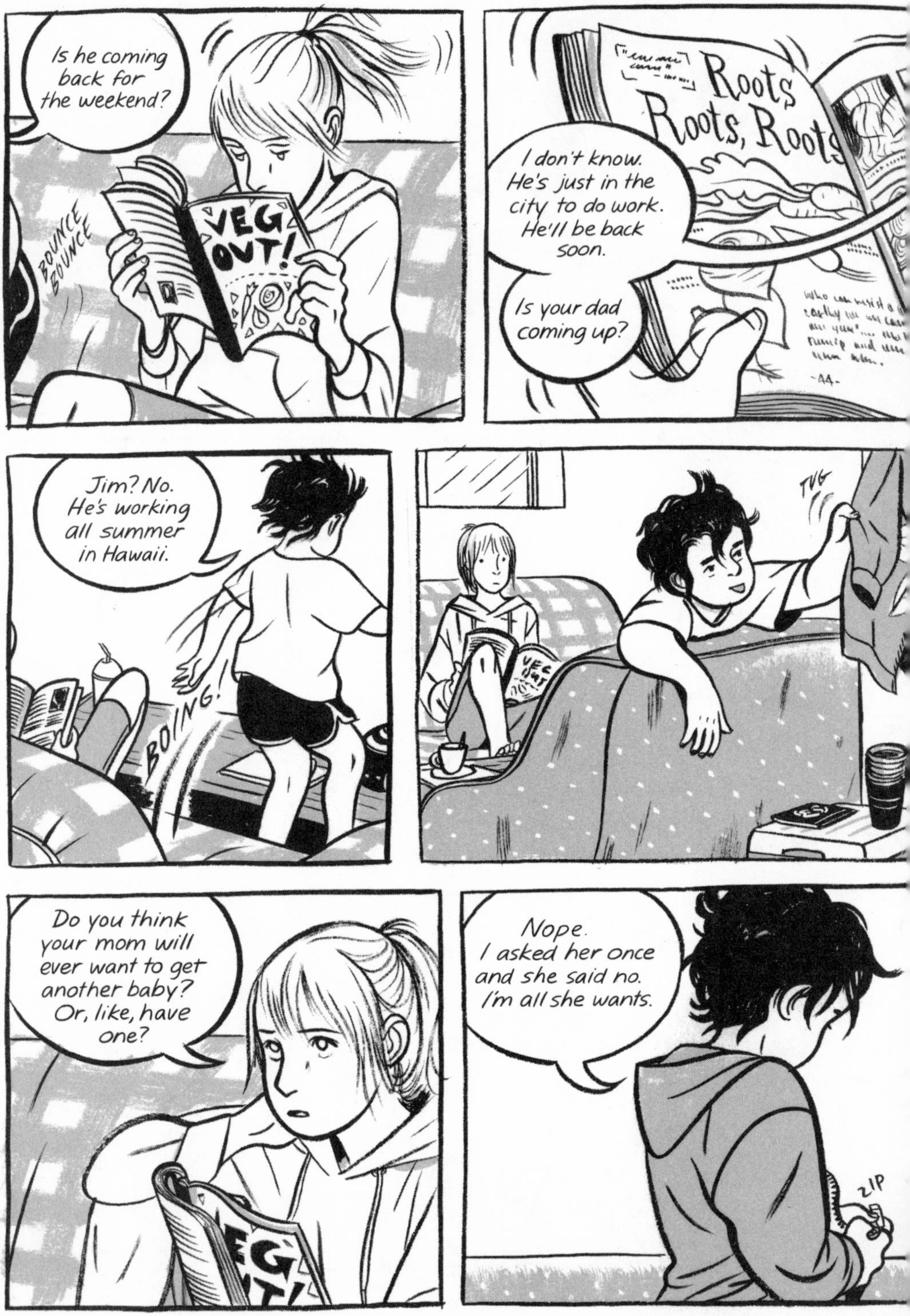

Is he coming back for the weekend?
BOUNCE BOUNCE
VEG OUT!
Roots Roots, Roots
I don't know. He's just in the city to do work. He'll be back soon.
Is your dad coming up?
-44-
Jim? No. He's working all summer in Hawaii.
BOING!
TUG
Do you think your mom will ever want to get another baby? Or, like, have one?
Nope. I asked her once and she said no. I'm all she wants.
ZIP

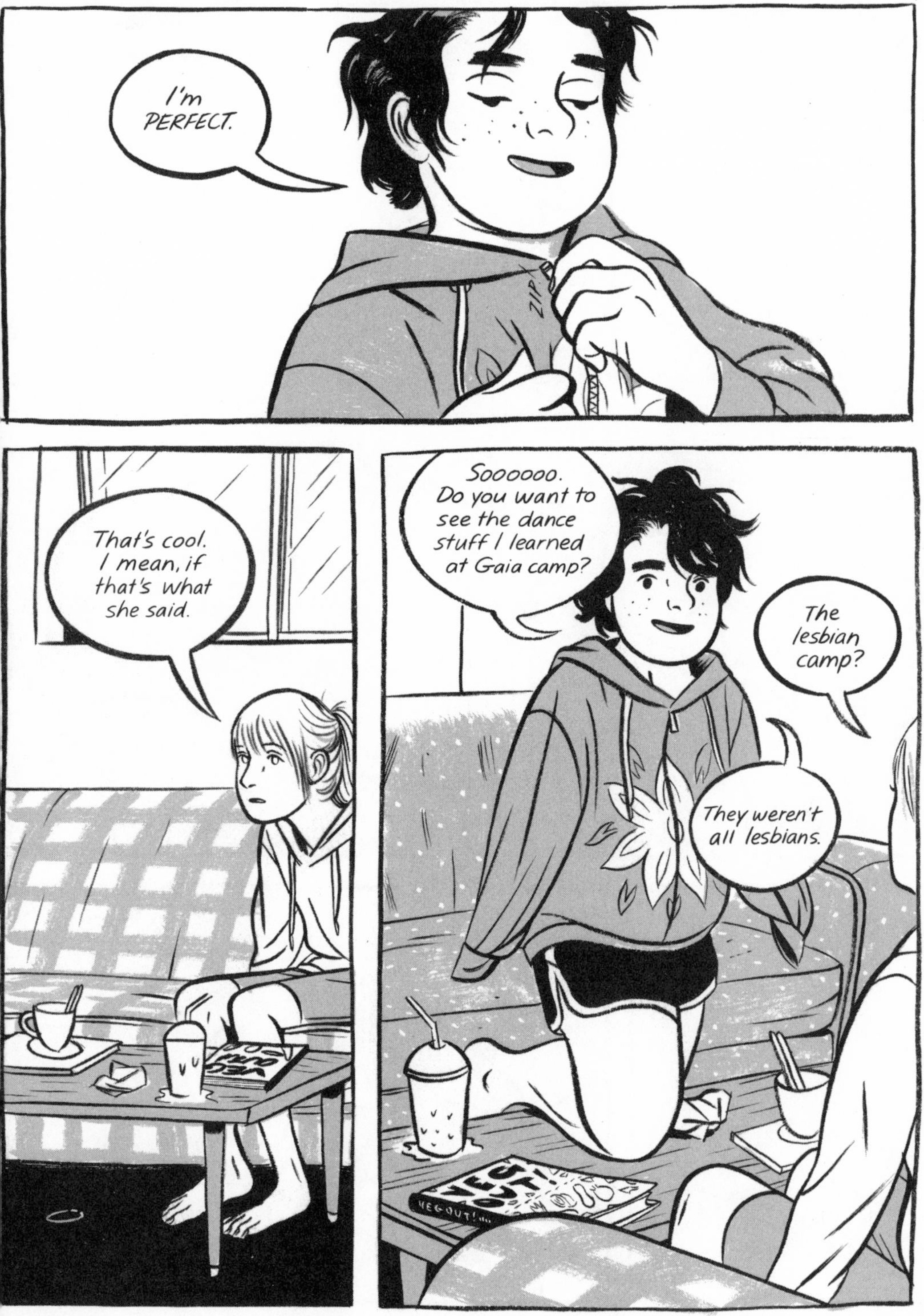
I'm PERFECT.
ZIP
That's cool. I mean, if that's what she said.
Soooooo. Do you want to see the dance stuff I learned at Gaia camp?
The lesbian camp?
They weren't all lesbians.

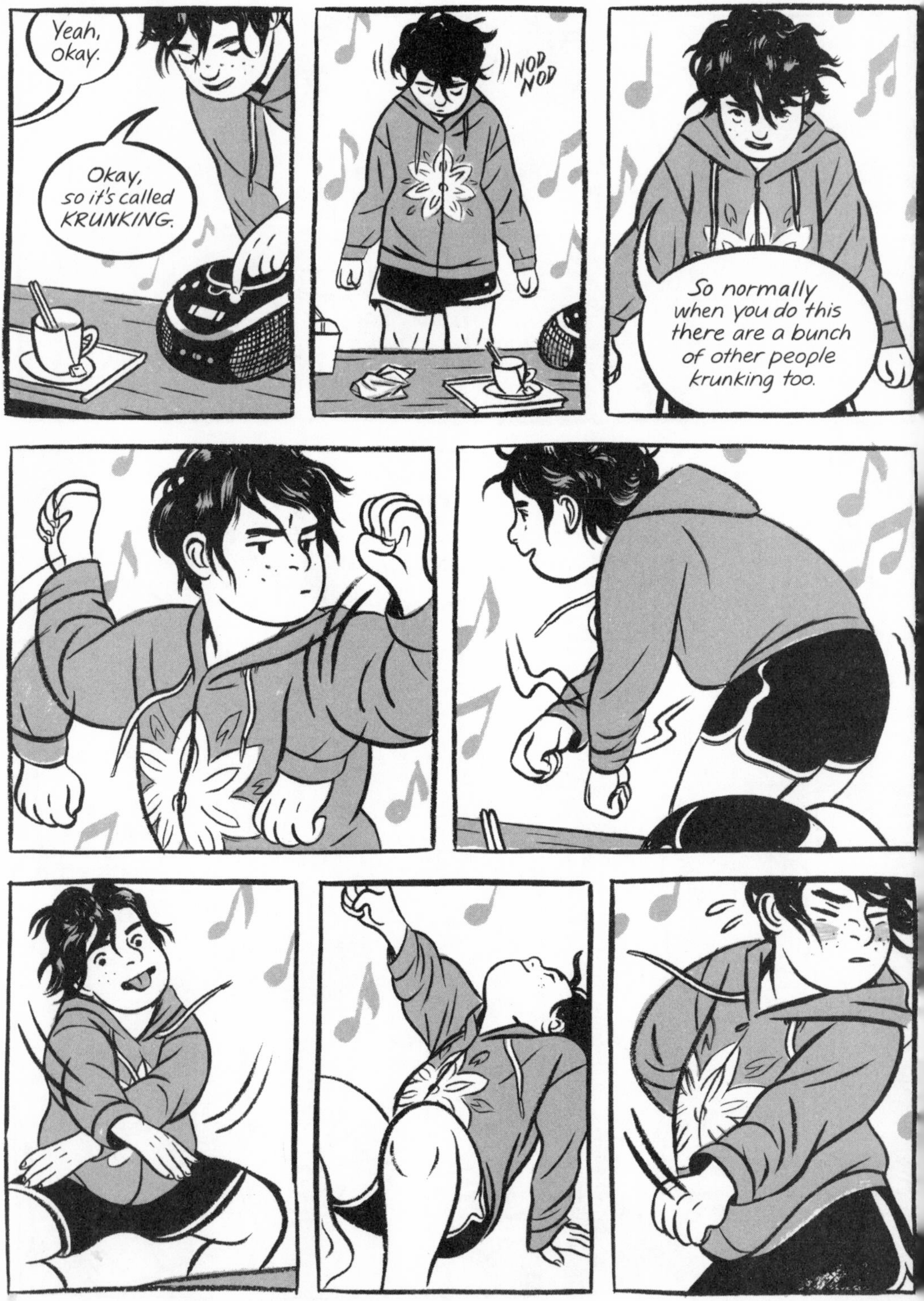
Yeah, okay.
Okay, so it's called KRUNKING.
NOD NOD
So normally when you do this there are a bunch of other people krunking too.

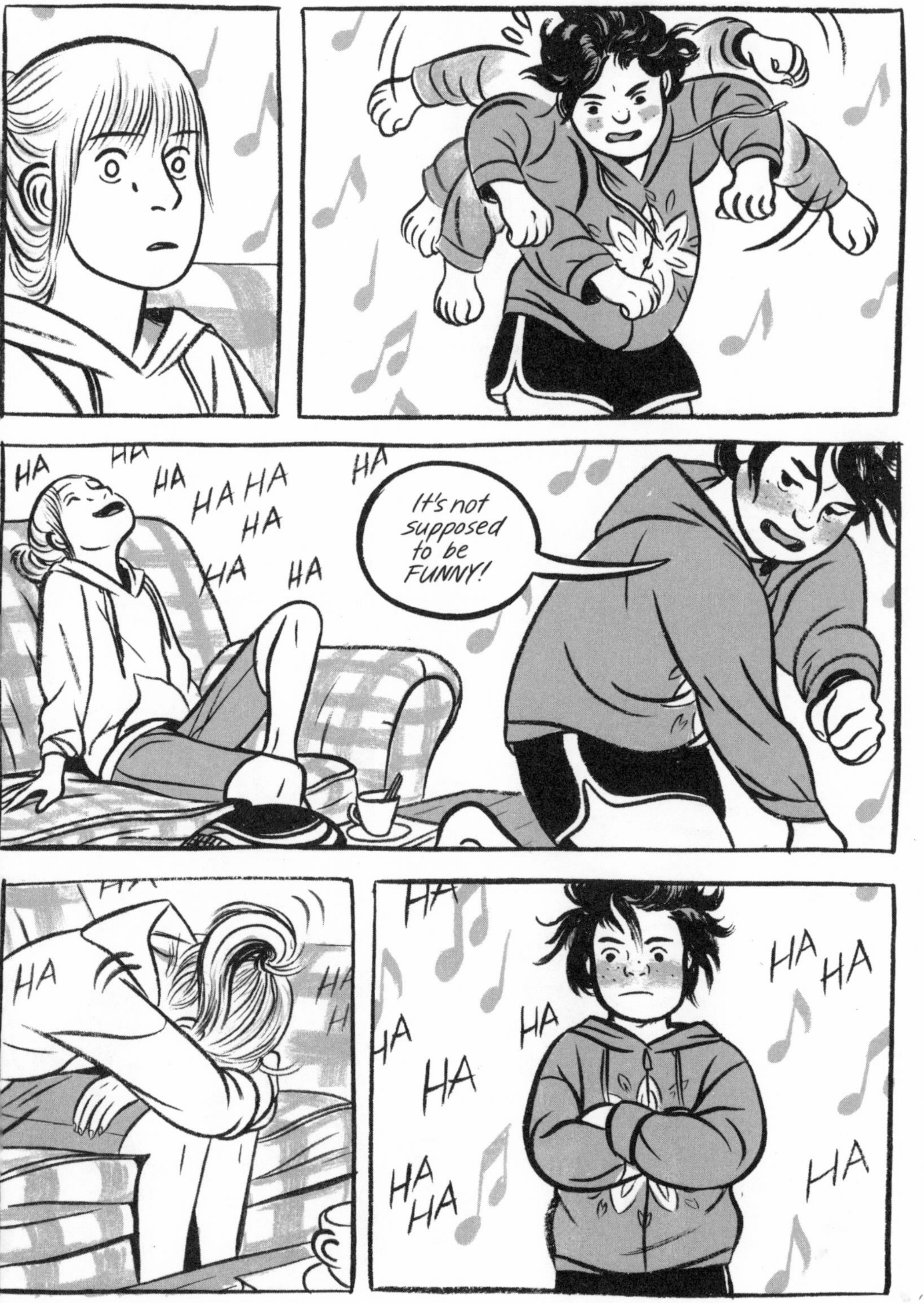
HA
HA
HA
HA HA
HA
HA
HA
HA
It's not supposed to be FUNNY!
HA
HA
HA HA
HA
HA
HA
HA HA
HA

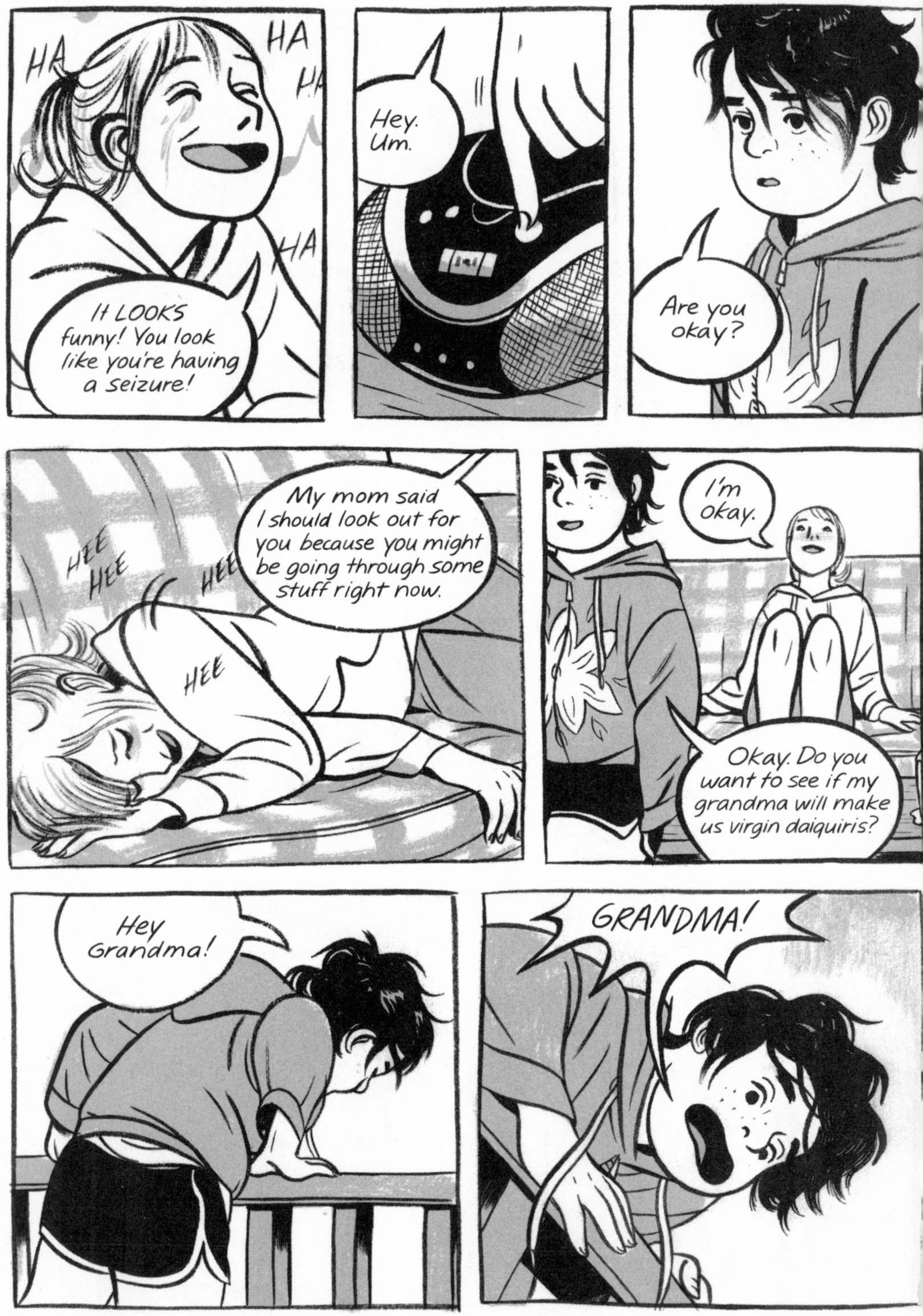
HA
HA
HA
HA
It LOOKS funny! You look like you're having a seizure!
Hey. Um.
Are you okay?
HEE
HEE
HEE
HEE
My mom said I should look out for you because you might be going through some stuff right now.
I'm okay.
Okay. Do you want to see if my grandma will make us virgin daiquiris?
Hey Grandma!
GRANDMA!

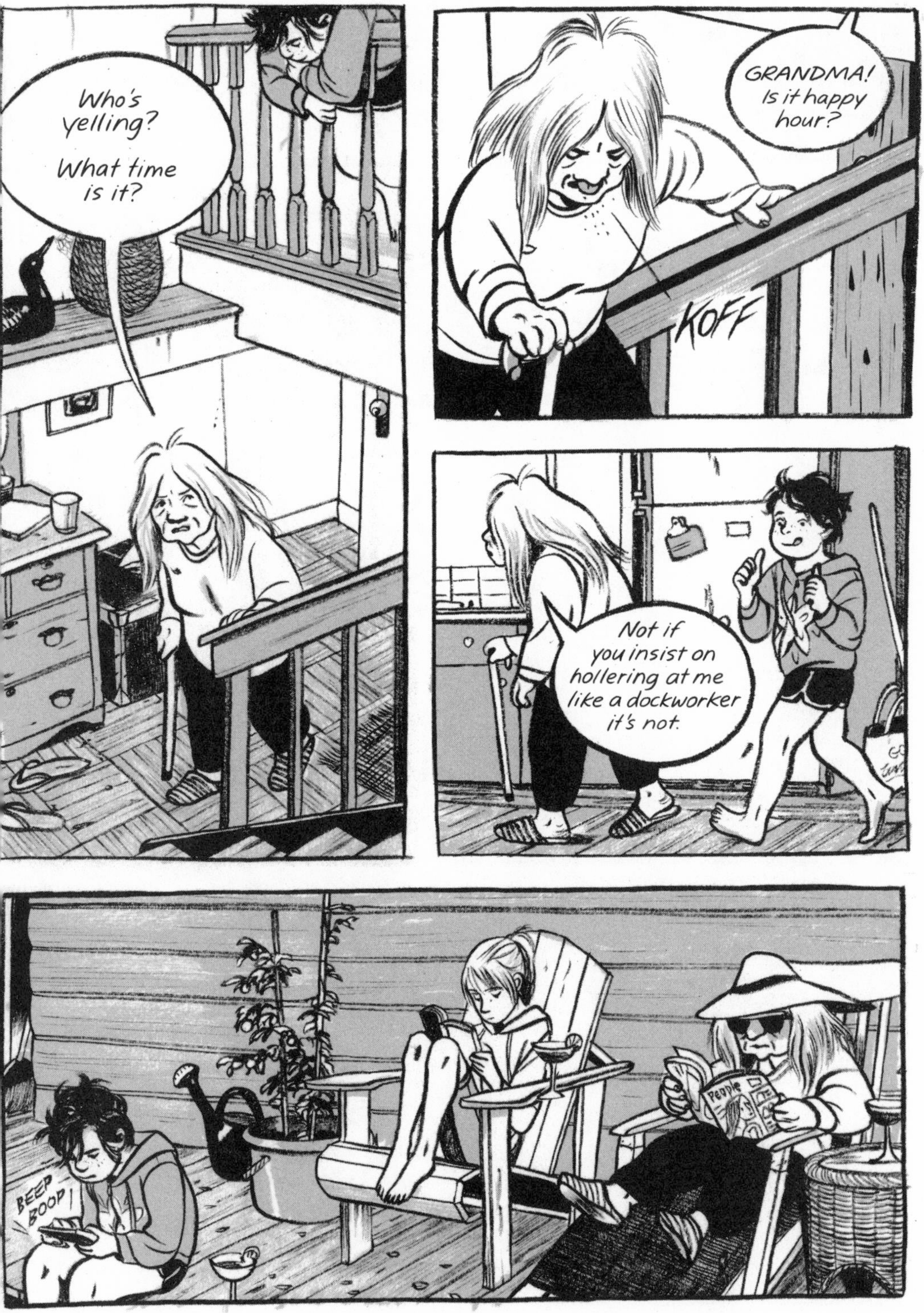

Who's yelling?
What time is it?
GRANDMA! Is it happy hour?
KOFF
Not if you insist on hollering at me like a dockworker it's not.
BEEP BOOP
People

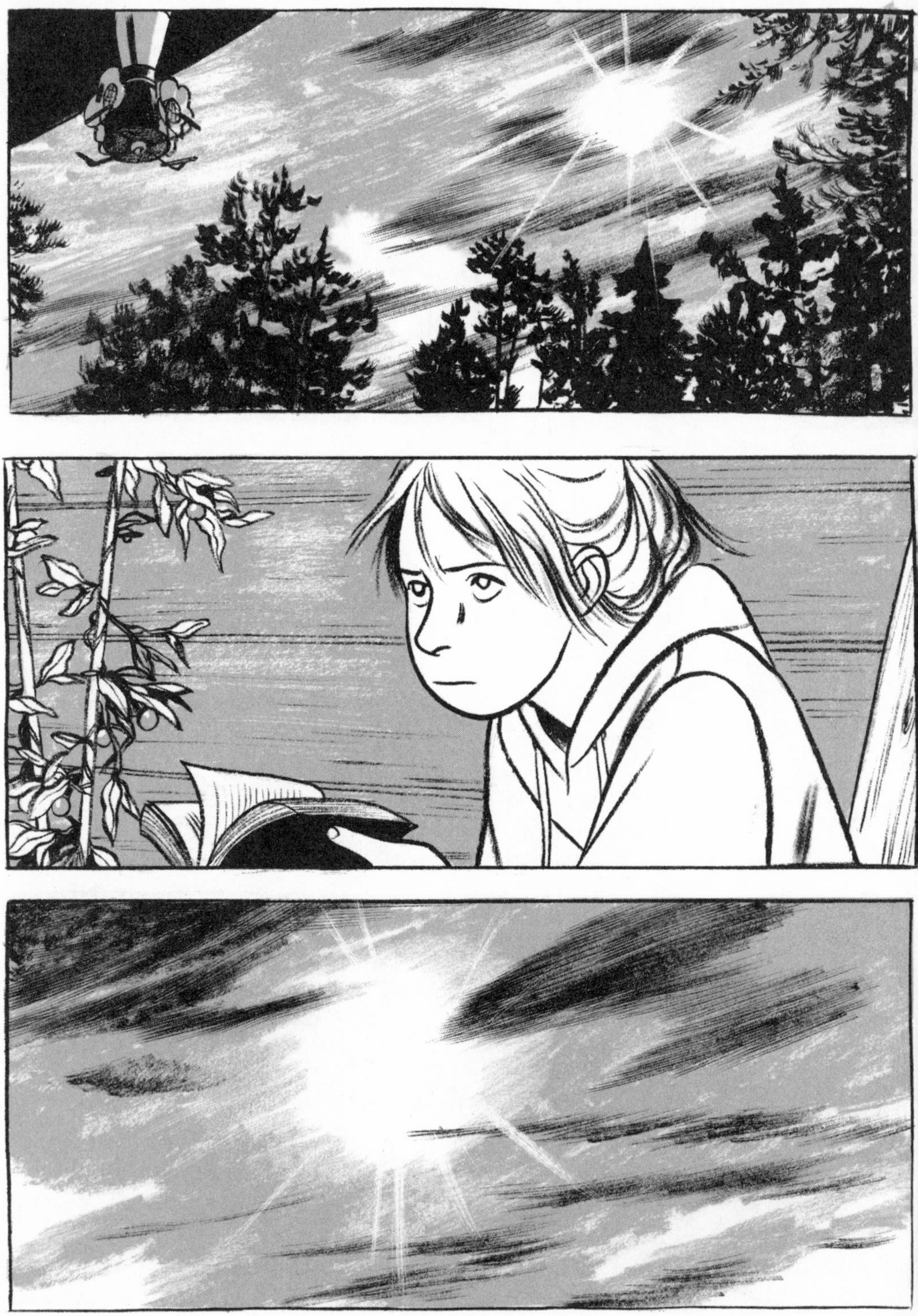

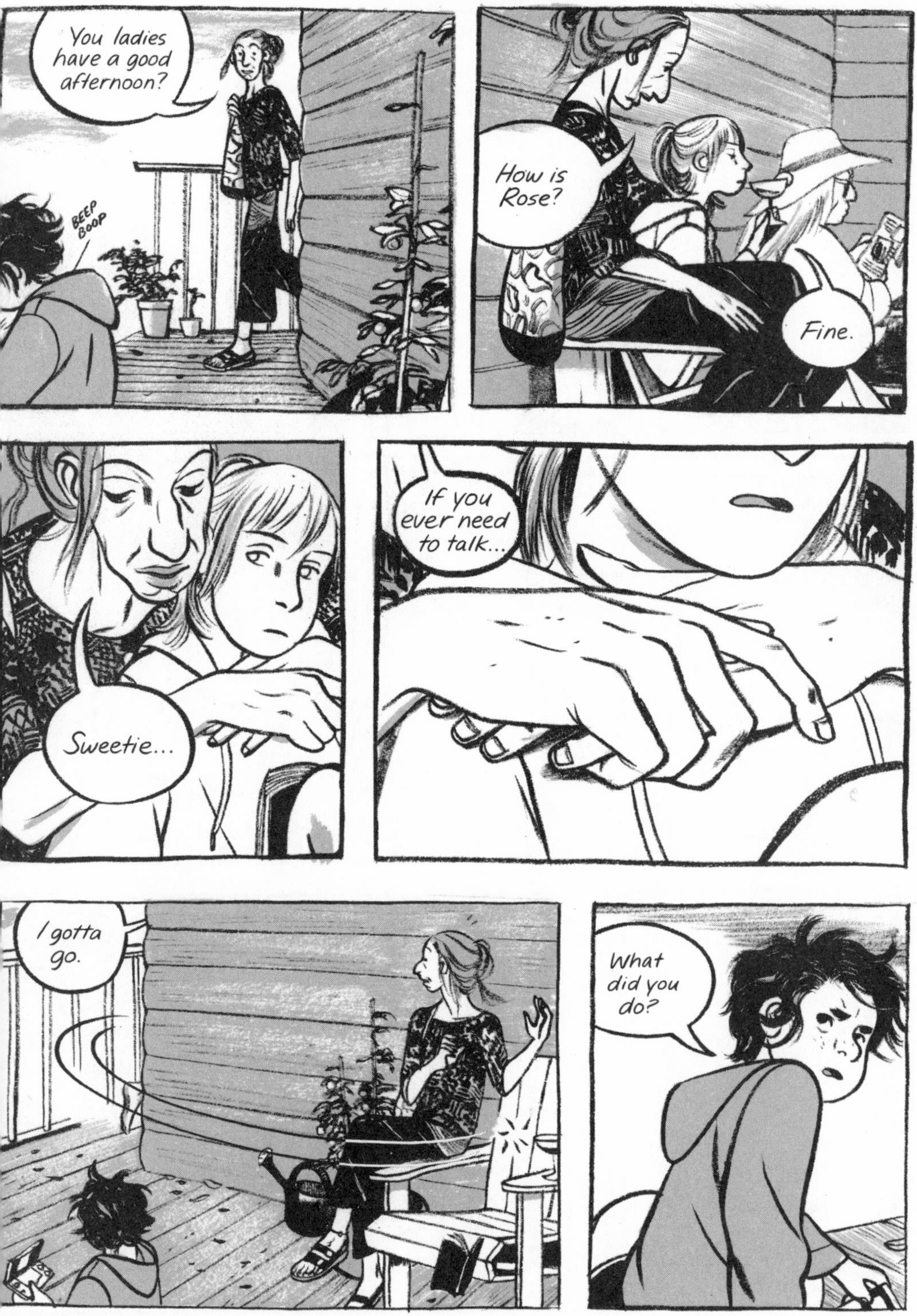
You ladies have a good afternoon?
BEEP BOOP
How is Rose?
Fine.
Sweetie...
If you ever need to talk...
I gotta go.
What did you do?

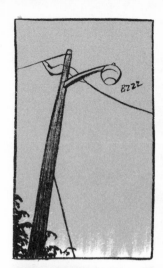

BZZZ

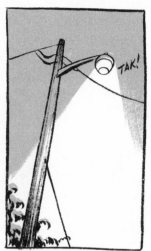

TAK!

SLAM!

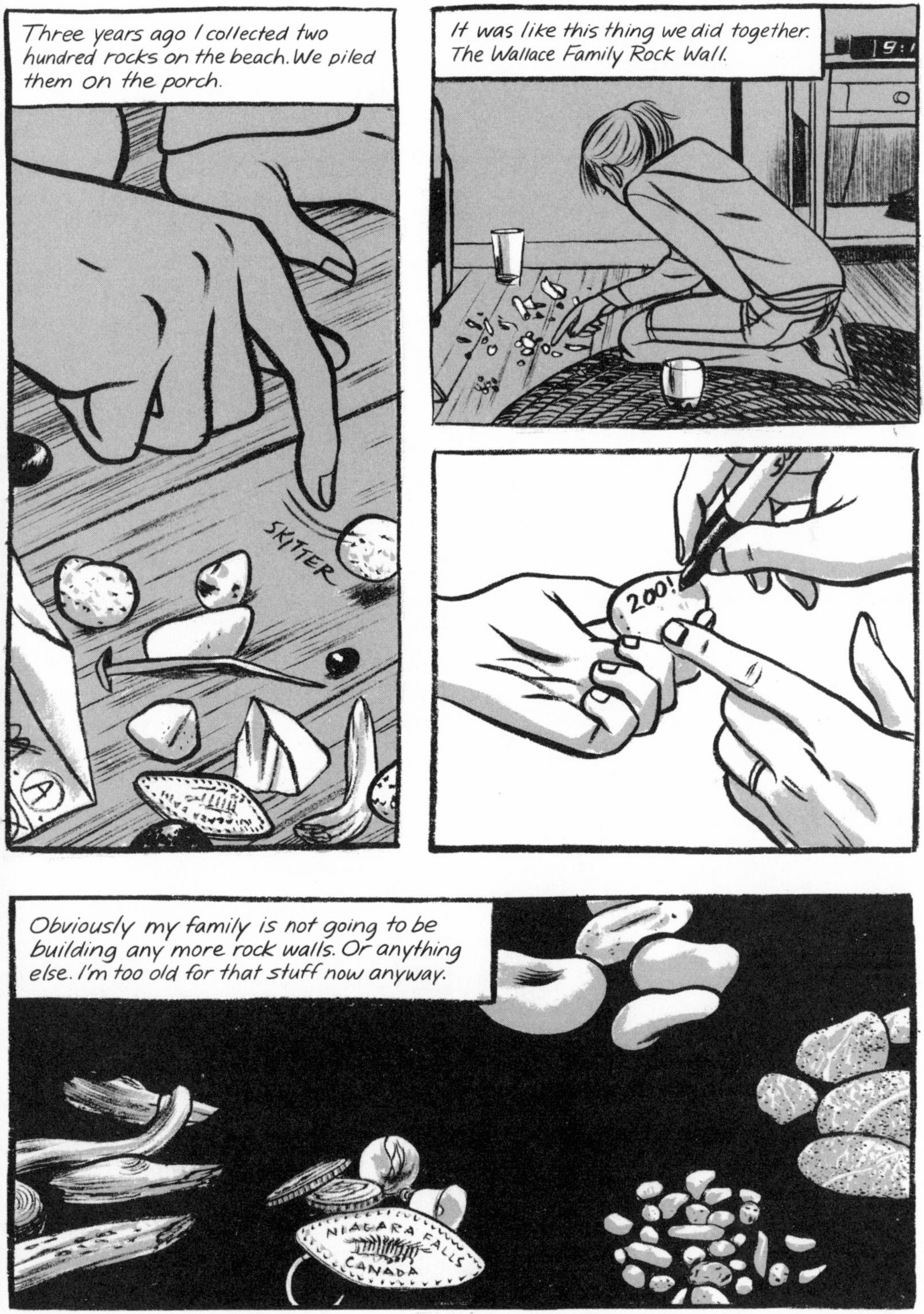
Three years ago I collected two hundred rocks on the beach. We piled them on the porch.
SKITTER
It was like this thing we did together. The Wallace Family Rock Wall.
200!
Obviously my family is not going to be building any more rock walls. Or anything else. I'm too old for that stuff now anyway.
NIAGARA FALLS CANADA

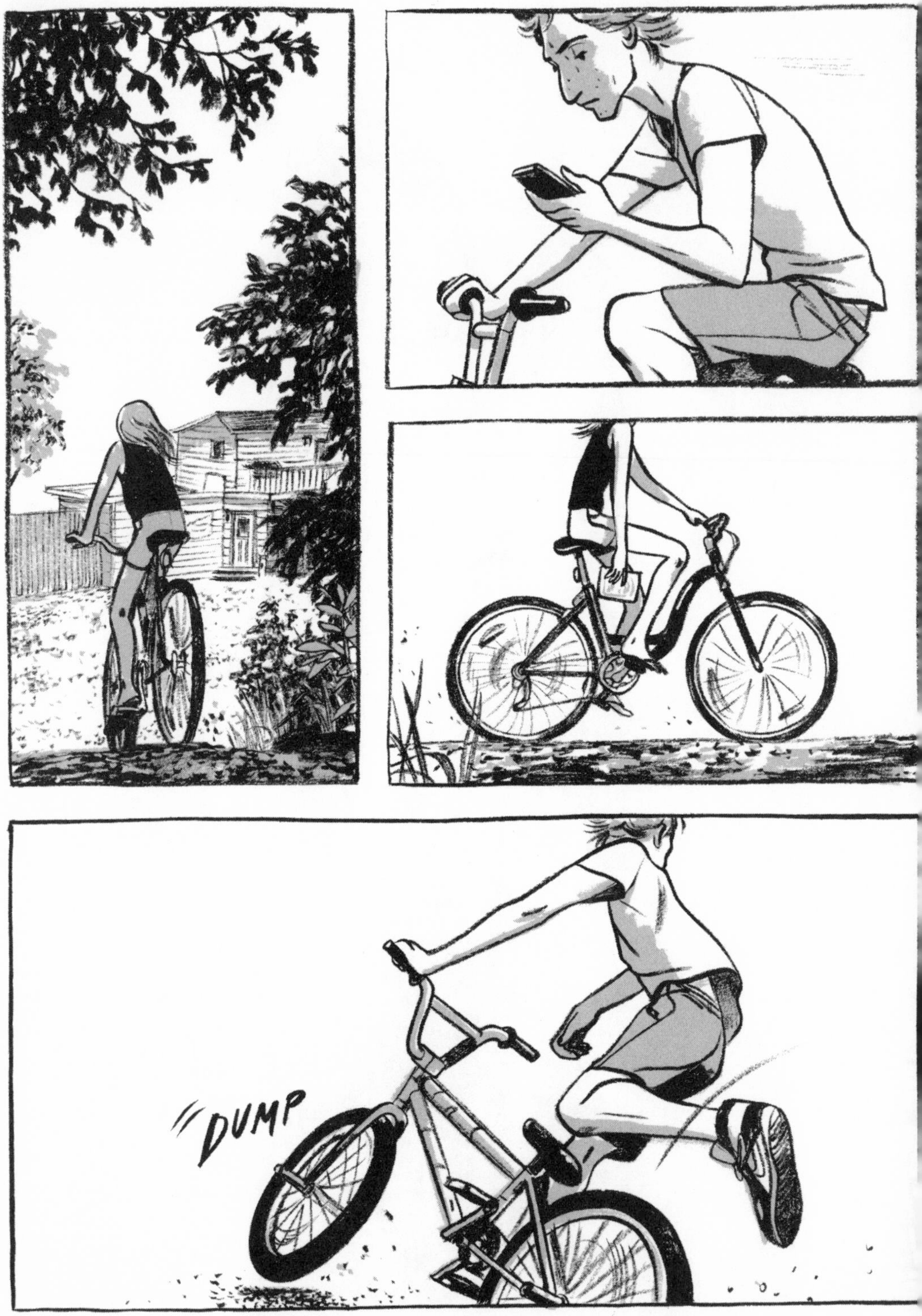
DUMP

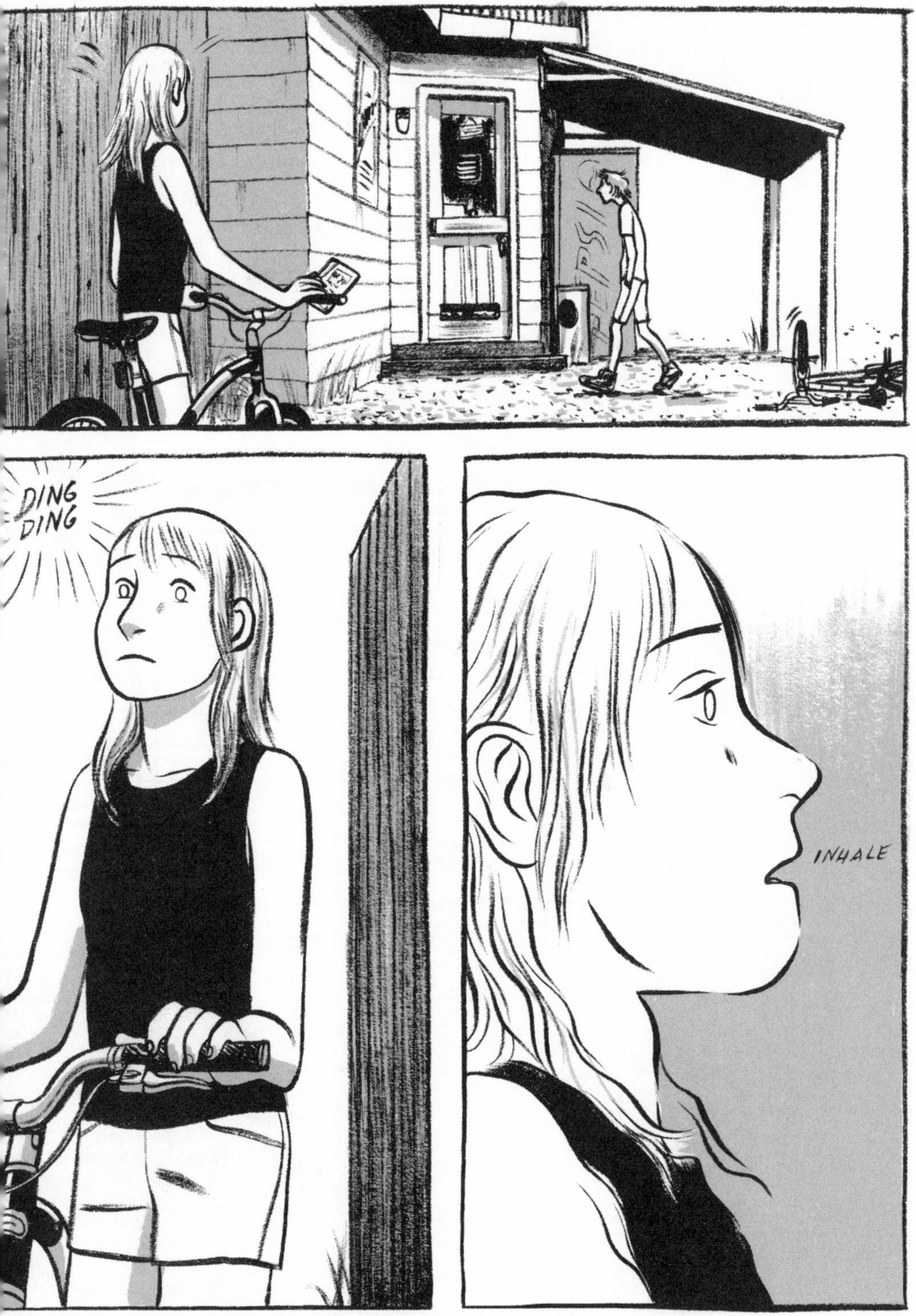
DING
DING
INHALE

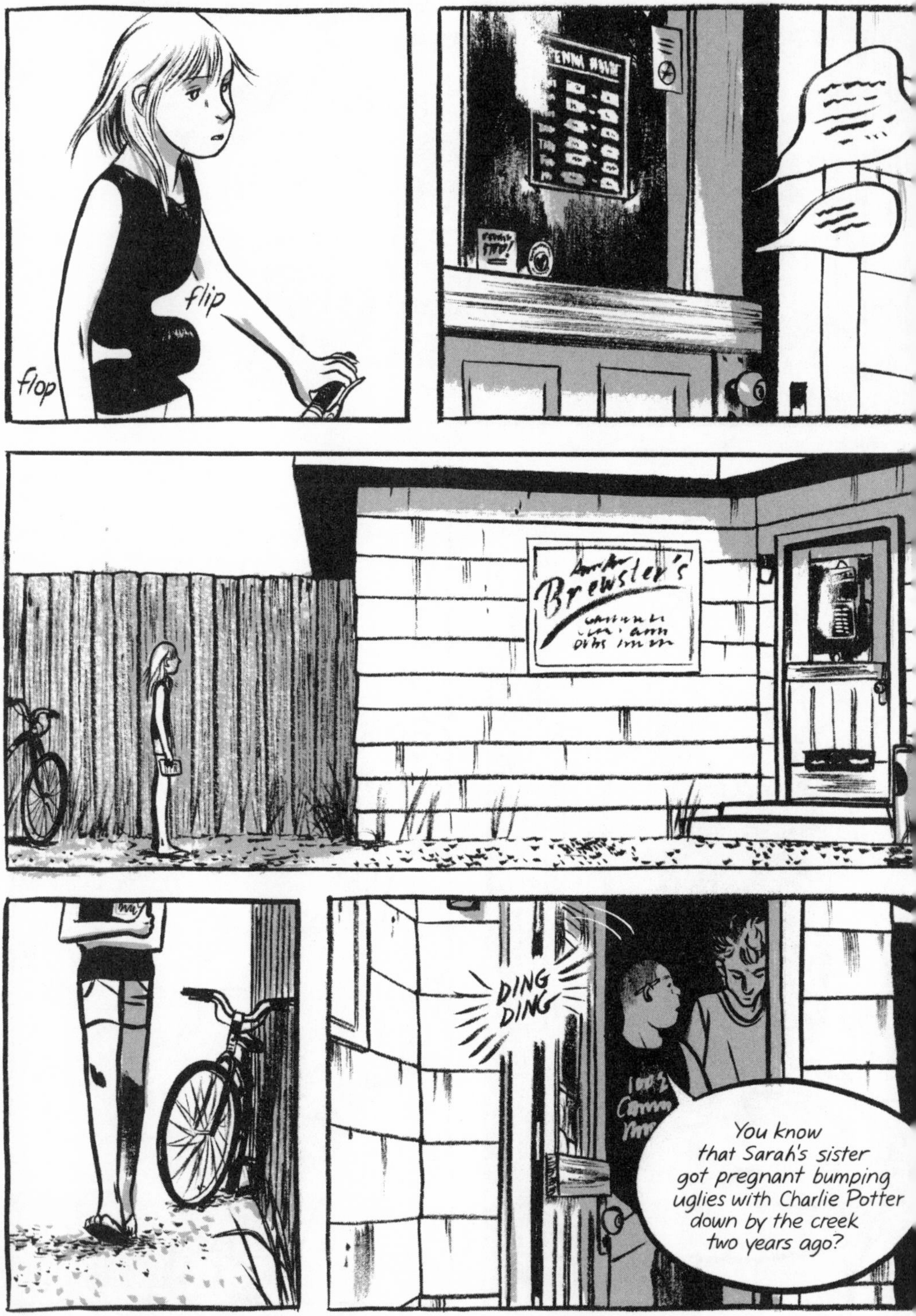
flip
flop
Brewster's
DING DING
You know that Sarah's sister got pregnant bumping uglies with Charlie Potter down by the creek two years ago?

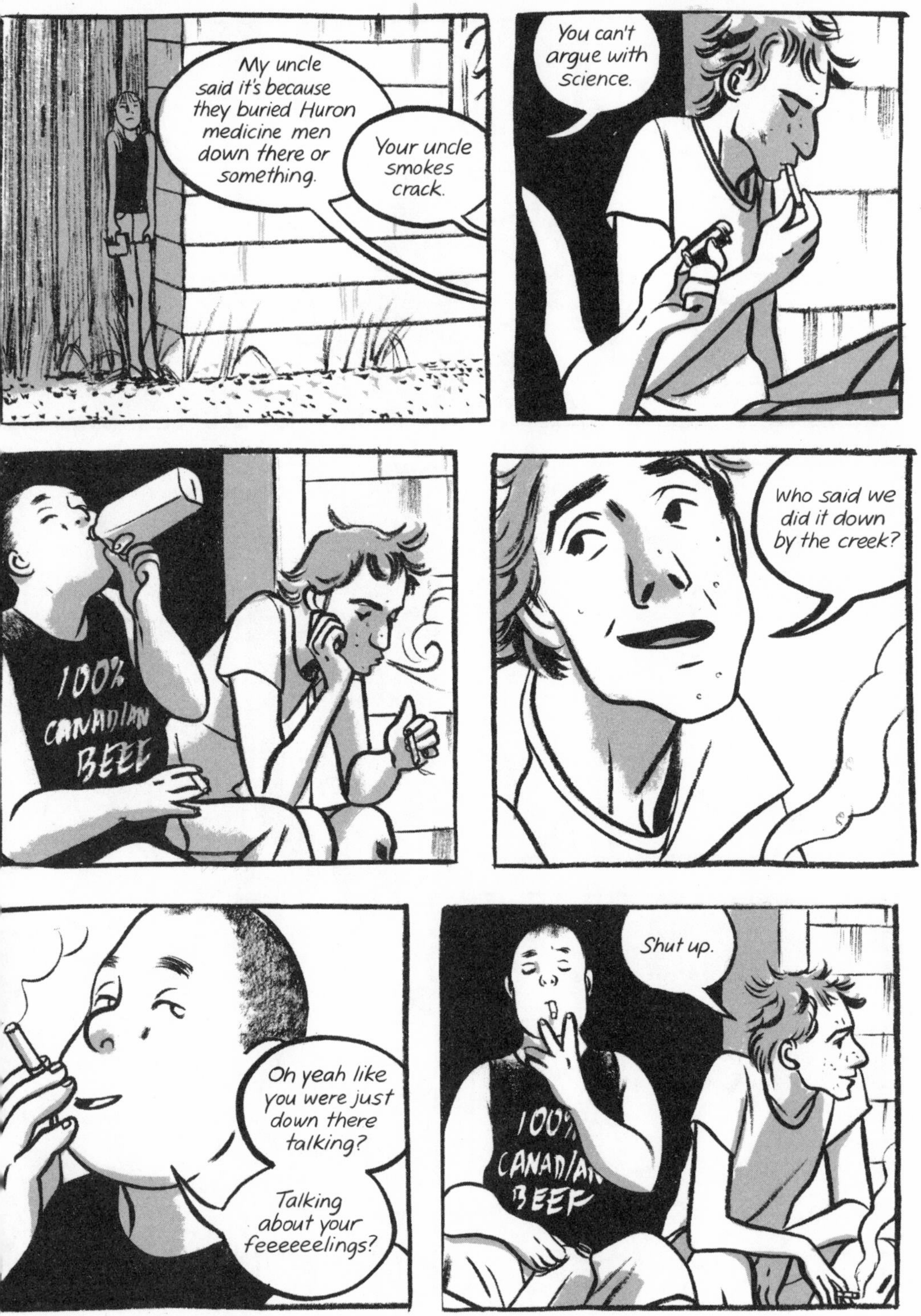
My uncle said it's because they buried Huron medicine men down there or something.
Your uncle smokes crack.
You can't argue with science.
100% CANADIAN BEEF
Who said we did it down by the creek?
Oh yeah like you were just down there talking?
Talking about your feeeeeelings?
Shut up.
100% CANADIAN BEEF

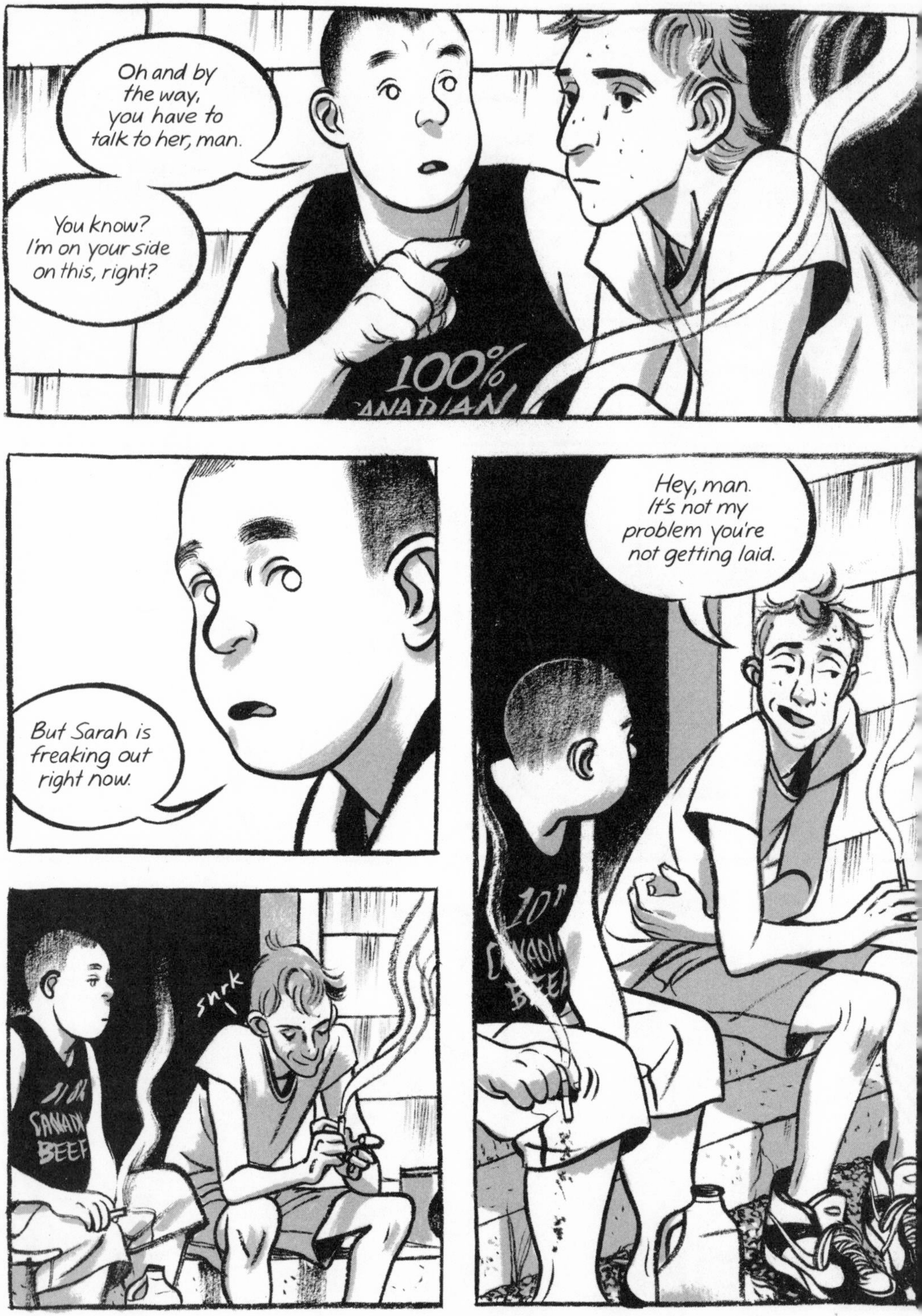
Oh and by the way, you have to talk to her, man.
You know? I'm on your side on this, right?
100% CANADIAN
But Sarah is freaking out right now.
Hey, man. It's not my problem you're not getting laid.
snrk
CANADIAN BEEF

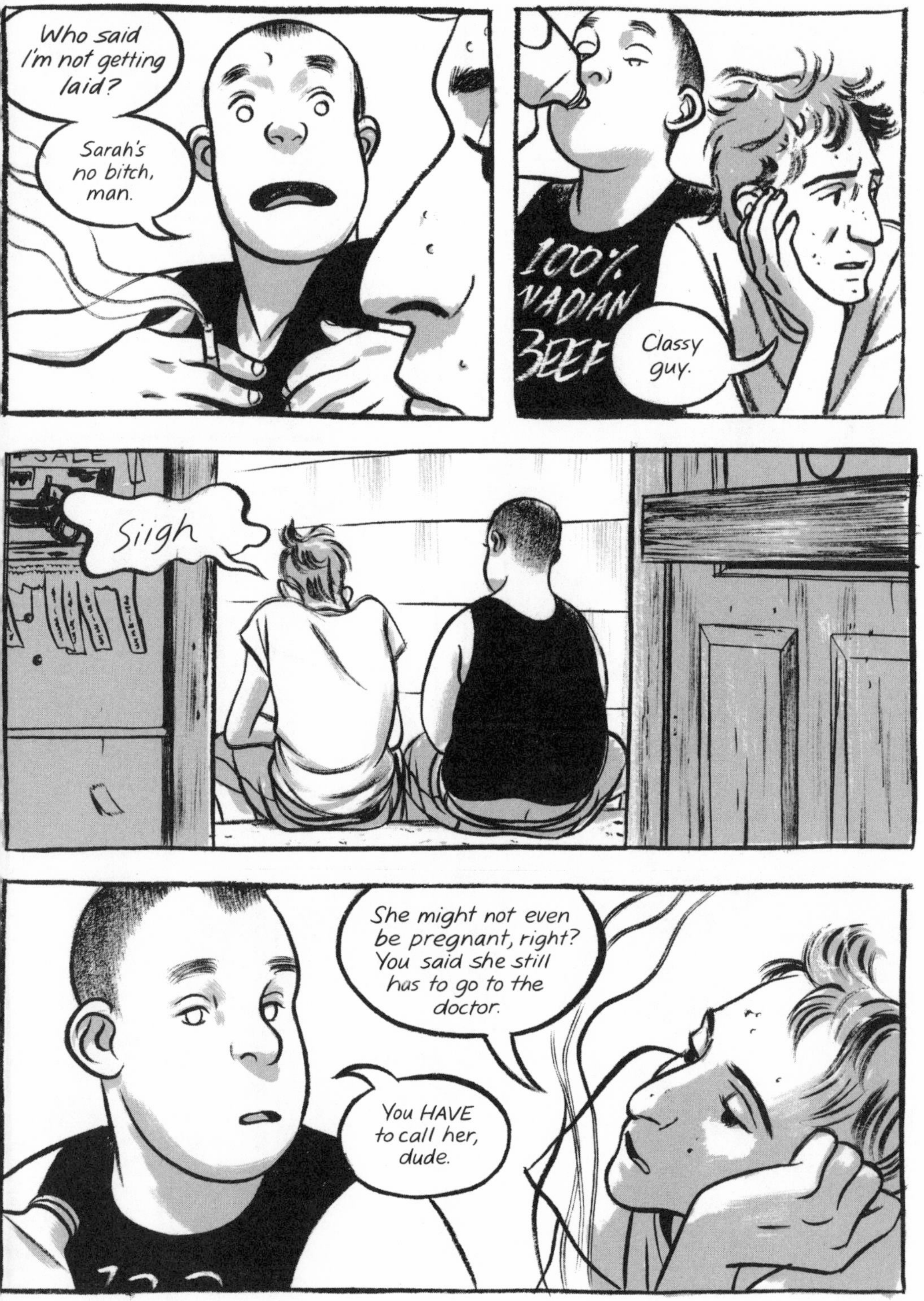

Who said I'm not getting laid?
Sarah's no bitch, man.
100% NADIAN BEEF
Classy guy.
Siigh
She might not even be pregnant, right? You said she still has to go to the doctor.
You HAVE to call her, dude.

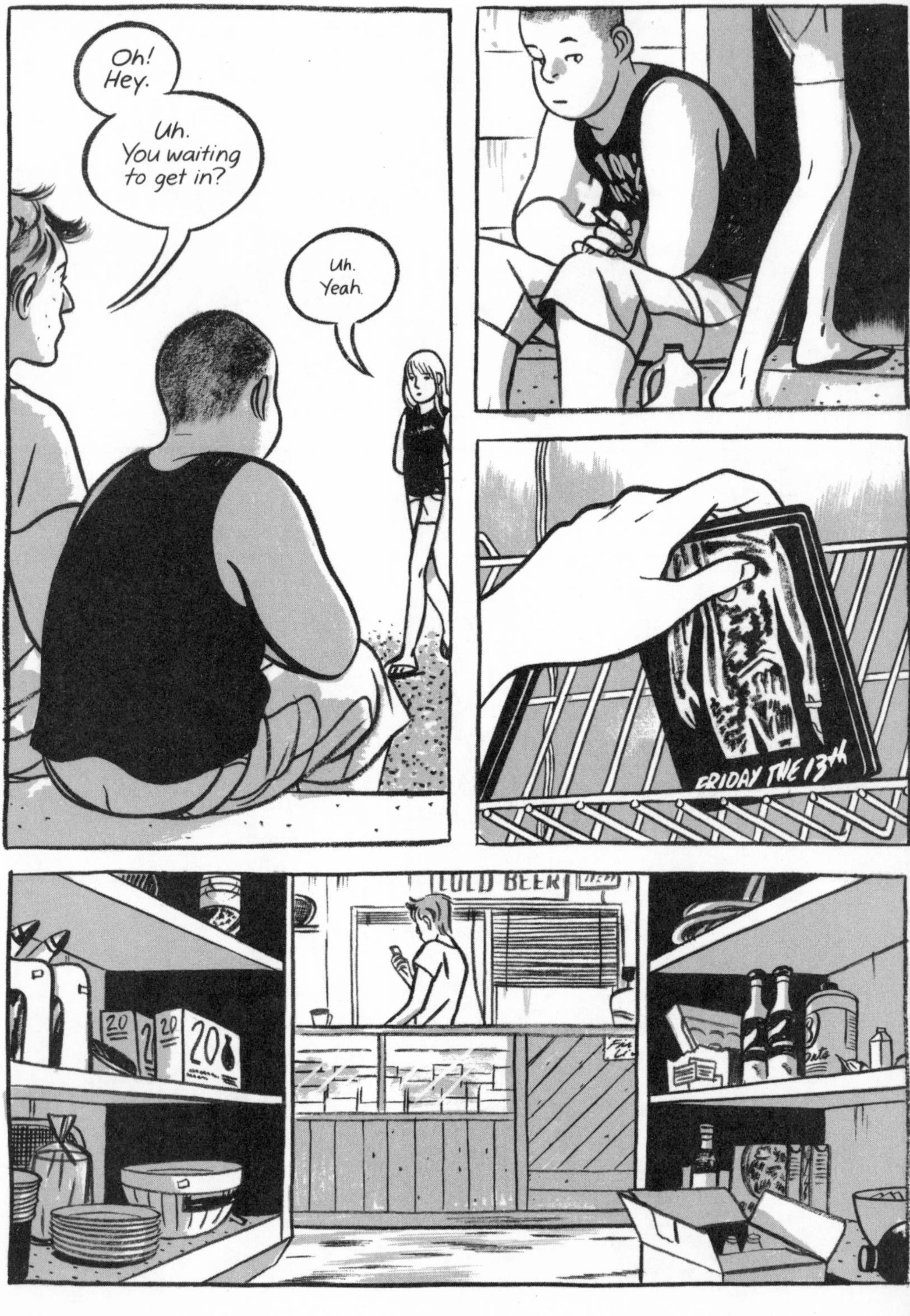
Oh! Hey.
Uh. You waiting to get in?
Uh. Yeah.
FRIDAY THE 13th
COLD BEER

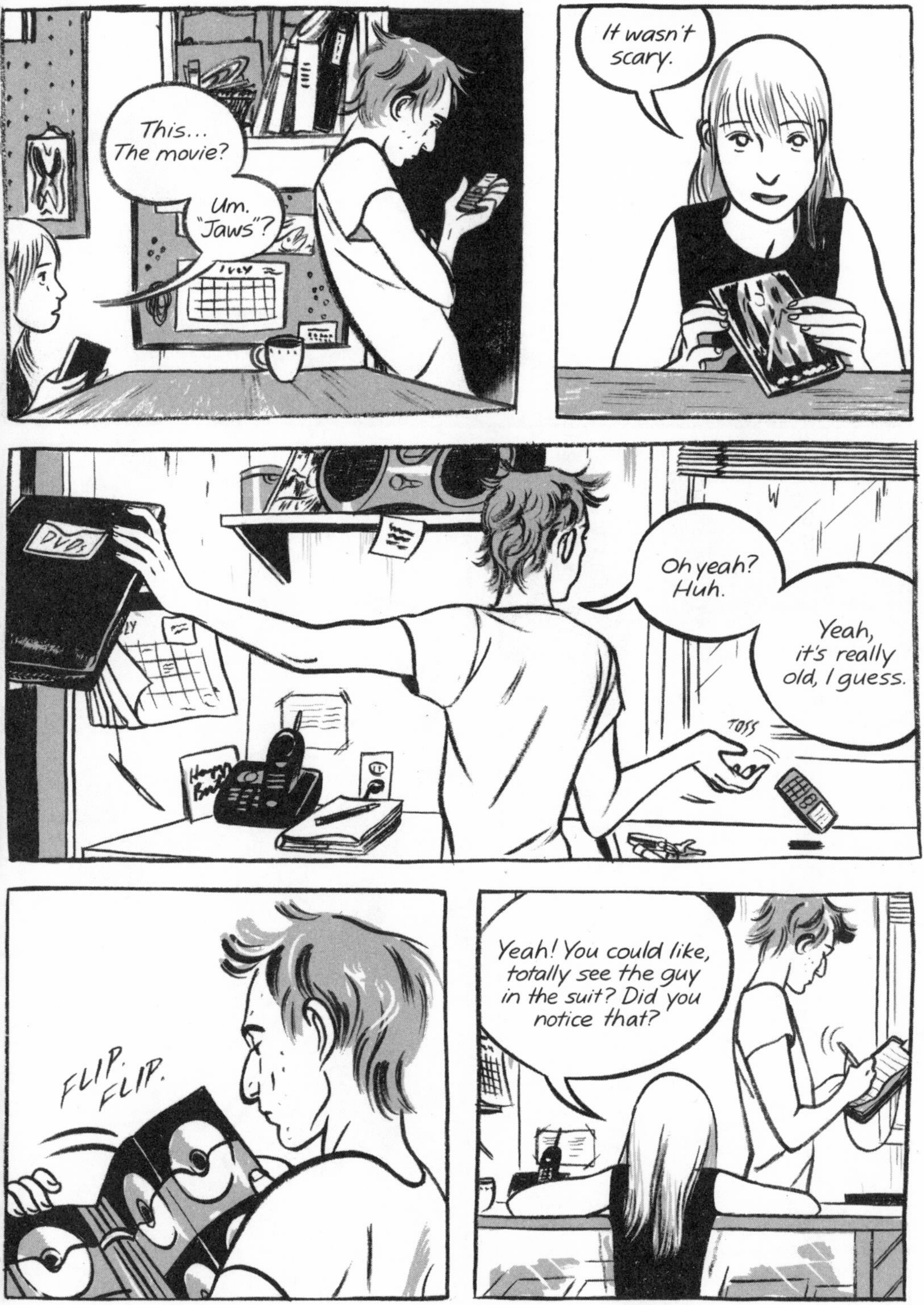
This... The movie?
Um. "Jaws"?
It wasn't scary.
DVDs
Oh yeah? Huh.
Yeah, it's really old, I guess.
TOSS
FLIP. FLIP.
Yeah! You could like, totally see the guy in the suit? Did you notice that?

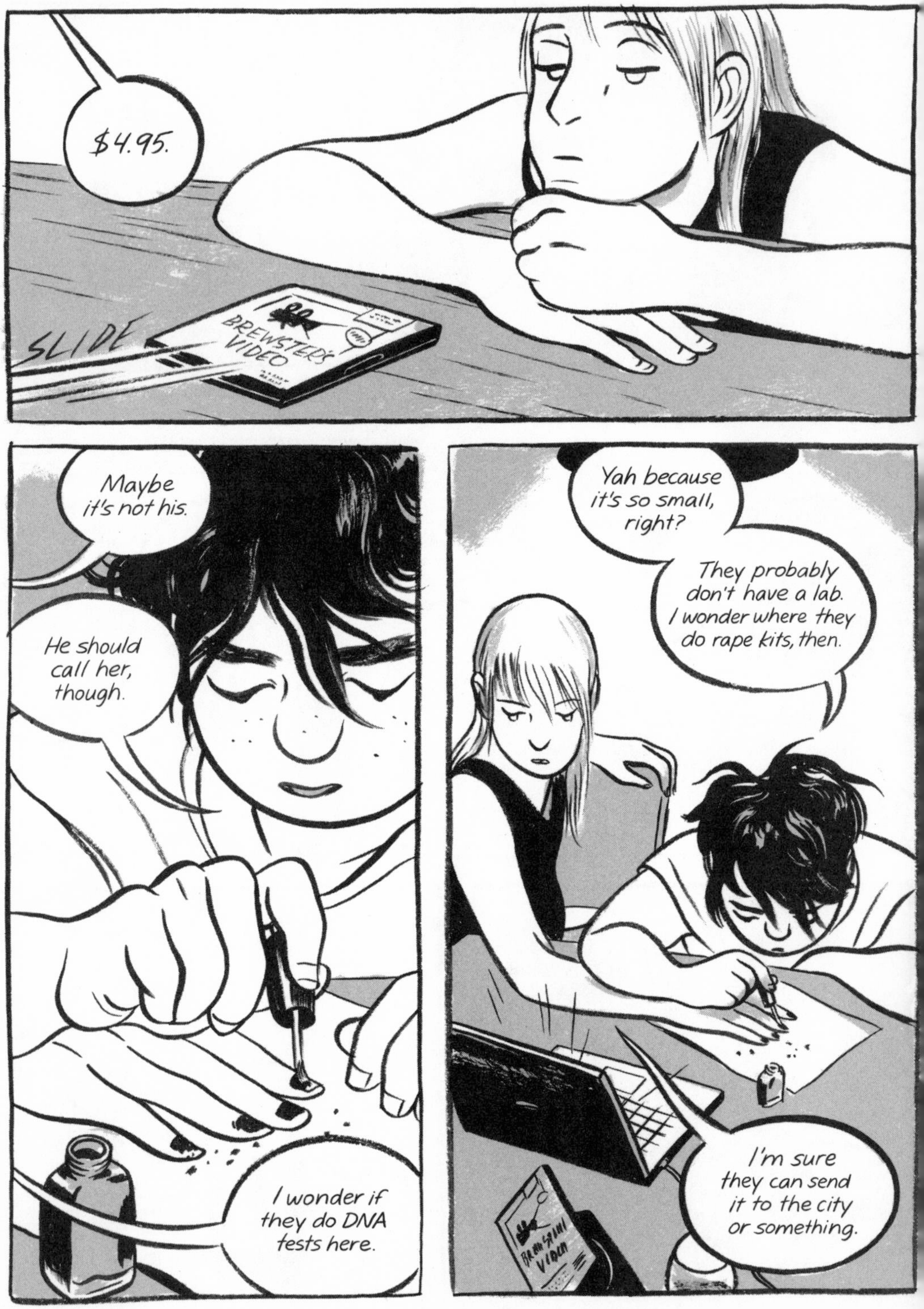
$4.95.
SLIDE
BREWSTER'S VIDEO
Maybe it's not his.
He should call her, though.
I wonder if they do DNA tests here.
Yah because it's so small, right?
They probably don't have a lab. I wonder where they do rape kits, then.
I'm sure they can send it to the city or something.

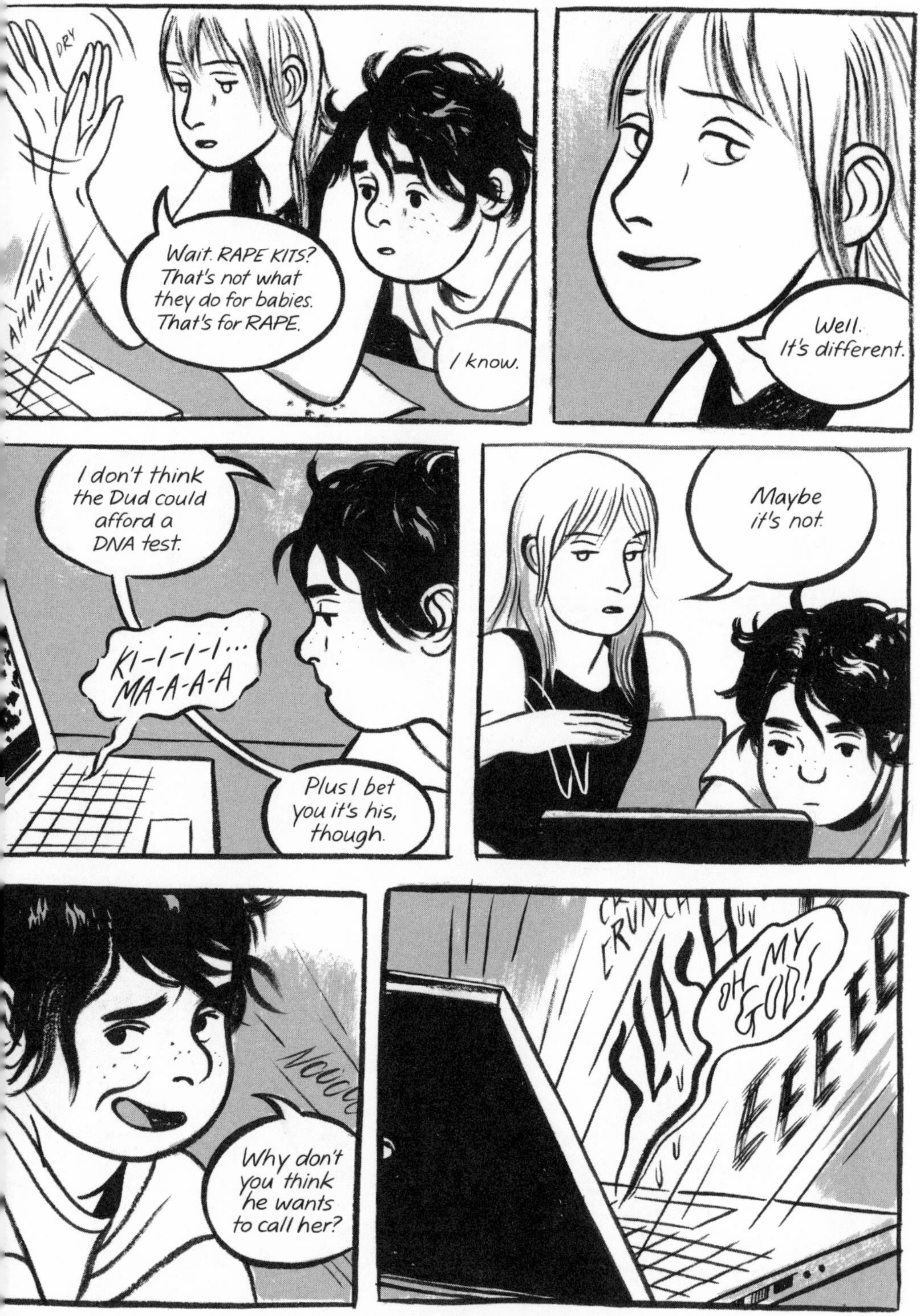
DRY
AHHH!
Wait. RAPE KITS? That's not what they do for babies. That's for RAPE.
I know.
Well. It's different.
I don't think the Dud could afford a DNA test.
KI-I-I-I... MA-A-A-A
Plus I bet you it's his, though.
Maybe it's not.
Why don't you think he wants to call her?
CRUNCH
OH MY GOD!
EEEEE

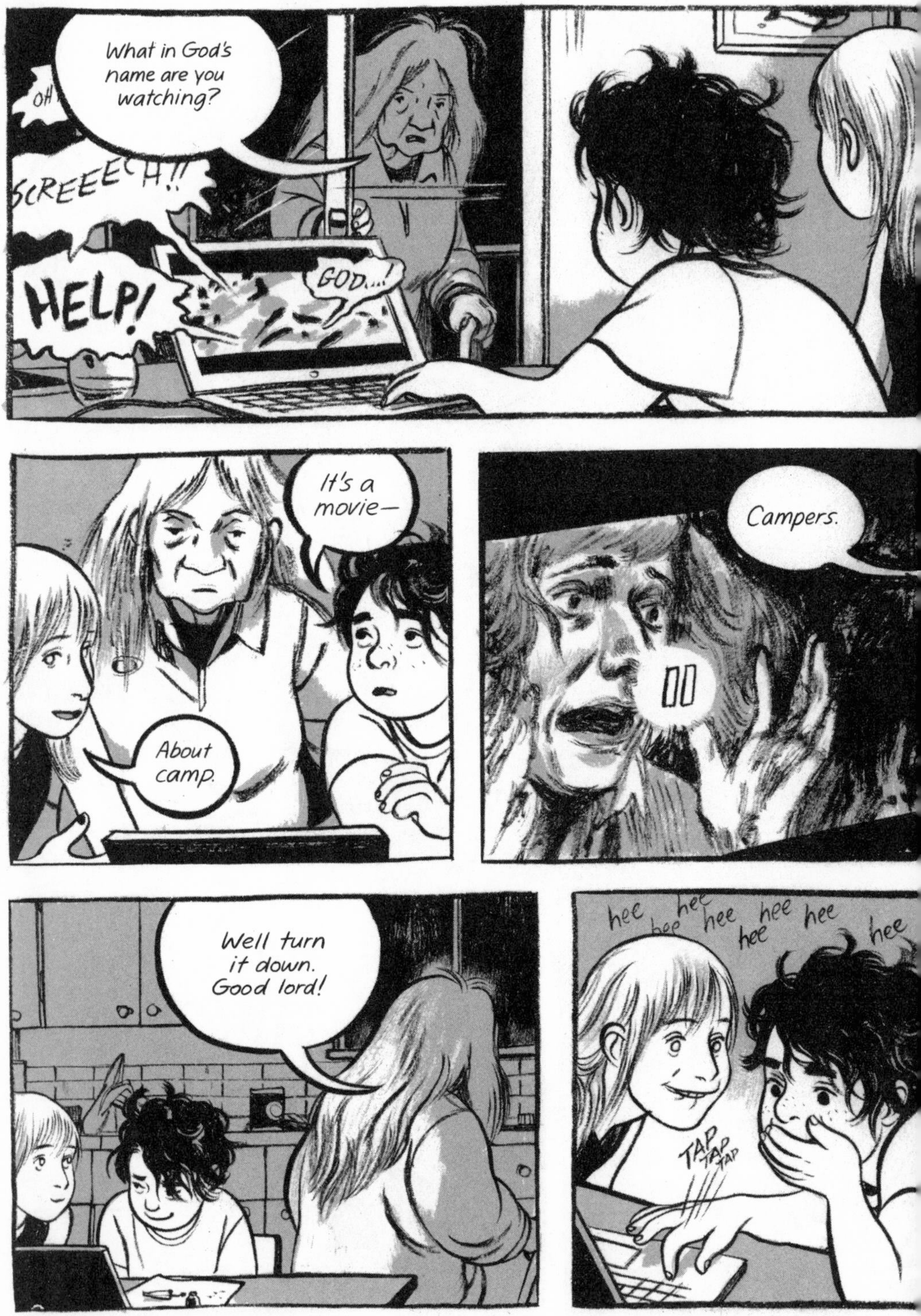
What in God's name are you watching?
OH
SCREEECH!!
HELP!
GOD...!
It's a movie—
About camp.
Campers.
Well turn it down. Good lord!
hee hee hee hee hee hee hee
TAP TAP TAP

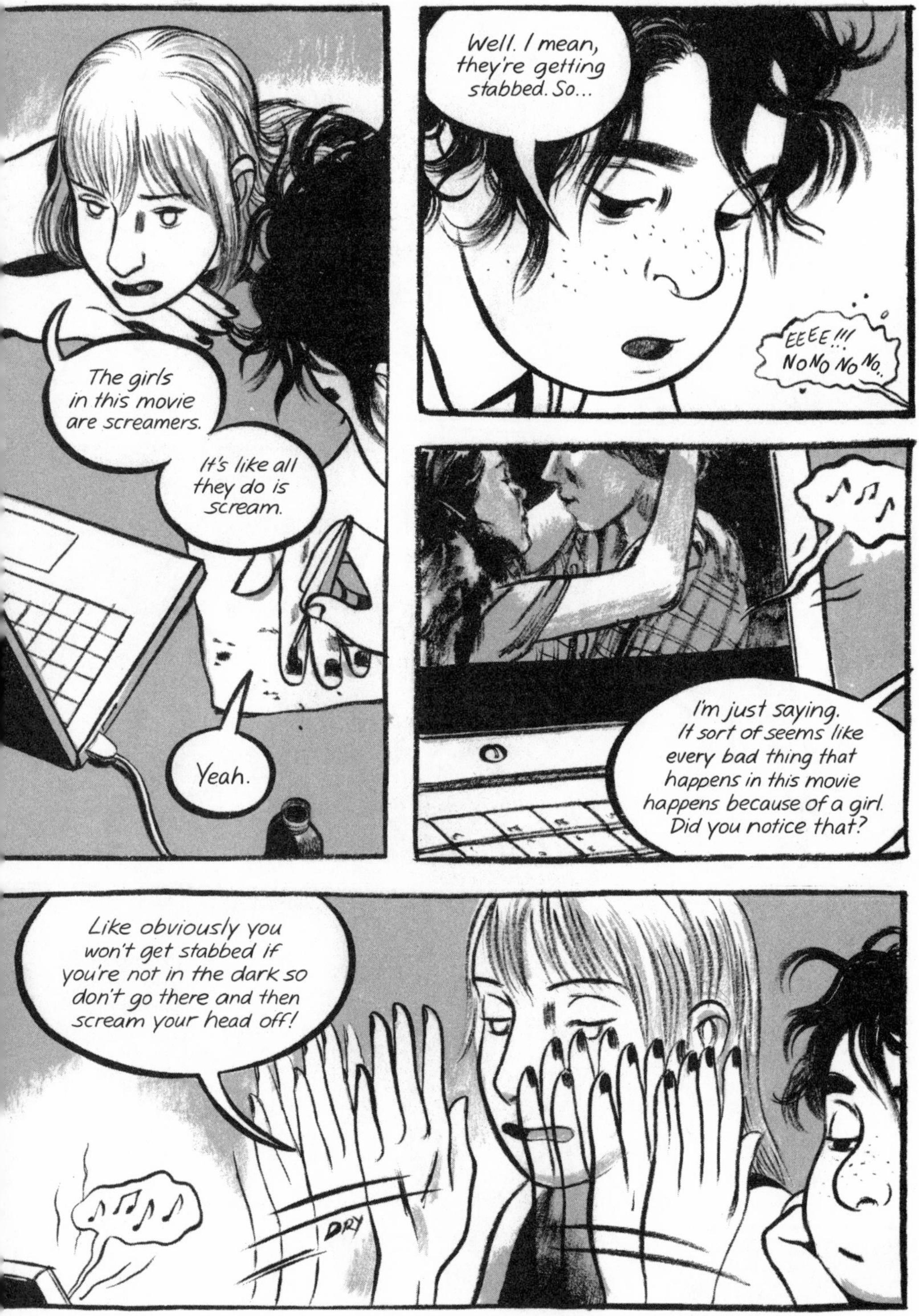
The girls in this movie are screamers.
It's like all they do is scream.
Yeah.
Well. I mean, they're getting stabbed. So...
EEEE!!! NoNo No No..
I'm just saying. It sort of seems like every bad thing that happens in this movie happens because of a girl. Did you notice that?
Like obviously you won't get stabbed if you're not in the dark so don't go there and then scream your head off!
DRY

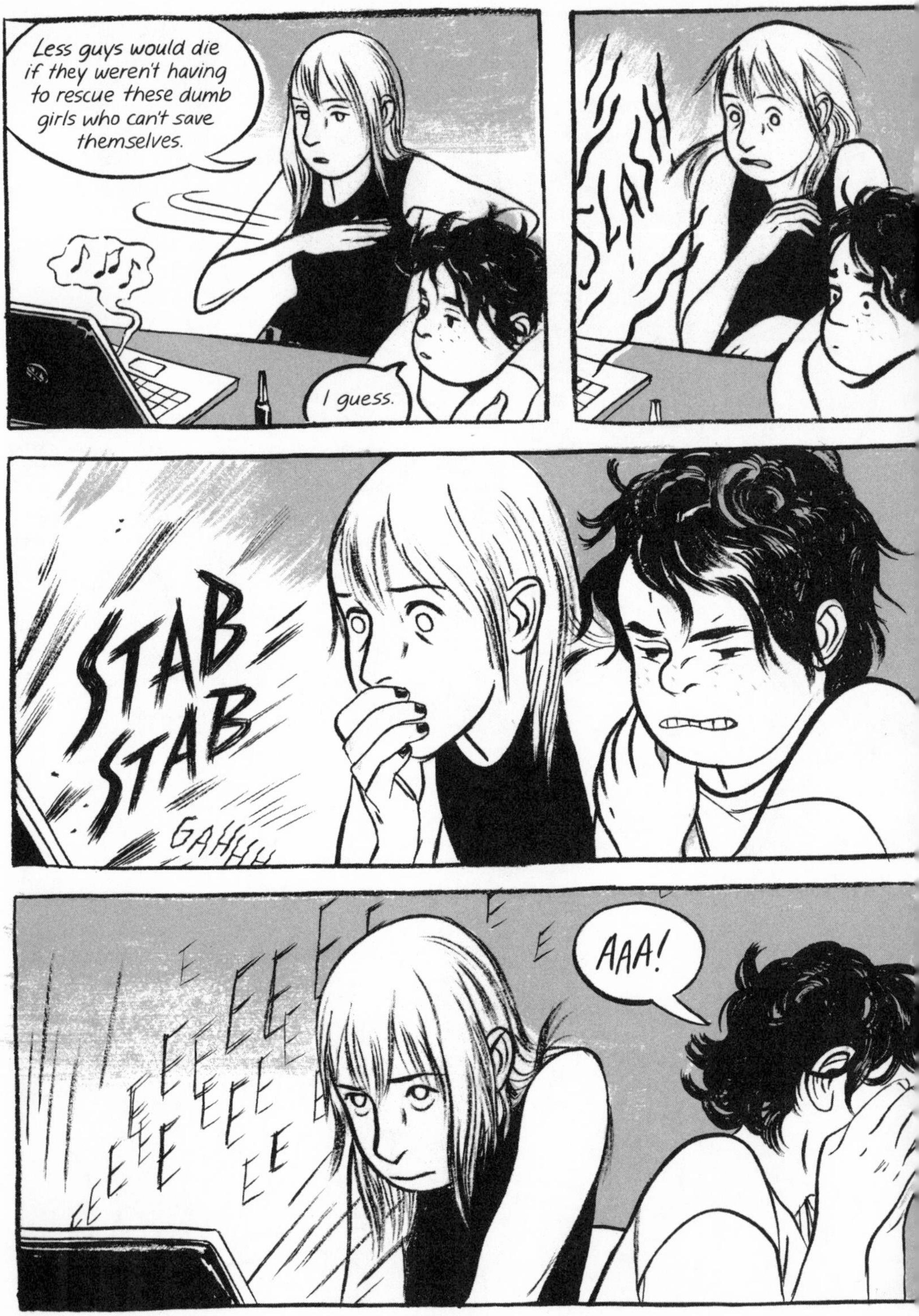
Less guys would die if they weren't having to rescue these dumb girls who can't save themselves.
I guess.
SLASH
STAB STAB
GAHHH
AAA!

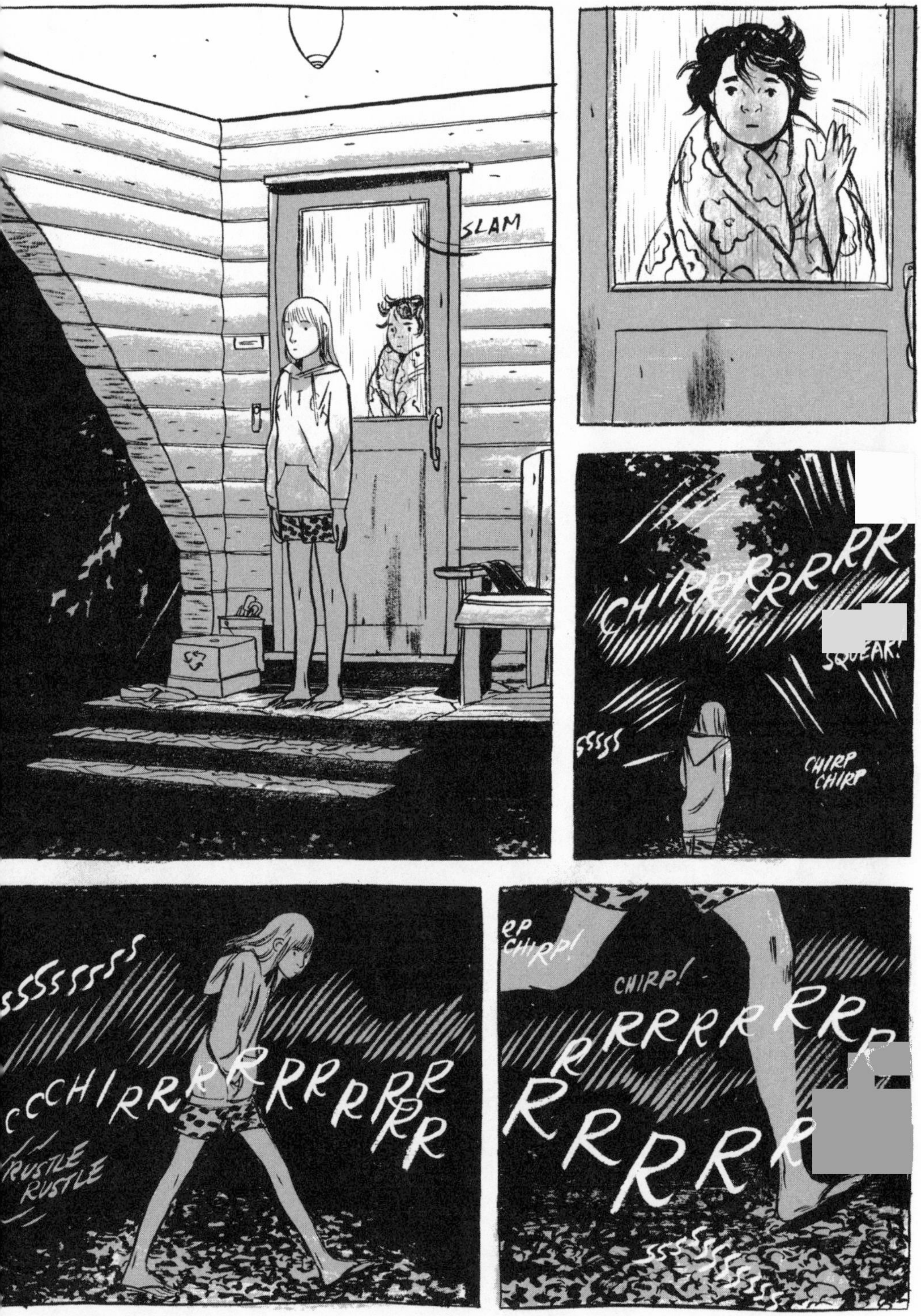
SLAM
CHIRRRRRRK
SQUEAK!
SSSSS
CHIRP
CHIRP
SSSSSSSSS
CCCHIRRRRRRRRRRR
RUSTLE
RUSTLE
ep
CHIRP!
CHIRP!
RRRRRRRR
RRRRR
SSSSSSSS

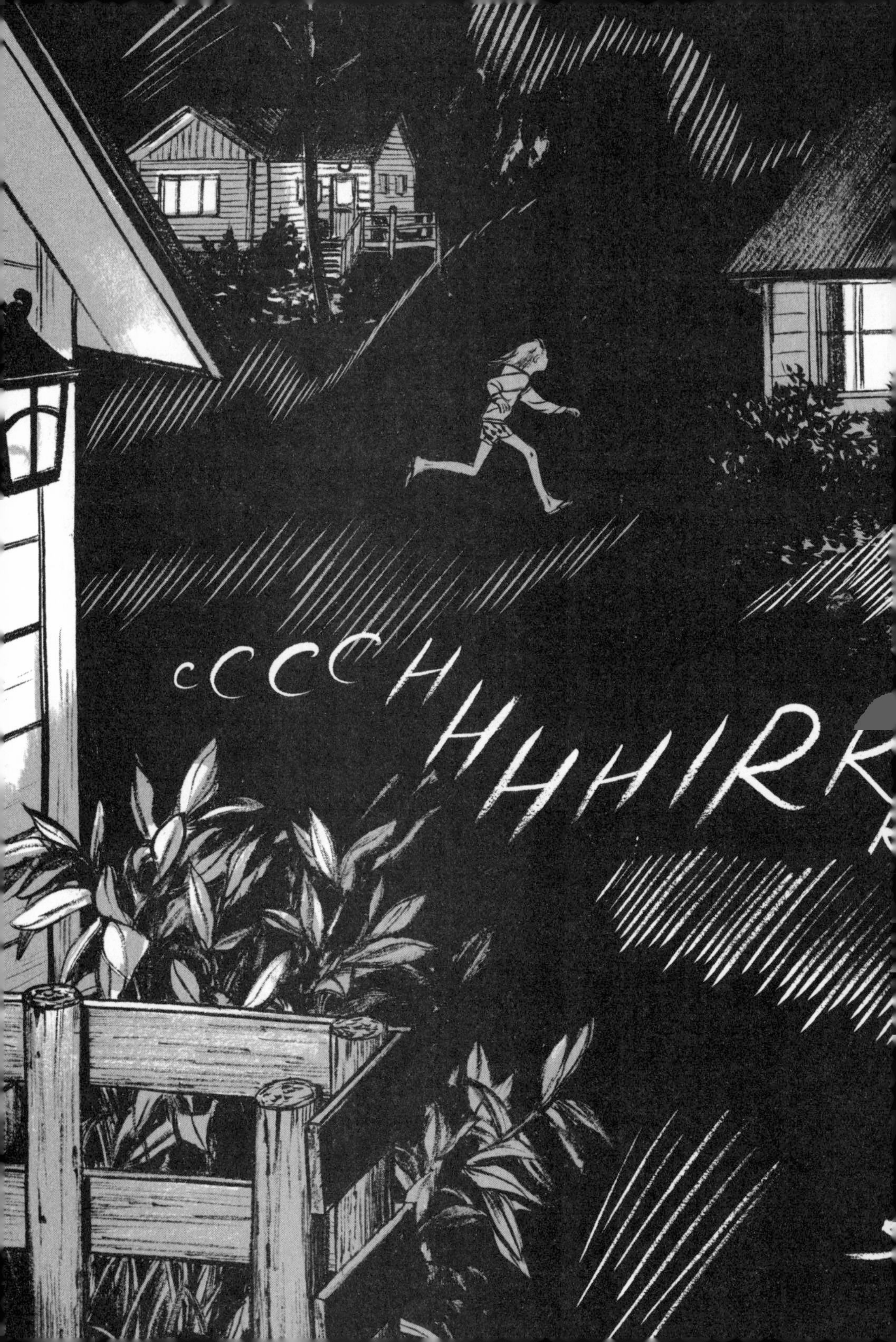
cCCCH
HHHIRR

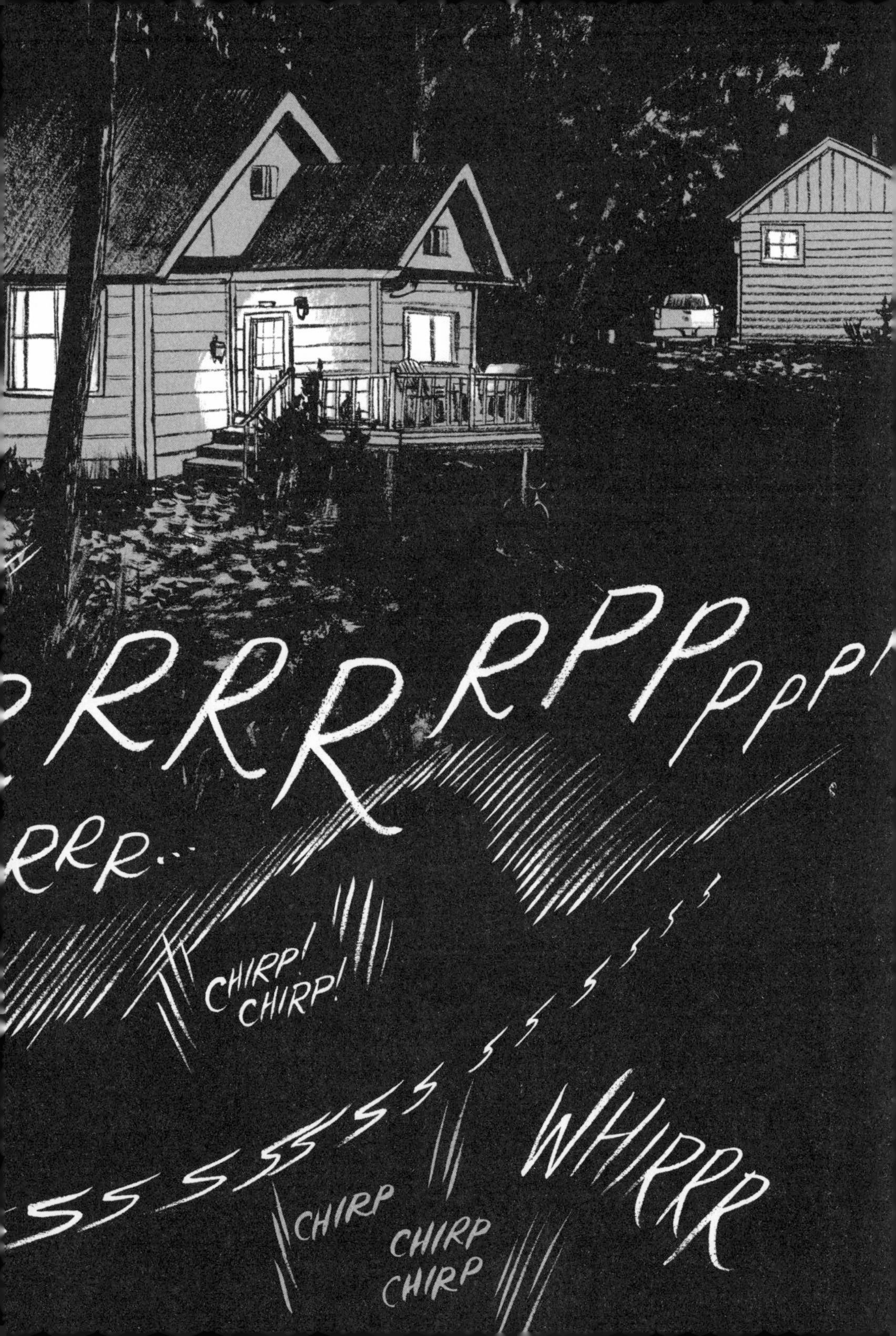
RRRRRPPppp
RRR...
CHIRP! CHIRP!
SSSSSSSSSSS
WHIRRR
CHIRP
CHIRP
CHIRP

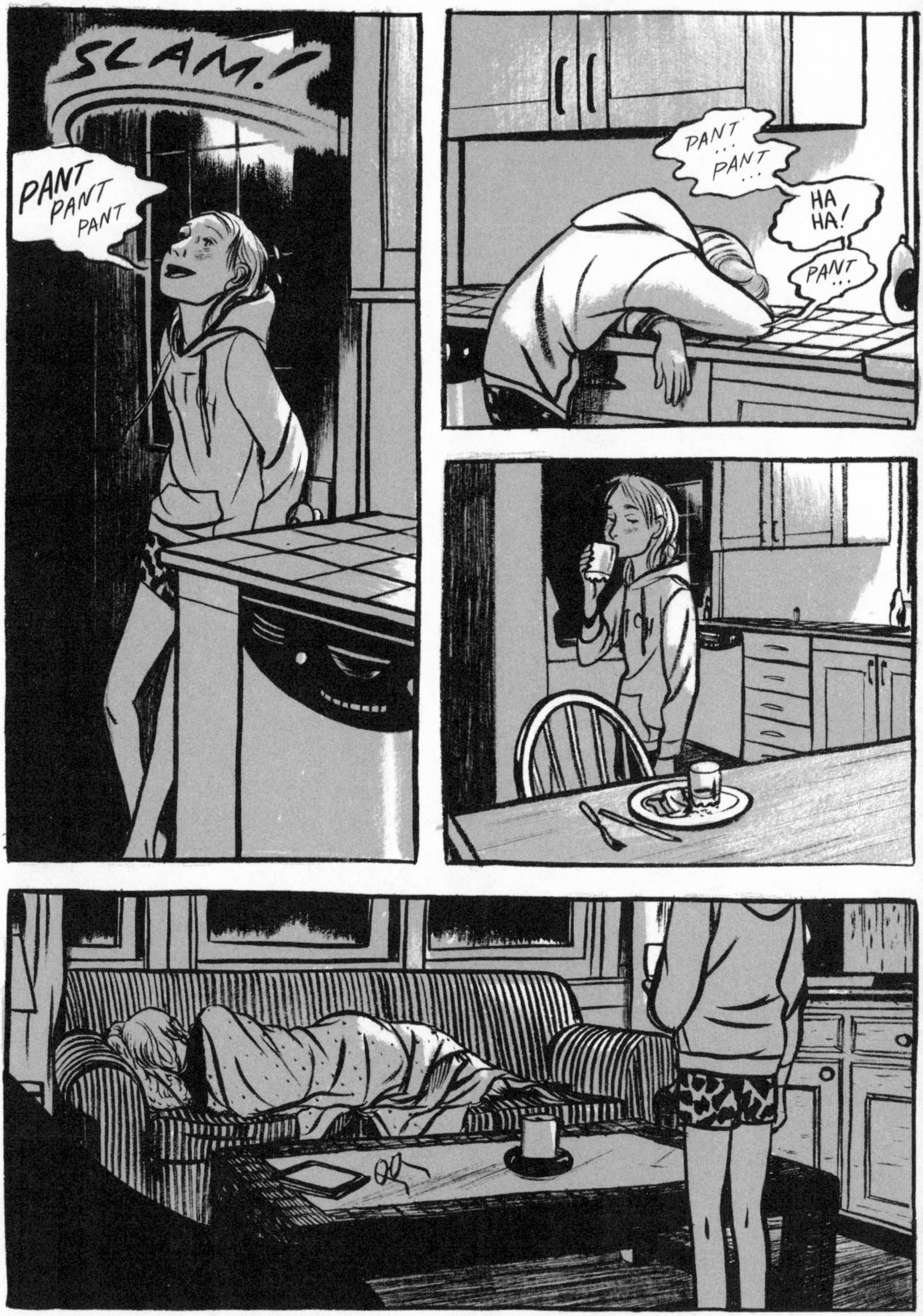
SLAM!
PANT PANT PANT
PANT ... PANT ...
HA HA!
PANT ...

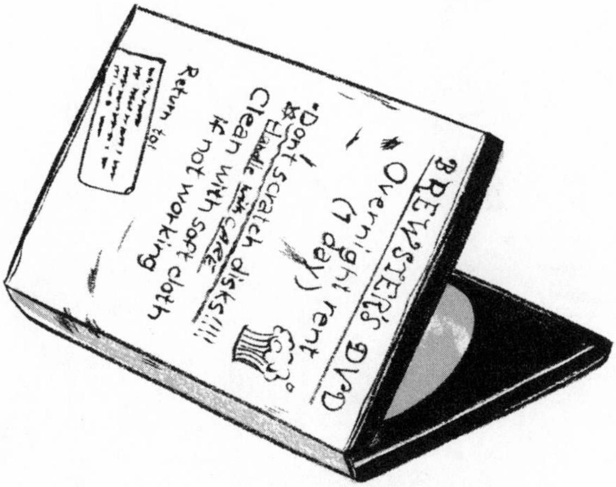
BREWSTER'S DVD
•Overnight rent (1 day)
•Don't scratch disks!!!!
☆Handle with CARE
Clean with soft cloth if not working
Return to:

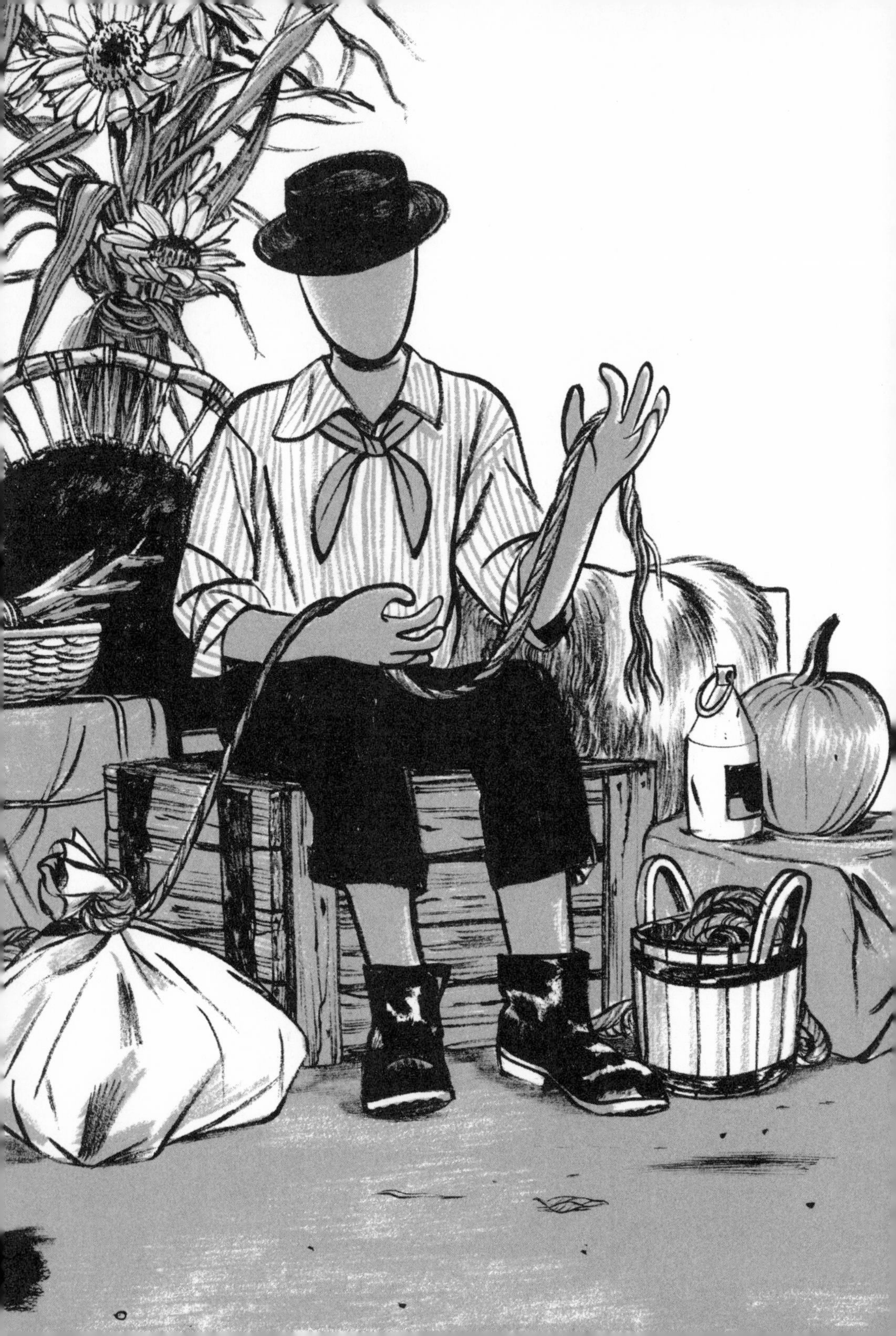

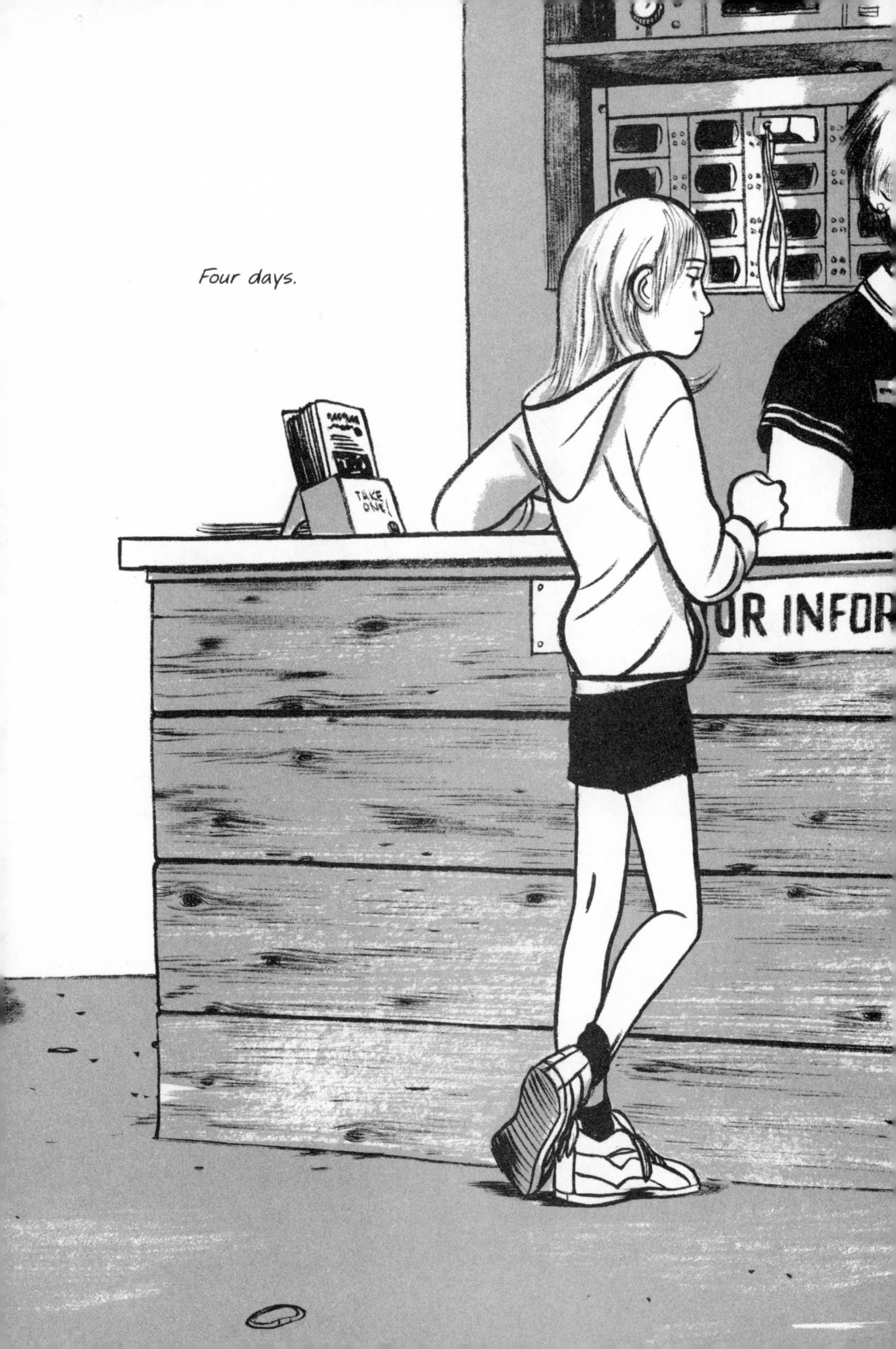
Four days.
TAKE ONE!
OR INFOR

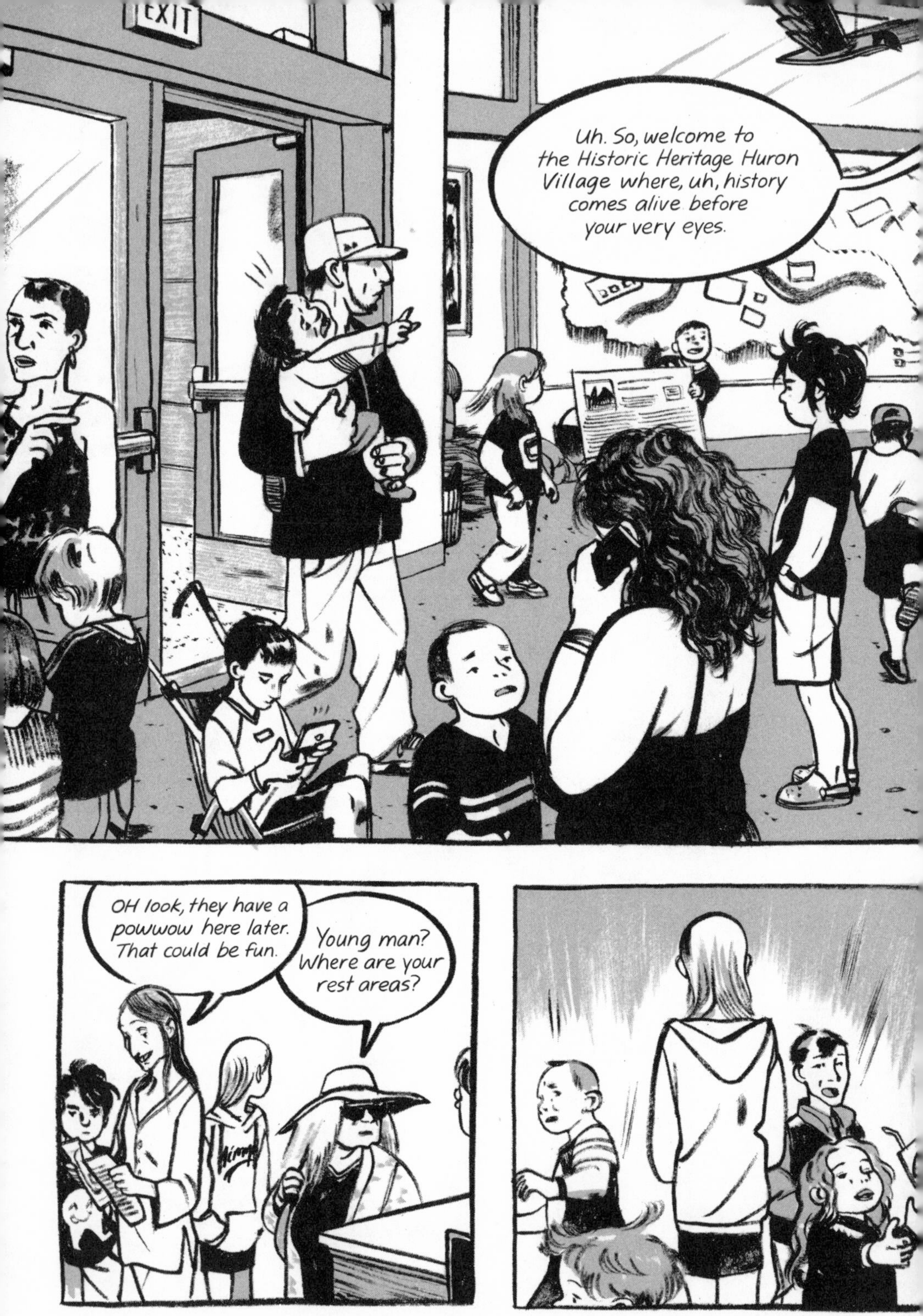
EXIT
Uh. So, welcome to the Historic Heritage Huron Village where, uh, history comes alive before your very eyes.
OH look, they have a powwow here later. That could be fun.
Young man? Where are your rest areas?

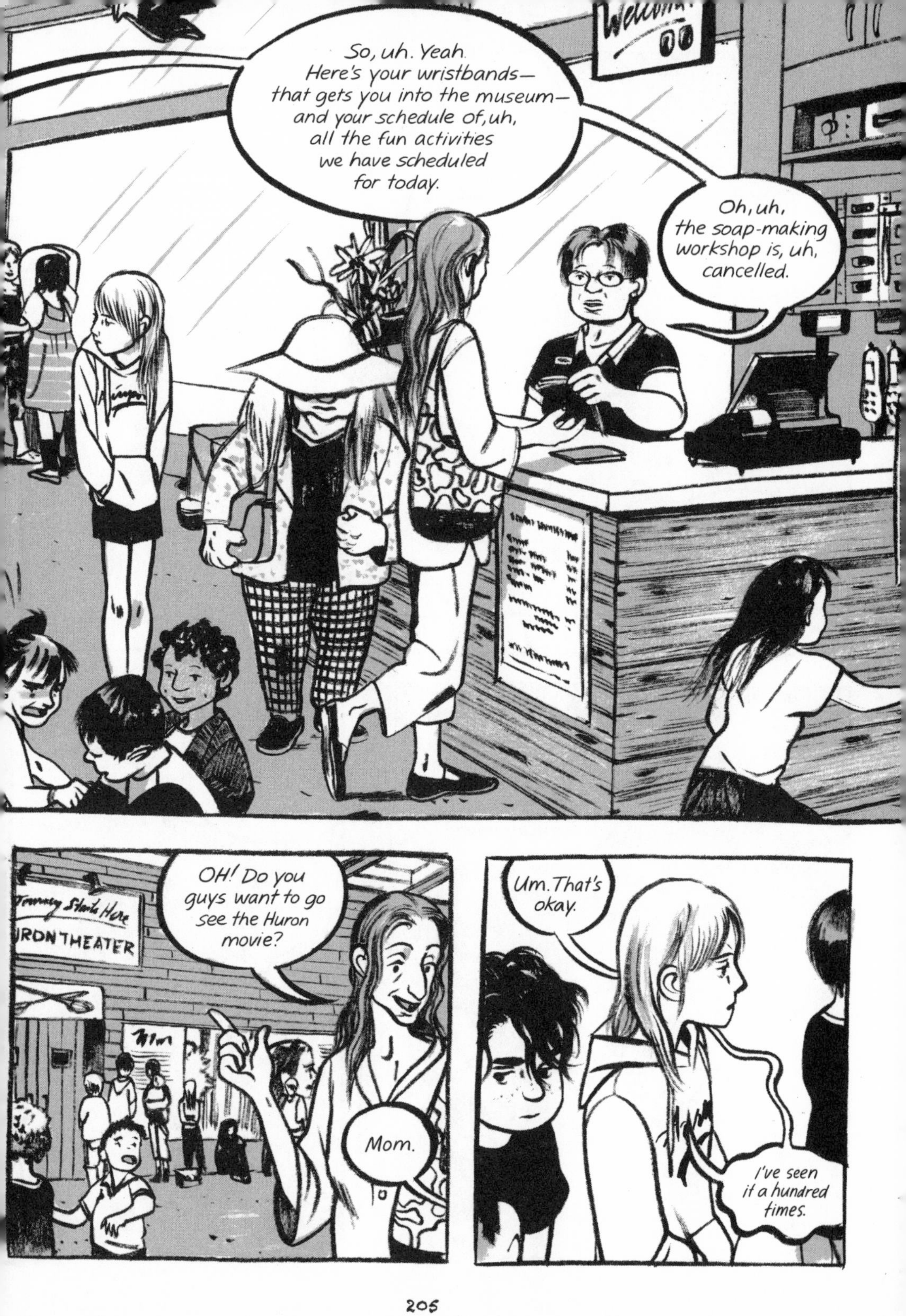
So, uh. Yeah. Here's your wristbands— that gets you into the museum— and your schedule of, uh, all the fun activities we have scheduled for today.
Oh, uh, the soap-making workshop is, uh, cancelled.
URON THEATER
OH! Do you guys want to go see the Huron movie?
Mom.
Um. That's okay.
I've seen it a hundred times.

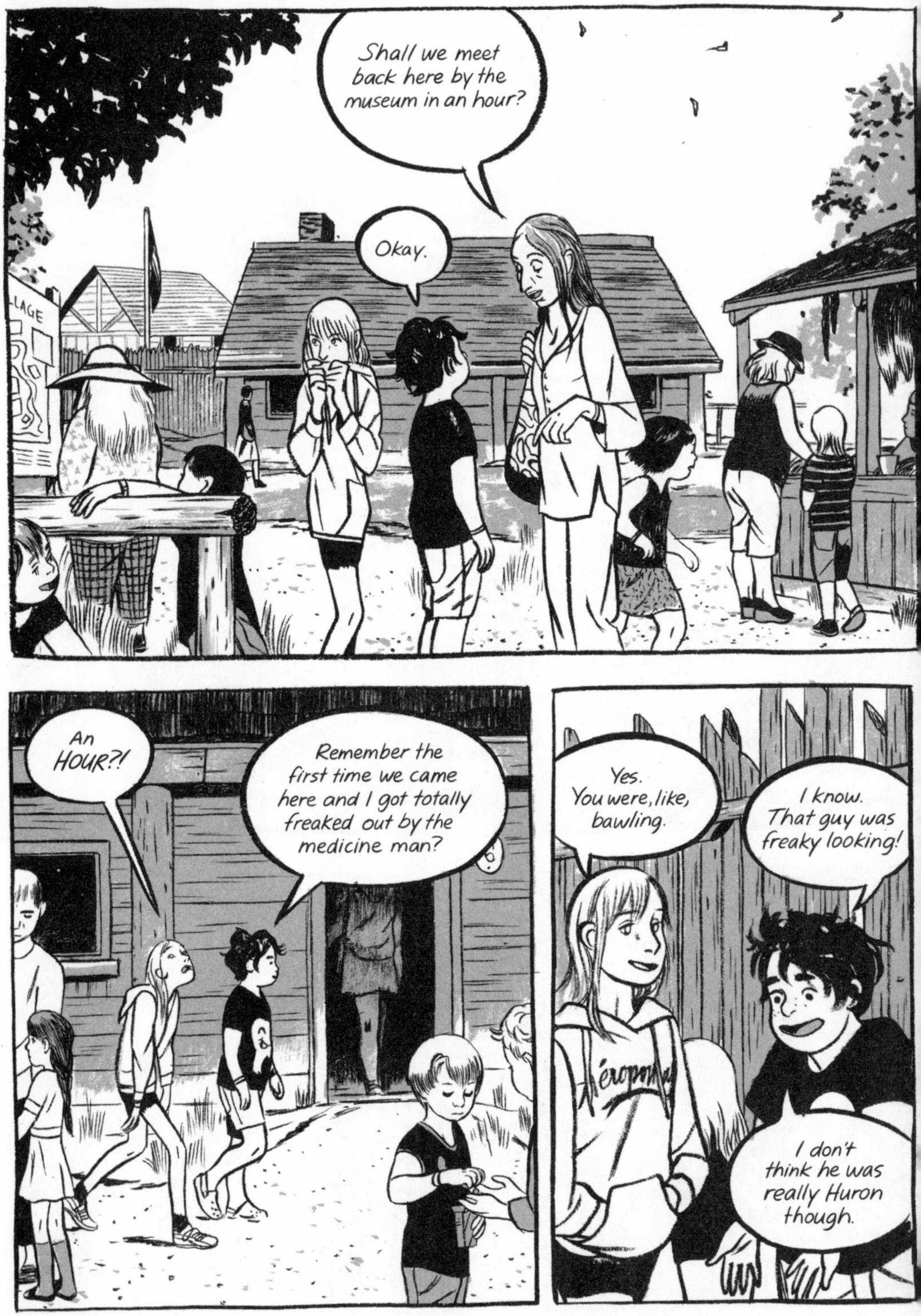
Shall we meet back here by the museum in an hour?
Okay.
LLAGE
An HOUR?!
Remember the first time we came here and I got totally freaked out by the medicine man?
Yes. You were, like, bawling.
I know. That guy was freaky looking!
I don't think he was really Huron though.

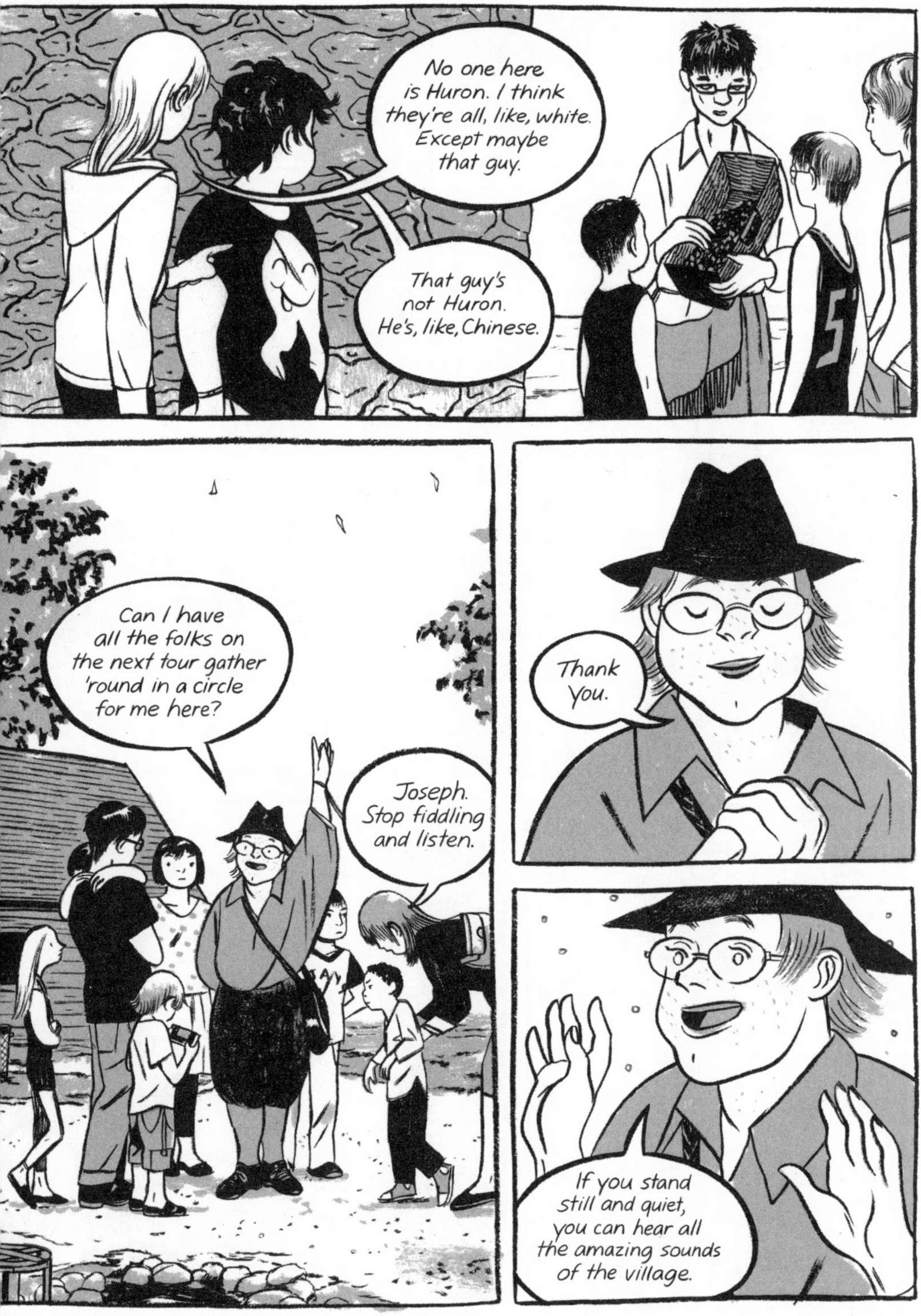
No one here is Huron. I think they're all, like, white. Except maybe that guy.
That guy's not Huron. He's, like, Chinese.
Can I have all the folks on the next tour gather 'round in a circle for me here?
Joseph. Stop fiddling and listen.
Thank You.
If you stand still and quiet, you can hear all the amazing sounds of the village.

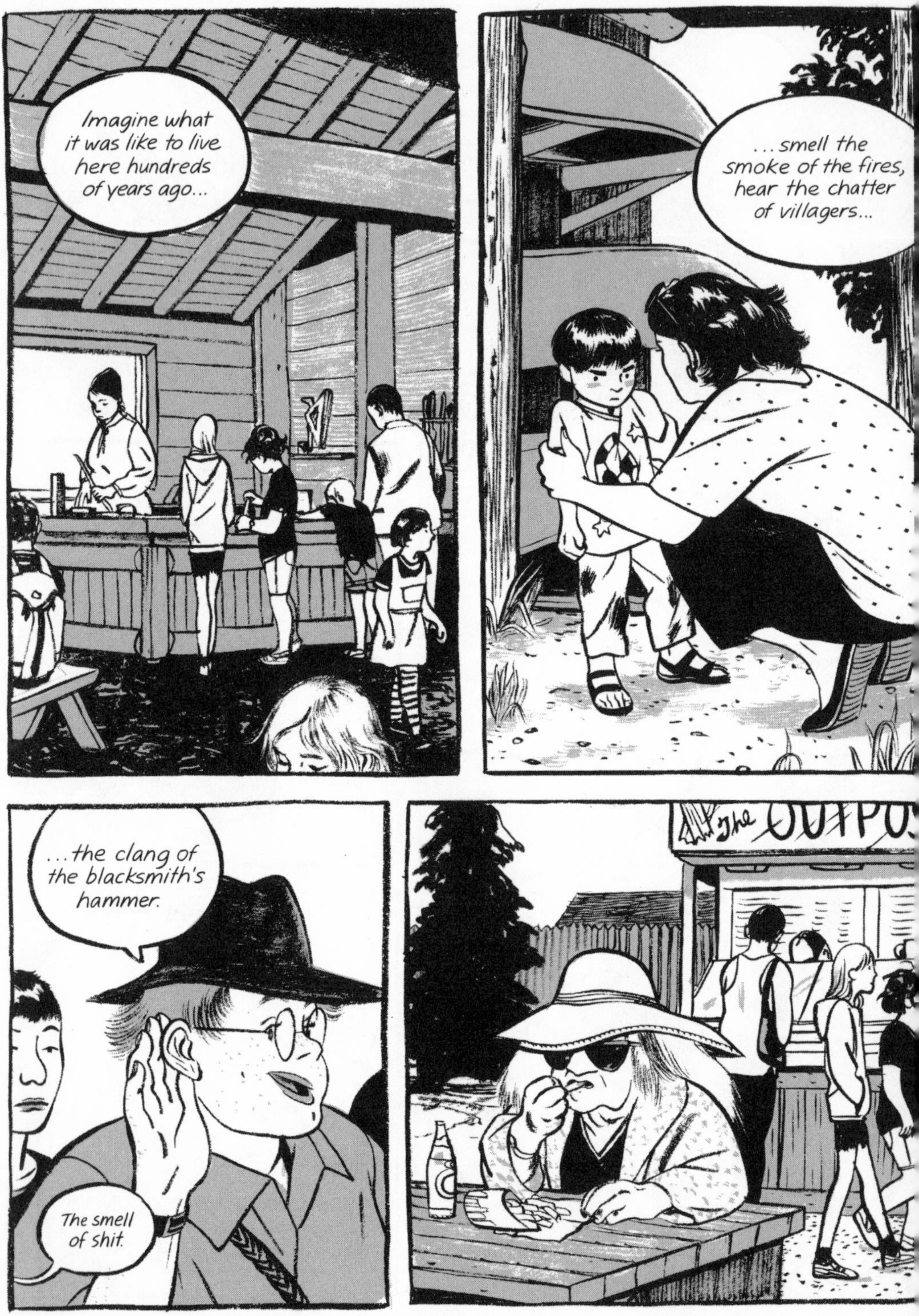
Imagine what it was like to live here hundreds of years ago...
...smell the smoke of the fires, hear the chatter of villagers...
...the clang of the blacksmith's hammer.
The smell of shit.
The OUTPOS

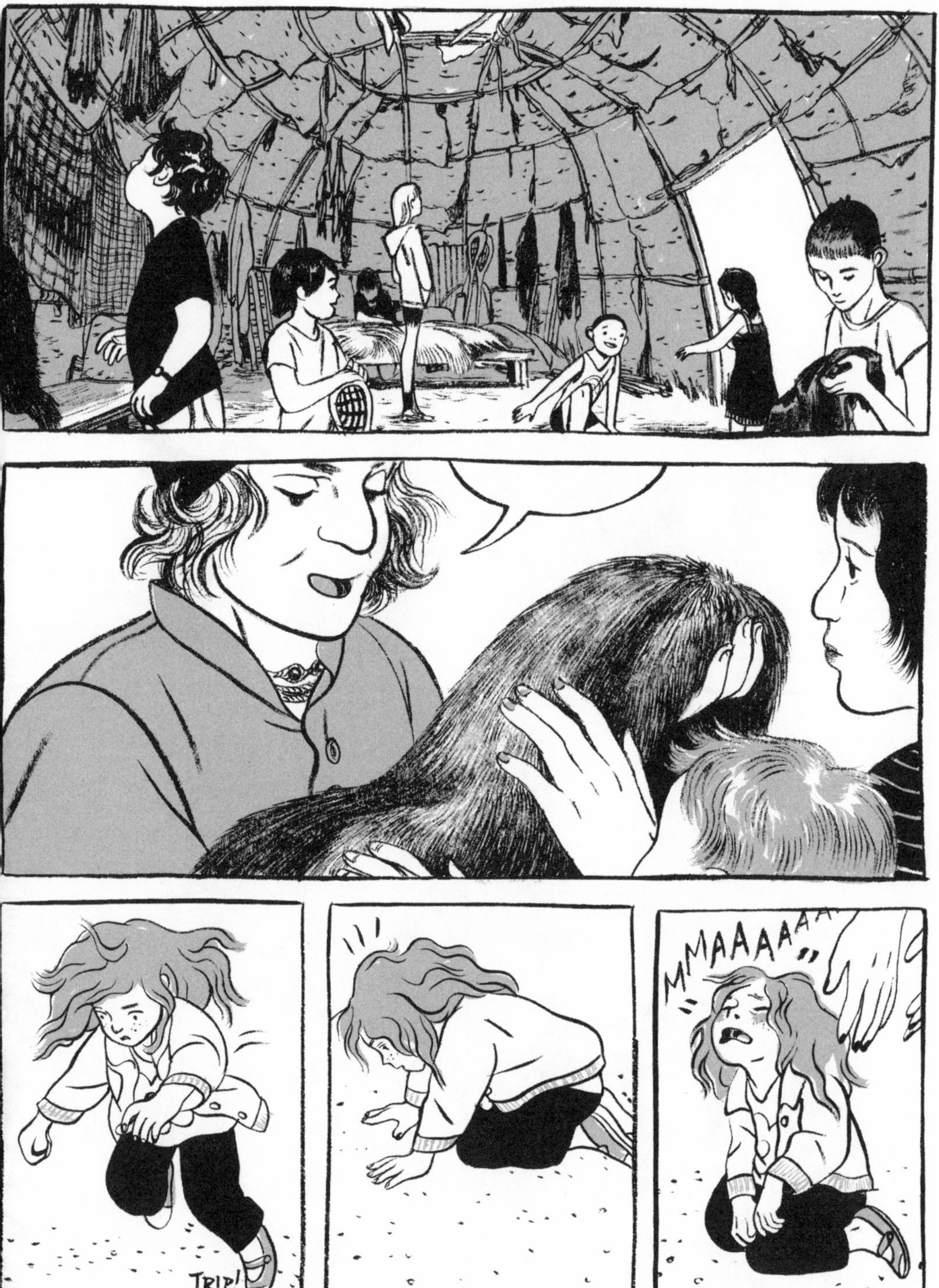
TRIP!
MMAAAAA

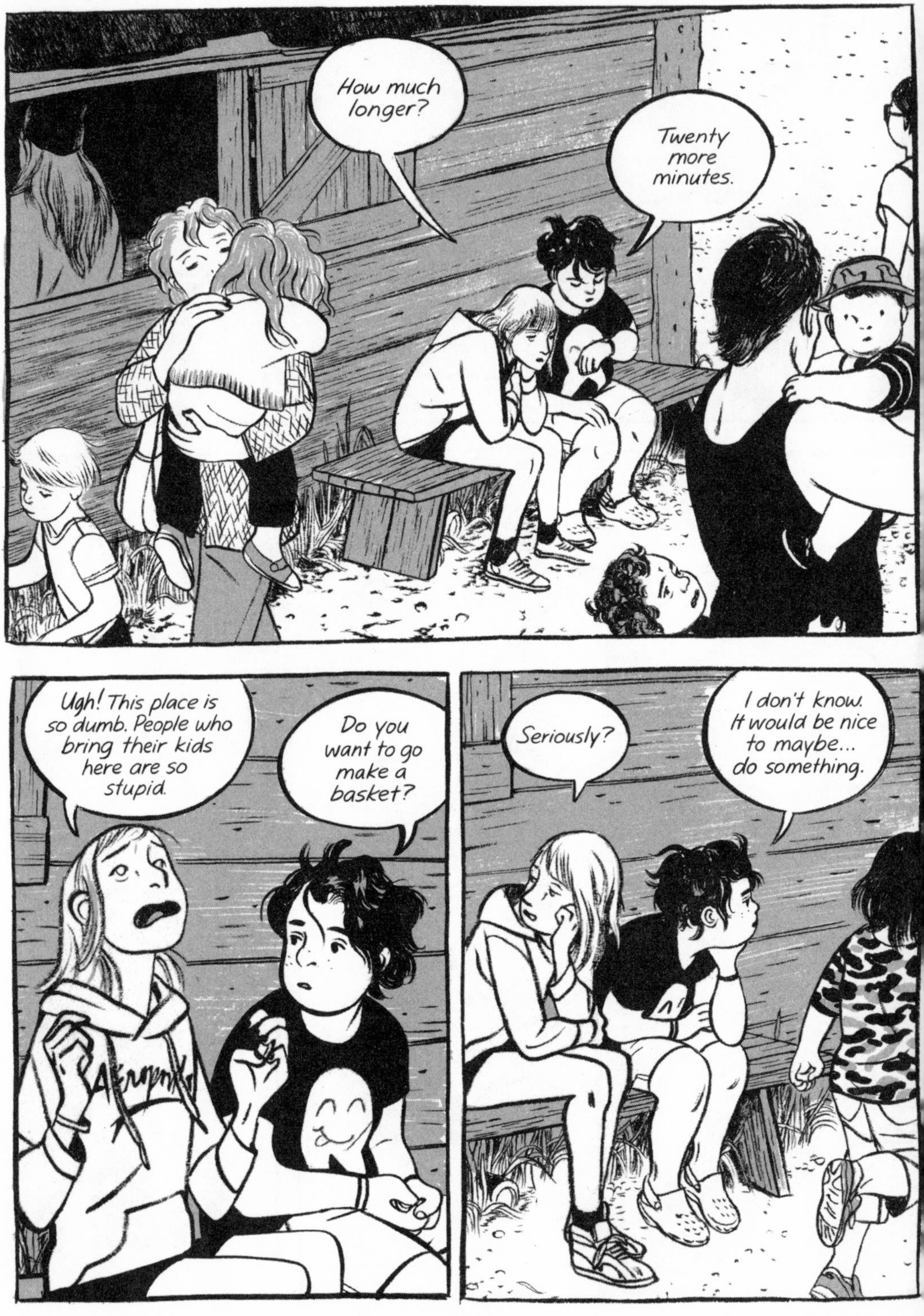
How much longer?
Twenty more minutes.
Ugh! This place is so dumb. People who bring their kids here are so stupid.
Do you want to go make a basket?
Seriously?
I don't know. It would be nice to maybe... do something.

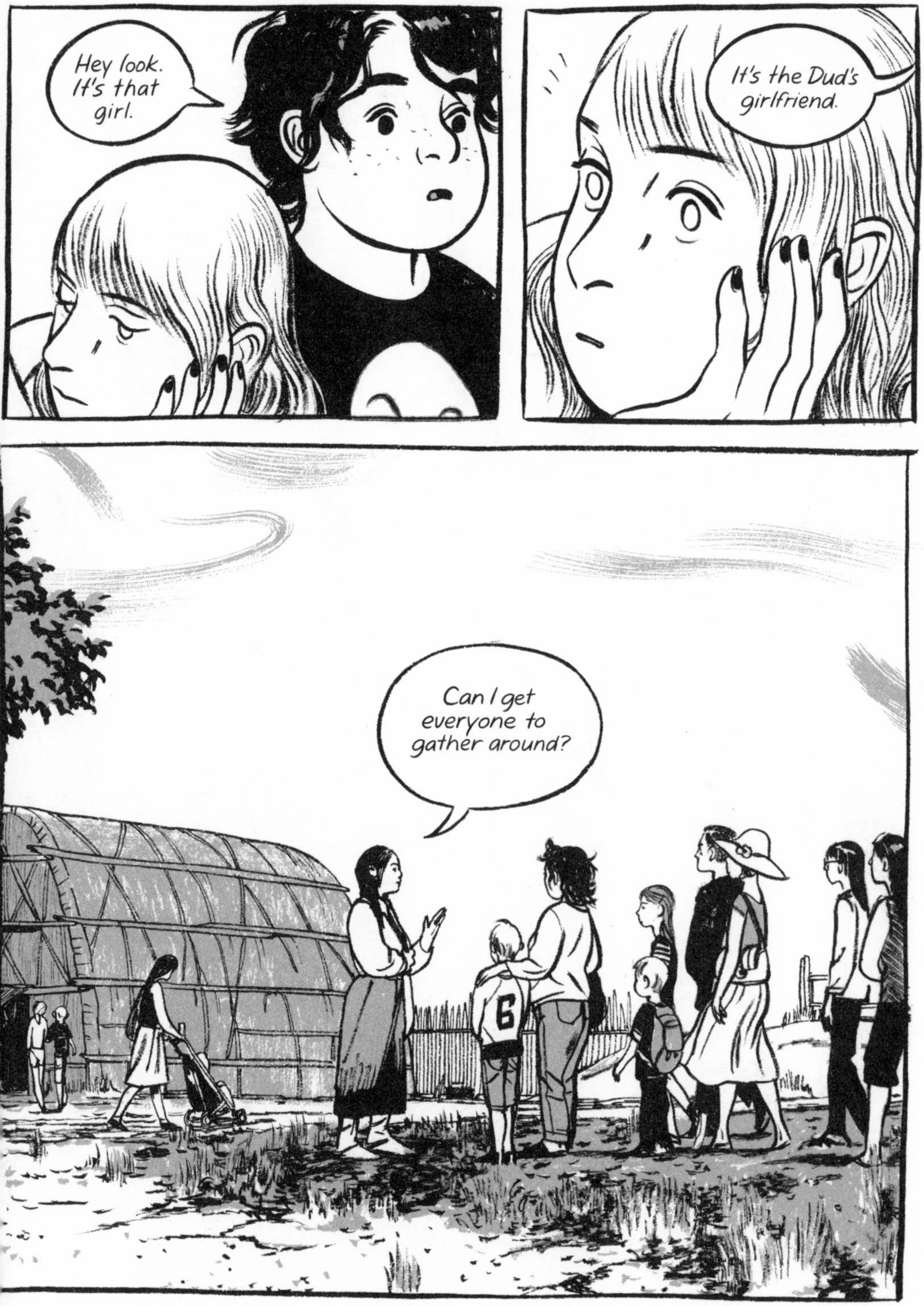
Hey look. It's that girl.
It's the Dud's girlfriend.
Can I get everyone to gather around?

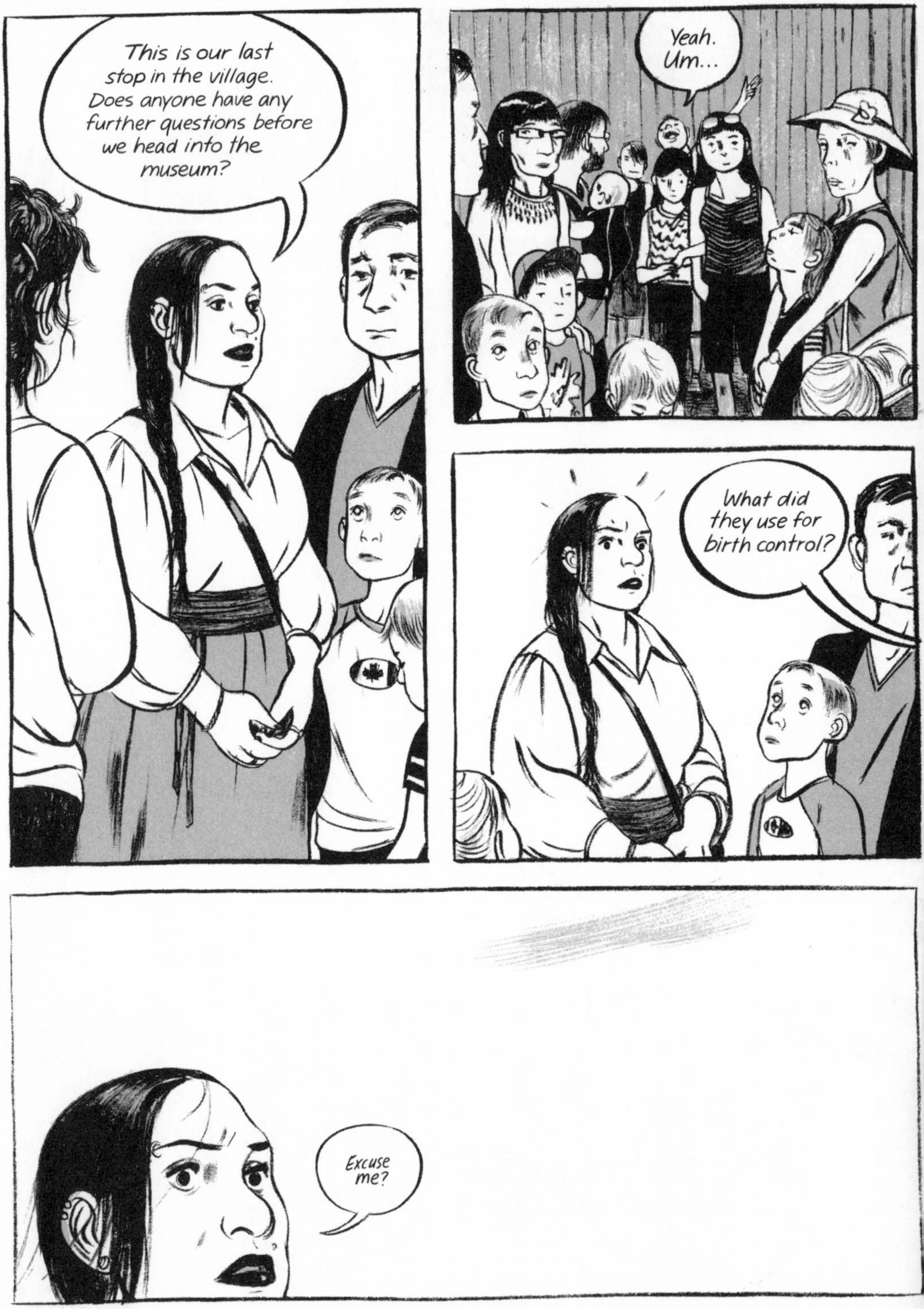
This is our last stop in the village. Does anyone have any further questions before we head into the museum?
Yeah. Um...
What did they use for birth control?
Excuse me?

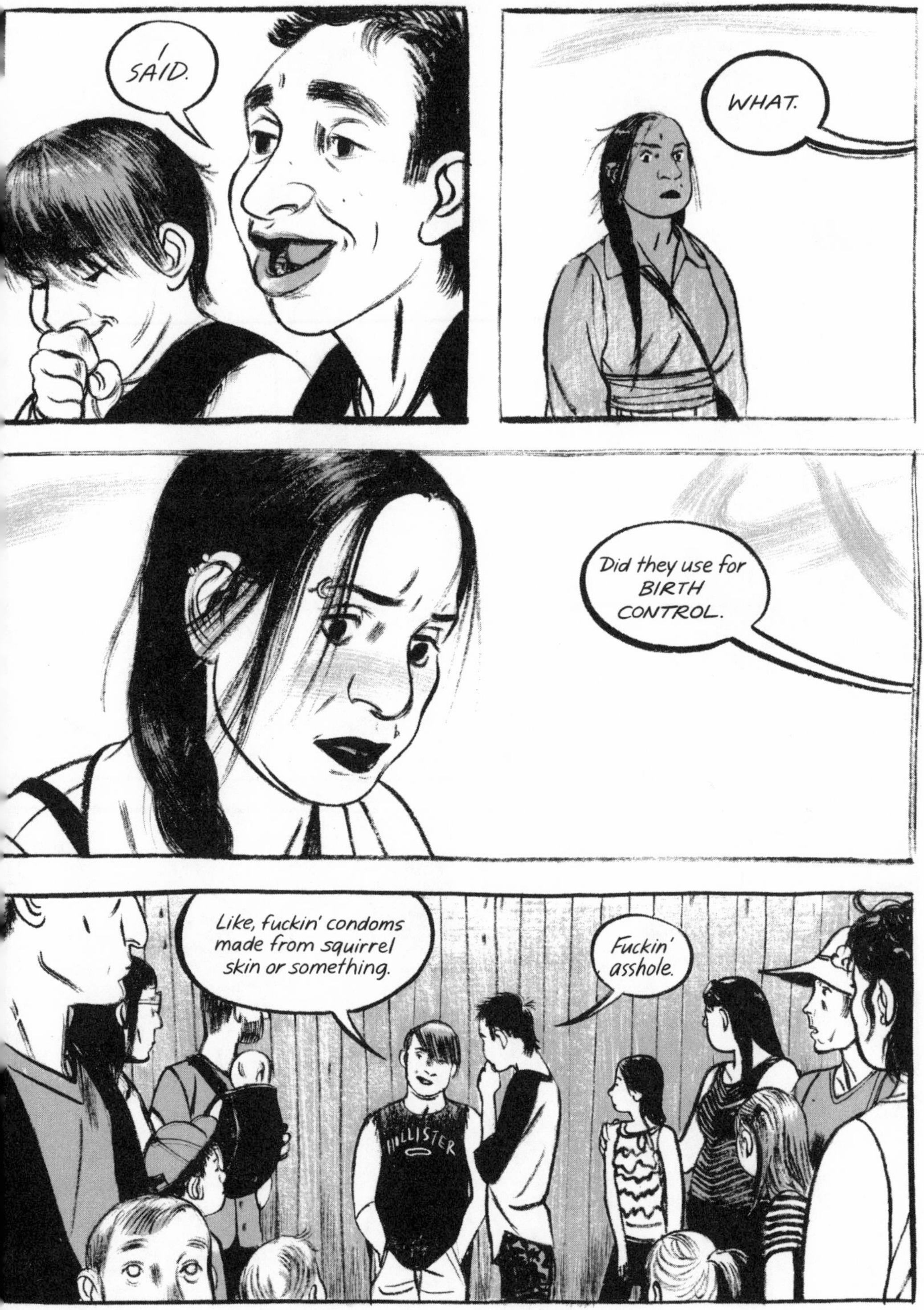
I SAID.
WHAT.
Did they use for BIRTH CONTROL.
Like, fuckin' condoms made from squirrel skin or something.
Fuckin' asshole.
HOLLISTER

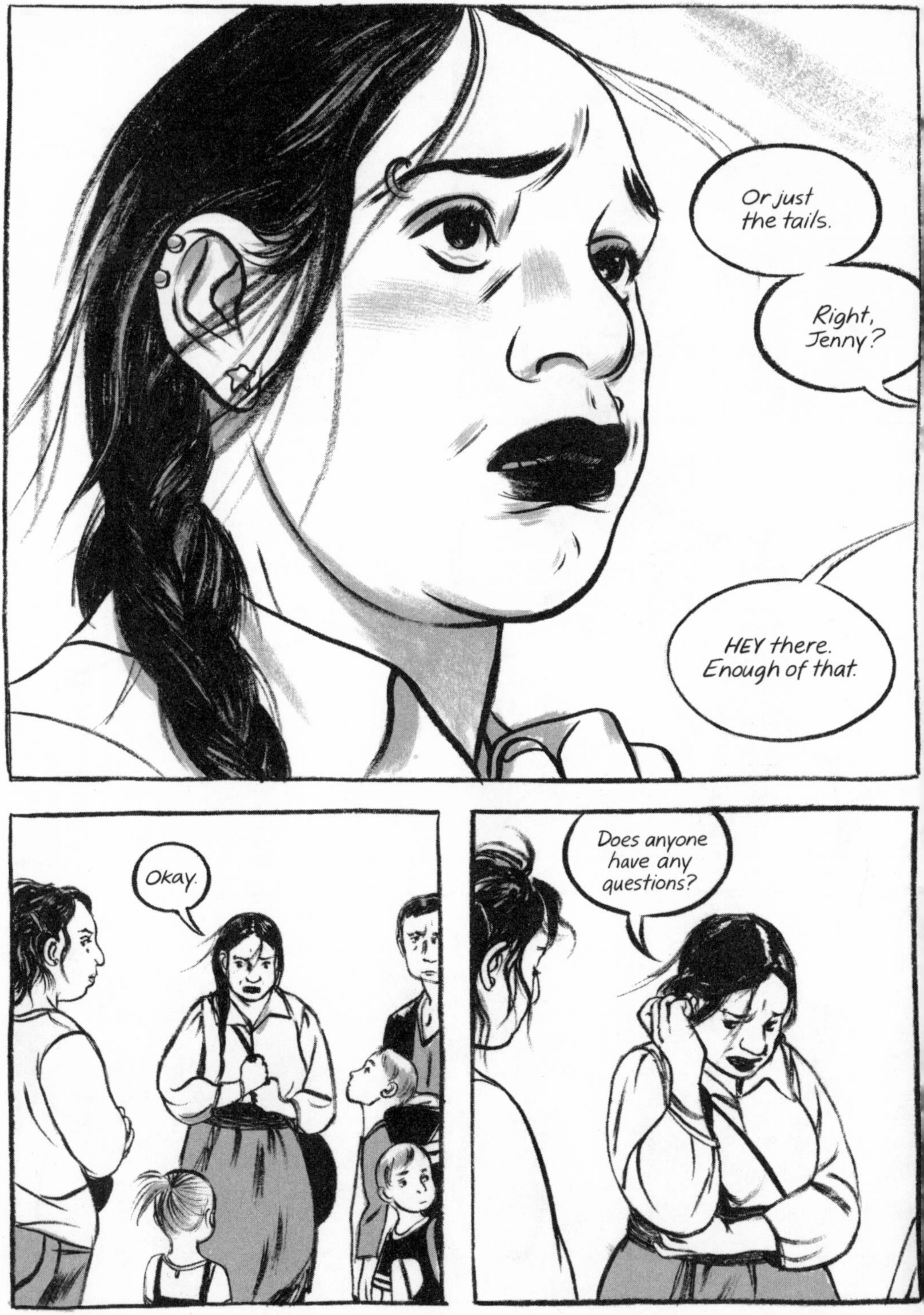
Or just the tails.
Right, Jenny?
HEY there. Enough of that.
Okay.
Does anyone have any questions?

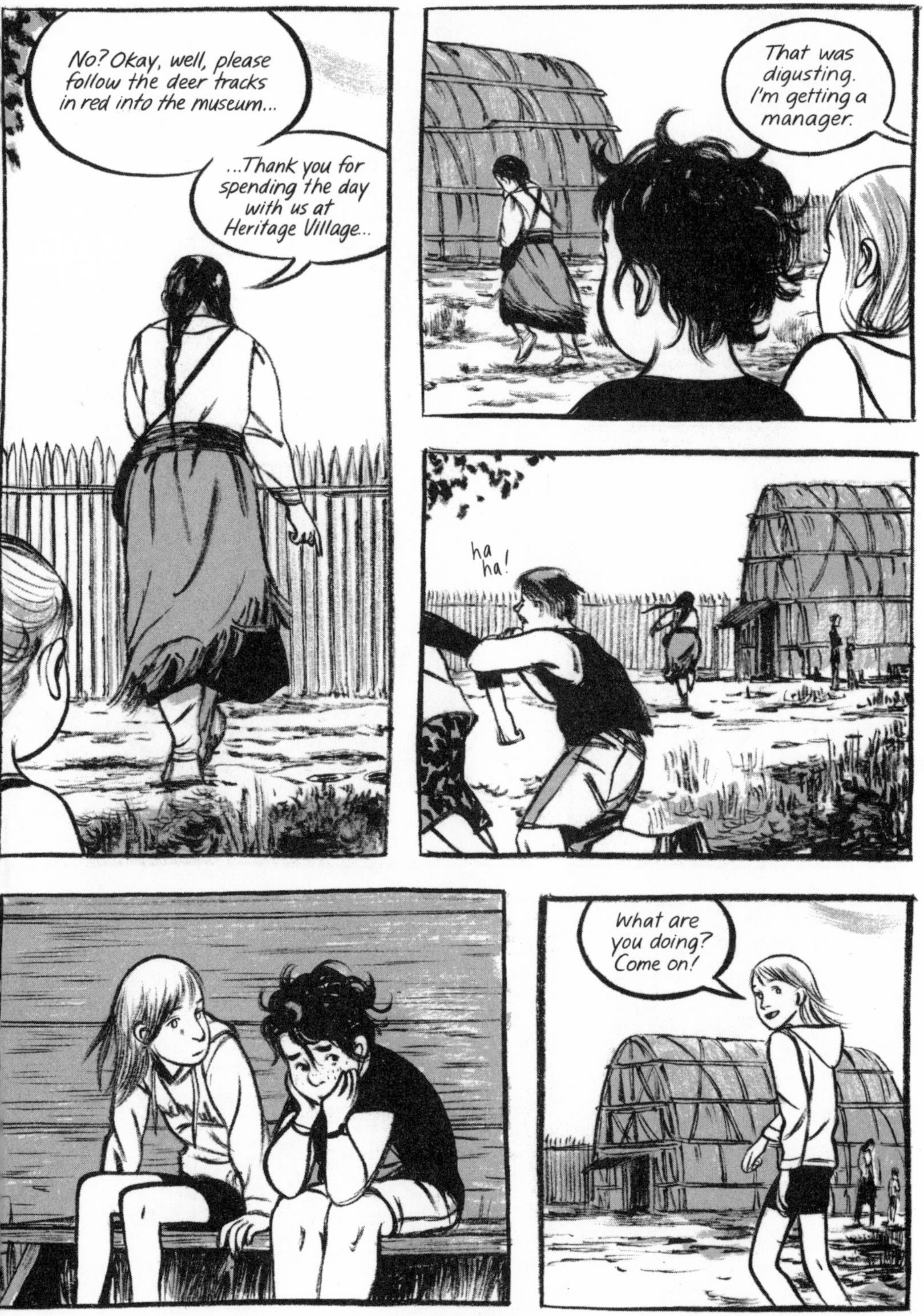
No? Okay, well, please follow the deer tracks in red into the museum...
...Thank you for spending the day with us at Heritage Village...
That was digusting. I'm getting a manager.
ha ha!
What are you doing? Come on!

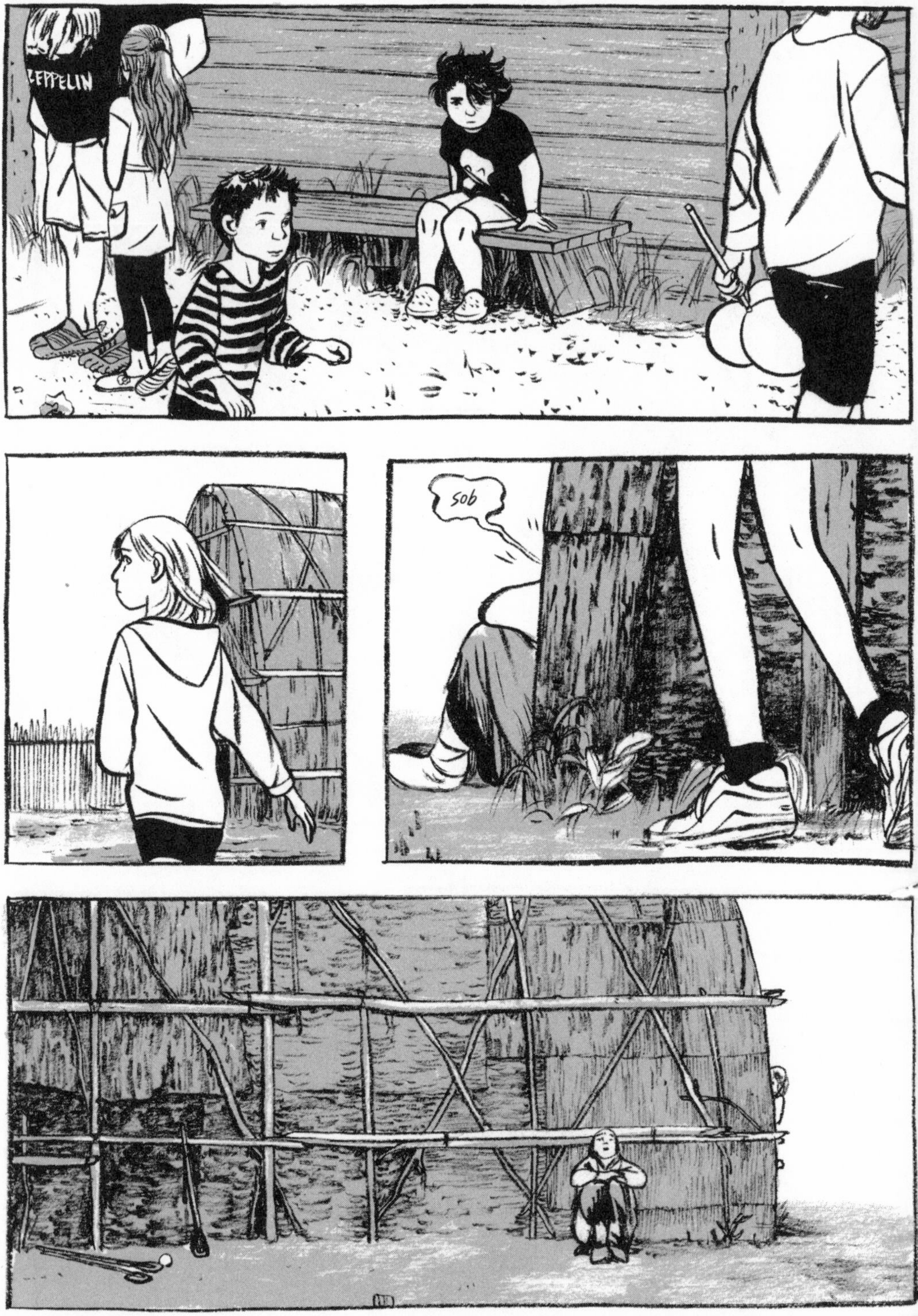
ZEPPELIN
sob

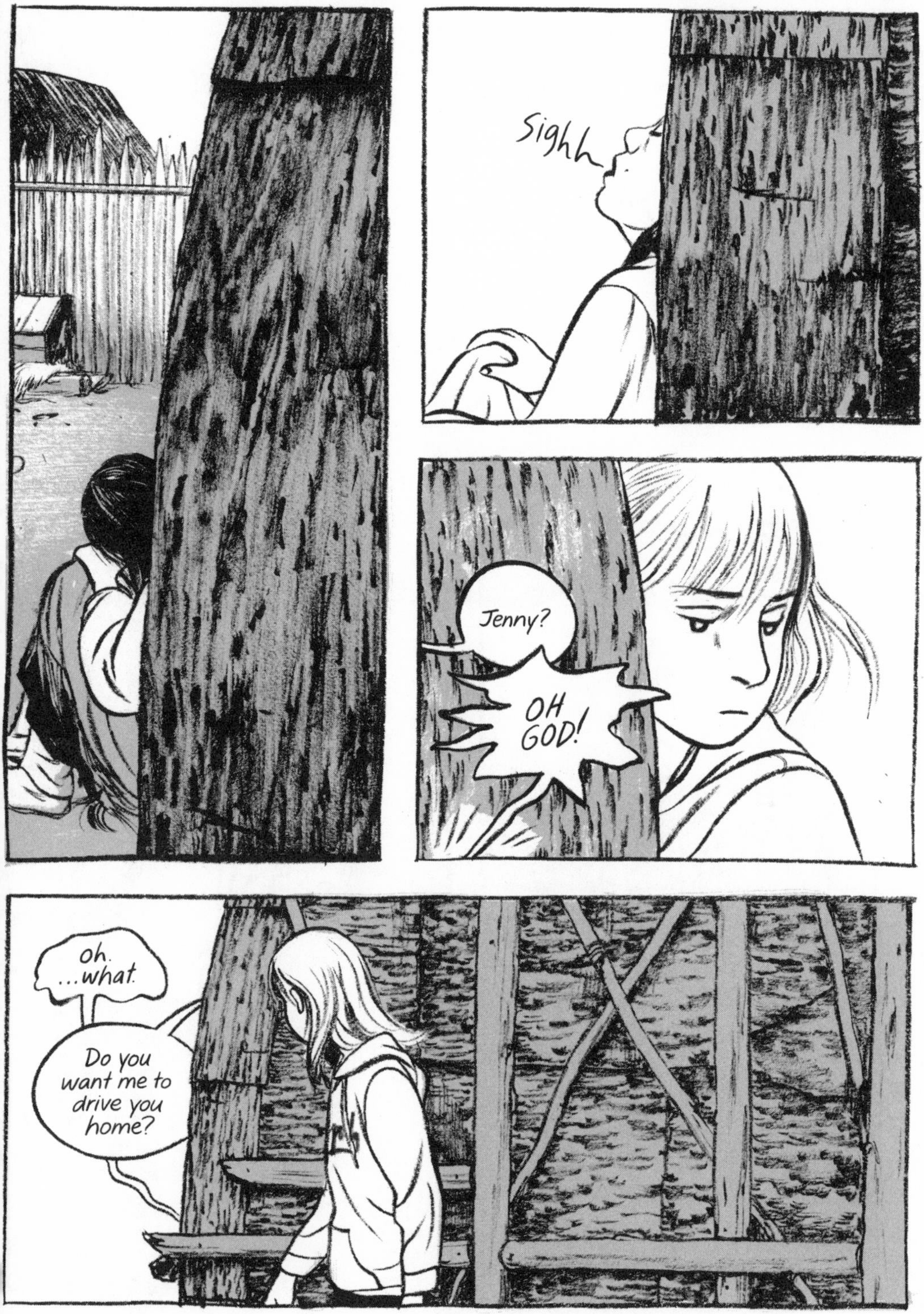
Sighh
Jenny?
OH GOD!
Oh. ...what.
Do you want me to drive you home?

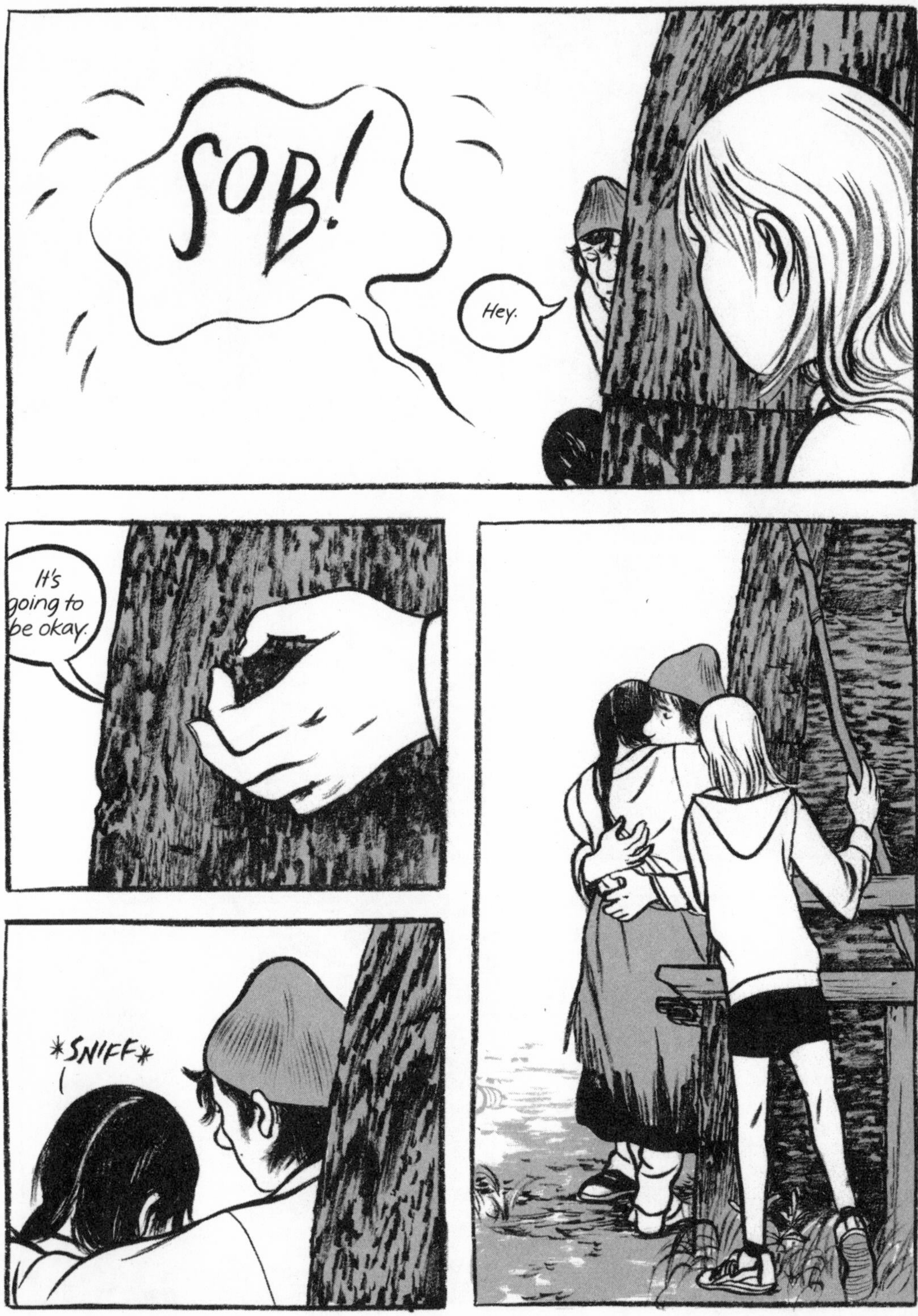
SOB!
Hey.
It's going to be okay.
SNIFF

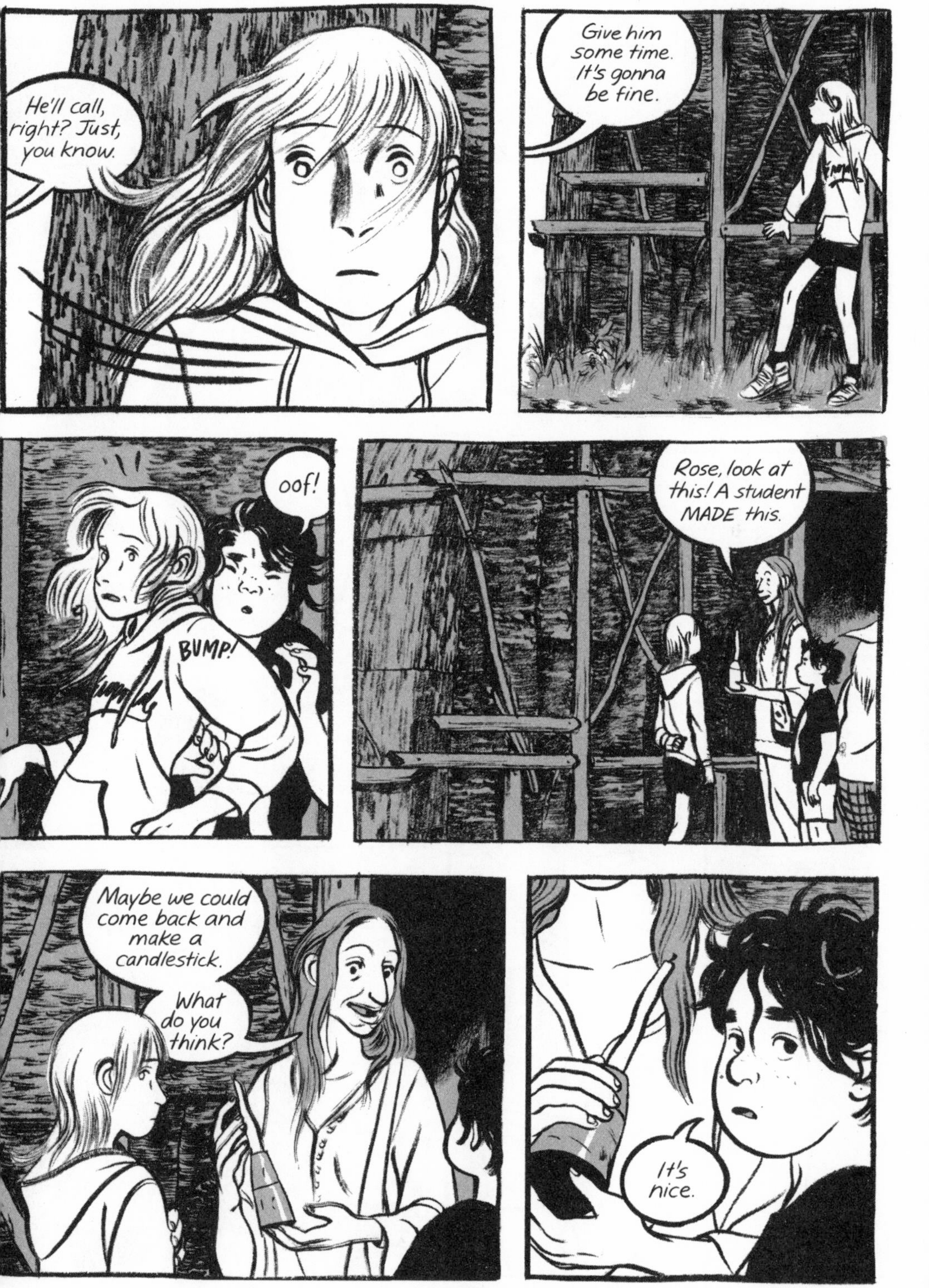
He'll call, right? Just, you know.
Give him some time. It's gonna be fine.
oof!
BUMP!
Rose, look at this! A student MADE this.
Maybe we could come back and make a candlestick.
What do you think?
It's nice.

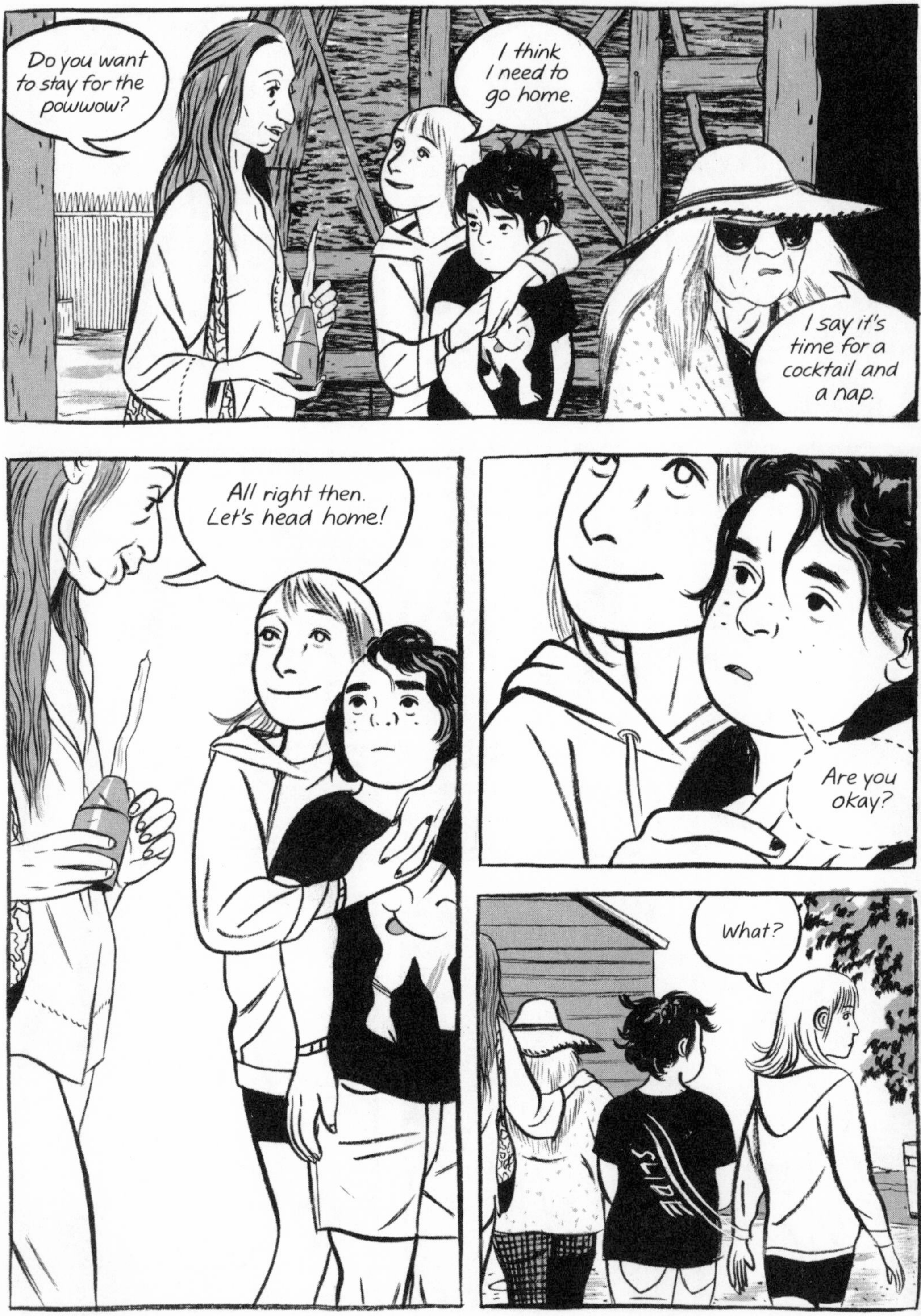
Do you want to stay for the powwow?
I think I need to go home.
I say it's time for a cocktail and a nap.
All right then. Let's head home!
Are you okay?
What?
SLIDE

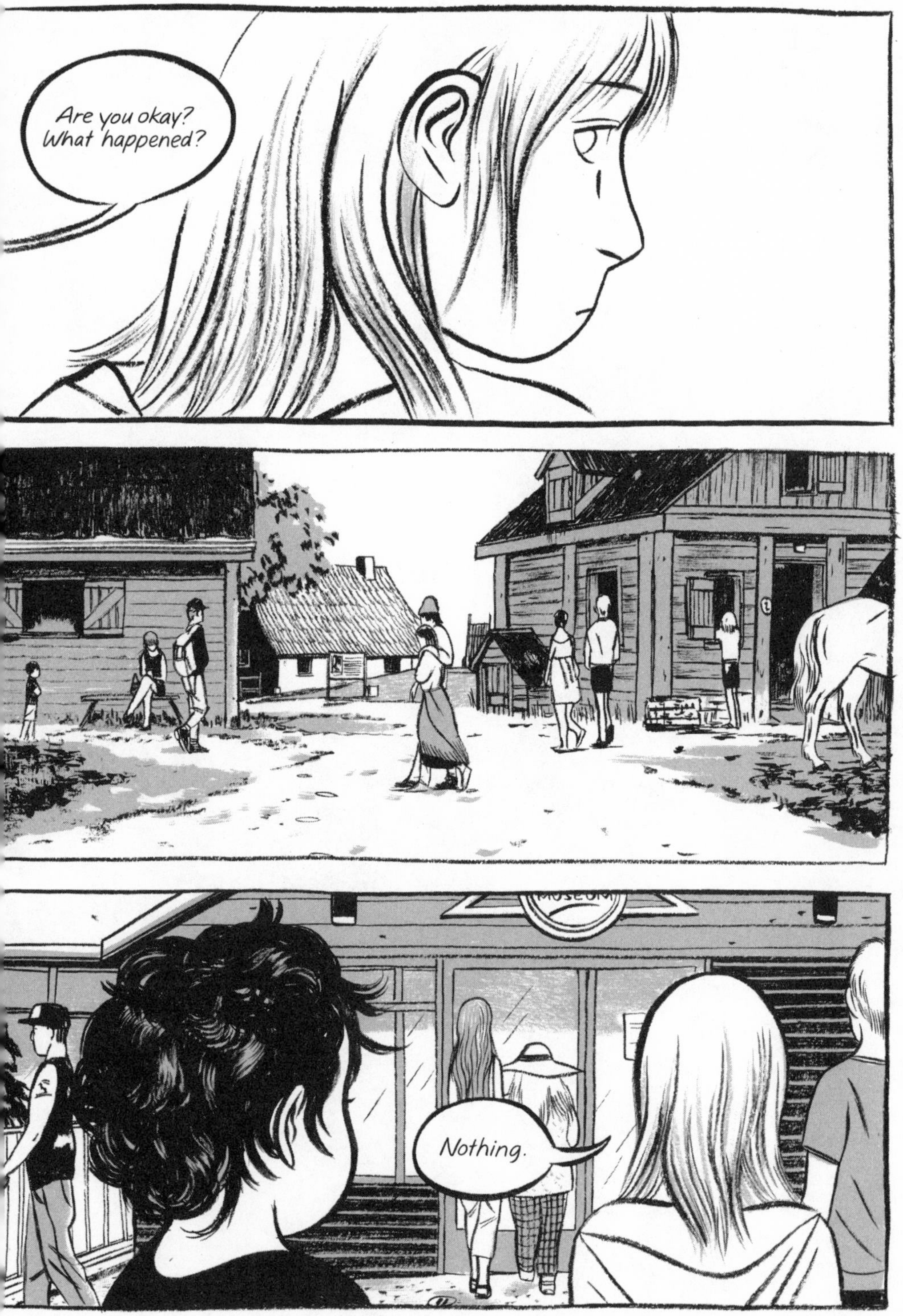
Are you okay? What happened?
Nothing.

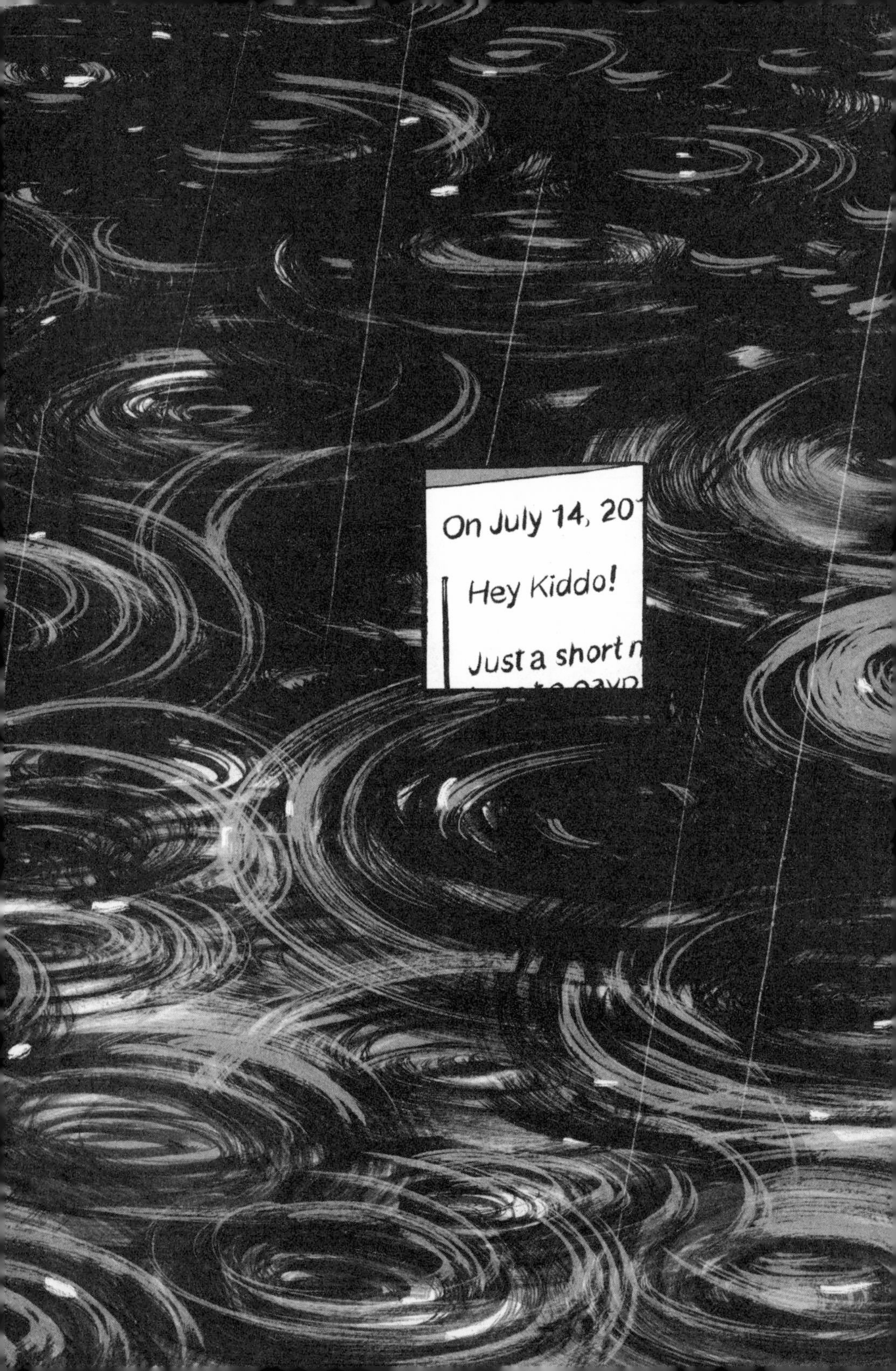
On July 14, 20
Hey Kiddo!
Just a short

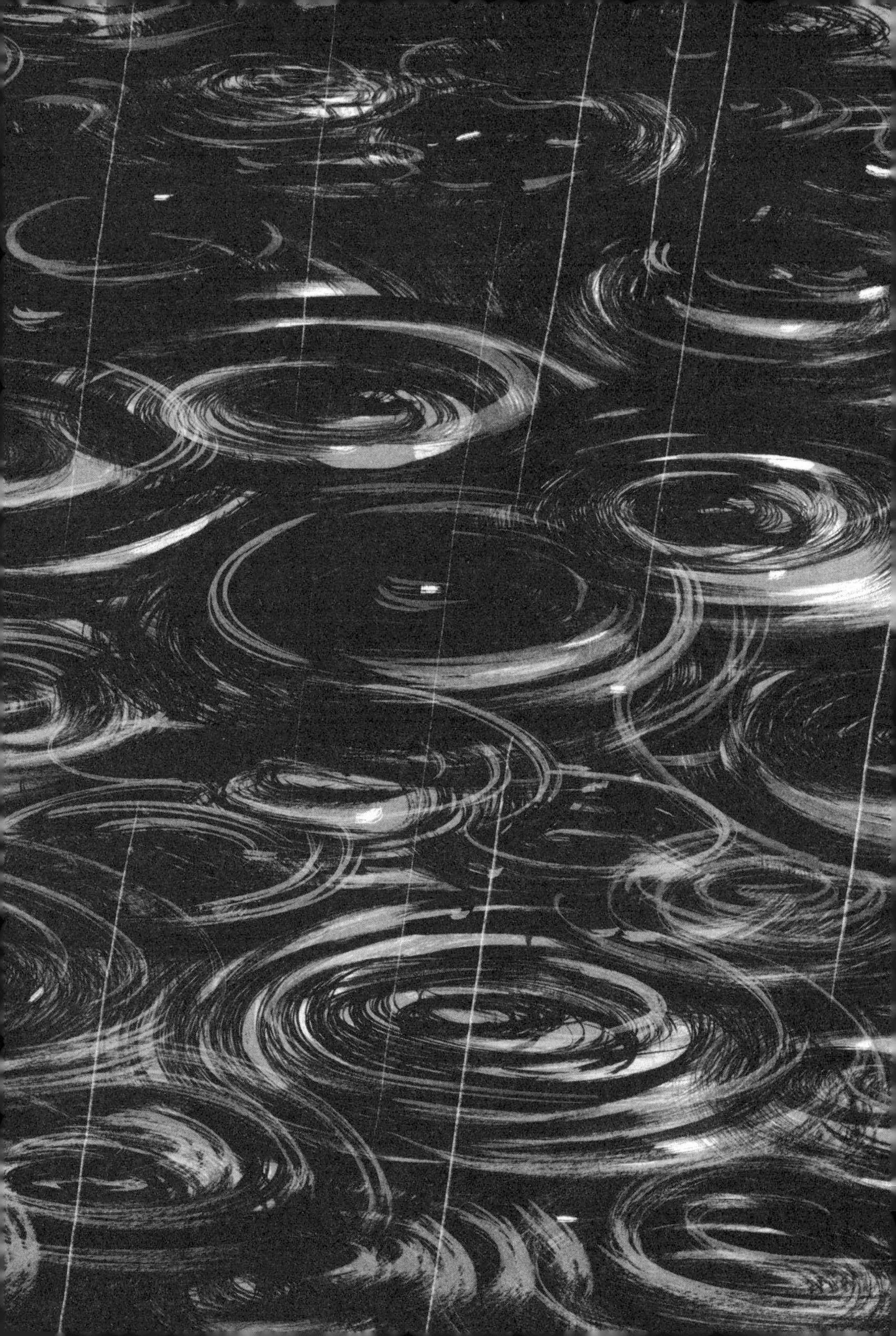

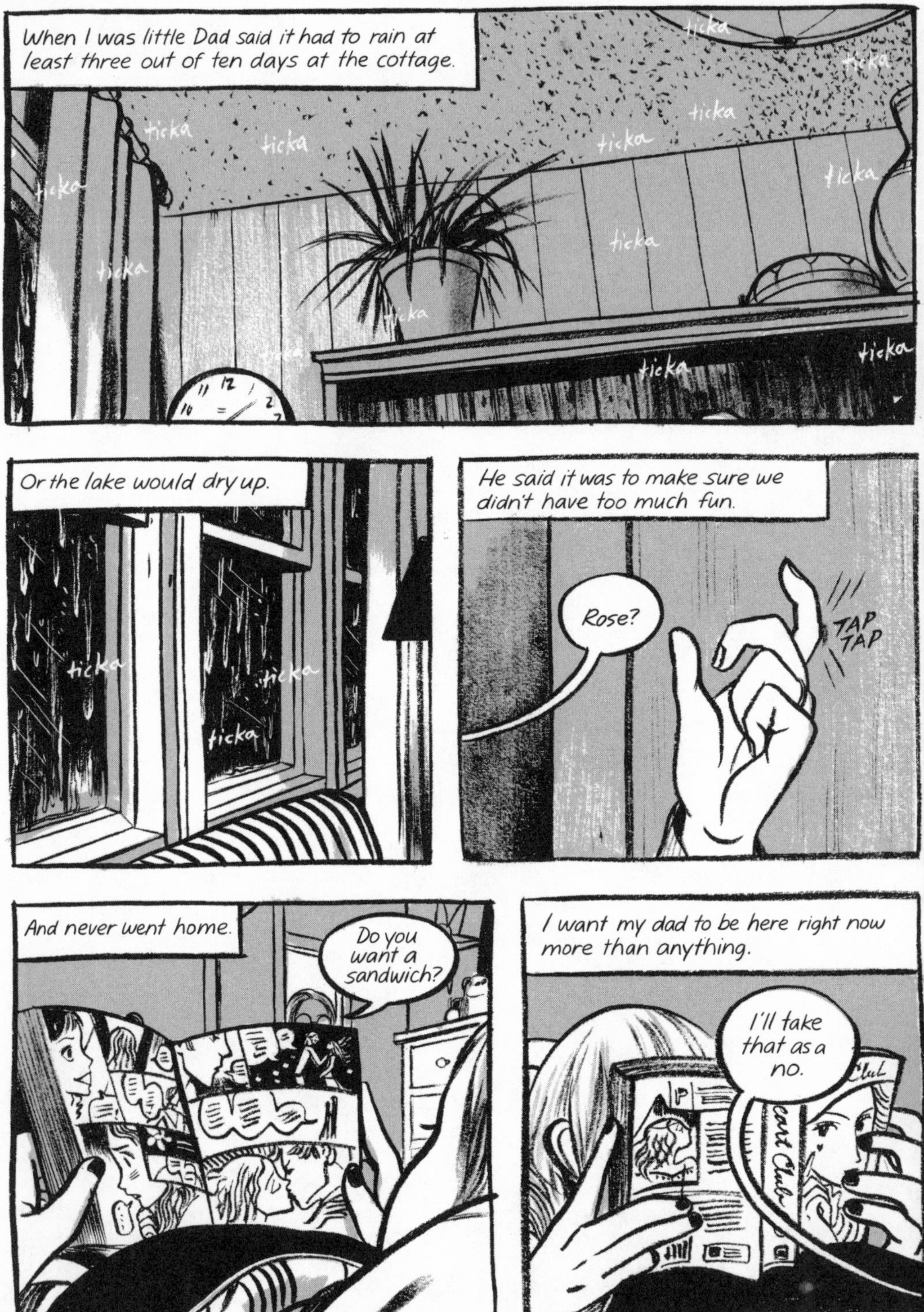
When I was little Dad said it had to rain at least three out of ten days at the cottage.
ticka
ticka
ticka
ticka
ticka
ticka
ticka
ticka
ticka
ticka
ticka
ticka
Or the lake would dry up.
ticka
ticka
ticka
He said it was to make sure we didn't have too much fun.
Rose?
TAP TAP
And never went home.
Do you want a sandwich?
I want my dad to be here right now more than anything.
I'll take that as a no.

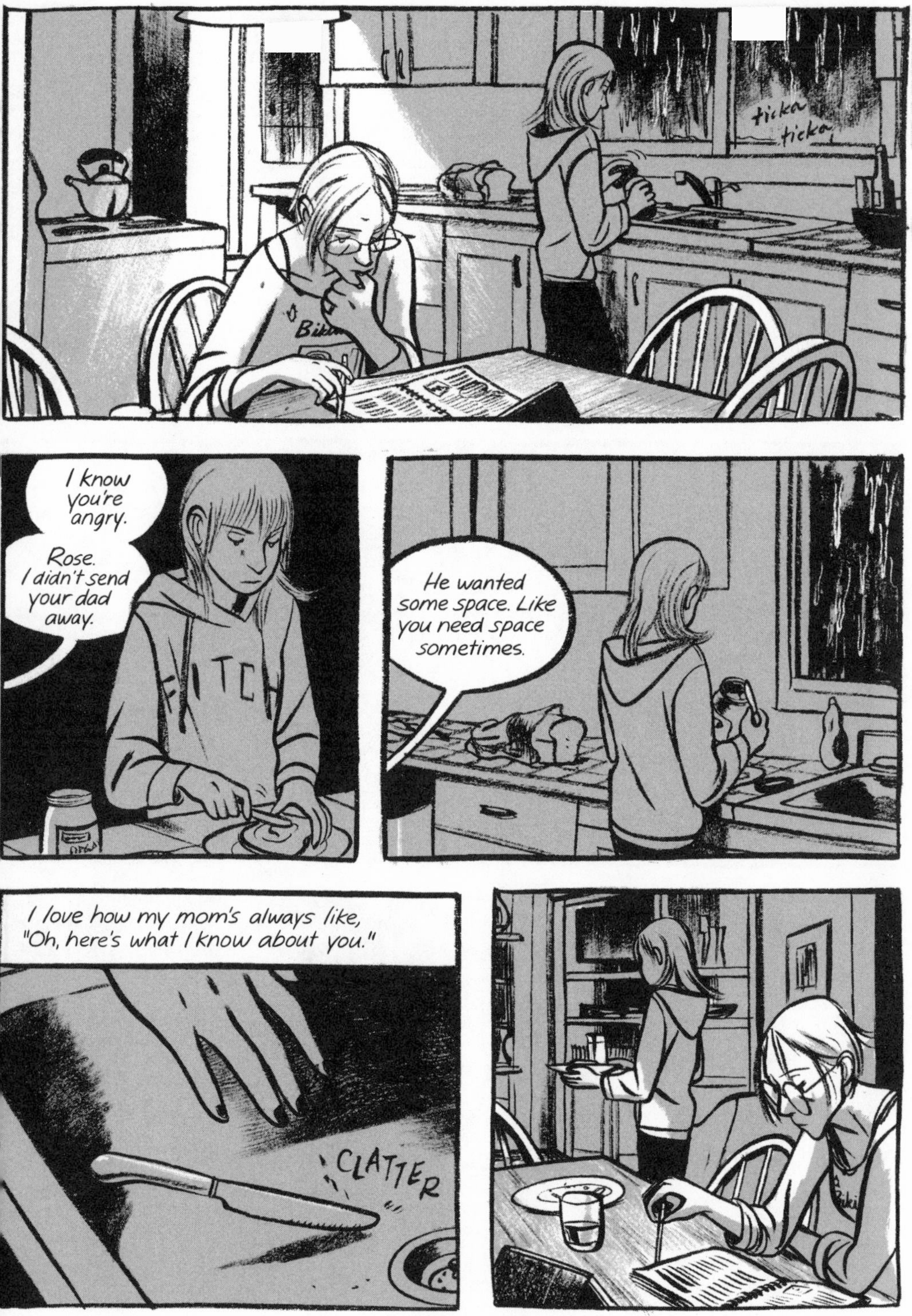
ticka ticka
I know you're angry.
Rose. I didn't send your dad away.
He wanted some space. Like you need space sometimes.
I love how my mom's always like, "Oh, here's what I know about you."
CLATTER

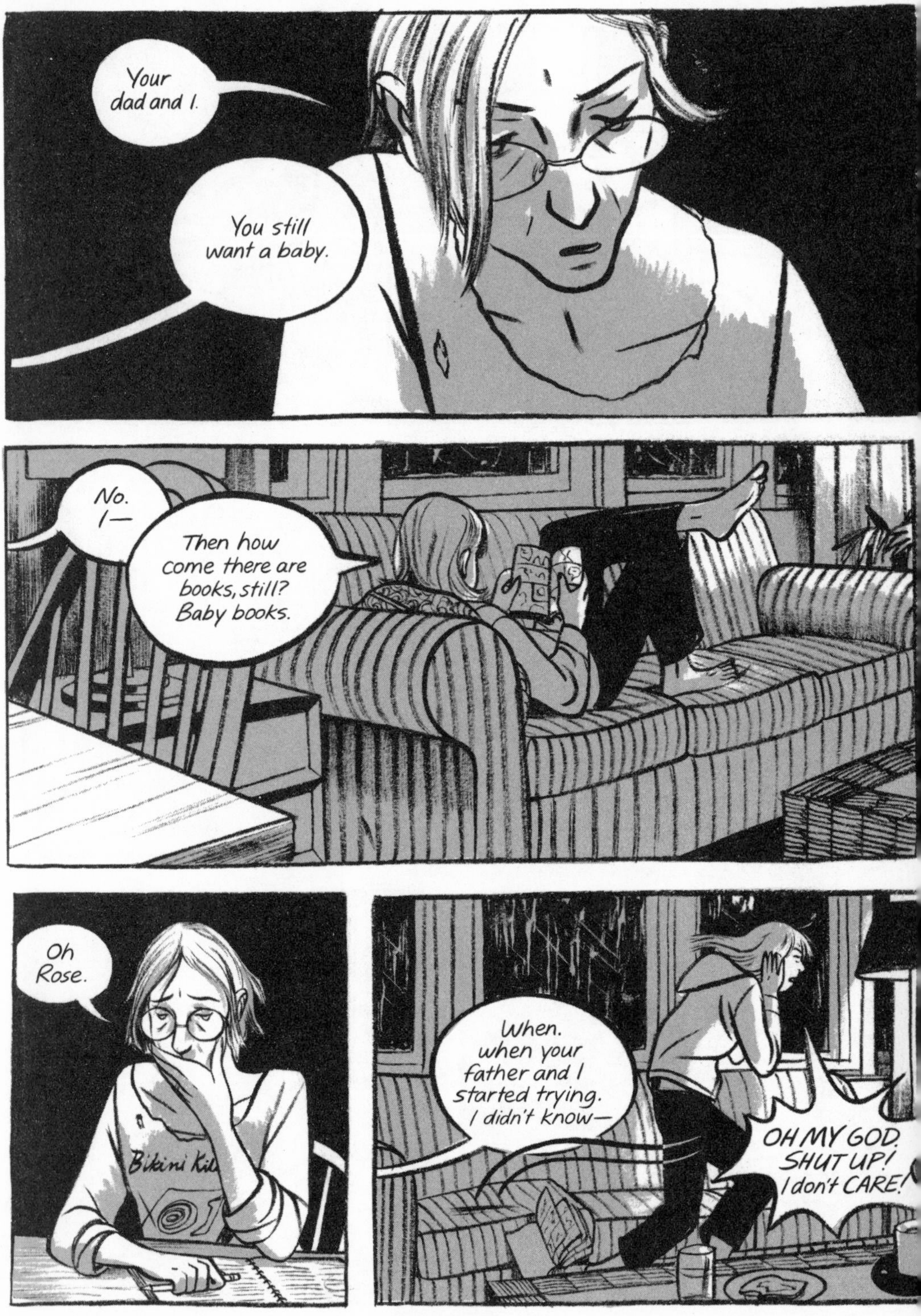
Your dad and I.
You still want a baby.
No. I—
Then how come there are books, still? Baby books.
Oh Rose.
When. when your father and I started trying. I didn't know—
OH MY GOD. SHUT UP! I don't CARE!

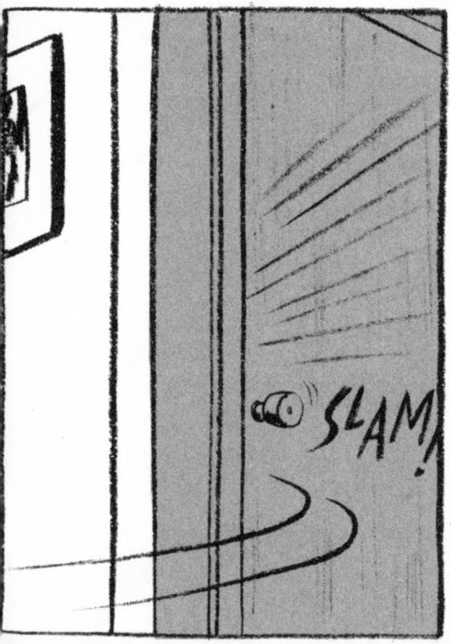
SLAM!

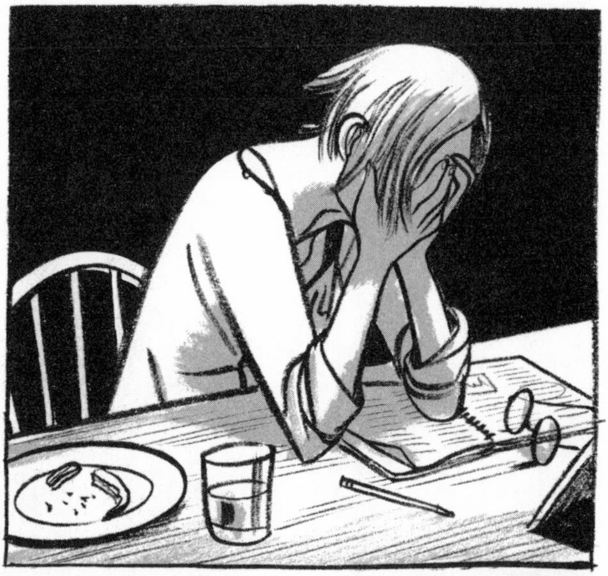

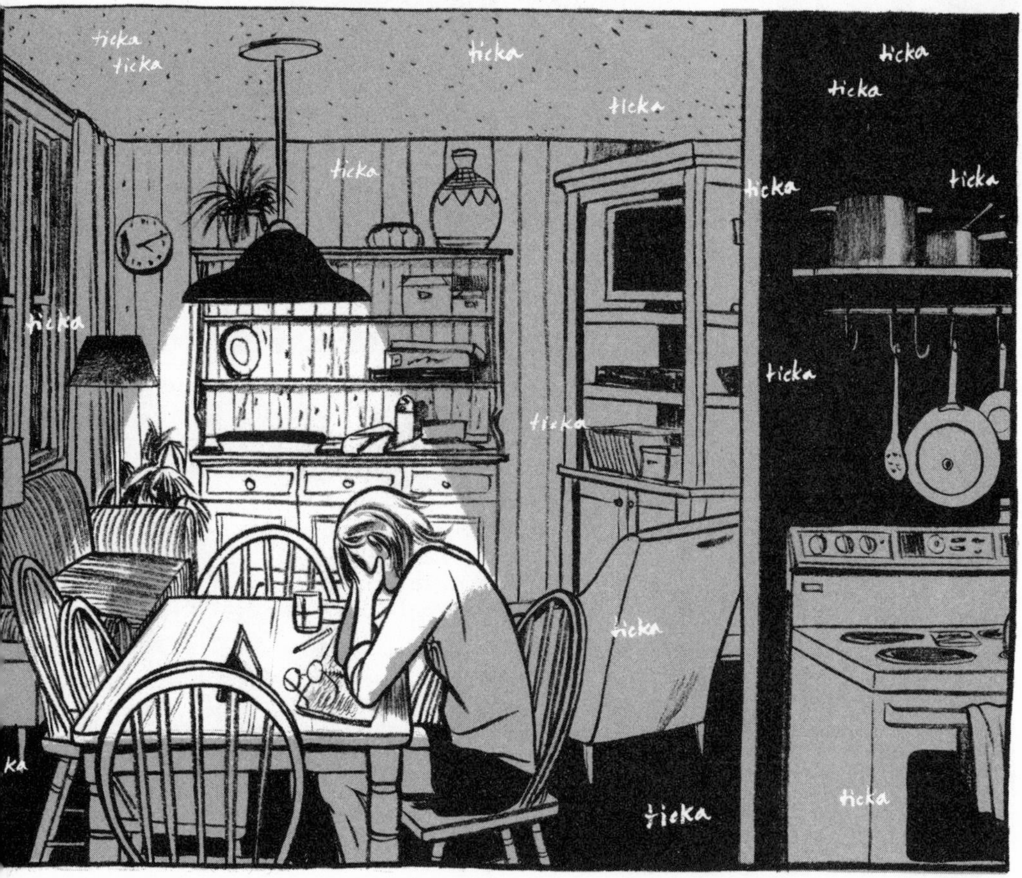
ticka
ticka
ticka
ticka
ticka
ticka
ticka
ticka
ticka
ticka
ticka
ticka
ticka
ka
ticka
ticka

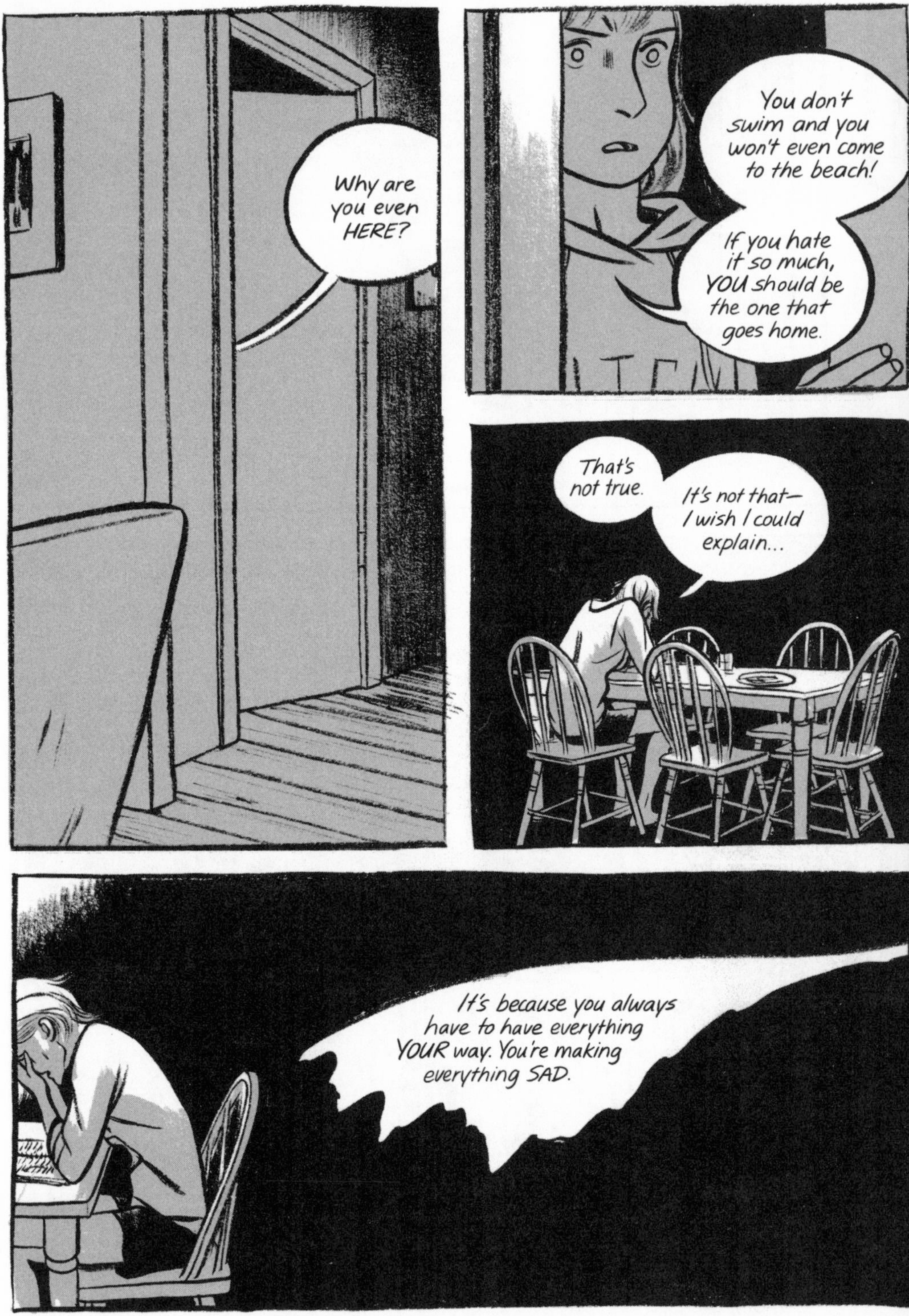
Why are you even HERE?
You don't swim and you won't even come to the beach!
If you hate it so much, YOU should be the one that goes home.
That's not true.
It's not that— I wish I could explain...
It's because you always have to have everything YOUR way. You're making everything SAD.

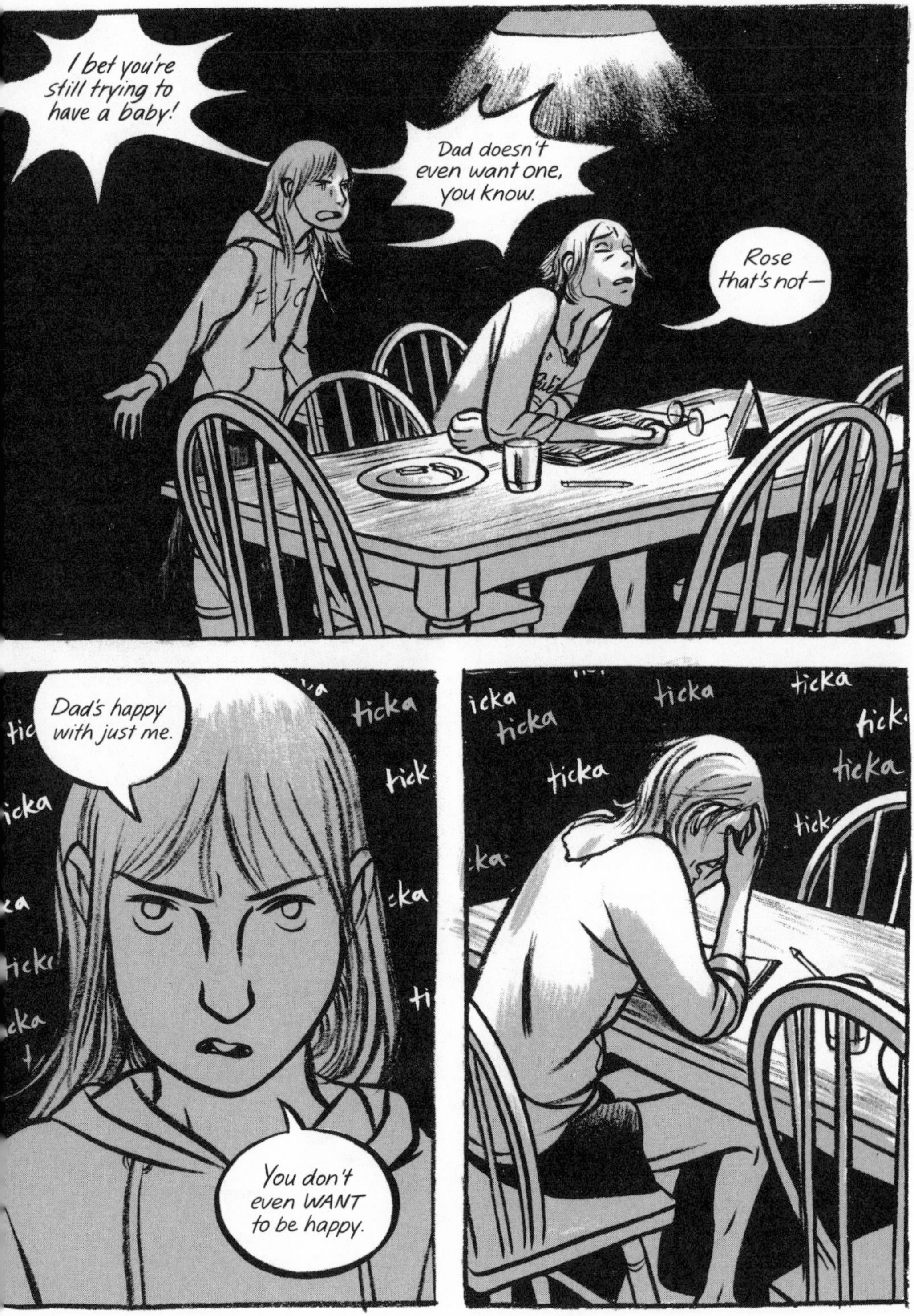
I bet you're still trying to have a baby!
Dad doesn't even want one, you know.
Rose that's not—
Dad's happy with just me.
You don't even WANT to be happy.
ticka ticka ticka ticka ticka ticka ticka

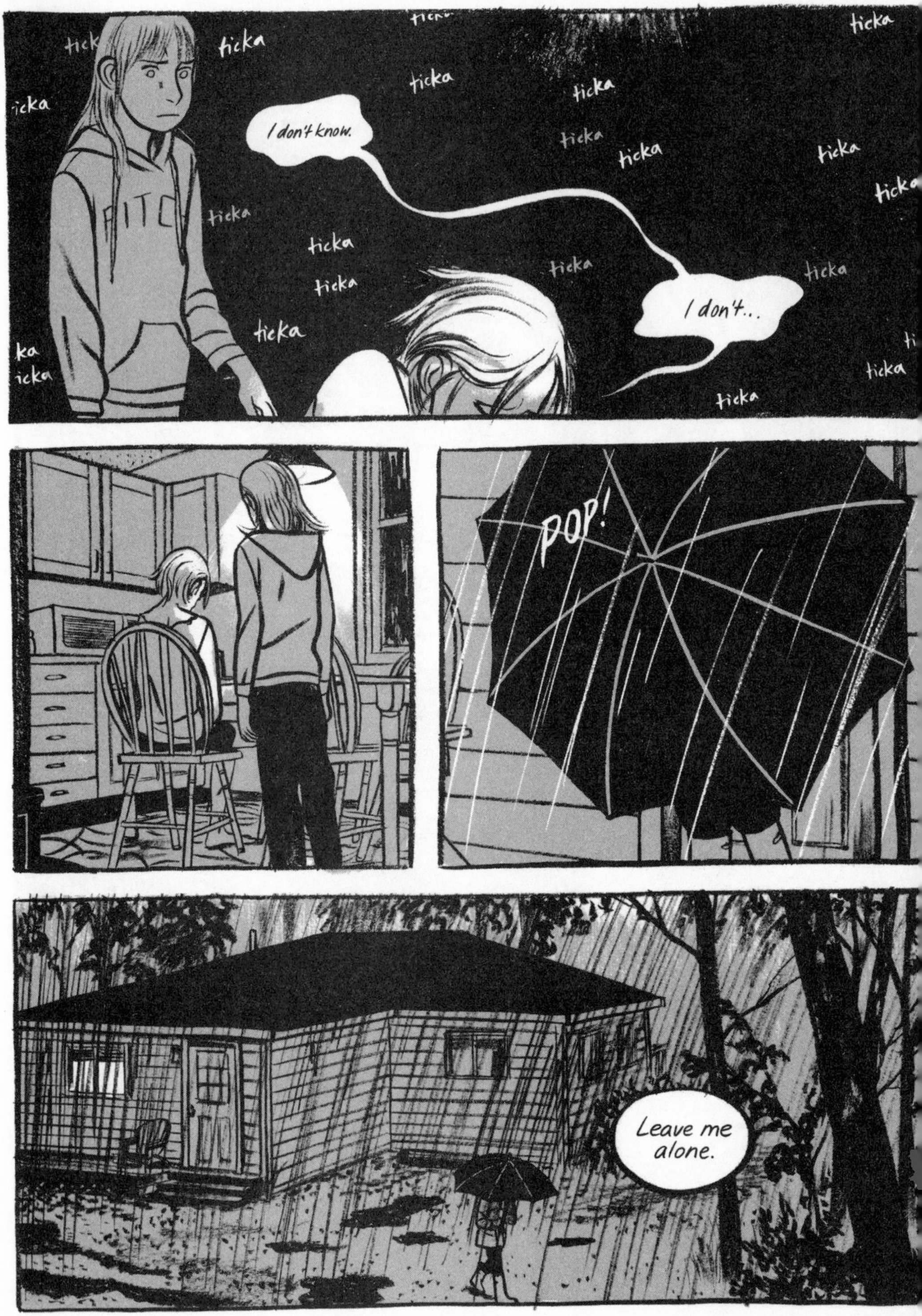
ticka
ticka
ticka
ticka
I don't know.
ticka
ticka
ticka
ticka
ticka
ticka
I don't...
ticka
ticka
ticka
POP!
Leave me
alone.

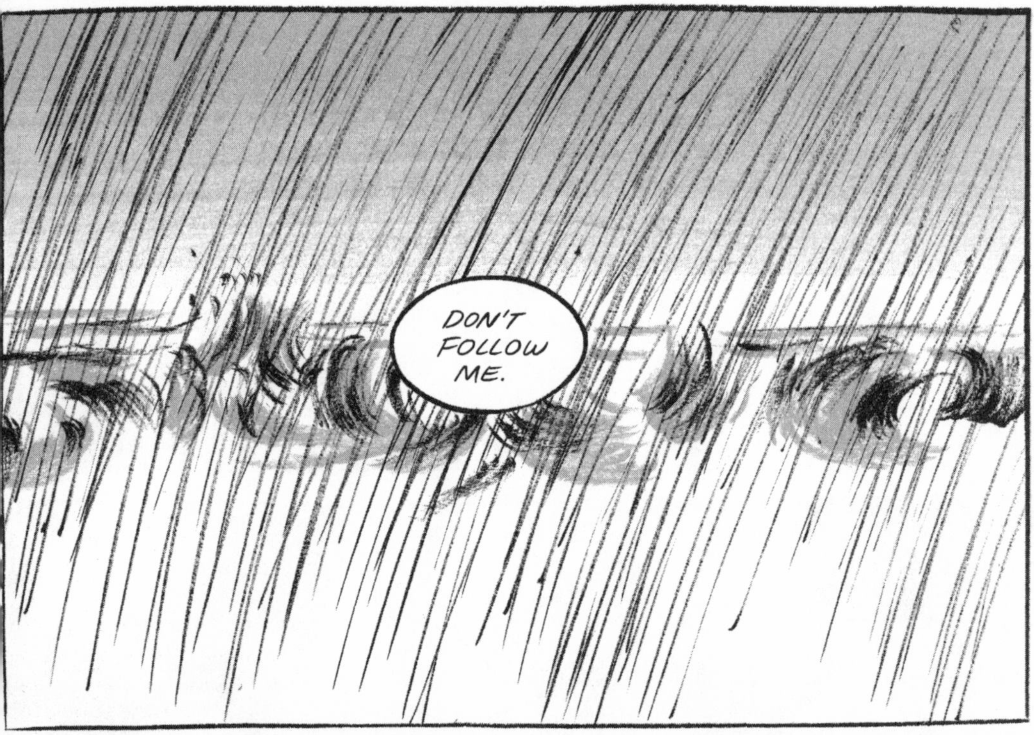
DON'T FOLLOW ME.

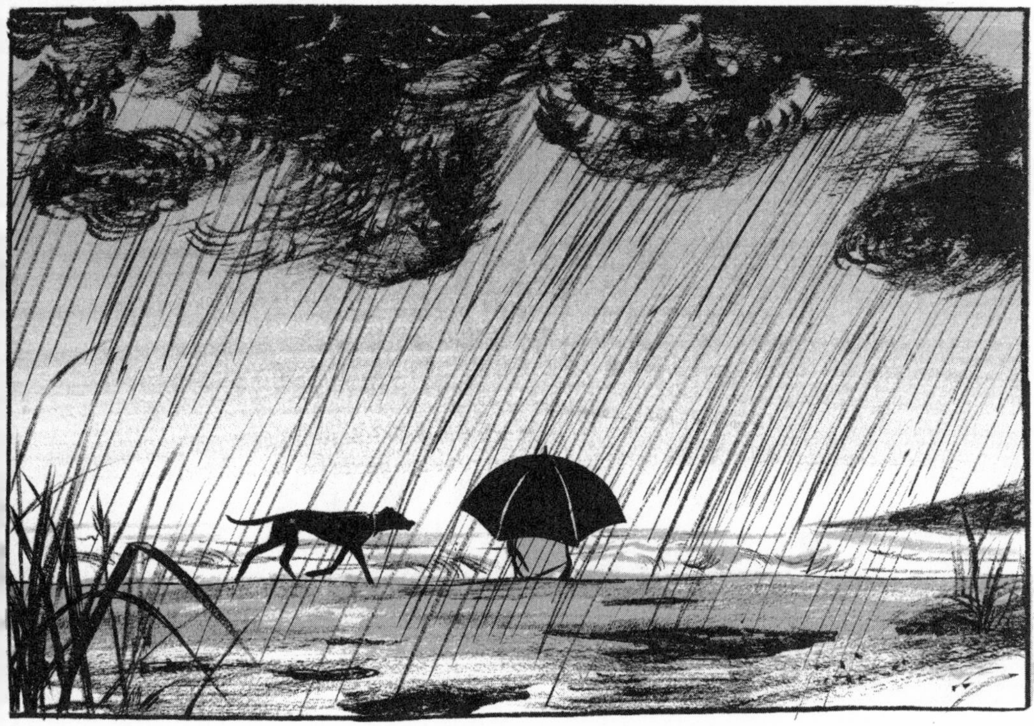

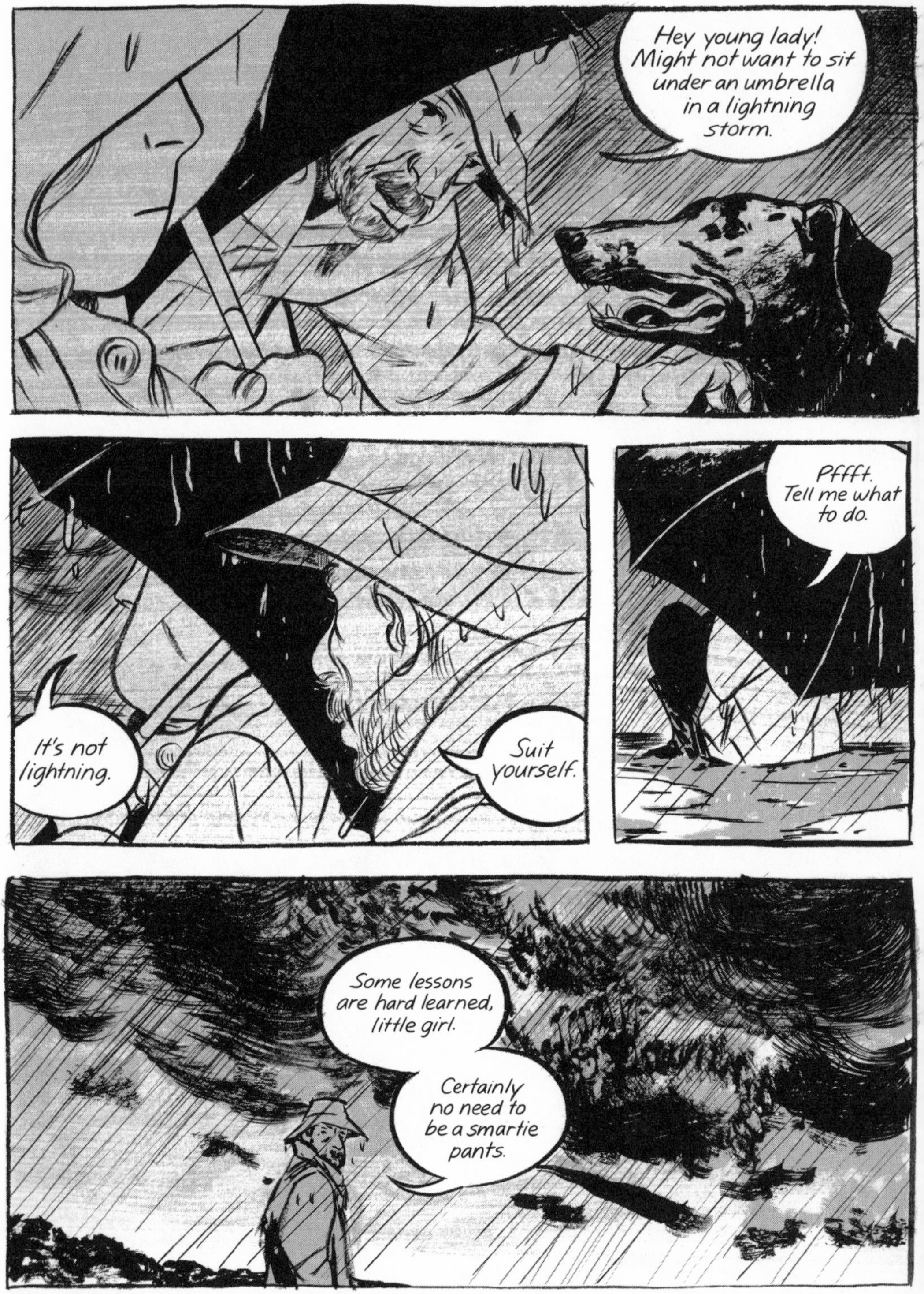
Hey young lady! Might not want to sit under an umbrella in a lightning storm.
It's not lightning.
Suit yourself.
Pffft. Tell me what to do.
Some lessons are hard learned, little girl.
Certainly no need to be a smartie pants.

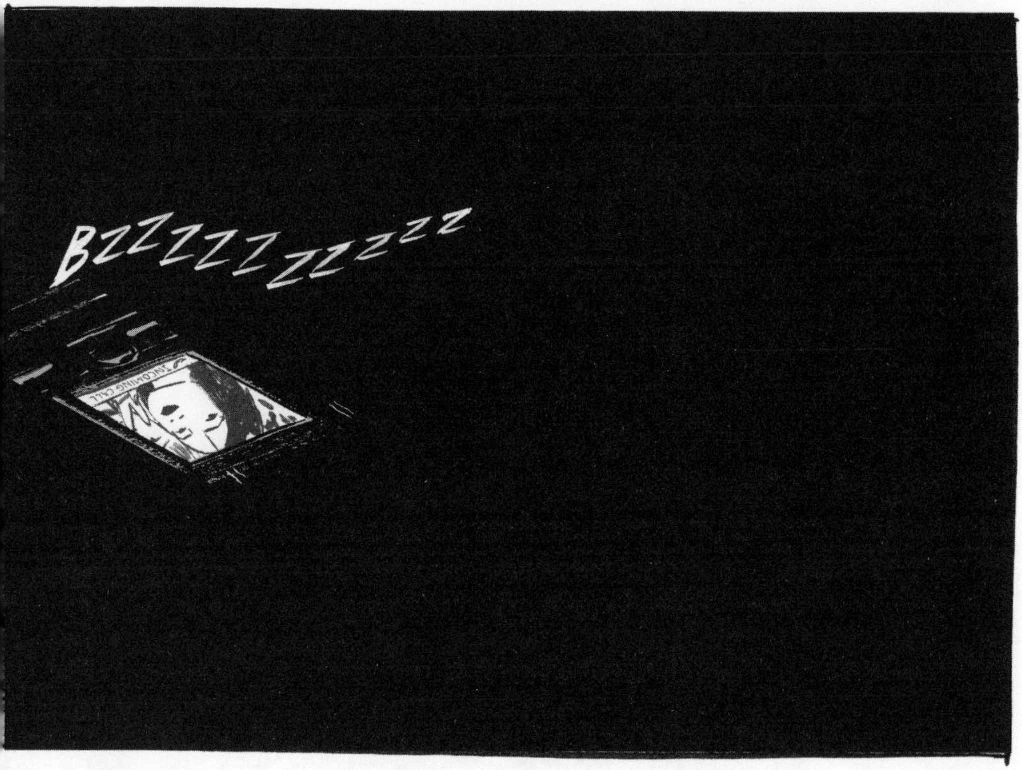
BZZZZZZZZZZZ
INCOMING CALL

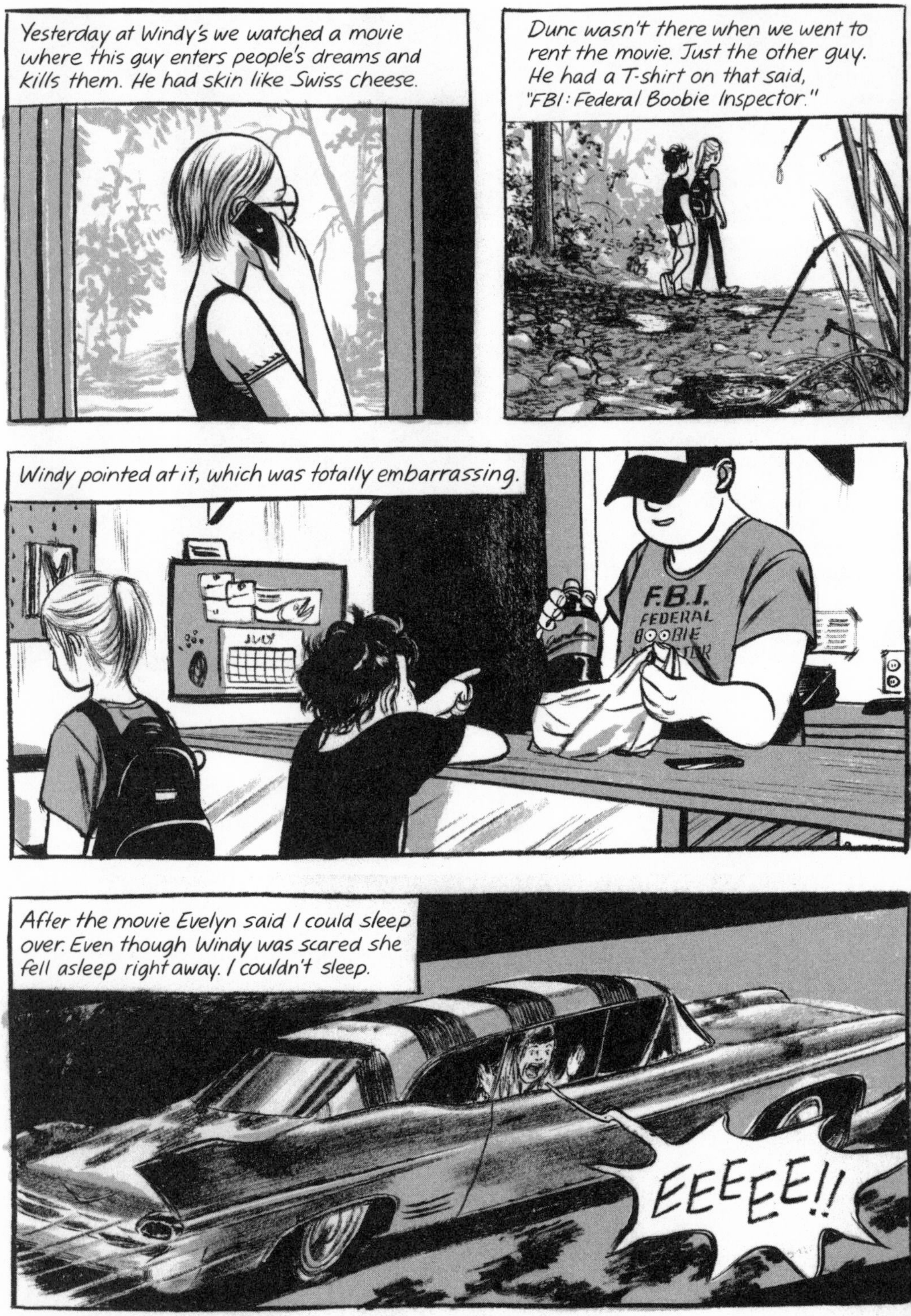
Yesterday at Windy's we watched a movie where this guy enters people's dreams and kills them. He had skin like Swiss cheese.
Dunc wasn't there when we went to rent the movie. Just the other guy. He had a T-shirt on that said, "FBI: Federal Boobie Inspector."
Windy pointed at it, which was totally embarrassing.
F.B.I.
FEDERAL
After the movie Evelyn said I could sleep over. Even though Windy was scared she fell asleep right away. I couldn't sleep.
EEEEE!!

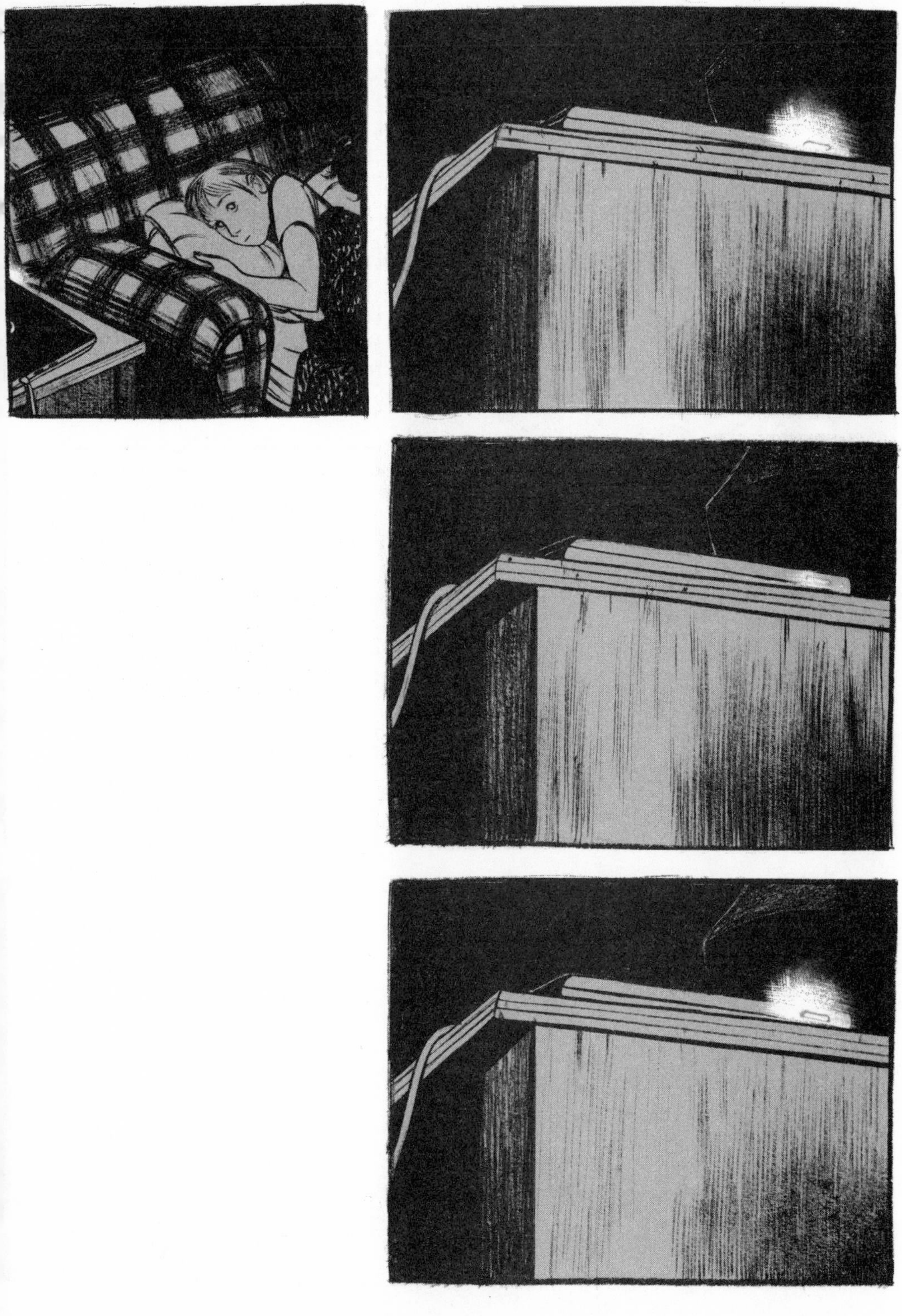

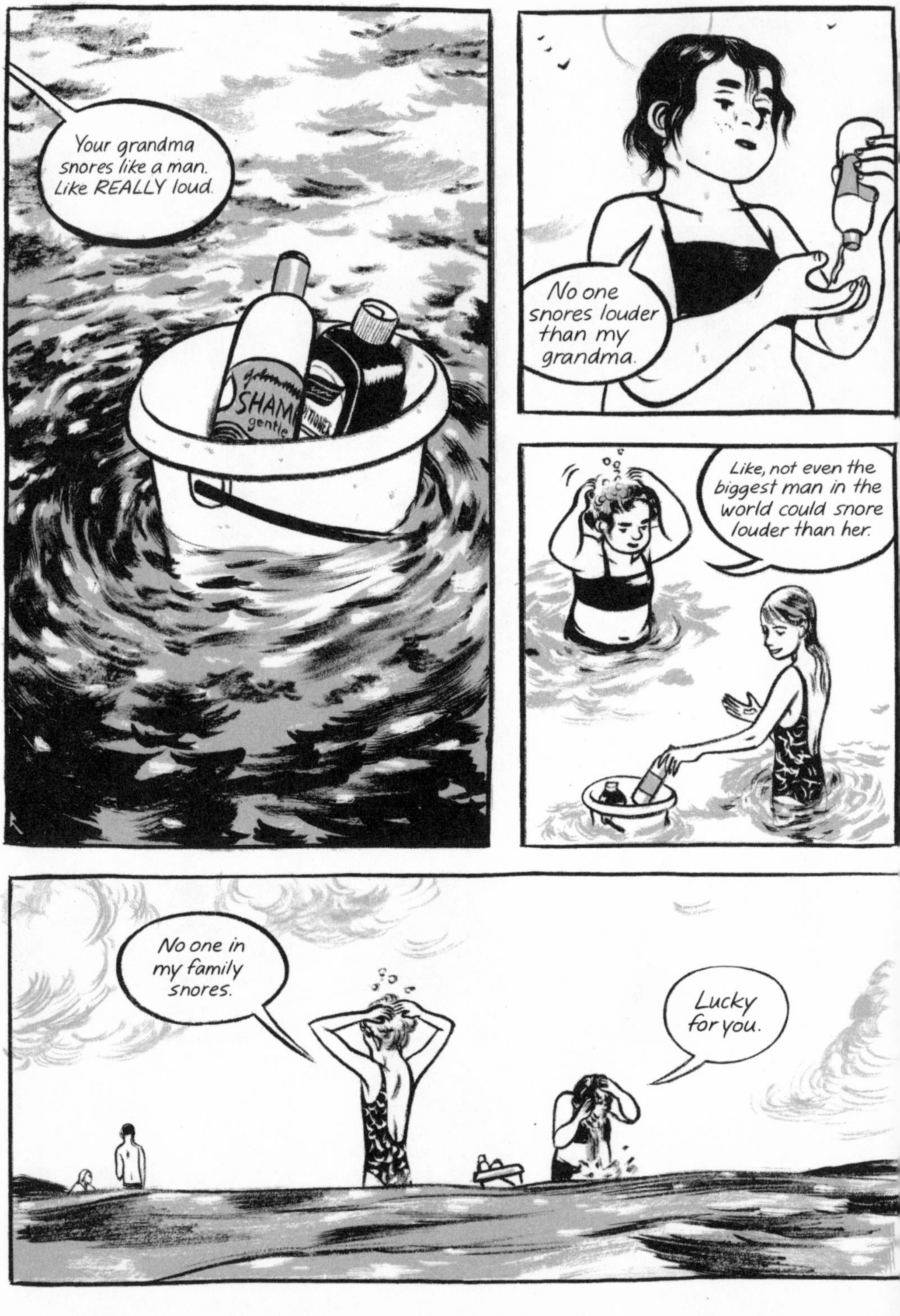
Your grandma snores like a man. Like REALLY loud.
No one snores louder than my grandma.
Like, not even the biggest man in the world could snore louder than her.
No one in my family snores.
Lucky for you.

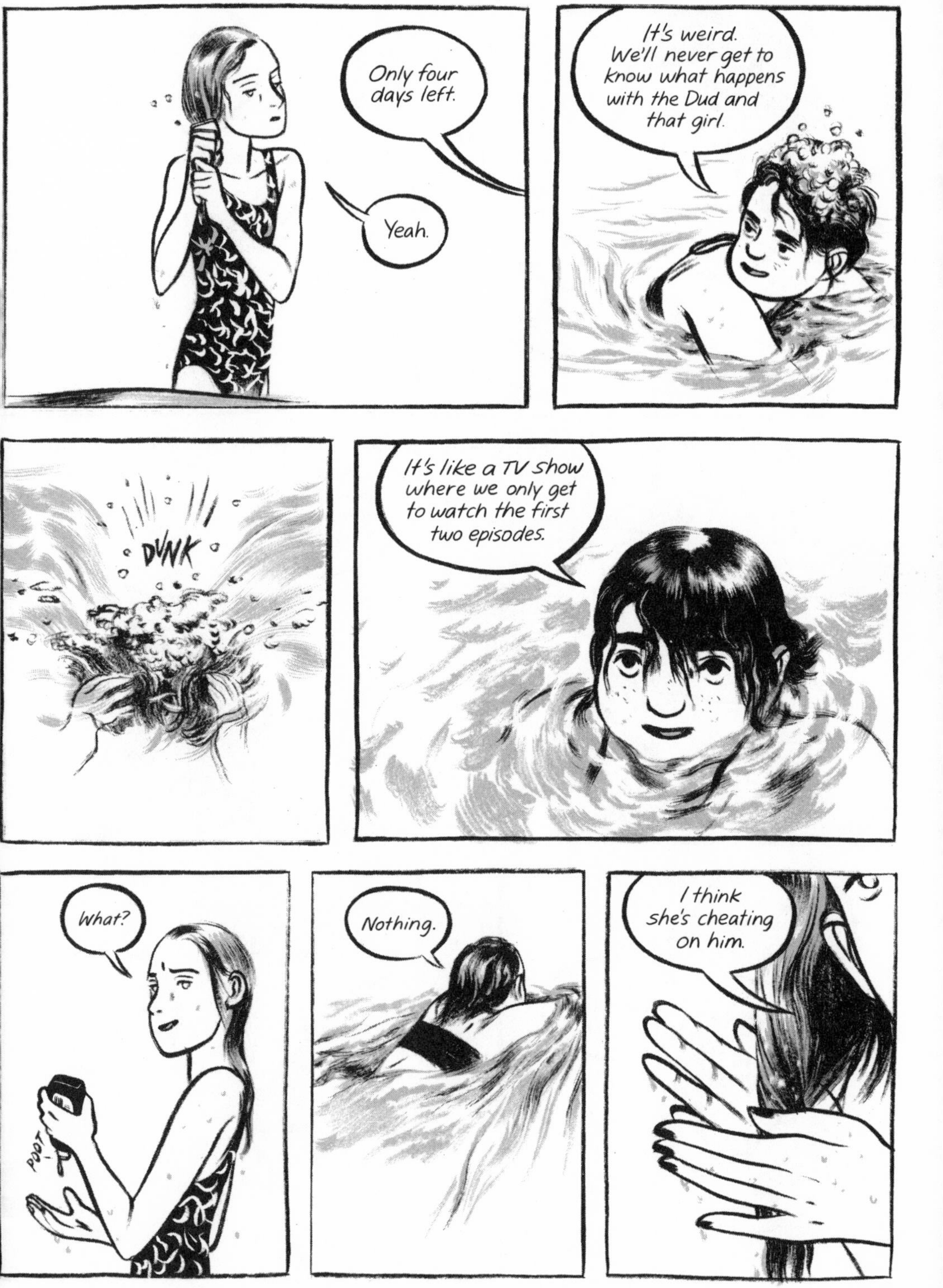

Only four days left.
Yeah.
It's weird. We'll never get to know what happens with the Dud and that girl.
DUNK
It's like a TV show where we only get to watch the first two episodes.
What?
POOT
Nothing.
I think she's cheating on him.

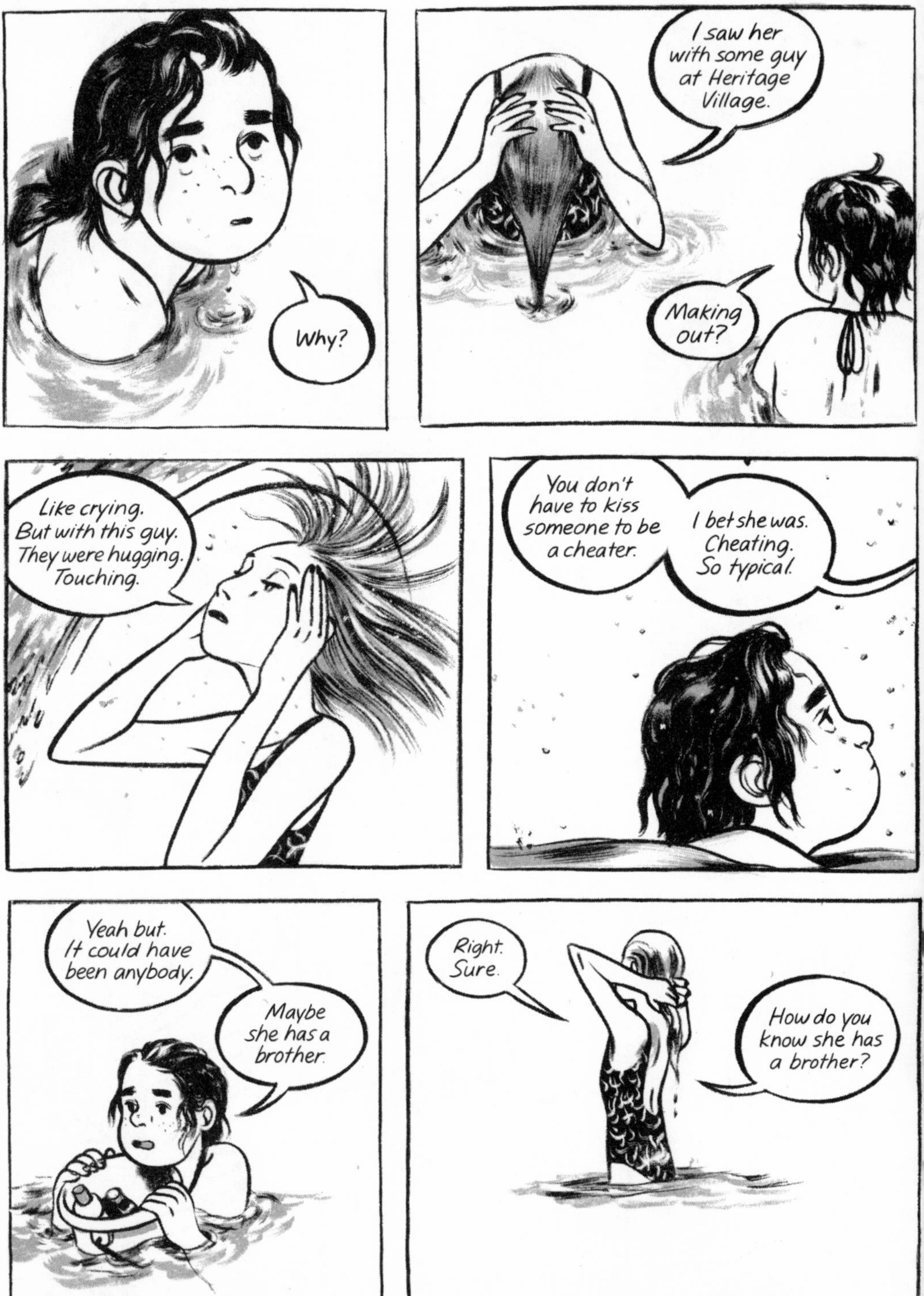
Why?
I saw her with some guy at Heritage Village.
Making out?
Like crying. But with this guy. They were hugging. Touching.
You don't have to kiss someone to be a cheater.
I bet she was. Cheating. So typical.
Yeah but. It could have been anybody.
Maybe she has a brother.
Right. Sure.
How do you know she has a brother?

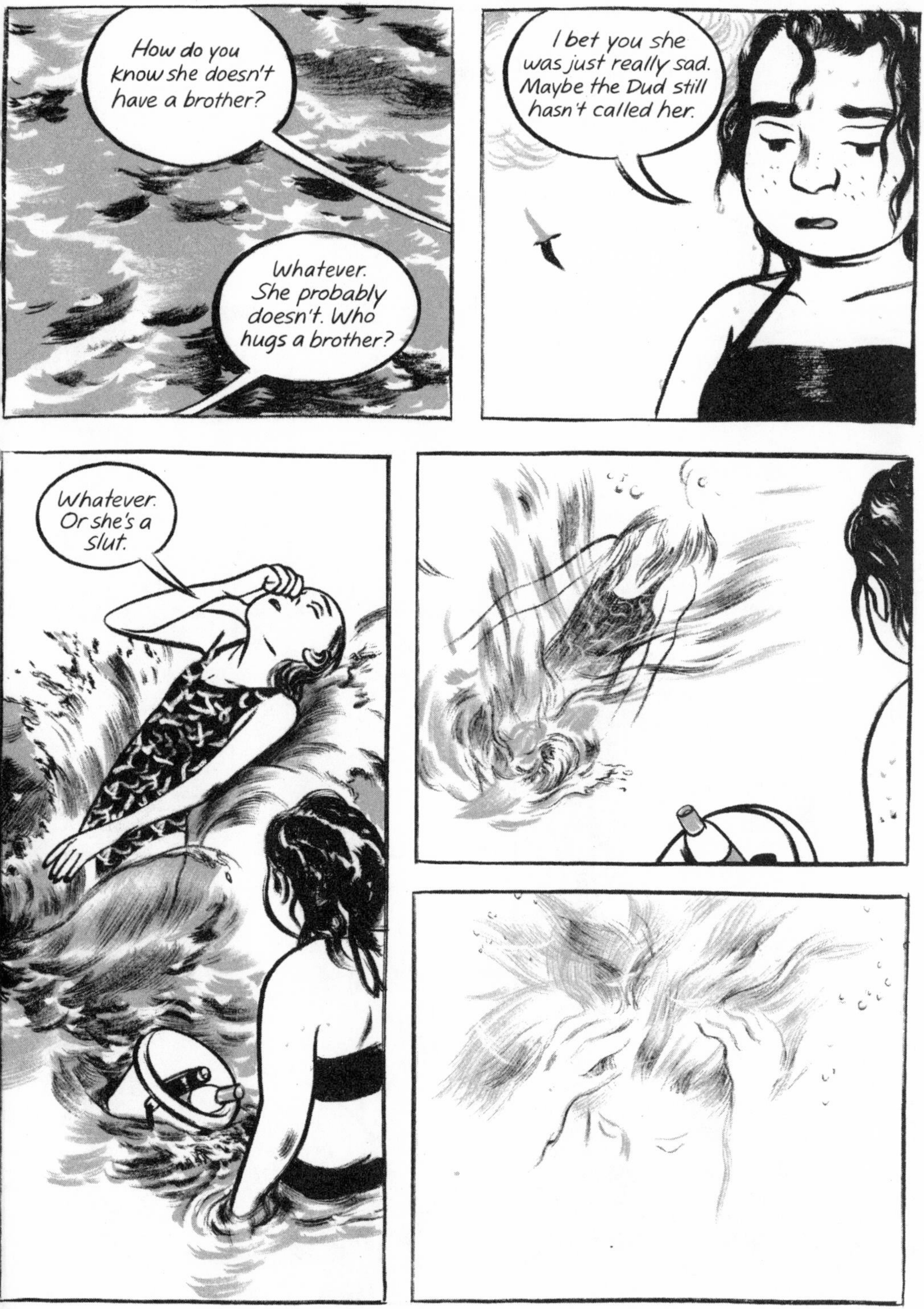
How do you know she doesn't have a brother?
Whatever. She probably doesn't. Who hugs a brother?
I bet you she was just really sad. Maybe the Dud still hasn't called her.
Whatever. Or she's a slut.

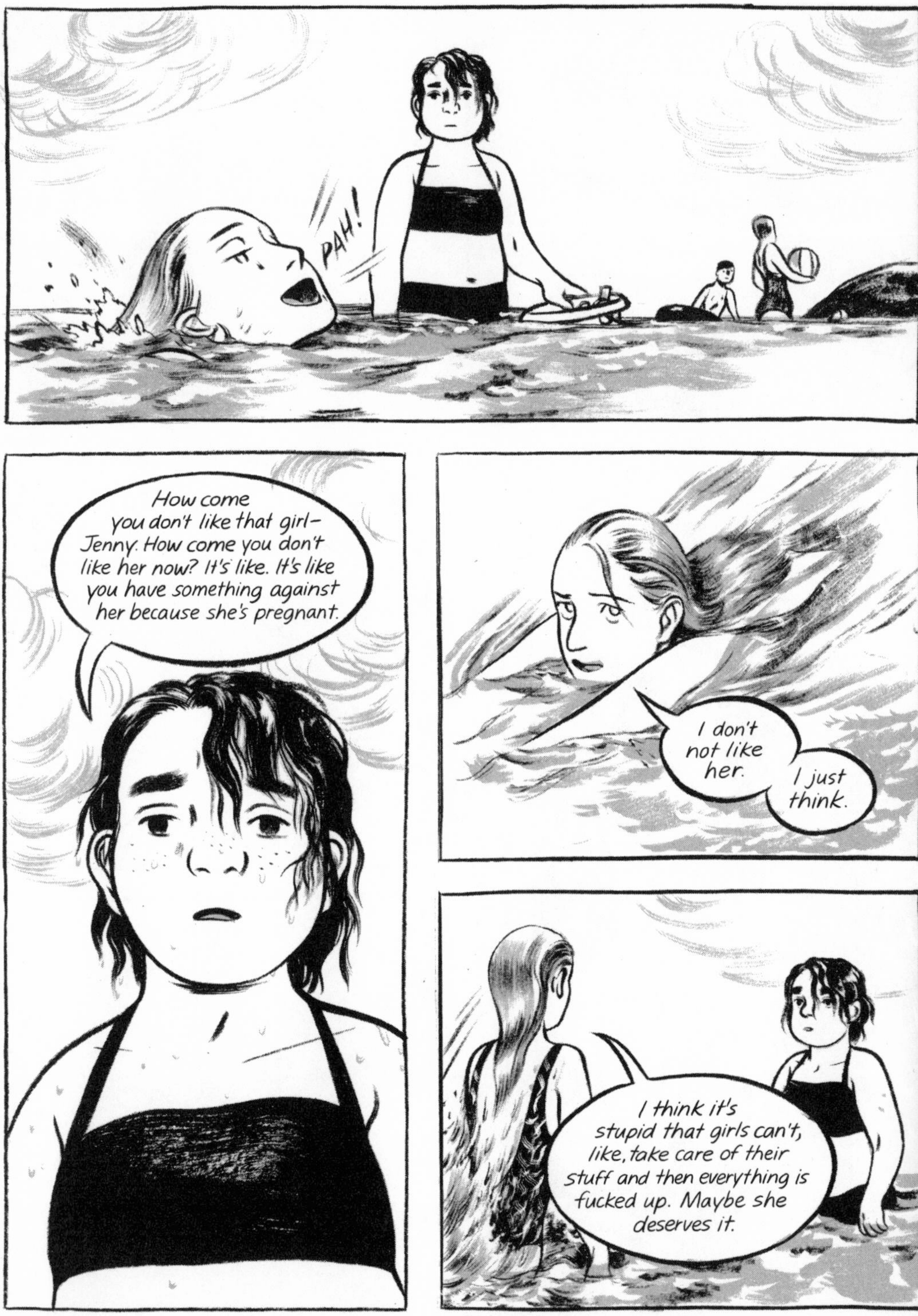
PAH!
How come you don't like that girl– Jenny. How come you don't like her now? It's like. It's like you have something against her because she's pregnant.
I don't not like her.
I just think.
I think it's stupid that girls can't, like, take care of their stuff and then everything is fucked up. Maybe she deserves it.

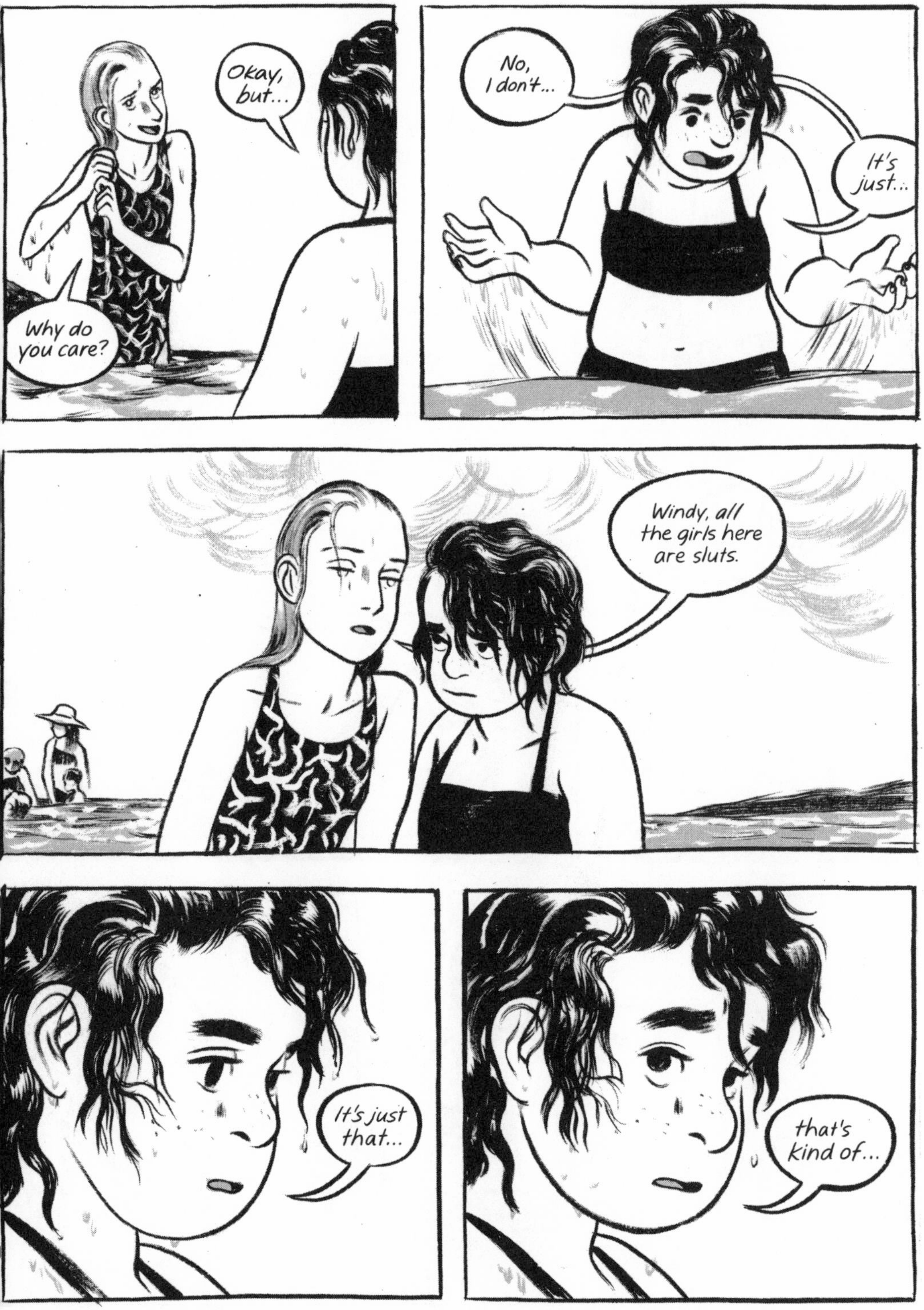
Okay, but...
Why do you care?
No, I don't...
It's just...
Windy, all the girls here are sluts.
It's just that...
that's kind of...

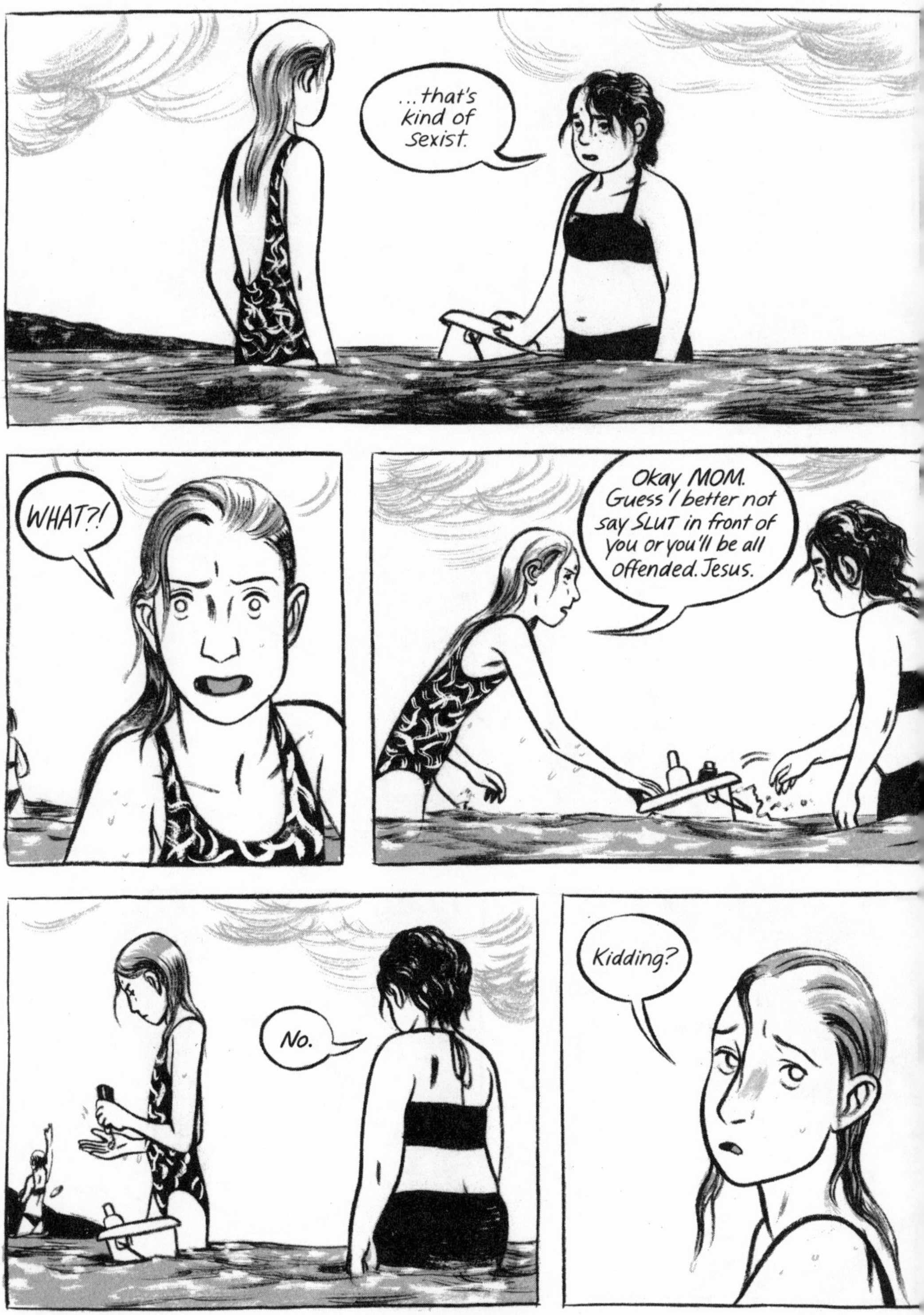
...that's kind of sexist.
WHAT?!
Okay MOM. Guess I better not say SLUT in front of you or you'll be all offended. Jesus.
No.
Kidding?

Where are you going?

I have soap in my eyes.

DUNK

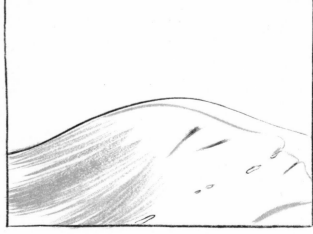

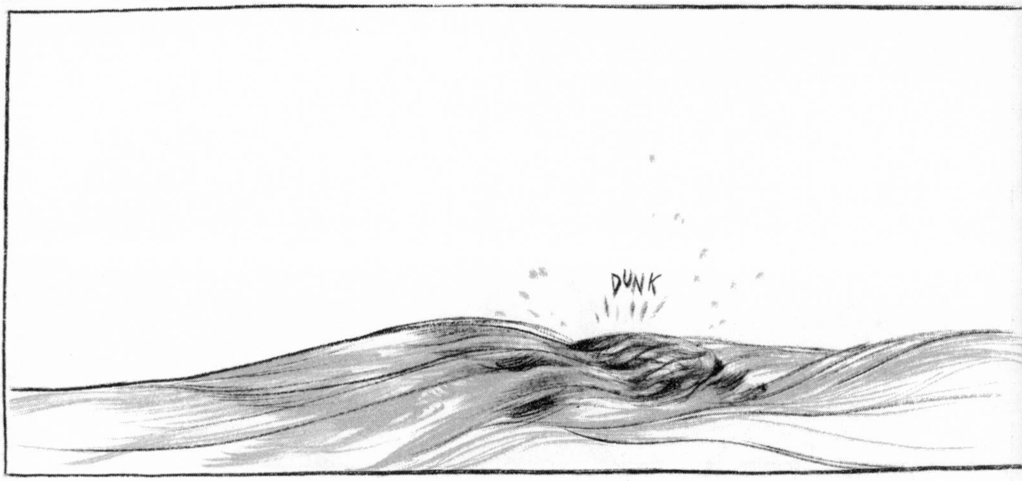
DUNK

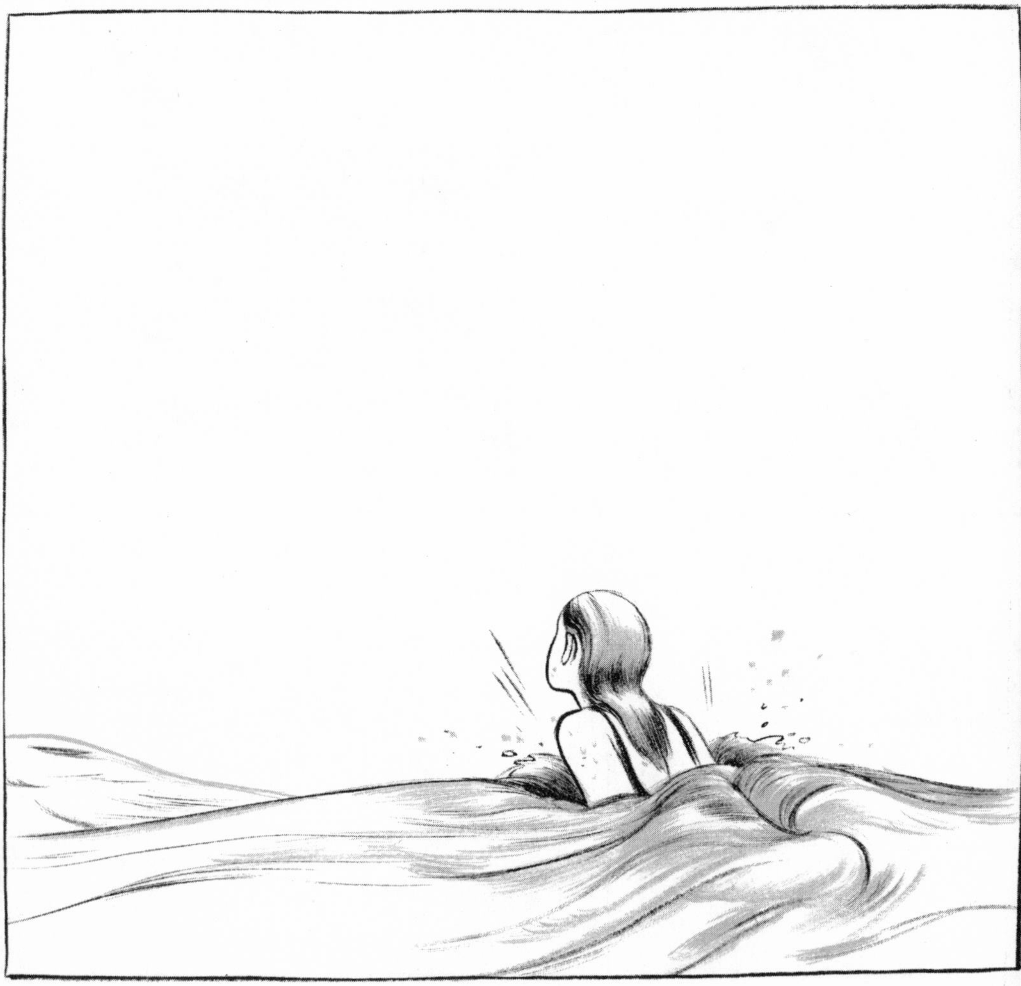

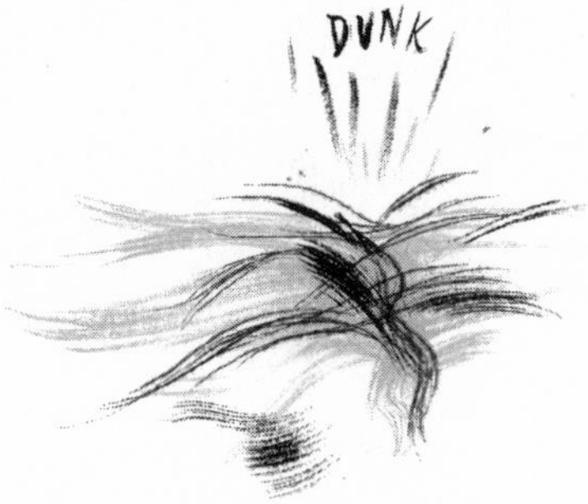
DUNK

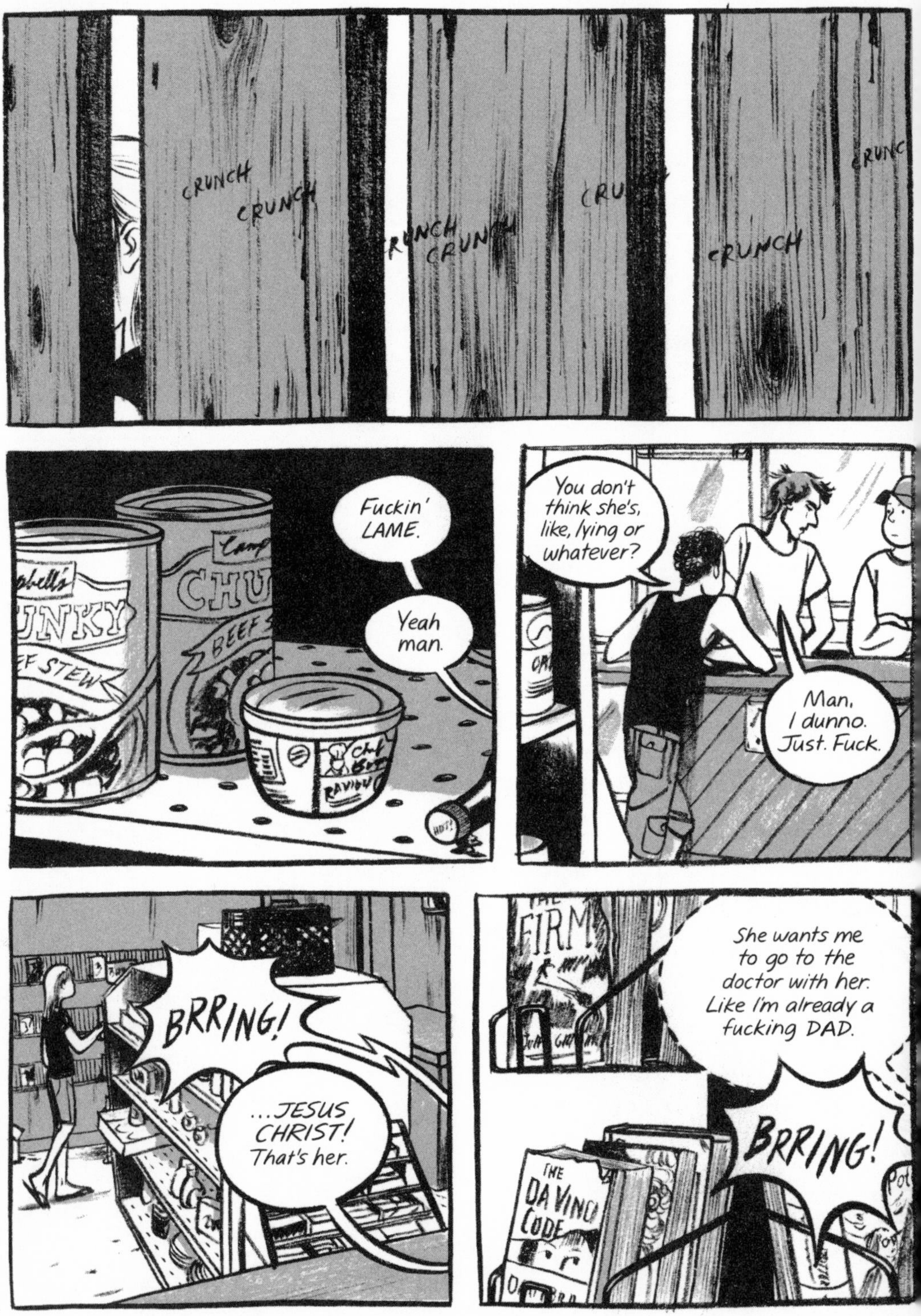
CRUNCH
CRUNCH
CRUNCH
CRUNCH
Fuckin' LAME.
Yeah man.
You don't think she's, like, lying or whatever?
Man, I dunno. Just. Fuck.
BRRING!
...JESUS CHRIST! That's her.
She wants me to go to the doctor with her. Like I'm already a fucking DAD.
BRRING!

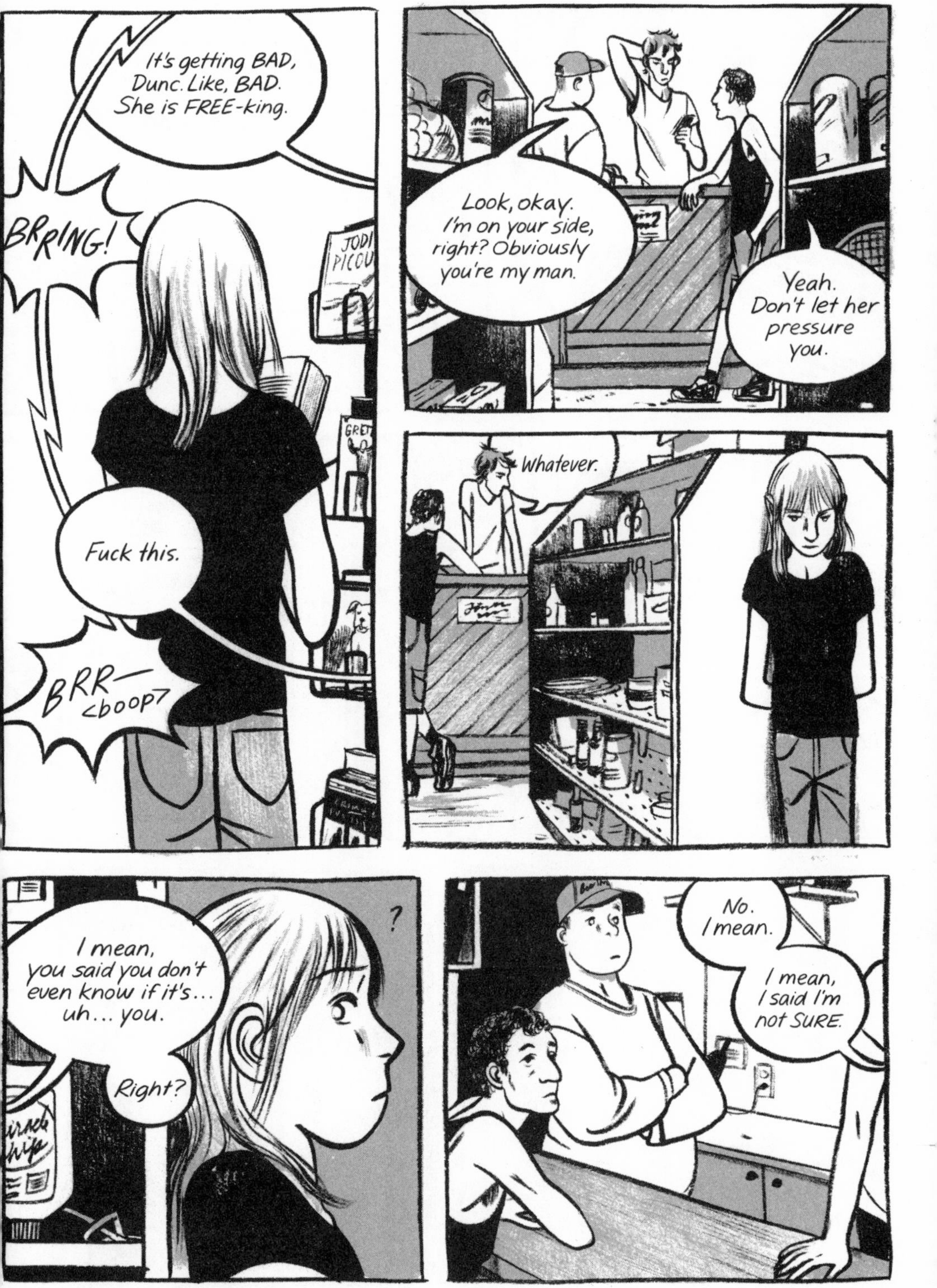

It's getting BAD, Dunc. Like, BAD. She is FREE-king.
BRRING!
Fuck this.
BRR—
<boop>
Look, okay. I'm on your side, right? Obviously you're my man.
Yeah. Don't let her pressure you.
Whatever.
?
I mean, you said you don't even know if it's... uh... you.
Right?
No. I mean.
I mean, I said I'm not SURE.

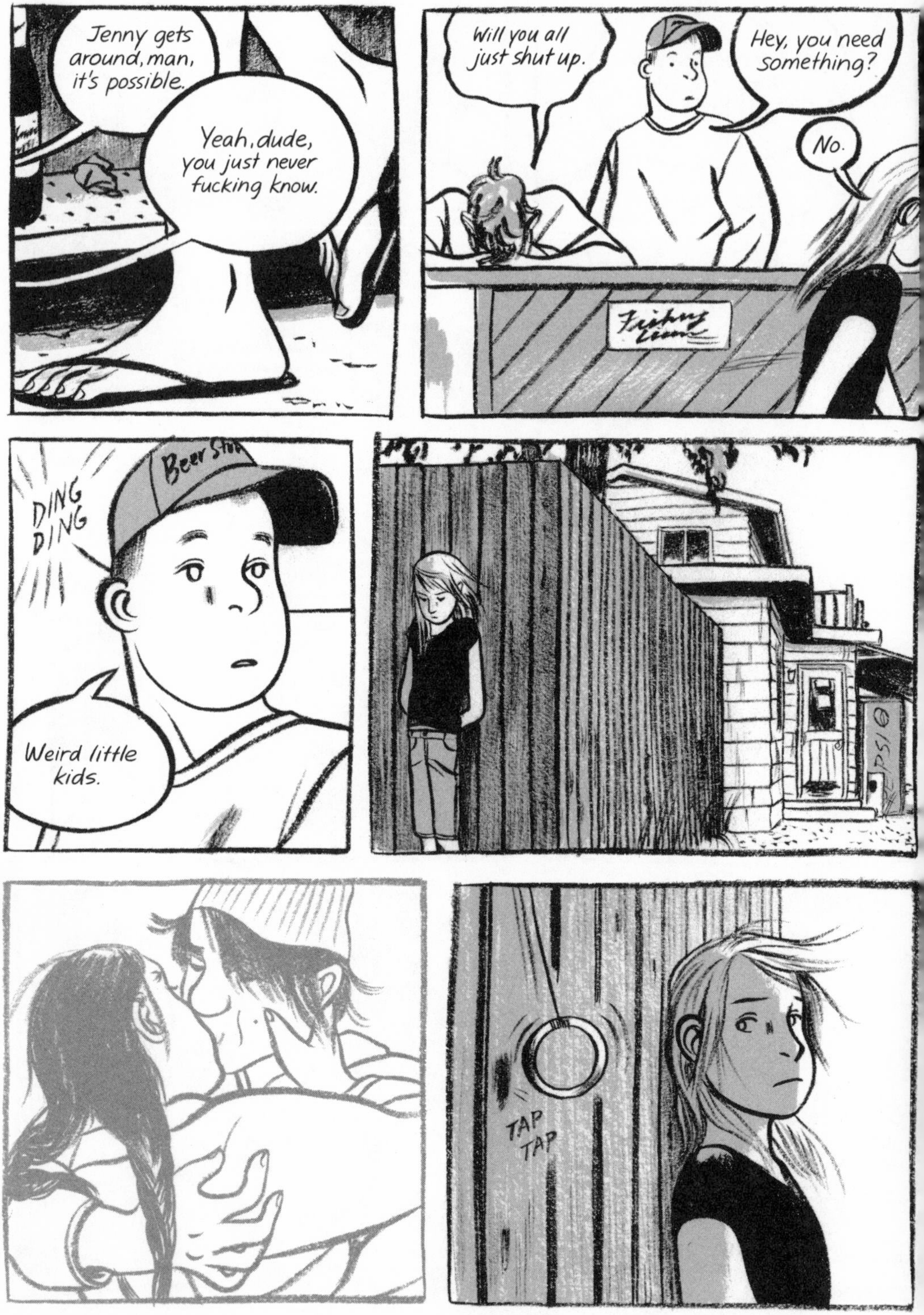
Jenny gets around, man, it's possible.
Yeah, dude, you just never fucking know.
Will you all just shut up.
Hey, you need something?
No.
Beer Sto
DING DING
Weird little kids.
TAP TAP

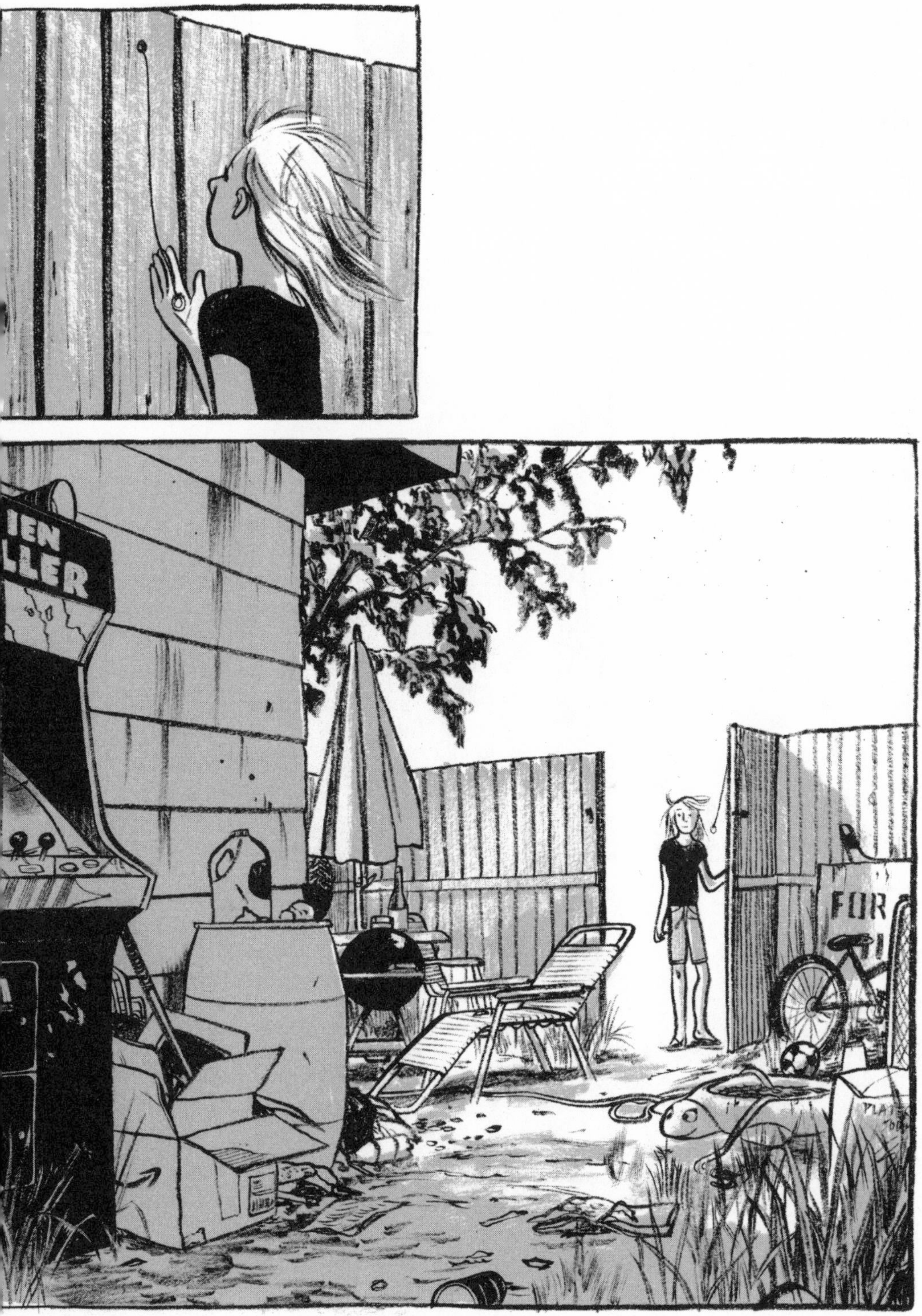
IEN
LLER
FOR

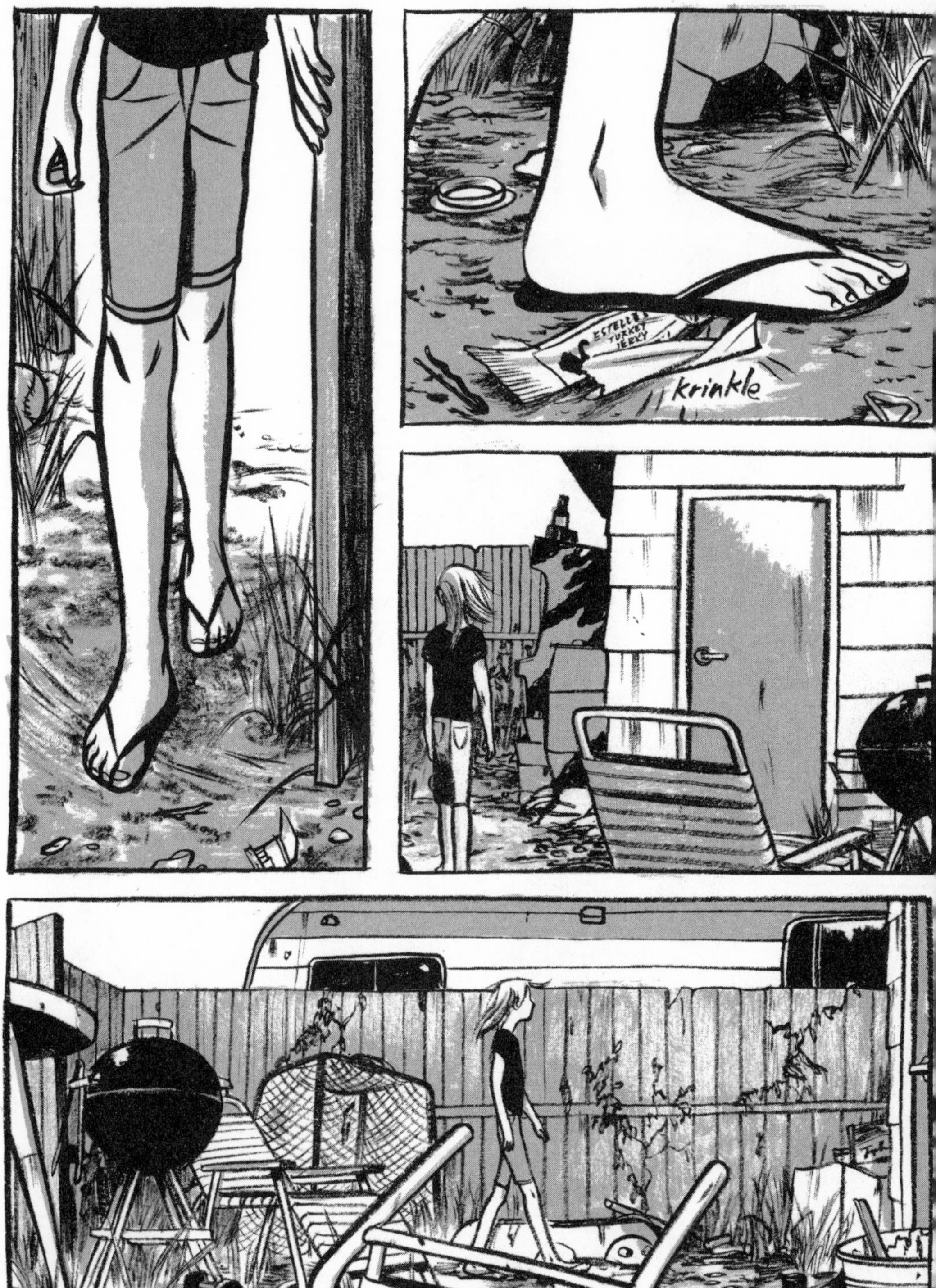
ESTELLE'S
TURKEY
JERKY
krinkle

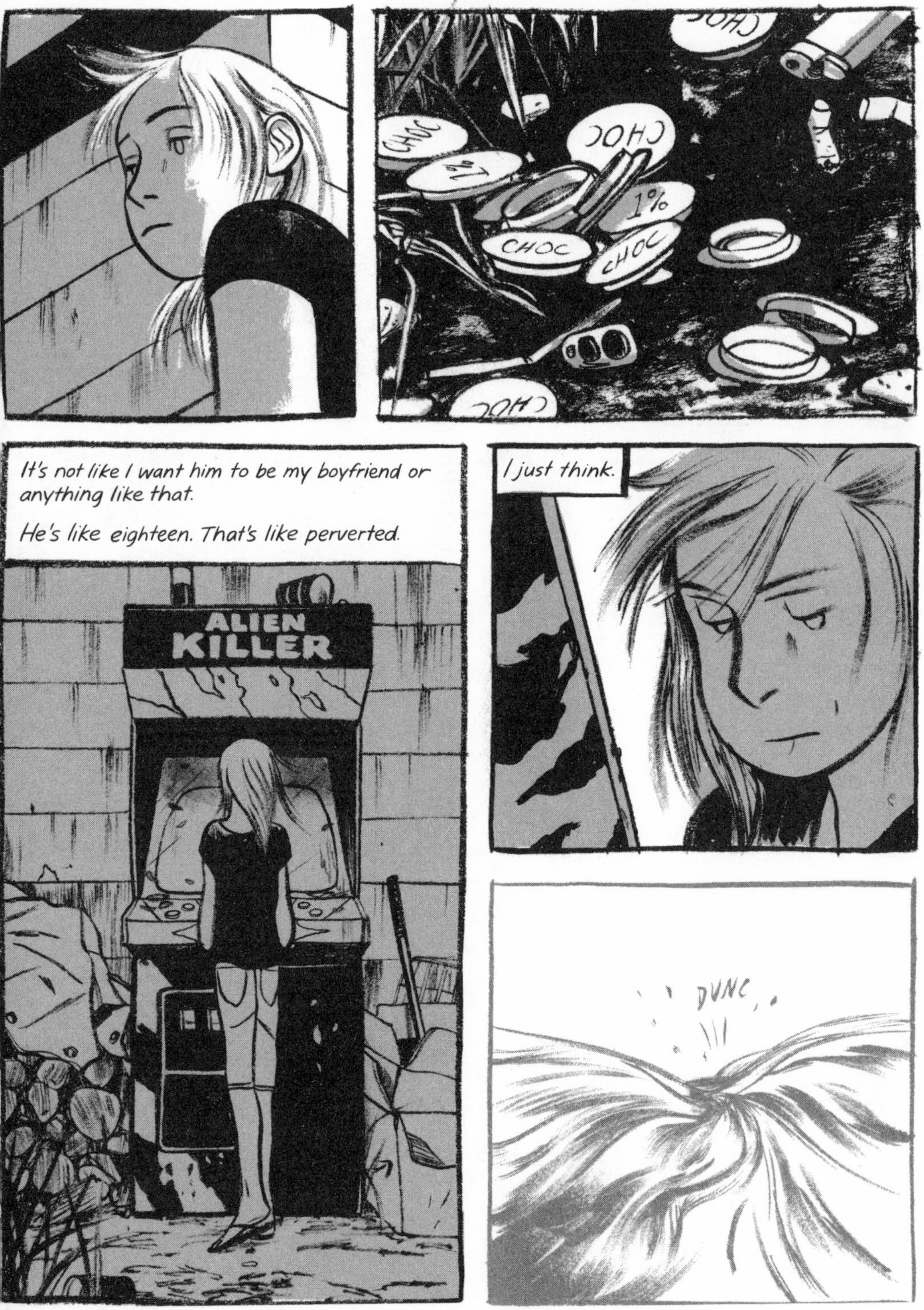

CHOC
1%
CHOC
It's not like I want him to be my boyfriend or anything like that.
He's like eighteen. That's like perverted.
ALIEN KILLER
I just think.
DUNC

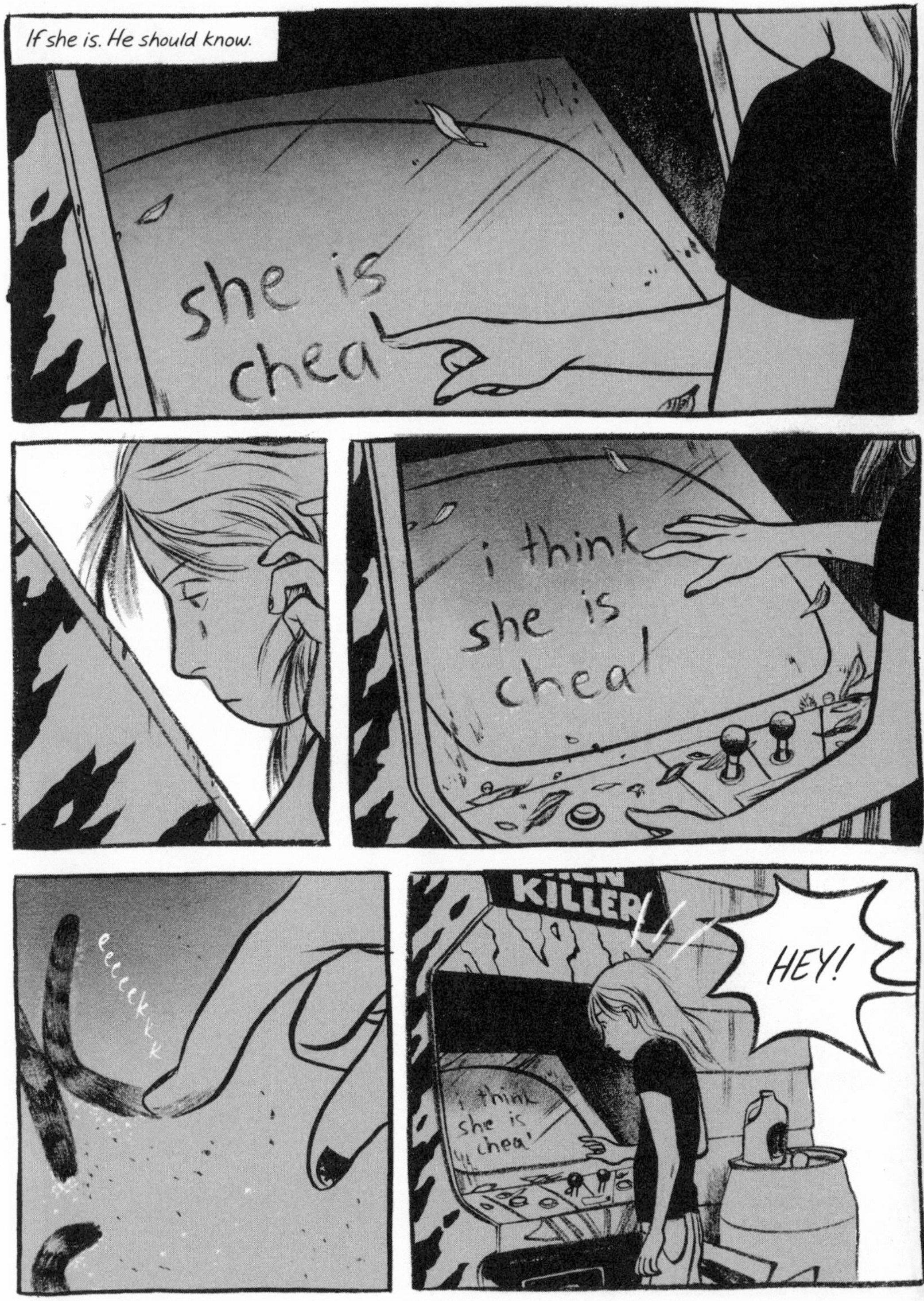
If she is. He should know.
she is chea
i think she is chea
KILLER
HEY!
i think she is chea

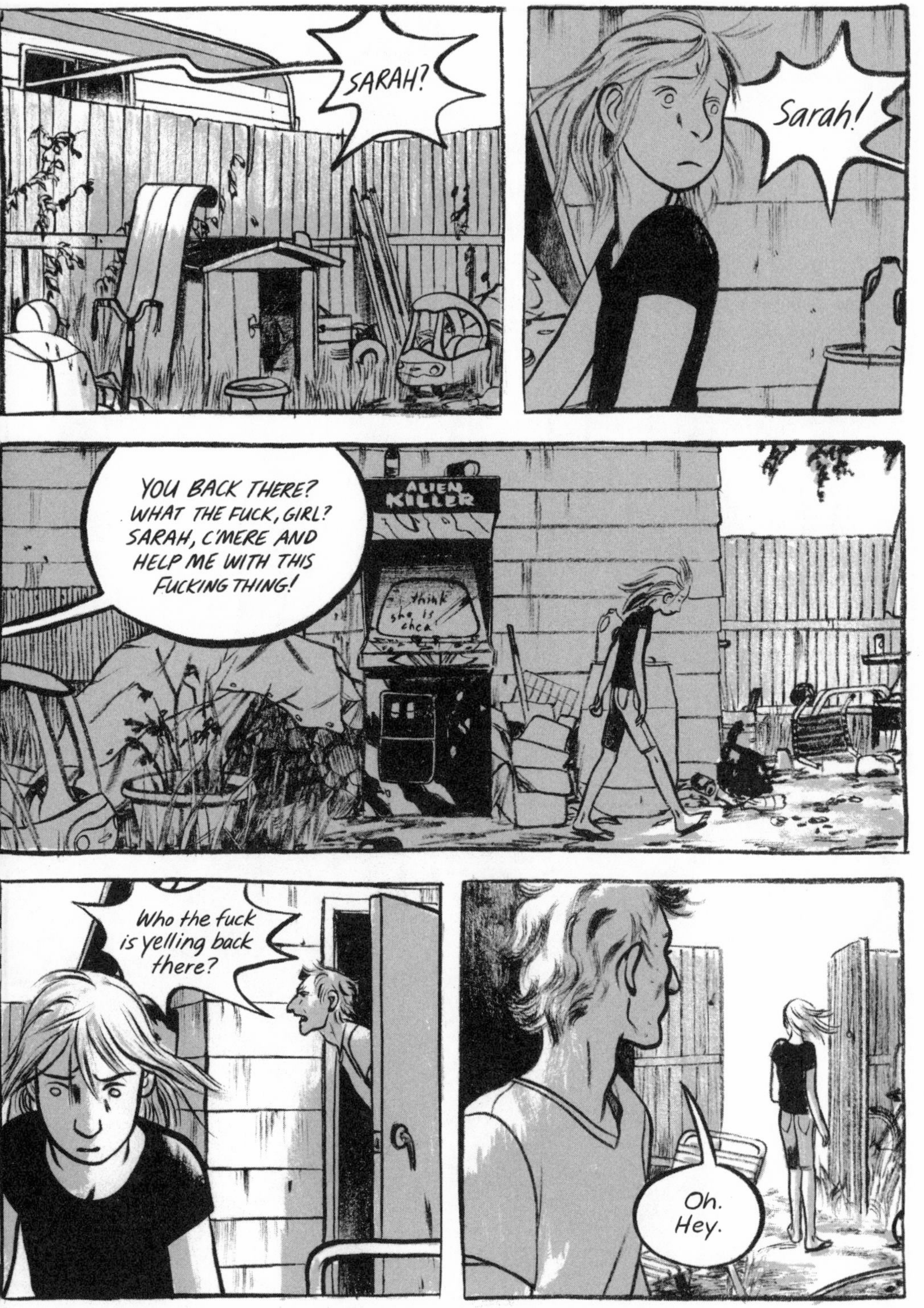
SARAH?
Sarah!
YOU BACK THERE? WHAT THE FUCK, GIRL? SARAH, C'MERE AND HELP ME WITH THIS FUCKING THING!
ALIEN KILLER
Who the fuck is yelling back there?
Oh. Hey.

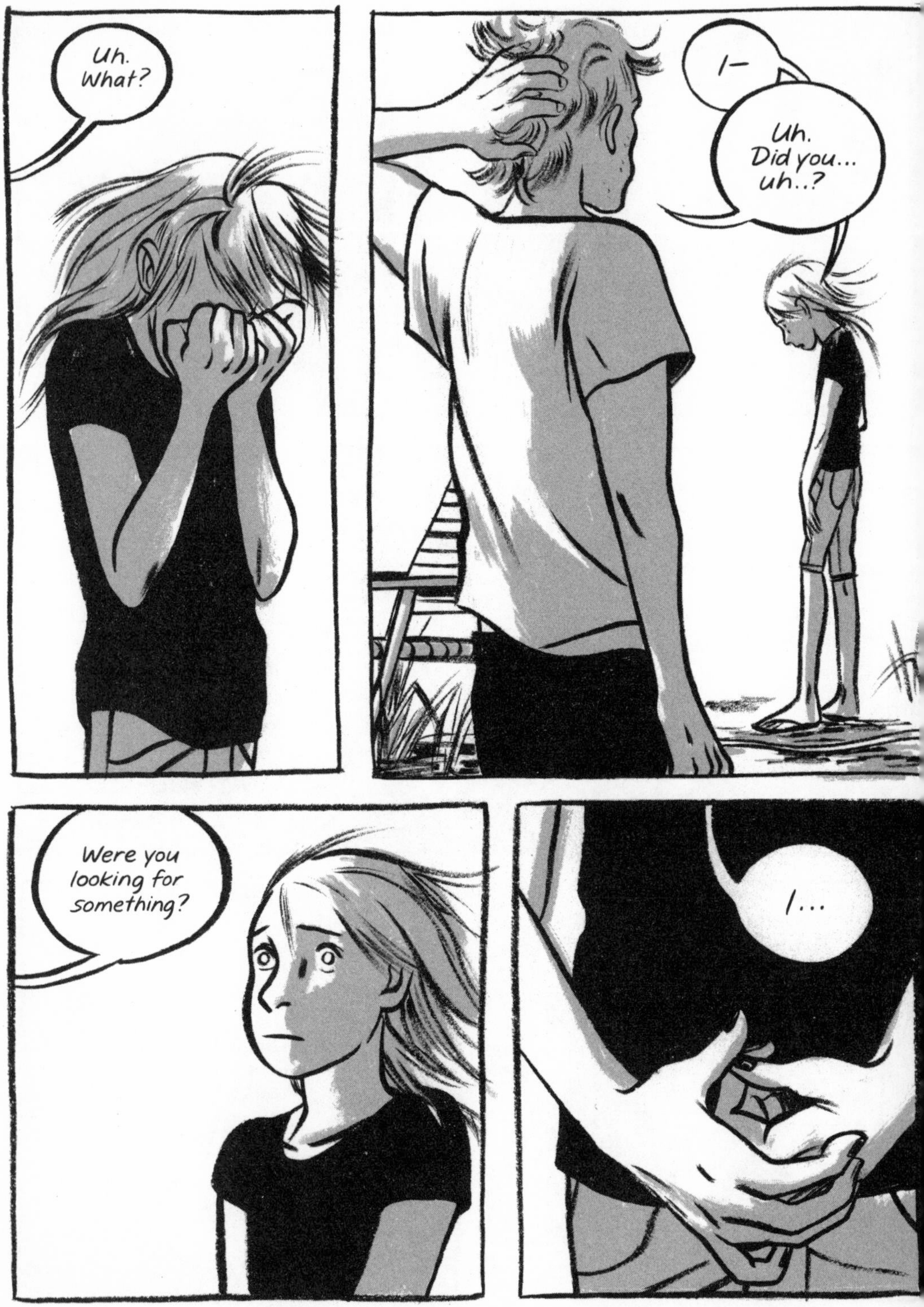
Uh.
What?
I-
Uh.
Did you...
uh..?
Were you
looking for
something?
I...

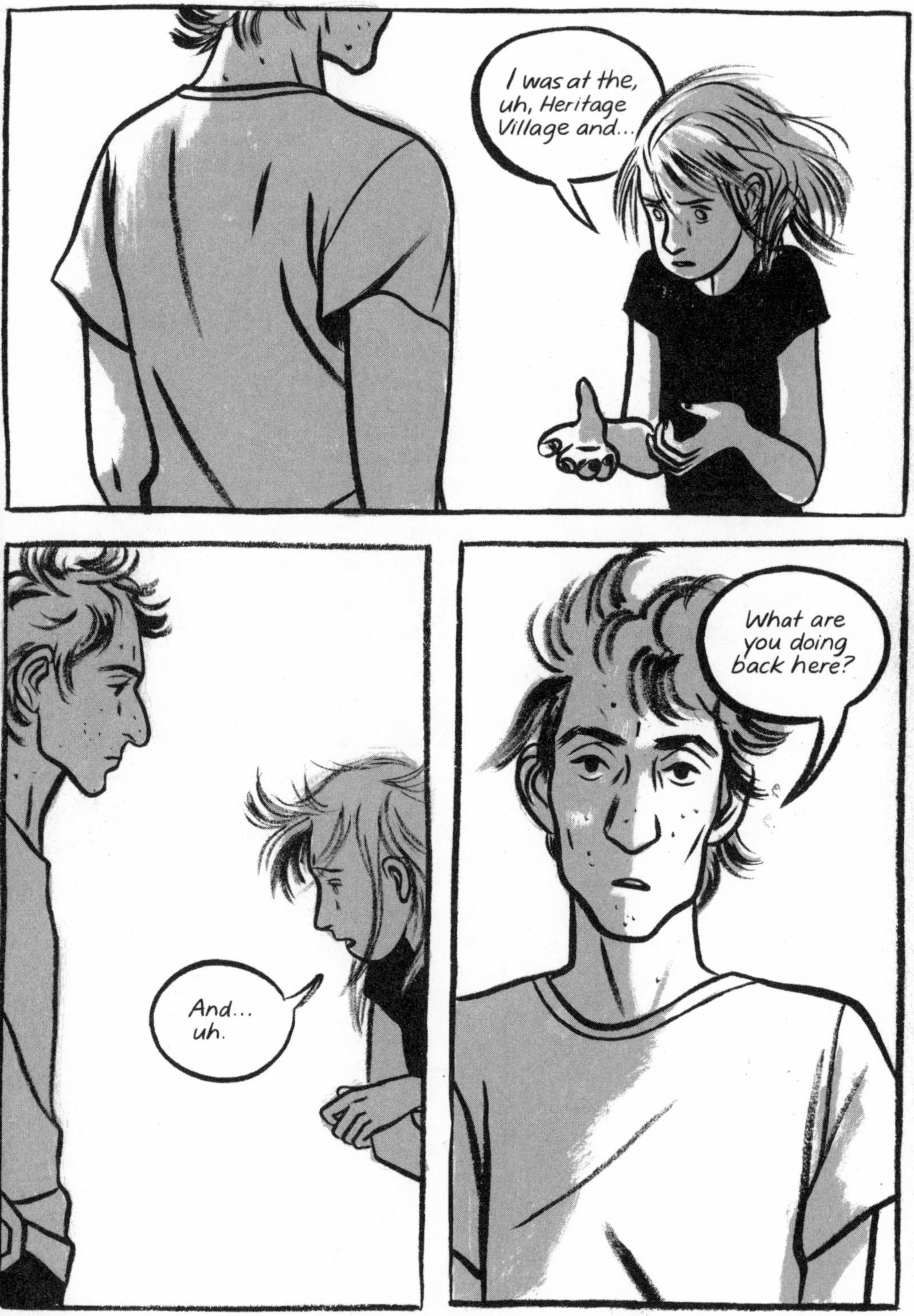
I was at the, uh, Heritage Village and...
And... uh.
What are you doing back here?

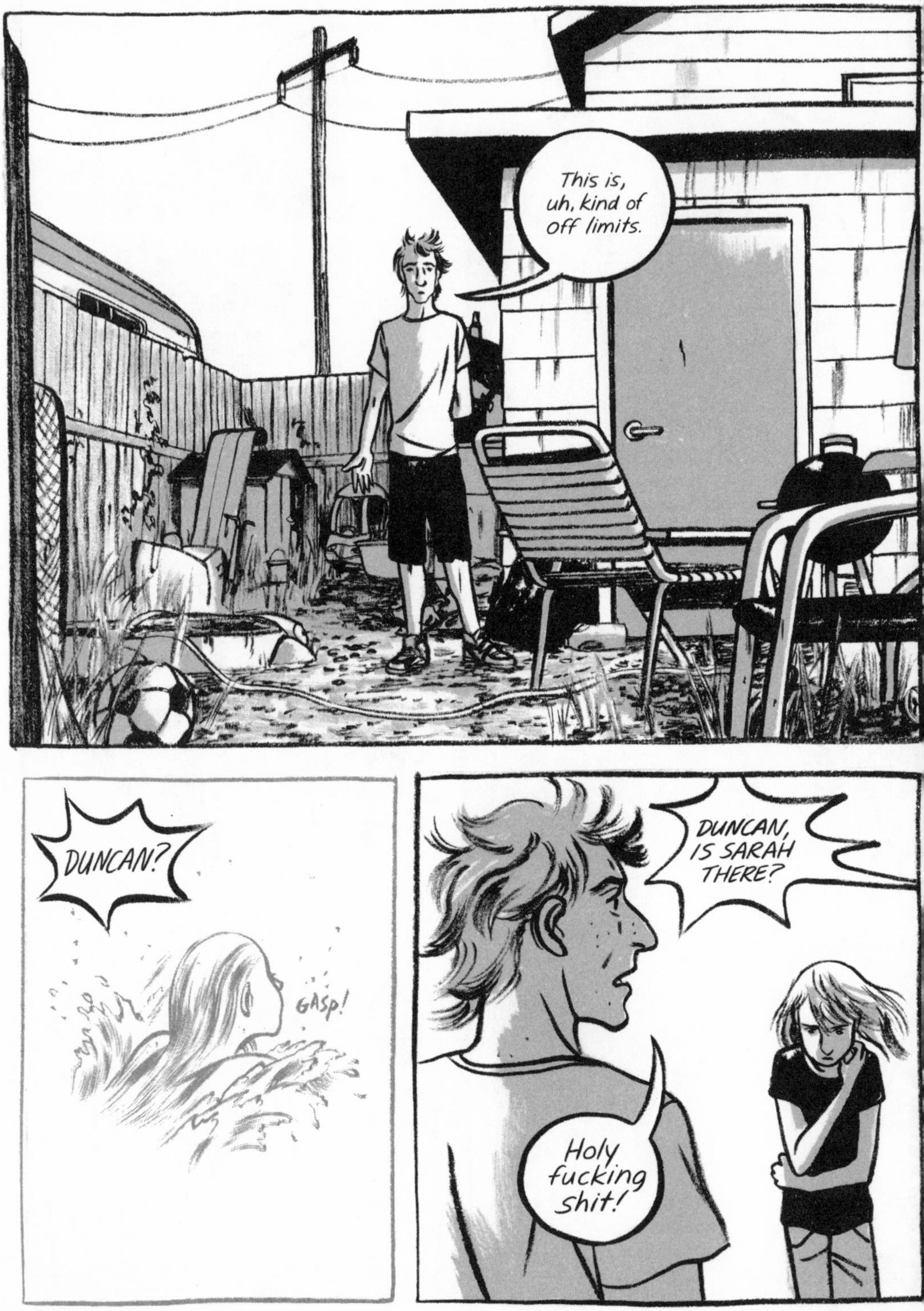
This is, uh, kind of off limits.
DUNCAN?
GASP!
DUNCAN, IS SARAH THERE?
Holy fucking shit!

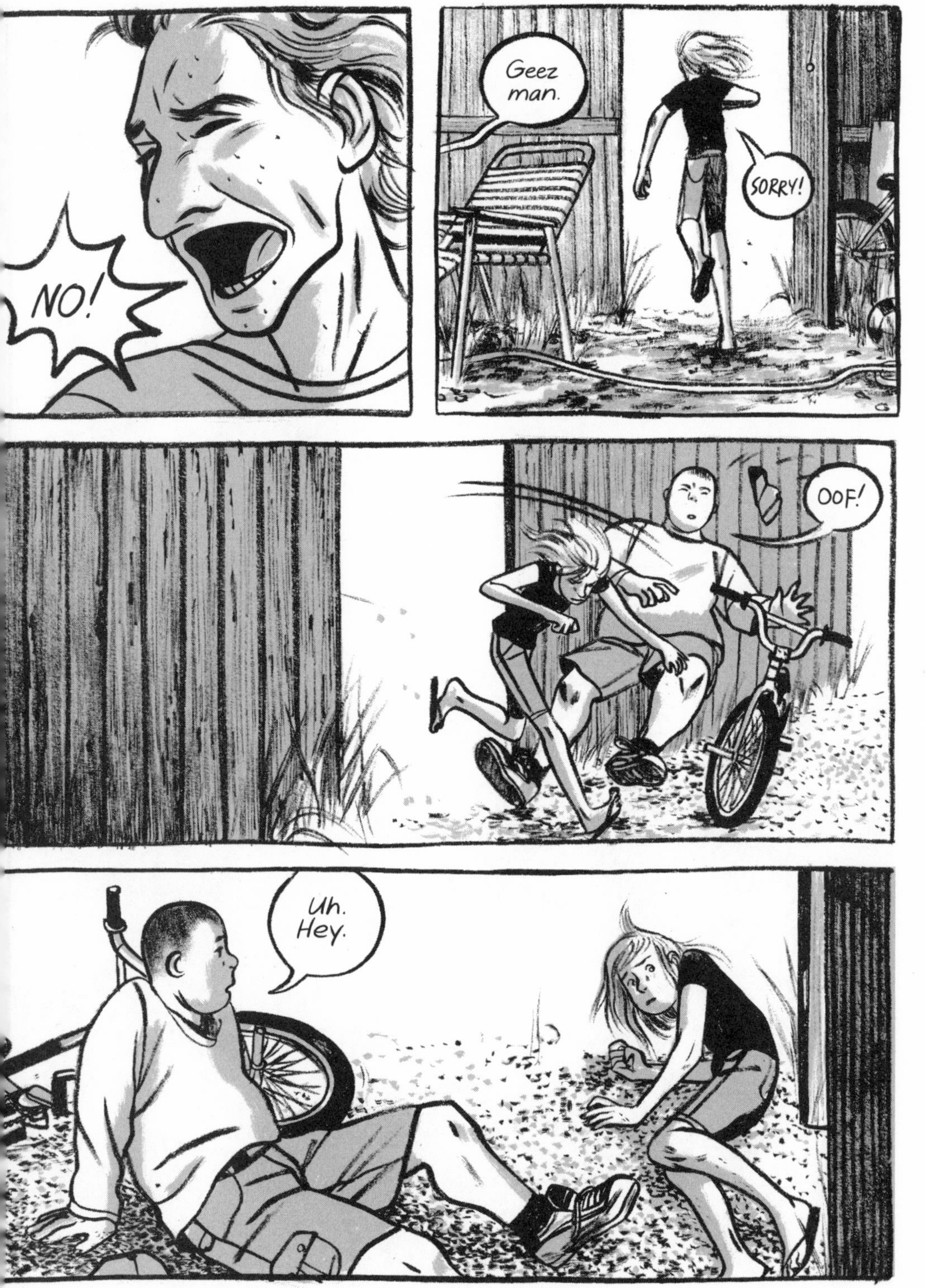
NO!
Geez man.
SORRY!
OOF!
Uh. Hey.

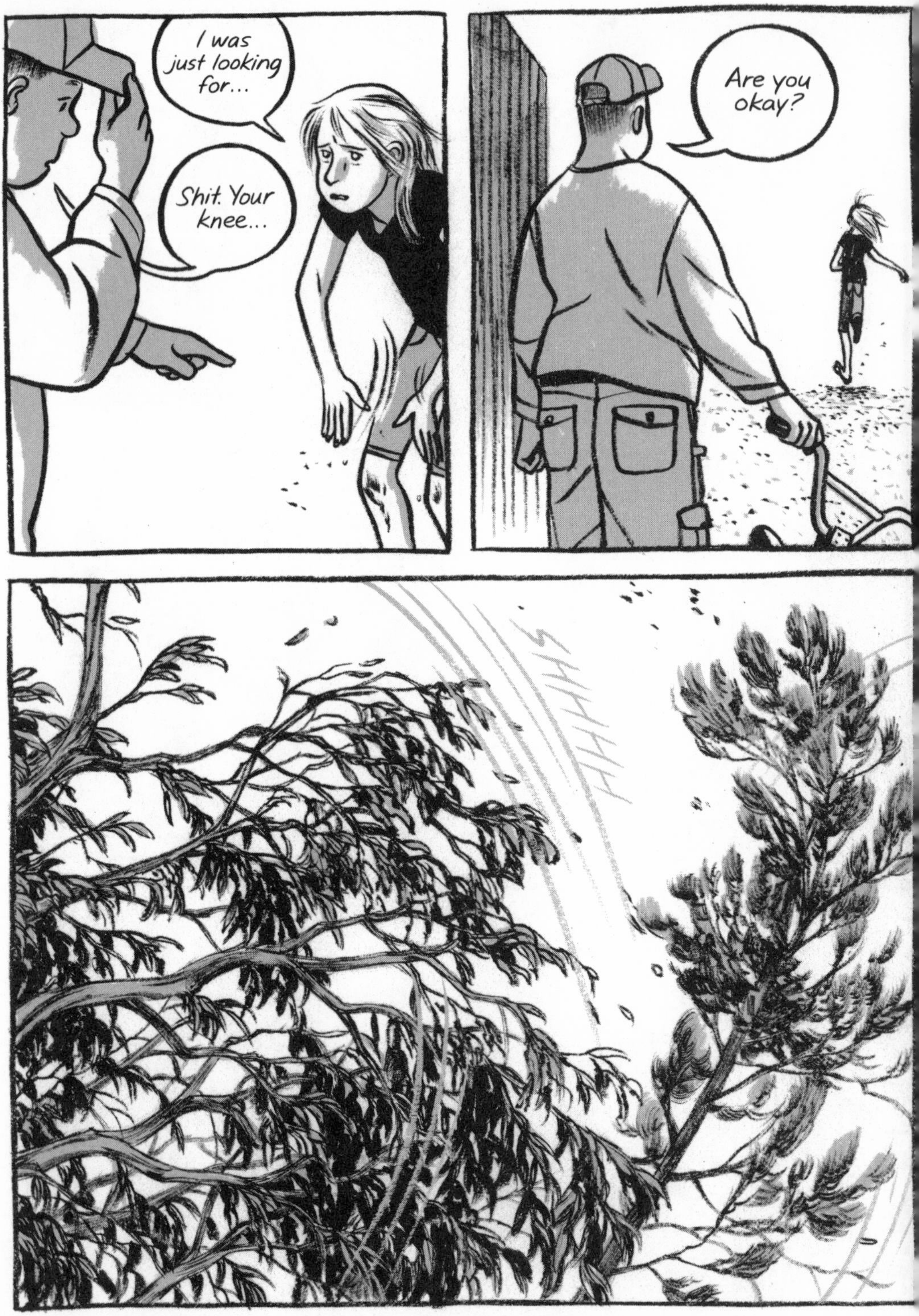
I was just looking for...
Shit. Your knee...
Are you okay?
SHHHHH

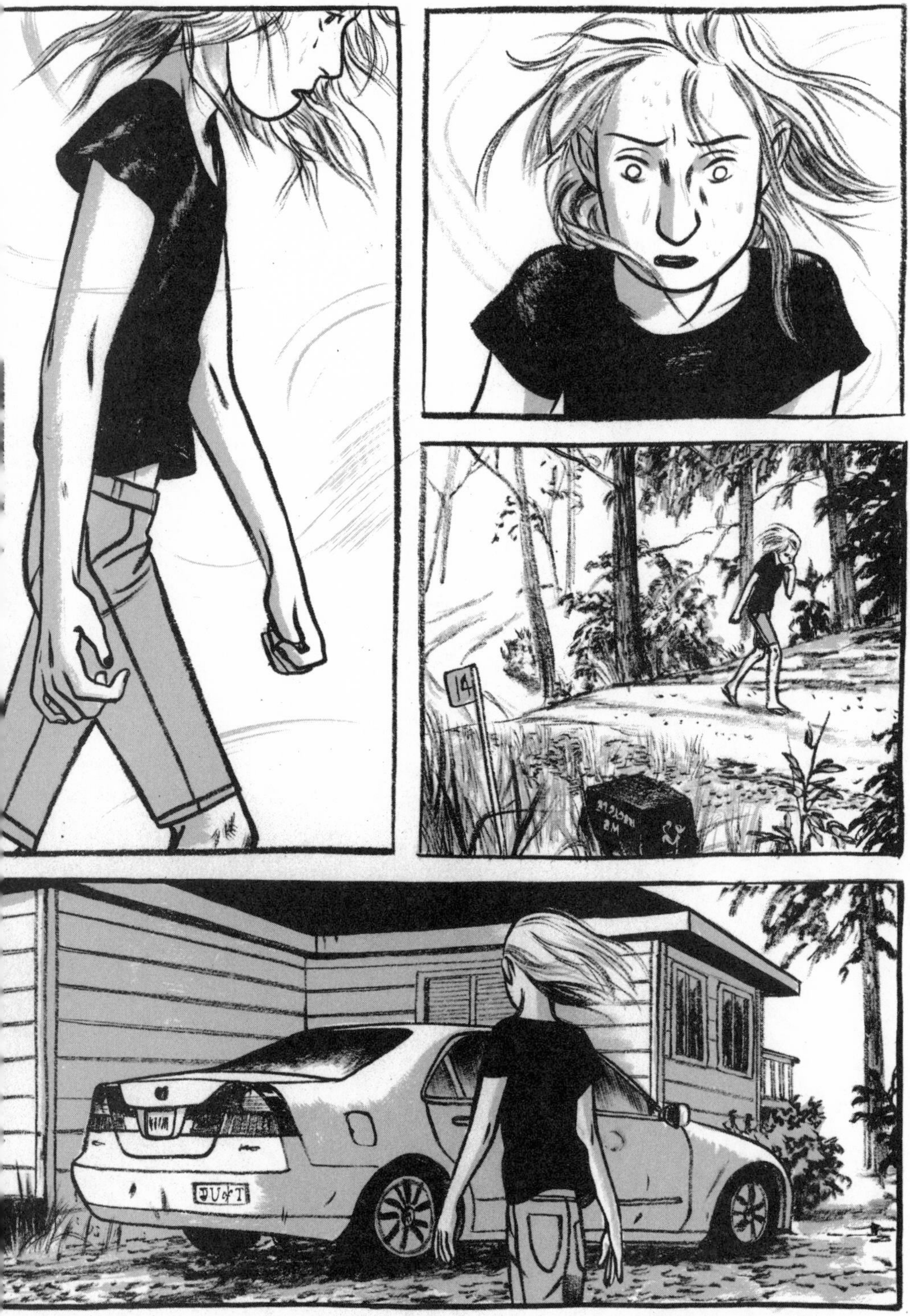
14

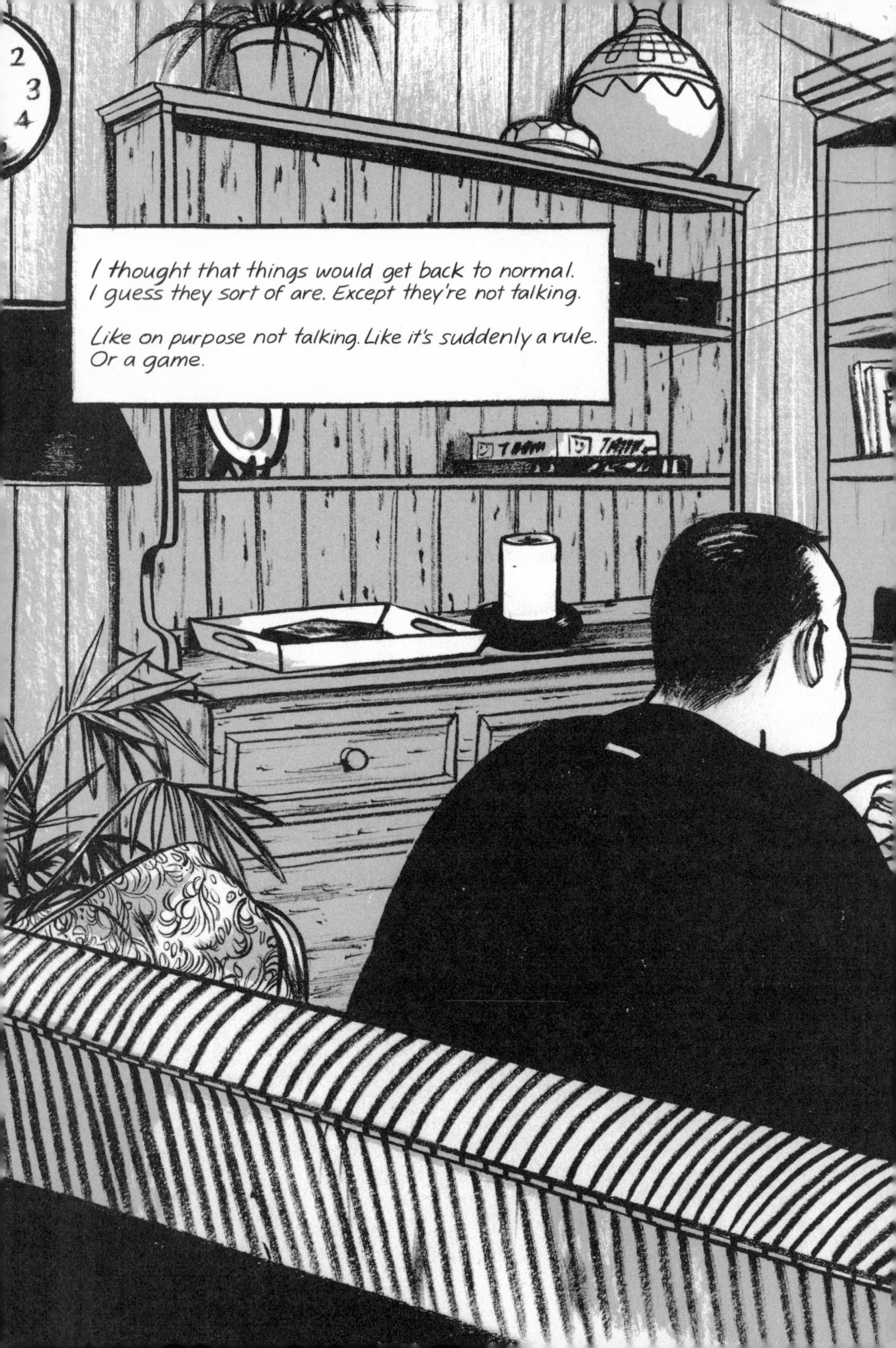
I thought that things would get back to normal. I guess they sort of are. Except they're not talking.
Like on purpose not talking. Like it's suddenly a rule. Or a game.

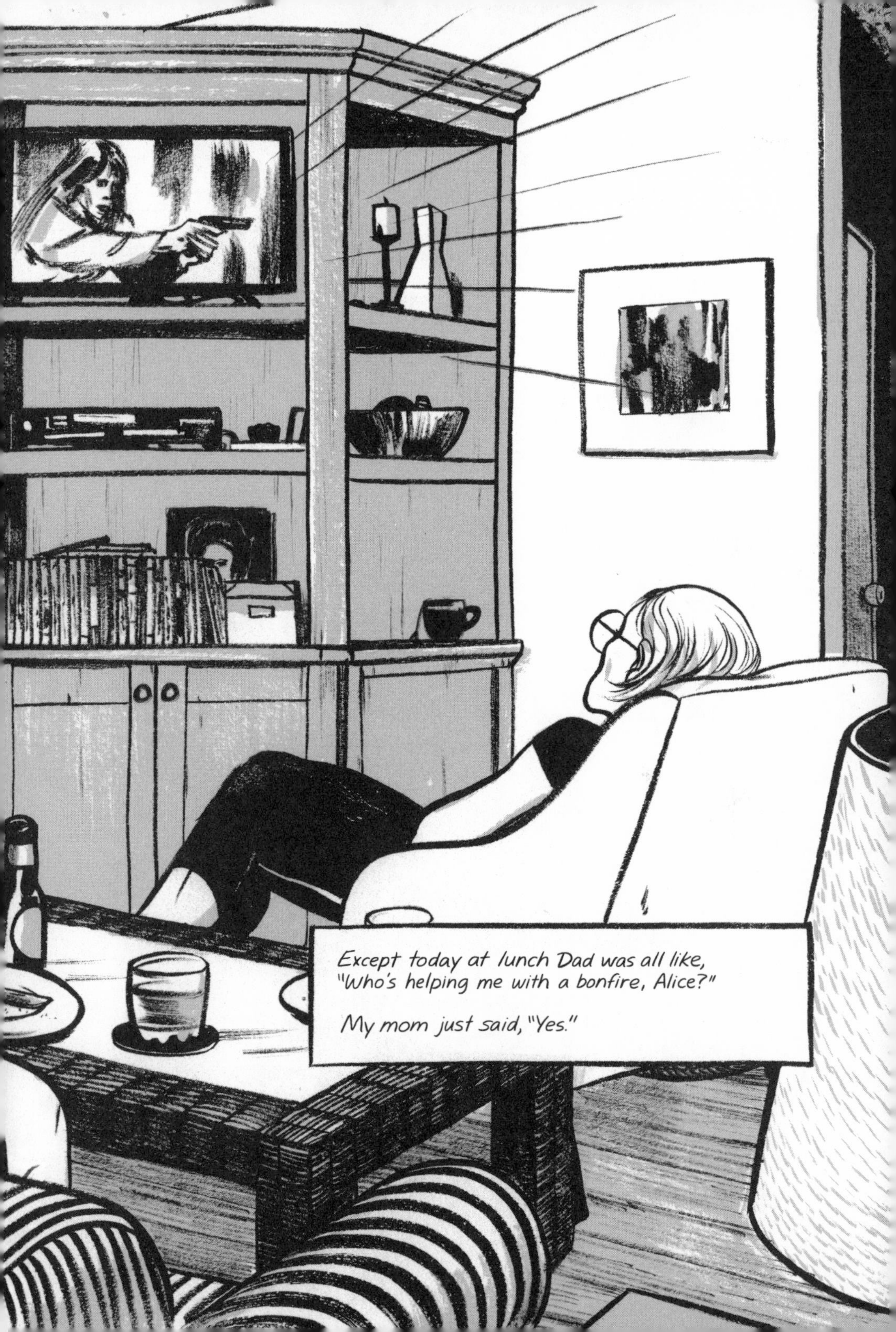
Except today at lunch Dad was all like, "Who's helping me with a bonfire, Alice?"
My mom just said, "Yes."

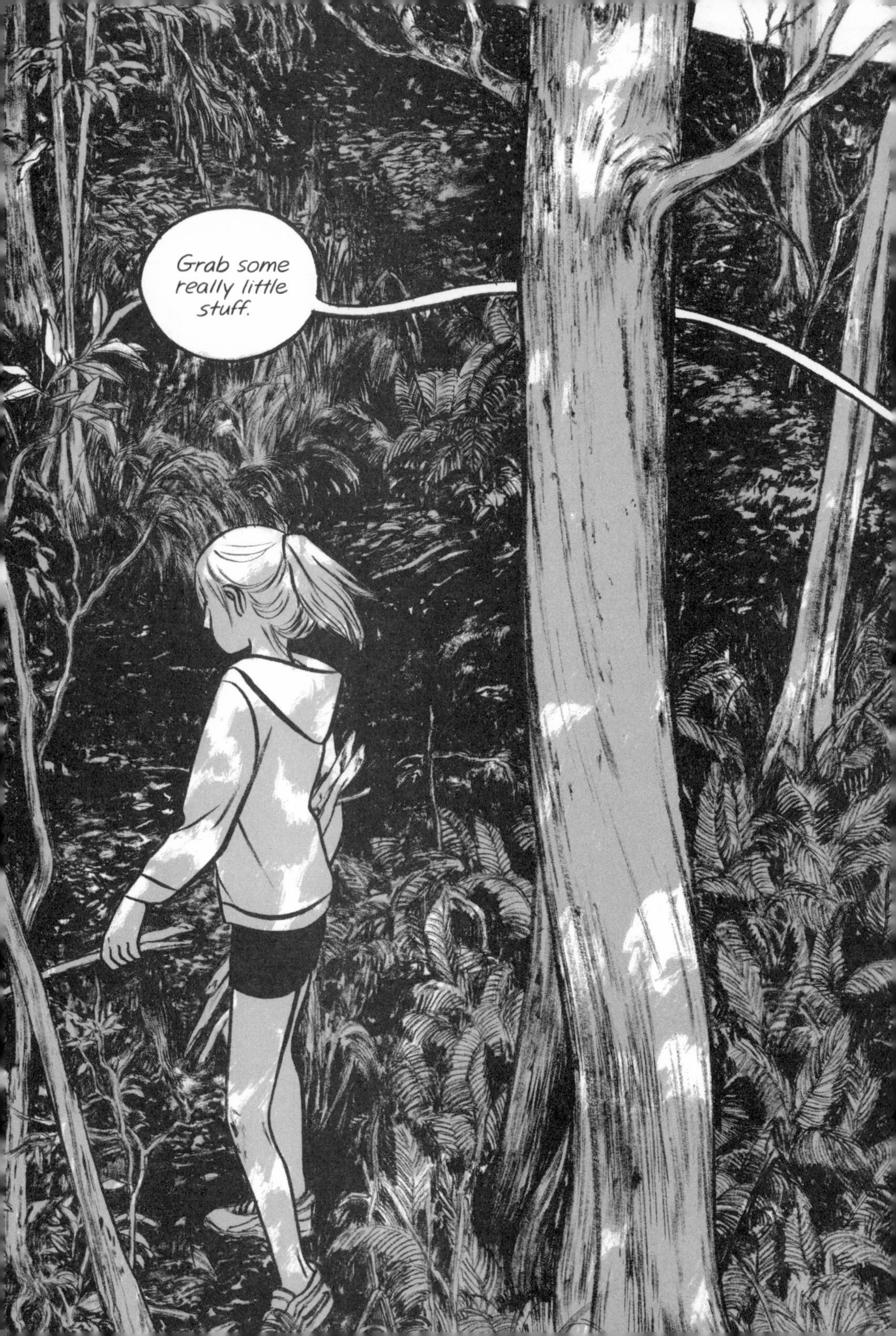
Grab some really little stuff.

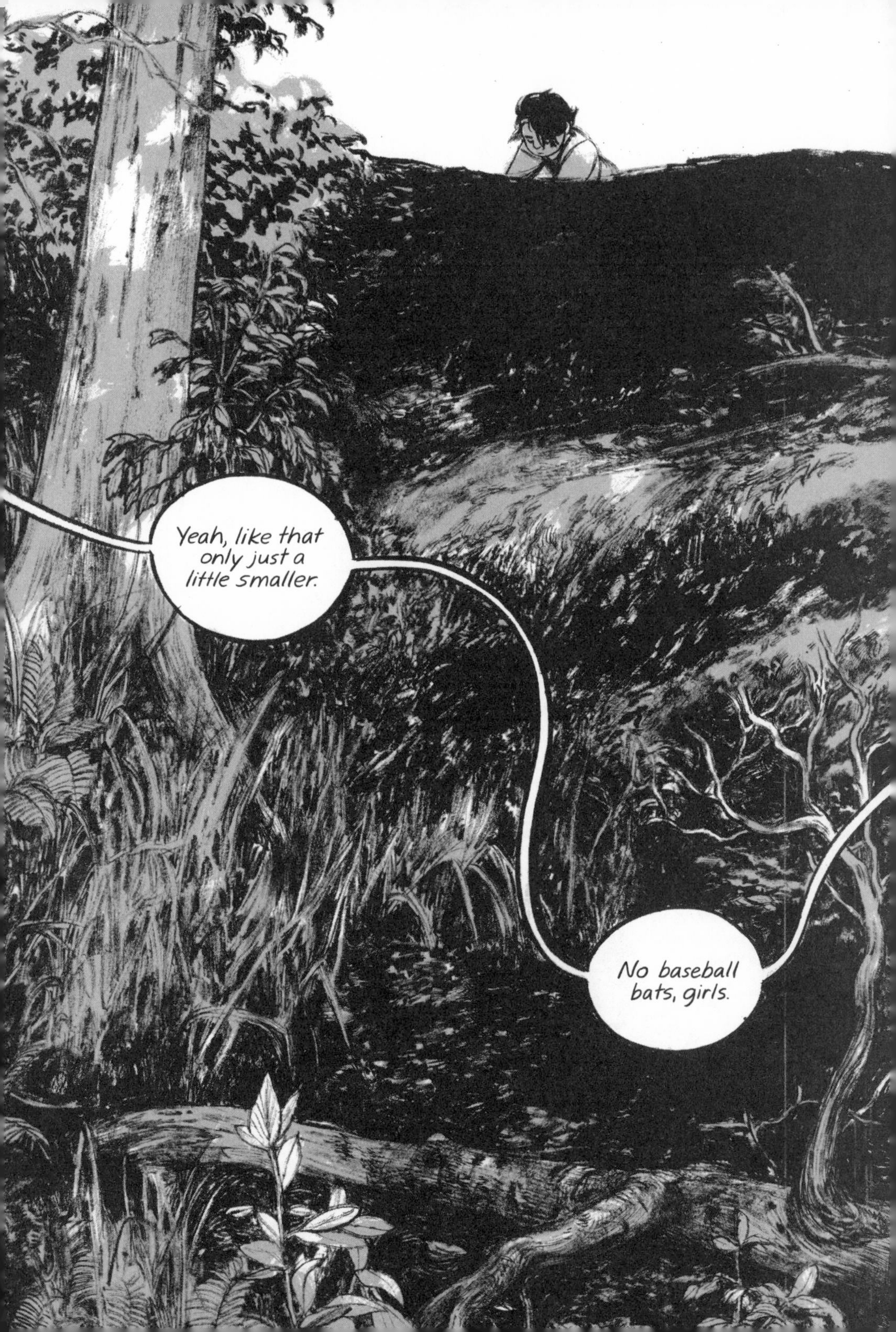
Yeah, like that only just a little smaller.
No baseball bats, girls.

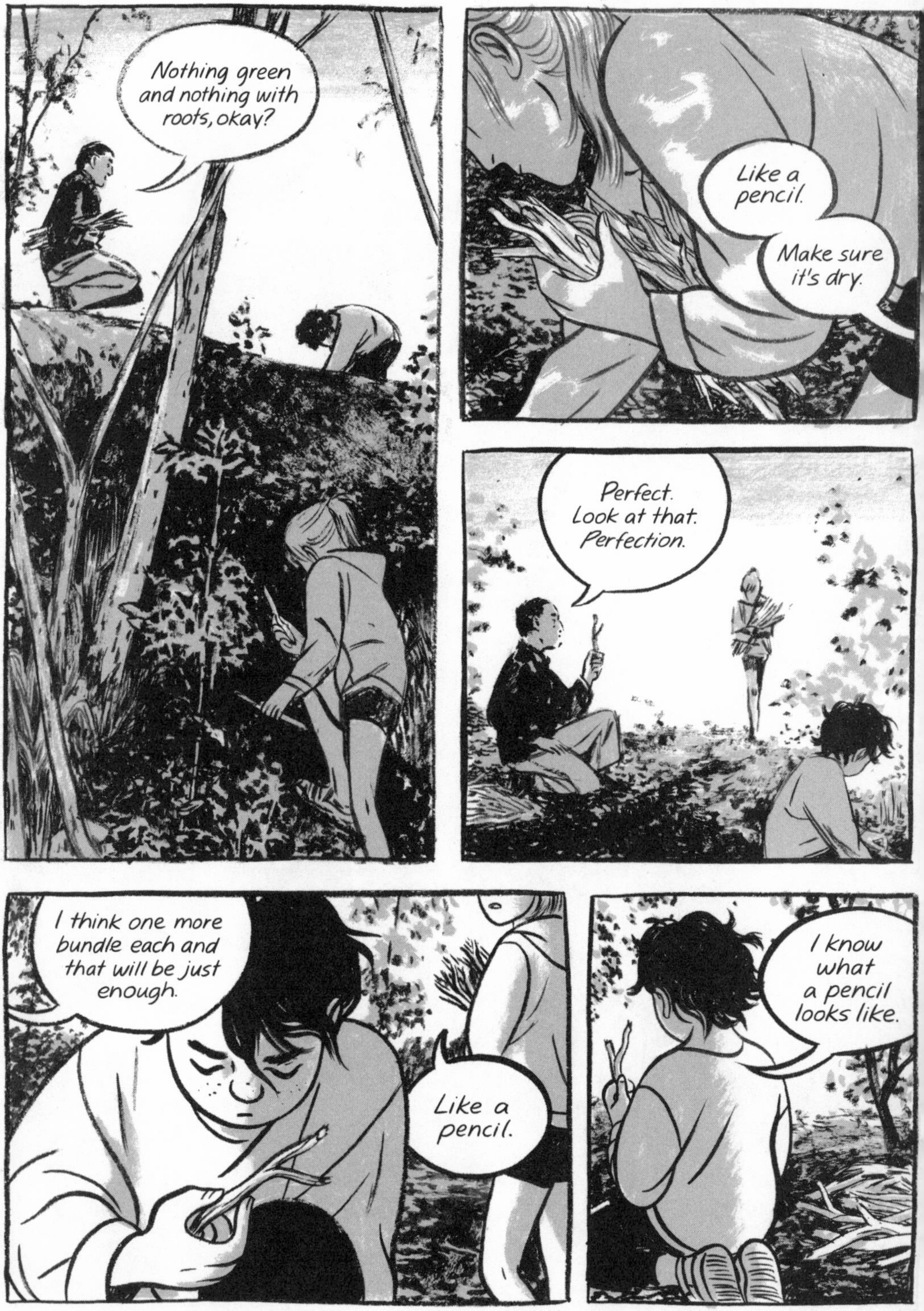
Nothing green and nothing with roots, okay?
Like a pencil.
Make sure it's dry.
Perfect. Look at that. Perfection.
I think one more bundle each and that will be just enough.
Like a pencil.
I know what a pencil looks like.

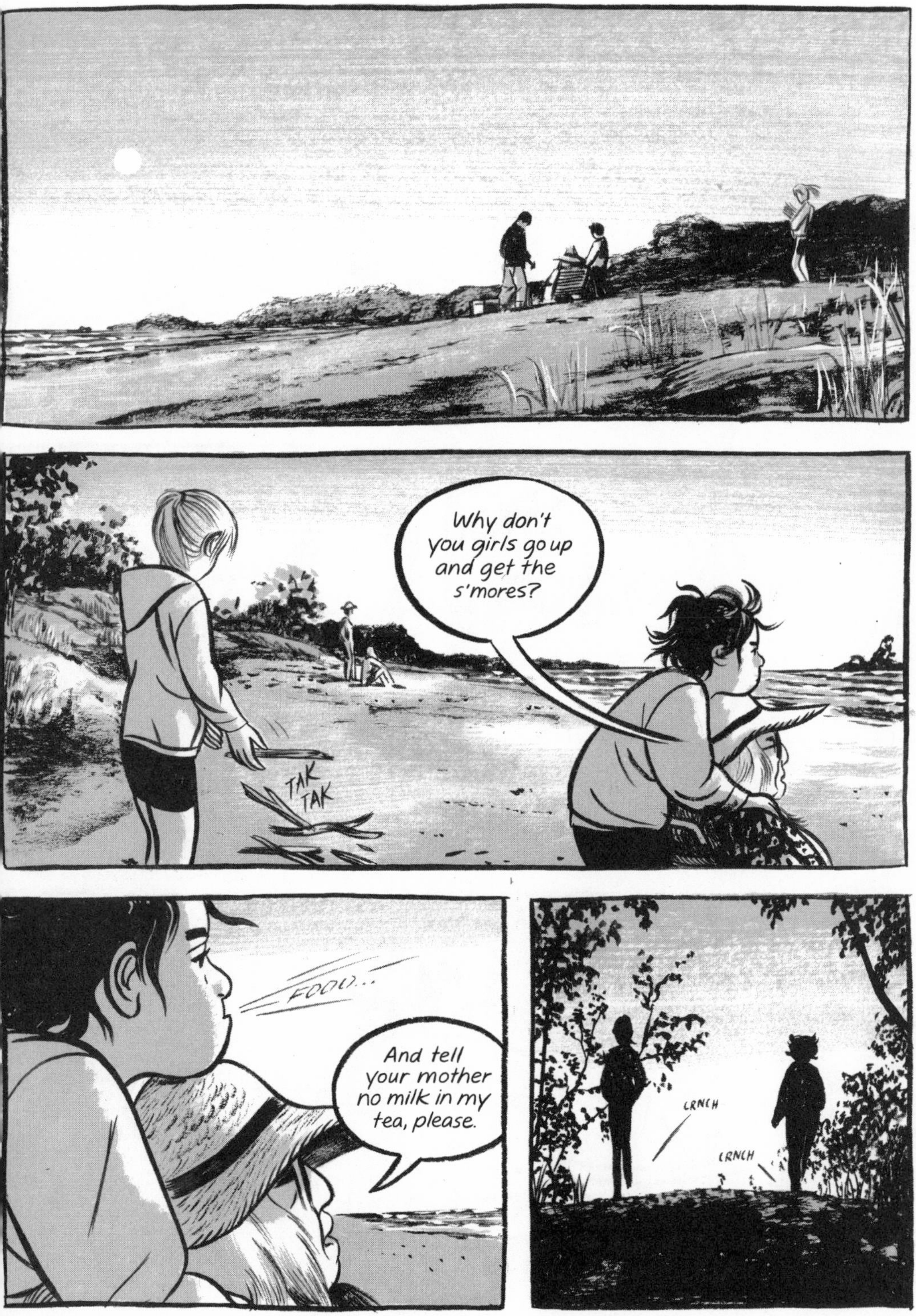
Why don't you girls go up and get the s'mores?
TAK TAK
FOOO...
And tell your mother no milk in my tea, please.
CRNCH
CRNCH

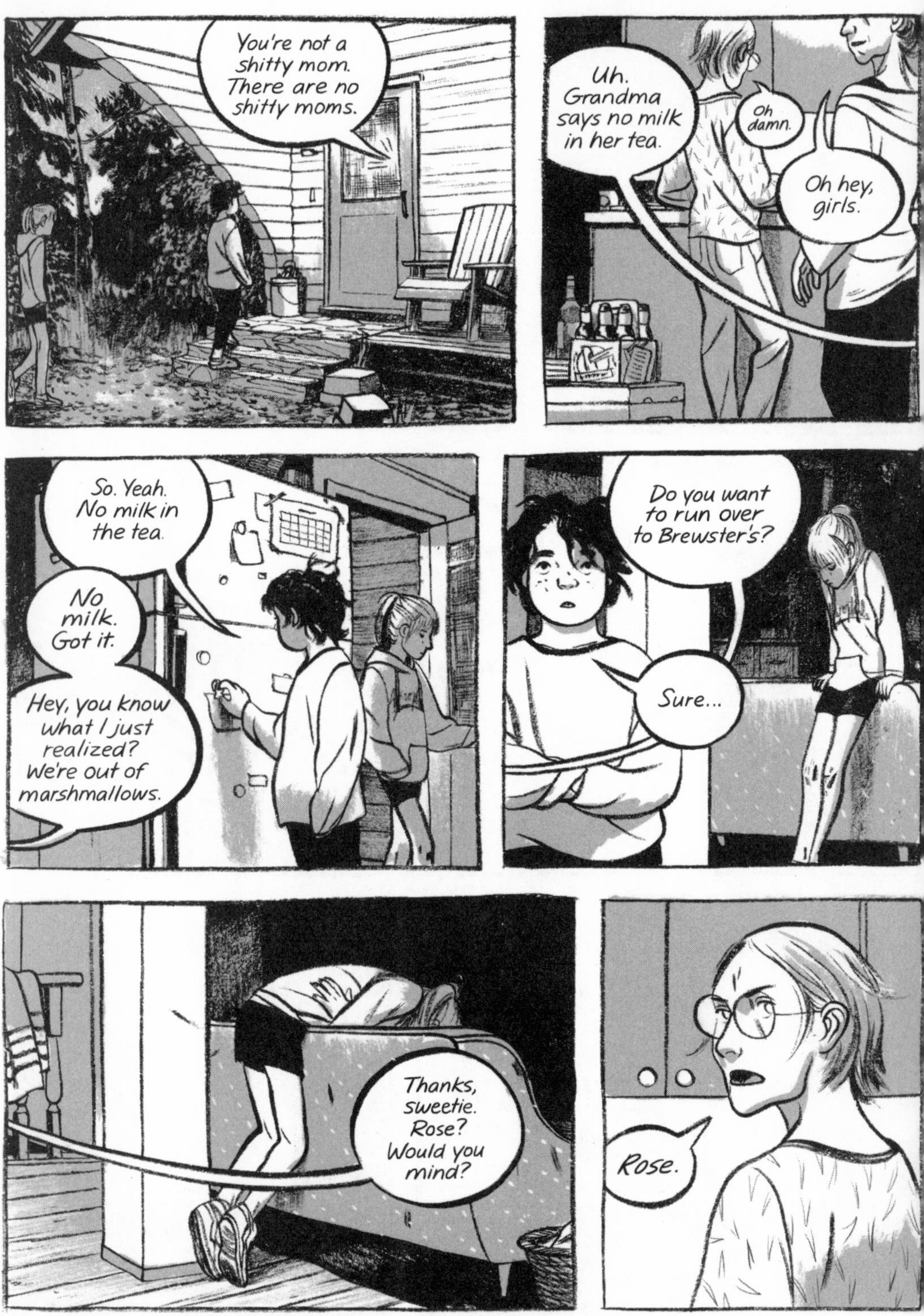
You're not a shitty mom. There are no shitty moms.
Uh. Grandma says no milk in her tea.
Oh damn.
Oh hey, girls.
So. Yeah. No milk in the tea.
No milk. Got it.
Hey, you know what I just realized? We're out of marshmallows.
Do you want to run over to Brewster's?
Sure...
Thanks, sweetie. Rose? Would you mind?
Rose.

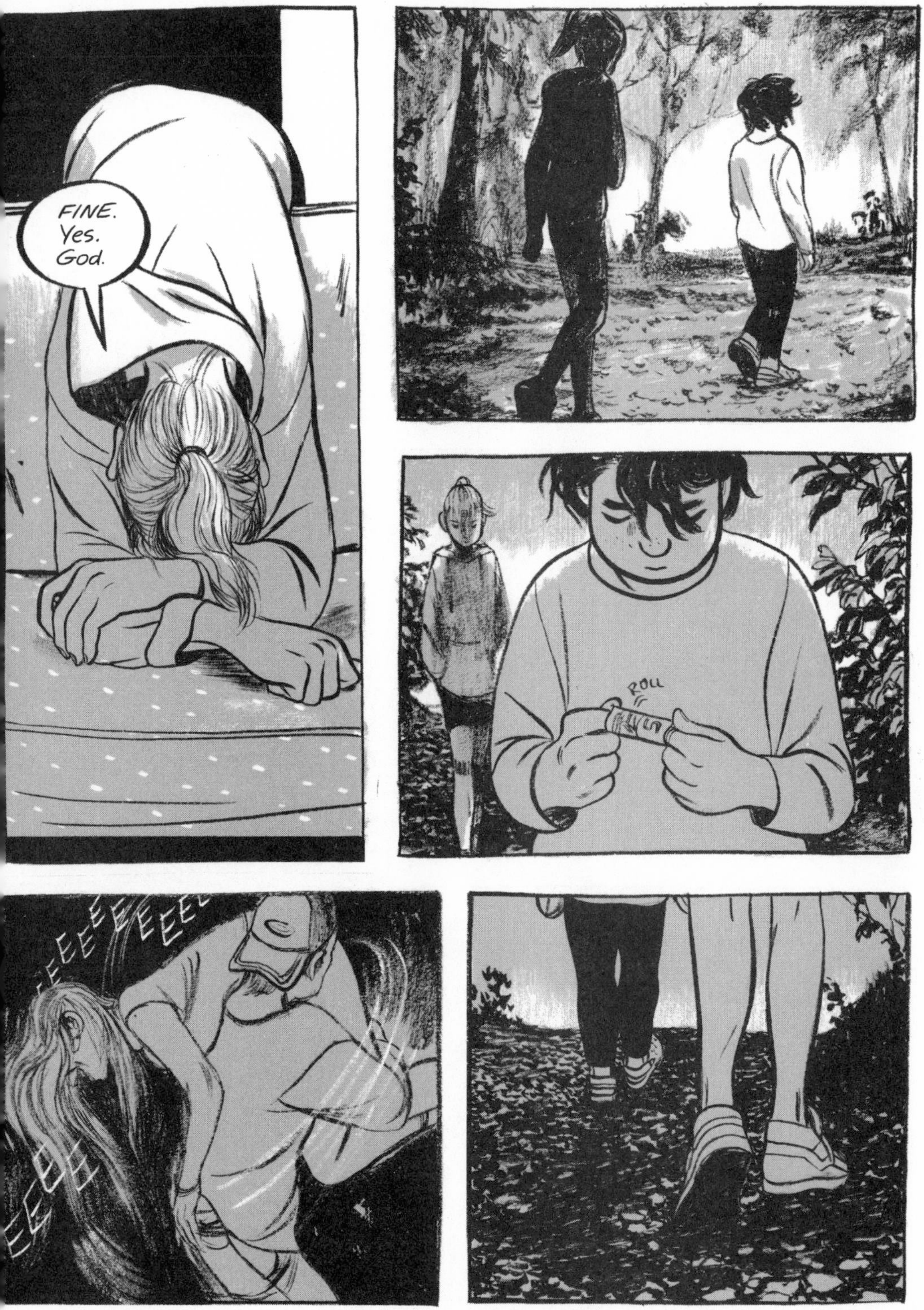
FINE. Yes. God.
ROLL

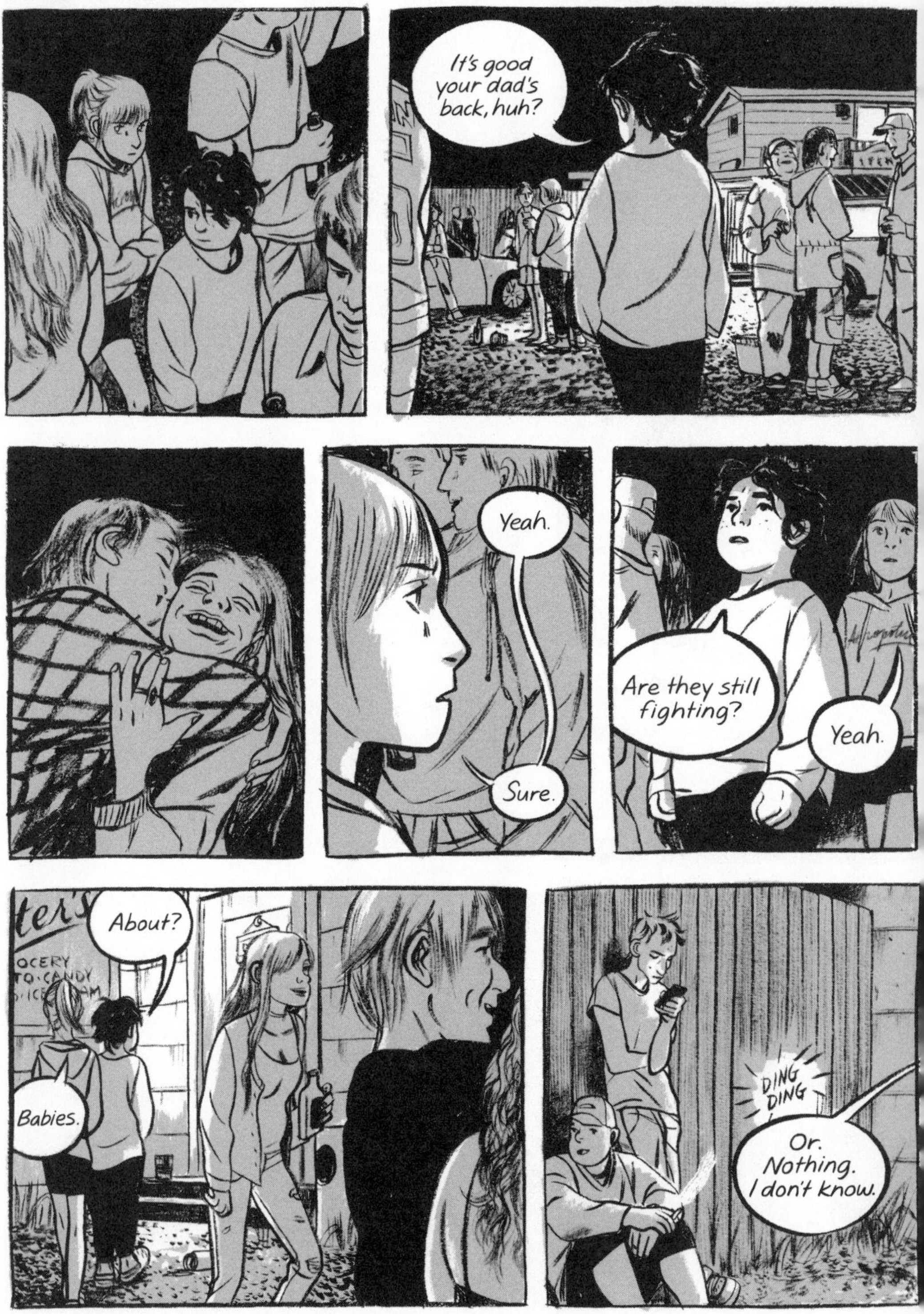
It's good your dad's back, huh?
Yeah.
Sure.
Are they still fighting?
Yeah.
About?
Babies.
DING DING
Or. Nothing. I don't know.

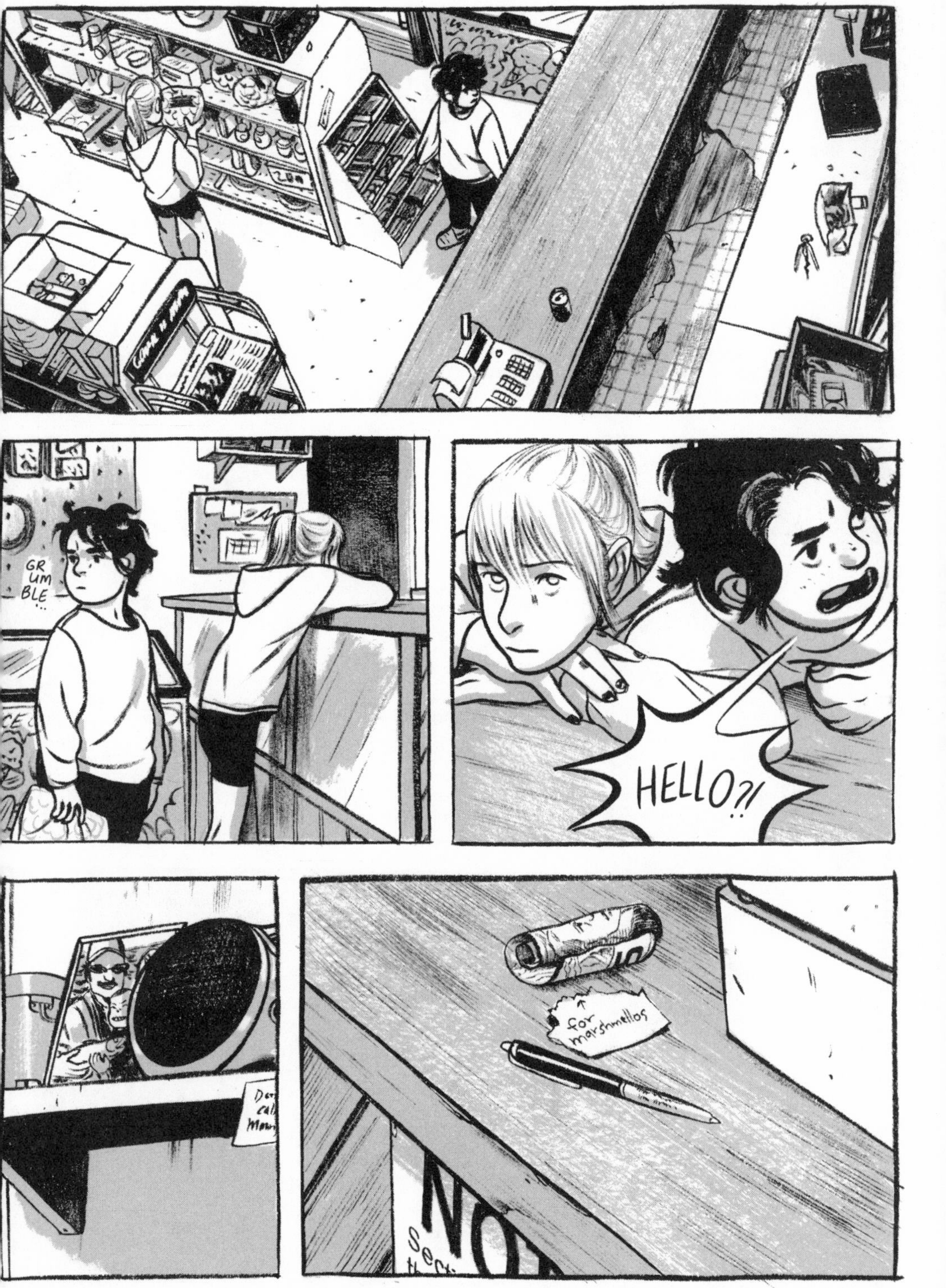
GR UM BLE ...
HELLO?!
for marshmellos

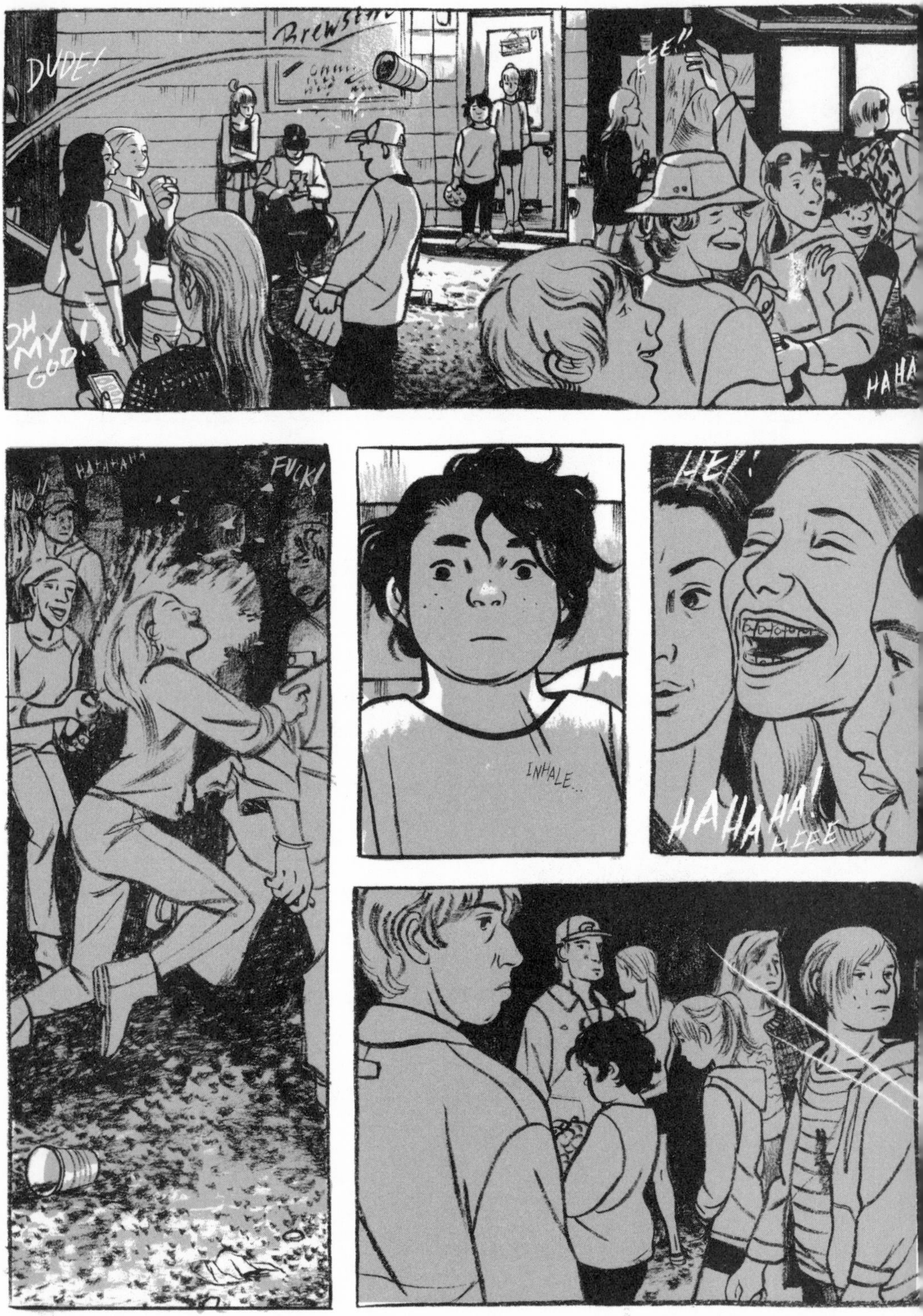
DUDE!
EEE!!
OH MY GOD!
HAHA
NO!!
HAHAHAHA
FUCK!
INHALE...
HEY!
HAHAHA!

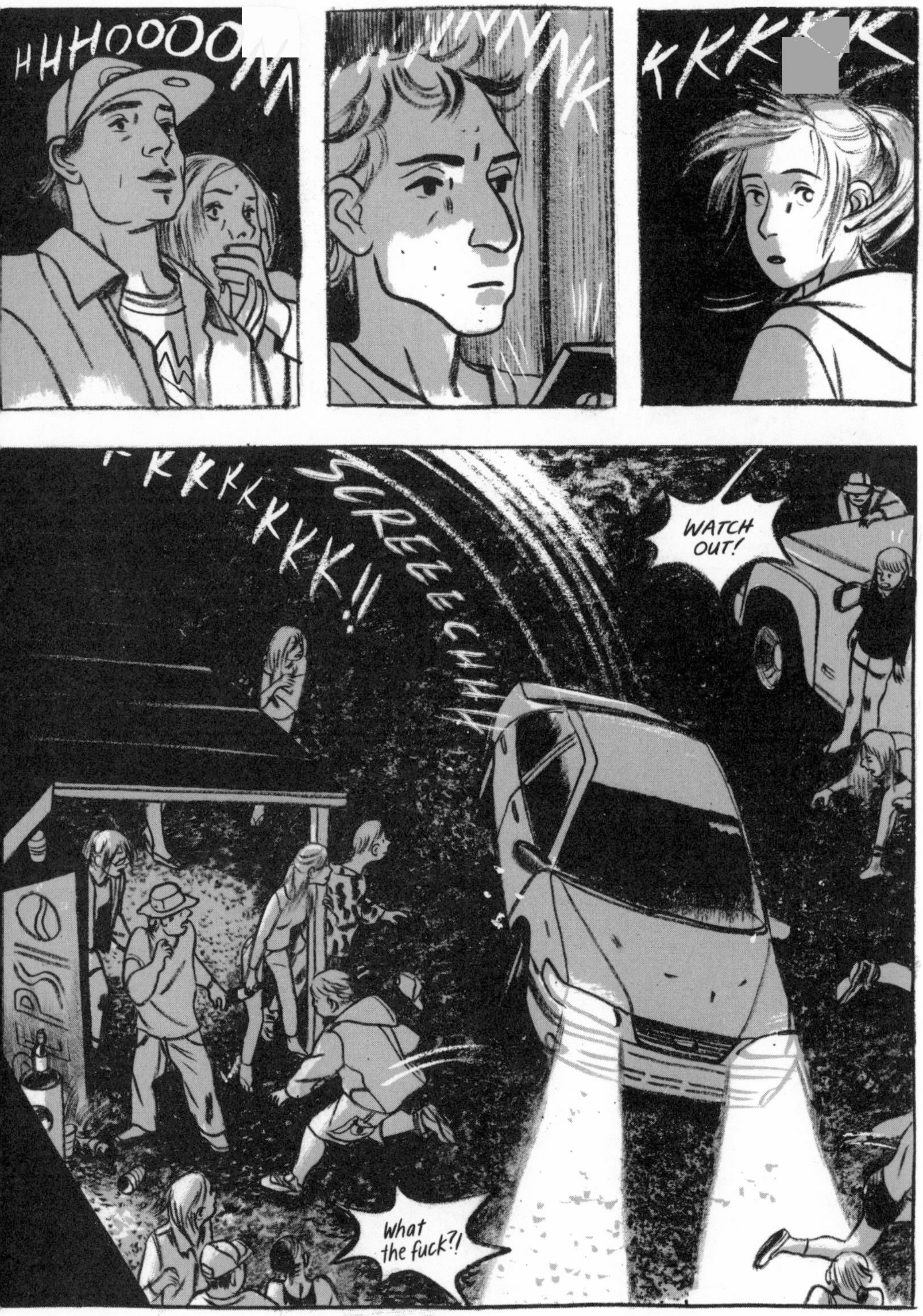
HHHOOOON
NNNNK
KKKKK
KKKKKKKKK!!
SCREEECHHH
WATCH OUT!
What the fuck?!

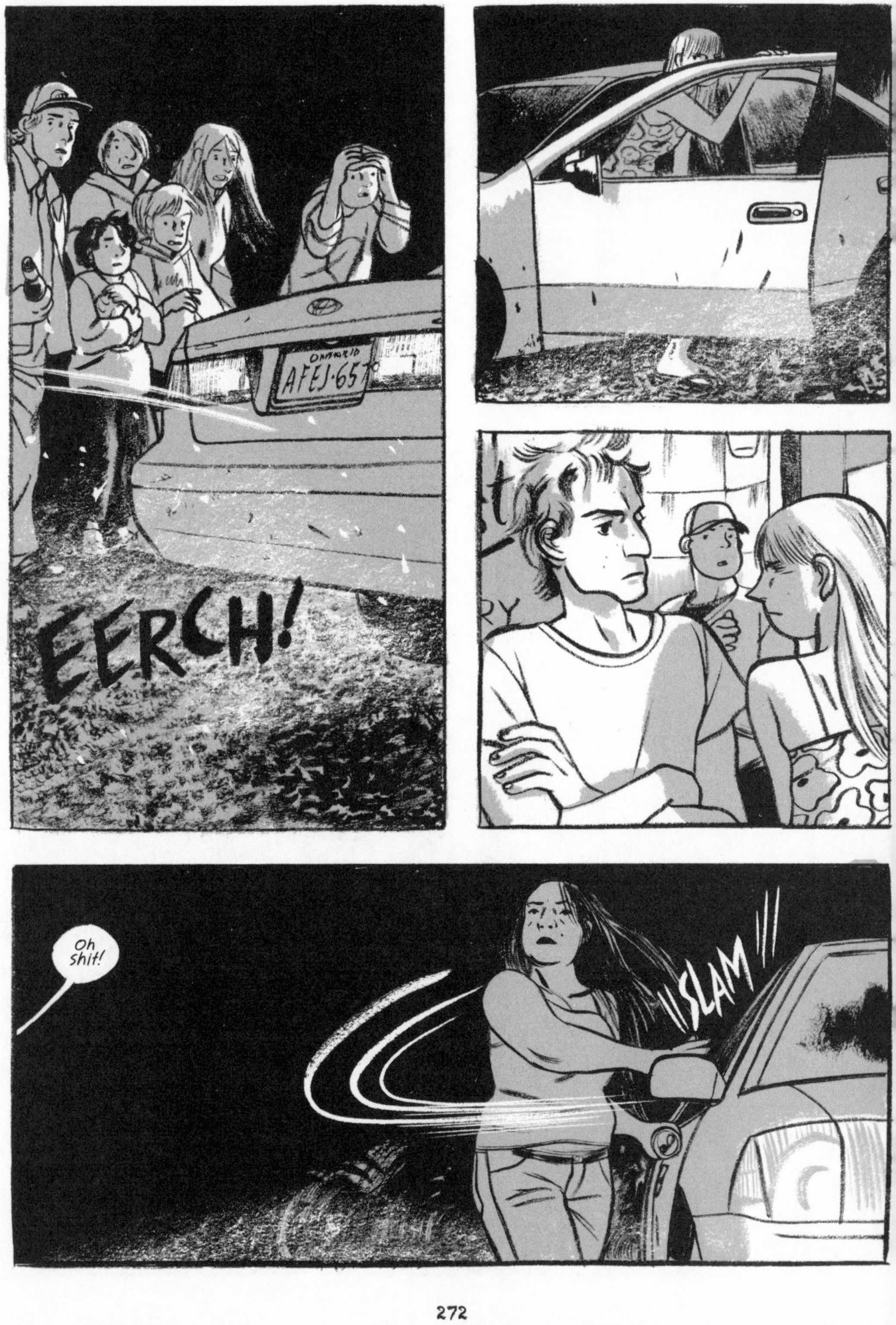
EERCH!
Oh shit!
SLAM

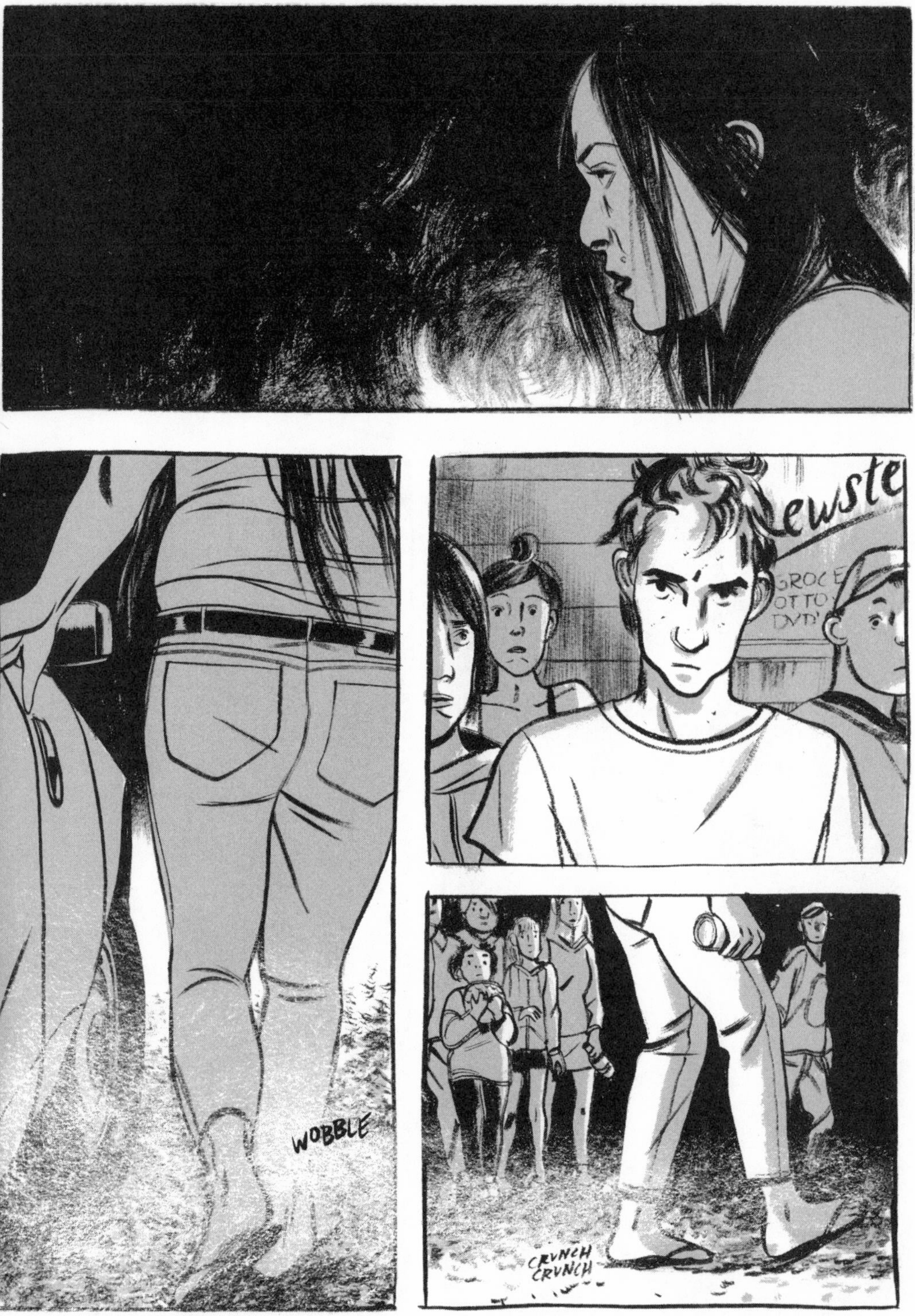
WOBBLE
CRUNCH
CRUNCH

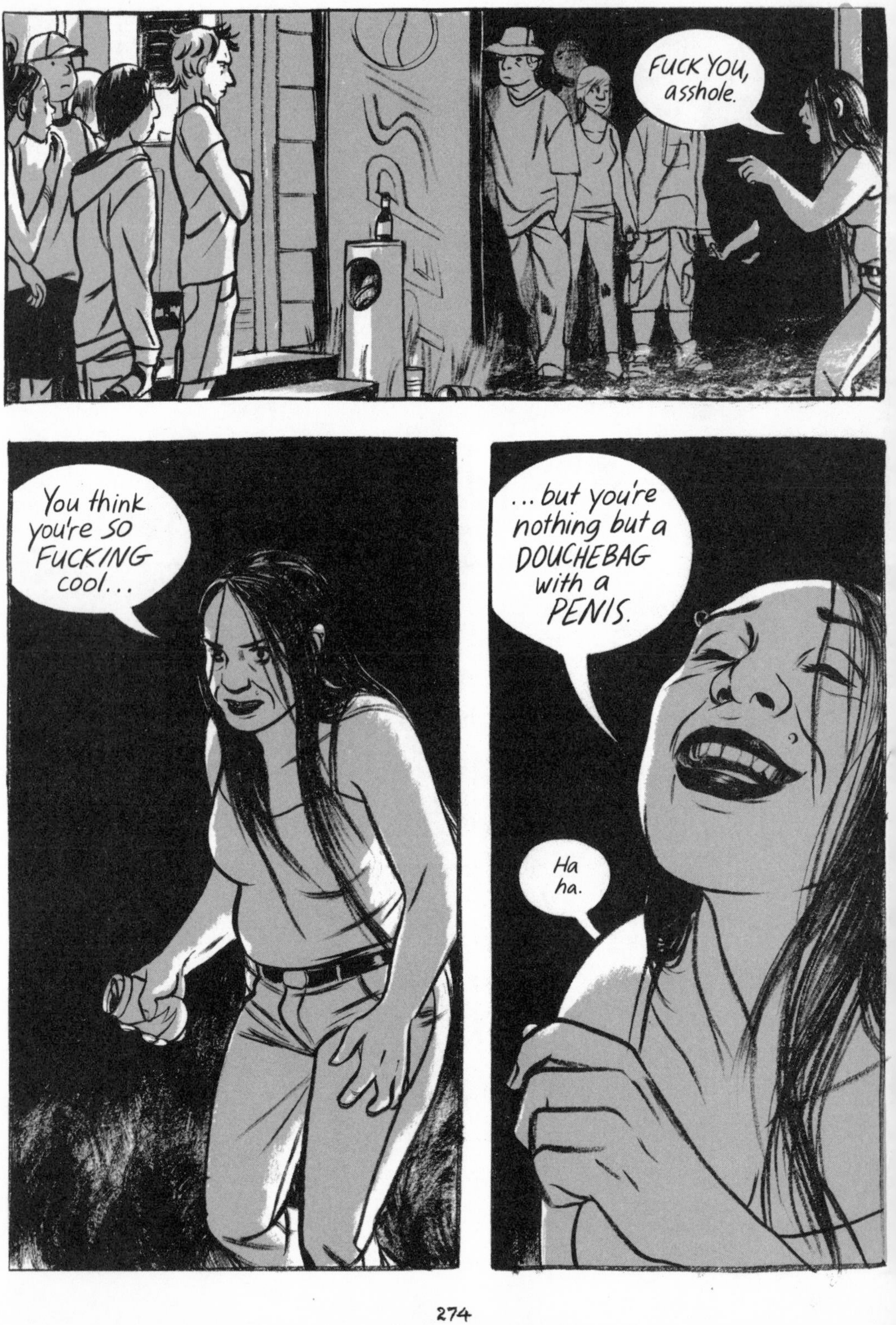
FUCK YOU, asshole.
You think you're SO FUCKING cool...
...but you're nothing but a DOUCHEBAG with a PENIS.
Ha ha.

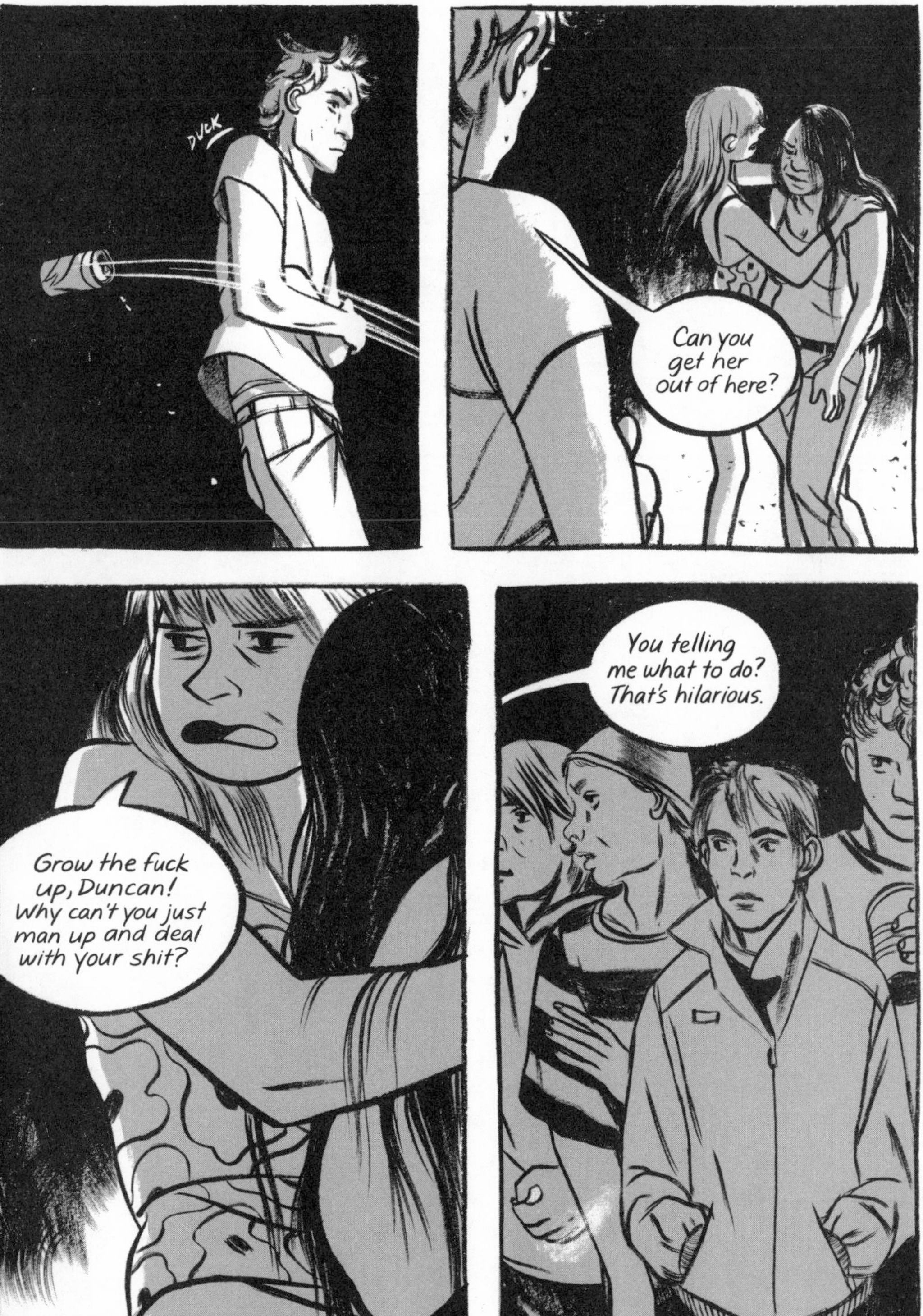
DUCK
Can you get her out of here?
Grow the fuck up, Duncan! Why can't you just man up and deal with your shit?
You telling me what to do? That's hilarious.

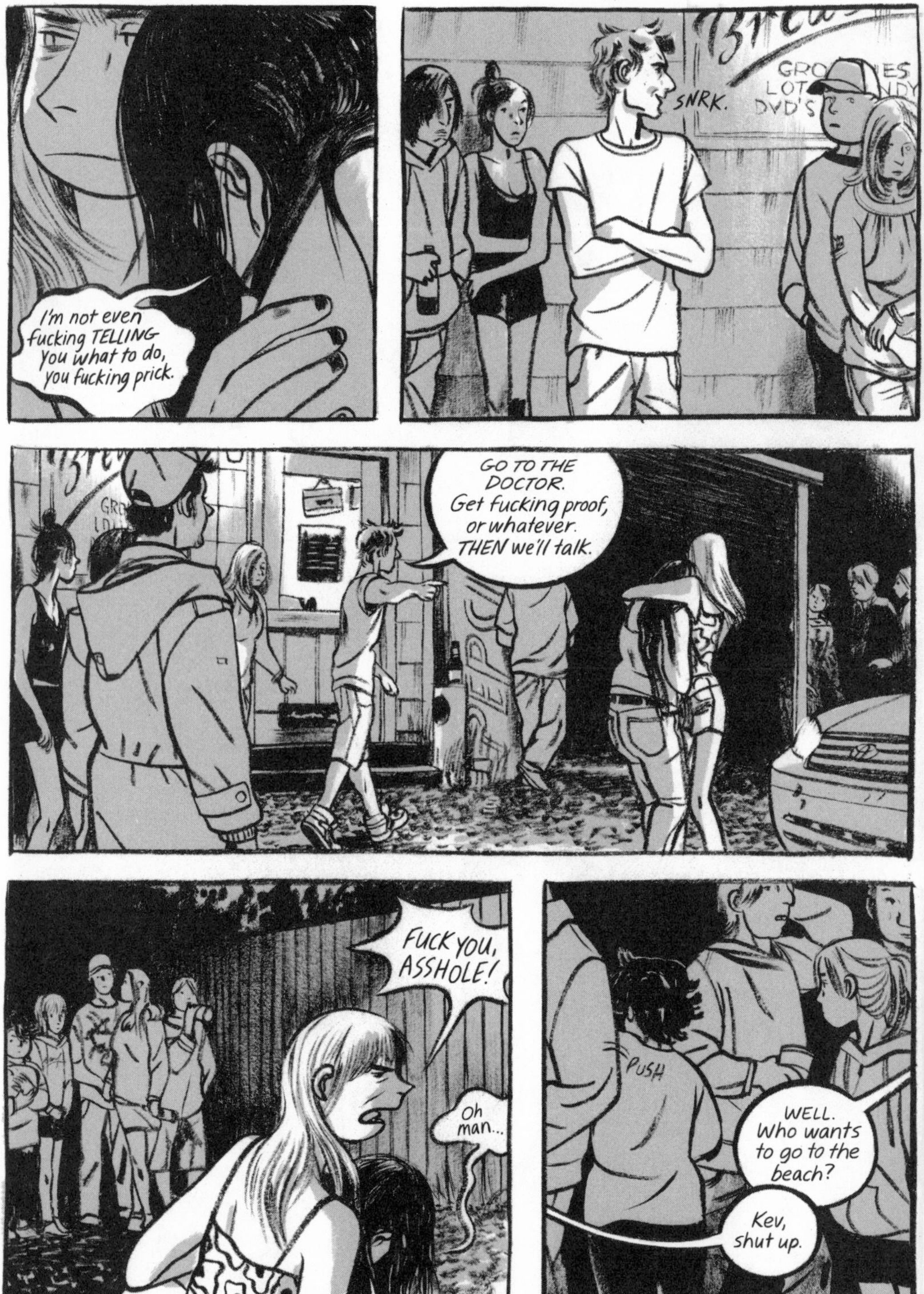
I'm not even fucking TELLING you what to do, you fucking prick.
SNRK.
GROCERIES LOTTO CANDY DVD'S
GO TO THE DOCTOR. Get fucking proof, or whatever. THEN we'll talk.
FUCK YOU, ASSHOLE!
Oh man...
PUSH
WELL. Who wants to go to the beach?
Kev, shut up.

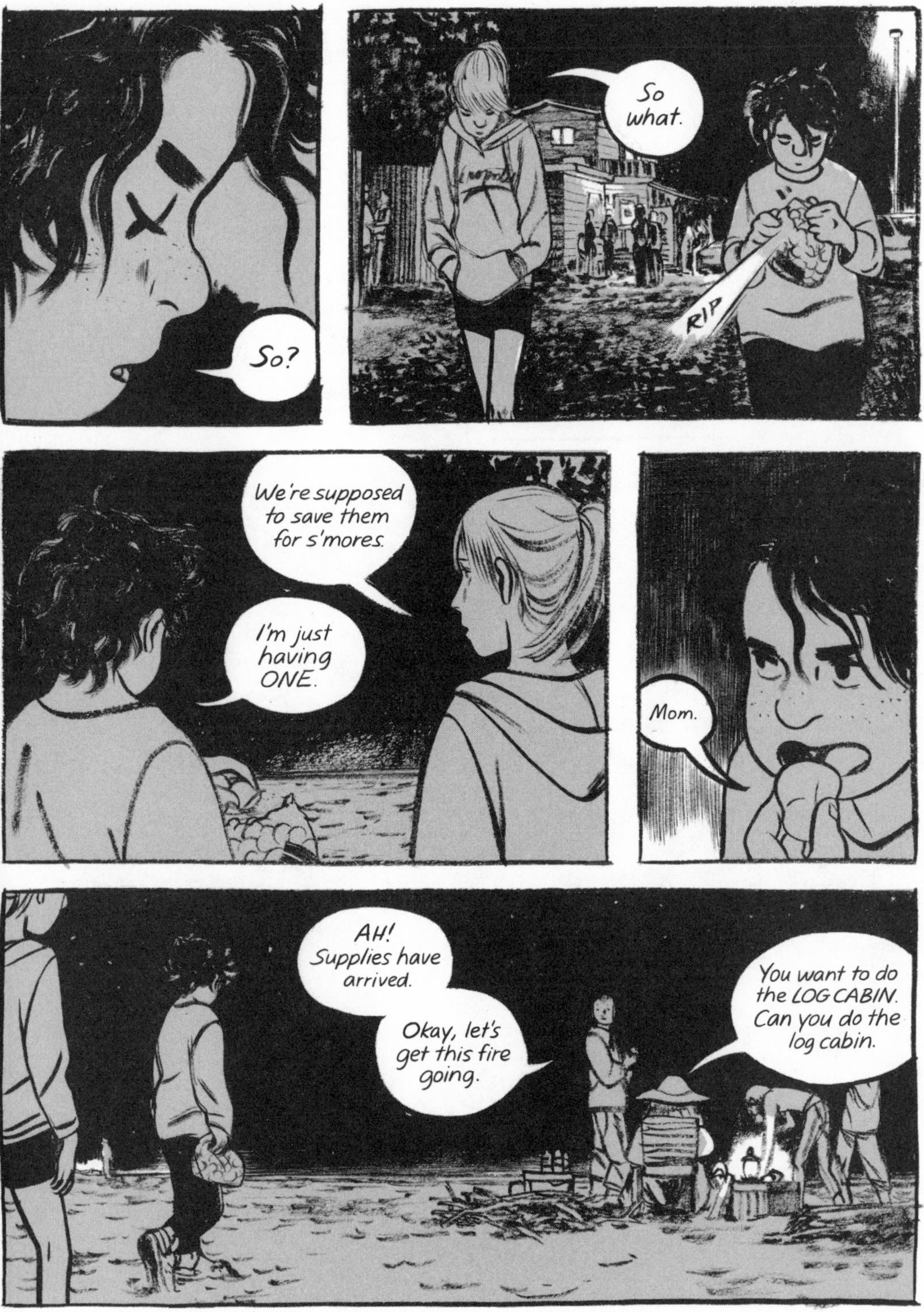
So?
So what.
RIP
We're supposed to save them for s'mores.
I'm just having ONE.
Mom.
AH! Supplies have arrived.
Okay, let's get this fire going.
You want to do the LOG CABIN. Can you do the log cabin.

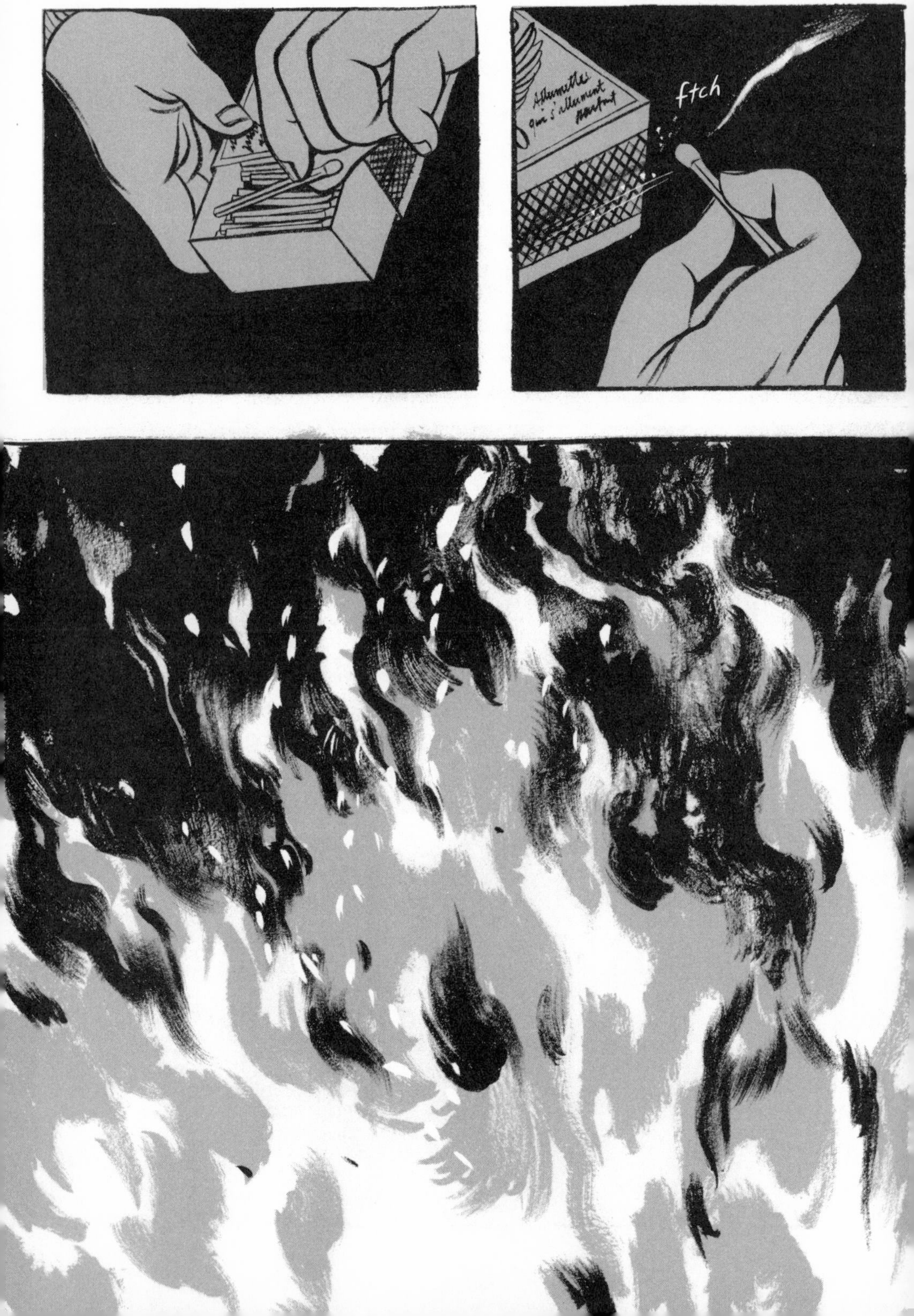
Allumettes qui s'allument partout
ftch

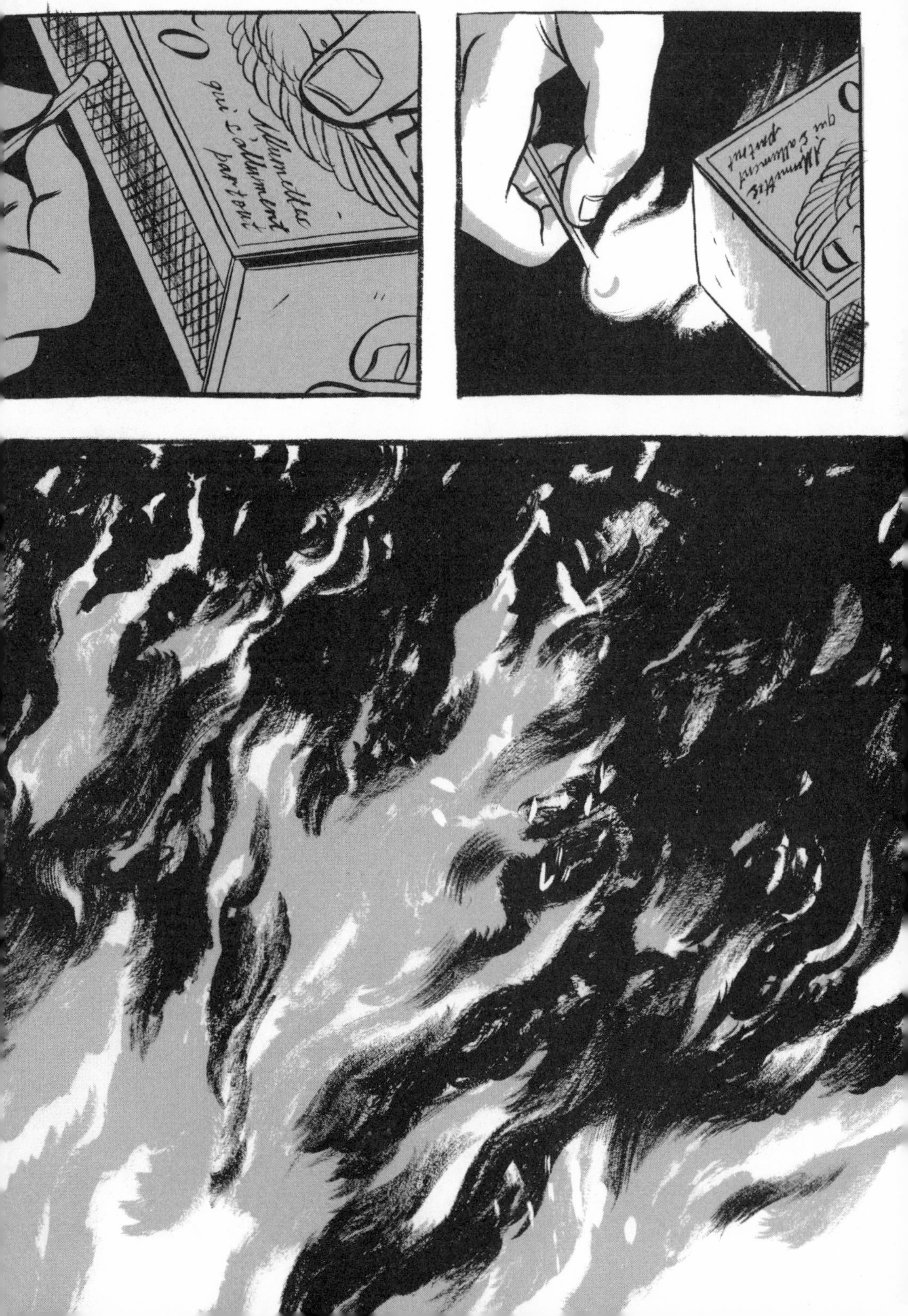

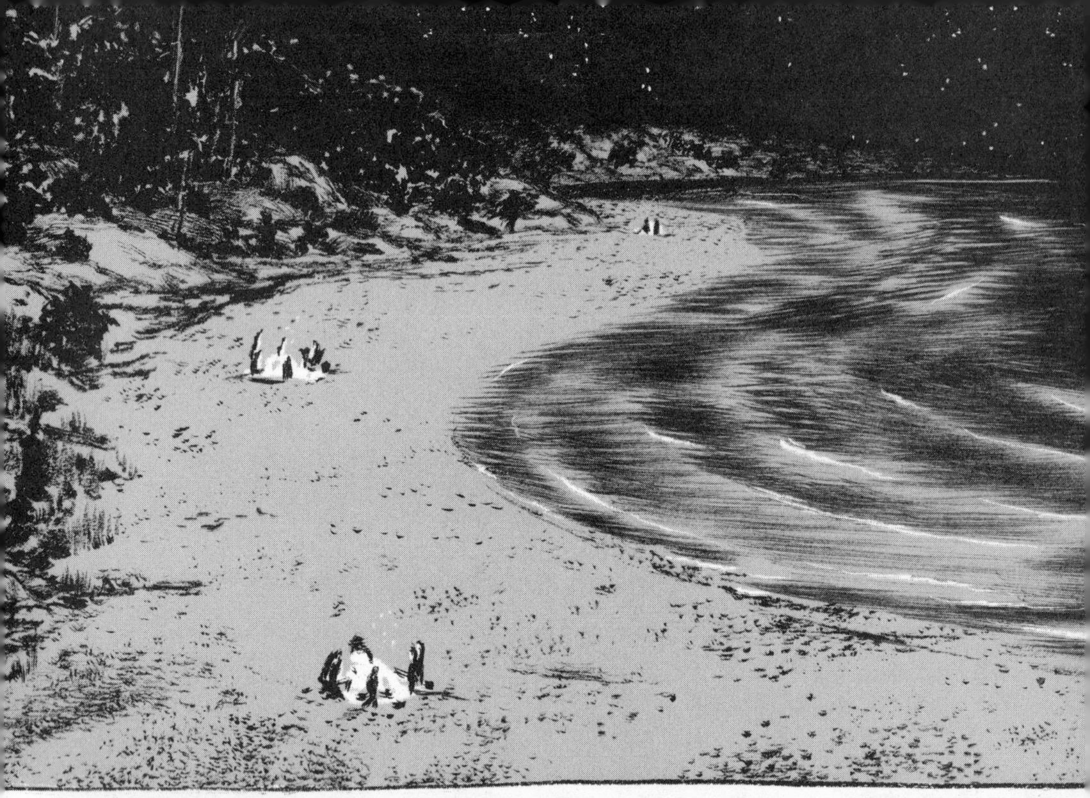

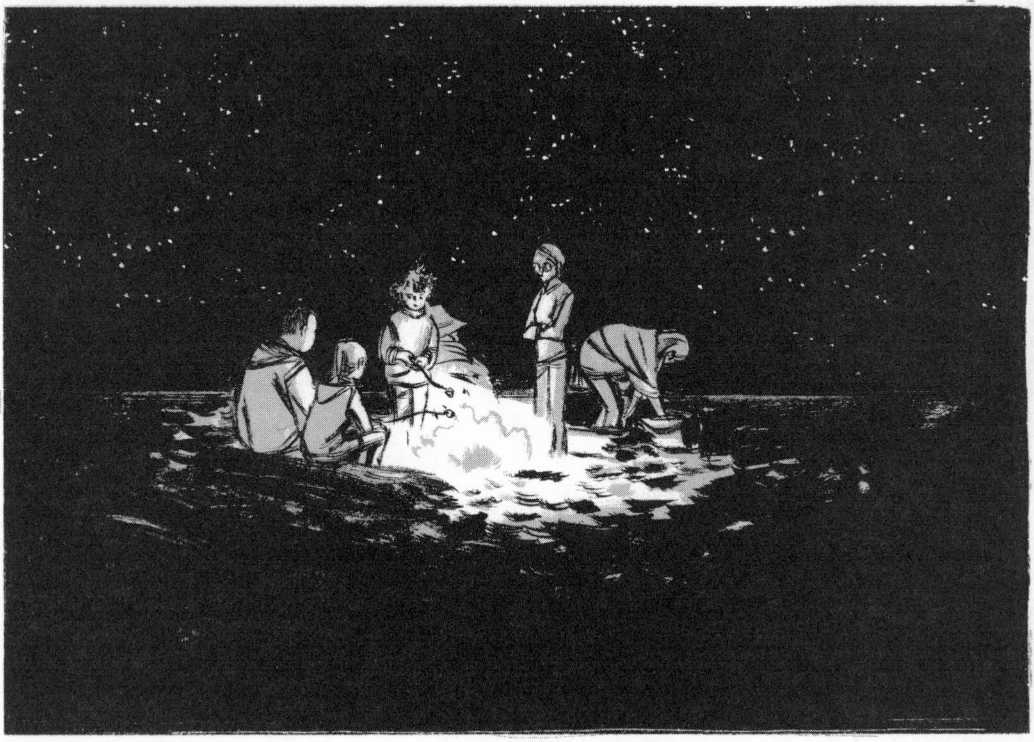

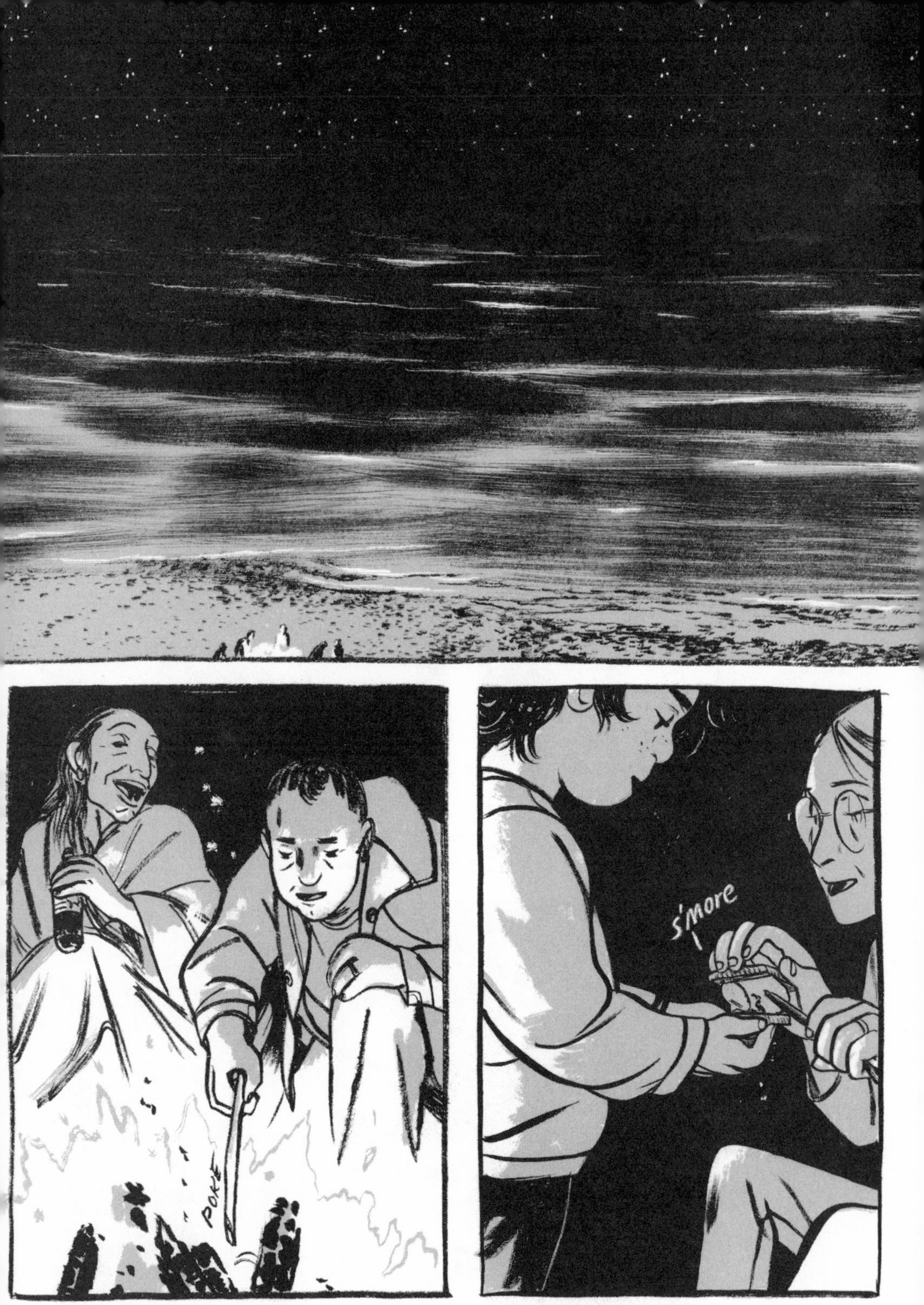
POKE
s'more

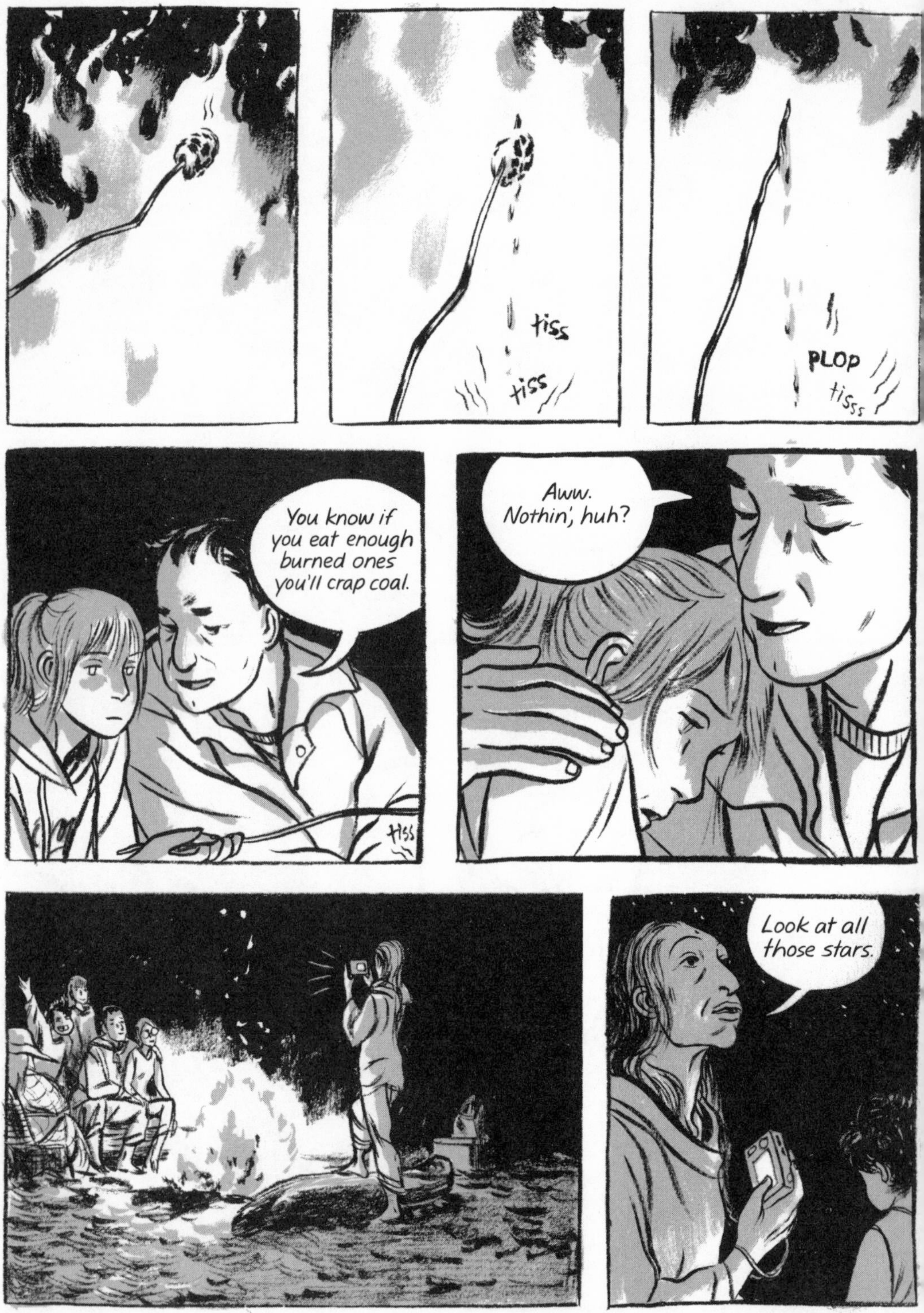
tiss
tiss
PLOP
tisss
You know if you eat enough burned ones you'll crap coal.
tiss
Aww. Nothin', huh?
Look at all those stars.

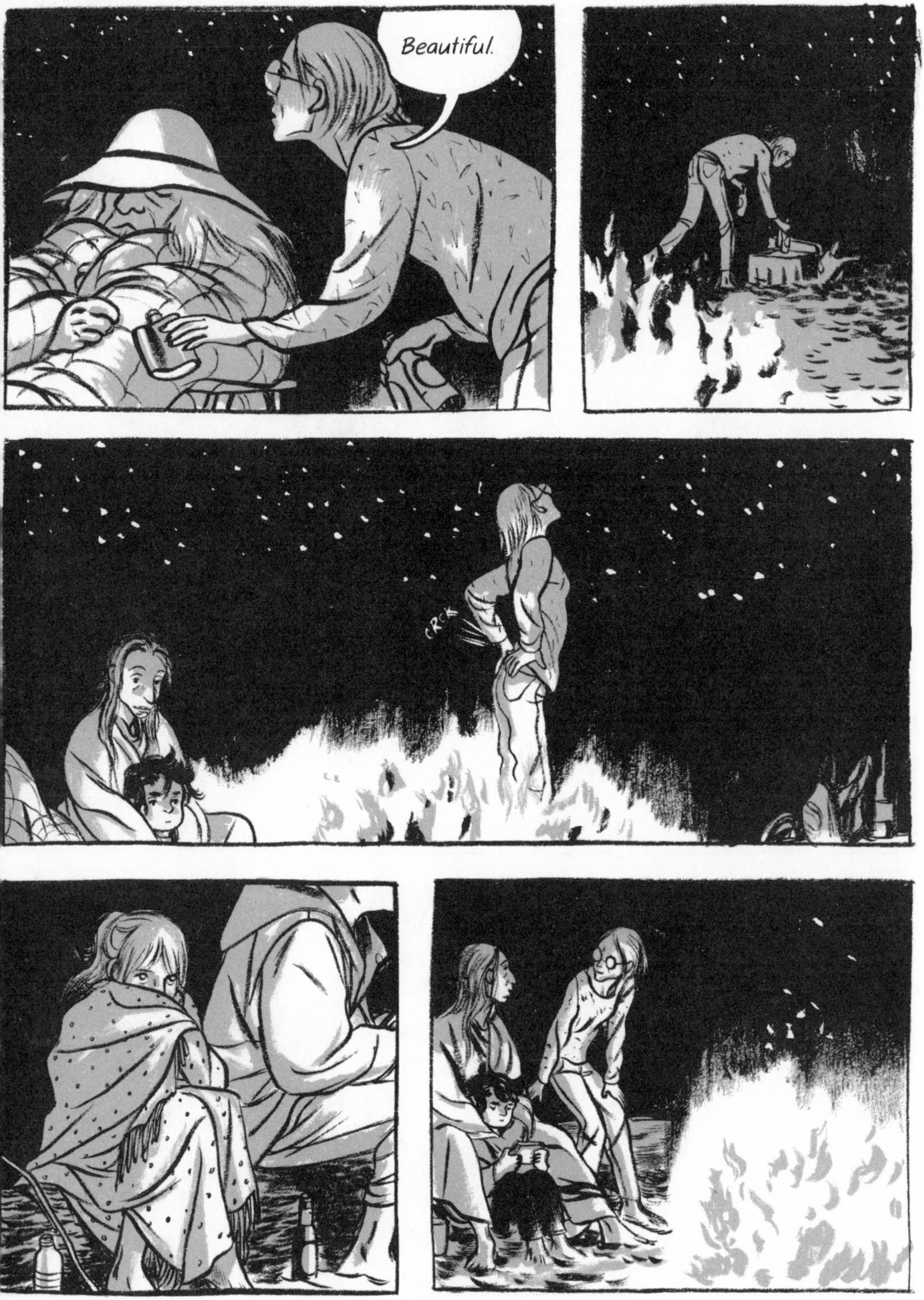

Beautiful.
CRCK

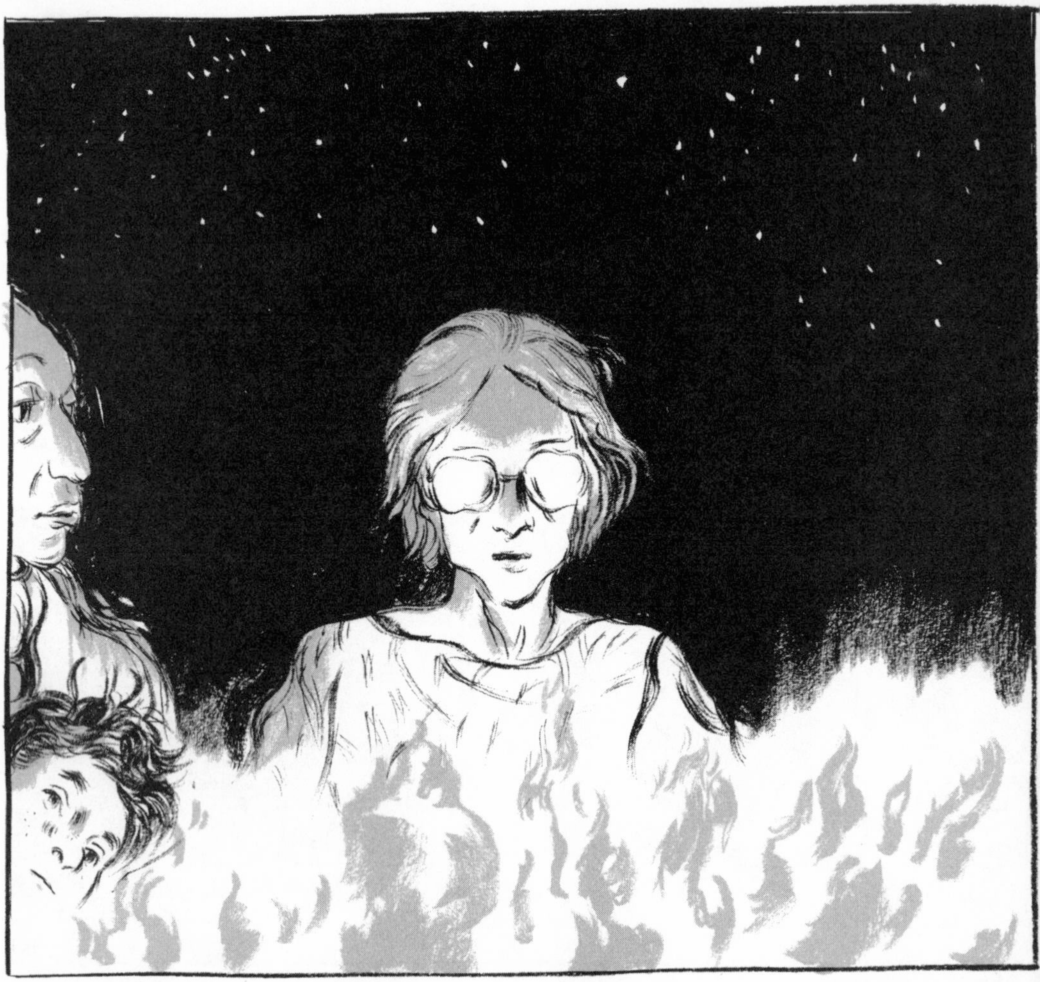

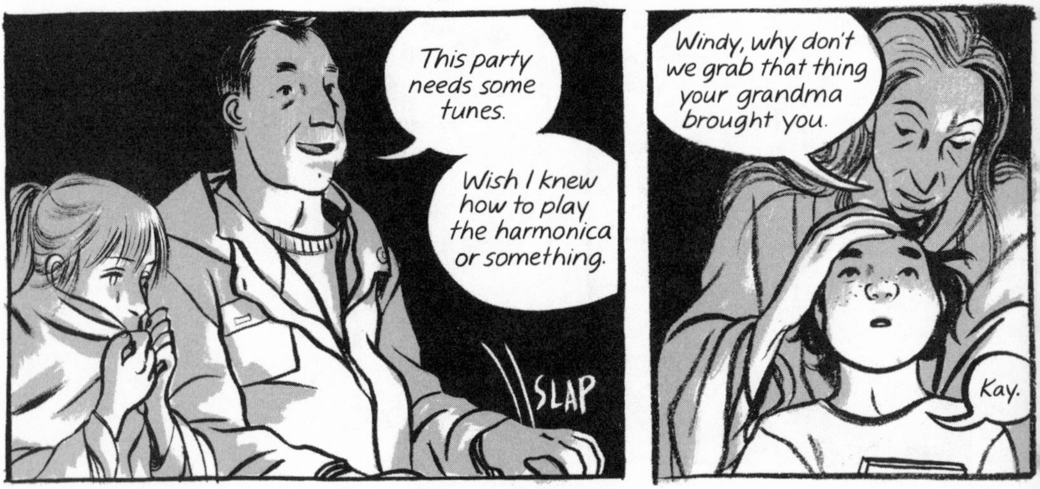
This party needs some tunes.
Wish I knew how to play the harmonica or something.
SLAP
Windy, why don't we grab that thing your grandma brought you.
Kay.

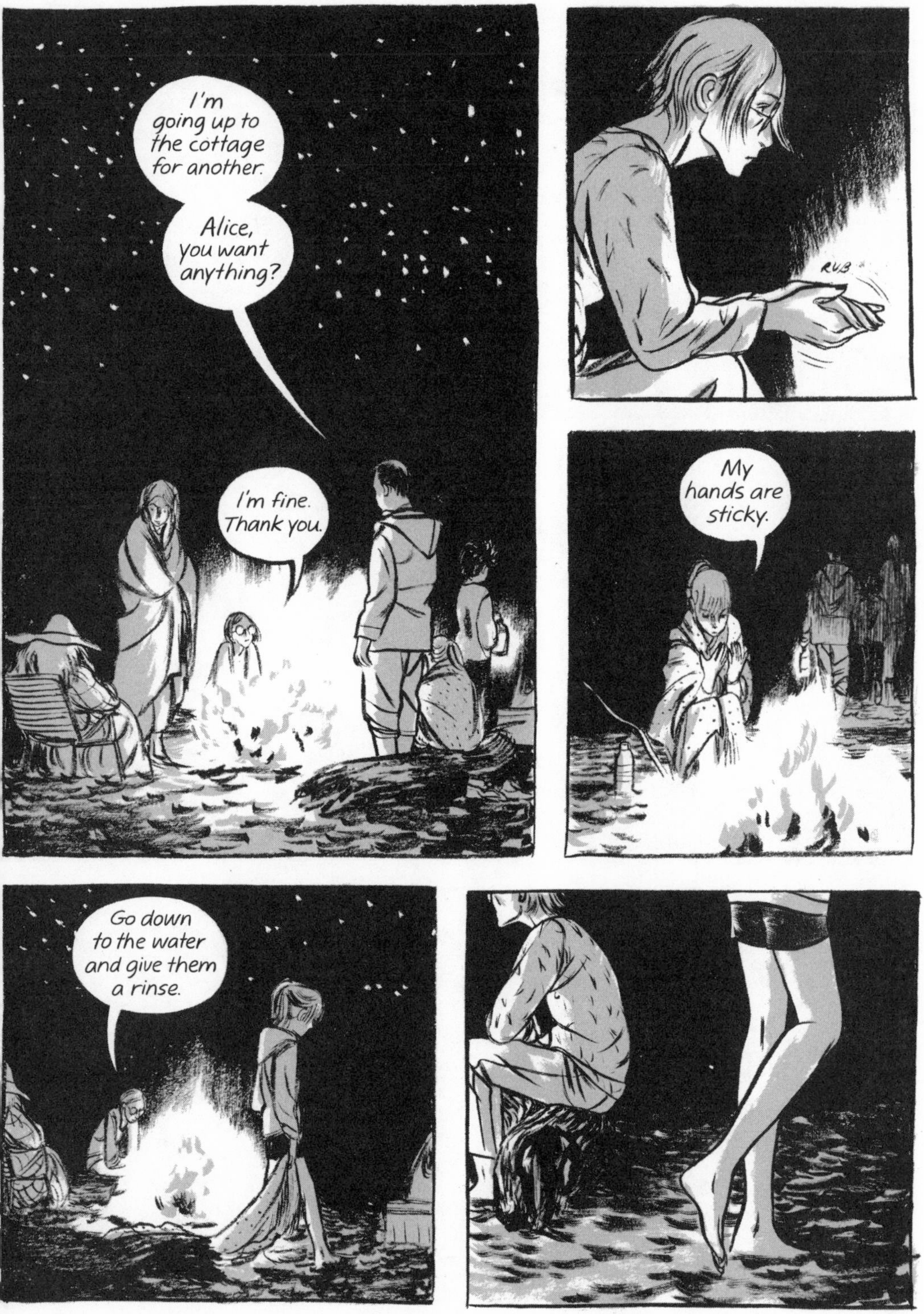
I'm going up to the cottage for another.
Alice, you want anything?
I'm fine. Thank you.
RUB
My hands are sticky.
Go down to the water and give them a rinse.

Babies.

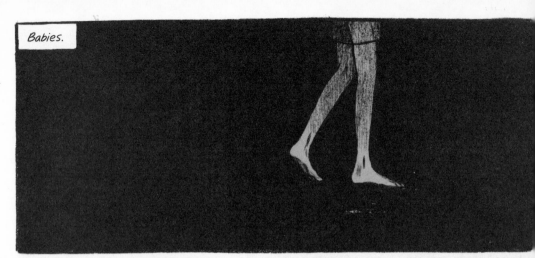

RUB
RUB

Or. Nothing.

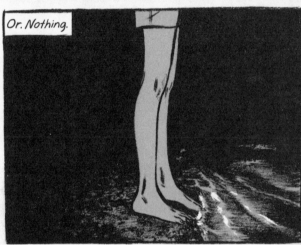

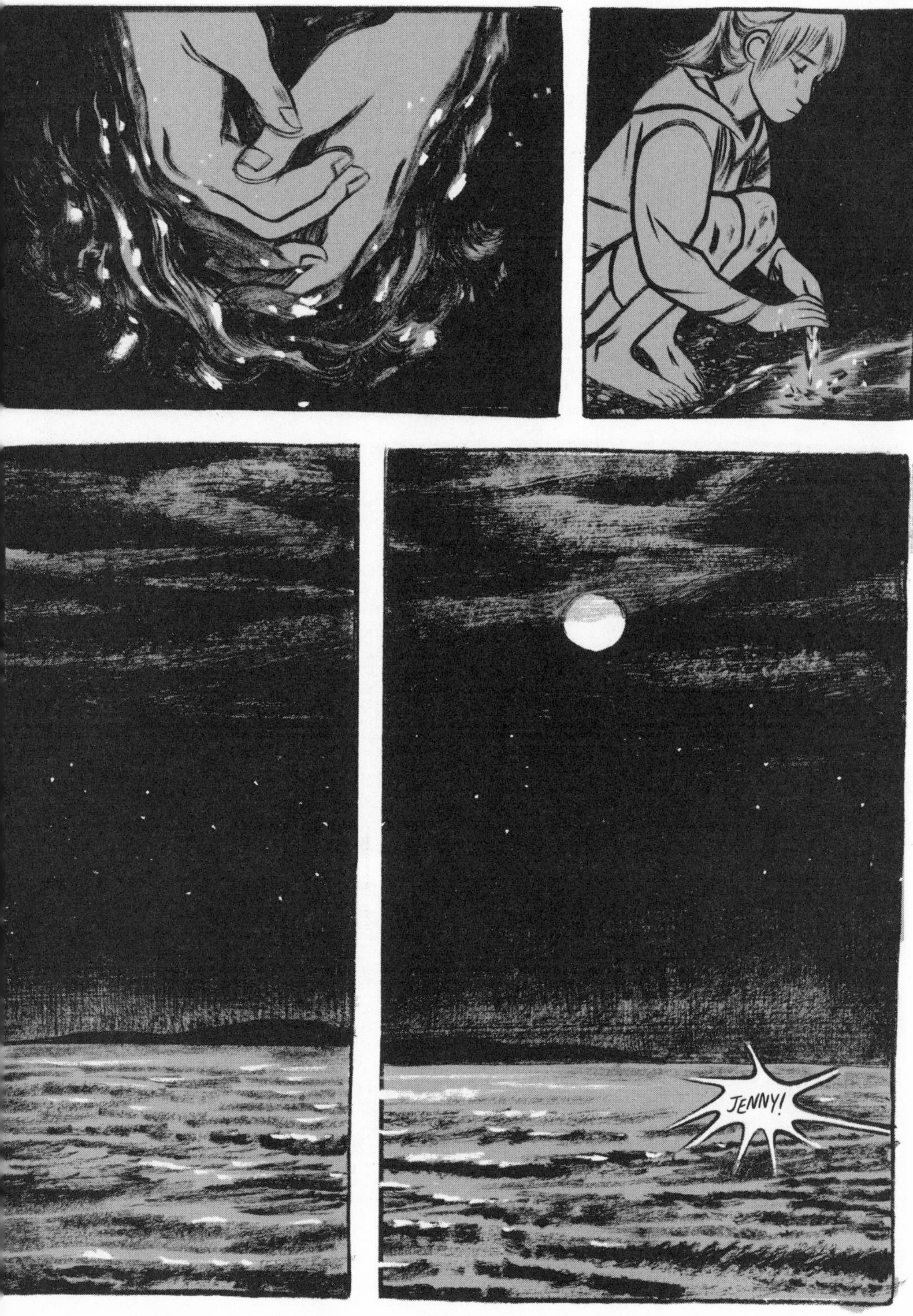
JENNY!

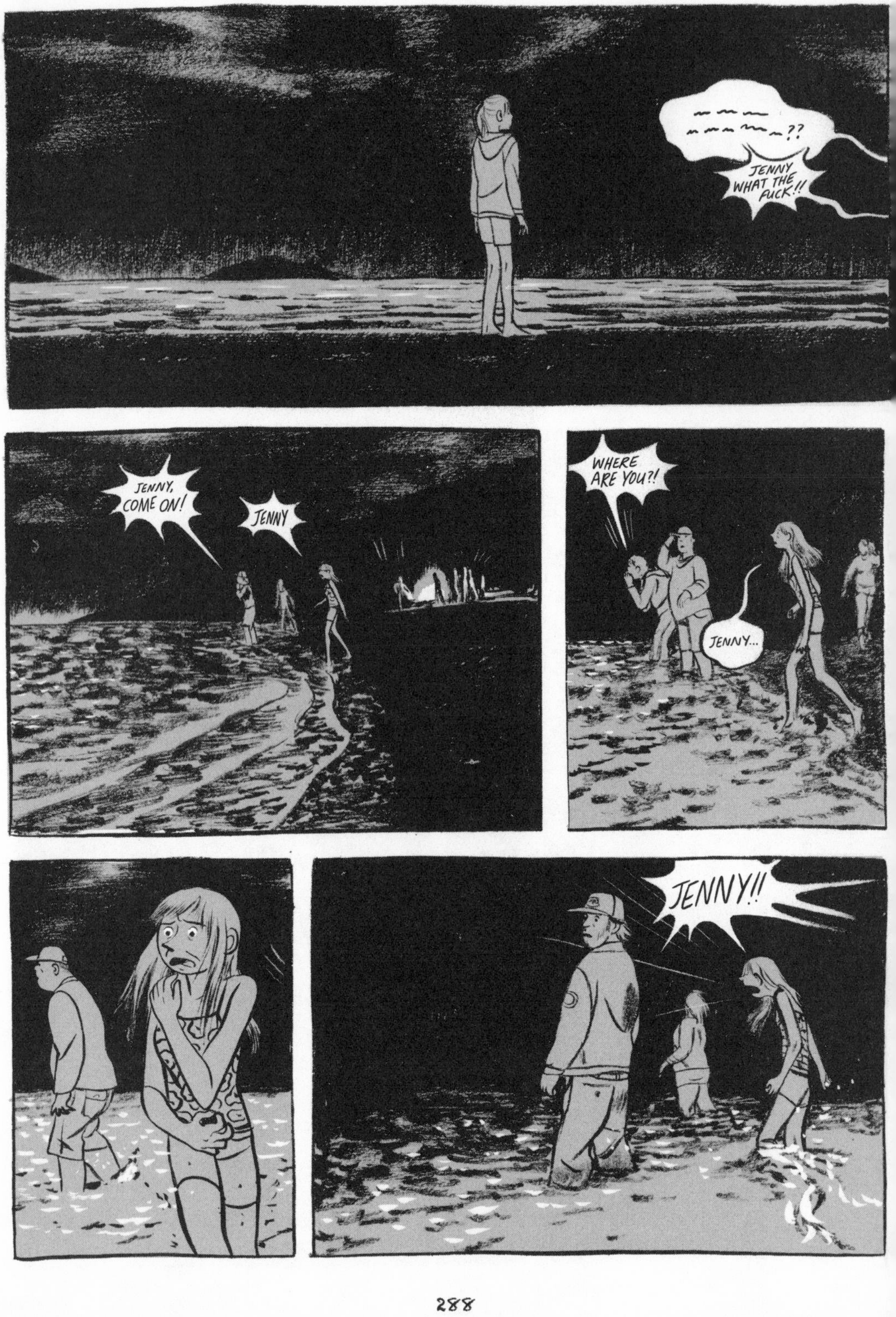

JENNY WHAT THE FUCK!!
JENNY, COME ON!
JENNY
WHERE ARE YOU?!
JENNY...
JENNY!!

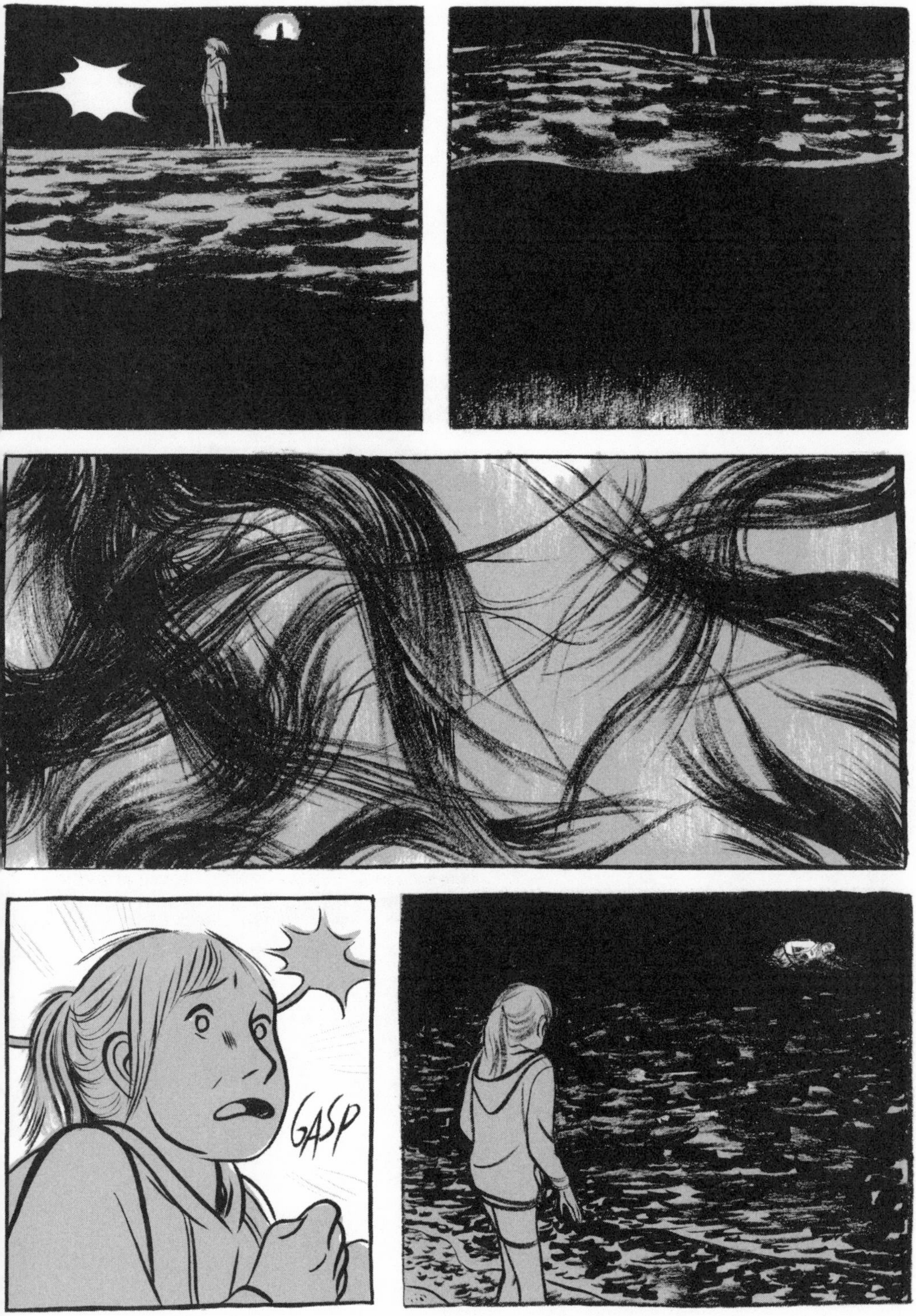
GASP

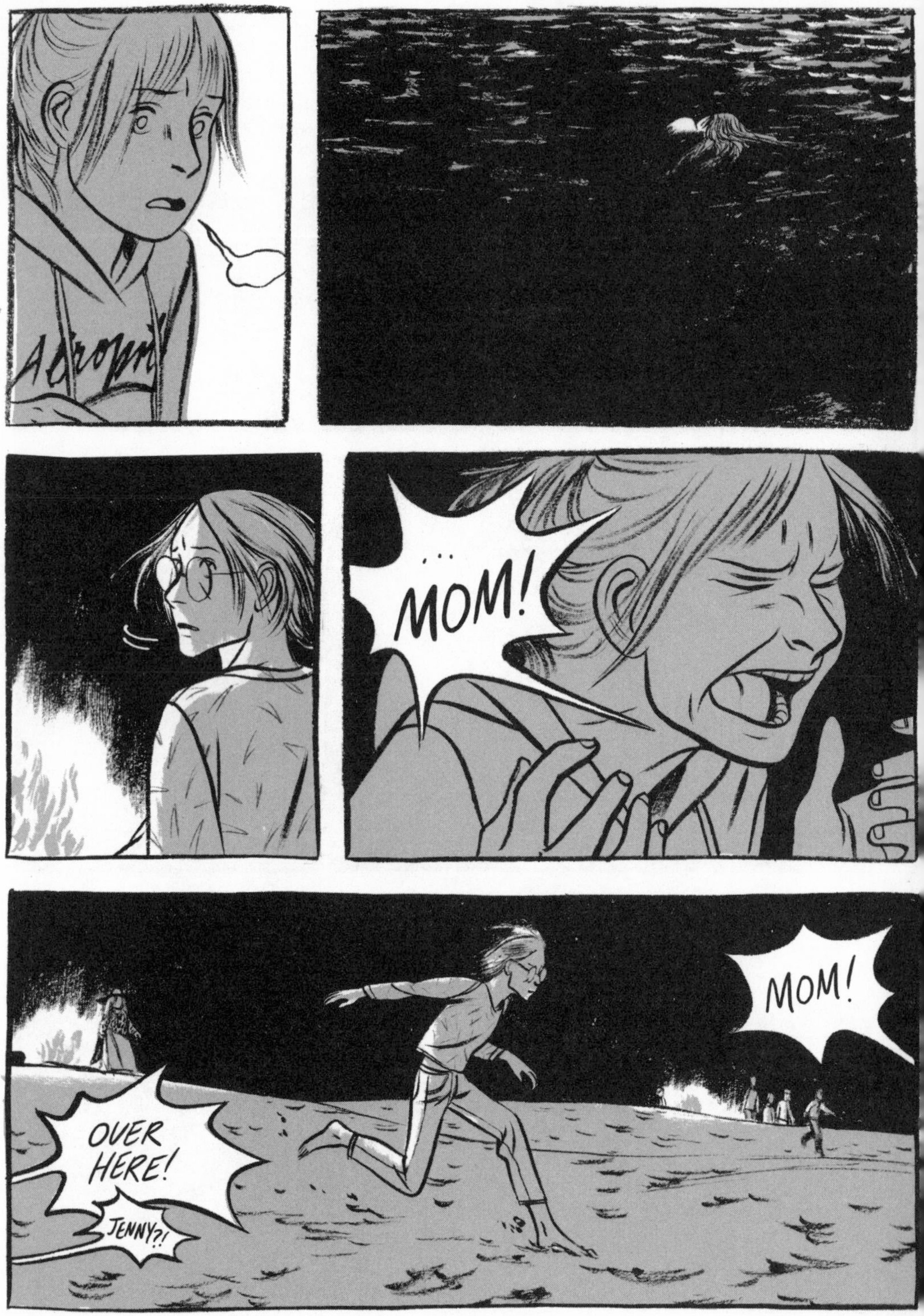
...
MOM!
MOM!
OVER HERE!
JENNY?!

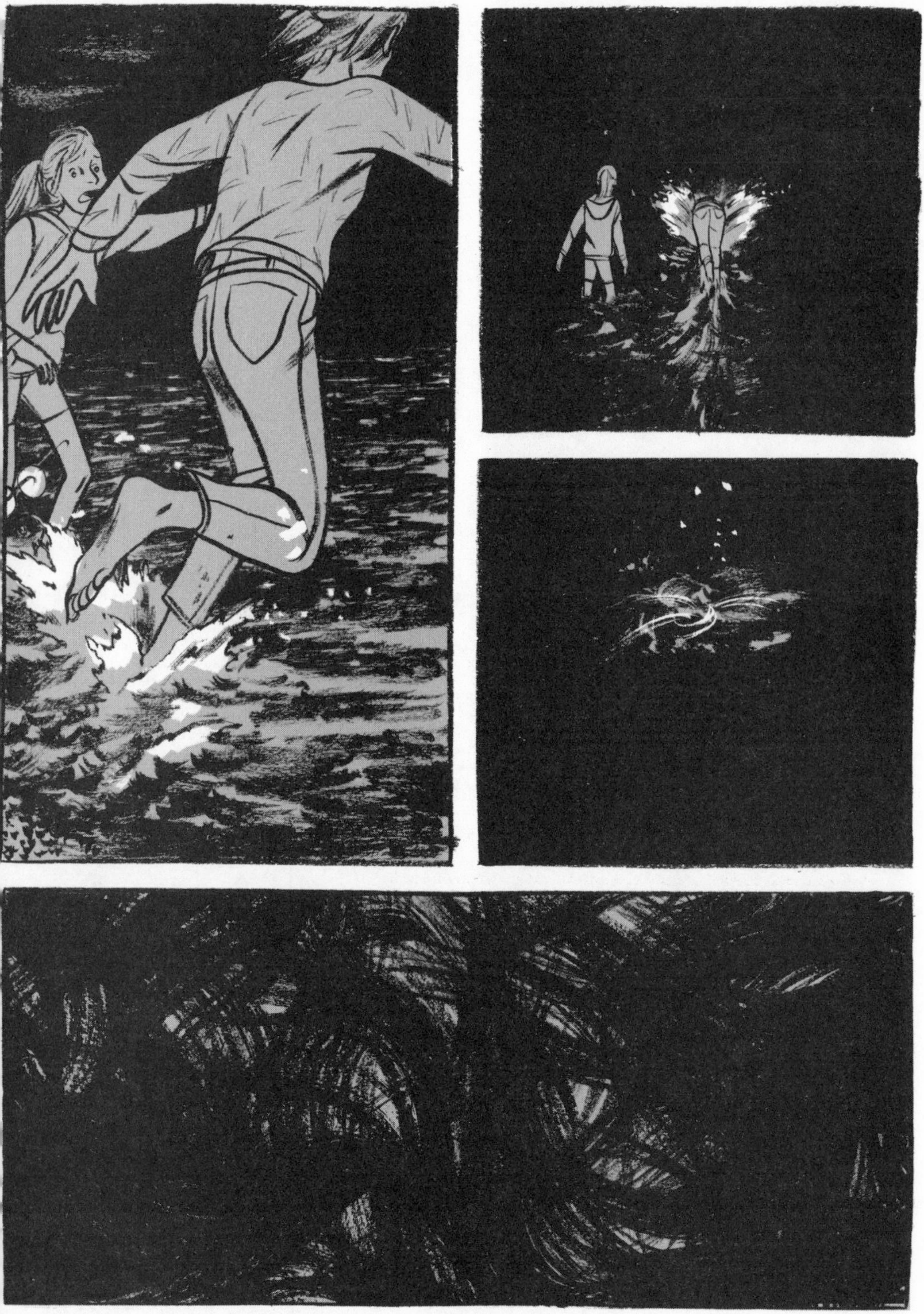

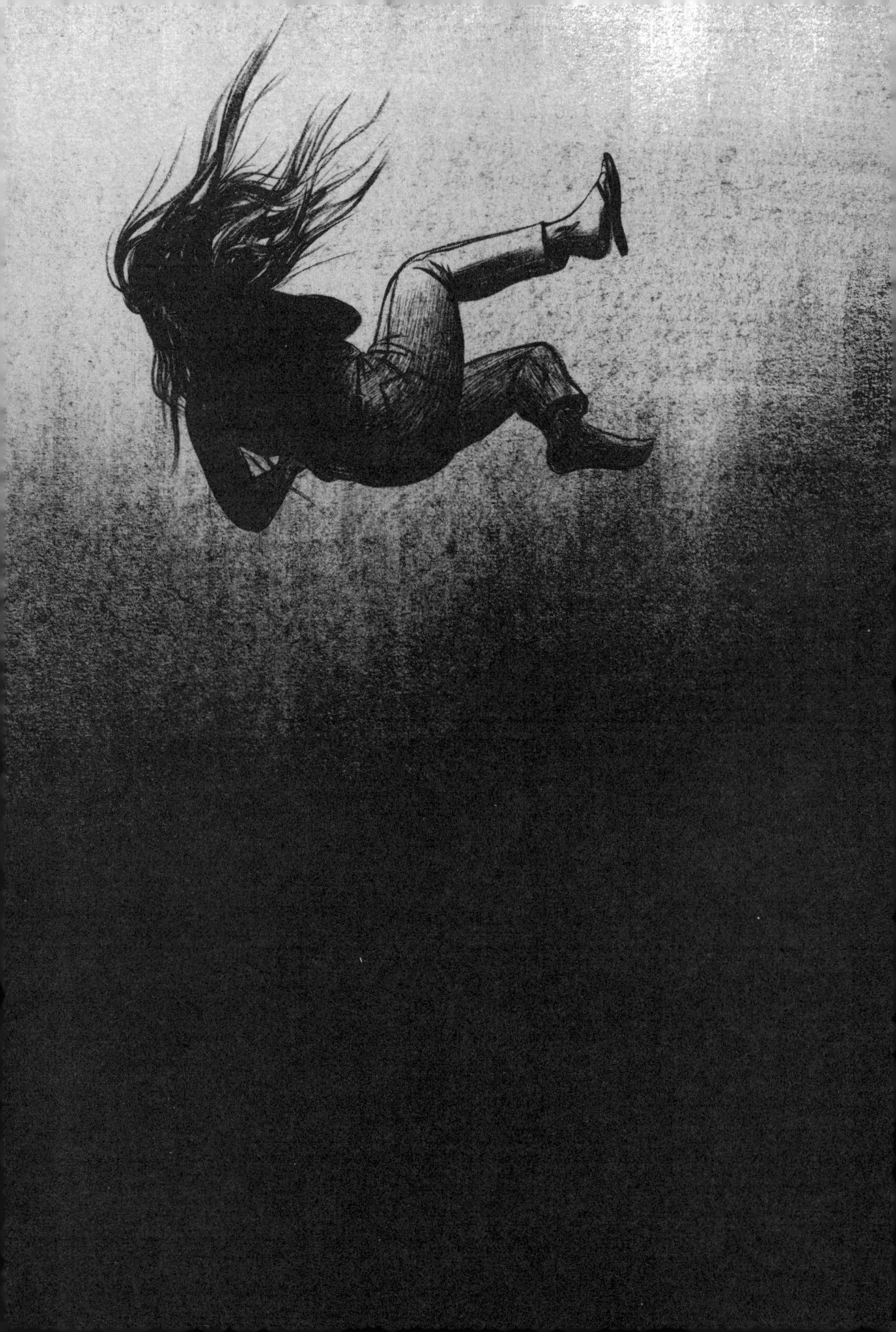

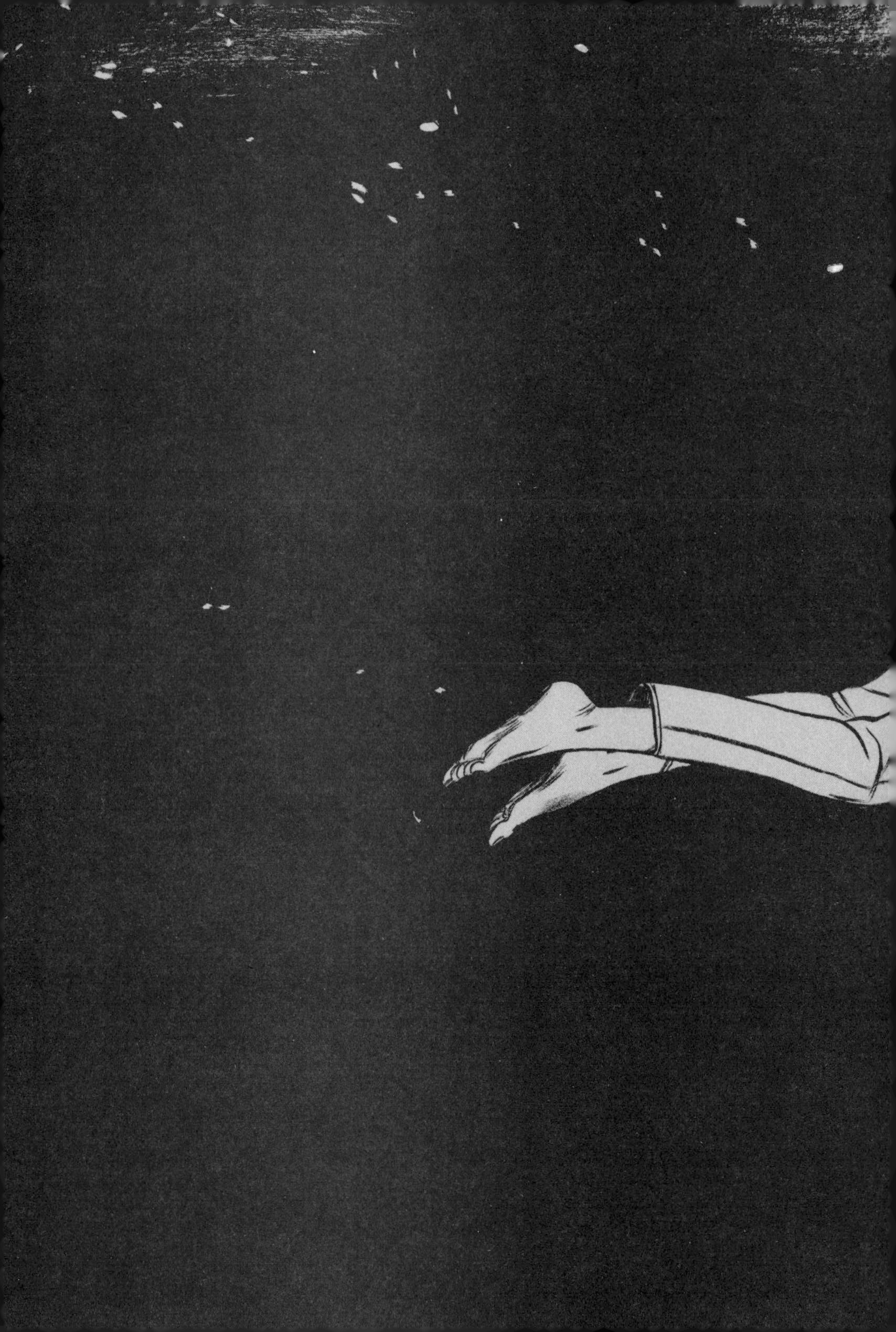

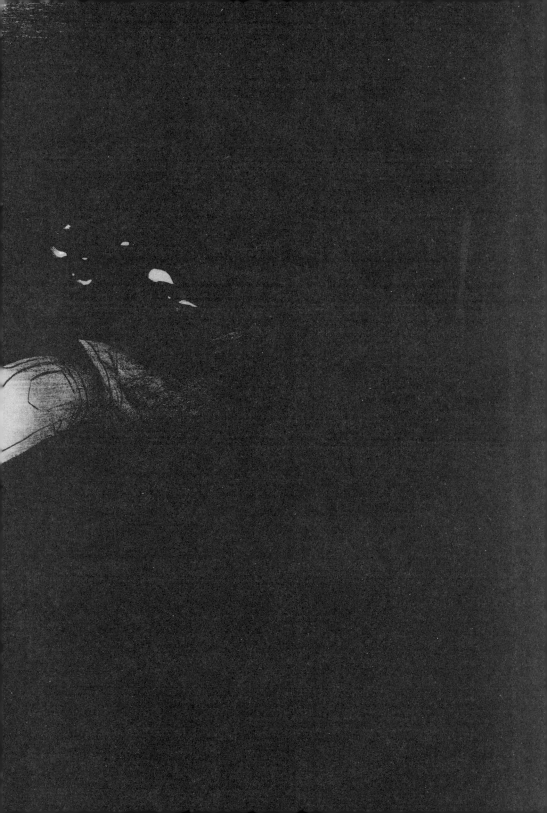

My mom told me.
Used to tell me all the time.
That she dreamed of me before I was born.

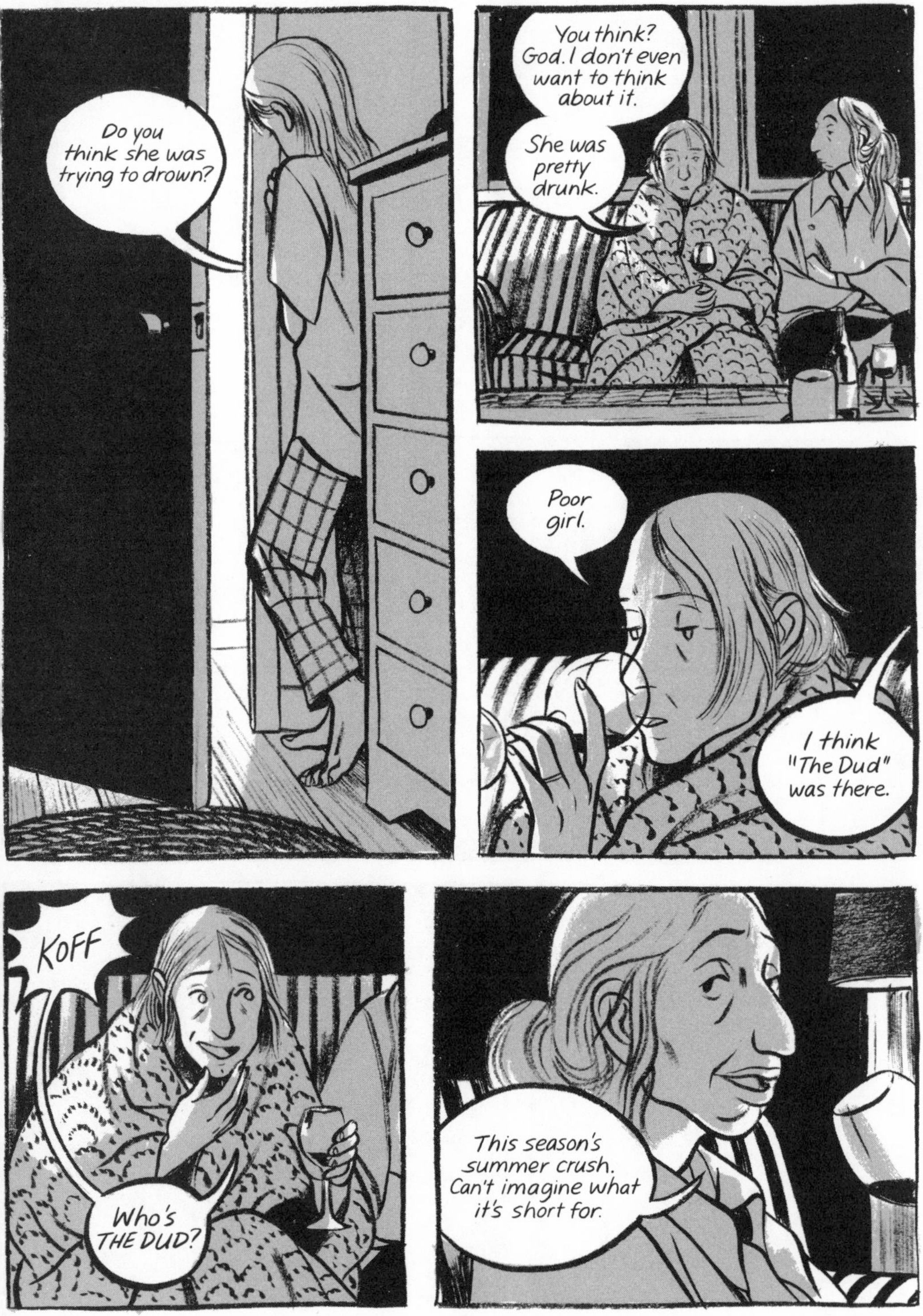
Do you think she was trying to drown?
You think? God. I don't even want to think about it.
She was pretty drunk.
Poor girl.
I think "The Dud" was there.
KOFF
Who's THE DUD?
This season's summer crush. Can't imagine what it's short for.

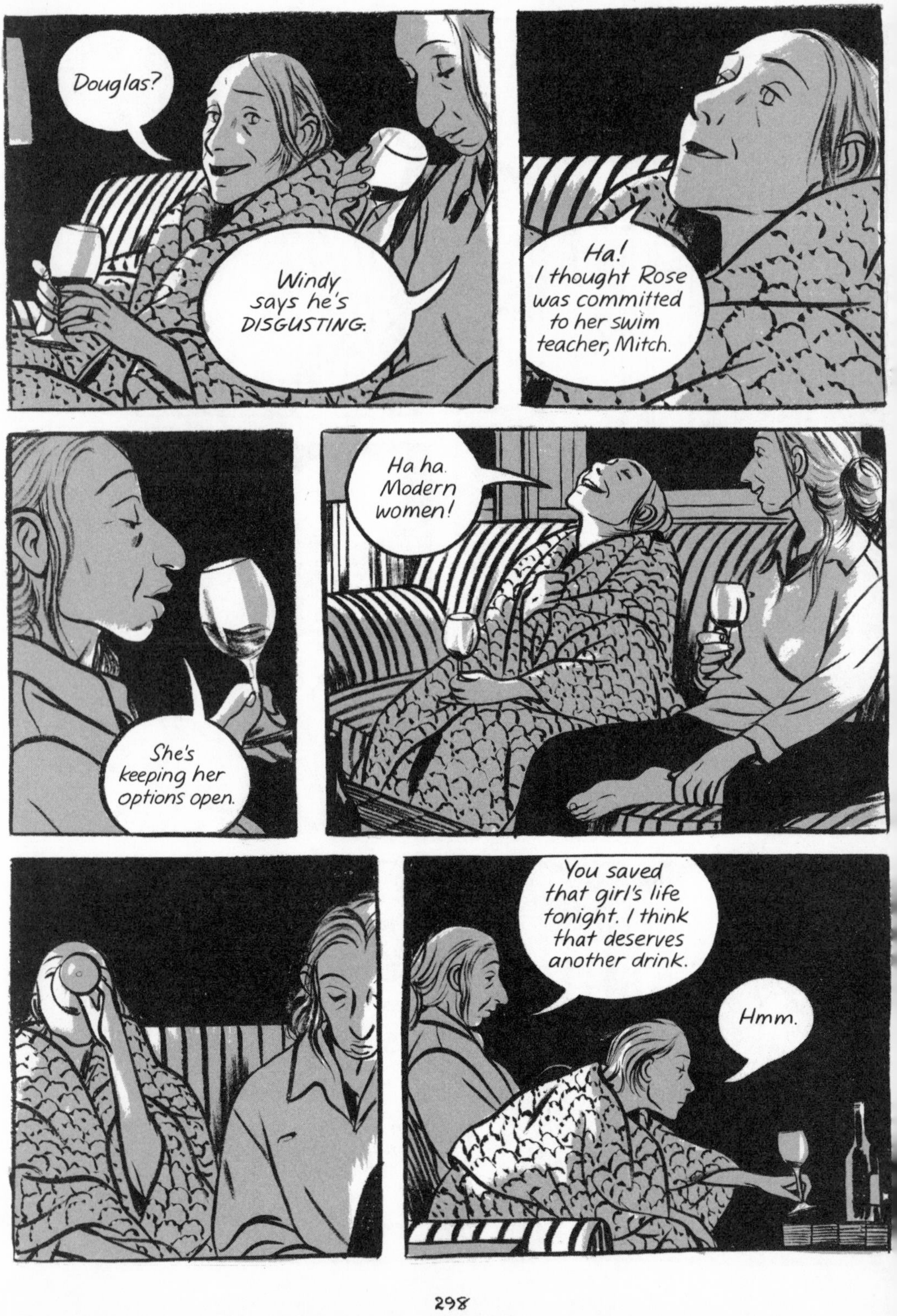
Douglas?
Windy says he's DISGUSTING.
Ha! I thought Rose was committed to her swim teacher, Mitch.
She's keeping her options open.
Ha ha. Modern women!
You saved that girl's life tonight. I think that deserves another drink.
Hmm.

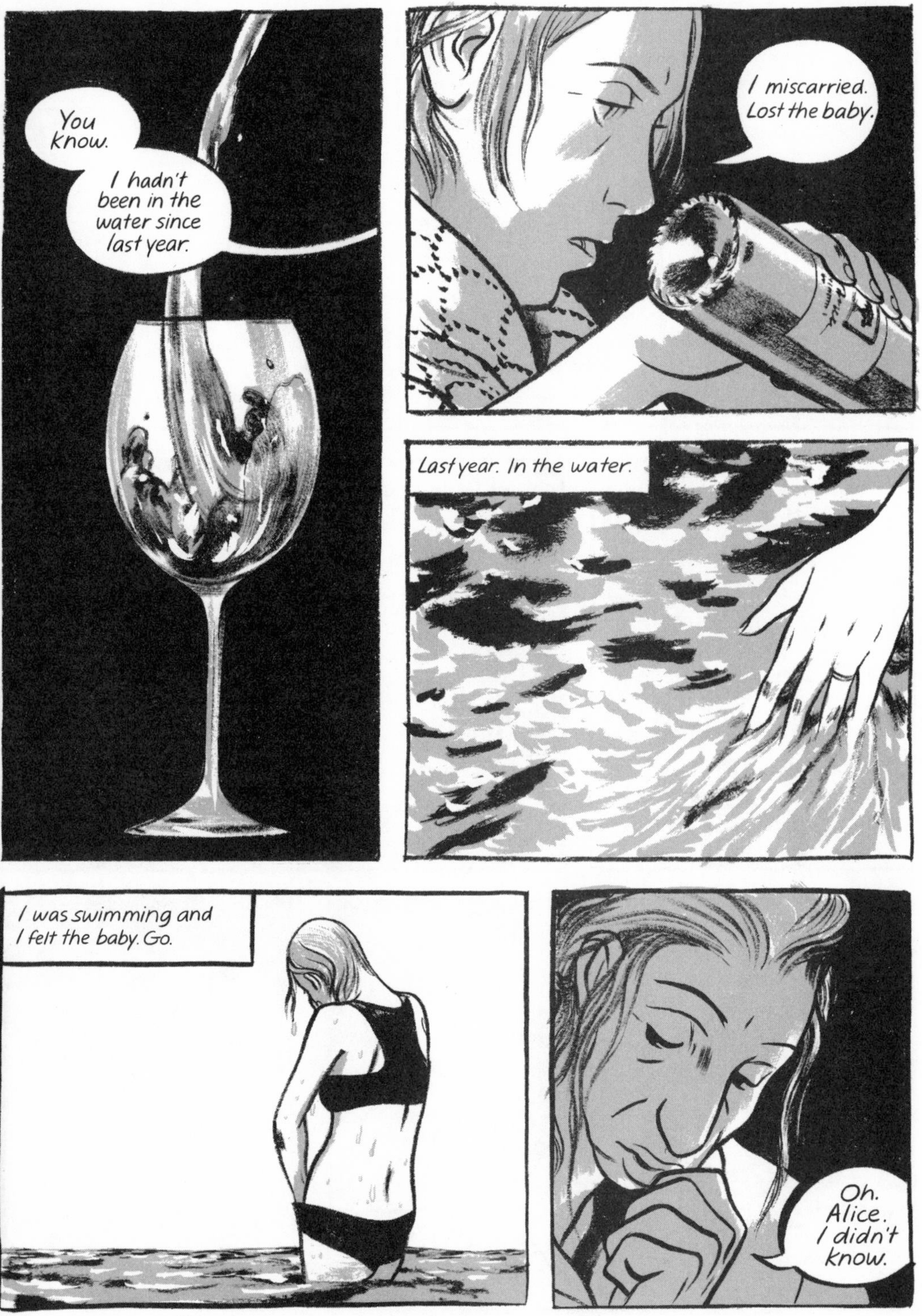
You know.
I hadn't been in the water since last year.
I miscarried. Lost the baby.
Last year. In the water.
I was swimming and I felt the baby. Go.
Oh. Alice. I didn't know.

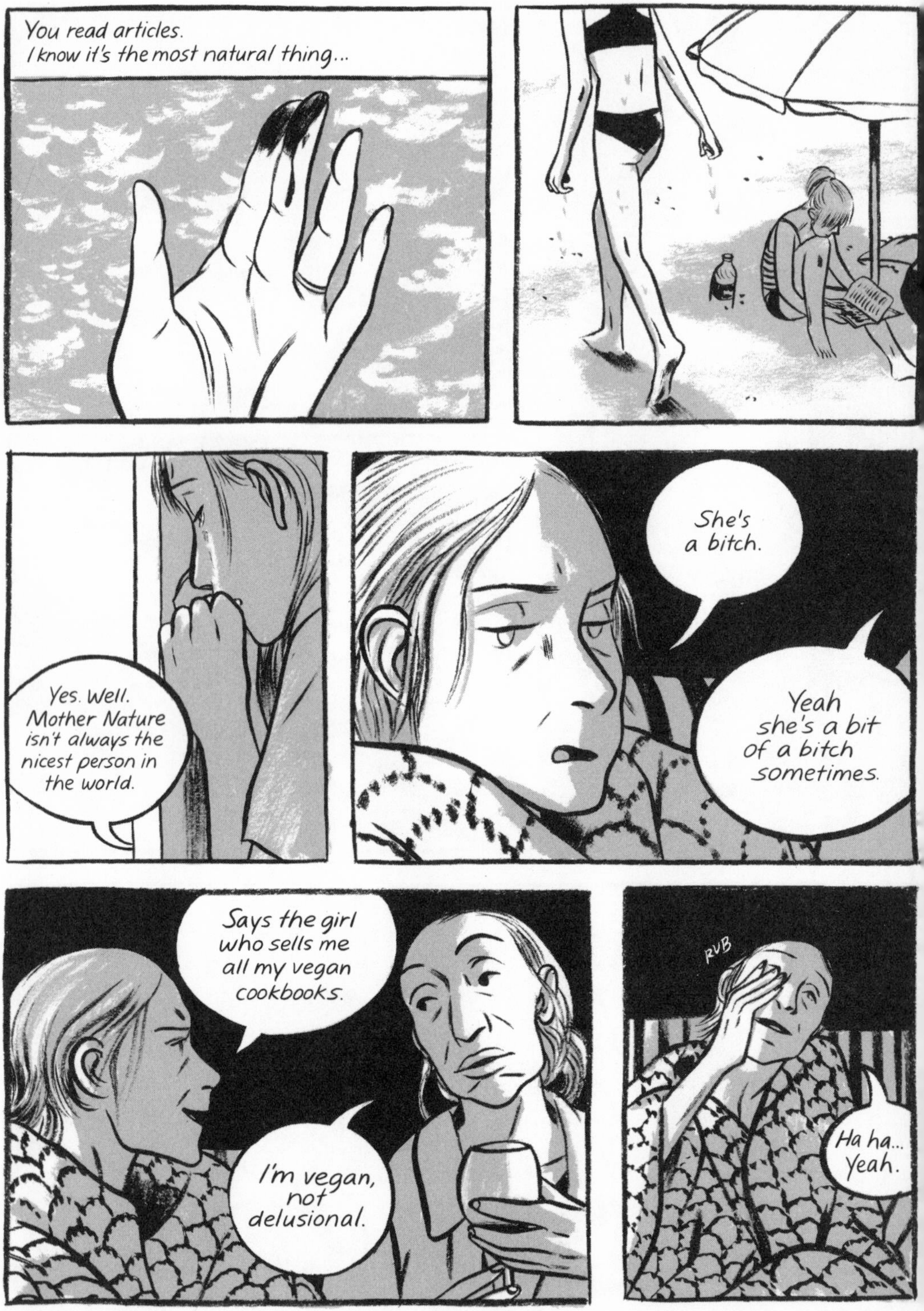
You read articles.
I know it's the most natural thing...
Yes. Well. Mother Nature isn't always the nicest person in the world.
She's a bitch.
Yeah she's a bit of a bitch sometimes.
Says the girl who sells me all my vegan cookbooks.
I'm vegan, not delusional.
RUB
Ha ha... Yeah.

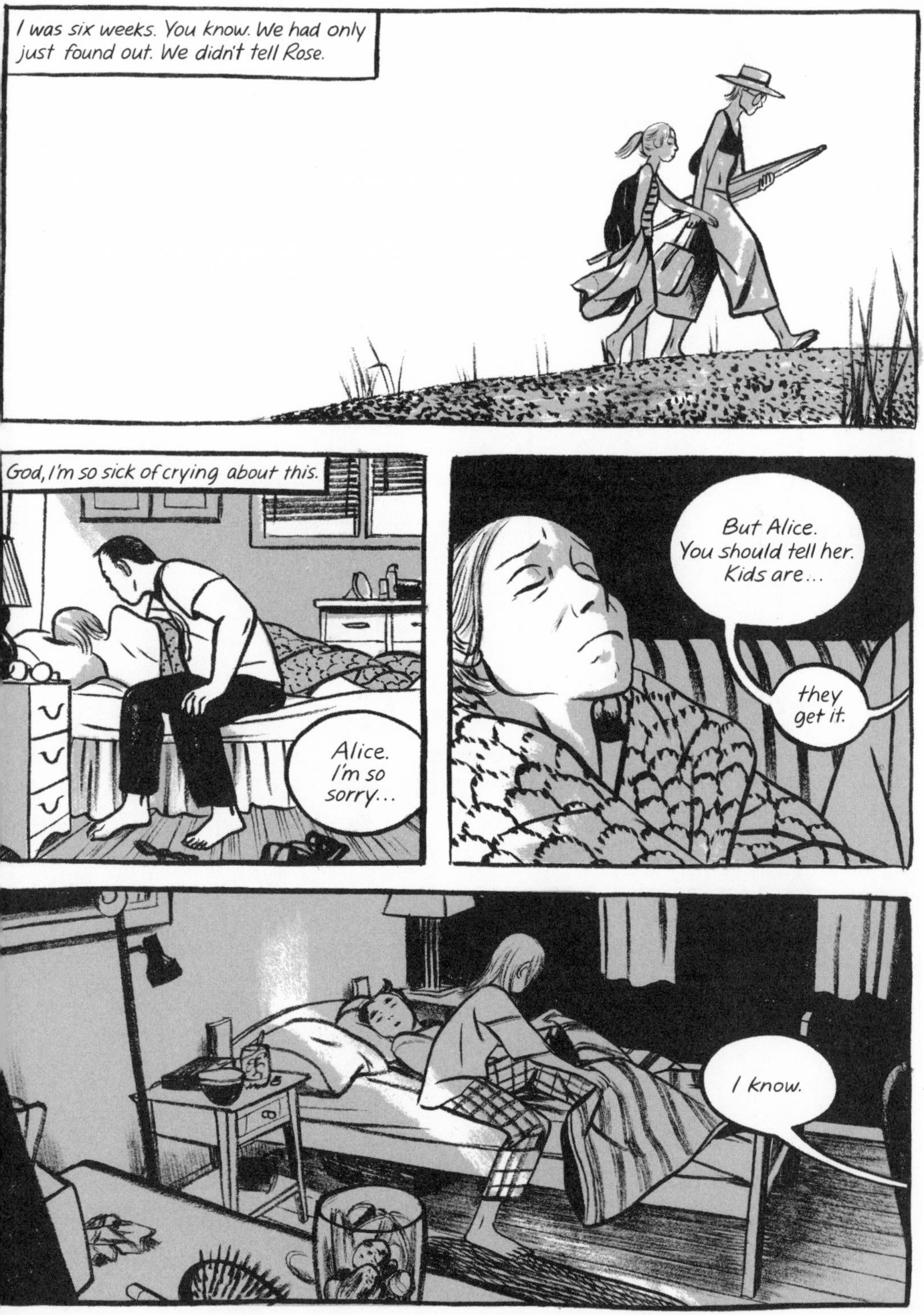
I was six weeks. You know. We had only just found out. We didn't tell Rose.
God, I'm so sick of crying about this.
Alice. I'm so sorry...
But Alice. You should tell her. Kids are...
they get it.
I know.

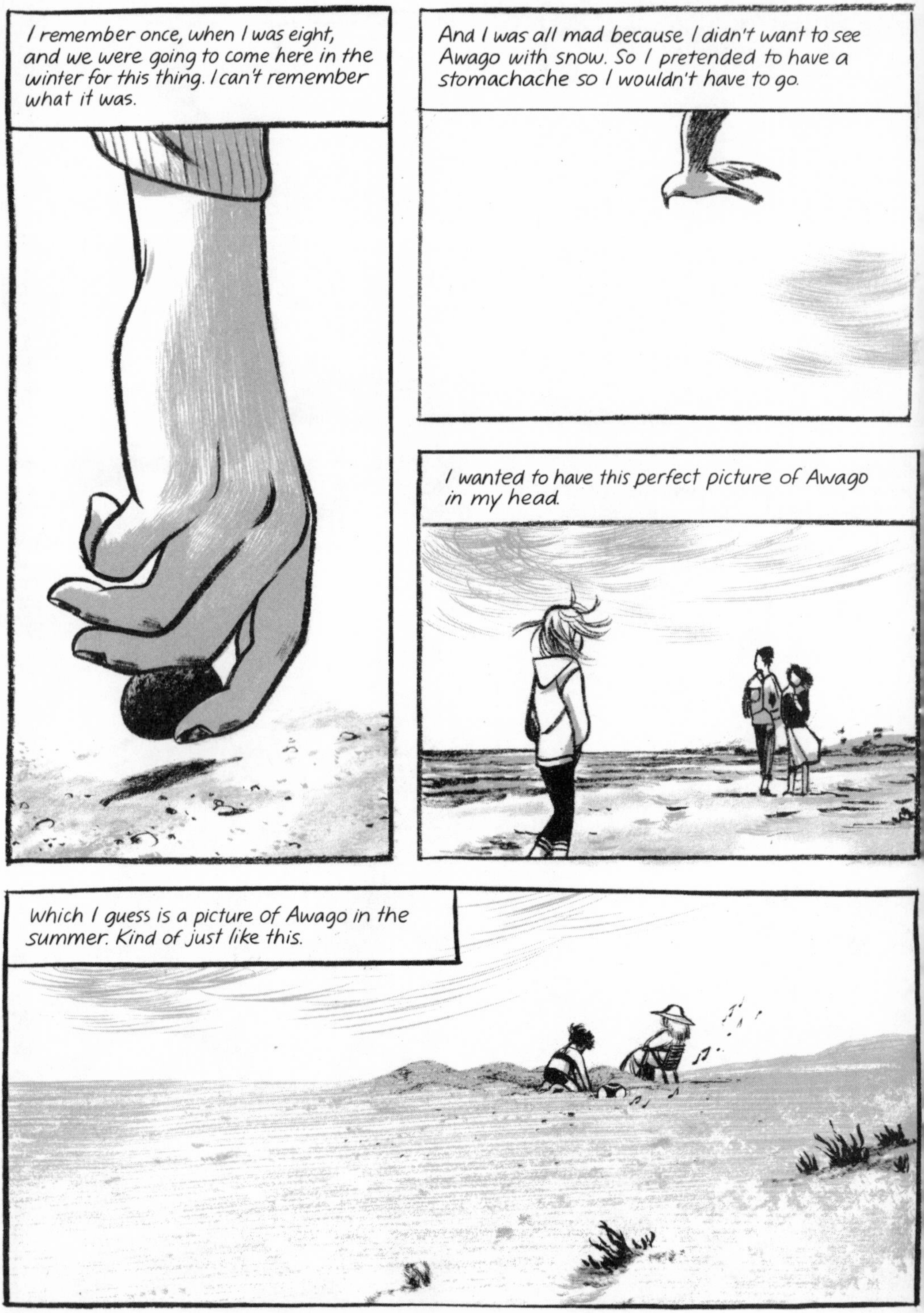
I remember once, when I was eight, and we were going to come here in the winter for this thing. I can't remember what it was.
And I was all mad because I didn't want to see Awago with snow. So I pretended to have a stomachache so I wouldn't have to go.
I wanted to have this perfect picture of Awago in my head.
Which I guess is a picture of Awago in the summer. Kind of just like this.

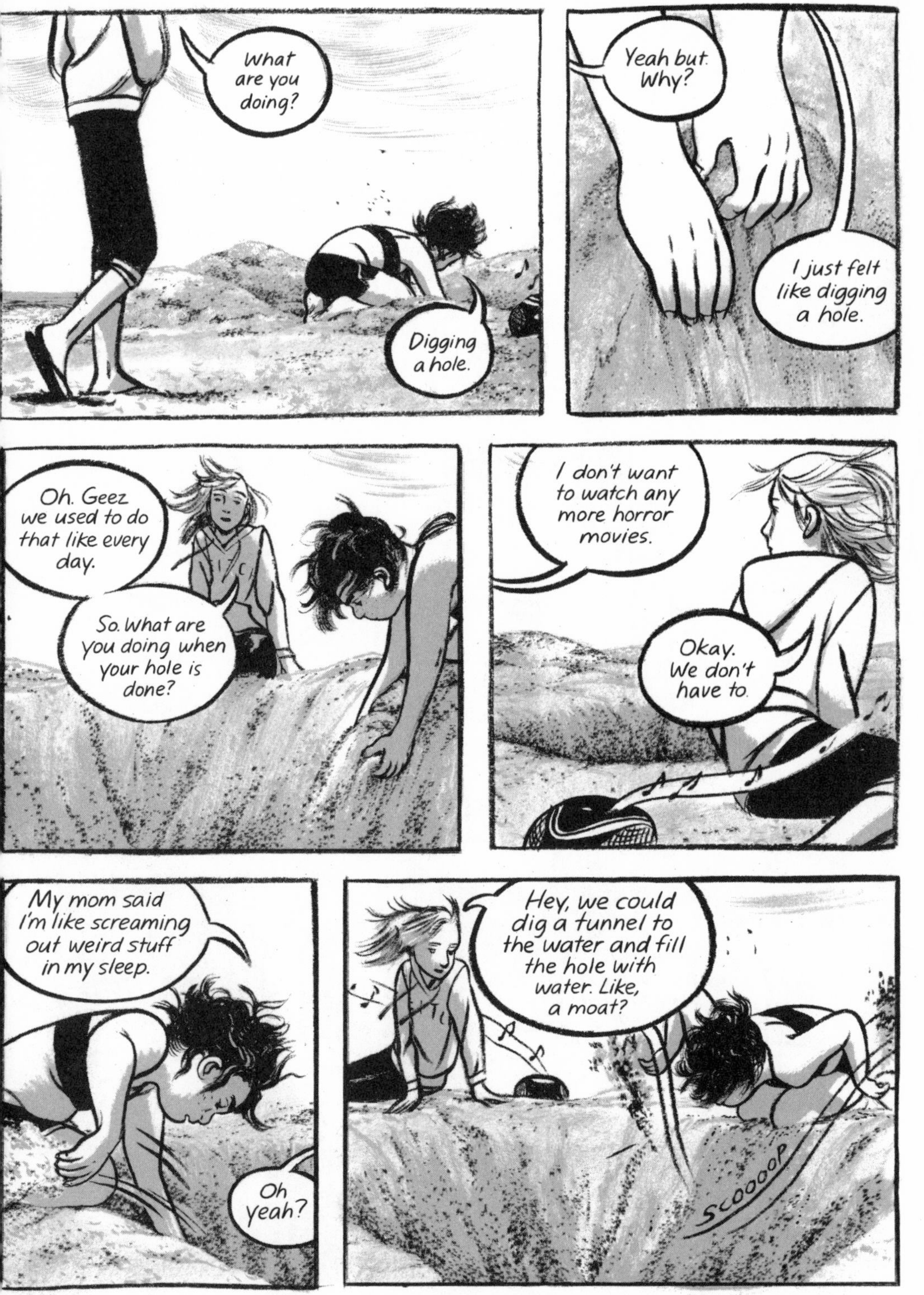
What are you doing?
Digging a hole.
Yeah but. Why?
I just felt like digging a hole.
Oh. Geez we used to do that like every day.
So. What are you doing when your hole is done?
I don't want to watch any more horror movies.
Okay. We don't have to.
My mom said I'm like screaming out weird stuff in my sleep.
Oh yeah?
Hey, we could dig a tunnel to the water and fill the hole with water. Like, a moat?
SCOOOOP

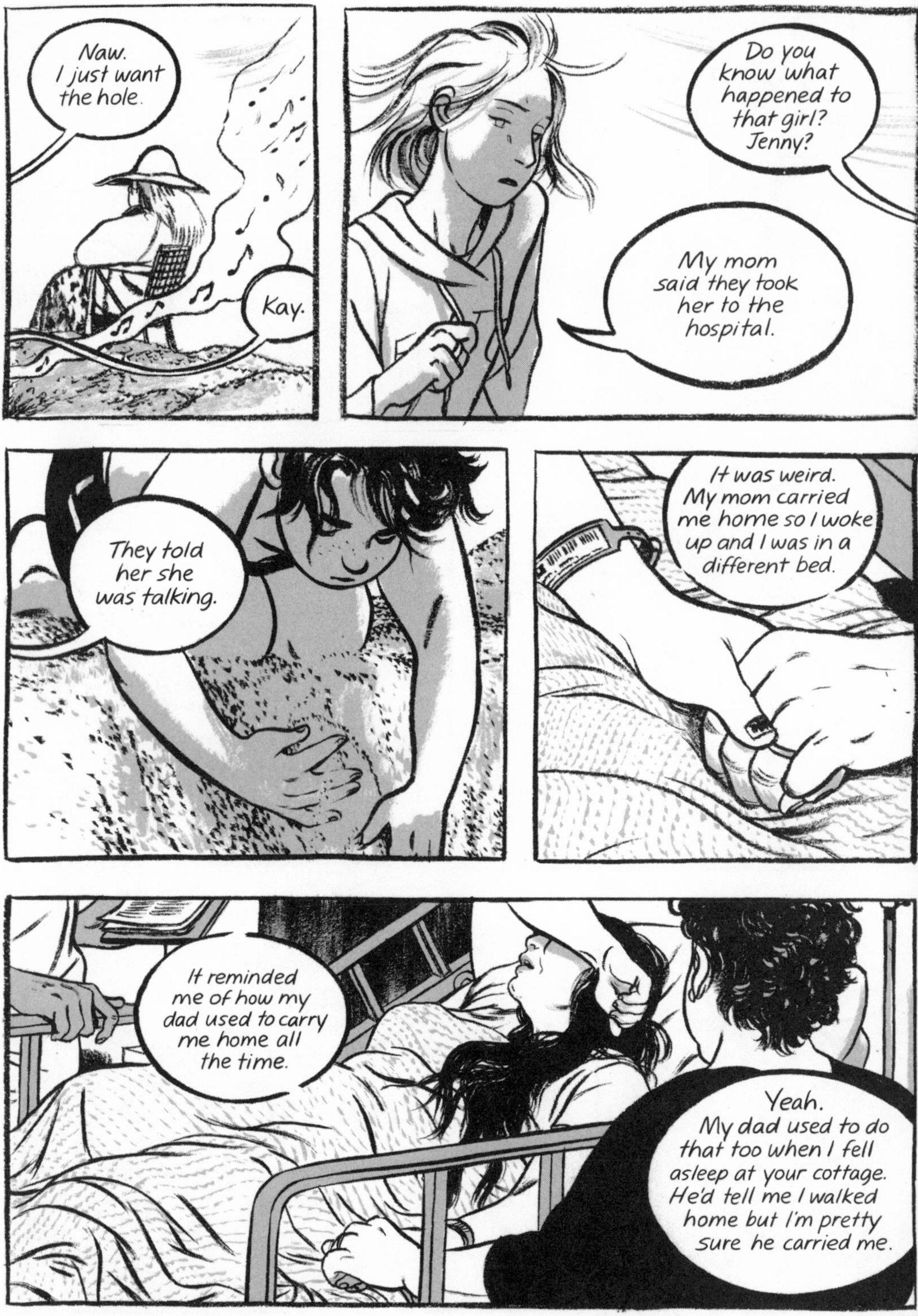
Naw. I just want the hole.
Kay.
Do you know what happened to that girl? Jenny?
My mom said they took her to the hospital.
They told her she was talking.
It was weird. My mom carried me home so I woke up and I was in a different bed.
It reminded me of how my dad used to carry me home all the time.
Yeah. My dad used to do that too when I fell asleep at your cottage. He'd tell me I walked home but I'm pretty sure he carried me.

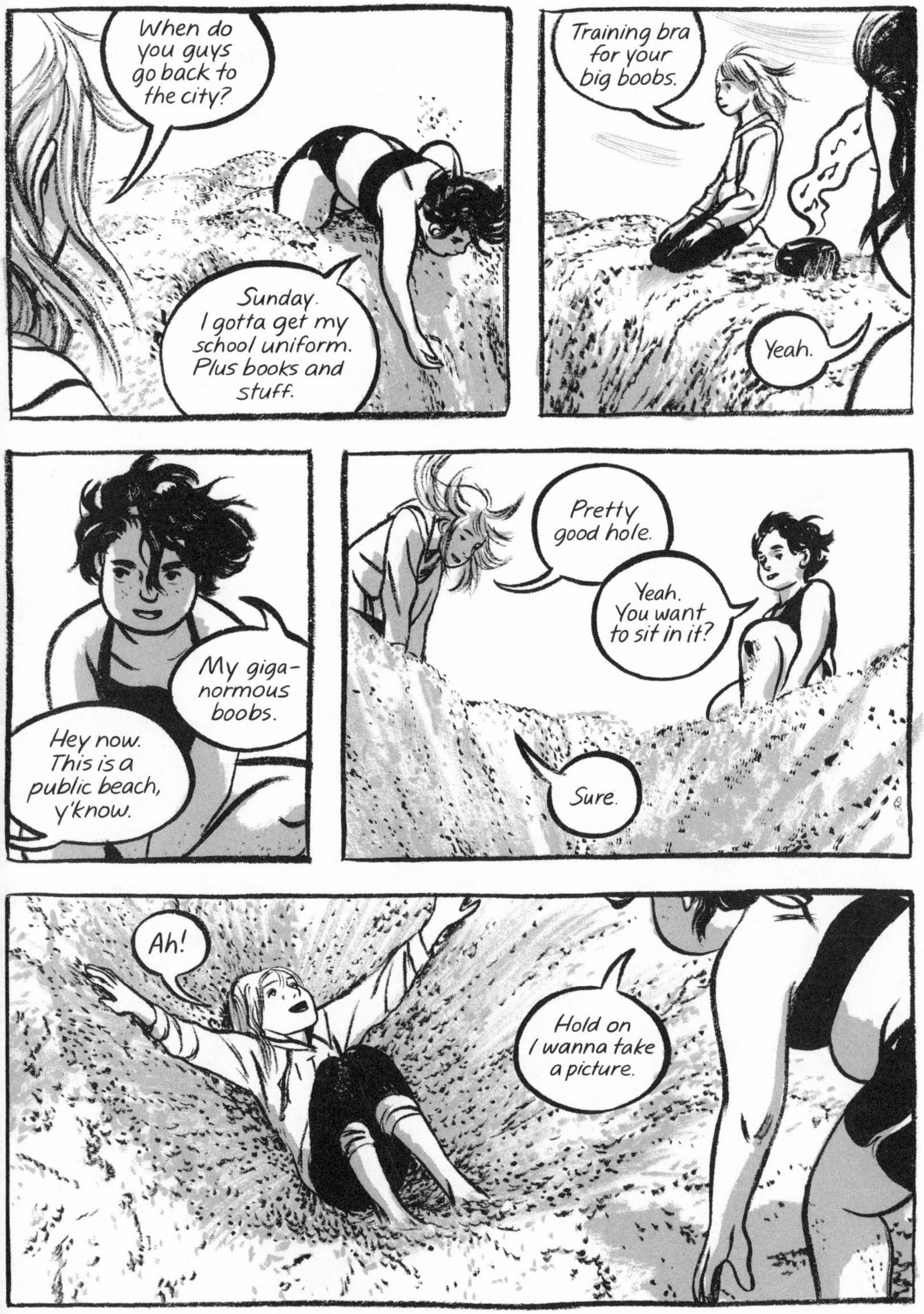
When do you guys go back to the city?
Sunday. I gotta get my school uniform. Plus books and stuff.
Training bra for your big boobs.
Yeah.
My giga-normous boobs.
Hey now. This is a public beach, y'know.
Pretty good hole.
Yeah. You want to sit in it?
Sure.
Ah!
Hold on I wanna take a picture.

Say "BOOBS!"

Kidding.

2:15

CPF

DING
DING

NOTICE

FISHING LICENSES SOLD HERE

BAIT

HO! You returning this?

Yes.

On time?

Uh, yes.

Let's see what we got here.

POP

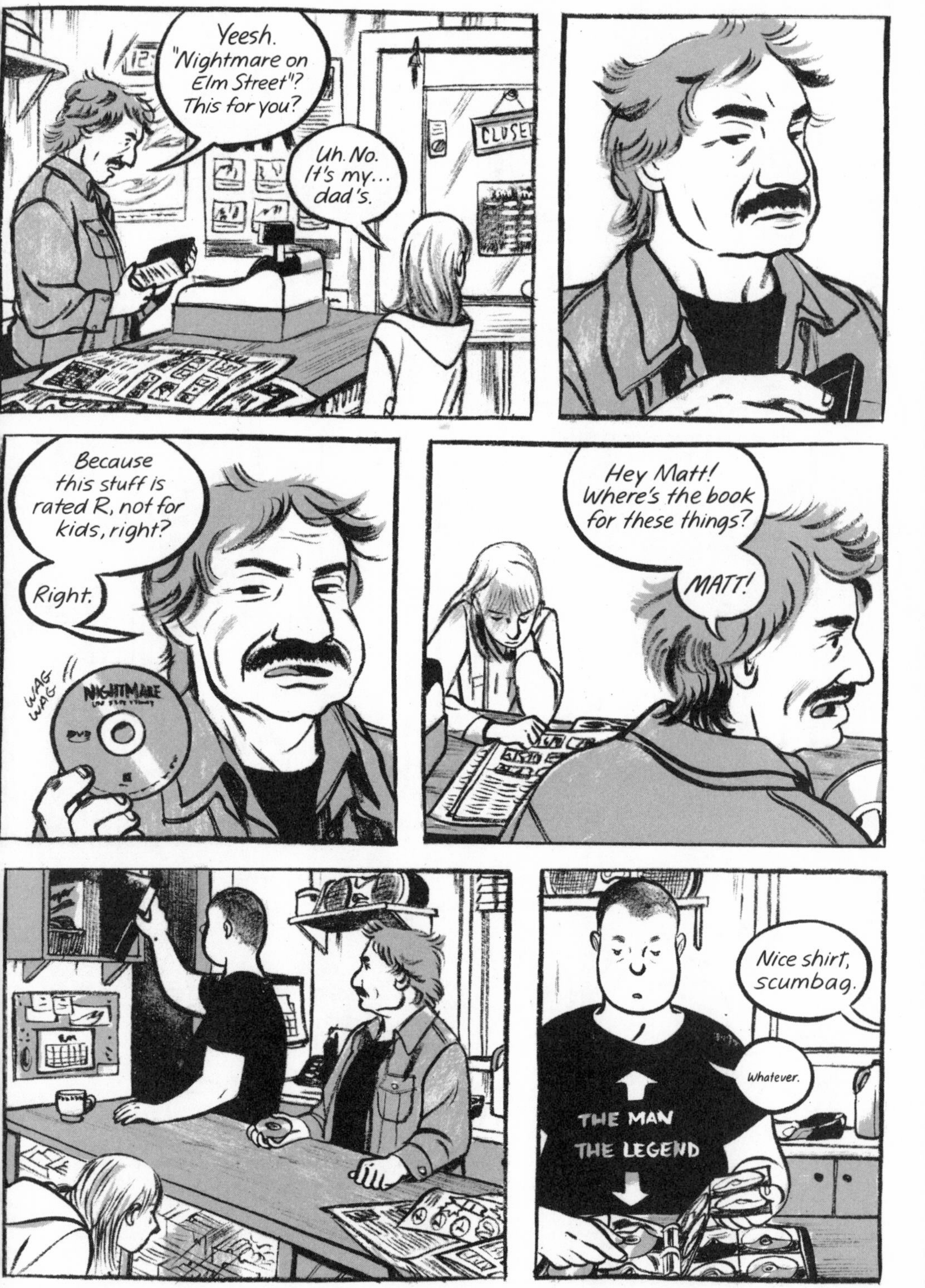
Yeesh. "Nightmare on Elm Street"? This for you?
Uh. No. It's my... dad's.
CLOSED
Because this stuff is rated R, not for kids, right?
Right.
WAG WAG
NIGHTMARE
DVD
Hey Matt! Where's the book for these things?
MATT!
Nice shirt, scumbag.
Whatever.
THE MAN
THE LEGEND

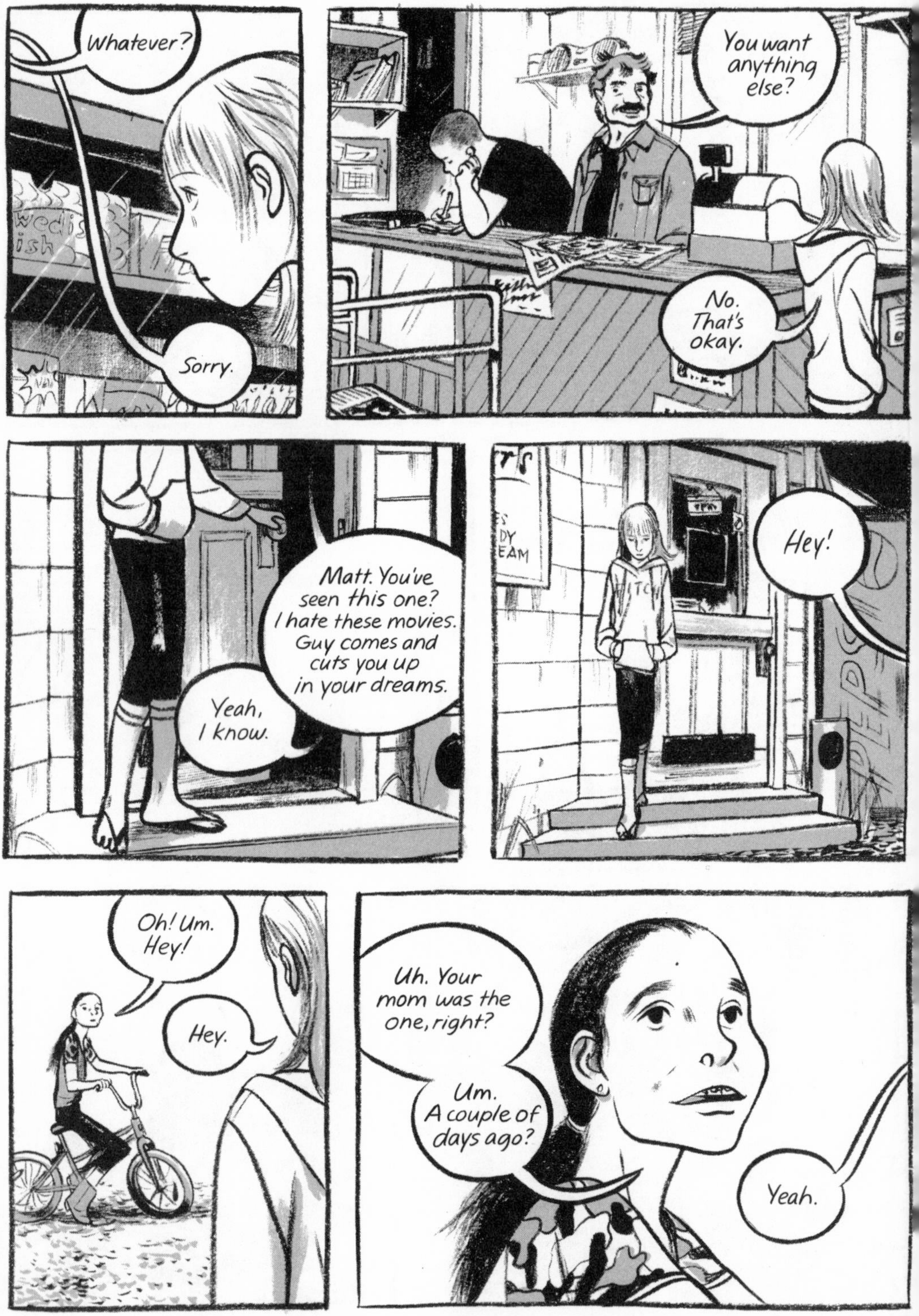

Whatever?
Sorry.
You want anything else?
No. That's okay.
Matt. You've seen this one? I hate these movies. Guy comes and cuts you up in your dreams.
Yeah, I know.
Hey!
Oh! Um. Hey!
Hey.
Uh. Your mom was the one, right?
Um. A couple of days ago?
Yeah.

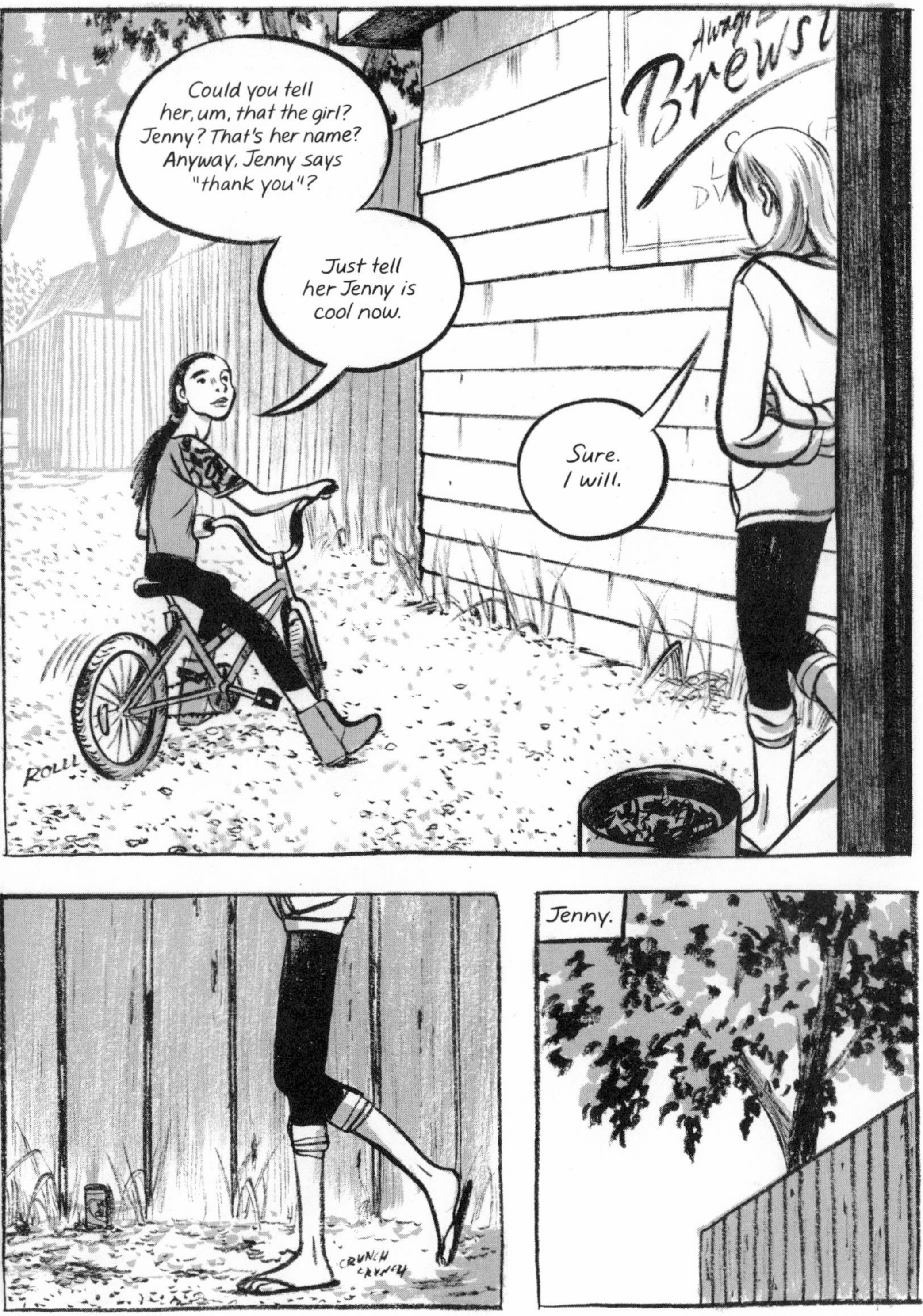
Could you tell her, um, that the girl? Jenny? That's her name? Anyway, Jenny says "thank you"?
Just tell her Jenny is cool now.
Sure. I will.
ROLL
CRUNCH CRUNCH
Jenny.

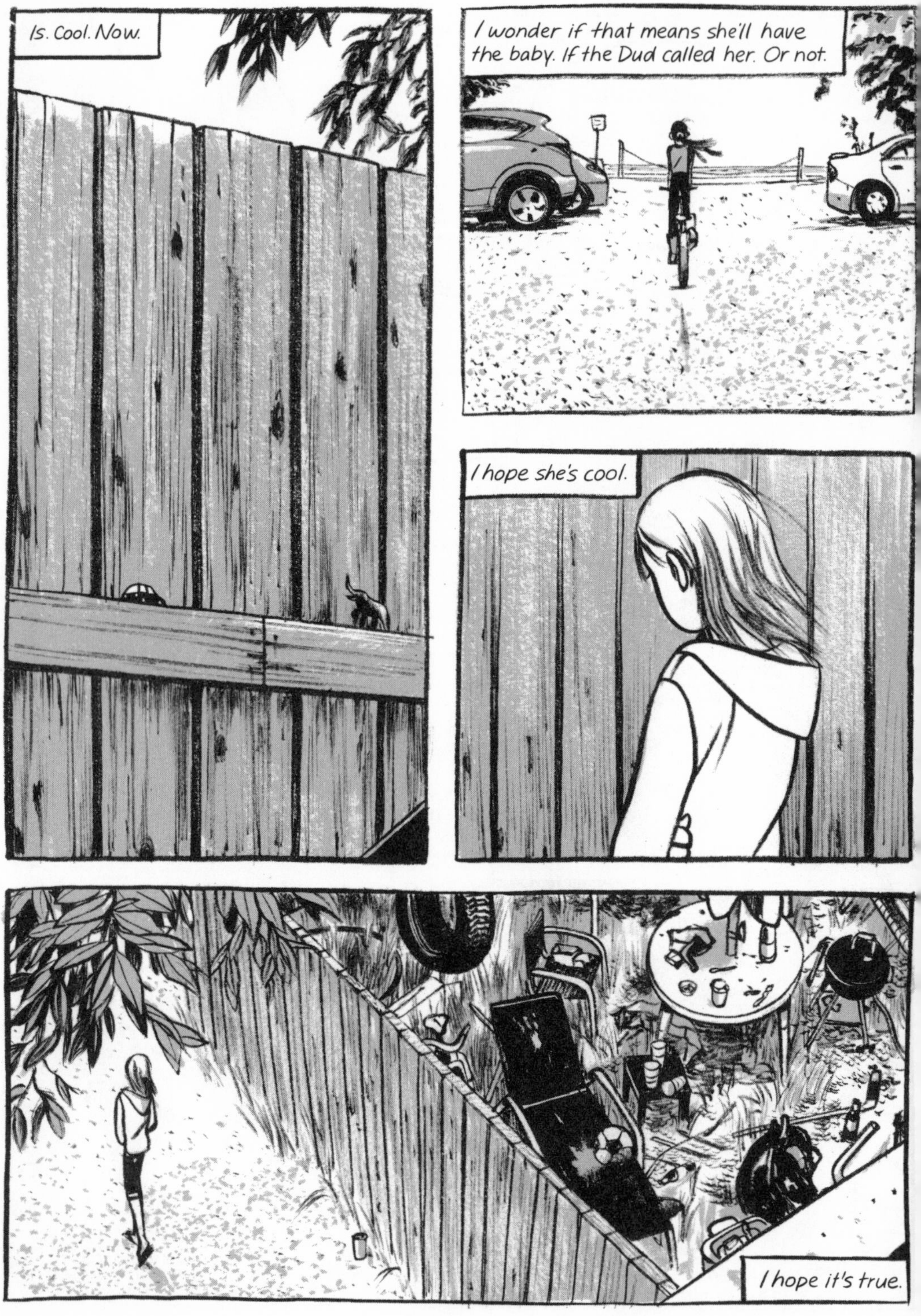
Is. Cool. Now.
I wonder if that means she'll have the baby. If the Dud called her. Or not.
I hope she's cool.
I hope it's true.

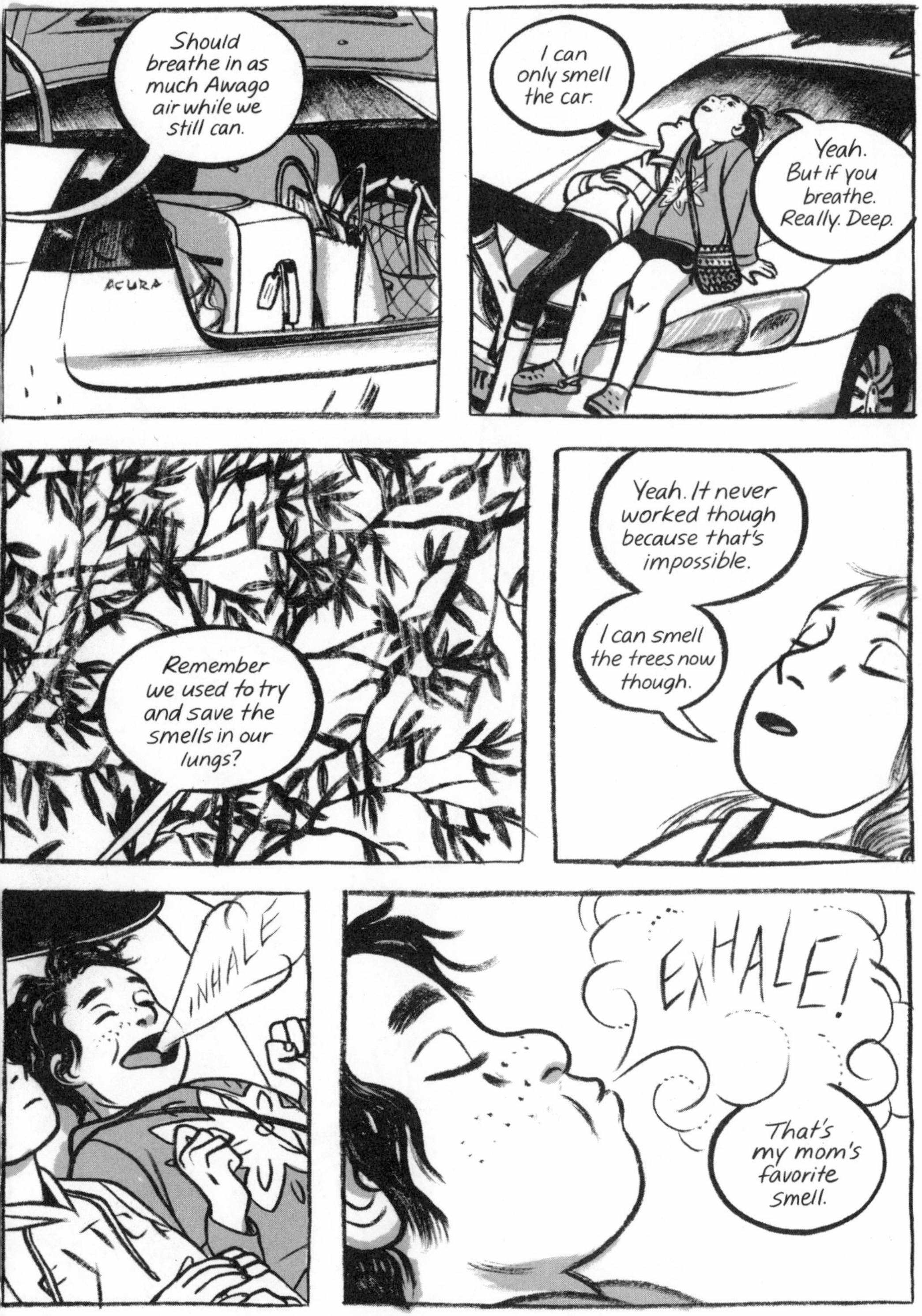
ACURA
Should breathe in as much Awago air while we still can.
I can only smell the car.
Yeah. But if you breathe. Really. Deep.
Remember we used to try and save the smells in our lungs?
Yeah. It never worked though because that's impossible.
I can smell the trees now though.
INHALE
EXHALE!
That's my mom's favorite smell.

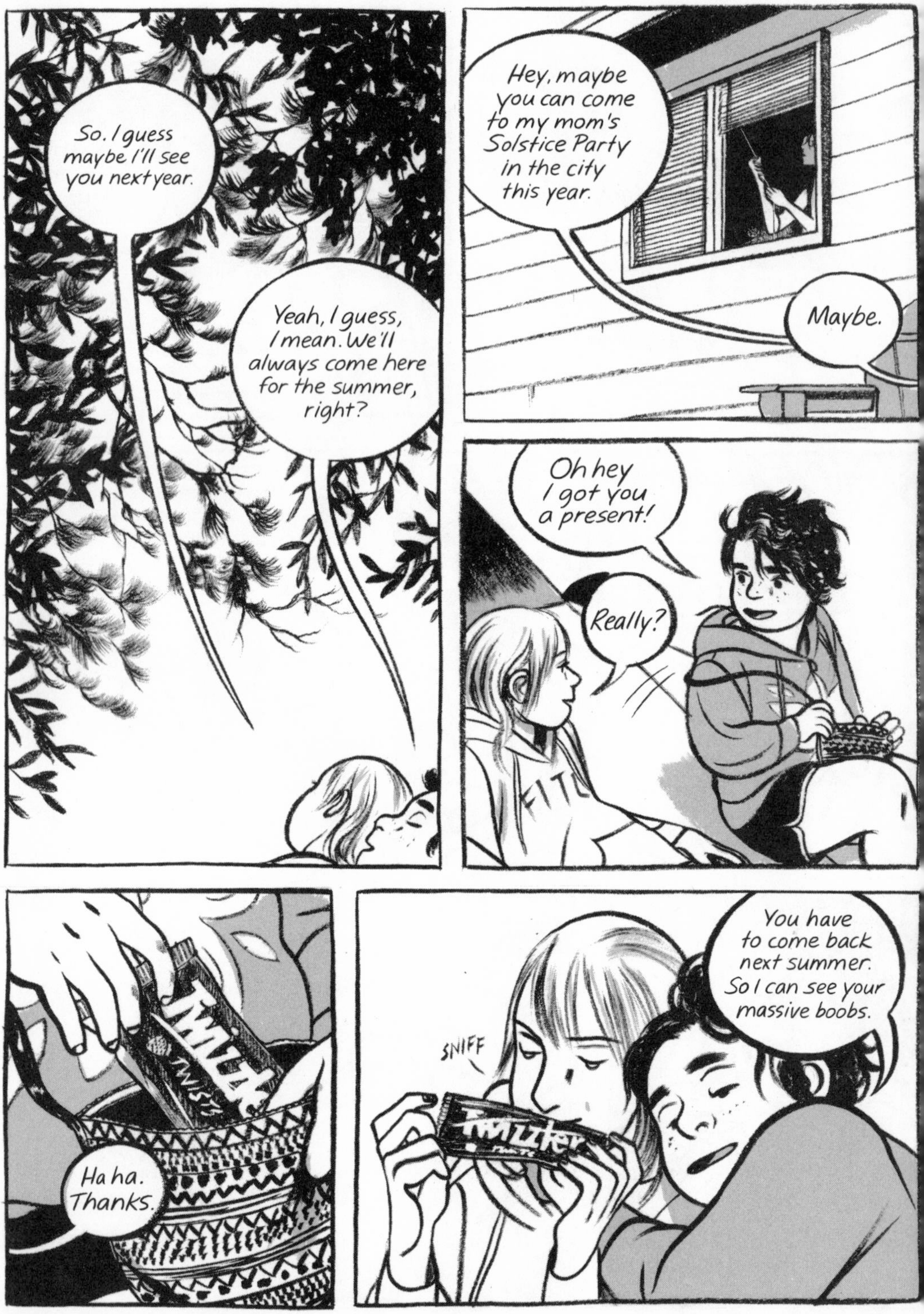
So. I guess maybe I'll see you next year.
Yeah, I guess, I mean. We'll always come here for the summer, right?
Hey, maybe you can come to my mom's Solstice Party in the city this year.
Maybe.
Oh hey I got you a present!
Really?
Ha ha. Thanks.
SNIFF
You have to come back next summer. So I can see your massive boobs.

Hey kiddo. You want to go and make sure you got everything?

Okay.

Bye Mr.Wallace.

Stay out of trouble, Windy.

Make sure you check the drawers and under the bed, okay?

Yup.

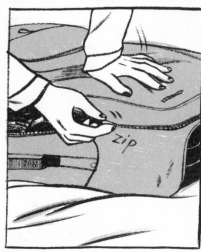

ZIP

THUNK

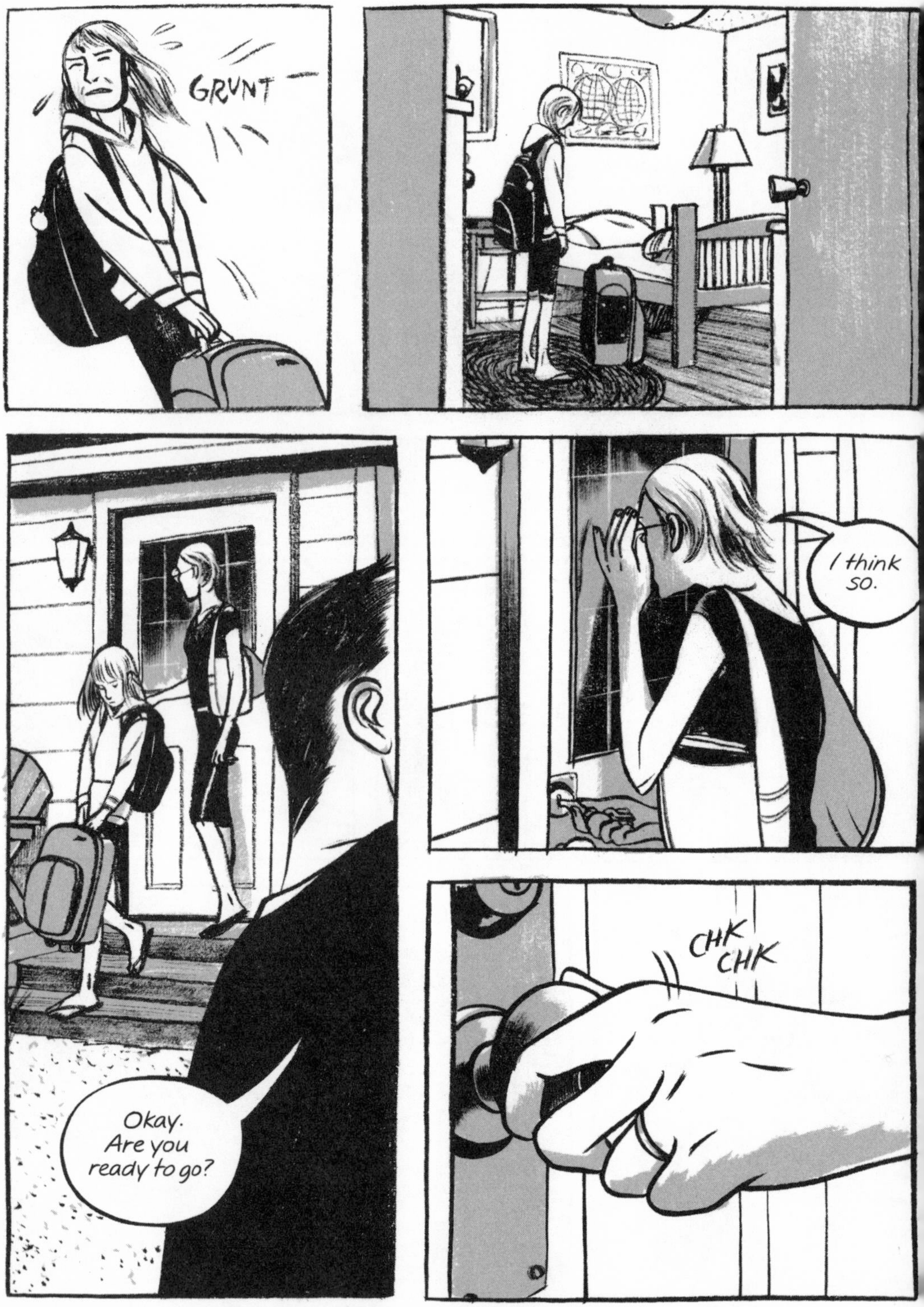
GRUNT
Okay. Are you ready to go?
I think so.
CHK CHK

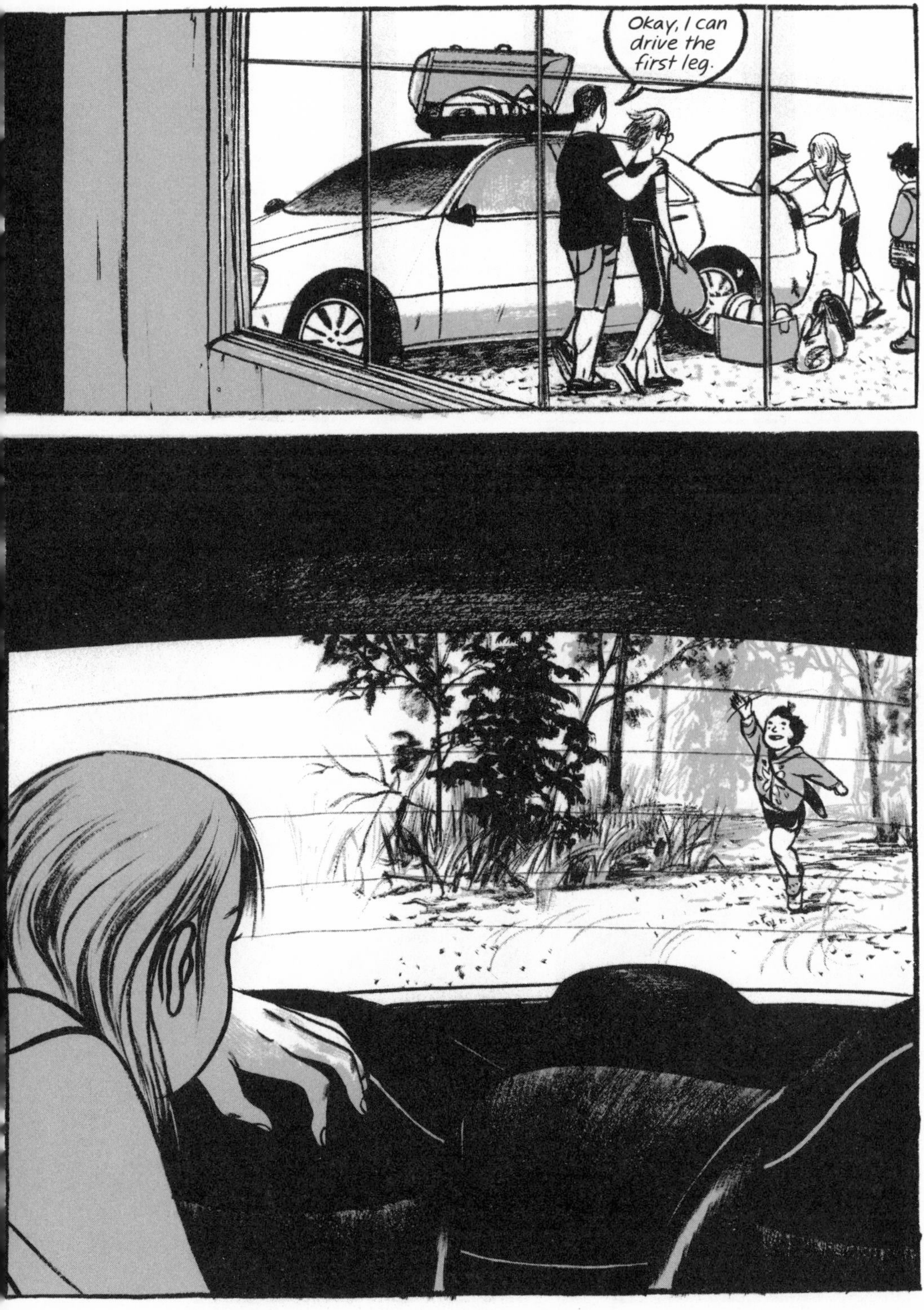
Okay, I can drive the first leg.

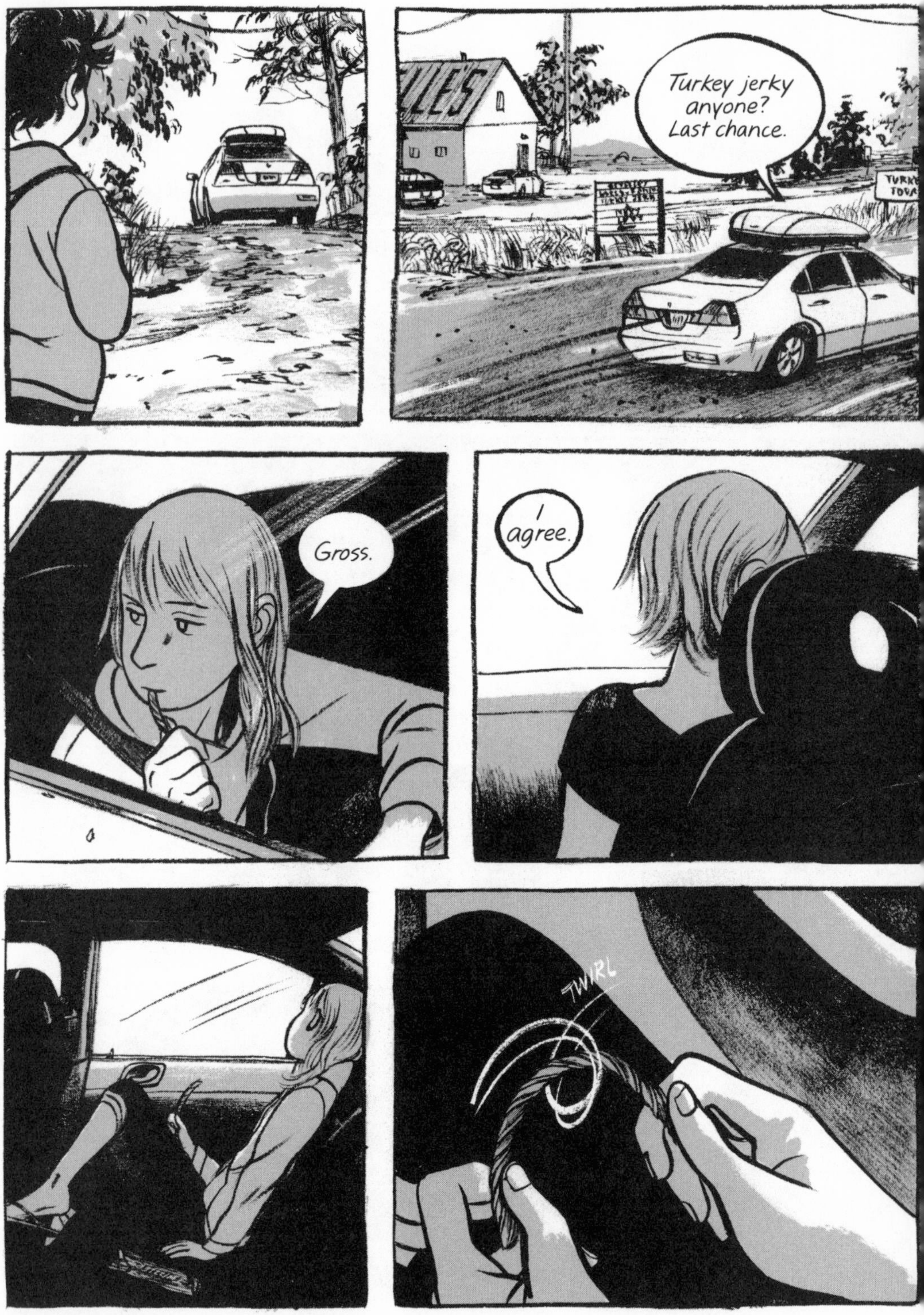
Turkey jerky anyone? Last chance.
Gross.
I agree.
TWIRL

tick tick tick tick tick

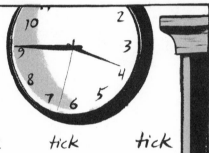

Maybe I will have massive boobs.

tick   tick   tick   tick   tick   tick

tick   tick   tick   tick

tick   tick   tick   tick

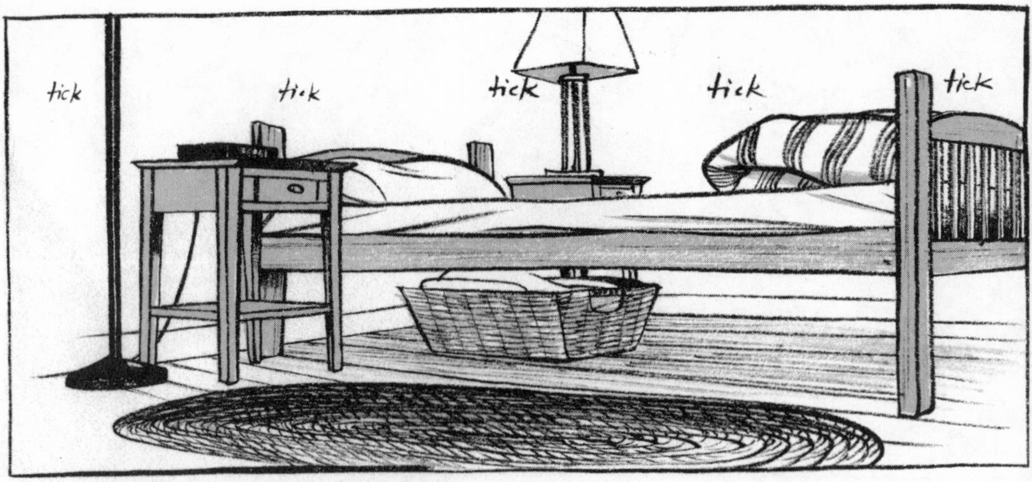
tick
tick
tick
tick
tick

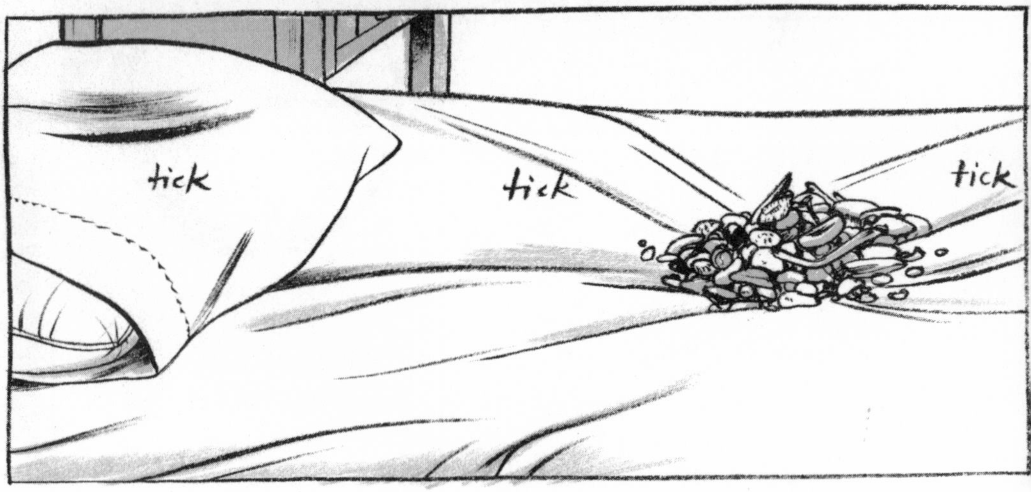
tick
tick
tick

tick.

*Boobs would
be cool.*

For Julia K. & Abi S.

To the Tamaki families; Sam Weber; Heather Gold; The Kelk family;
Tom Upchurch; Zoe Whittall; Anna Yoken for the manga help;
Sam Hiyate and Allison McDonald of The Rights Factory; Mark Siegel
and Calista Brill at First Second; Shelley Tanaka, Patsy Aldana,
and Sheila Barry at Groundwood Books; and Rush.

First Second

Text copyright © 2014 by Mariko Tamaki
Art copyright © 2014 by Jillian Tamaki

This is a work of fiction. Names, characters, places, and incidents are either a product
of the creators' imaginations or, if real, are used fictiously.

Published by First Second
First Second is an imprint of Roaring Brook Press,
a division of Holtzbrinck Publishing Holdings Limited Partnership
175 Fifth Avenue, New York, New York 10010

All rights reserved

Cataloging-in-Publication Data is on file at the Library of Congress.

Hardcover ISBN 978-1-62672-094-7
Paperback ISBN 978-1-59643-774-6

First Second books may be purchased for business or promotional use. For information
on bulk purchases please contact Macmillan Corporate and Premium Sales Department
at (800) 221-7945 x 5442 or by email at specialmarkets@macmillan.com.

First edition 2014
Book design by Rob Steen and Colleen AF Venable

Printed in the United States of America

Hardcover: 10 9 8 7 6 5 4 3 2 1
Paperback: 10 9 8 7 6 5 4 3 2 1

For Julia K. & Abi S.

To the Tamaki families; Sam Weber; Heather Gold; The Kelk family;
Tom Upchurch; Zoe Whittall; Anna Yoken for the manga help;
Sam Hiyate and Allison McDonald of The Rights Factory; Mark Siegel
and Calista Brill at First Second; Shelley Tanaka, Patsy Aldana,
and Sheila Barry at Groundwood Books; and Rush.

Firŝt Second

Text copyright © 2014 by Mariko Tamaki
Art copyright © 2014 by Jillian Tamaki

This is a work of fiction. Names, characters, places, and incidents are either a product
of the creators' imaginations or, if real, are used fictiously.
Published by First Second
First Second is an imprint of Roaring Brook Press,
a division of Holtzbrinck Publishing Holdings Limited Partnership
175 Fifth Avenue, New York, New York 10010
All rights reserved

Cataloging-in-Publication Data is on file at the Library of Congress.

Hardcover ISBN 978-1-62672-094-7
Paperback ISBN 978-1-59643-774-6

First Second books may be purchased for business or promotional use. For information
on bulk purchases please contact Macmillan Corporate and Premium Sales Department
at (800) 221-7945 x 5442 or by email at specialmarkets@macmillan.com.

First edition 2014
Book design by Rob Steen and Colleen AF Venable

Printed in the United States of America

Hardcover: 10 9 8 7 6 5 4 3 2 1
Paperback: 10 9 8 7 6 5 4 3 2 1

tick.

*Boobs would
be cool.*